I0824250

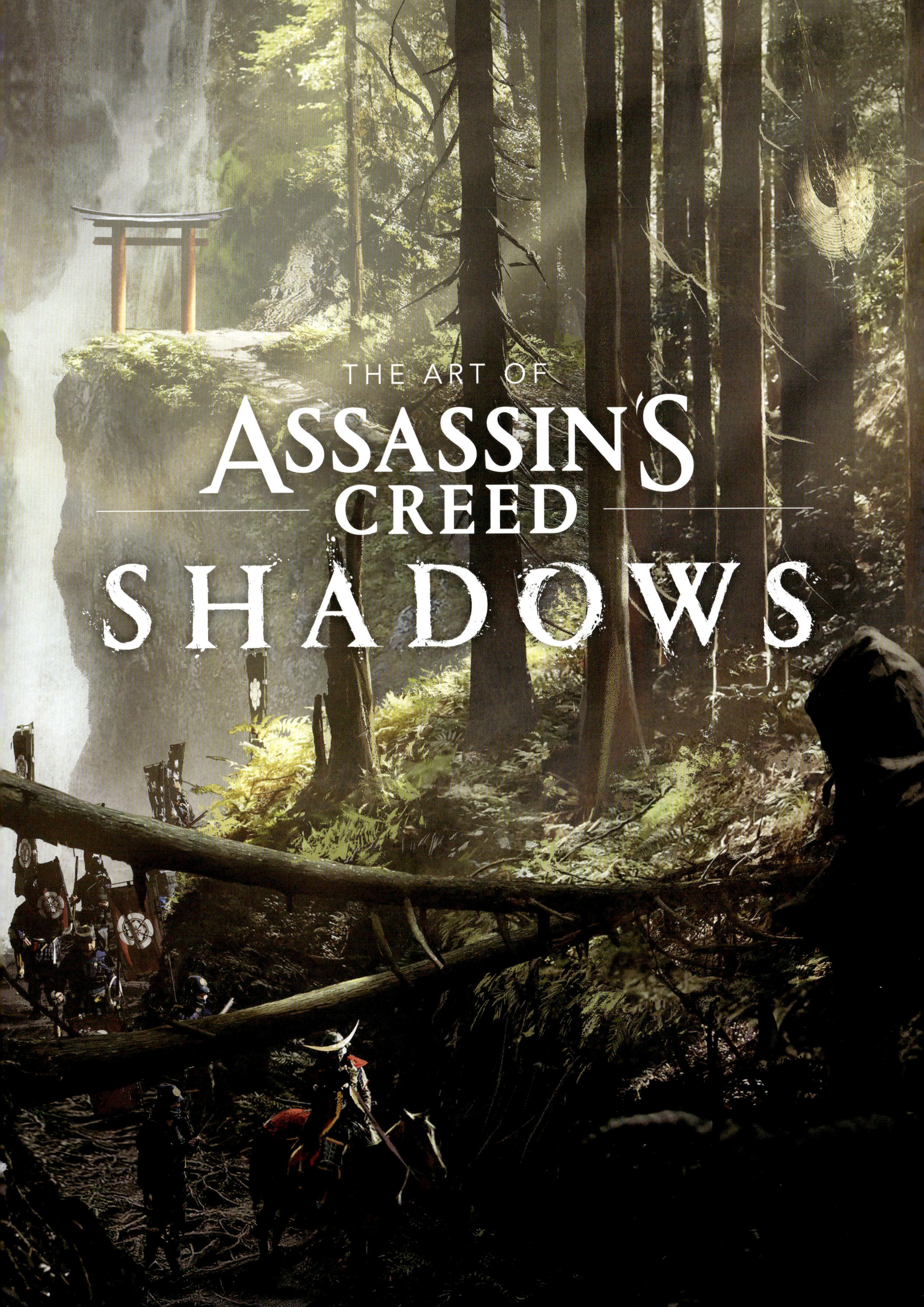
THE ART OF
ASSASSIN'S CREED
SHADOWS

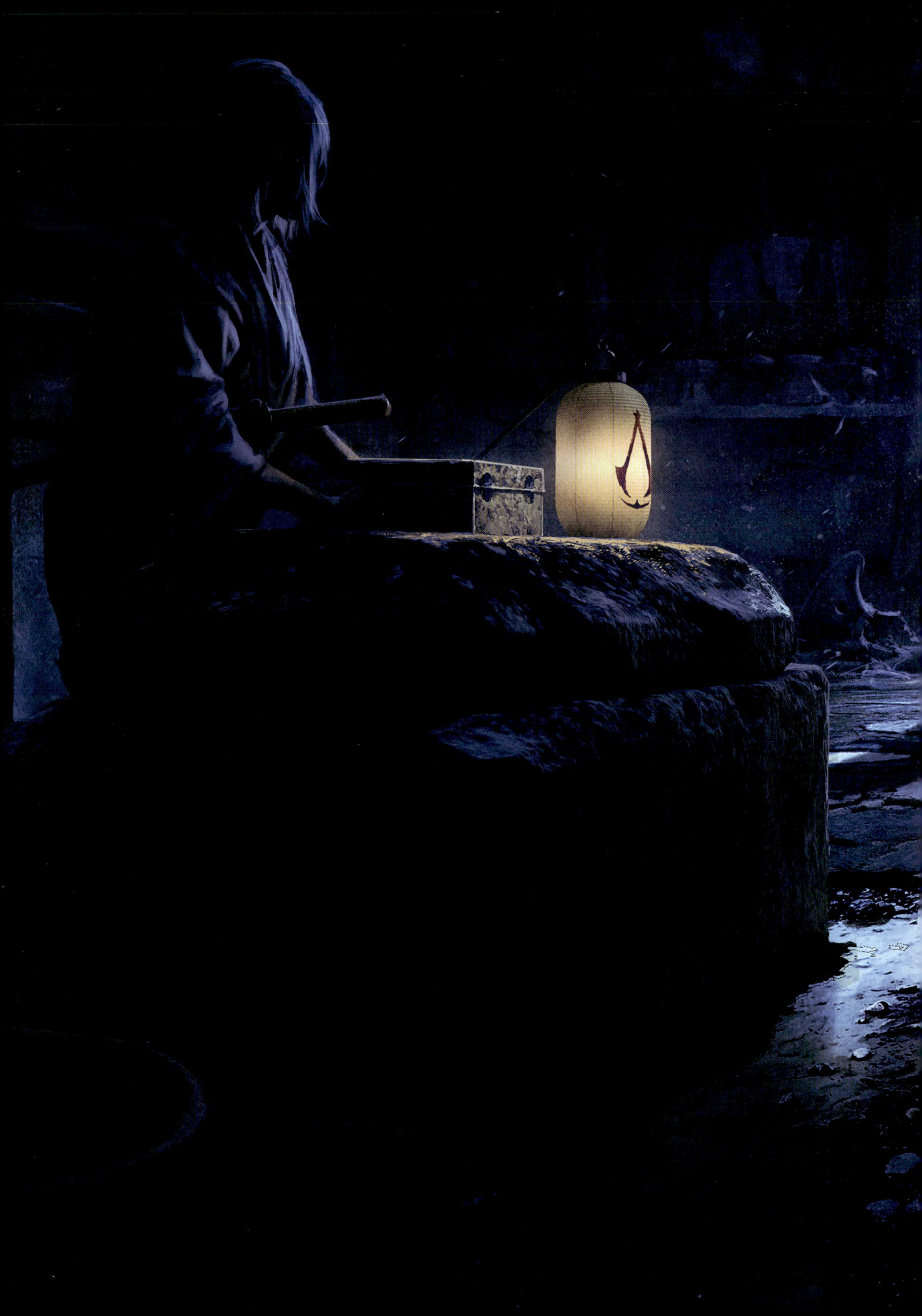

THE ART OF ASSASSIN'S CREED® SHADOWS

WRITTEN BY

RICK BARBA

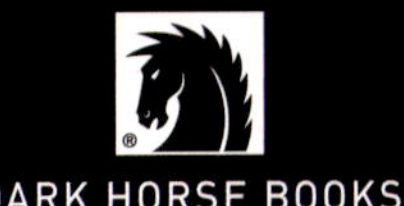

DARK HORSE BOOKS

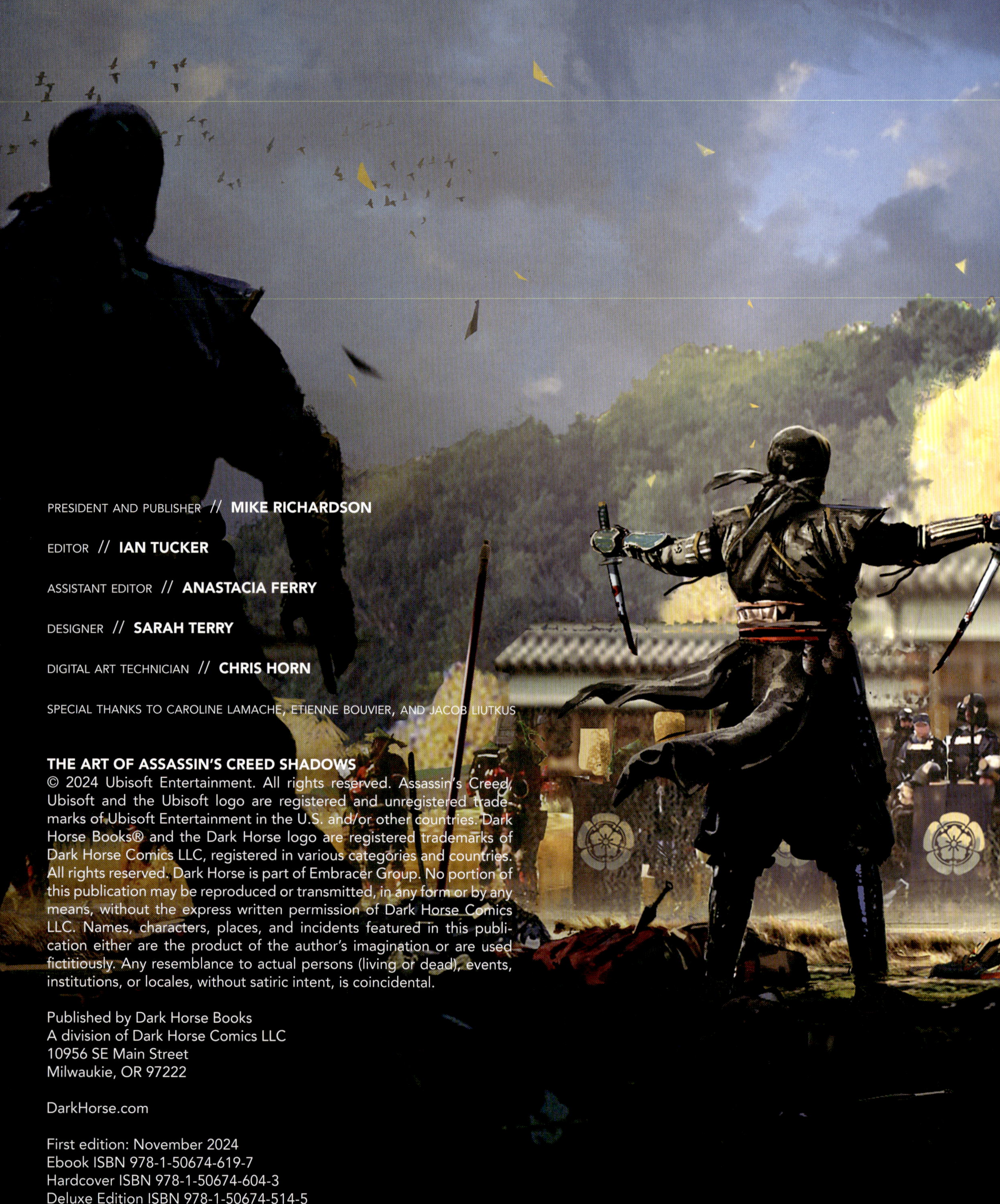

PRESIDENT AND PUBLISHER // **MIKE RICHARDSON**

EDITOR // **IAN TUCKER**

ASSISTANT EDITOR // **ANASTACIA FERRY**

DESIGNER // **SARAH TERRY**

DIGITAL ART TECHNICIAN // **CHRIS HORN**

SPECIAL THANKS TO CAROLINE LAMACHE, ETIENNE BOUVIER, AND JACOB LIUTKUS

THE ART OF ASSASSIN'S CREED SHADOWS

Published by Dark Horse Books
A division of Dark Horse Comics LLC
10956 SE Main Street
Milwaukie, OR 97222

DarkHorse.com

First edition: November 2024
Ebook ISBN 978-1-50674-619-7
Hardcover ISBN 978-1-50674-604-3
Deluxe Edition ISBN 978-1-50674-514-5

10 9 8 7 6 5 4 3 2 1
Printed in China

MIX
Paper | Supporting responsible forestry
FSC® C189328

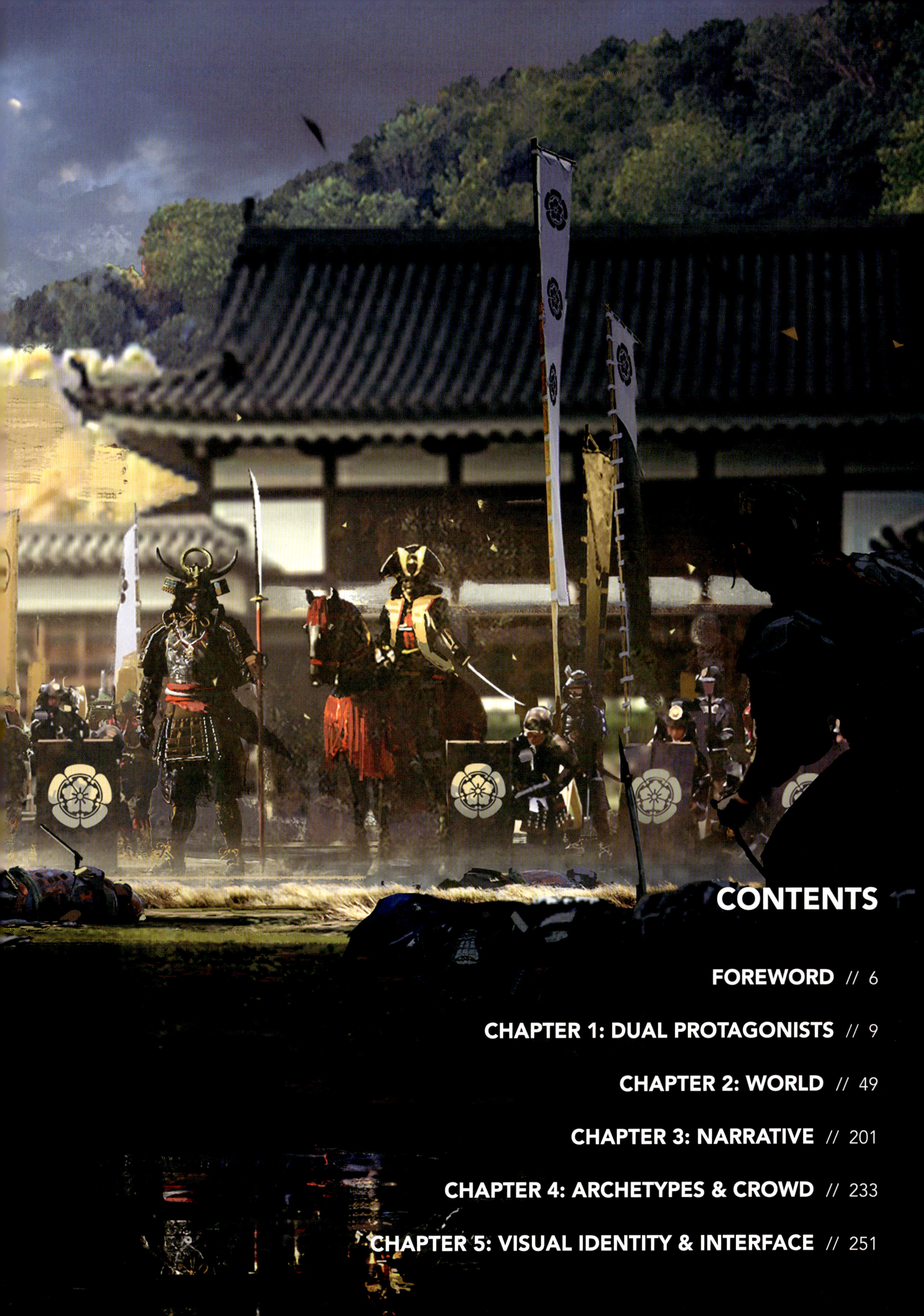

CONTENTS

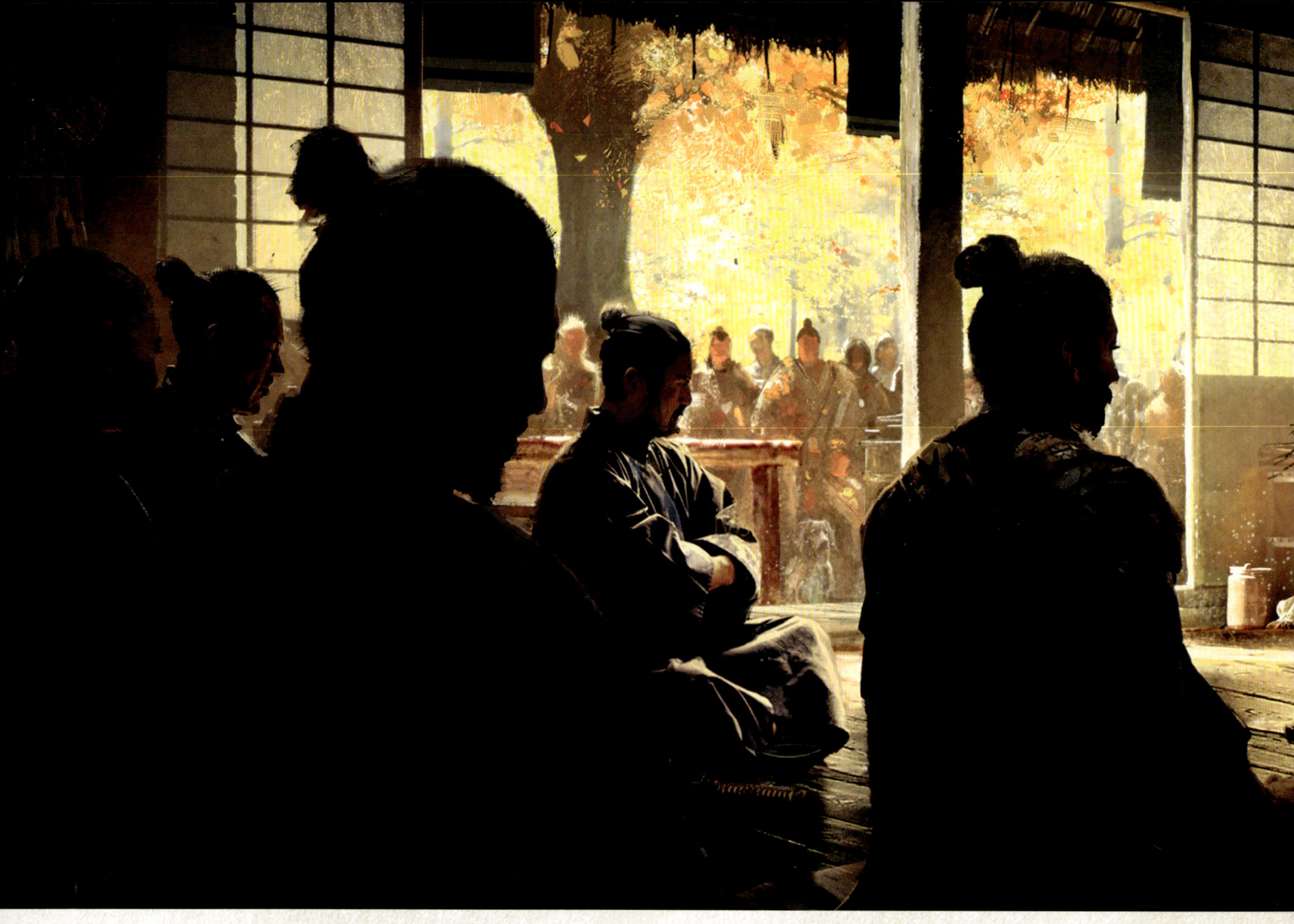

MARKING A FIRST in the *Assassin's Creed* series, we are thrilled to present *Assassin's Creed Shadows*, unfolding in an era our players have been keenly anticipating: feudal Japan!

The game takes place during the unification of Japan in the late sixteenth century, more precisely in the Azuchi-Momoyama era, from 1579 to 1584. This is a fascinating period to explore and an occasion to meet legendary historical figures such as Oda Nobunaga, Akechi Mitshuhide, Sen no Rikyu, Hattori Hanzo, and many more.

To get the opportunity to create an *Assassin's Creed* game set in Japan was a dream come true for many of us. It gave us a fantastic setting and an incredible fantasy to make an amazing game. However, we were also very aware of the high expectations our players and the gaming community rightfully held.

History has always been the playground of *Assassin's Creed*, and we take great pride in being accurate and true to the historical timeline and culture. For this game we've doubled, if not tripled, the effort to make sure that we had a thorough understanding of the Japanese culture of this time period. We worked with historians, experts, and Ubisoft local team members to ensure our game was respectful of Japanese culture and the historical background.

All our research and a field trip led us to define what kind of world we wanted to create. It became clear to us that we needed to make a postcard of Japan.

Japan is incredibly beautiful. Its diverse landscapes filled with mountain chains and coastlines are stunning. The architecture, urbanism, and harmony with nature are mesmerizing and awe inspiring. Japan is, without a doubt, one of the most beautiful countries and cultures in the world.

In *Assassin's Creed Shadows*, players will explore a dynamic and ever-changing open world, all of which is affected by dynamic seasons and weather systems and is directly impacted by their actions. As we progress from one location to another, we wanted to highlight the diverse themes and distinct moods: From secluded countryside vistas to peaceful shrines to lively and bustling merchant districts and from a dense and mysterious forest to the height of iconic castle towns, feudal Japan offers a vast variety of environments and landmarks.

The game introduces a novel dual-protagonist system, featuring Naoe, an adept *shinobi* Assassin from Iga, and

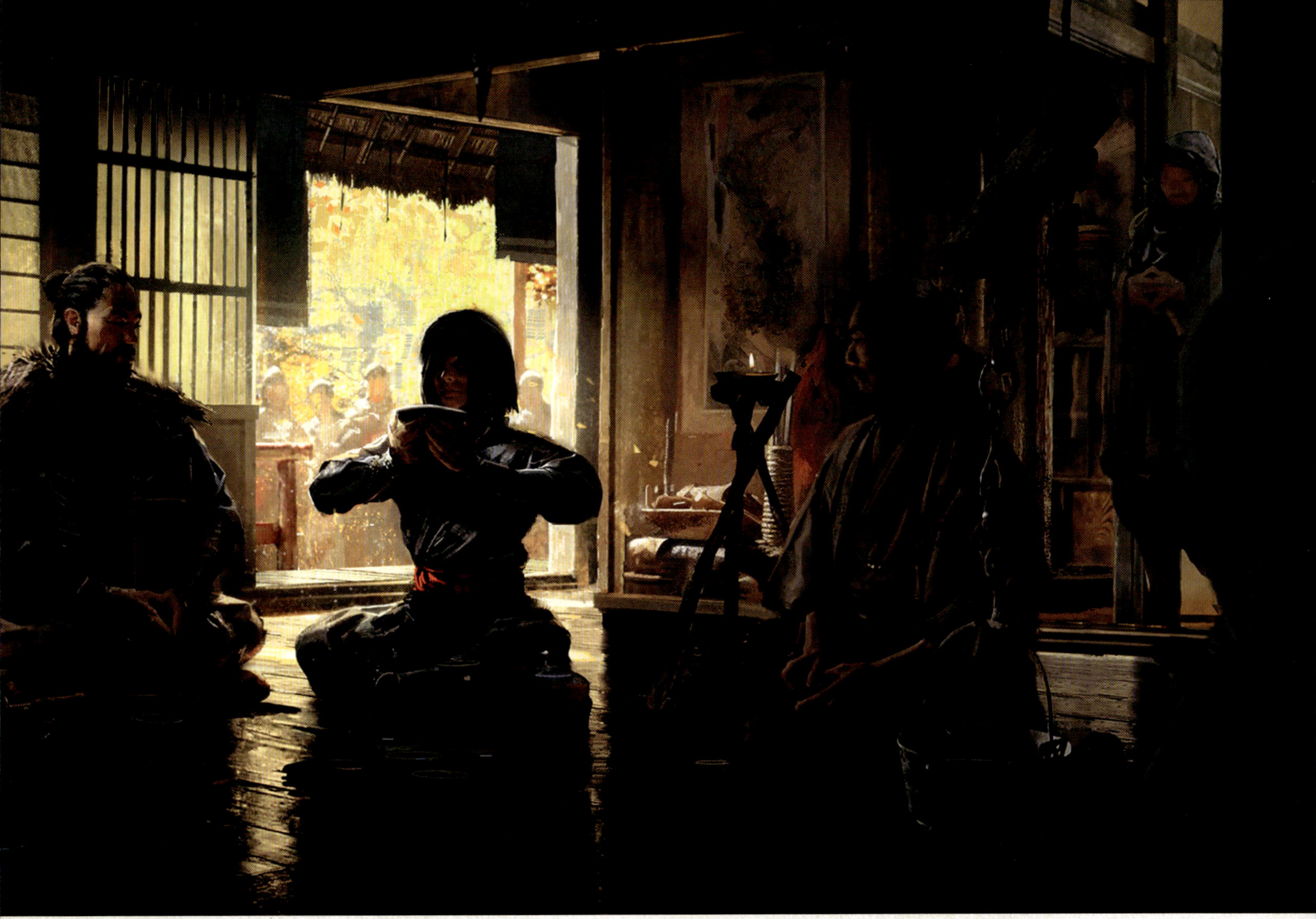

Yasuke, the powerful African samurai of historical legend. Naoe is an agile, stealth-focused *shinobi*, who will use noise, light, and shadows to evade detection as enemies respond to their changing surroundings. Yasuke is a charismatic combat-oriented samurai, striking his foes with brutal precision. He was the first African ever seen by the great daimyo Oda Nobunaga, who made him a samurai and brought him into his service. As a newcomer, Yasuke brings an interesting and complementary angle to Naoe's take on feudal Japan.

The making of *Assassin's Creed Shadows* was an incredible adventure filled with challenges. It required a massive collective effort to make it possible and many people had a huge positive impact on its making. I'm taking this opportunity to highlight the exceptional work of Gabriel Tan and Sina Hayati, who enriched and defined the art direction of the game through some of the best environmental concept art that I've seen. Their passionate work greatly contributed to making us all dream about the amazing potential that this game could reach.

Enough writing! Let's let the images speak for themselves! You have now in your hands a sample of the passion and hard work of a group of incredibly talented and devoted game developers.

On behalf of the whole *Assassin's Creed Shadows* team, thank you for your support and for playing our game!

Thierry Dansereau, Art Director

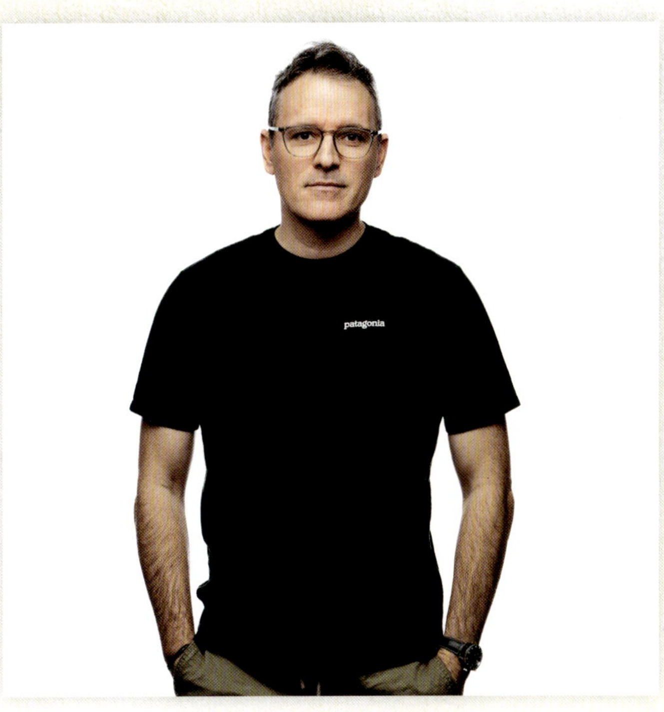

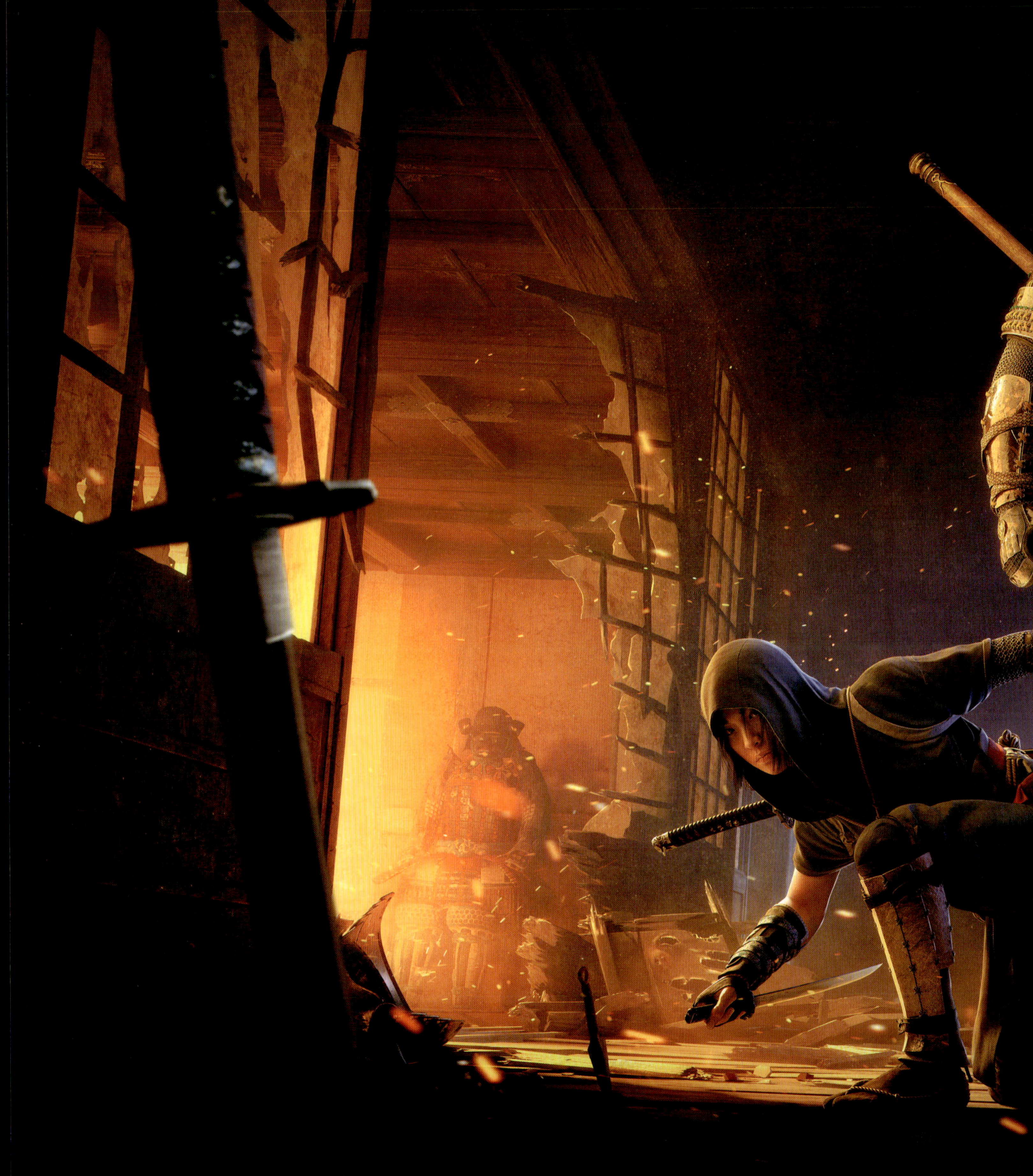

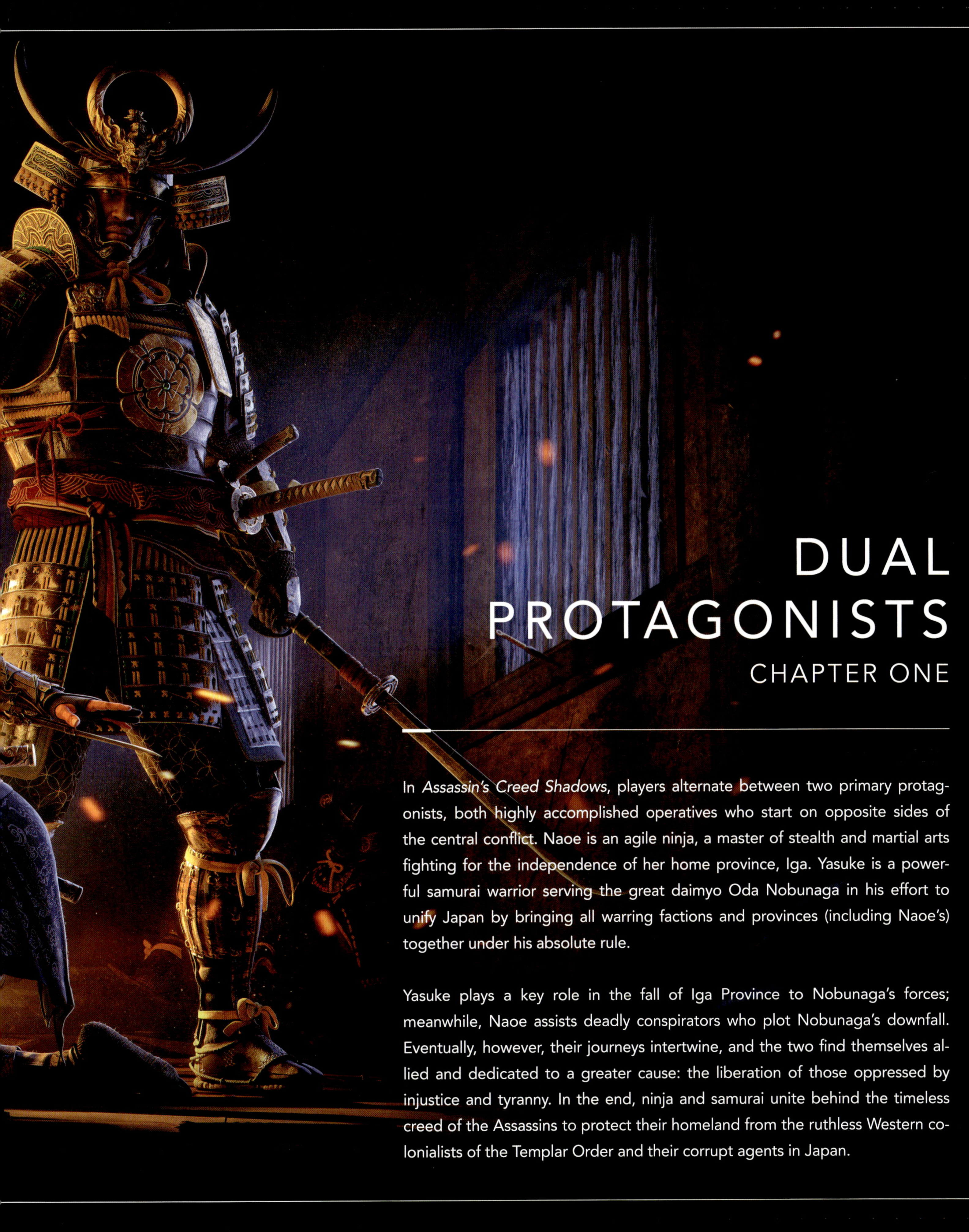

DUAL PROTAGONISTS

CHAPTER ONE

In *Assassin's Creed Shadows*, players alternate between two primary protagonists, both highly accomplished operatives who start on opposite sides of the central conflict. Naoe is an agile ninja, a master of stealth and martial arts fighting for the independence of her home province, Iga. Yasuke is a powerful samurai warrior serving the great daimyo Oda Nobunaga in his effort to unify Japan by bringing all warring factions and provinces (including Naoe's) together under his absolute rule.

Yasuke plays a key role in the fall of Iga Province to Nobunaga's forces; meanwhile, Naoe assists deadly conspirators who plot Nobunaga's downfall. Eventually, however, their journeys intertwine, and the two find themselves allied and dedicated to a greater cause: the liberation of those oppressed by injustice and tyranny. In the end, ninja and samurai unite behind the timeless creed of the Assassins to protect their homeland from the ruthless Western colonialists of the Templar Order and their corrupt agents in Japan.

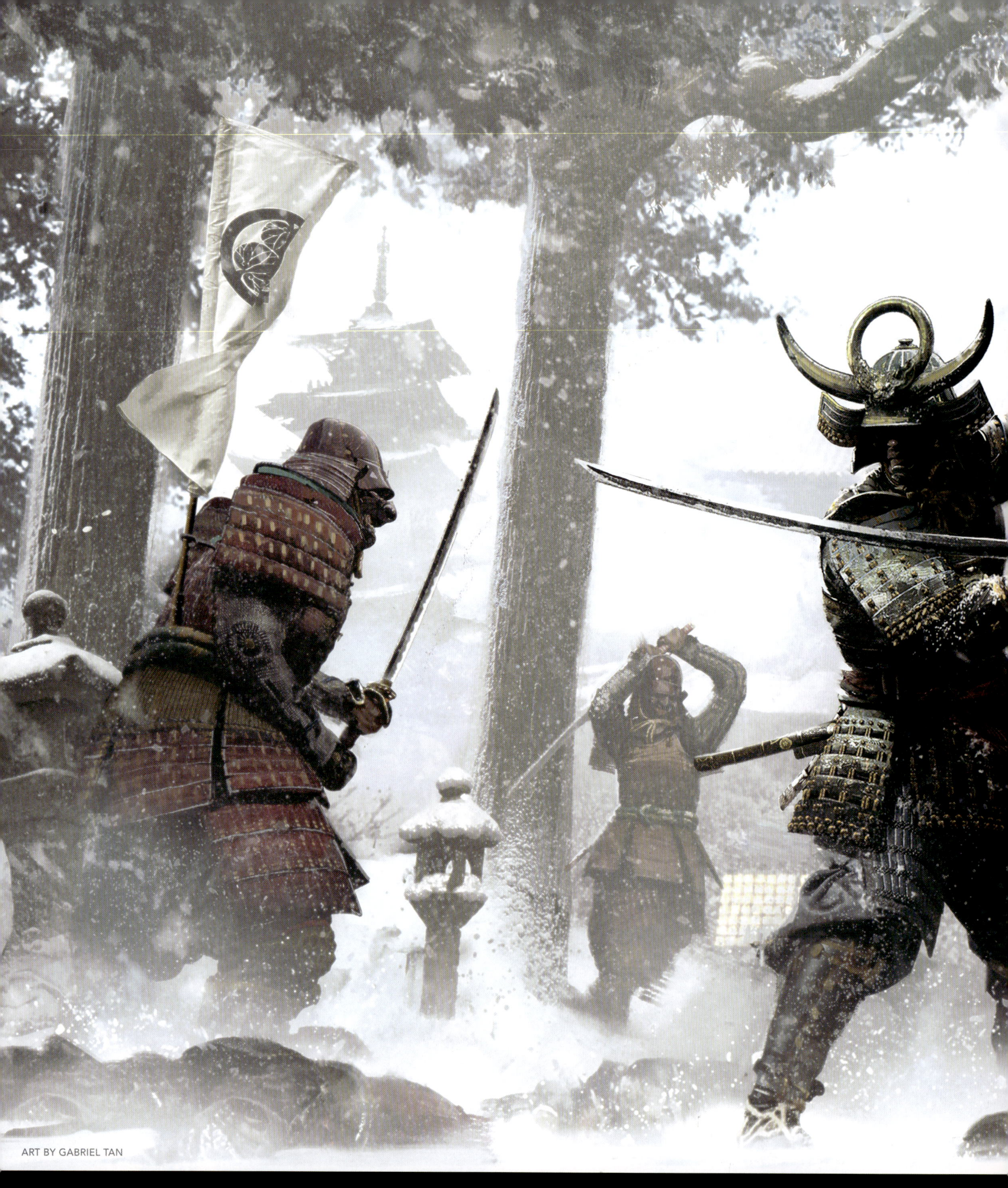

ART BY GABRIEL TAN

POWER AND AGILITY

Yasuke and Naoe are coequal protagonists. Each has their own skill set and their own collection of weapons, outfits, and gear

"Their skills are quite complementary," says *Shadows* lead art director Thierry Dansereau. Naoe can climb almost anything

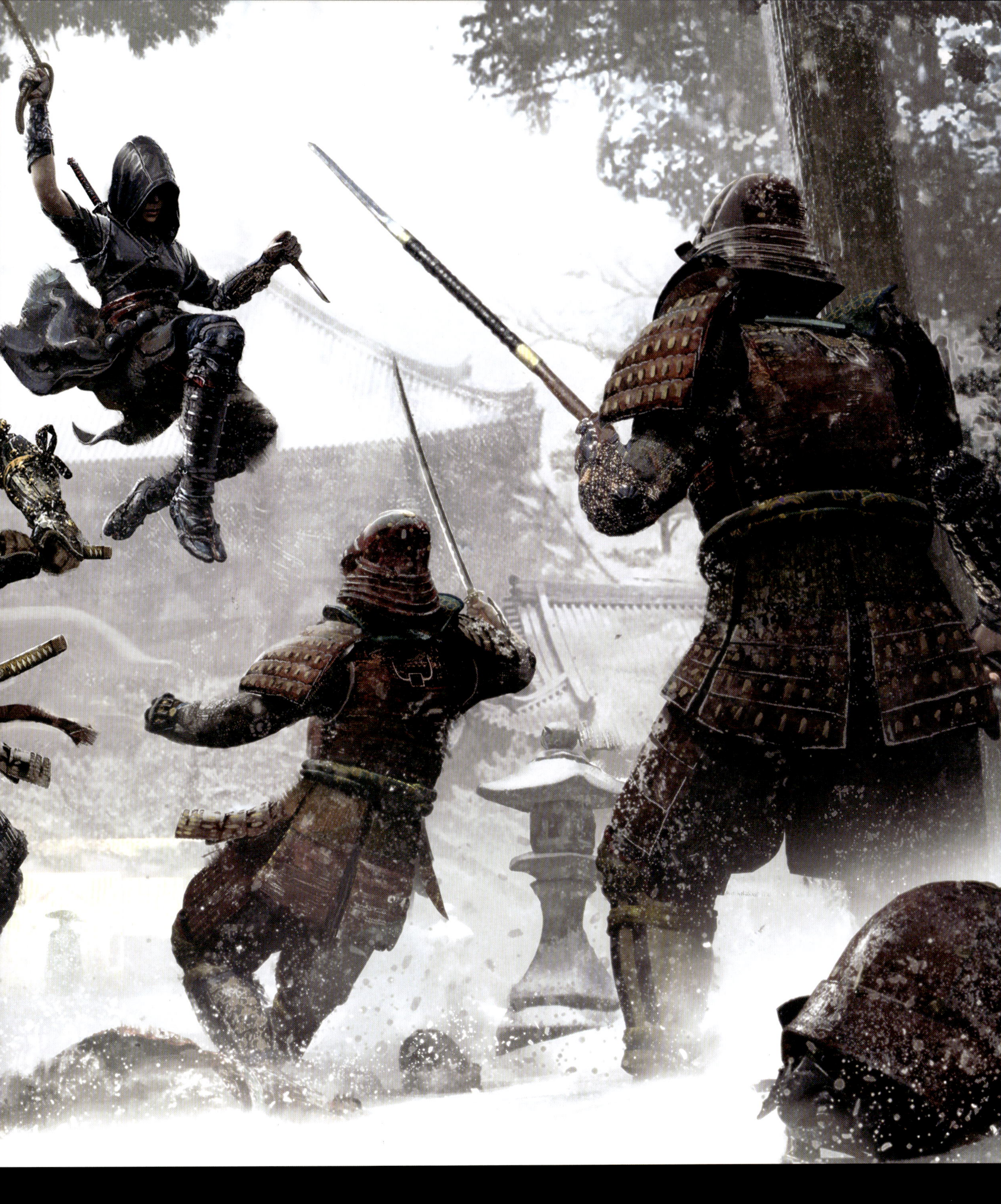

so she finds entry through high portals for covert navigation or silent assassination. Yasuke, on the other hand, may just bash through the front door and hammer foes with his heavy weapons.

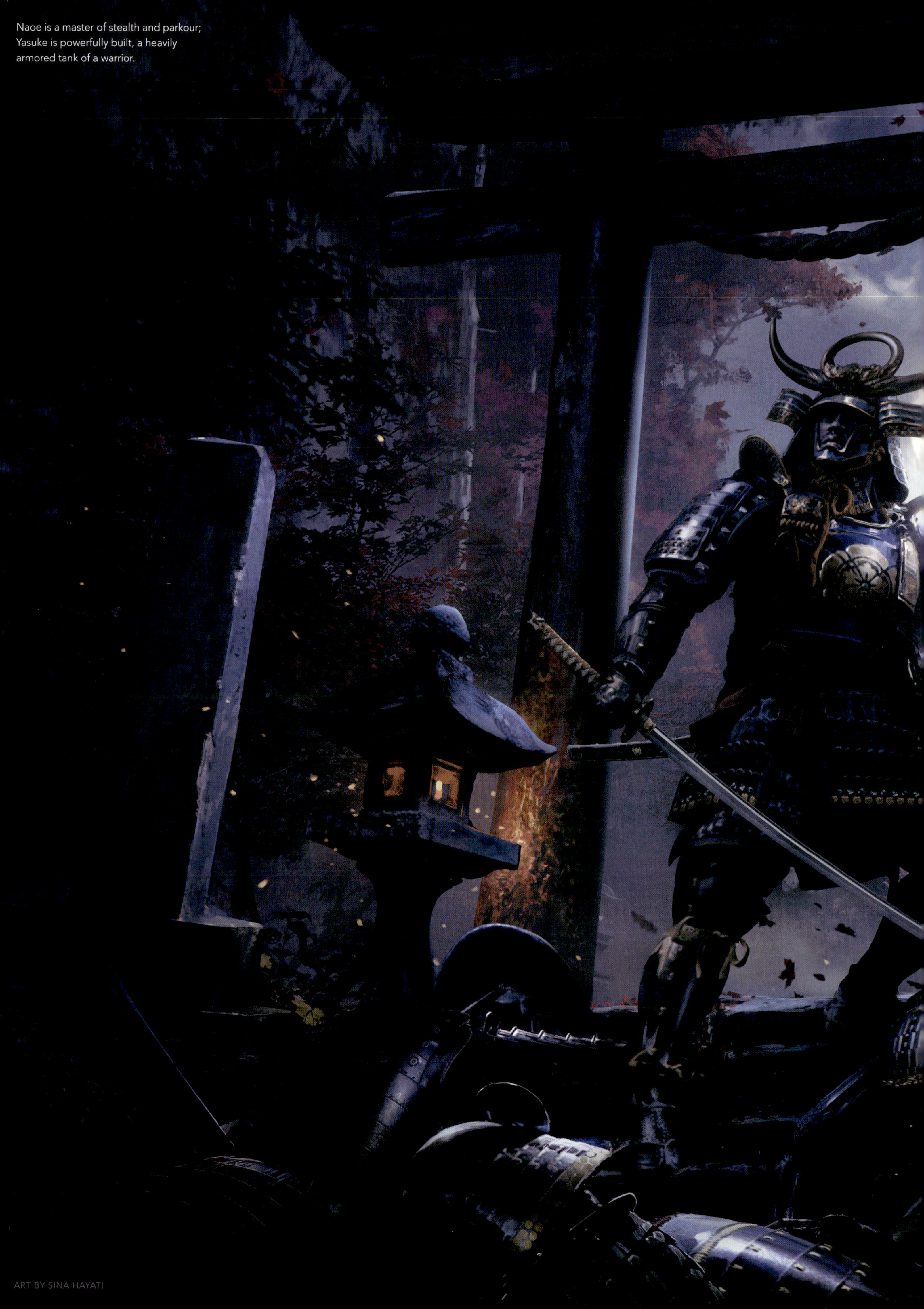

Naoe is a master of stealth and parkour; Yasuke is powerfully built, a heavily armored tank of a warrior.

ART BY SINA HAYATI

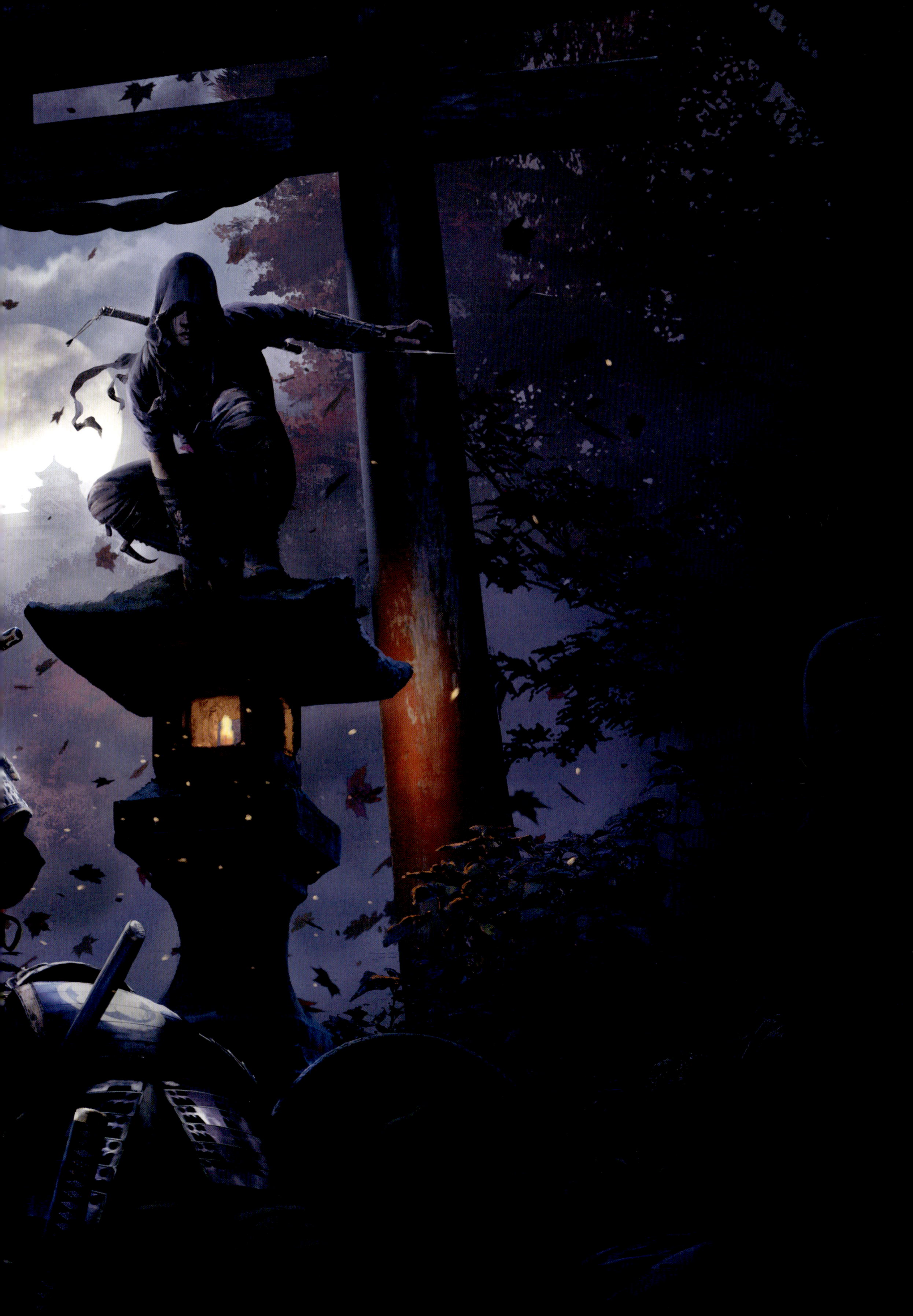

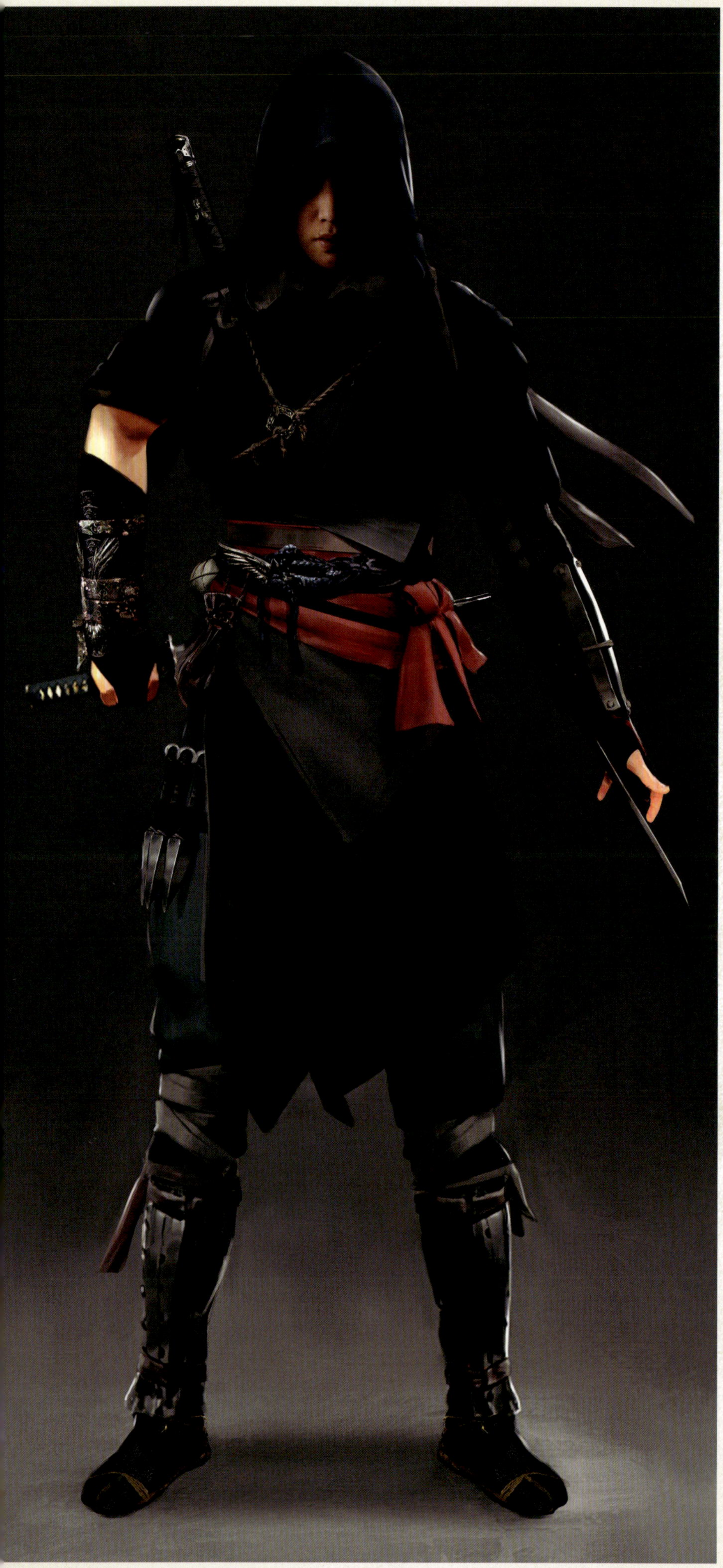

NAOE

Raised in the moutainous Iga Province, Naoe is the daughter of Fujibayashi Nagato, a legendary ninja warrior and a leader of the Iga *ikki*—a military confederation of farmer-warrior clans, masters of stealth and guerrilla warfare known as *shinobi*. Training under her father, Naoe masters many of his peerless skills. But she also inherits his inner fire as he instills core *shinobi* values of valor, compassion, and wisdom.

Naoe's iconic Assassin Shinobi outfit, seen here, grants her a unique assassination perk and a bonus to her ability to hide.

ART BY TYLER RYAN AND FRED RAMBAUD

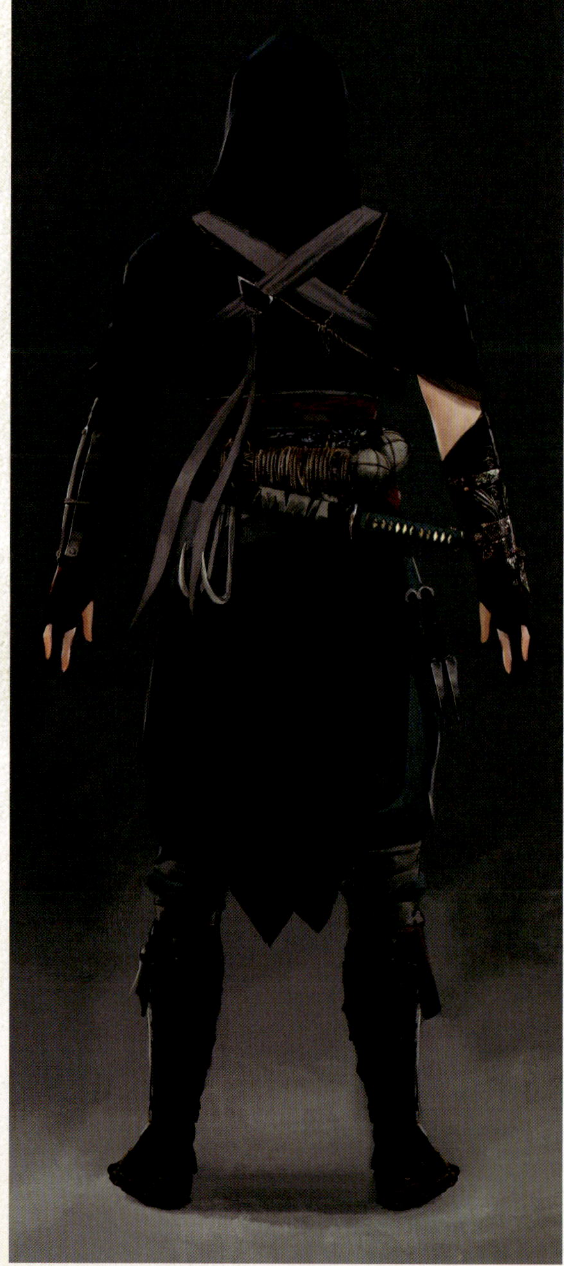

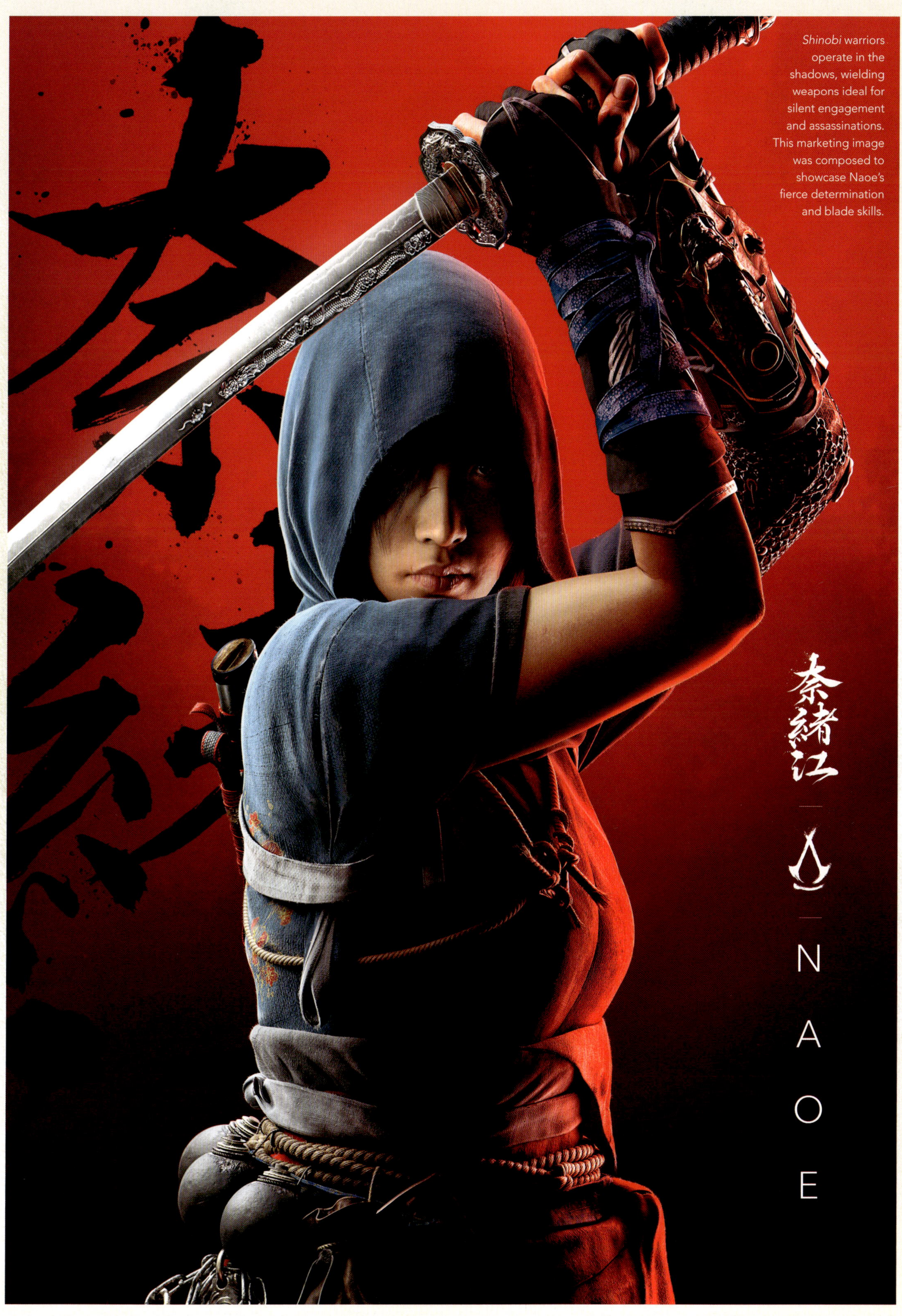

Shinobi warriors operate in the shadows, wielding weapons ideal for silent engagement and assassinations. This marketing image was composed to showcase Naoe's fierce determination and blade skills.

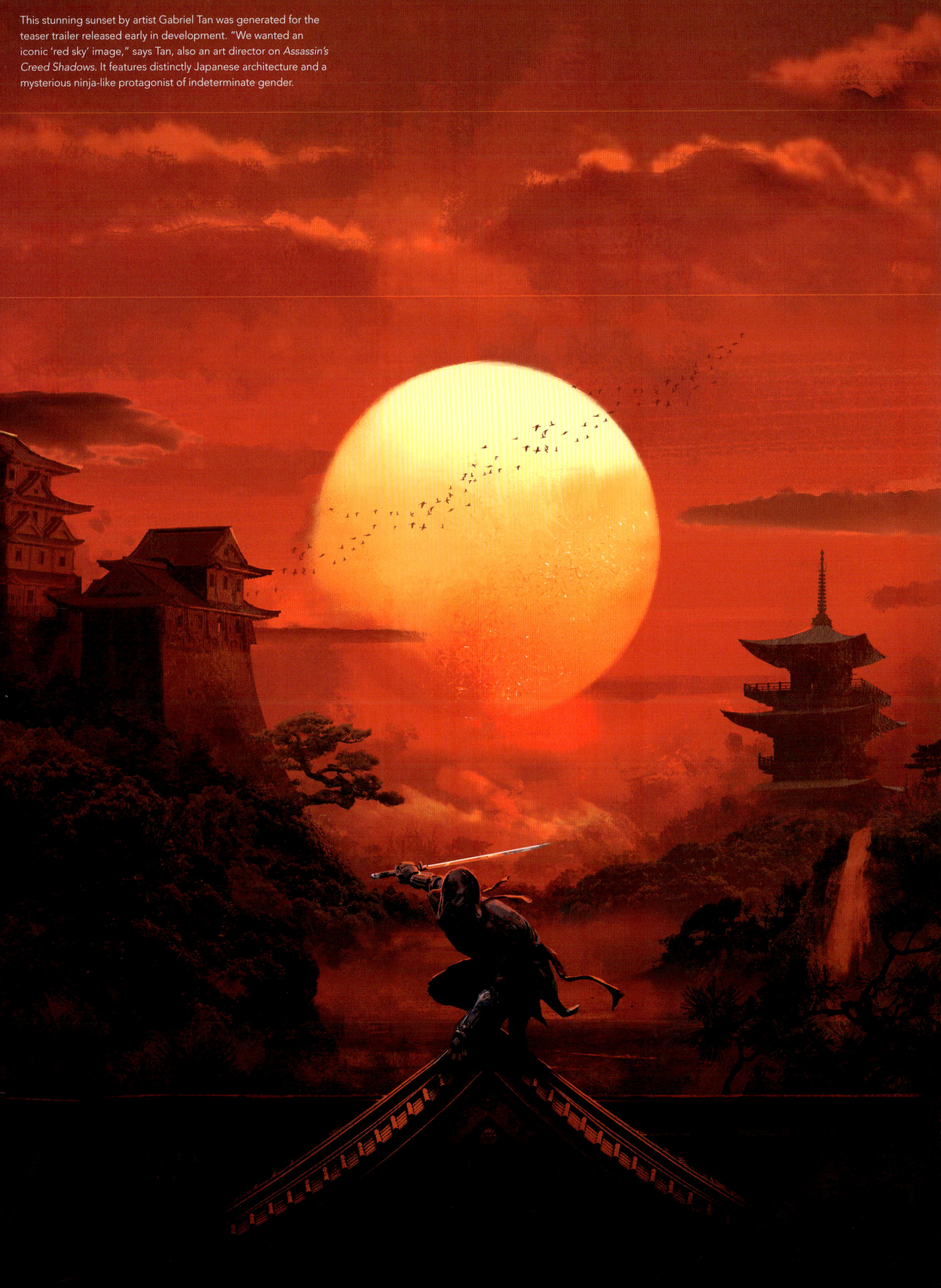

This stunning sunset by artist Gabriel Tan was generated for the teaser trailer released early in development. "We wanted an iconic 'red sky' image," says Tan, also an art director on *Assassin's Creed Shadows*. It features distinctly Japanese architecture and a mysterious ninja-like protagonist of indeterminate gender.

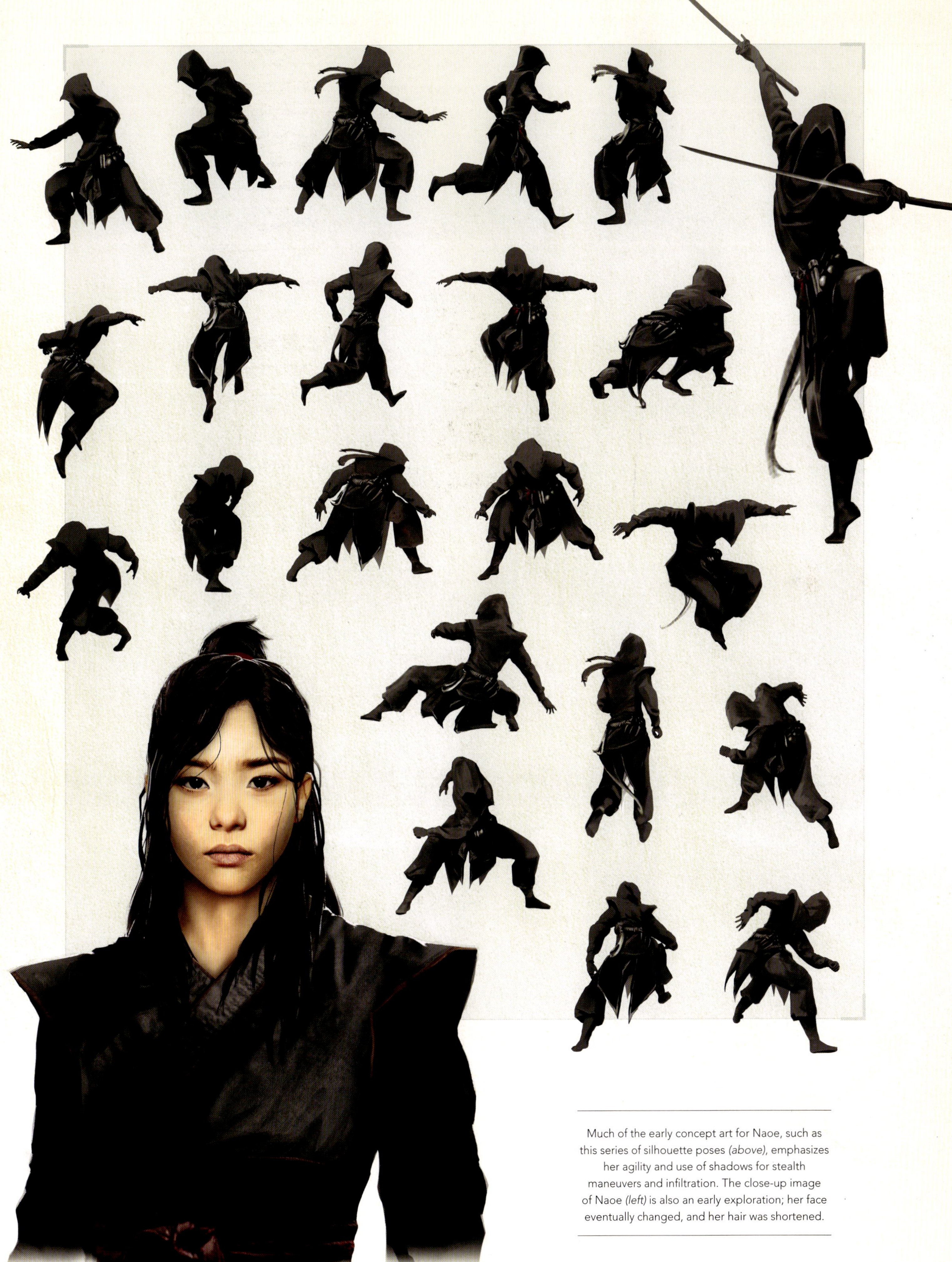

Much of the early concept art for Naoe, such as this series of silhouette poses *(above)*, emphasizes her agility and use of shadows for stealth maneuvers and infiltration. The close-up image of Naoe *(left)* is also an early exploration; her face eventually changed, and her hair was shortened.

ART BY VALERII ORLOV AND KEVIN MACIO

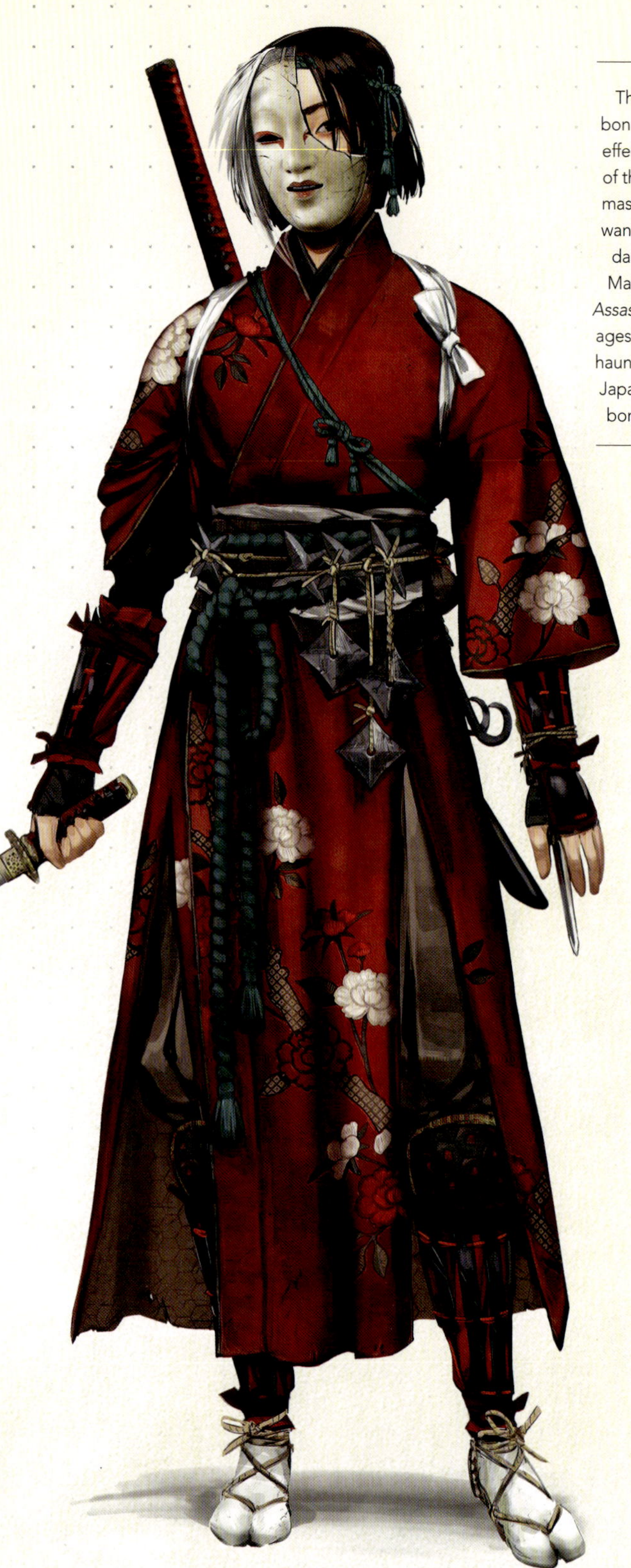

This Noh Artist outfit imparts bonuses to Naoe's bleeding tool effects, and is inspired by a form of theater with bright colors and masks like those seen here. "We wanted a sharp contrast with her dark *shinobi* gear," says Kevin Macio, assistant art director for *Assassin's Creed Shadows*. The images below are versions of Naoe's haunting Onryō outfit—the classic Japanese ghost. This outfit lends bonuses to Naoe's survivability.

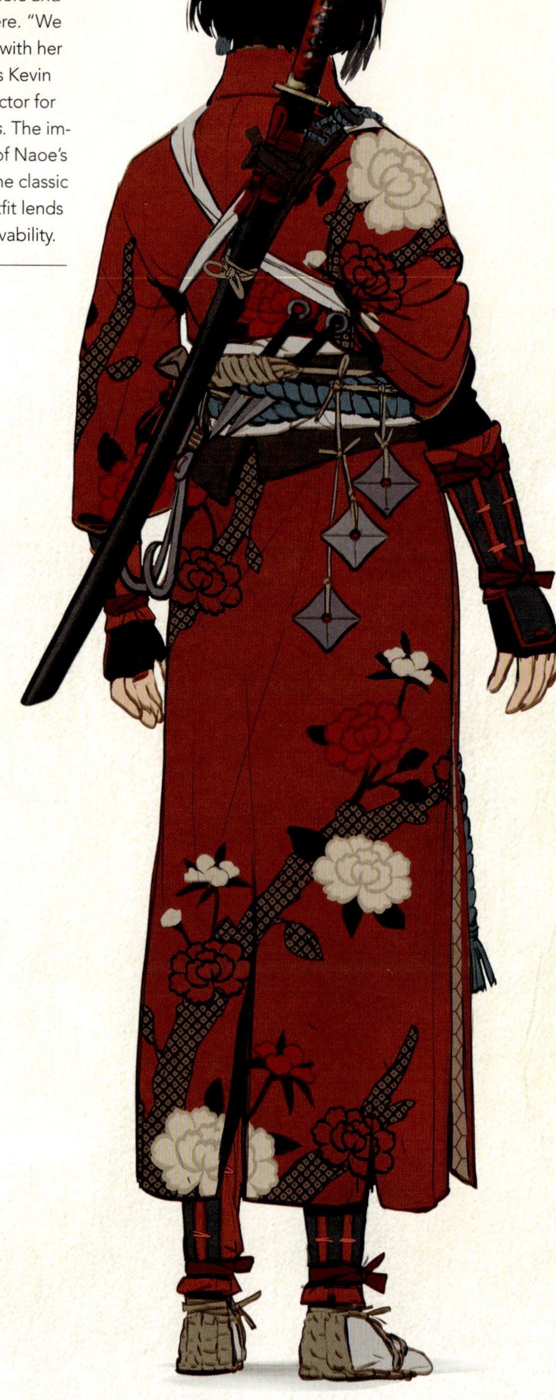

ART BY KONI (AMANDINE GIRARD)

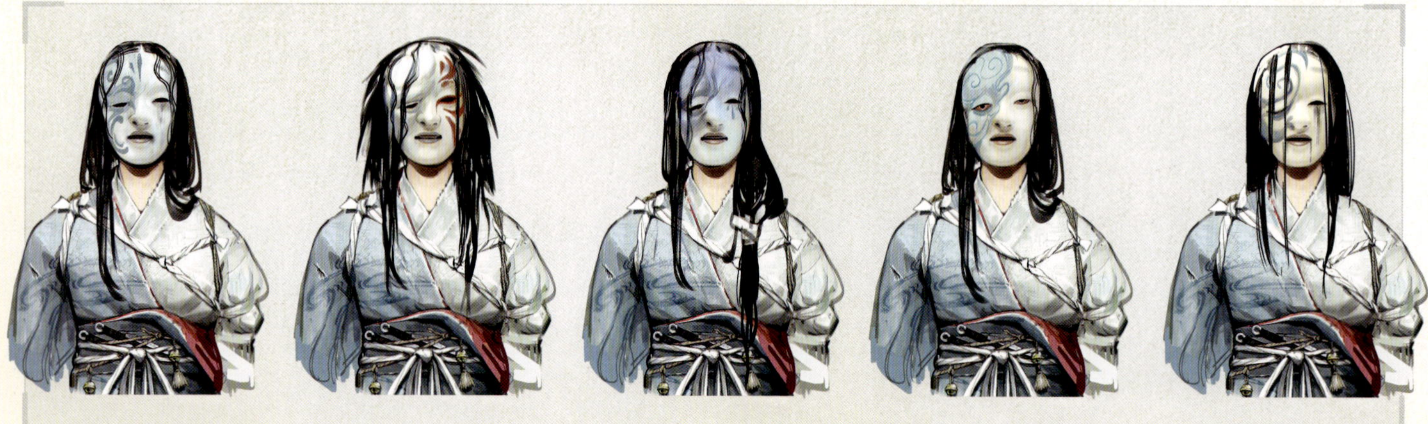

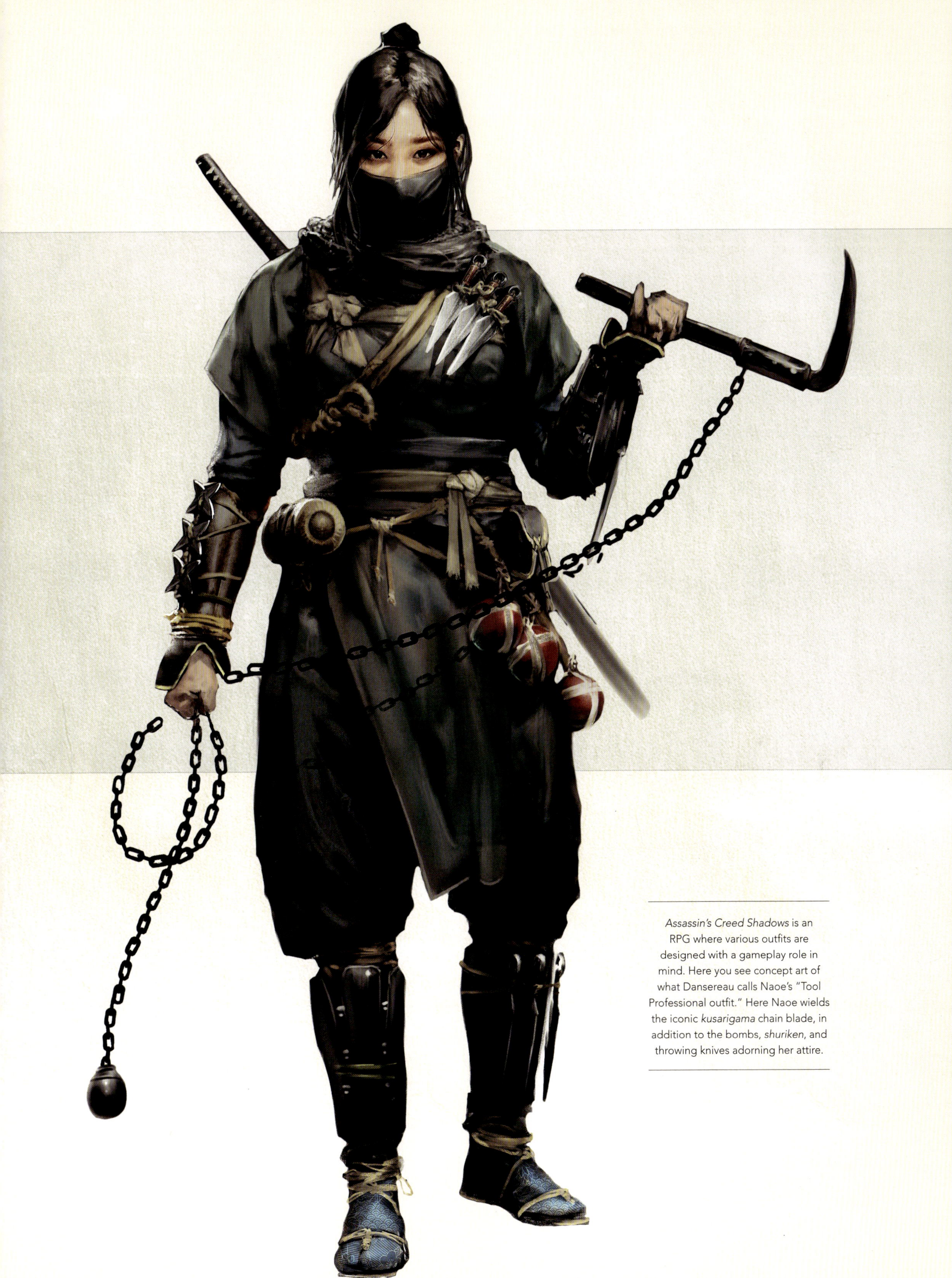

Assassin's Creed Shadows is an RPG where various outfits are designed with a gameplay role in mind. Here you see concept art of what Dansereau calls Naoe's "Tool Professional outfit." Here Naoe wields the iconic *kusarigama* chain blade, in addition to the bombs, *shuriken*, and throwing knives adorning her attire.

ART BY VINCENT GAIGNEUX

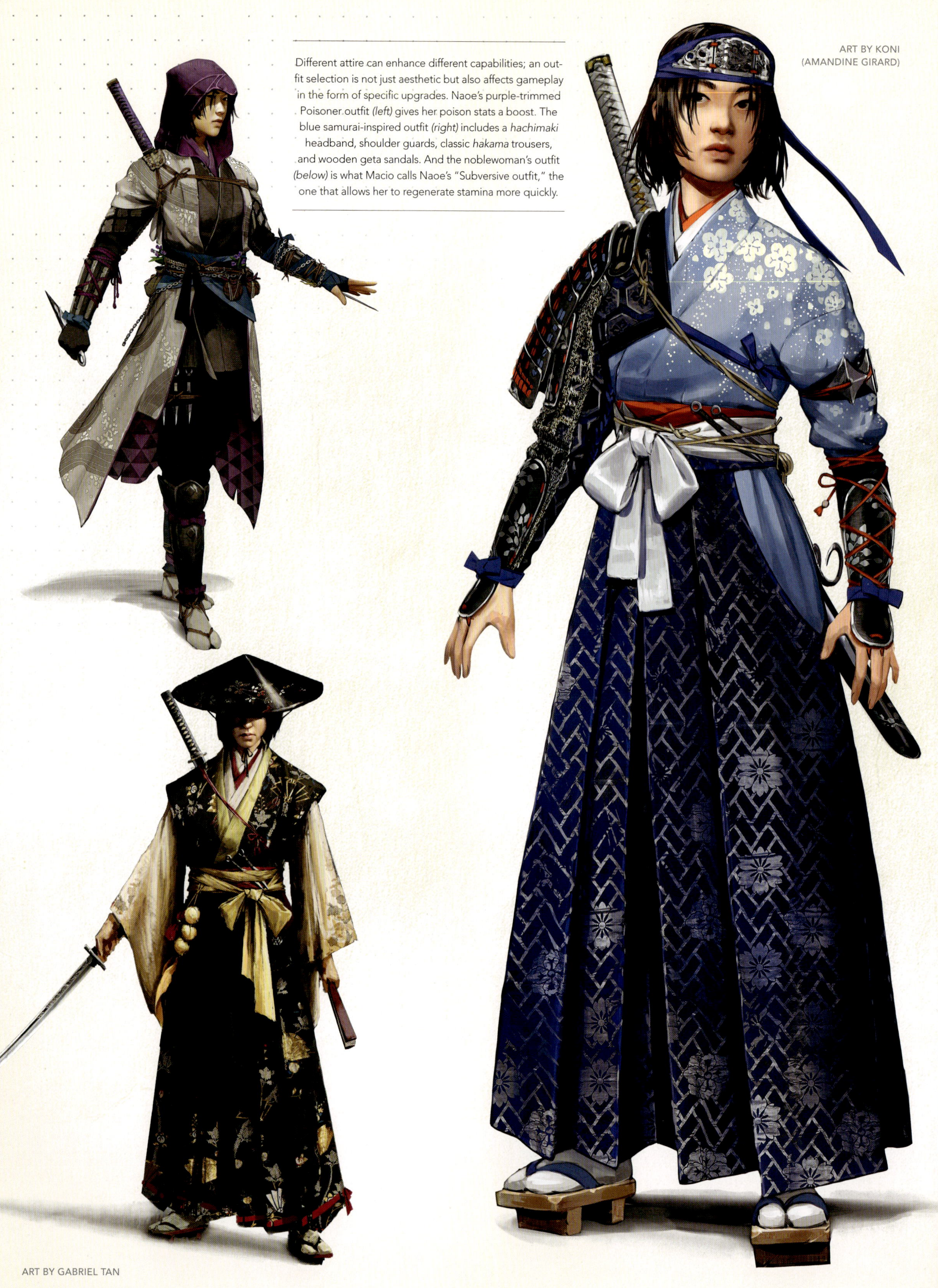

ART BY KONI (AMANDINE GIRARD)

Different attire can enhance different capabilities; an outfit selection is not just aesthetic but also affects gameplay in the form of specific upgrades. Naoe's purple-trimmed Poisoner outfit *(left)* gives her poison stats a boost. The blue samurai-inspired outfit *(right)* includes a *hachimaki* headband, shoulder guards, classic *hakama* trousers, and wooden geta sandals. And the noblewoman's outfit *(below)* is what Macio calls Naoe's "Subversive outfit," the one that allows her to regenerate stamina more quickly.

ART BY GABRIEL TAN

ART BY TYLER RYAN

This concept image is a study of Naoe's initial outfit. "It's a peasant farmer's attire, true to the time period and Naoe's station in life as the game begins," says Macio. As such, it's more subtle and less colorful. The Peasant outfit grants Naoe a combat bonus.

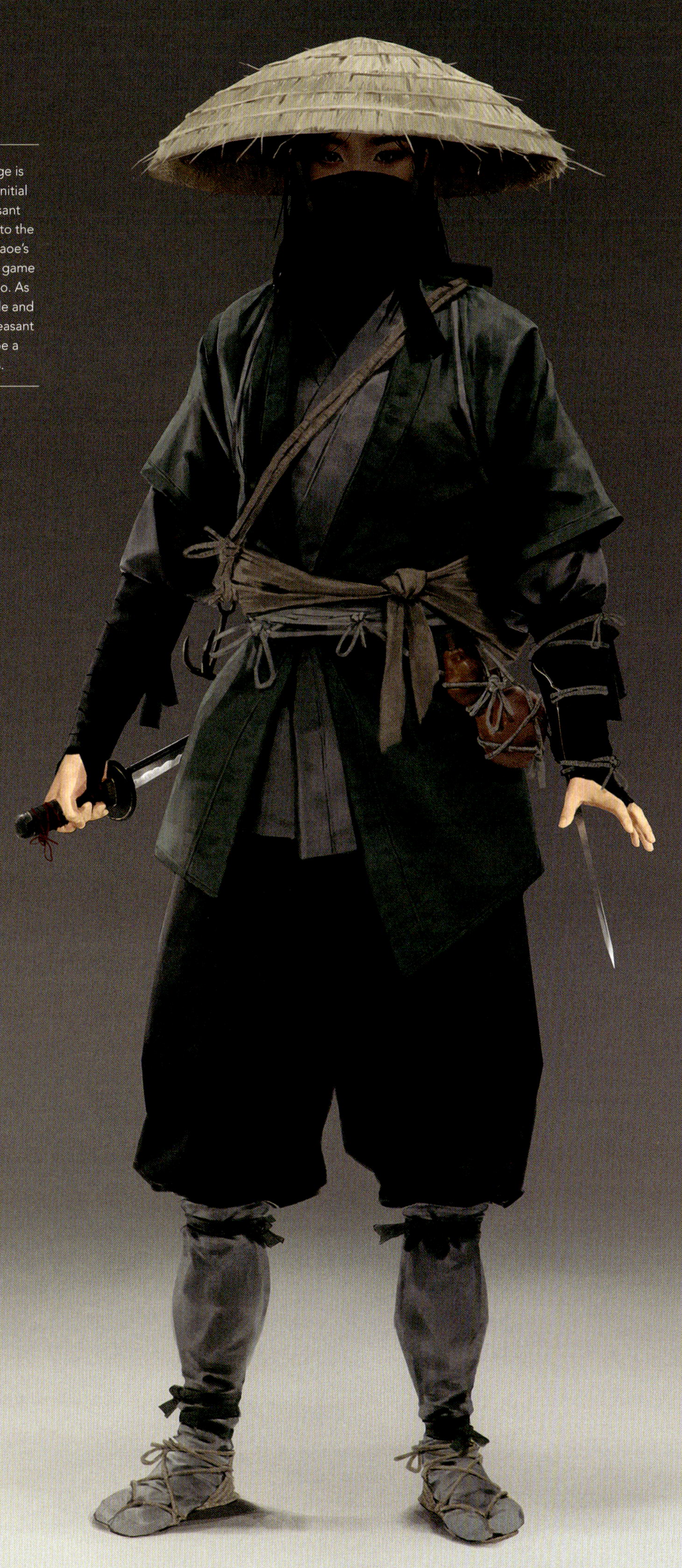

ART BY FRED RAMBAUD

This is Naoe's Shadow Stealth outfit: the classic ninja in a face mask. It features more black than her other attire and adds the traditional *shinobi* hood. "It's about being invisible in the night," Macio says. Naturally, this outfit grants a bonus to Naoe's stealth abilities and enables her to move more quietly.

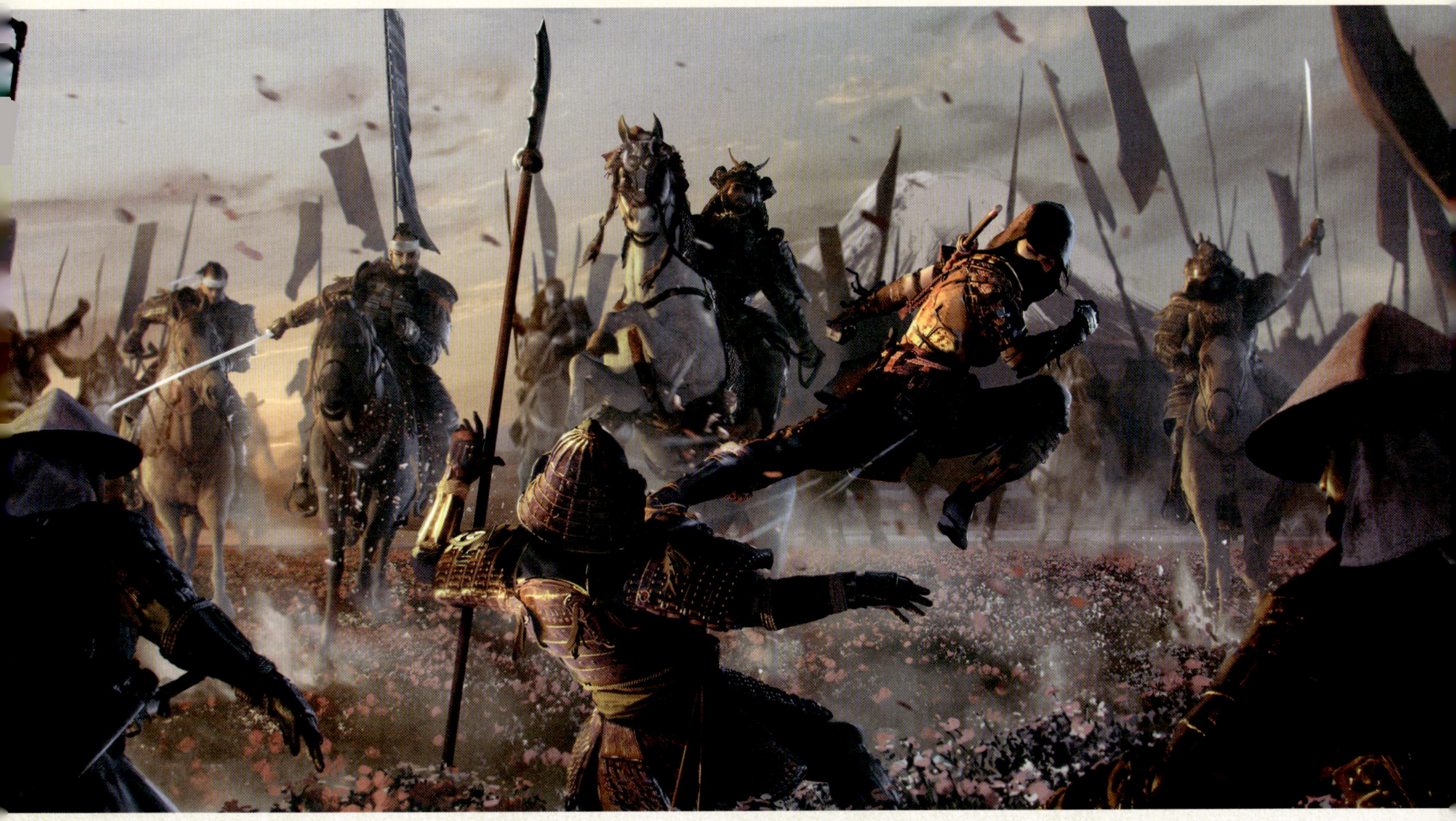

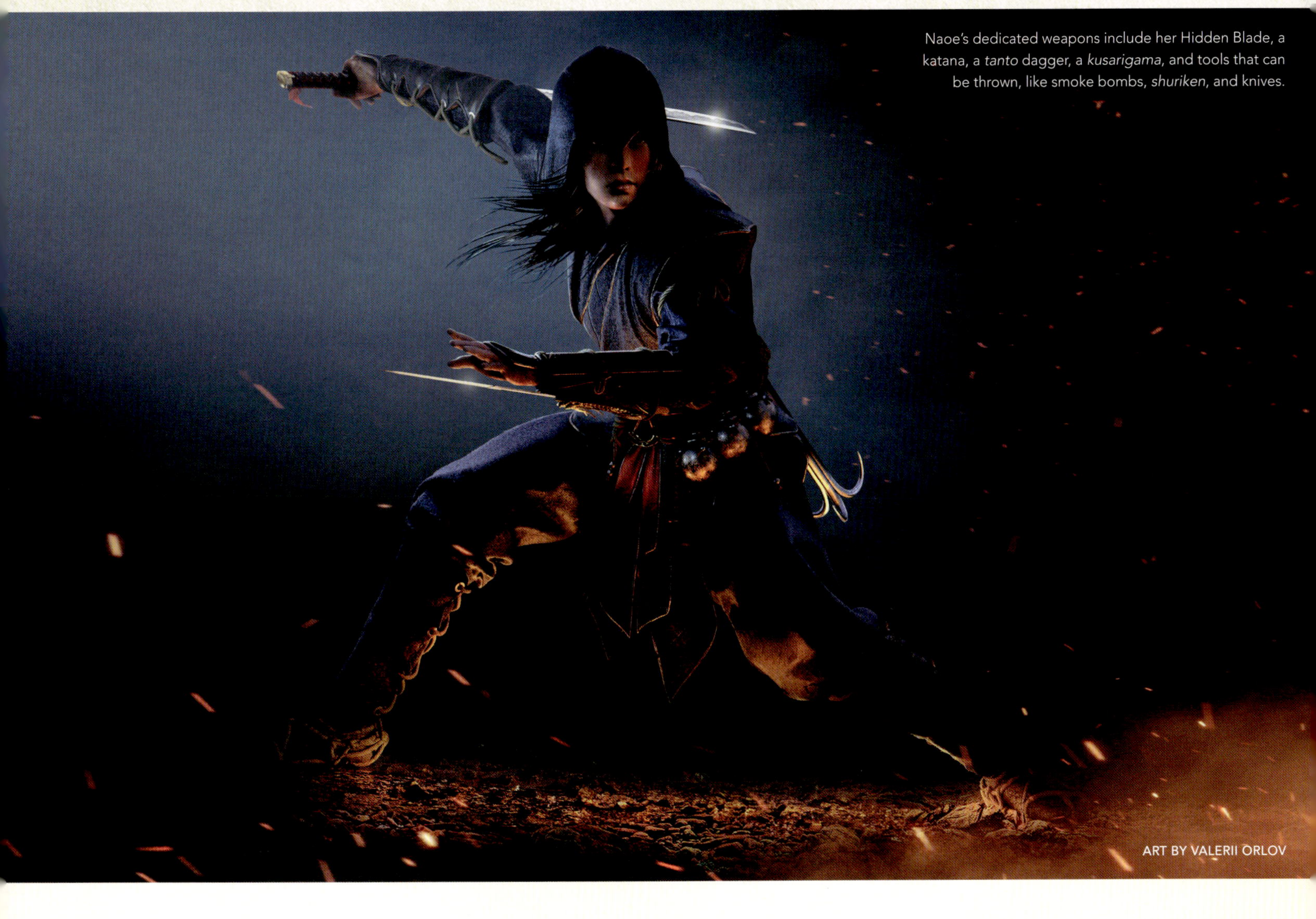

Naoe's dedicated weapons include her Hidden Blade, a katana, a *tanto* dagger, a *kusarigama*, and tools that can be thrown, like smoke bombs, *shuriken*, and knives.

ART BY VALERII ORLOV

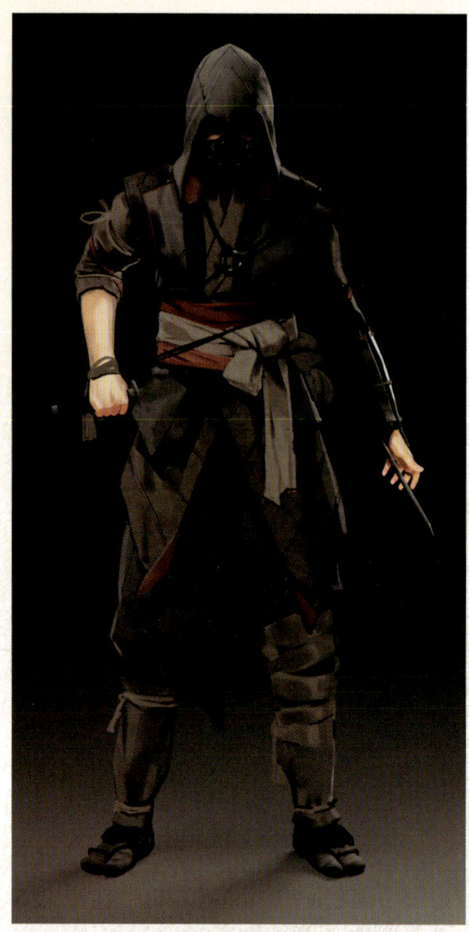

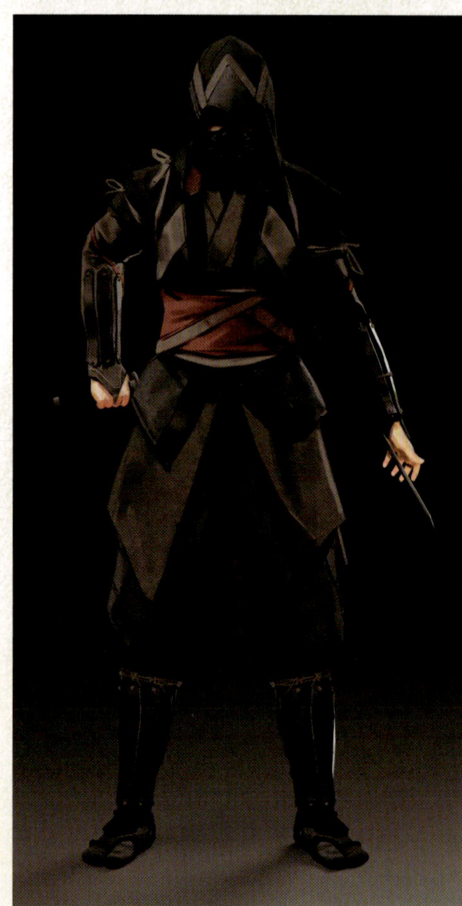

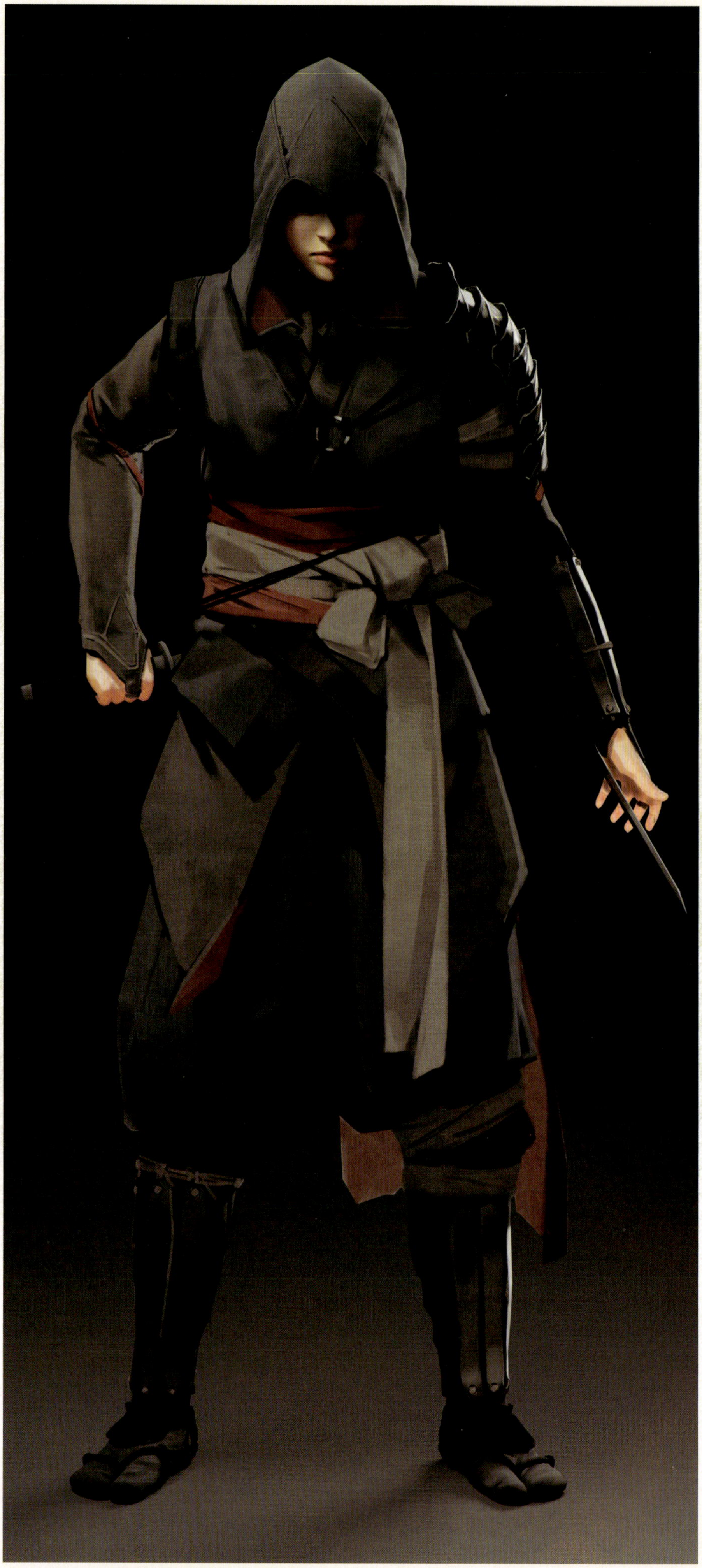

In these early studies, the art team researches ideas for Naoe's iconic outfit—i.e., her standard attire in *Shadows*.

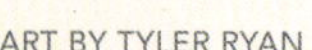

ART BY TYLER RYAN

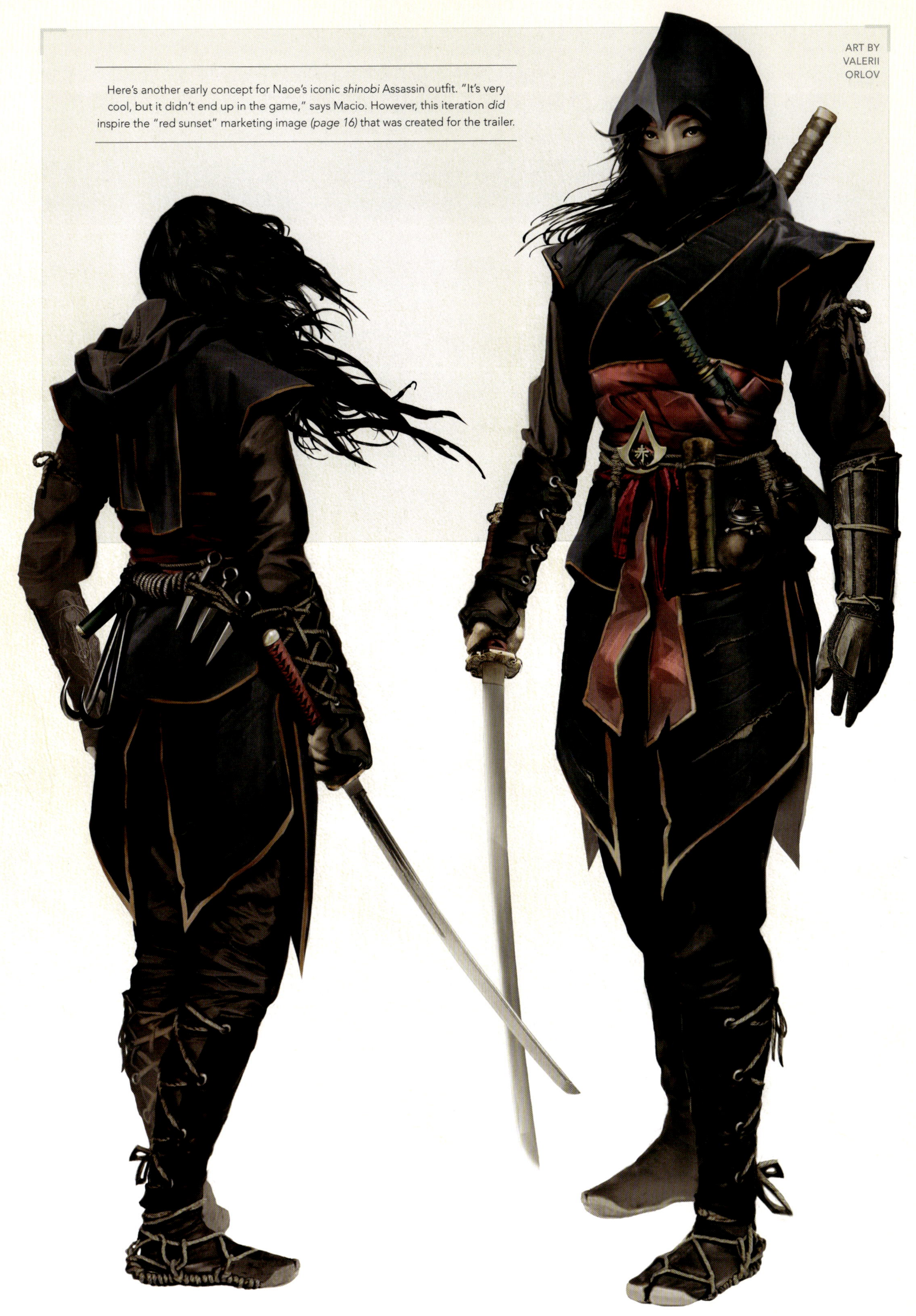

ART BY
VALERII
ORLOV

Here's another early concept for Naoe's iconic *shinobi* Assassin outfit. "It's very cool, but it didn't end up in the game," says Macio. However, this iteration *did* inspire the "red sunset" marketing image *(page 16)* that was created for the trailer.

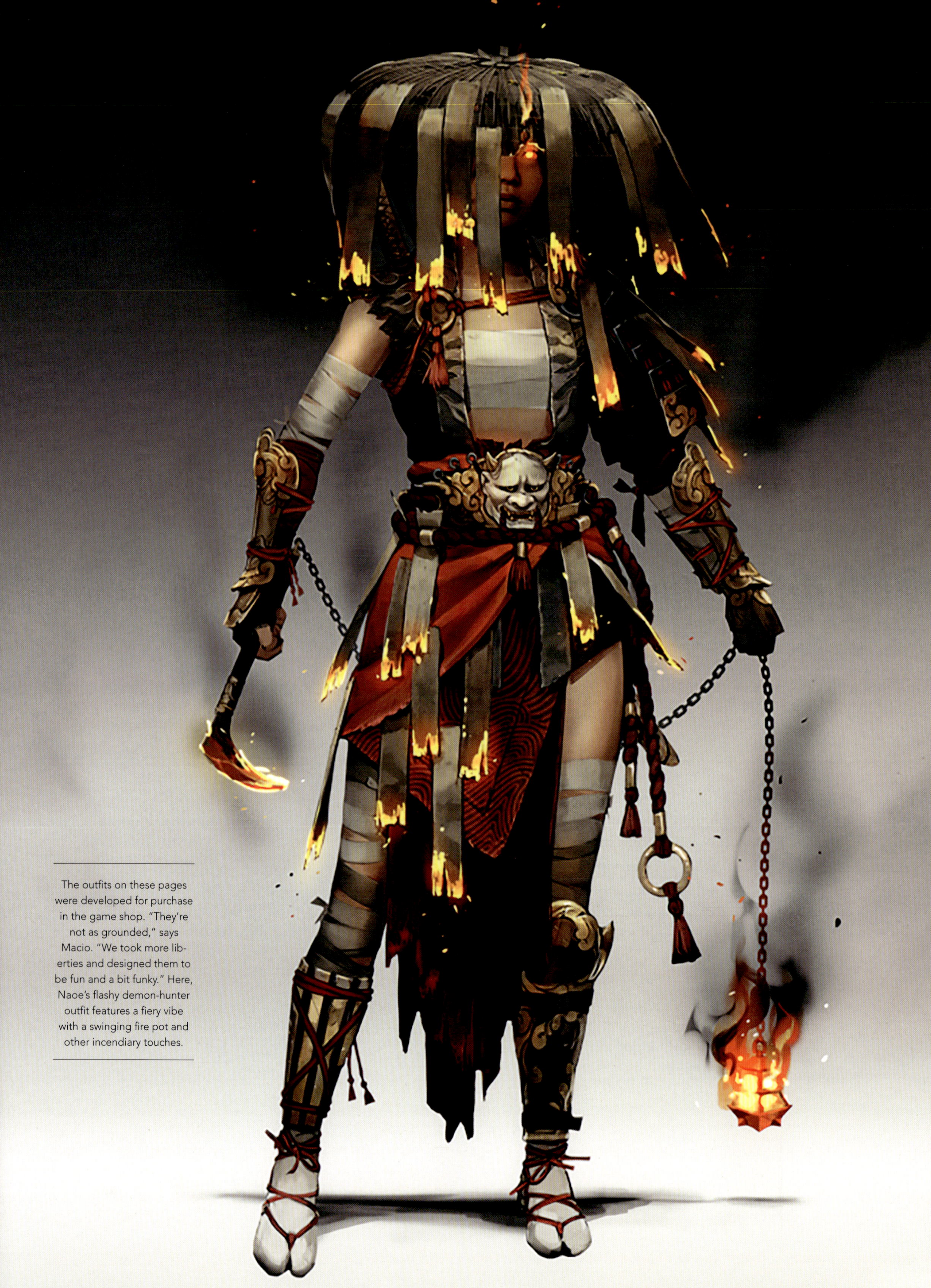

The outfits on these pages were developed for purchase in the game shop. "They're not as grounded," says Macio. "We took more liberties and designed them to be fun and a bit funky." Here, Naoe's flashy demon-hunter outfit features a fiery vibe with a swinging fire pot and other incendiary touches.

ART BY KONI (AMANDINE GIRARD)

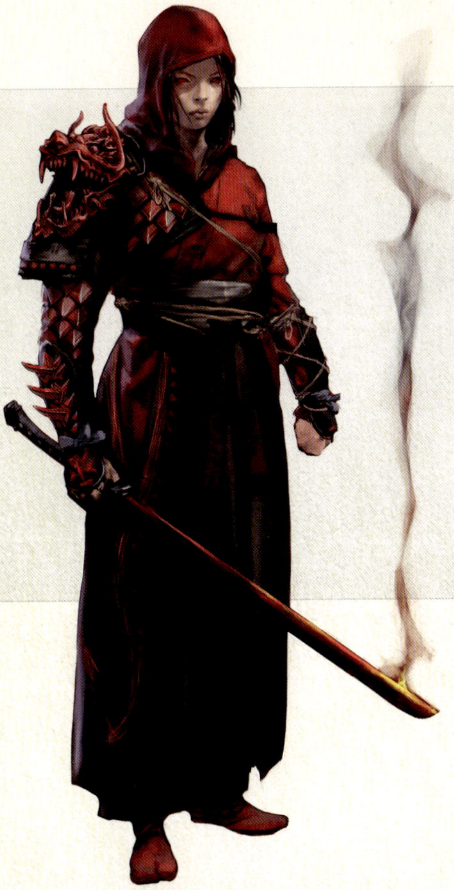

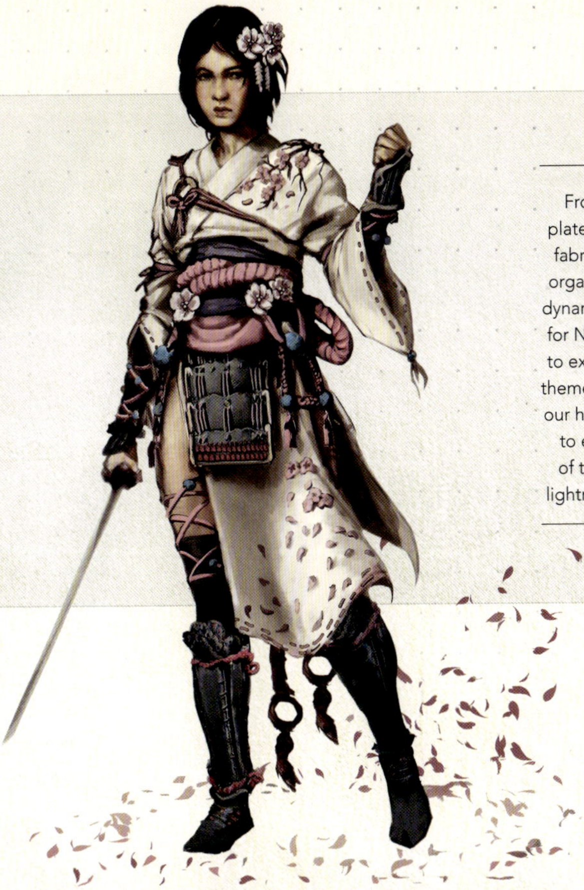

From geometric metal plates for dragon scales to fabrics embroidered with organic patterns and long, dynamic ropes, these outfits for Naoe allowed the team to explore more freely with theme and shape. This gives our heroine the opportunity to embody the strength of the red dragon or the lightness of a *sakura* flower.

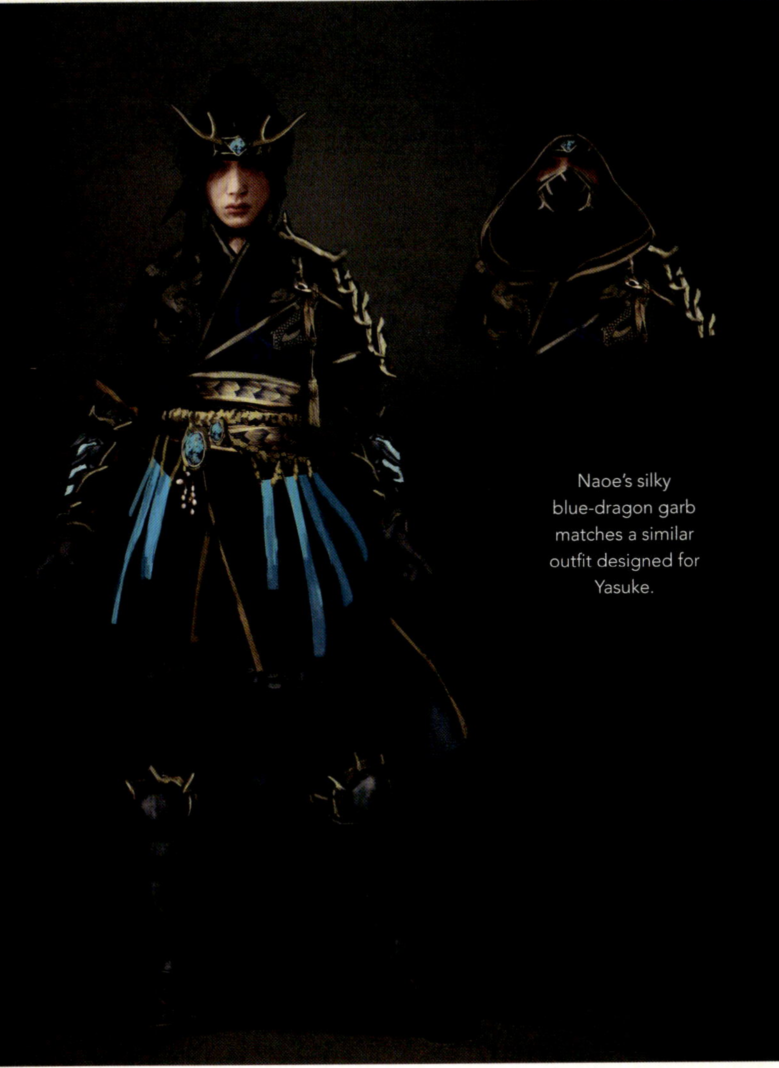

Naoe's silky blue-dragon garb matches a similar outfit designed for Yasuke.

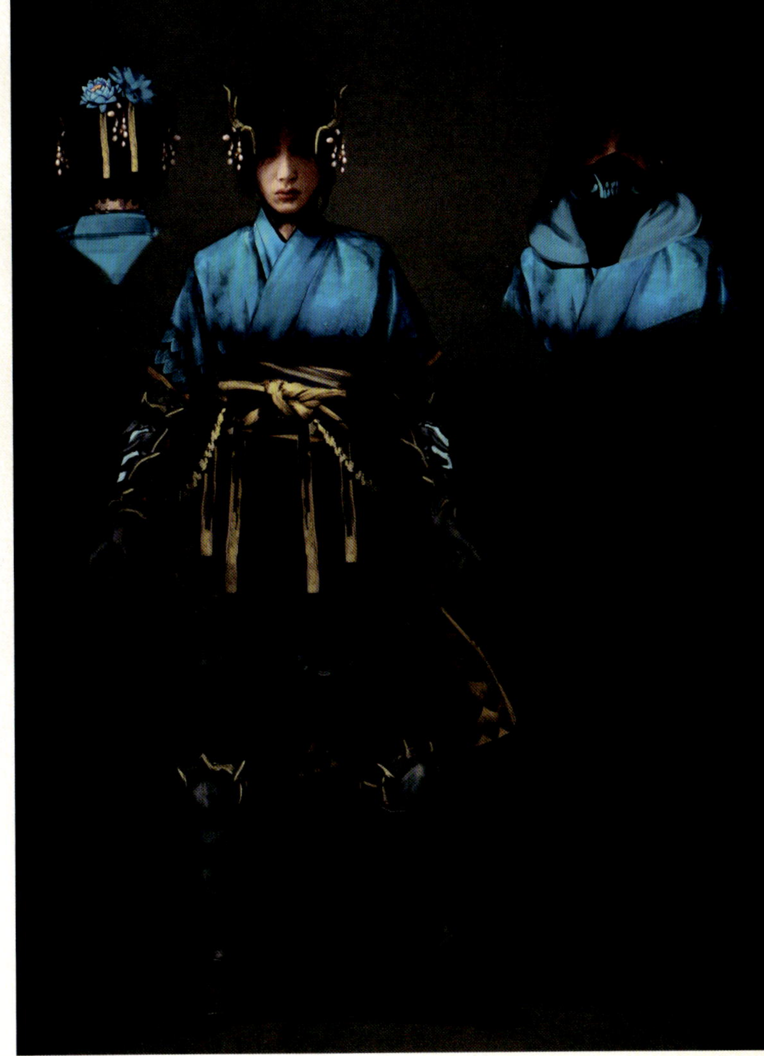

WEAPONS

Naoe uses a combination of classic Japanese weapons and *shinobi* tools. She even uses the famous Assassin's Hidden Blade in direct combat. She has a unique fighting style that combines flips, kicks, and slashes, enabling her to be agile and evasive. Naoe uses a short katana in an unconventional stance to take full advantage of her agility. This is also what allows her to augment her style with kicks and flips. She uses the classic *shinobi* fantasy weapon, the *kusarigama*, which combines ranged attacks from the weighted chain with quick blows from the sickle. The combination of *tanto* and Hidden Blade is the perfect way to land quick blows, evade a returning strike, then quickly counterattack. These different *shinobi* tools are lethally effective for this master of stealth.

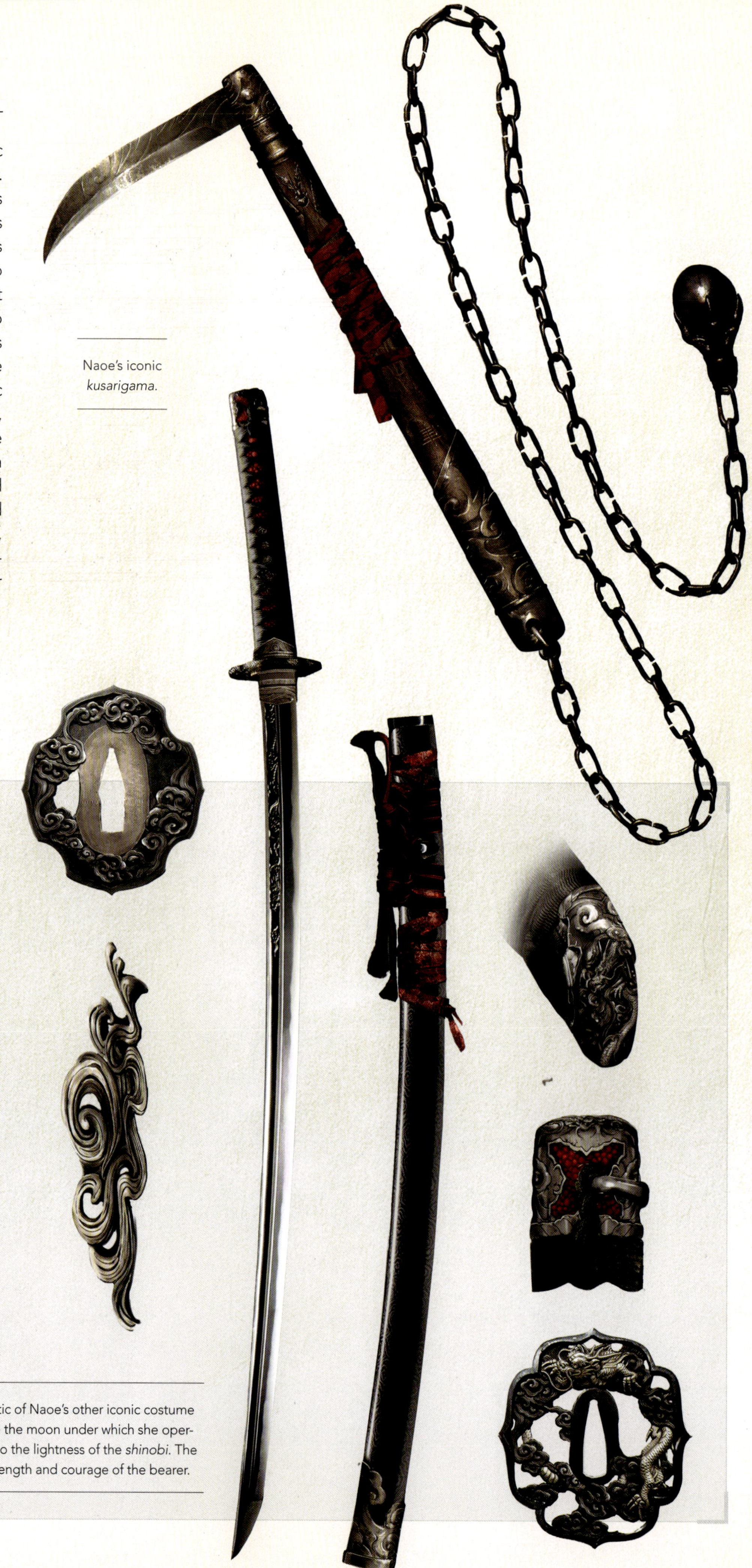

Naoe's iconic *kusarigama*.

The dark tones with hints of red are emblematic of Naoe's other iconic costume elements, and the silver-colored metals evoke the moon under which she operates. The airy shapes of clouds and smoke echo the lightness of the *shinobi*. The dragon figure on the katana illustrates the strength and courage of the bearer.

ART BY JOSHUA PEDRON

The classic Hidden Blade of the Assassins features a dragon arm sheath and brings back a vintage feature—it can rotate ninety degrees when gripped as a dagger in "*tanto* mode."

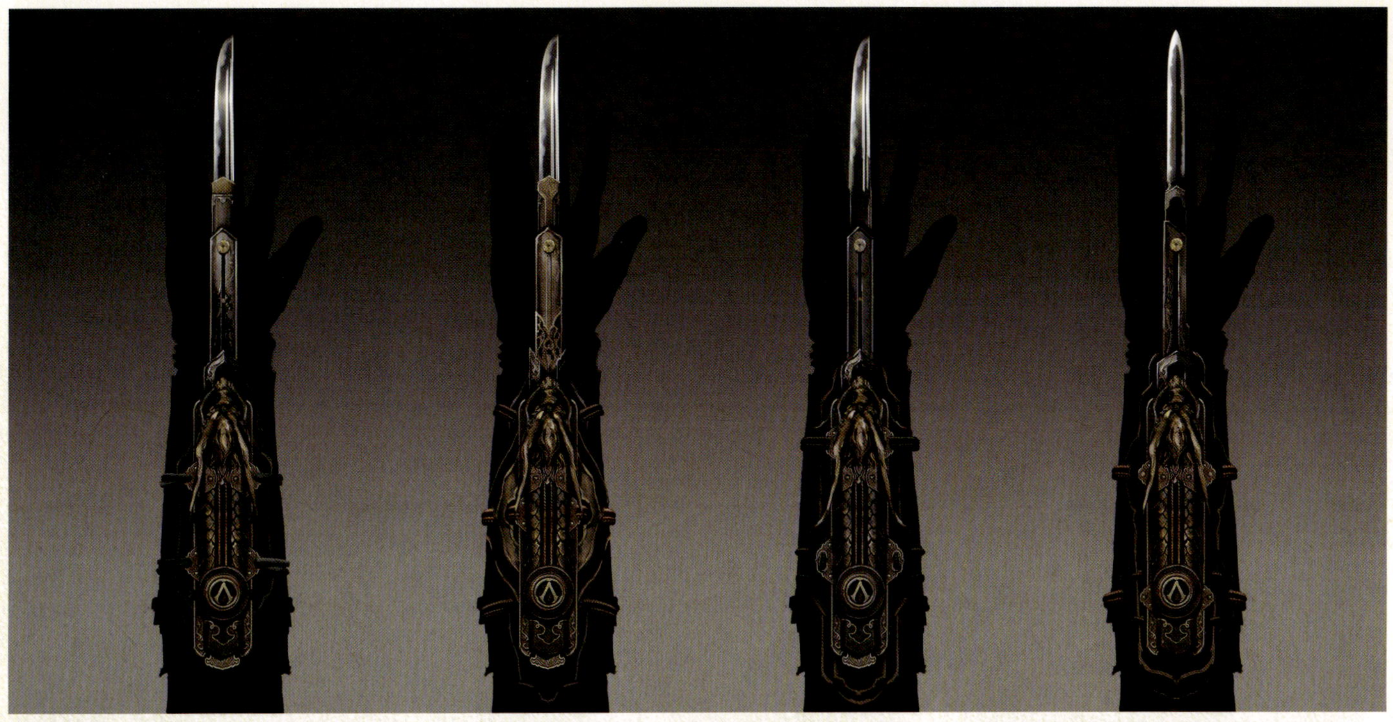

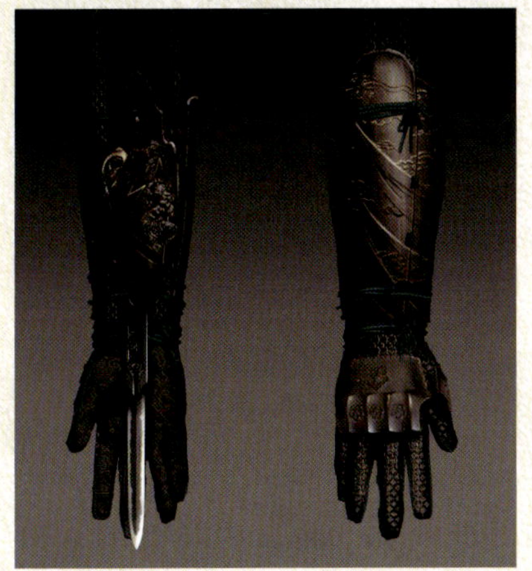

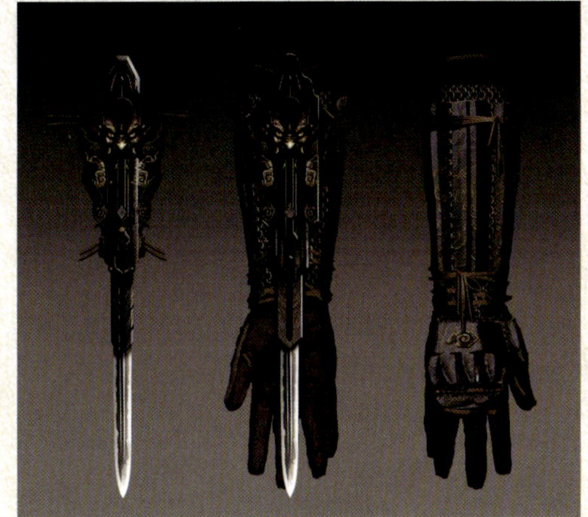

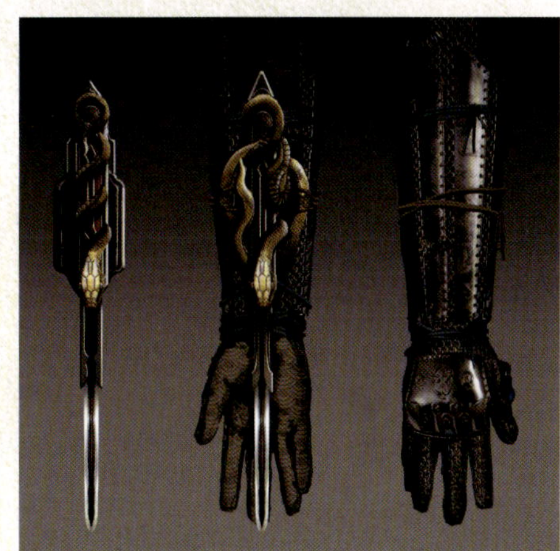

ART BY KATE CRUZ

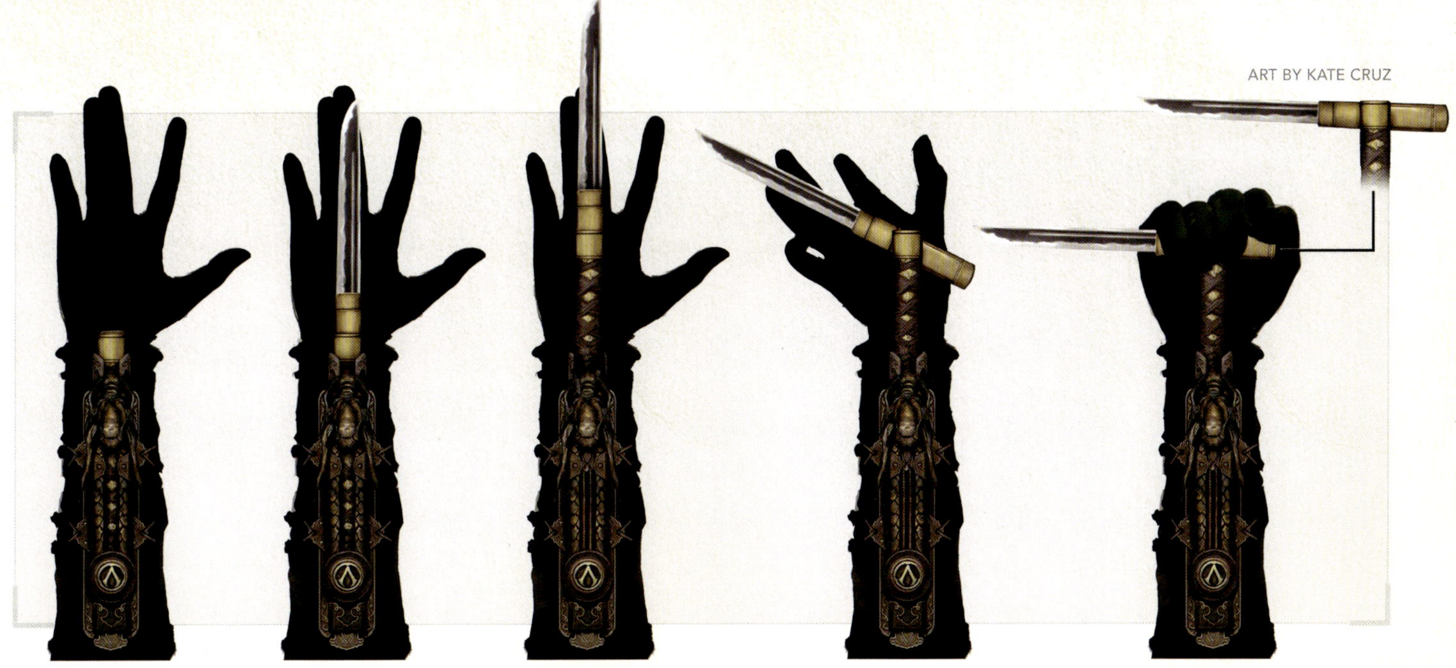

Naoe's various katanas also include versions that inflict special damage. The hand guards, called *tsuba*, feature decorative designs that reflect game themes.

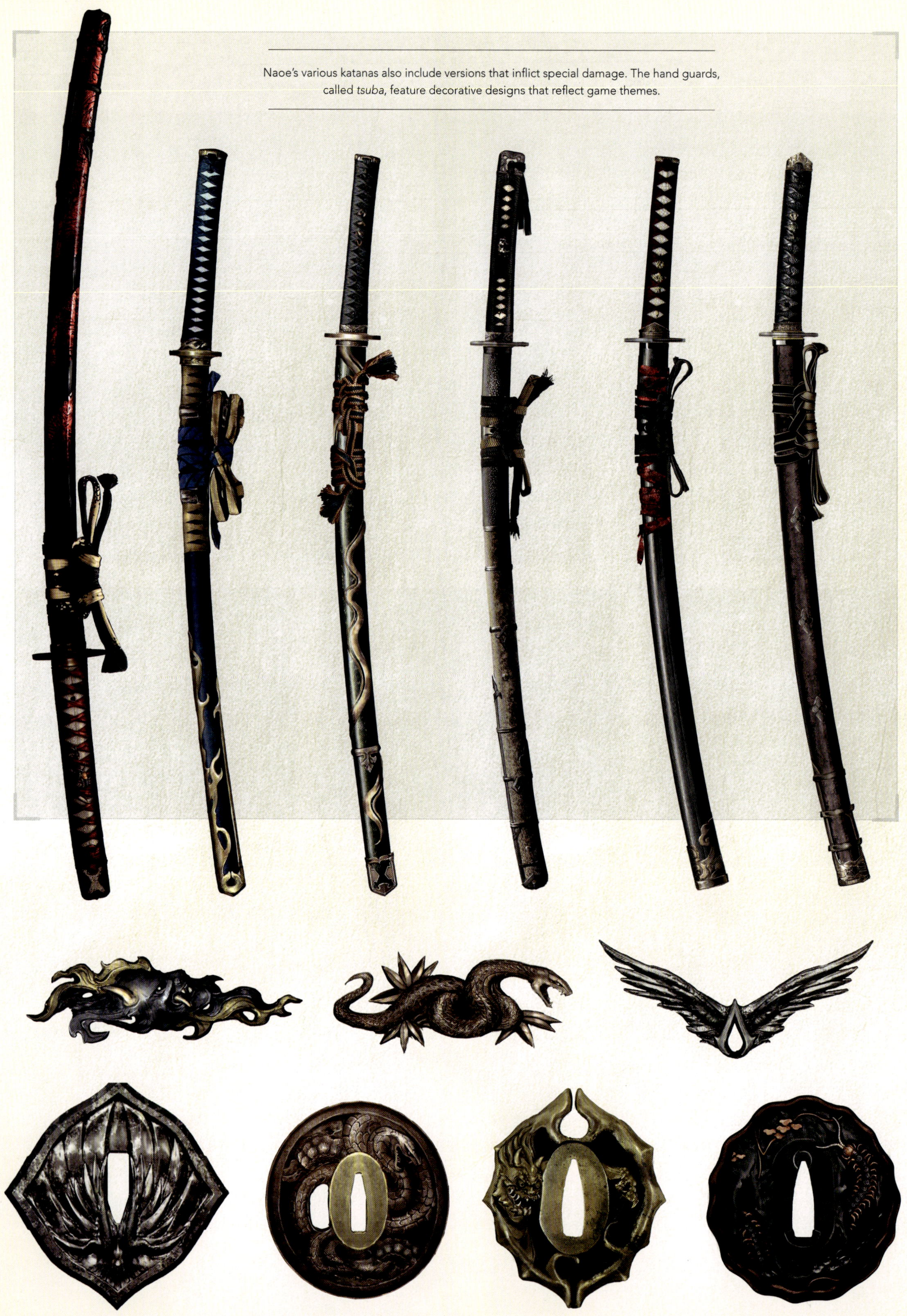

ART BY RUBY LOPEZ AND JOSHUA PEDRON

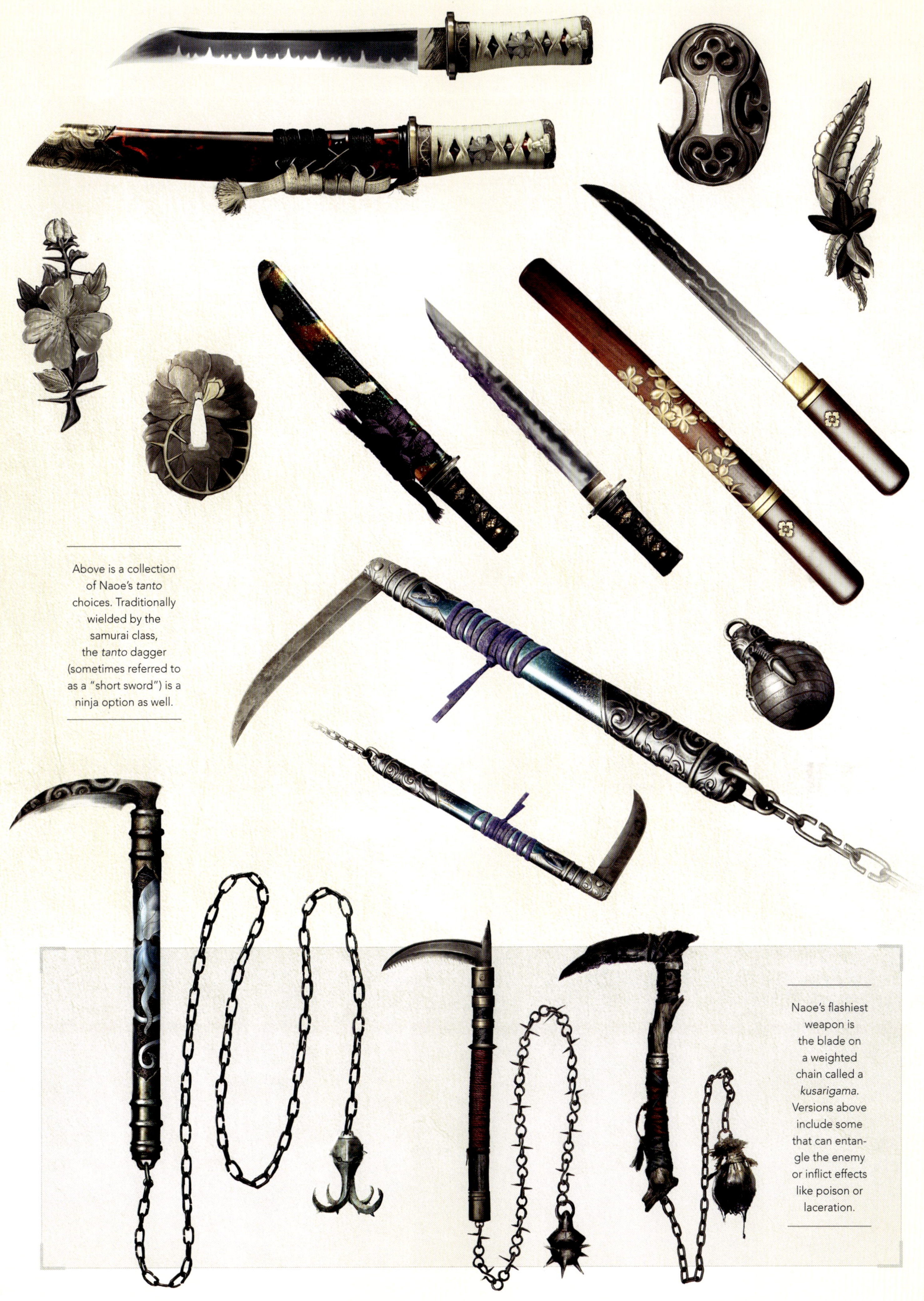

Above is a collection of Naoe's *tanto* choices. Traditionally wielded by the samurai class, the *tanto* dagger (sometimes referred to as a "short sword") is a ninja option as well.

Naoe's flashiest weapon is the blade on a weighted chain called a *kusarigama*. Versions above include some that can entangle the enemy or inflict effects like poison or laceration.

ART BY JOSHUA PEDRON, KURT NUÑEZ, AND DANI VILLACORTE

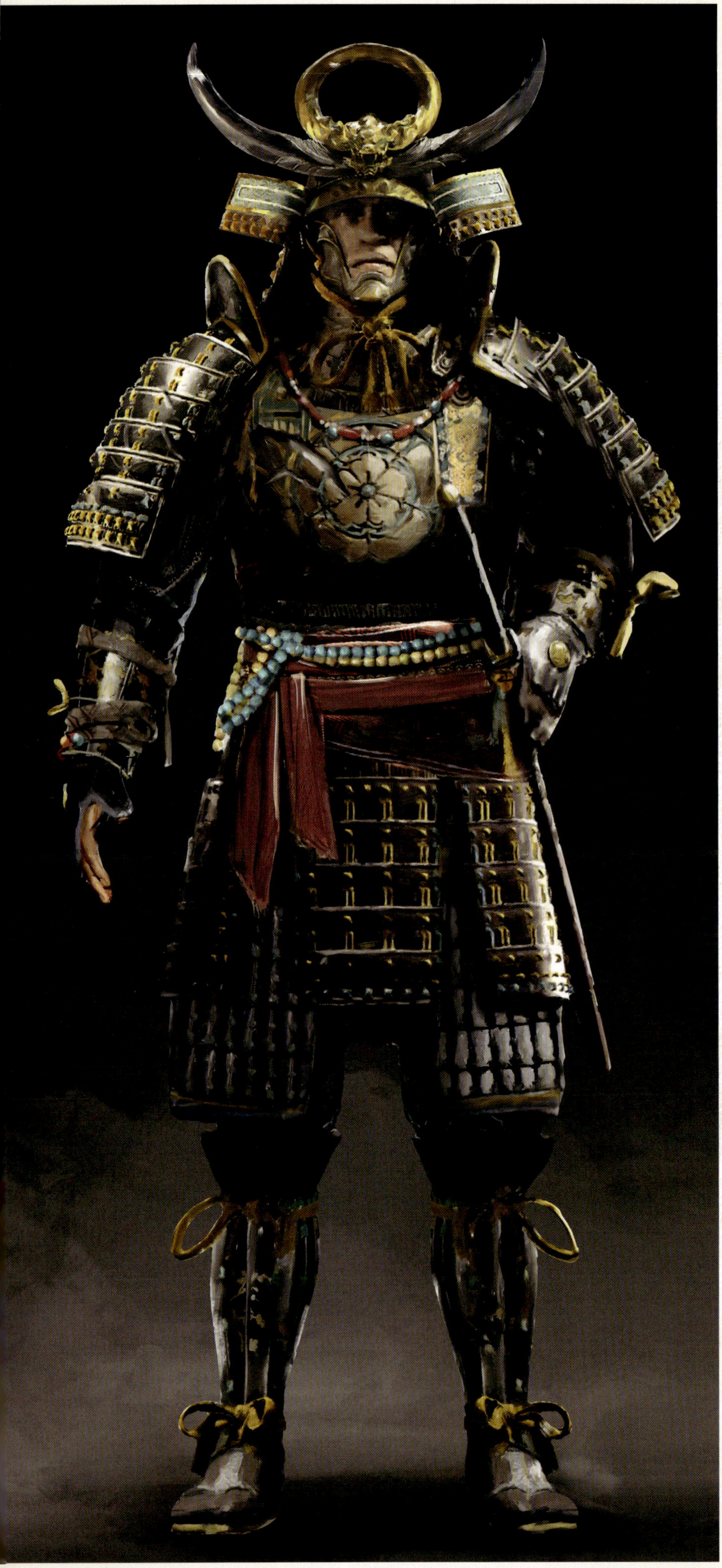

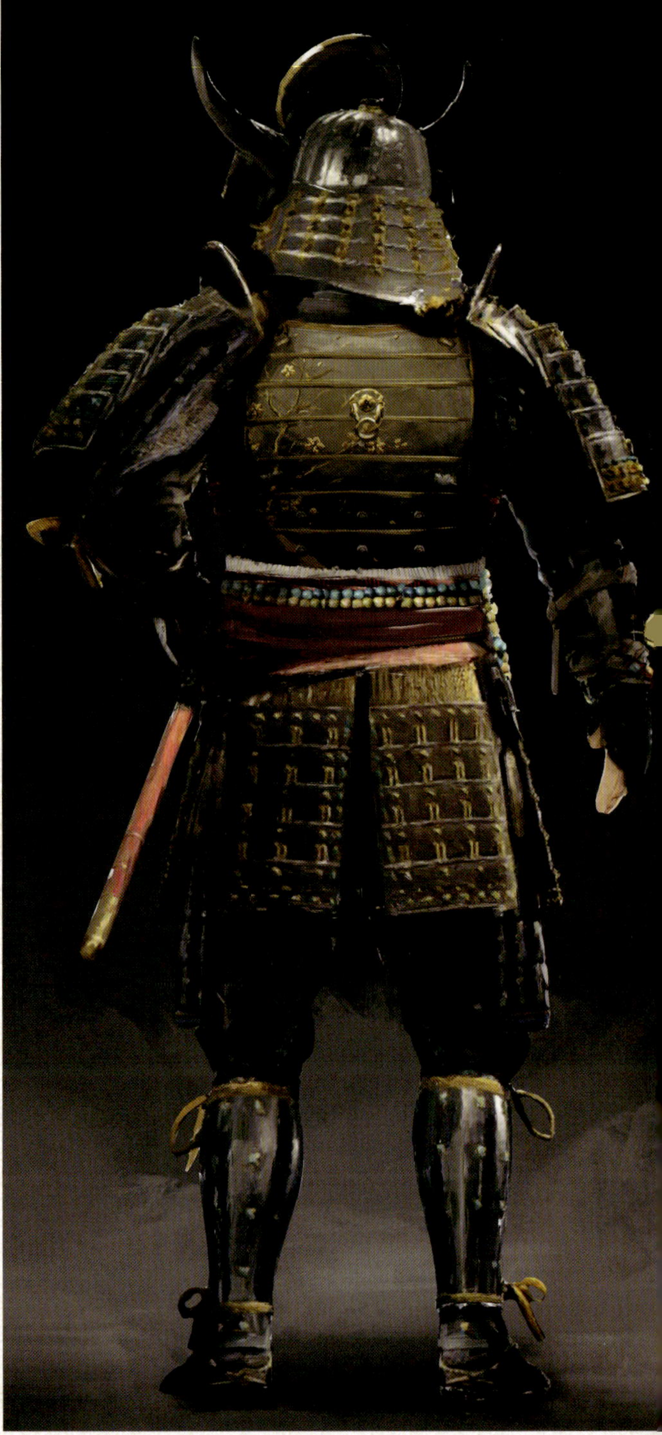

YASUKE

Yasuke is a former African slave who came to Japan as a bodyguard in service to Catholic Jesuit missionaries from Europe. When the priests meet Oda Nobunaga at a formal reception for central Japan's ruling elite, the powerful daimyo is deeply impressed by Yasuke's size, demeanor, and intelligence—he speaks fluent Japanese! Nobunaga brings Yasuke into his service for samurai training at Azuchi Castle, the daimyo's grand seat of power overlooking Lake Biwa. Yasuke excels and becomes a formidable, dominating warrior—a true juggernaut in combat.

ART BY FRED RAMBAUD

The art team worked on various helmet options for Yasuke. "Reports from the period say that Yasuke was more than six feet tall, and he was described as having the strength of ten men," says Dansereau. "At that time, the typical Japanese male was about five two, so he was already like a giant to them." Add an intimidating horned helmet on top, and you have a terrifying, bull-like figure. Early versions of the helmet design are shown below. Yasuke's iconic Samurai outfit, seen here, grants him a bonus to health regeneration.

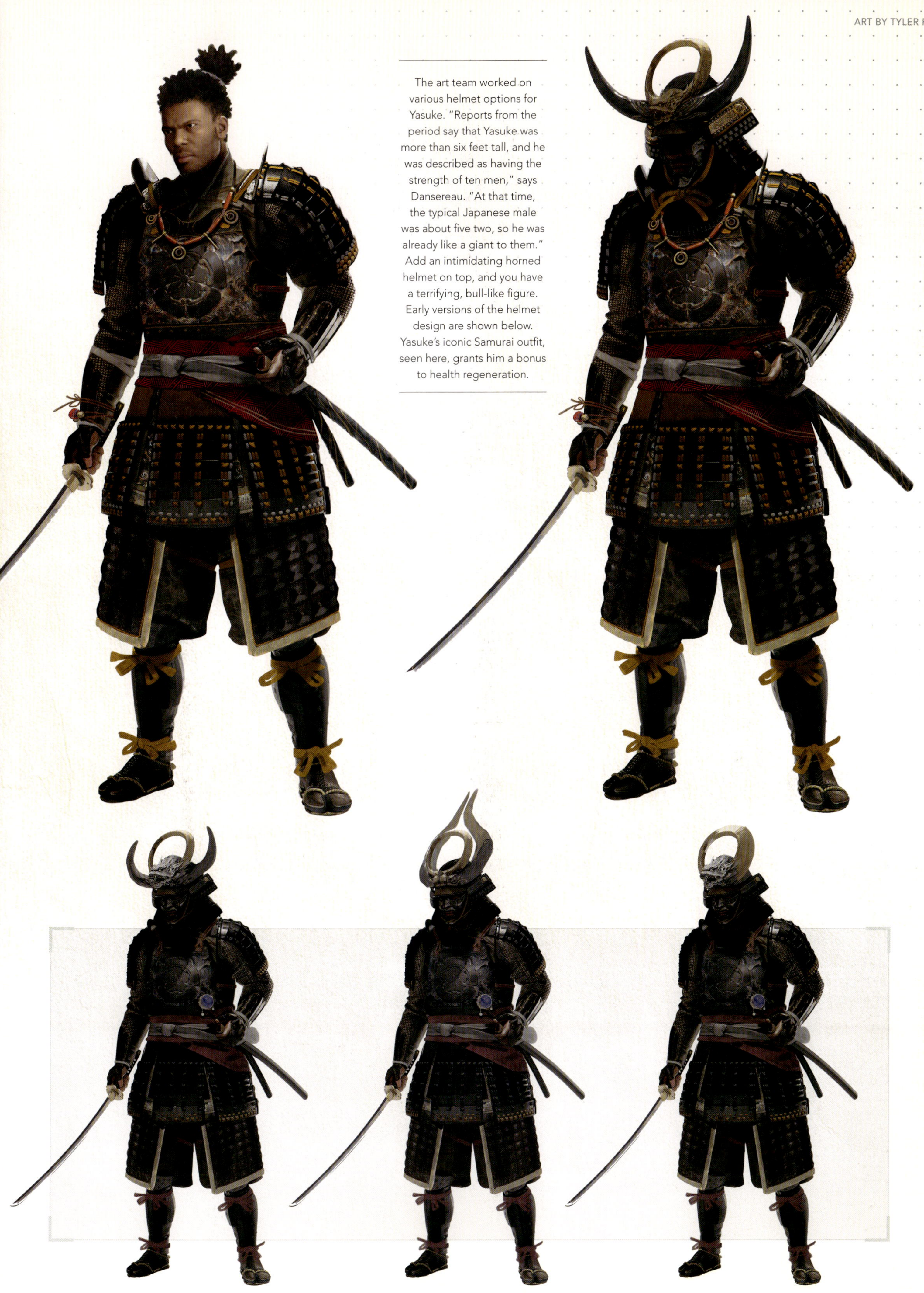

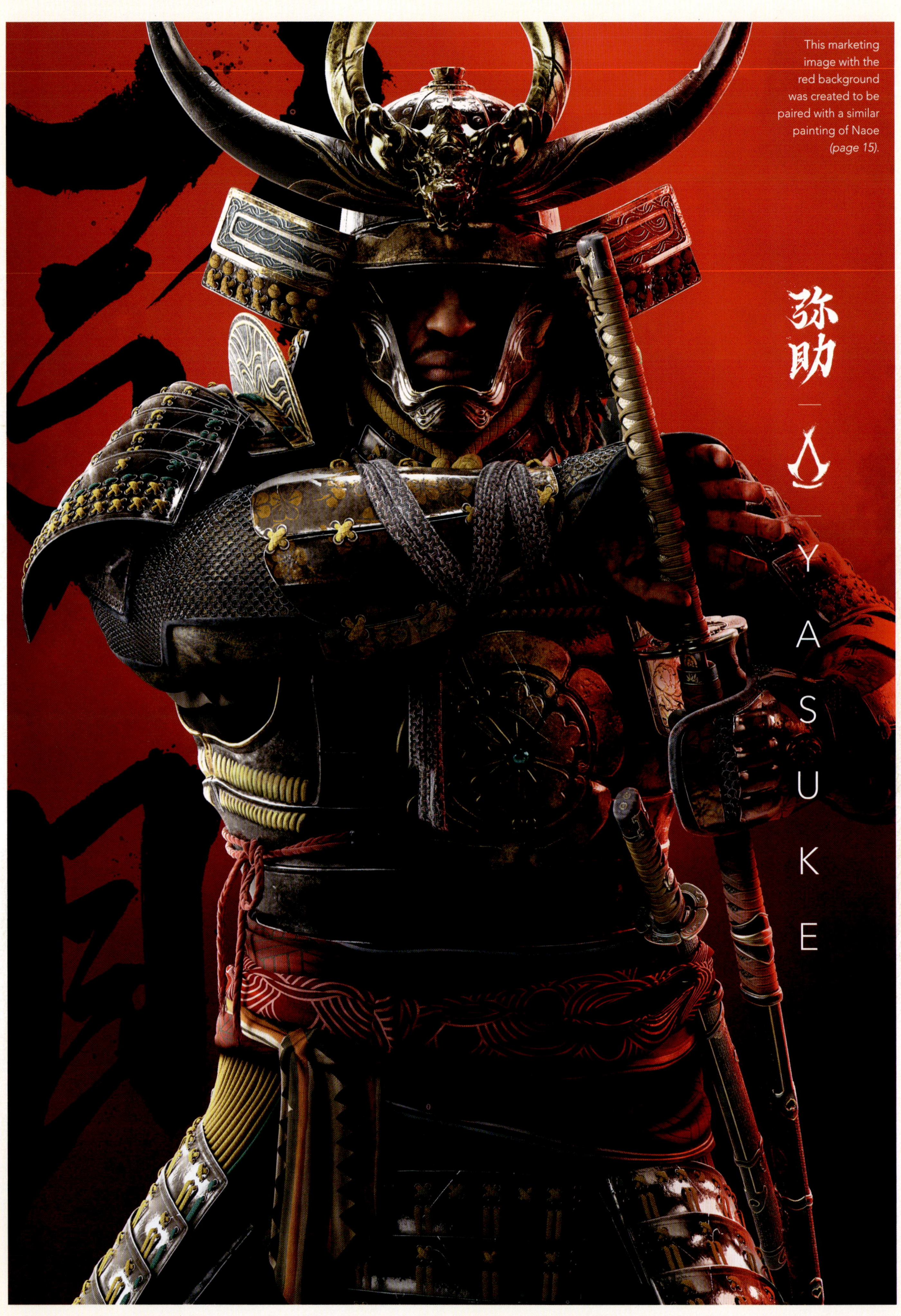

This marketing image with the red background was created to be paired with a similar painting of Naoe *(page 15)*.

ART BY VINCENT GAIGNEUX

These studies explore the concept that Macio calls "Yasuke the ronin." In *Shadows'* time period, a ronin was a samurai who served no lord or master—a lone, wandering warrior who followed his own path, seeking ways to redeem himself. The Ronin outfit grants a bonus to Yasuke's brutal assassinations.

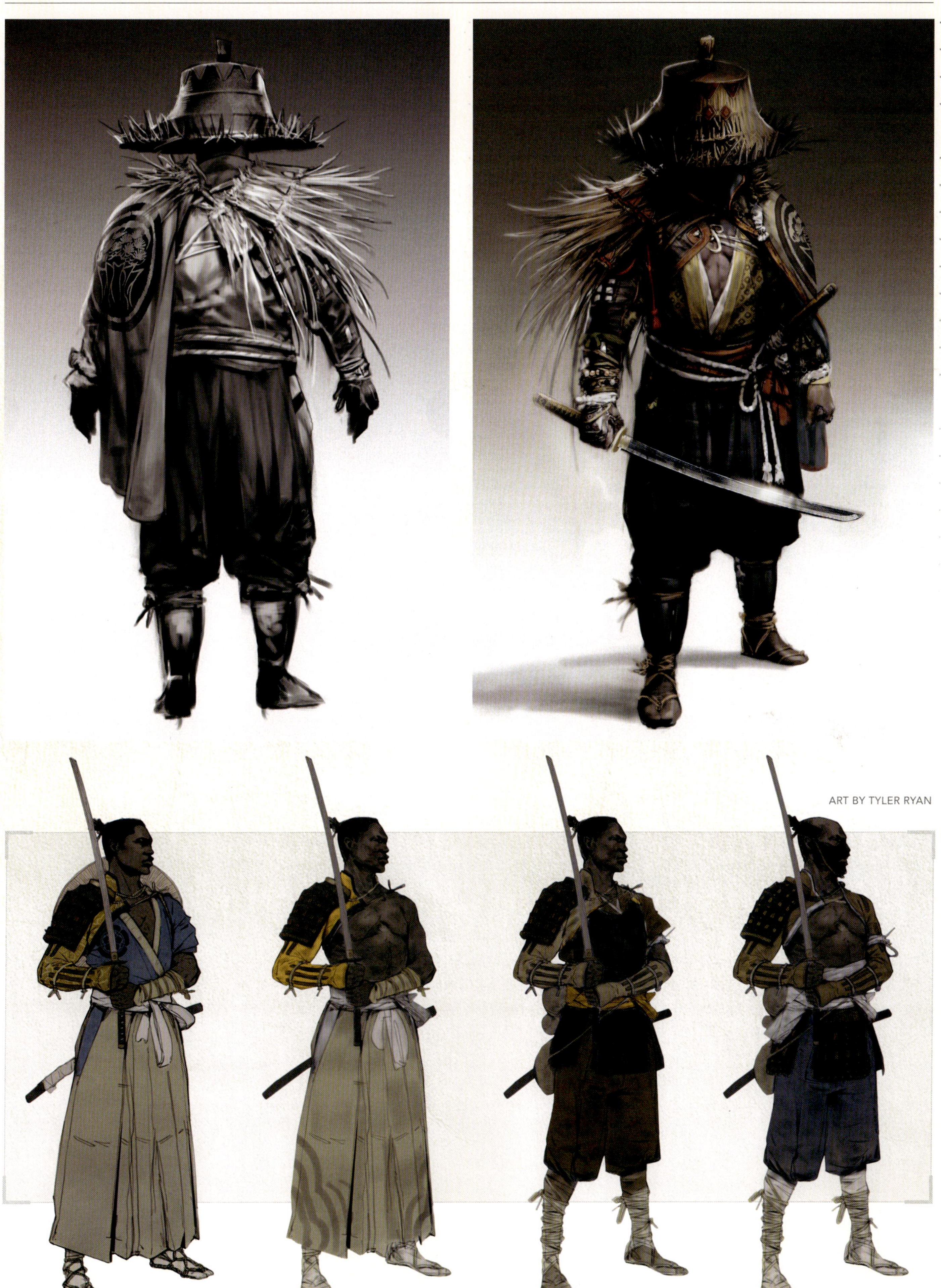

ART BY TYLER RYAN

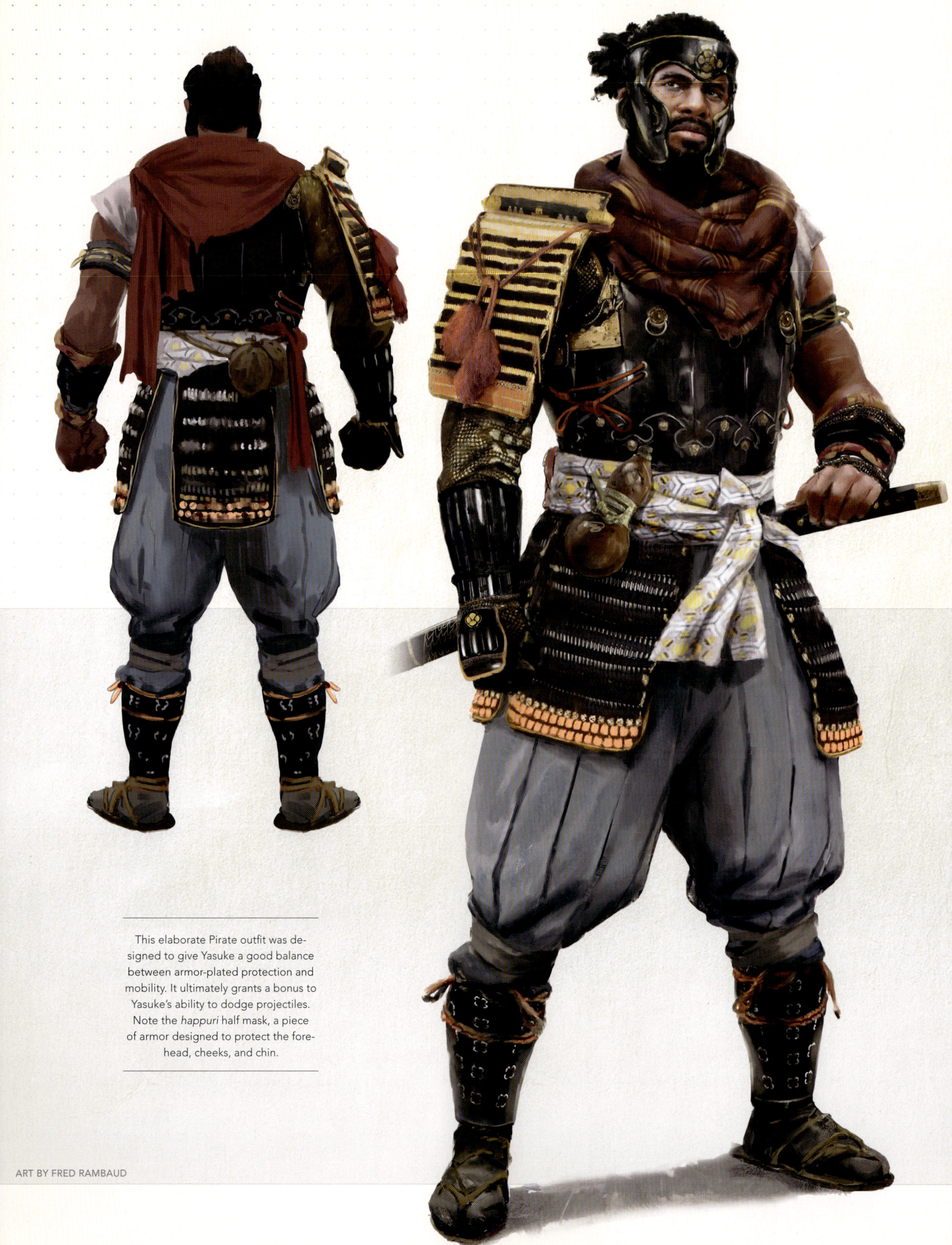

This elaborate Pirate outfit was designed to give Yasuke a good balance between armor-plated protection and mobility. It ultimately grants a bonus to Yasuke's ability to dodge projectiles. Note the *happuri* half mask, a piece of armor designed to protect the forehead, cheeks, and chin.

ART BY FRED RAMBAUD

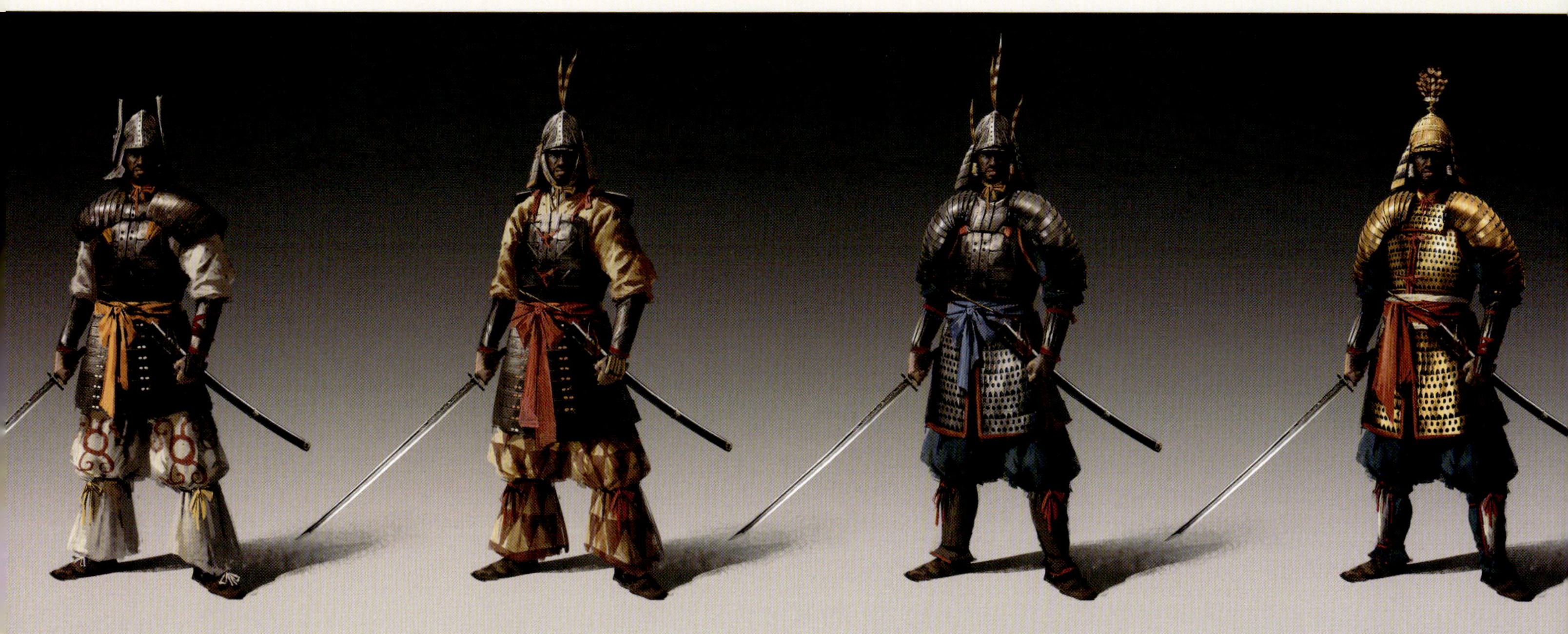

Above is a series of ancient armor sets that can be looted from *kofun* (megalithic tombs) during the game. This Guardian outfit grants a bonus to Yasuke's ability to parry.

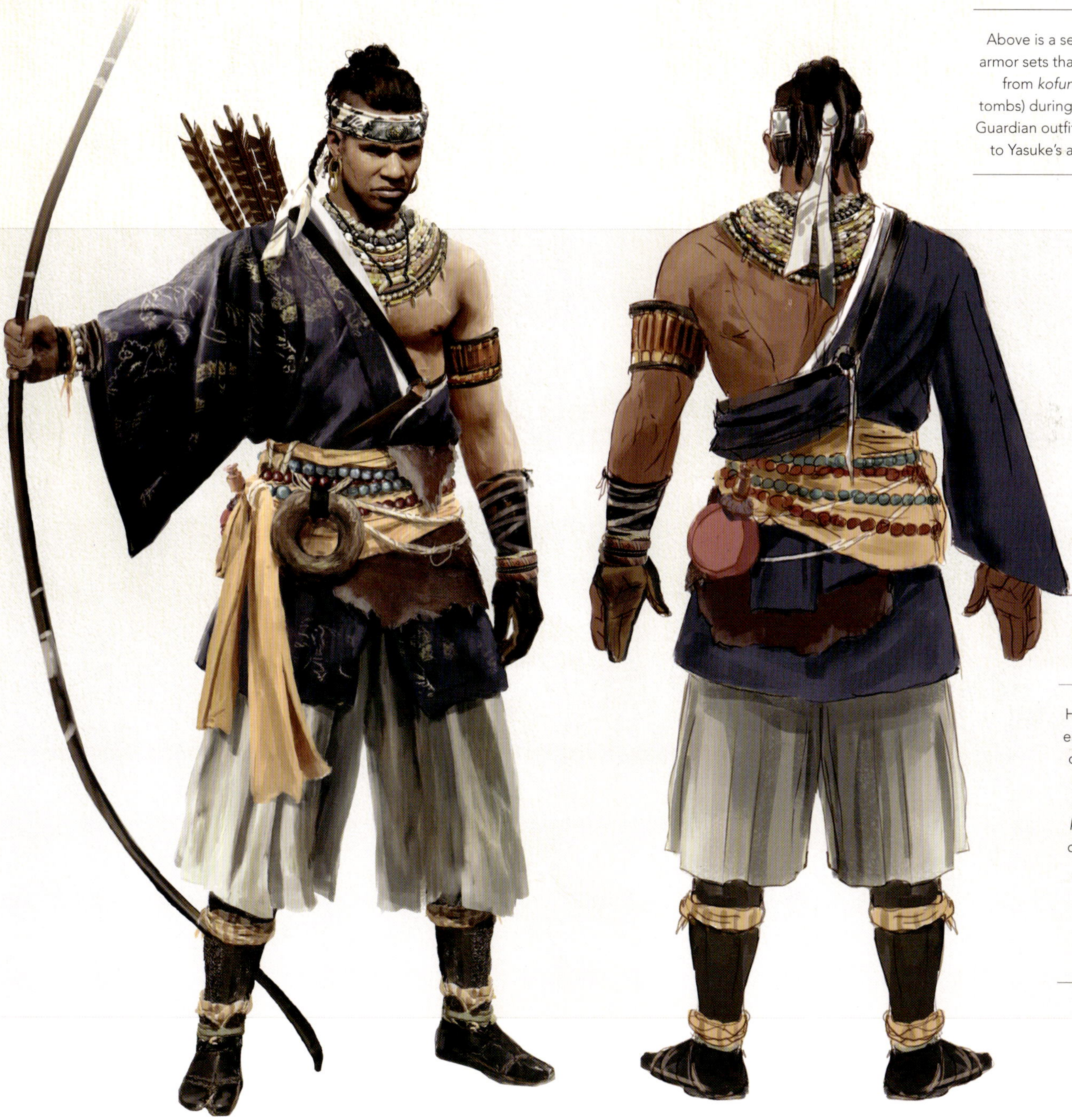

Here you see an early exploration of Yasuke as an archer clad in a one-sleeved *kosode*, a type of kimono. This Archer outfit makes Yasuke even deadlier with ranged weapons.

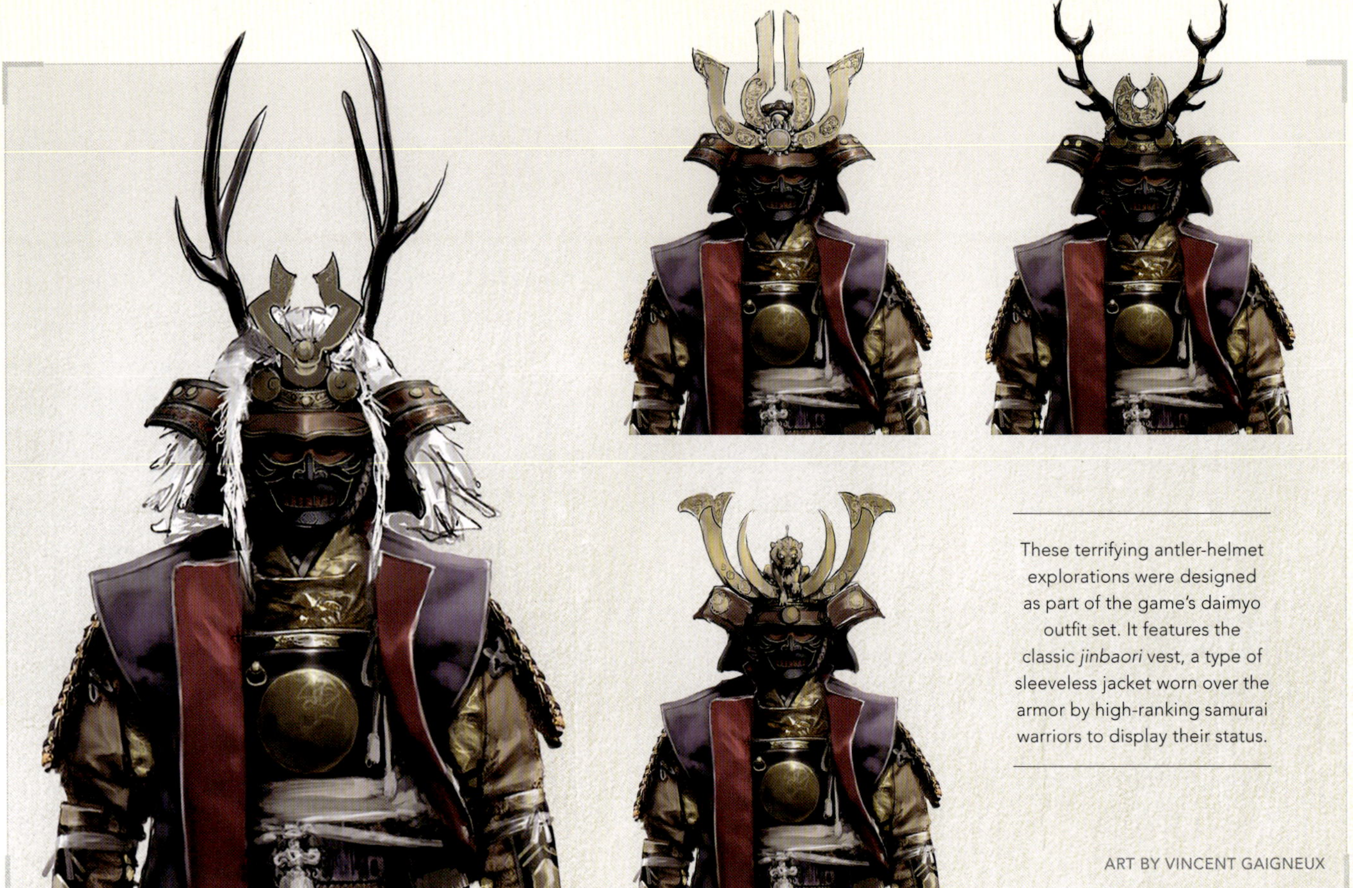

These terrifying antler-helmet explorations were designed as part of the game's daimyo outfit set. It features the classic *jinbaori* vest, a type of sleeveless jacket worn over the armor by high-ranking samurai warriors to display their status.

ART BY VINCENT GAIGNEUX

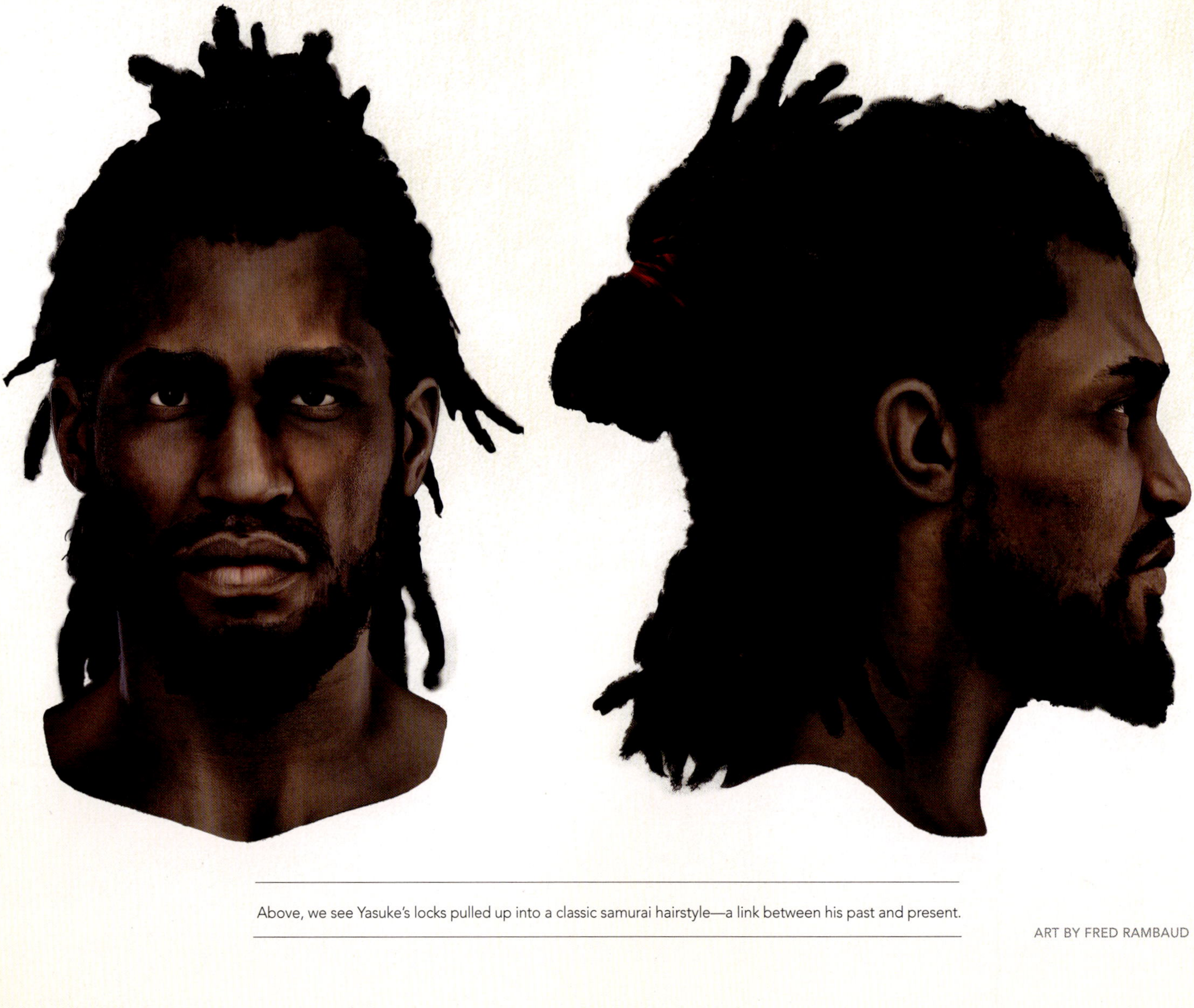

Above, we see Yasuke's locks pulled up into a classic samurai hairstyle—a link between his past and present.

ART BY FRED RAMBAUD

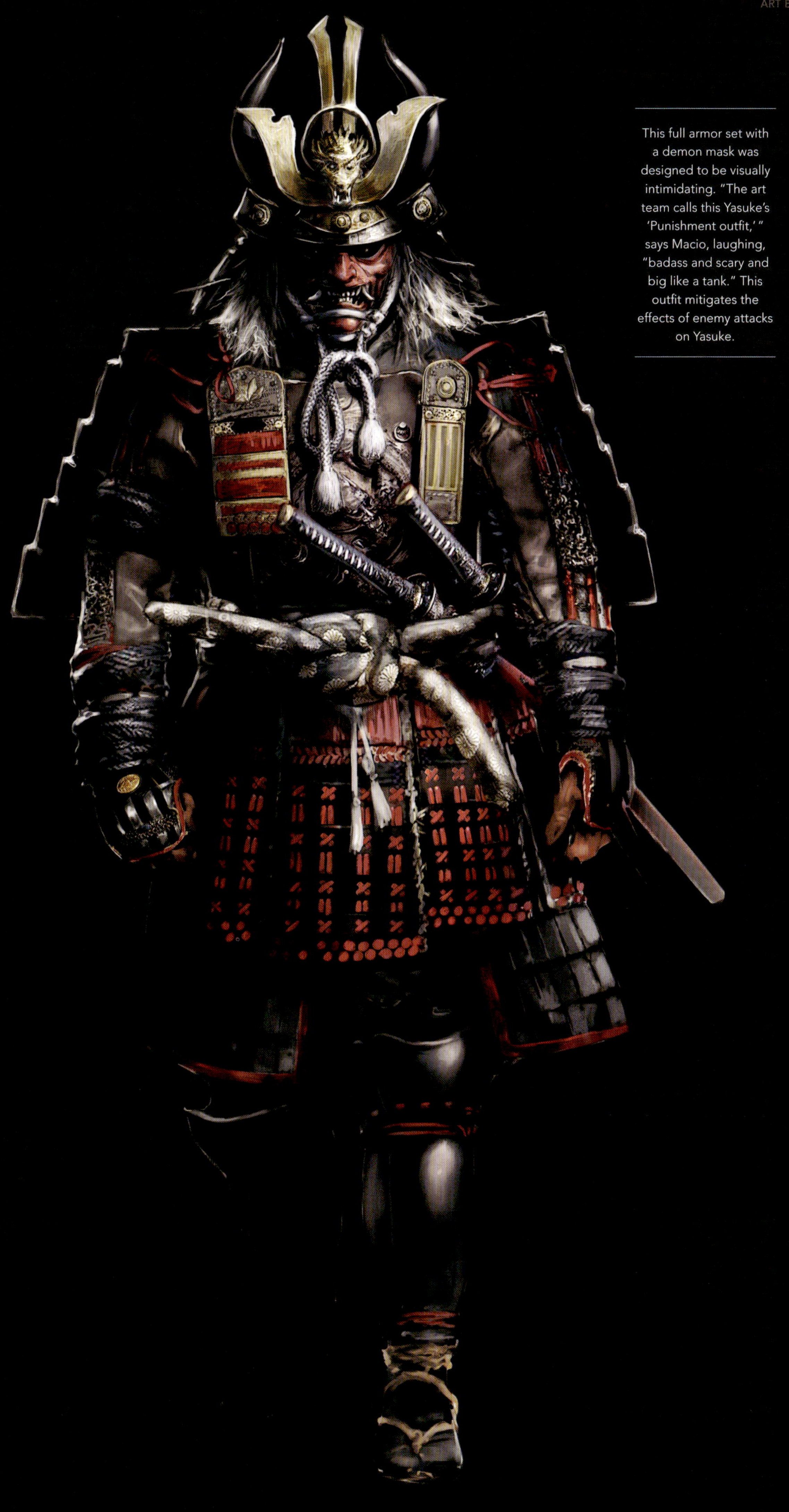

This full armor set with a demon mask was designed to be visually intimidating. "The art team calls this Yasuke's 'Punishment outfit,'" says Macio, laughing, "badass and scary and big like a tank." This outfit mitigates the effects of enemy attacks on Yasuke.

This concept piece explores Yasuke's flamboyant Kabukimono garb made with high-quality fabrics. *Kabukimono* were wandering gangs of samurai ronin who dressed and spoke in deliberately outrageous ways. This outfit grants bonuses to Yasuke's execution abilities.

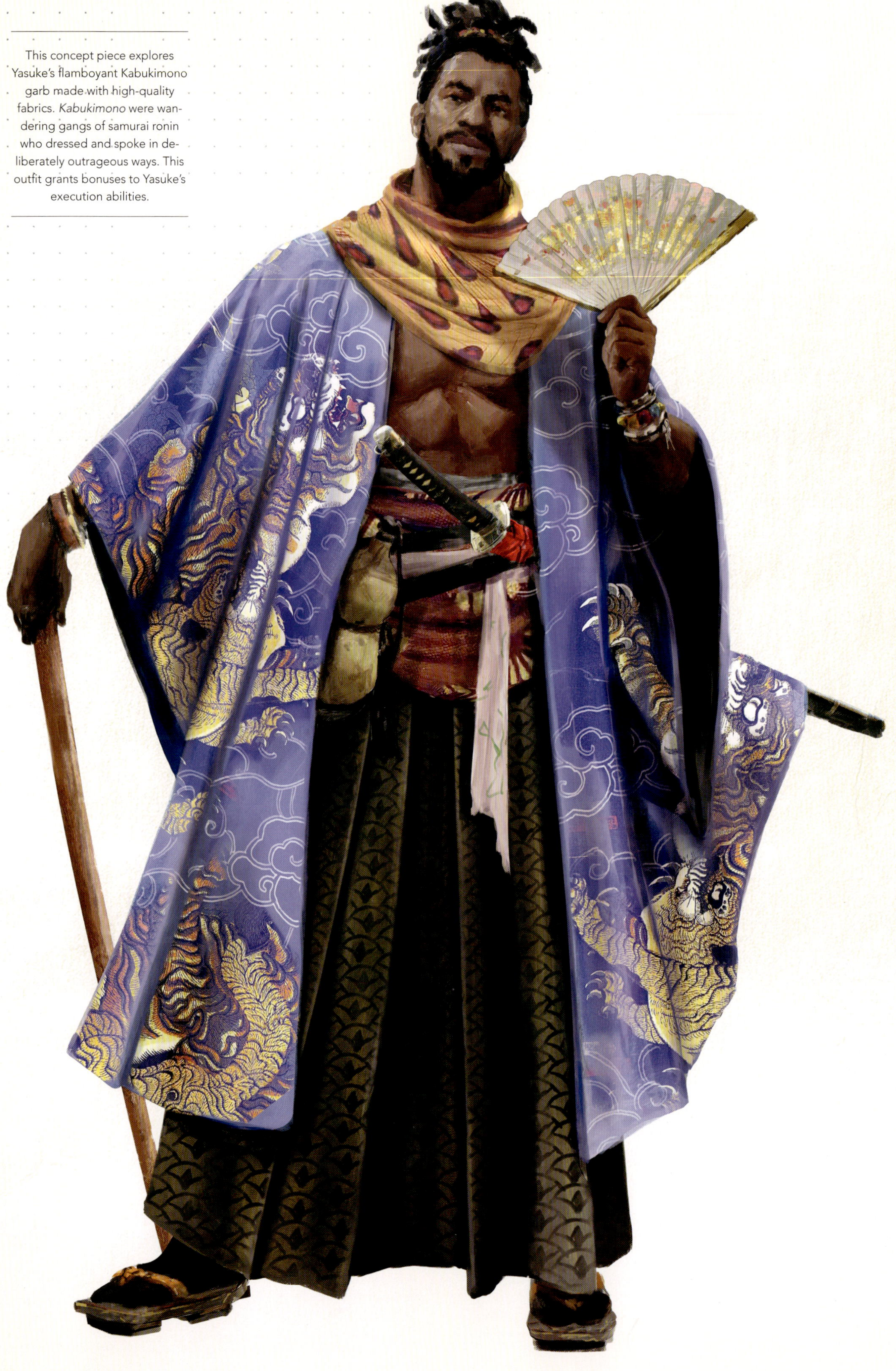

ART BY VINCENT GAIGNEUX AND TYLER RYAN

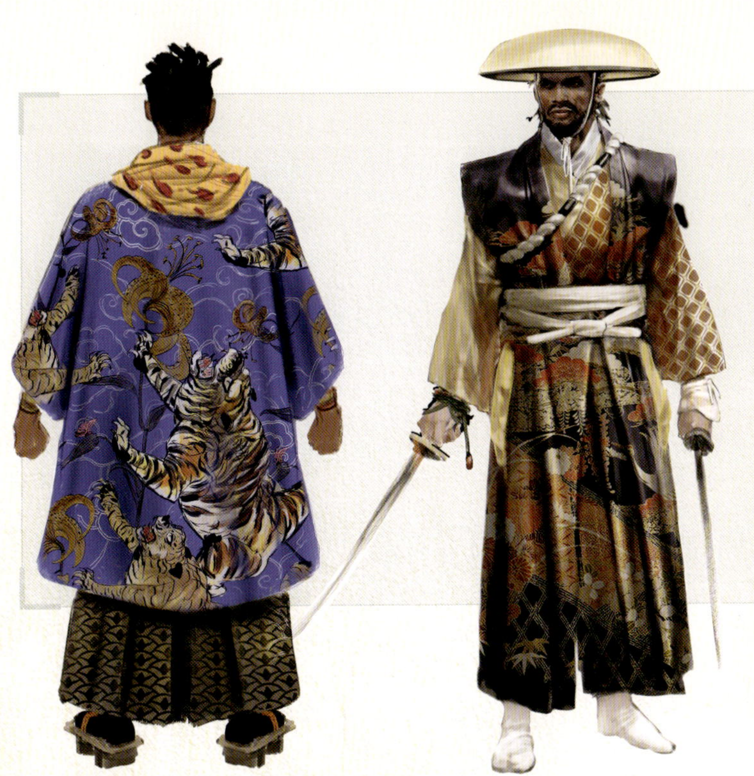

Left to right: A back view of the Kabukimono outfit; a study of the light samurai outfit worn by high-ranking samurai members, which bestows Yasuke with greater agility; and an early concept rendering of Yasuke's iconic outfit.

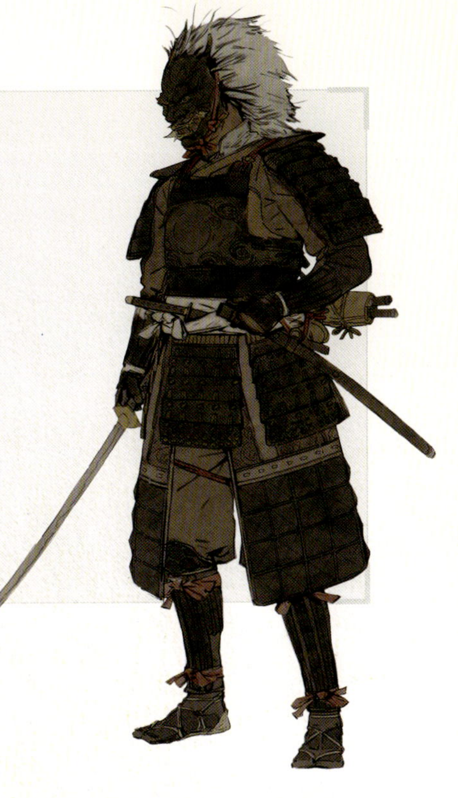

ART BY FRED RAMBAUD

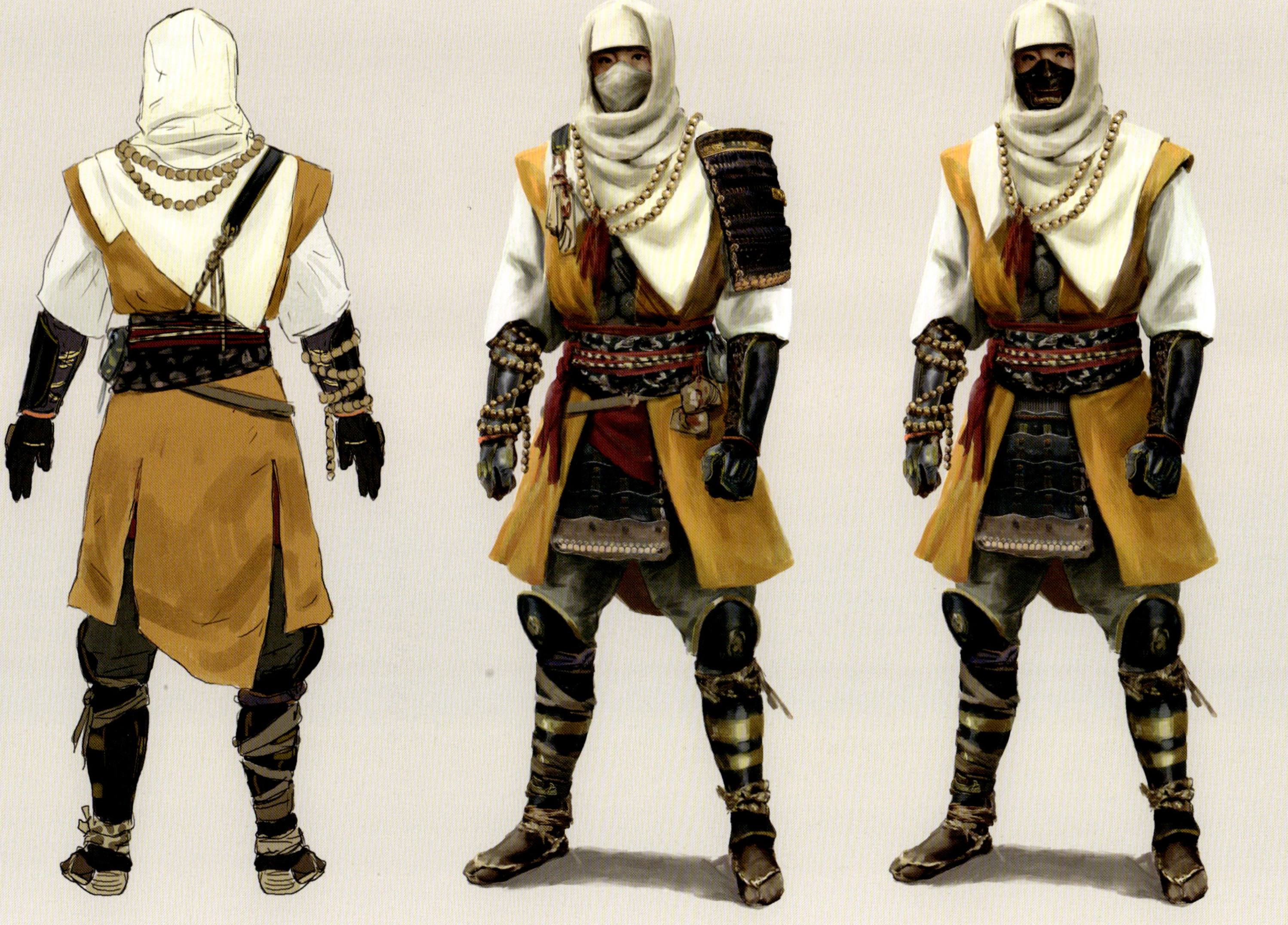

This set of images explores Yasuke's Sōhei (warrior-monk) outfit. Many such monks were fighting for various ideological purposes during the Azuchi-Momoyama period.

Here we see Yasuke's flaming red-dragon armor. On the opposite page is his demon-hunter outfit, a good match for Naoe's *(page 26)*. At the bottom are studies for Yasuke's version of Naoe's stunning blue-dragon outfit.

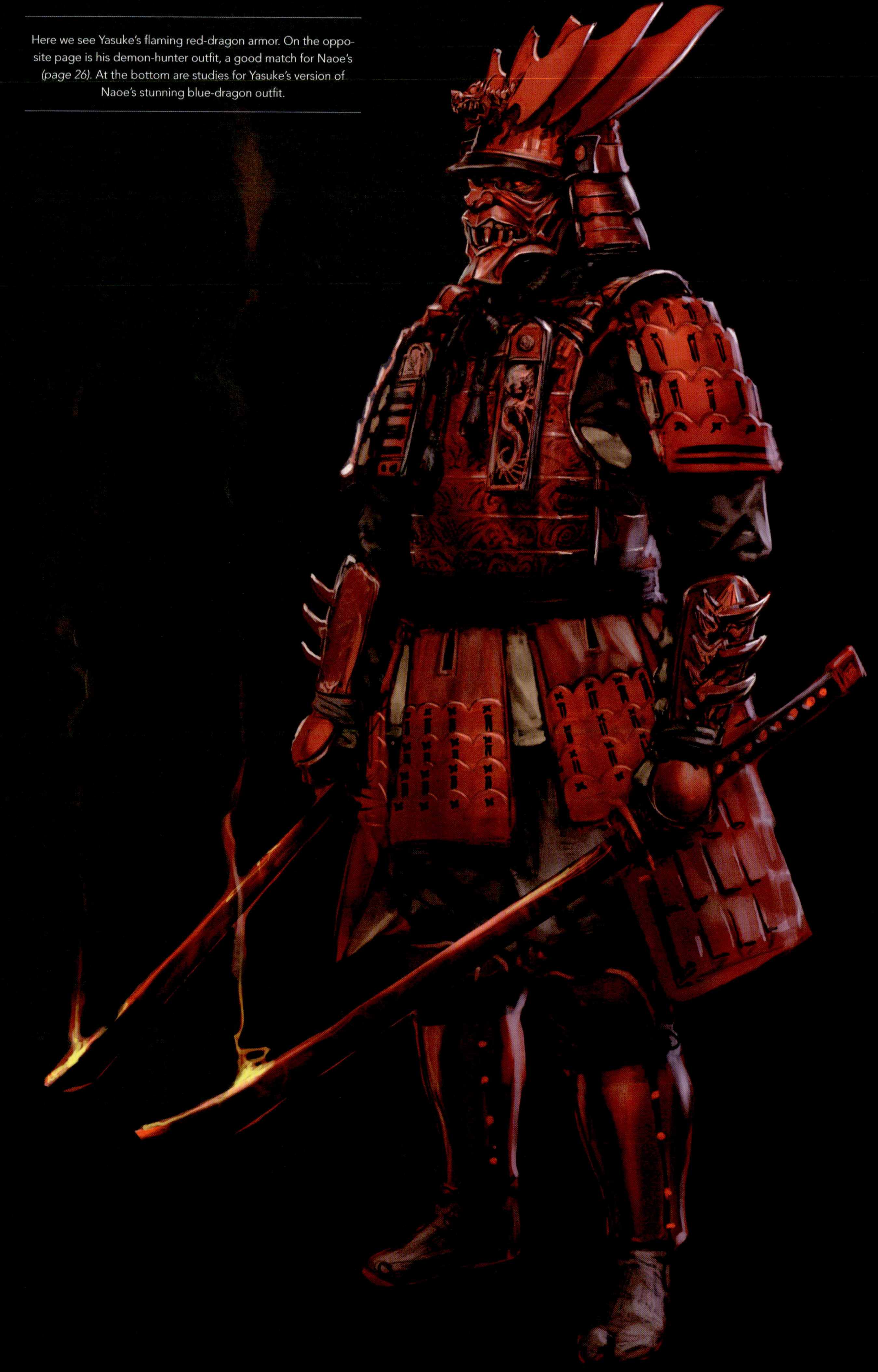

ART BY KONI (AMANDINE GIRARD)

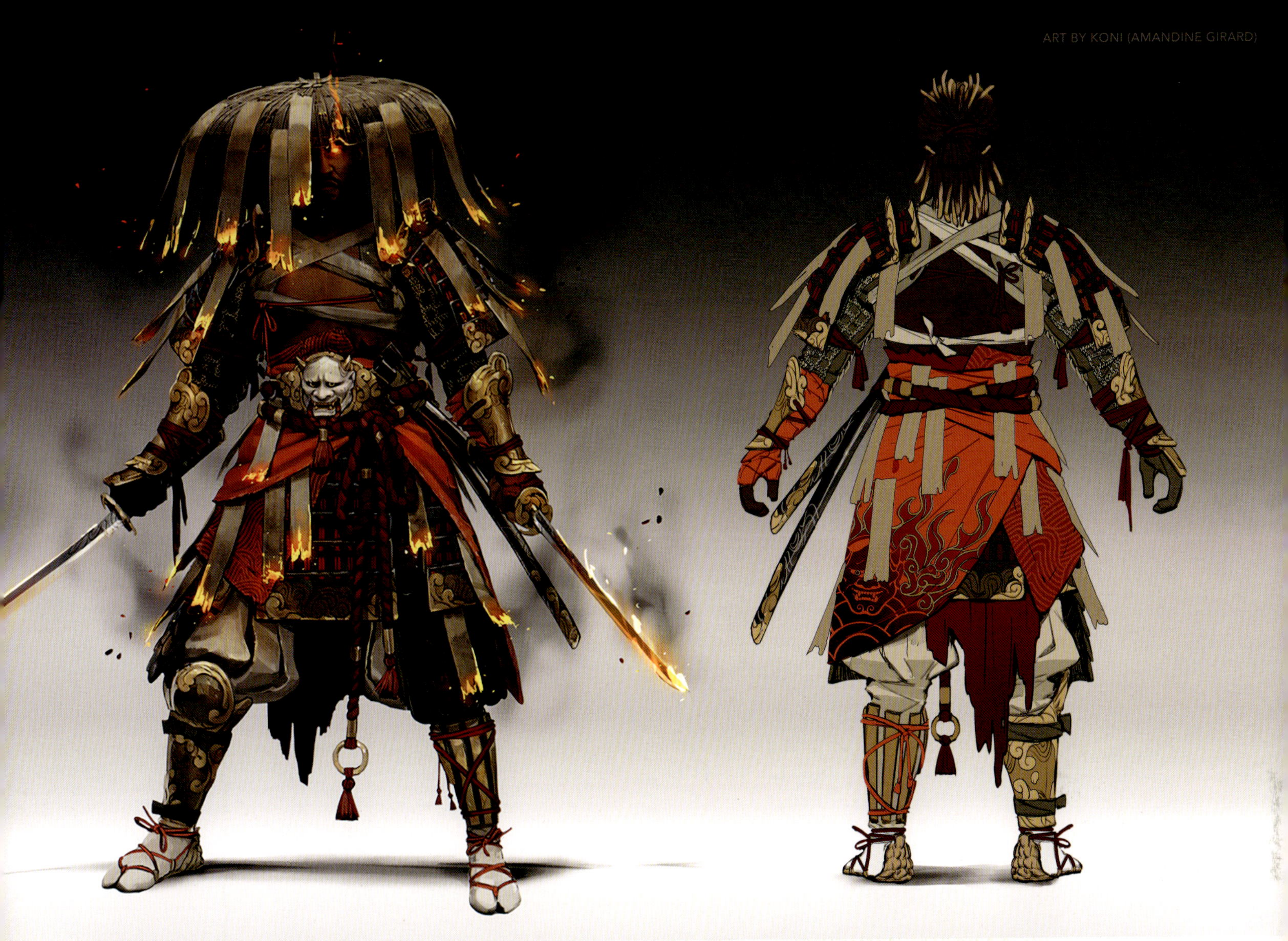

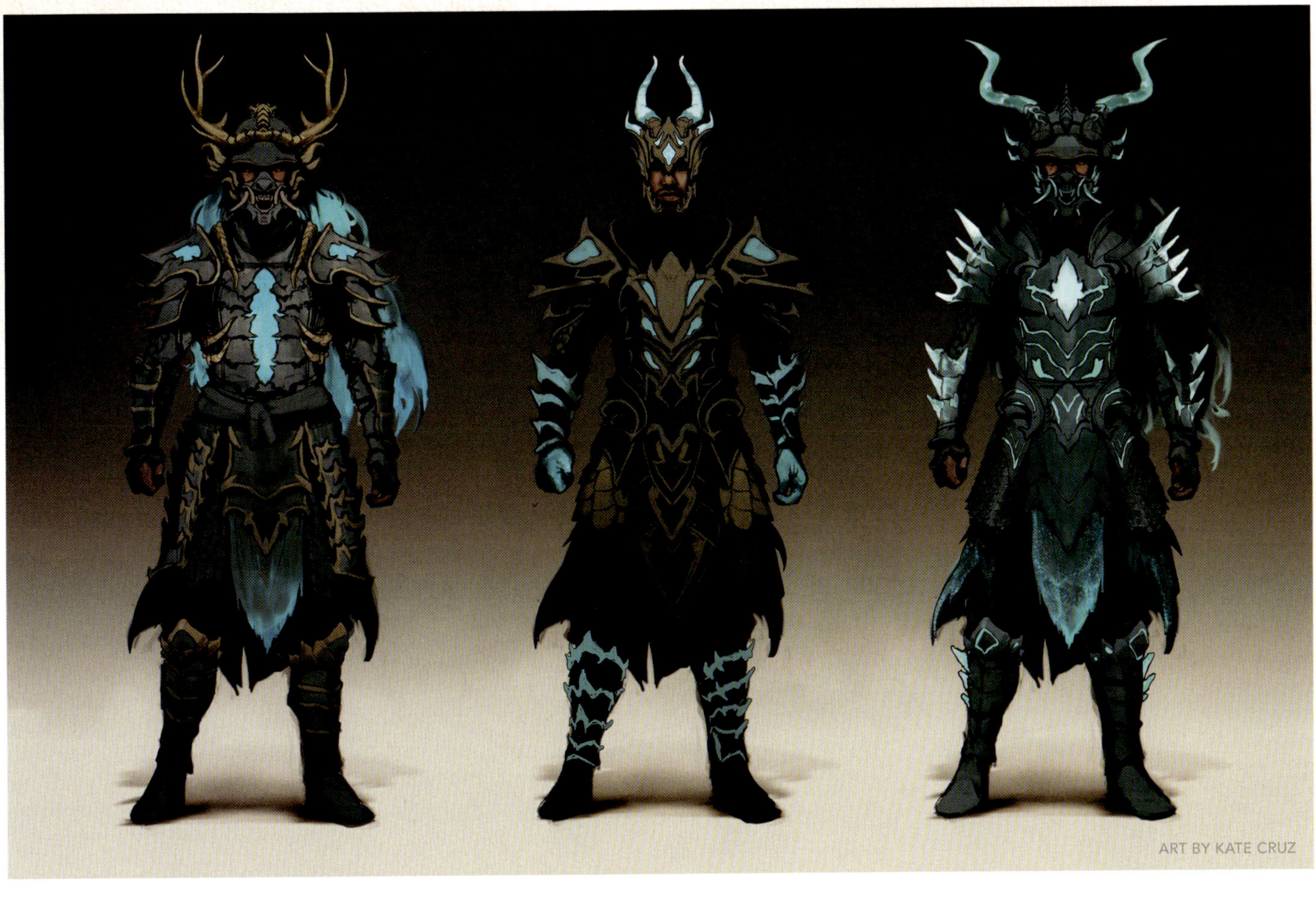

ART BY KATE CRUZ

ART BY ADRIEN GUIGUES, DMYTRO MOTUZ, ARNYLL DALE GACUSAN, AND FRANCIS FAURILLO

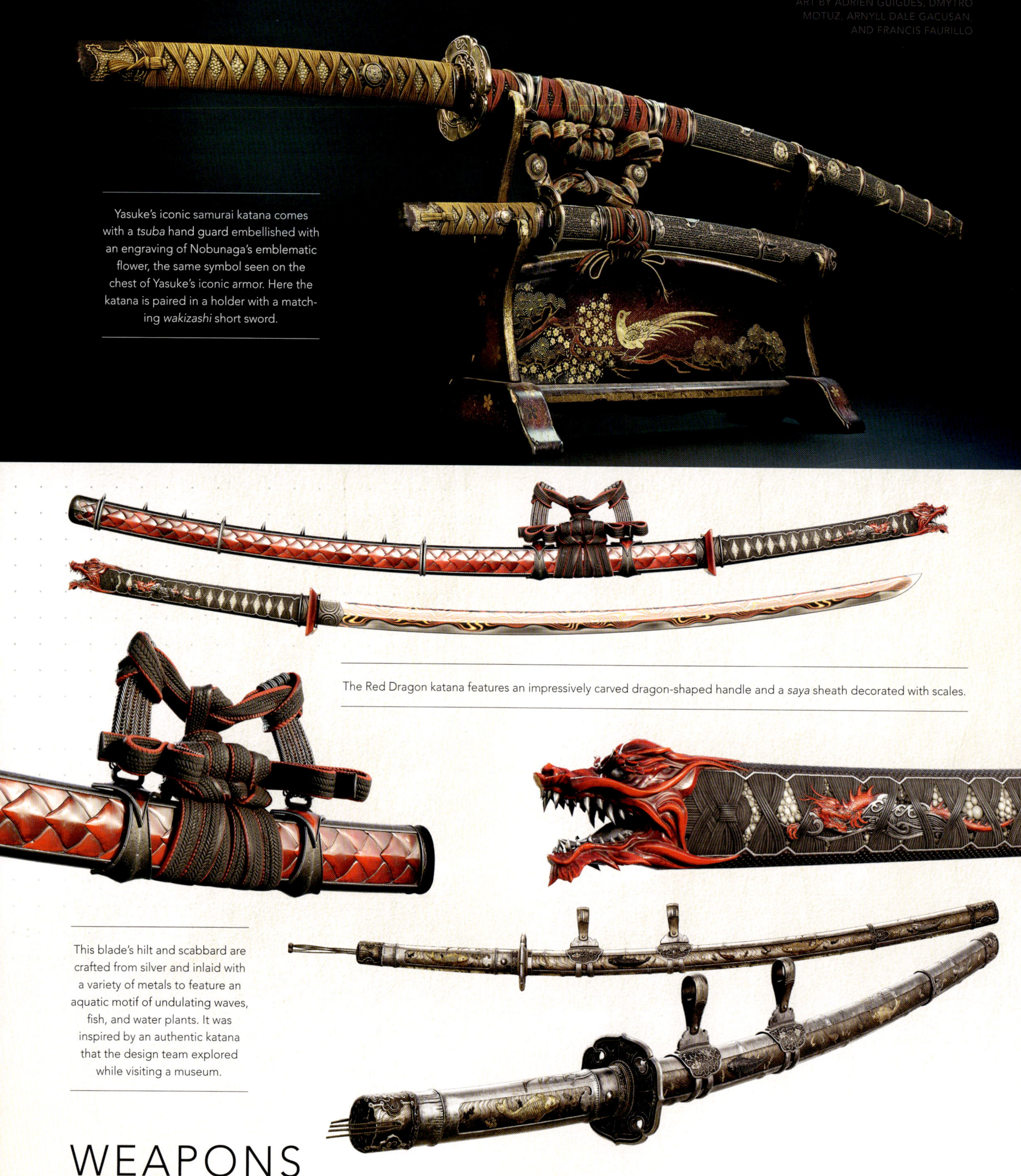

Yasuke's iconic samurai katana comes with a *tsuba* hand guard embellished with an engraving of Nobunaga's emblematic flower, the same symbol seen on the chest of Yasuke's iconic armor. Here the katana is paired in a holder with a matching *wakizashi* short sword.

The Red Dragon katana features an impressively carved dragon-shaped handle and a *saya* sheath decorated with scales.

This blade's hilt and scabbard are crafted from silver and inlaid with a variety of metals to feature an aquatic motif of undulating waves, fish, and water plants. It was inspired by an authentic katana that the design team explored while visiting a museum.

WEAPONS

Yasuke embodies the samurai fantasy with the ultimate Japanese weapon, the katana, but he can also wield a wide variety of melee and ranged weapons. The katana is the most balanced weapon, combining fast strikes and strong slashes that can cut through armor. Yasuke also has access to the *naginata*, an efficient weapon to use when fighting multiple foes at once. He also employs the unconventional *kanabō*, a massive bludgeoning weapon capable of knocking his enemies prone and breaking their armor. Finally, his ranged weapons are perfect for keeping enemies at bay. When attacking with the *yumi* bow or the harquebus, Yasuke's dexterity makes him as deadly at a distance as he is up close.

ART BY ADRIEN GUIGUES, DMYTRO MOTUZ, ARNYLL DALE GACUSAN, LEVI TORRE, JEMA MANALLO, AND DANI VILLACORTE

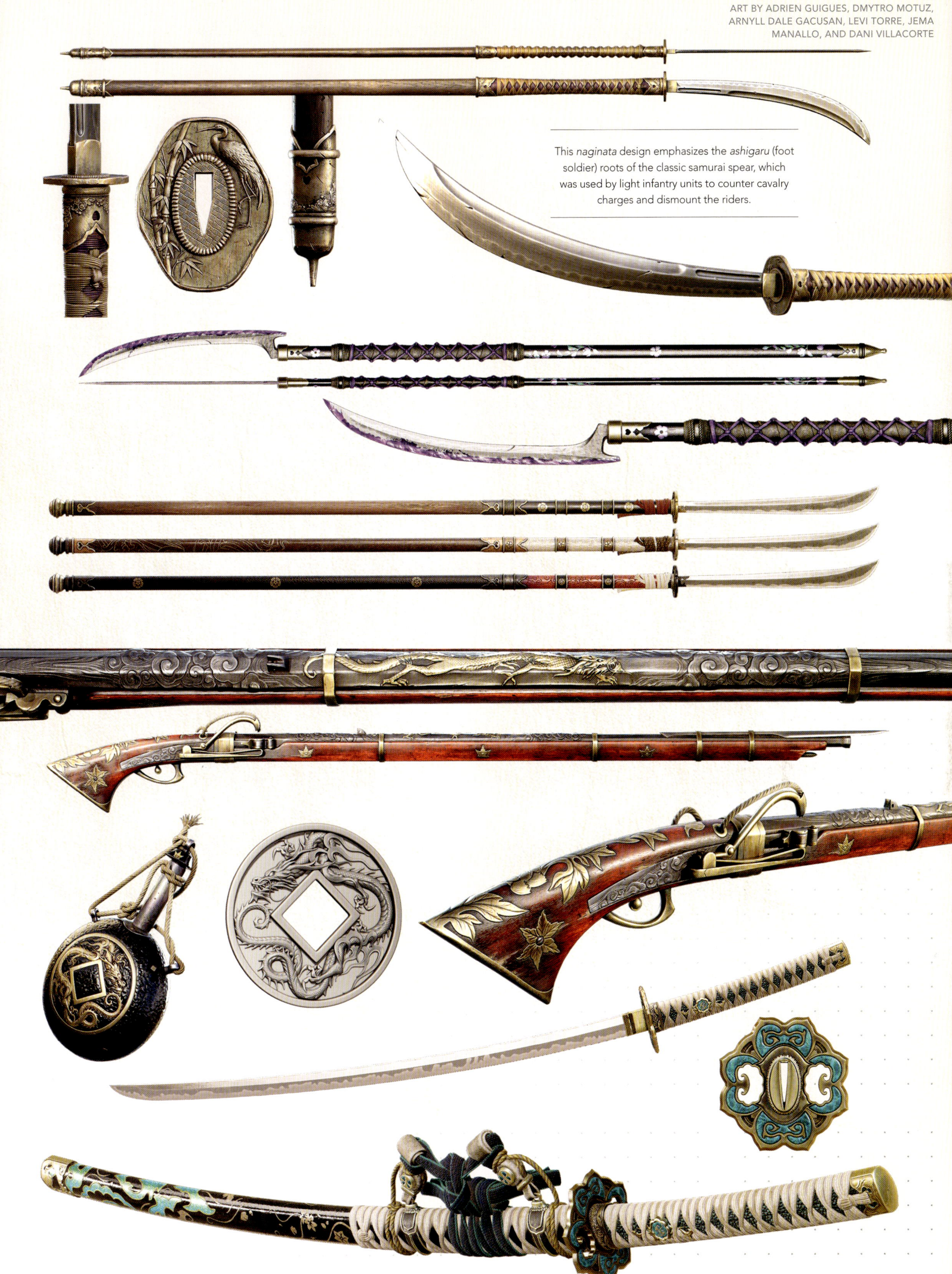

This *naginata* design emphasizes the *ashigaru* (foot soldier) roots of the classic samurai spear, which was used by light infantry units to counter cavalry charges and dismount the riders.

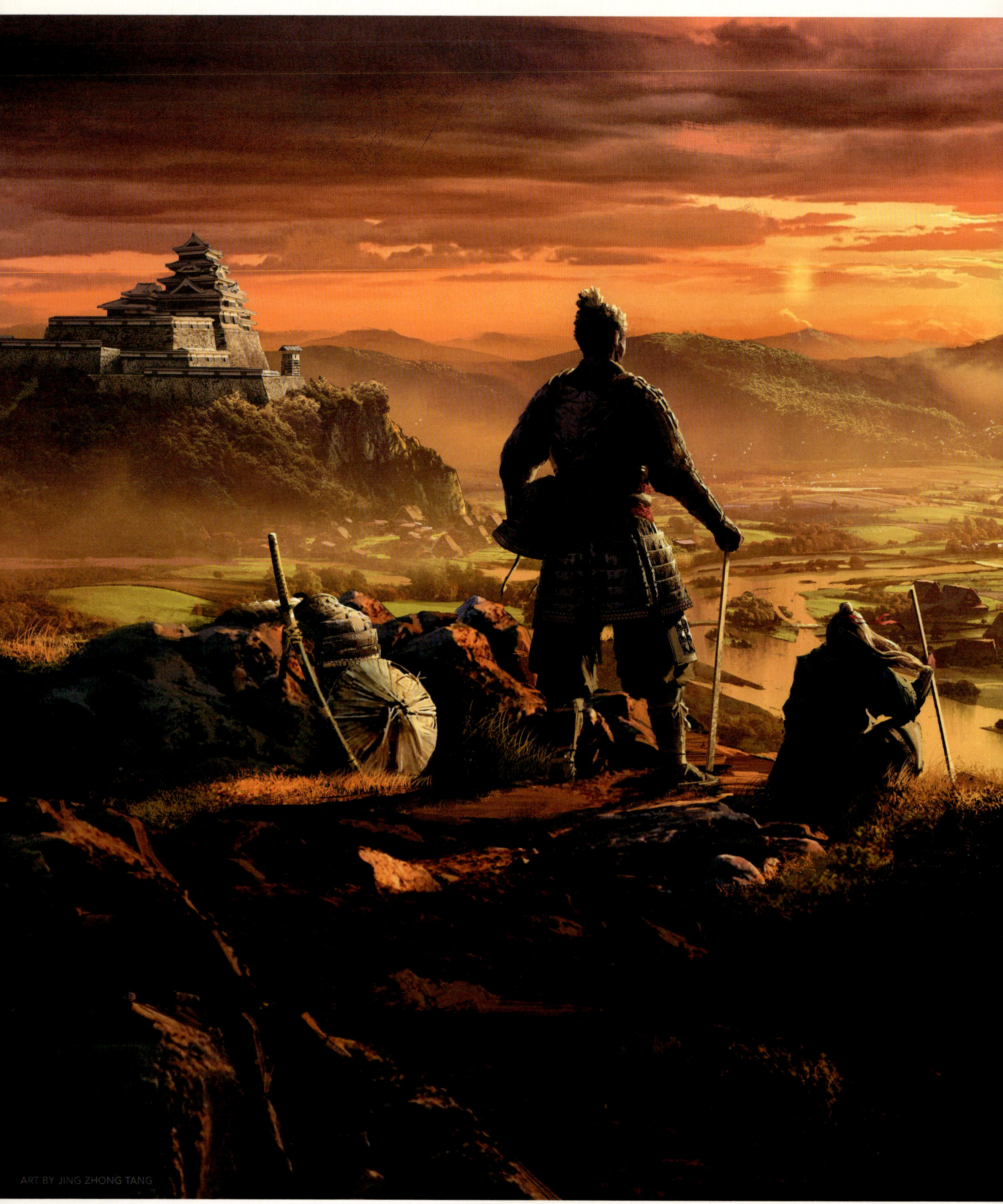

The eventual partnership of Yasuke and Naoe is based on a common goal: ending the bloody, warlord-fueled civil strife in Japan, a beautiful country built on centuries of both refined culture

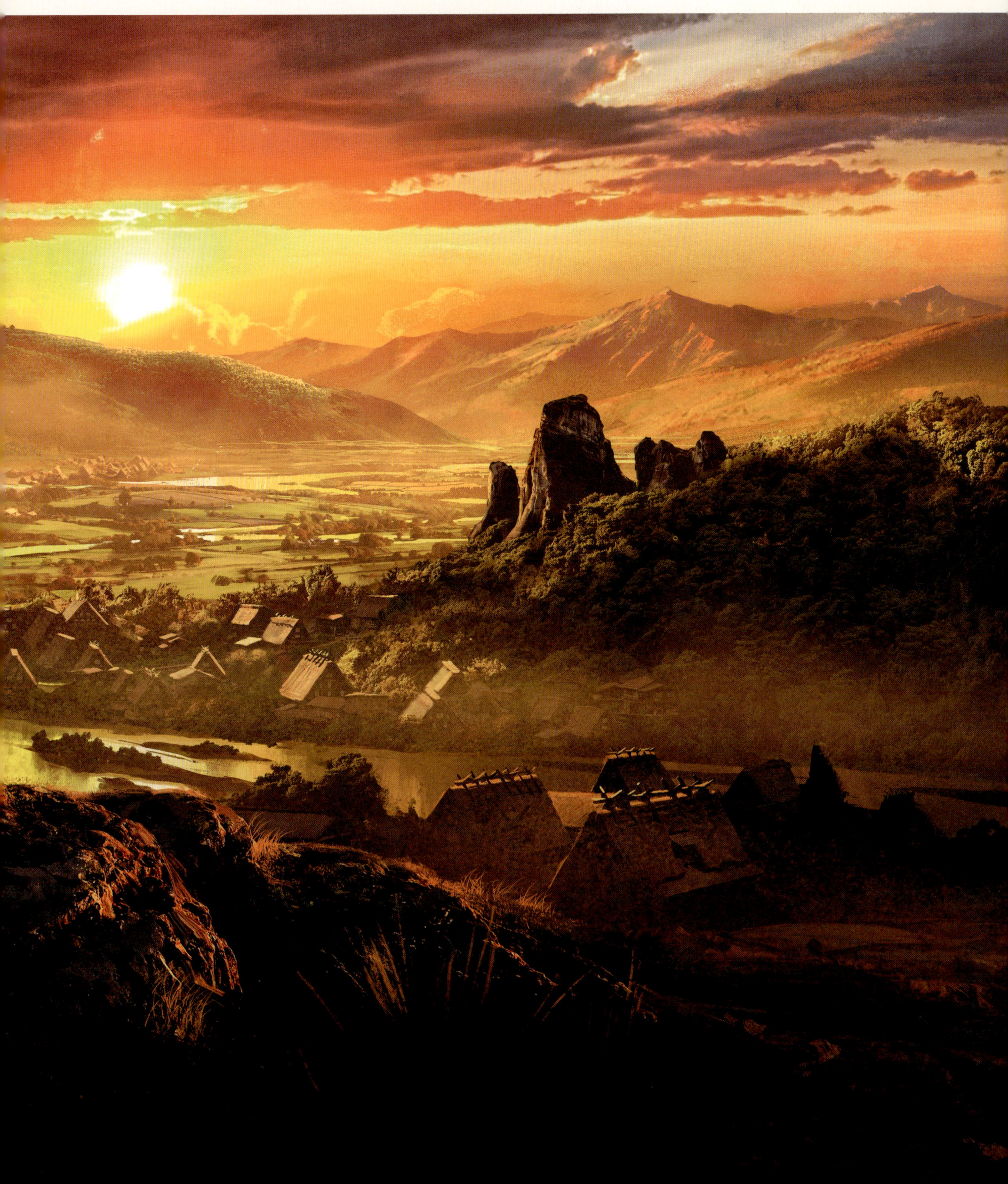

and agrarian communal values. This gorgeous concept image is meant to convey that hopeful theme as *Shadows'* dual protagonists gaze across a bucolic vision of the Japanese countryside.

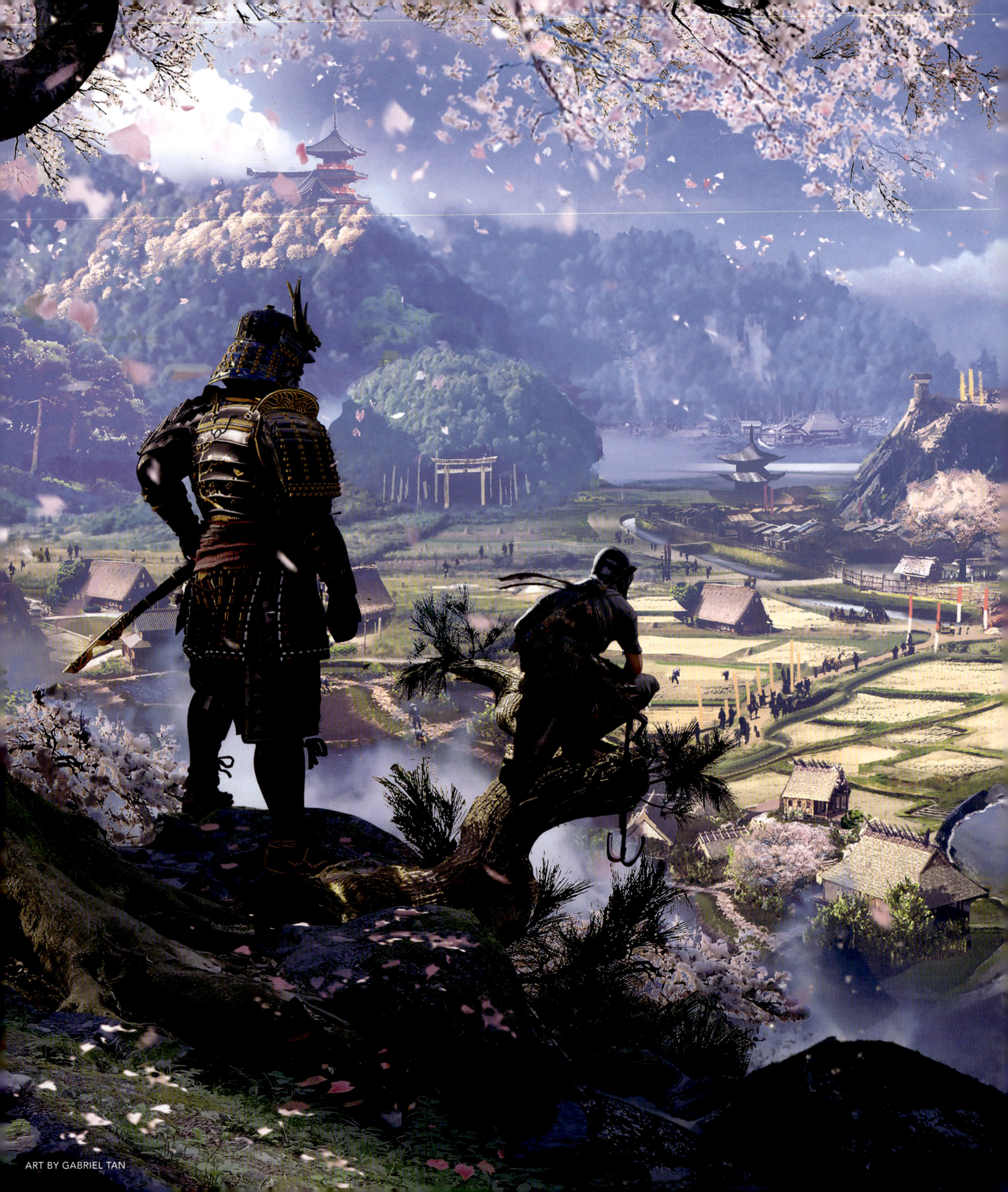

ART BY GABRIEL TAN

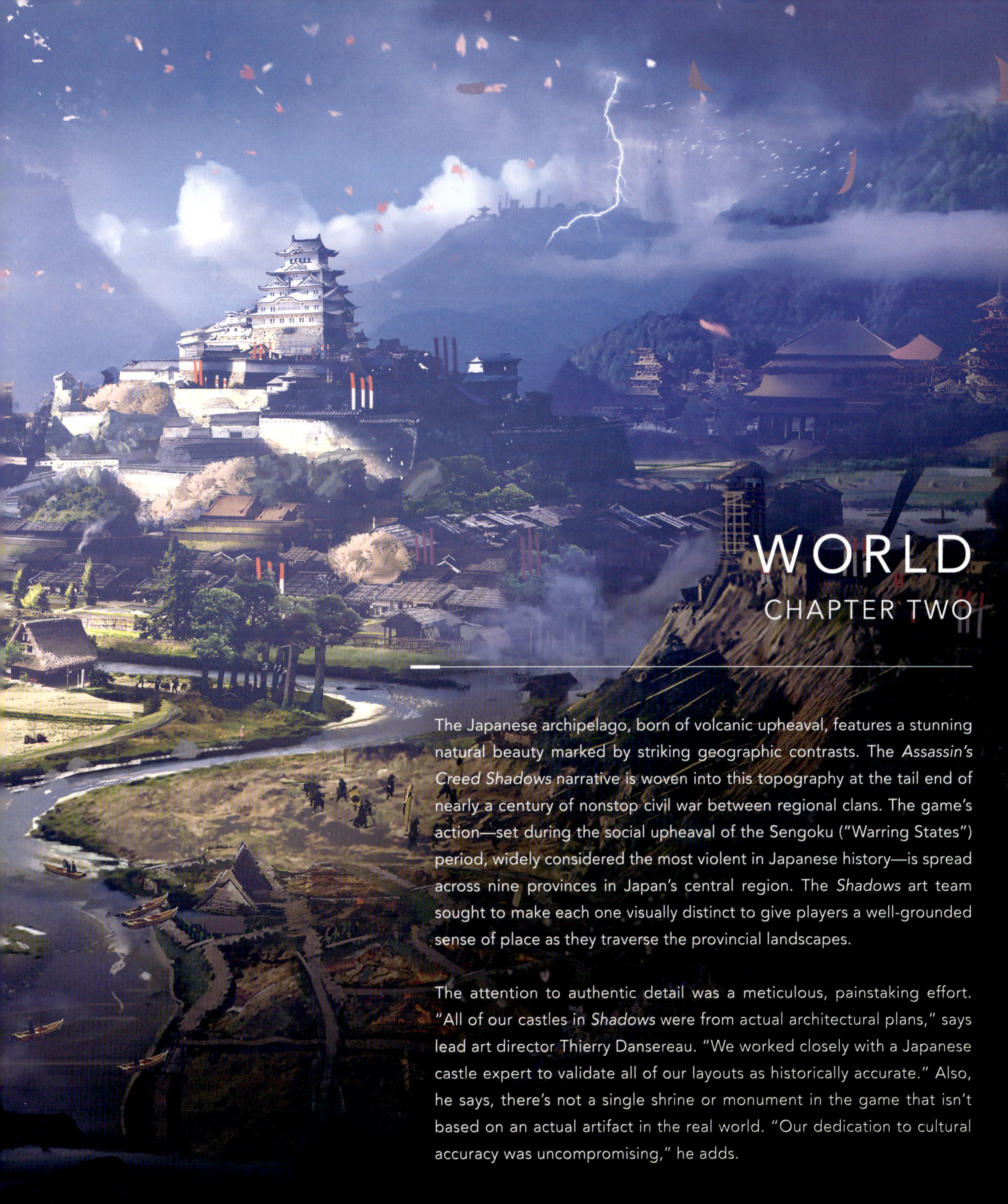

WORLD

CHAPTER TWO

The Japanese archipelago, born of volcanic upheaval, features a stunning natural beauty marked by striking geographic contrasts. The *Assassin's Creed Shadows* narrative is woven into this topography at the tail end of nearly a century of nonstop civil war between regional clans. The game's action—set during the social upheaval of the Sengoku ("Warring States") period, widely considered the most violent in Japanese history—is spread across nine provinces in Japan's central region. The *Shadows* art team sought to make each one visually distinct to give players a well-grounded sense of place as they traverse the provincial landscapes.

The attention to authentic detail was a meticulous, painstaking effort. "All of our castles in *Shadows* were from actual architectural plans," says lead art director Thierry Dansereau. "We worked closely with a Japanese castle expert to validate all of our layouts as historically accurate." Also, he says, there's not a single shrine or monument in the game that isn't based on an actual artifact in the real world. "Our dedication to cultural accuracy was uncompromising," he adds.

YAMASHIRO *THE IMPERIAL POWER*

The colorful imperial city of Kyoto *(seen below)*, throne of the emperor and largest population center in Japan, dominates Yamashiro Province. Largely untouched by Japan's sectional warfare, Kyoto has long played a crucial role in the development of Japanese cultural traditions—the city is renowned for the opulence of the imperial court, of course, but also for its

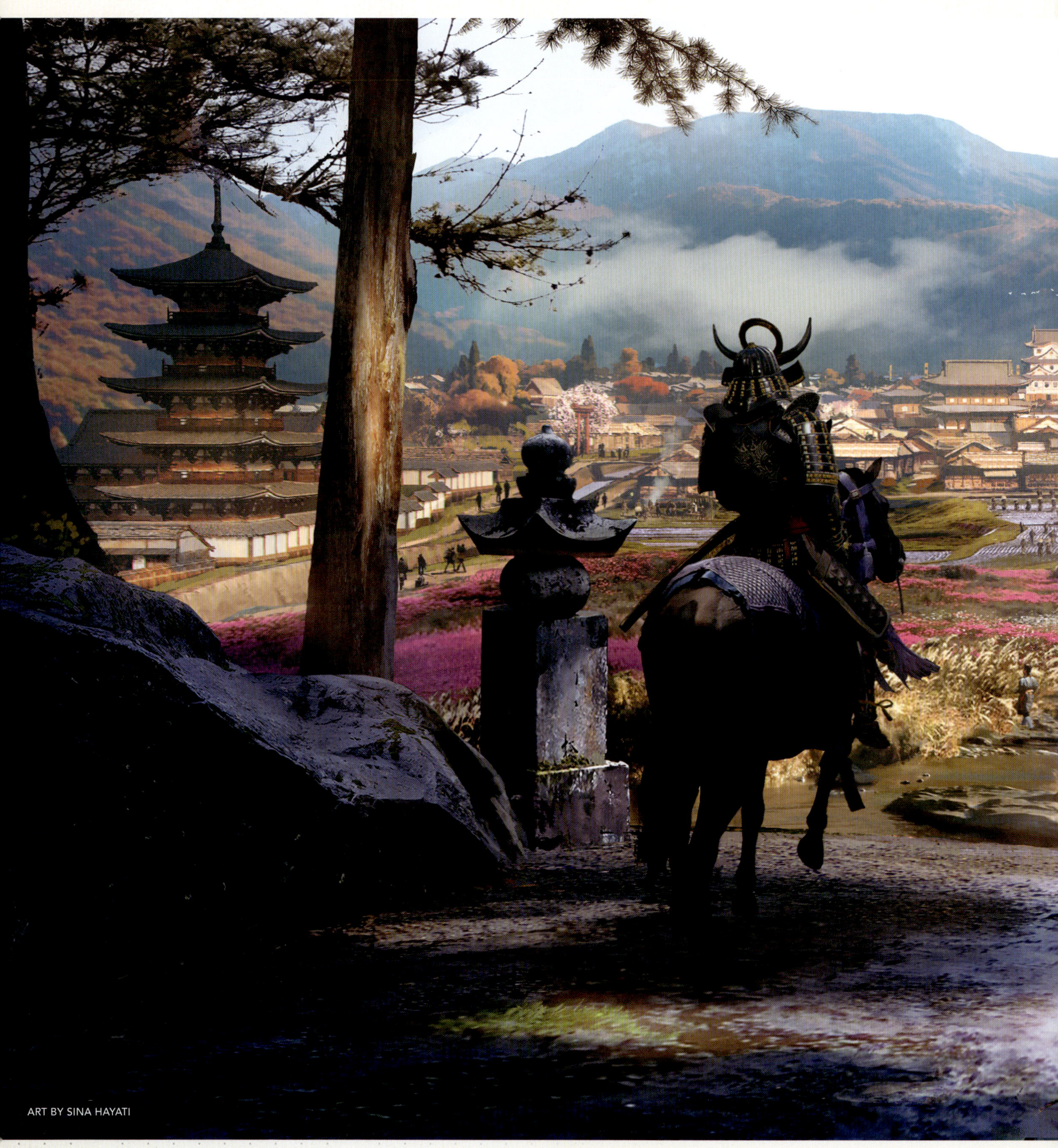

ART BY SINA HAYATI

art exhibits, luxury crafts, theater, libraries, and scholar-filled monasteries. This overview of Kyoto was created with historical accuracy in mind, including key sites such as the Buddhist temple of Honnō-ji, where a moment occurs in *Assassin's Creed Shadows*.

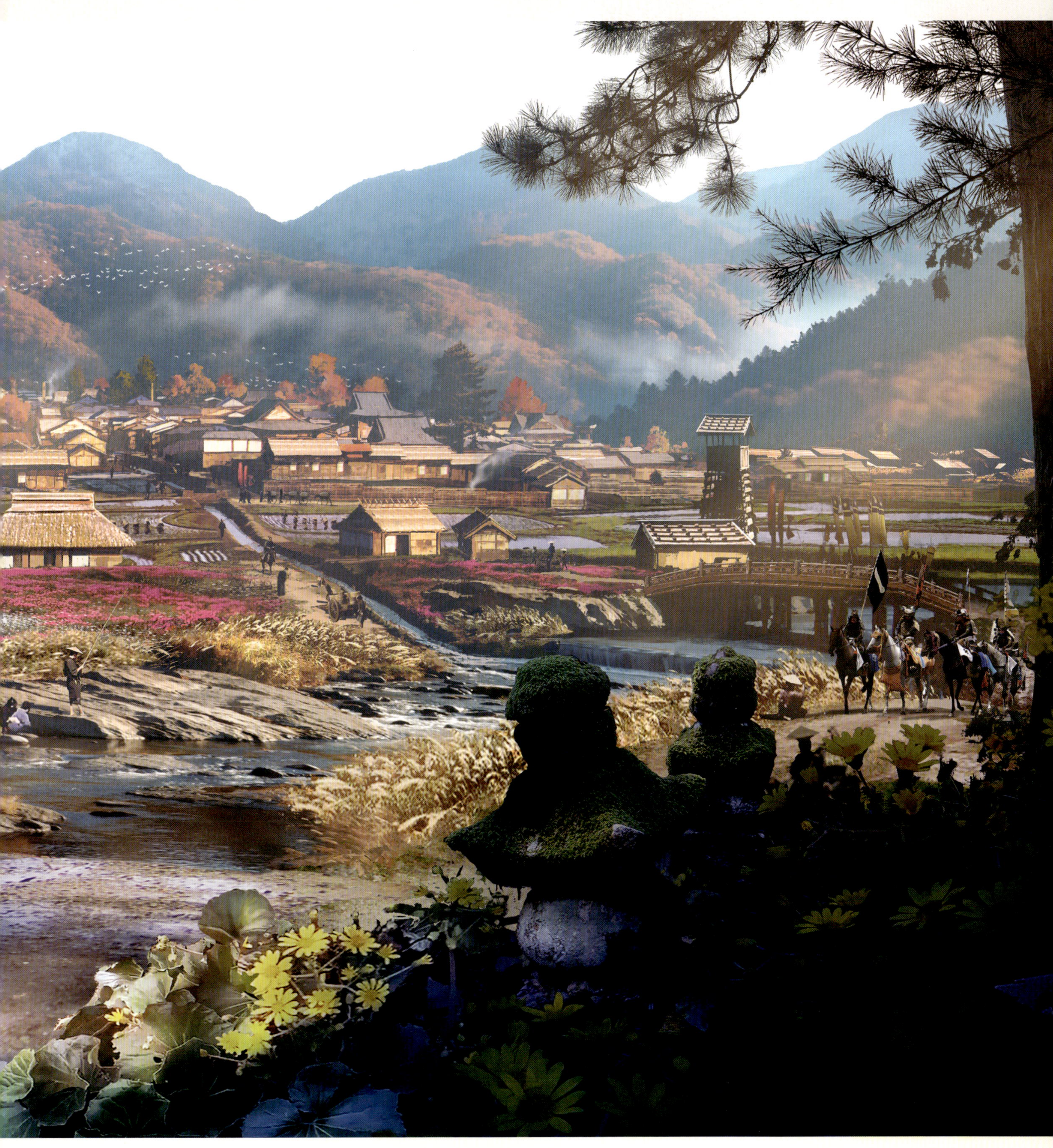

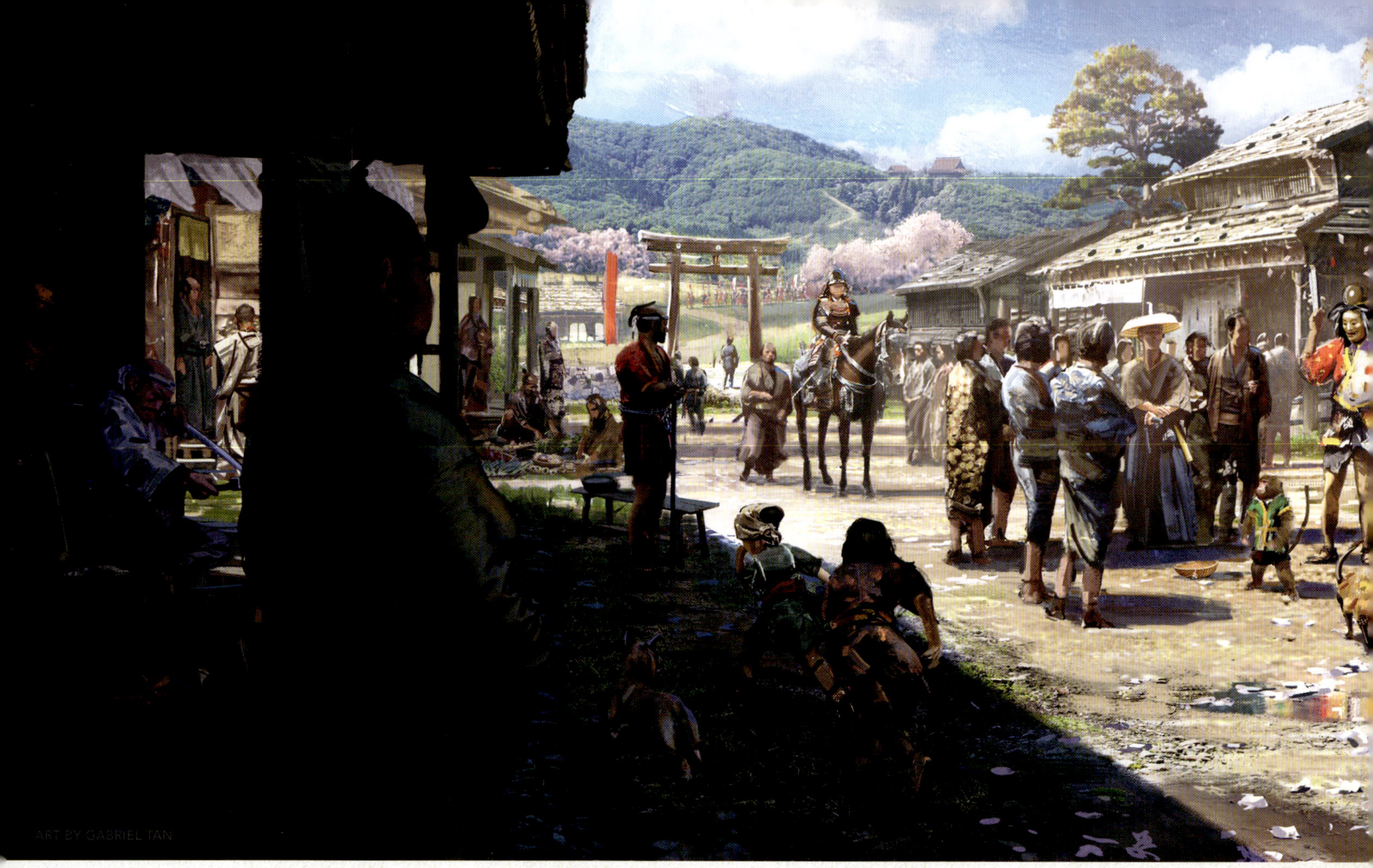

ART BY GABRIEL TAN

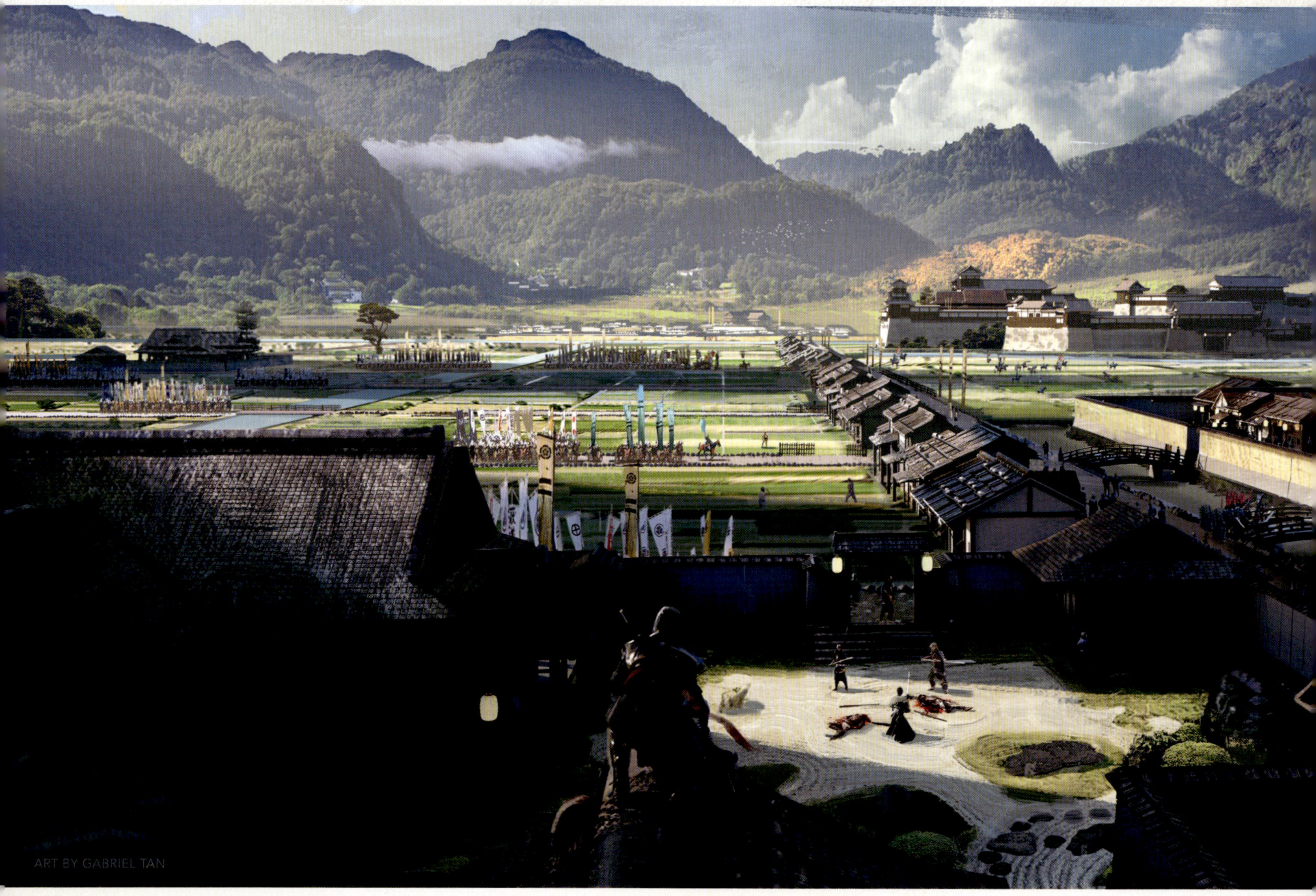

ART BY GABRIEL TAN

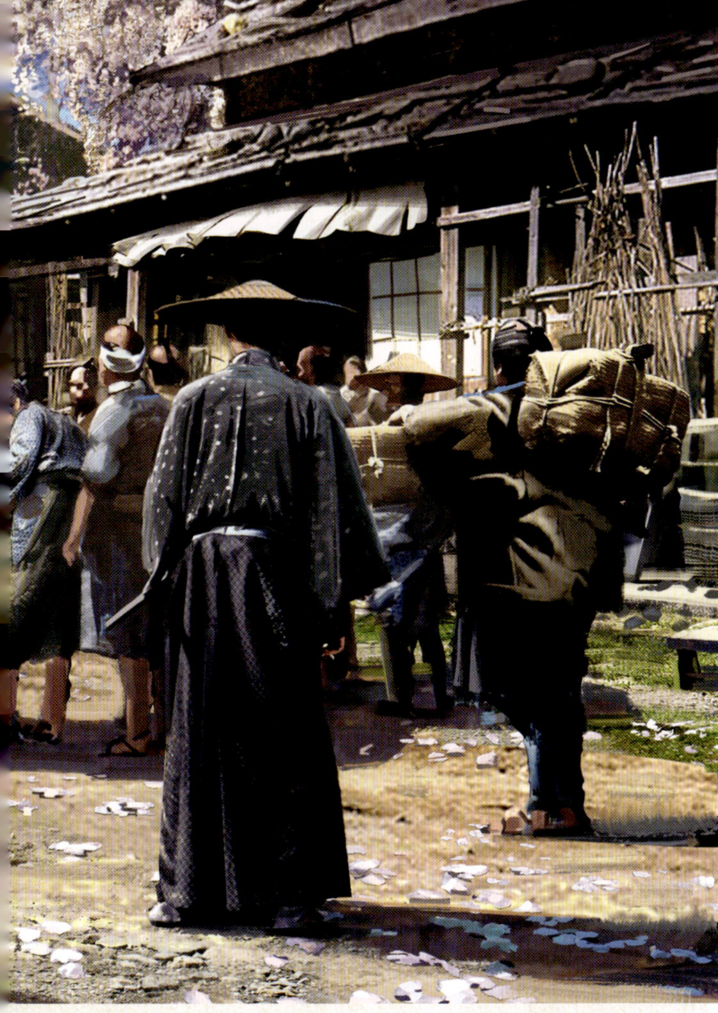

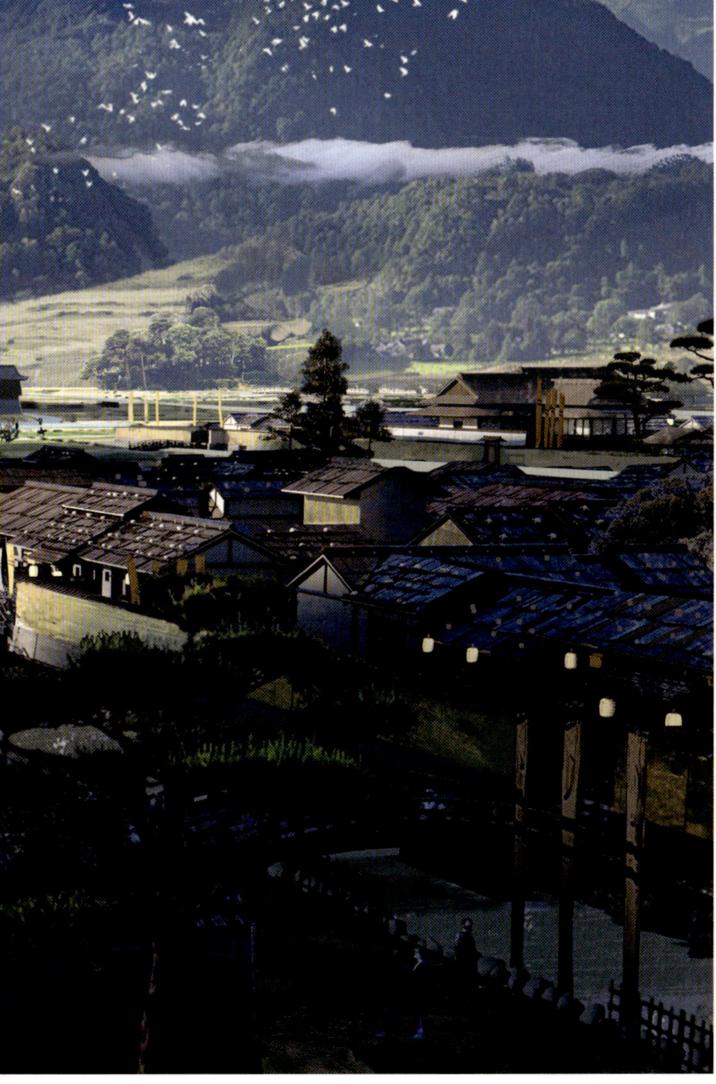

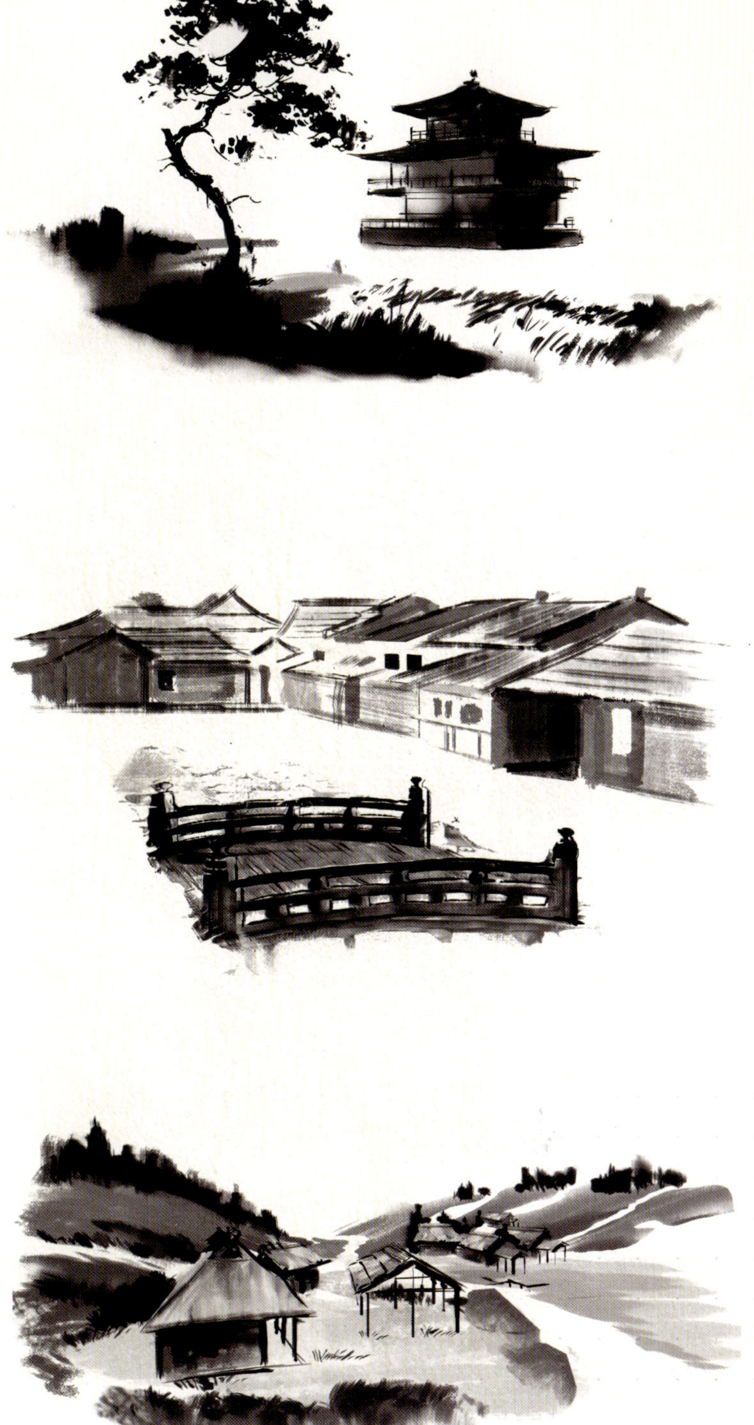

The great city of Kyoto is nestled in a wide plain encircled by mountains and dotted with agrarian villages. Sprawling tea plantations surround the capital and produce some of the most coveted brews in the world. These concept paintings explore the busy street life of a typical small village *(upper left)* and the expanse of the flat landscape outside Kyoto *(left)*. The distant troops in the lower image are Mitsuhide's soldiers marching with deadly intent toward Nobunaga's Honnō-ji temple sanctuary seen at far right. "We always try to include story elements like this in our environment concept art," says Gabriel Tan.

This spectacular view across a wintry Kyoto from the Honnō-ji pagoda is a paint-over image of an actual frame from the game. The palace complex is seen in the left distance.

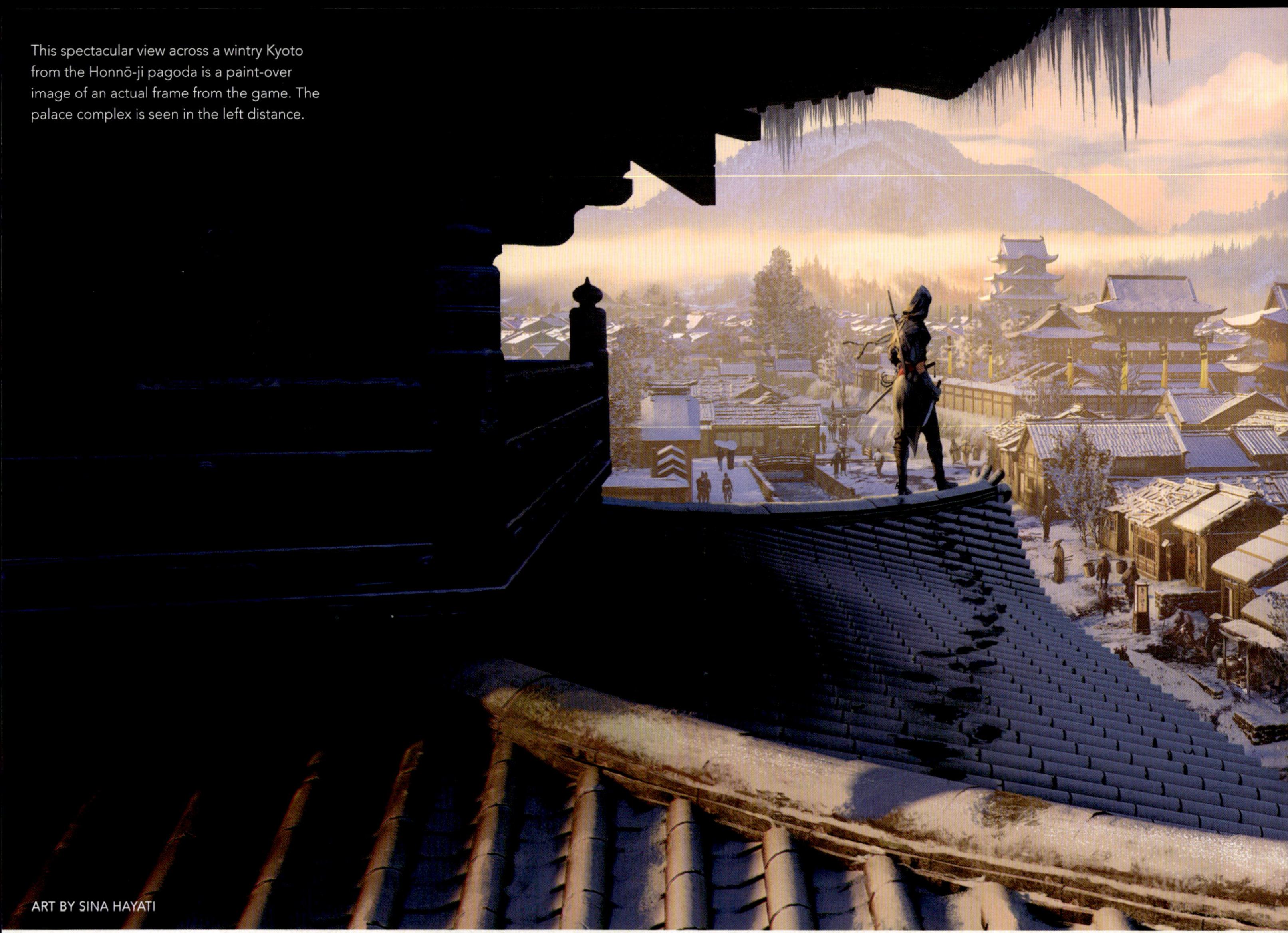

ART BY SINA HAYATI

The game's dynamic weather system prompted the art team to create concept images of key locations rendered in all four seasons. At right is a winter's panorama with the temple of Kiyomizu-dera in the foreground—a famous landmark that still stands today and was toured by the *Shadows* art team to ensure the accuracy of its depiction.

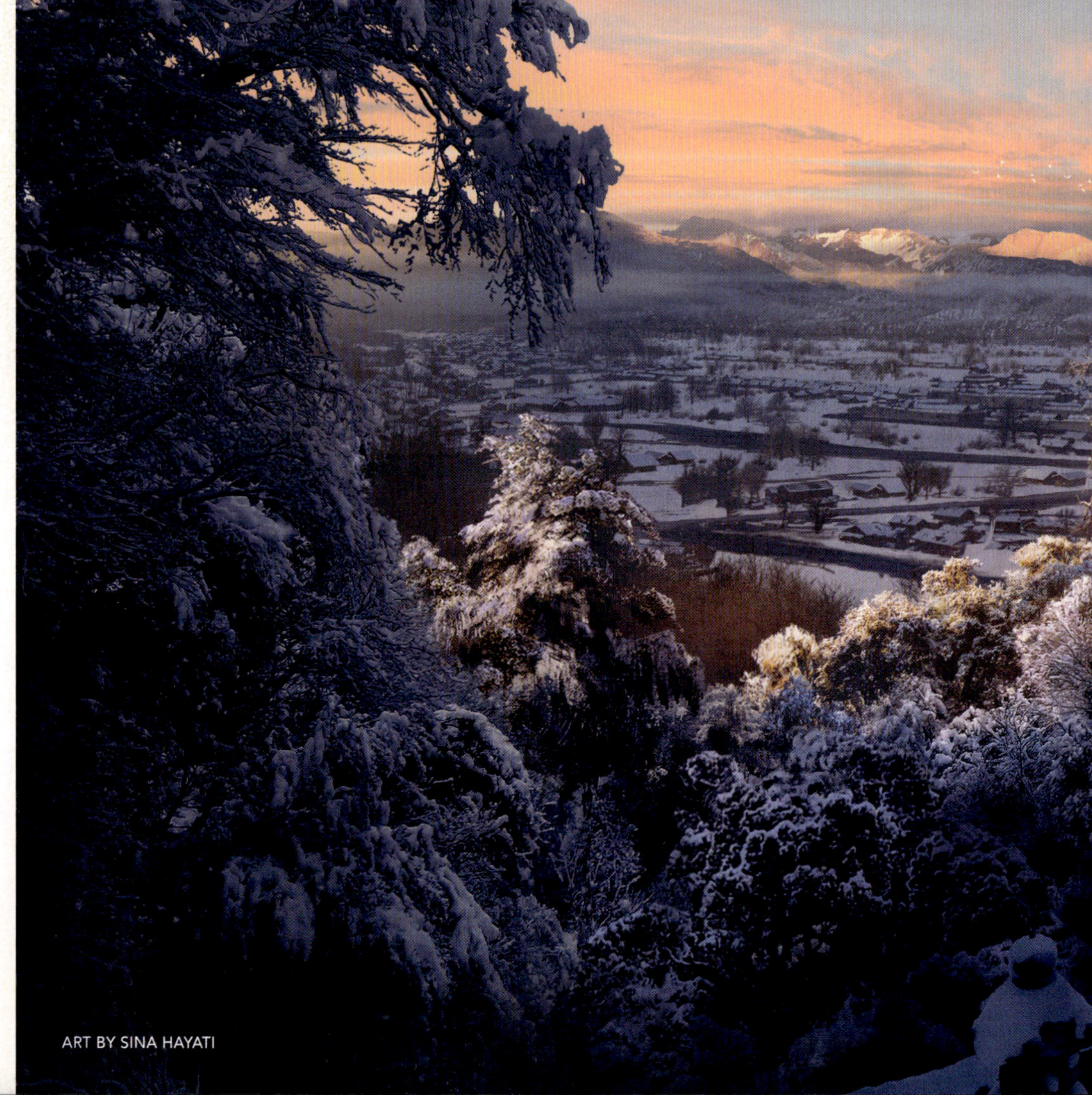

ART BY SINA HAYATI

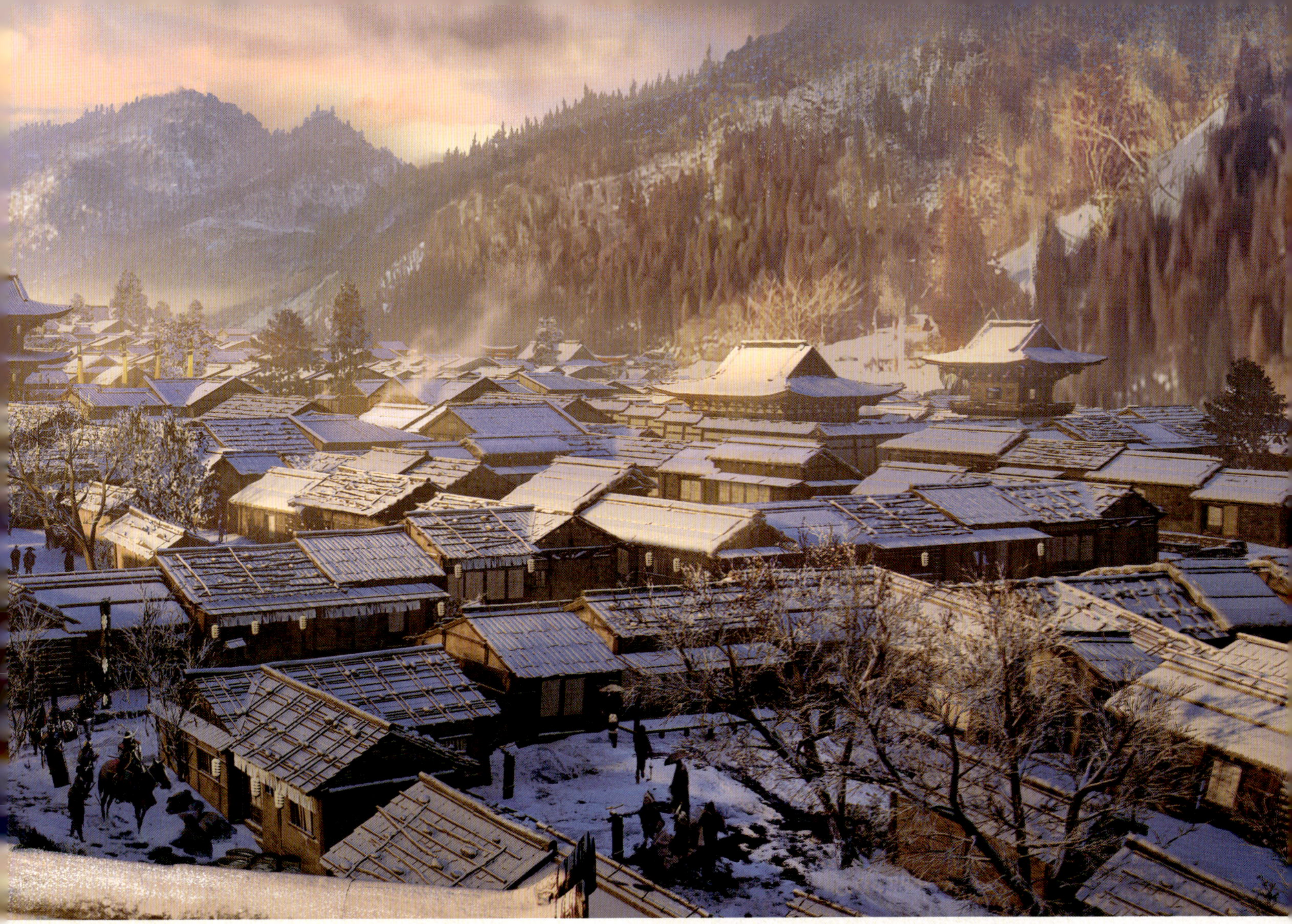

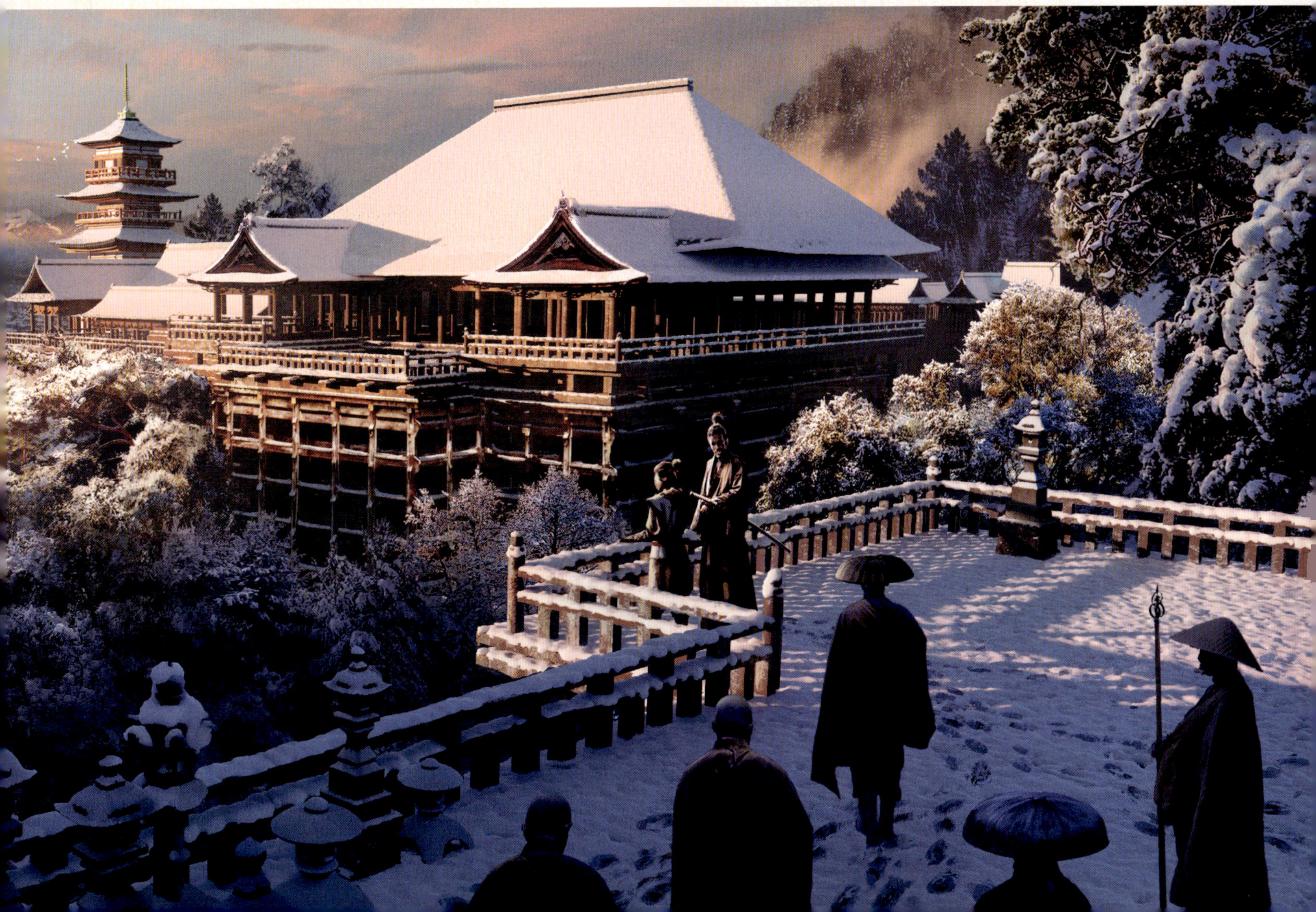

OMI *THE HEARTLAND*

Oda Nobunaga considers Omi the key province in his plan to unify the country. Its bountiful heartland is the breadbasket of Japan, and Lake Biwa serves as a strategic transit hub in the shipping of agricultural goods and other resources across

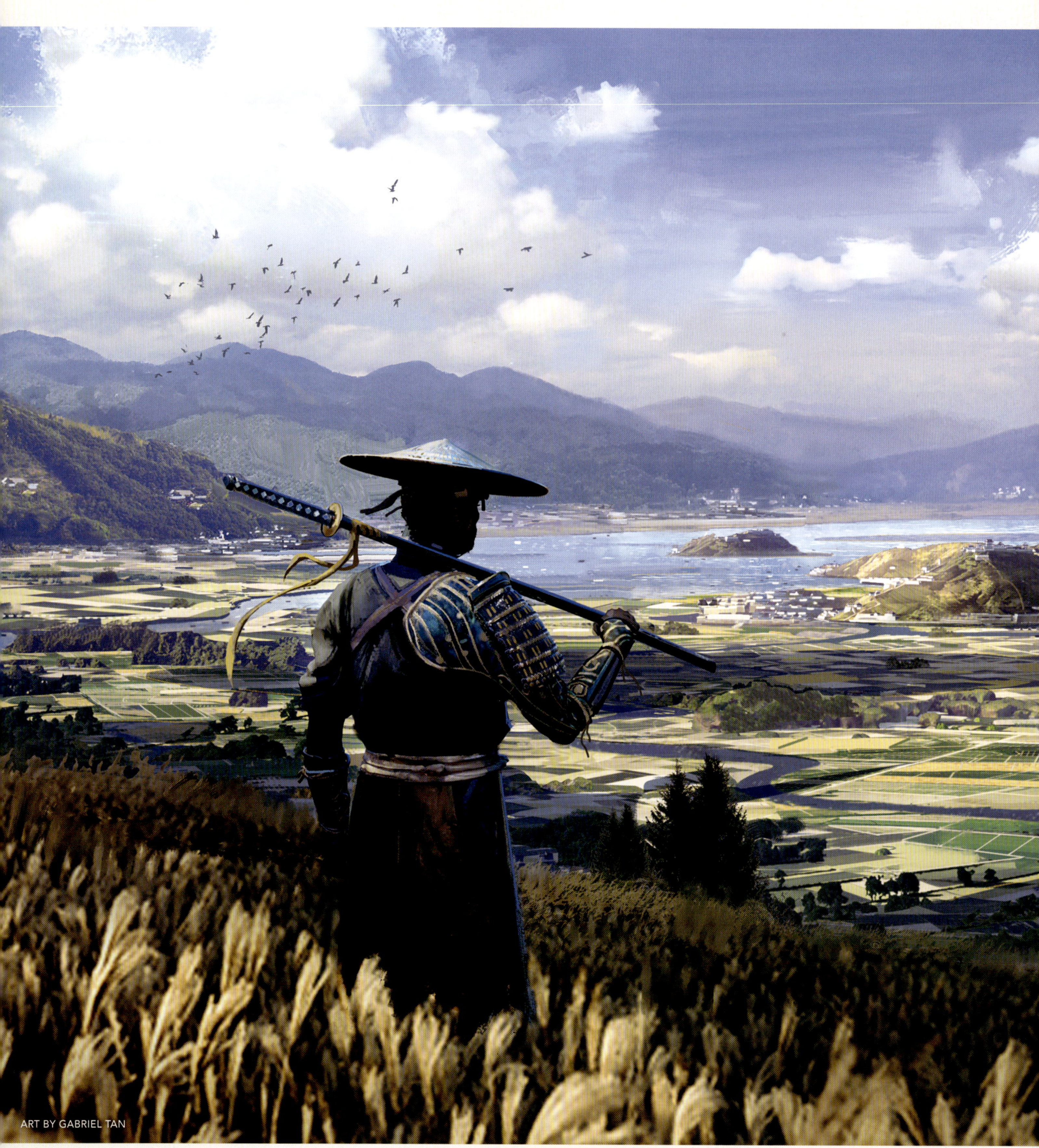

ART BY GABRIEL TAN

the entire region. A basin of fertile lowlands surrounds the great central lake and extends to the province's mountainous borders. This basin serves as one of Japan's largest areas of irrigated rice fields.

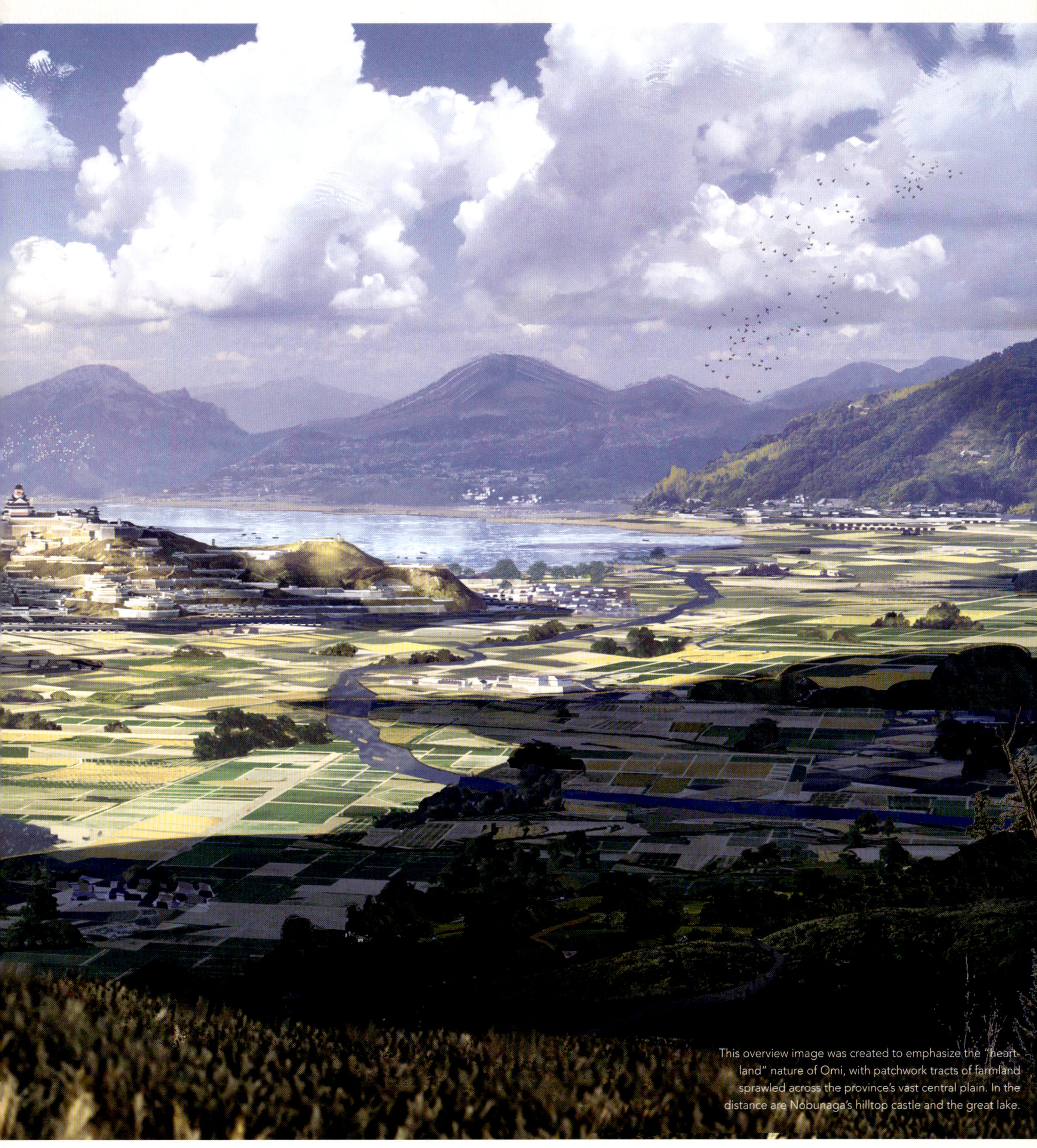

This overview image was created to emphasize the "heartland" nature of Omi, with patchwork tracts of farmland sprawled across the province's vast central plain. In the distance are Nobunaga's hilltop castle and the great lake.

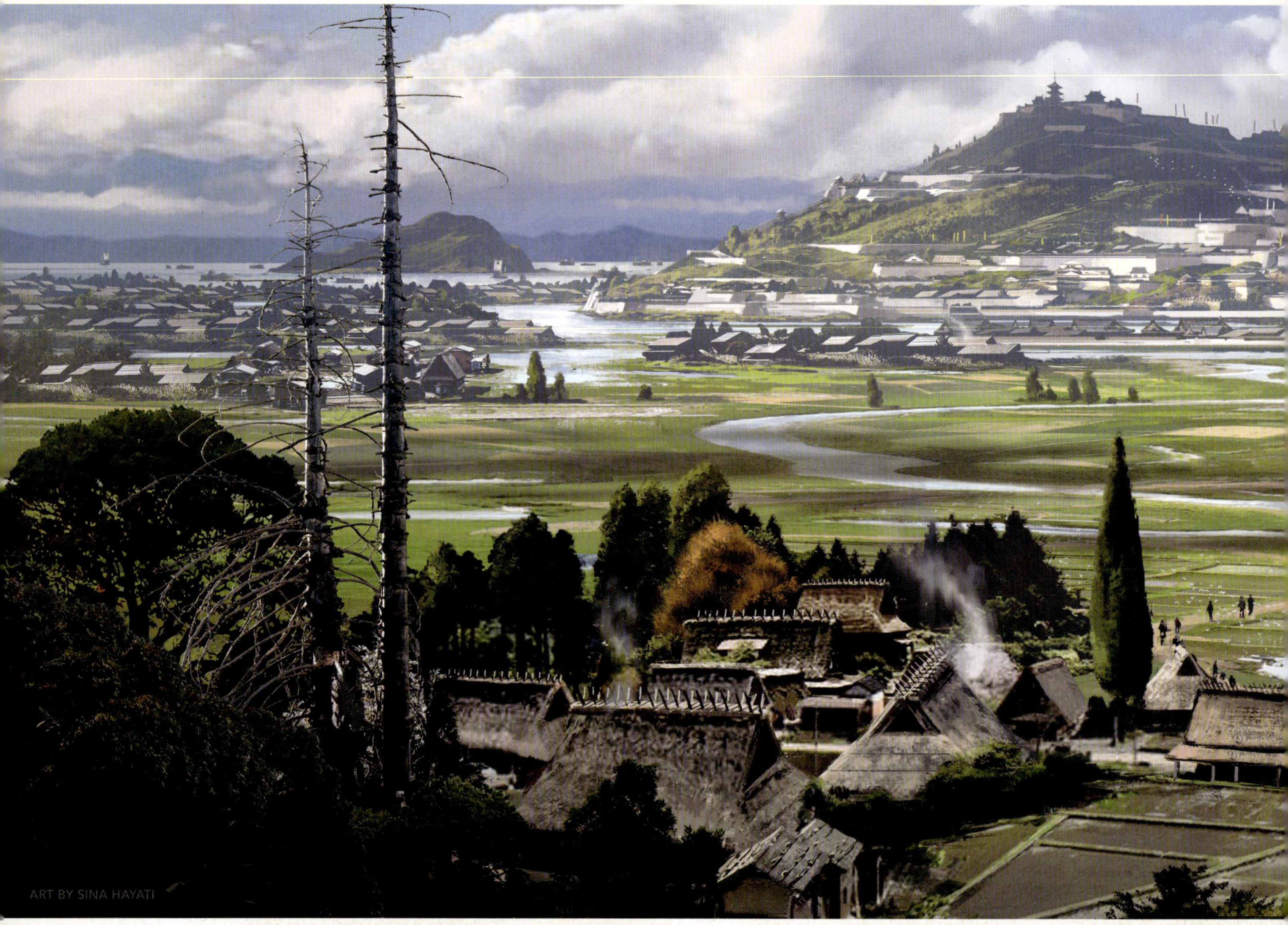

ART BY SINA HAYATI

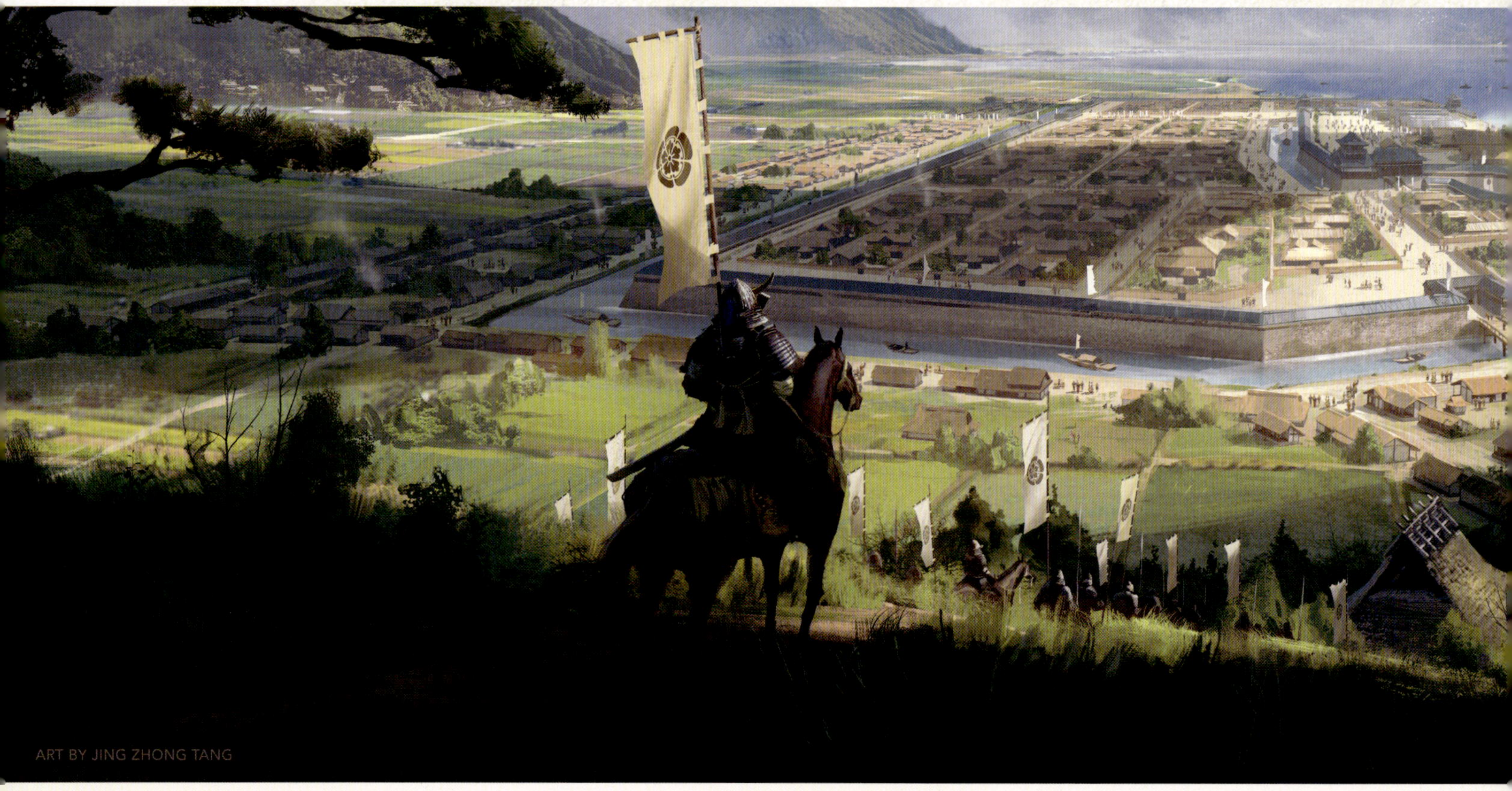

ART BY JING ZHONG TANG

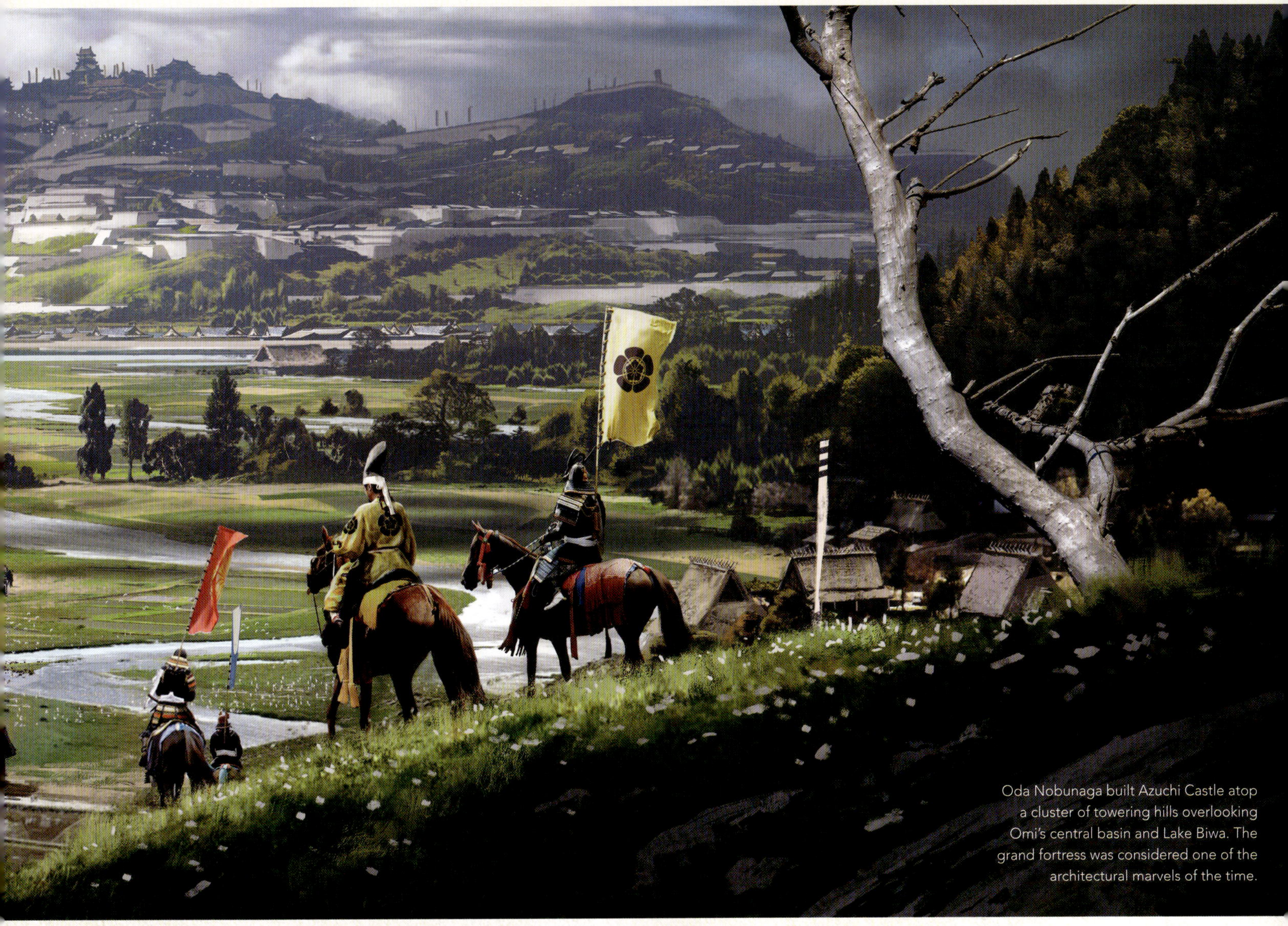

Oda Nobunaga built Azuchi Castle atop a cluster of towering hills overlooking Omi's central basin and Lake Biwa. The grand fortress was considered one of the architectural marvels of the time.

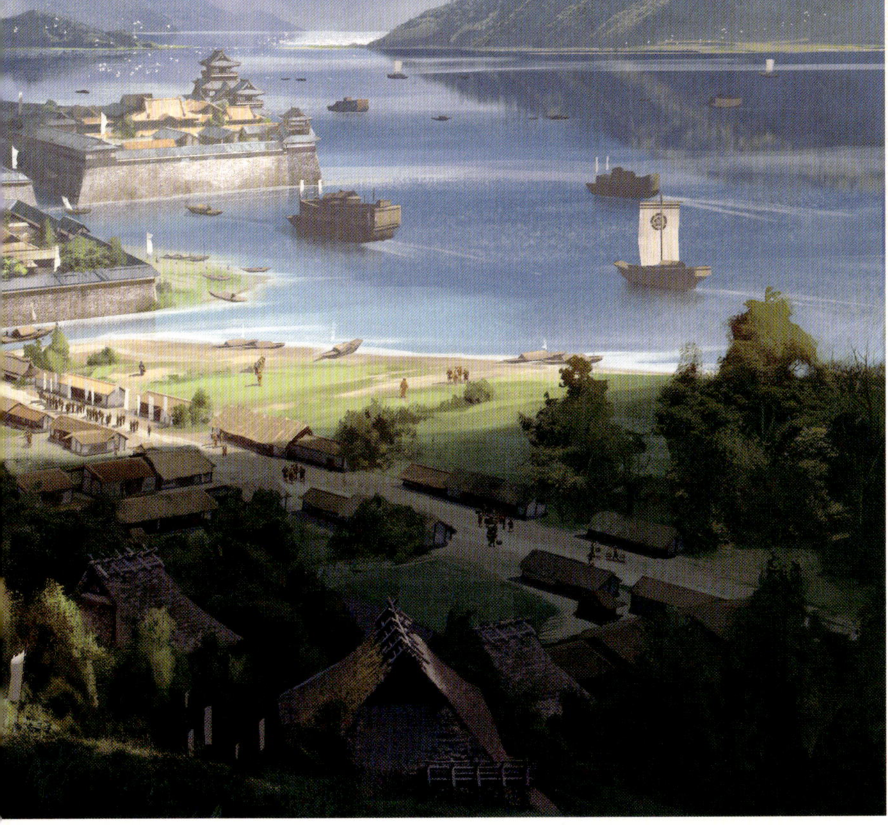

The walled fortress at Sakamoto serves as the castle of Akechi Mitsuhide, who, despite being one of the daimyo Oda Nobunaga's trusted samurai generals, nonetheless betrays his leader by orchestrating the Honnō-ji incident.

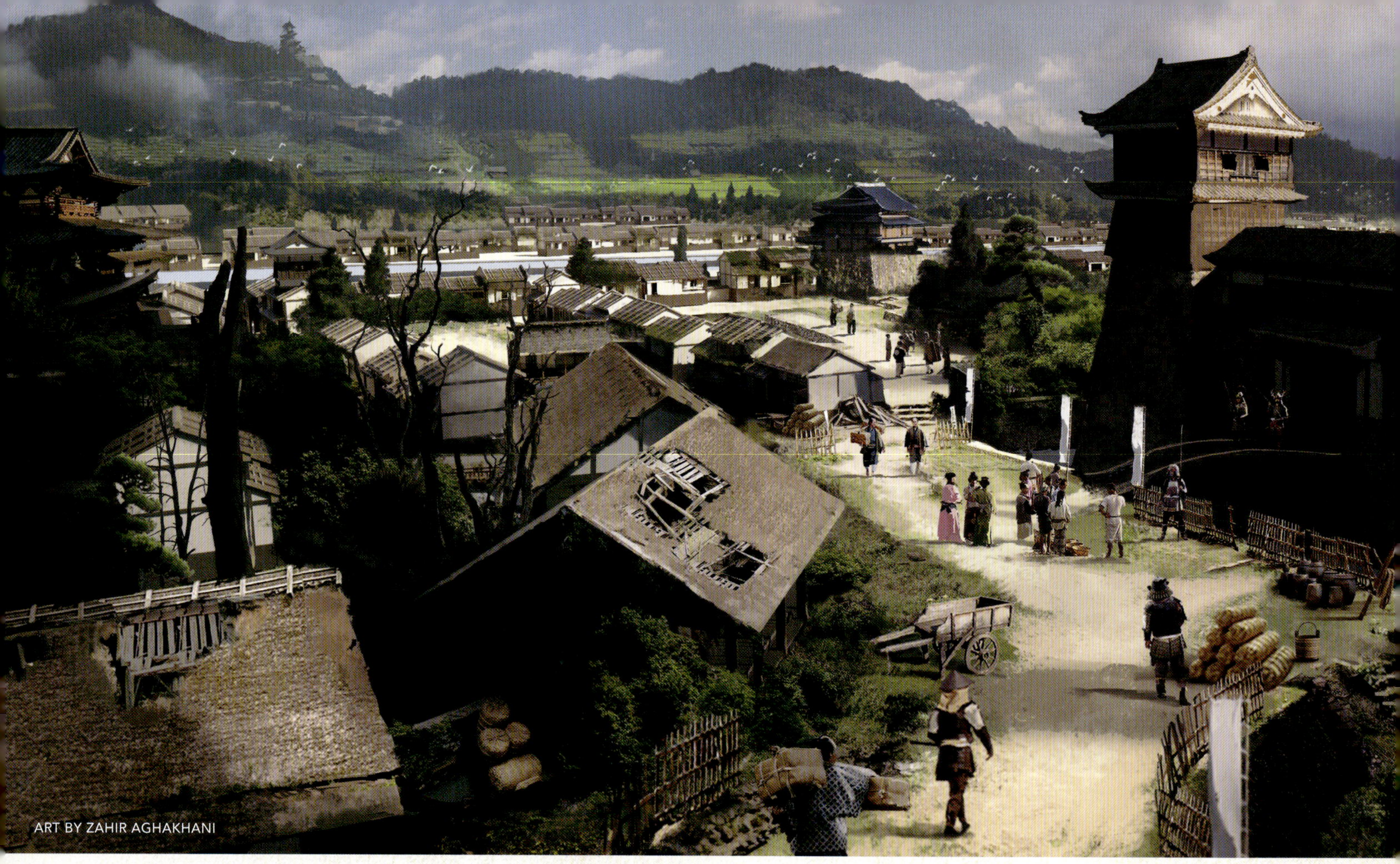

ART BY ZAHIR AGHAKHANI

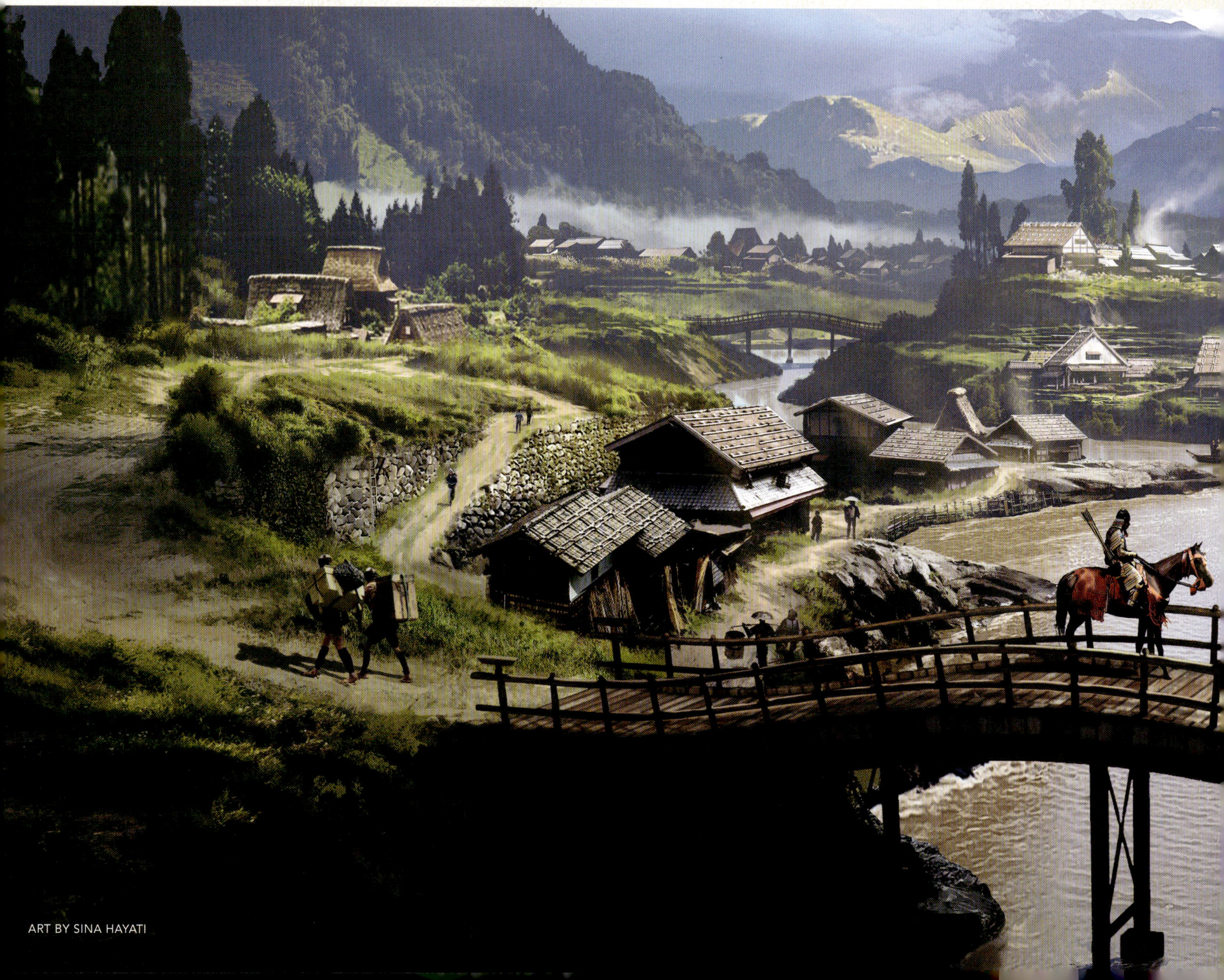

ART BY SINA HAYATI

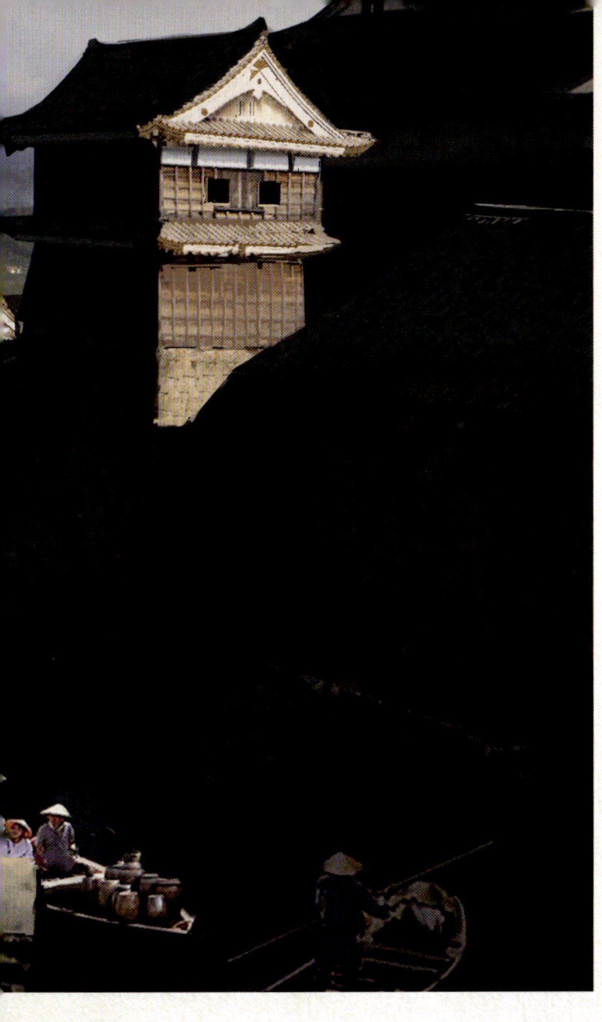

Left: This scene of the Sakamoto castle town depicts damaged huts outside the military gate leading into the main fortress. "We wanted to illustrate the contrast between hierarchies in those days," says Tan. "Commoners suffer devastation during a siege but often get no recovery aid from the warlord or his wealthy inner circle."

Below: Many Omi farming villages were connected by waterways like the Hachiman Canal. Here, Yasuke rides across a high-humped bridge, built to allow boat traffic to pass beneath it on the canal below.

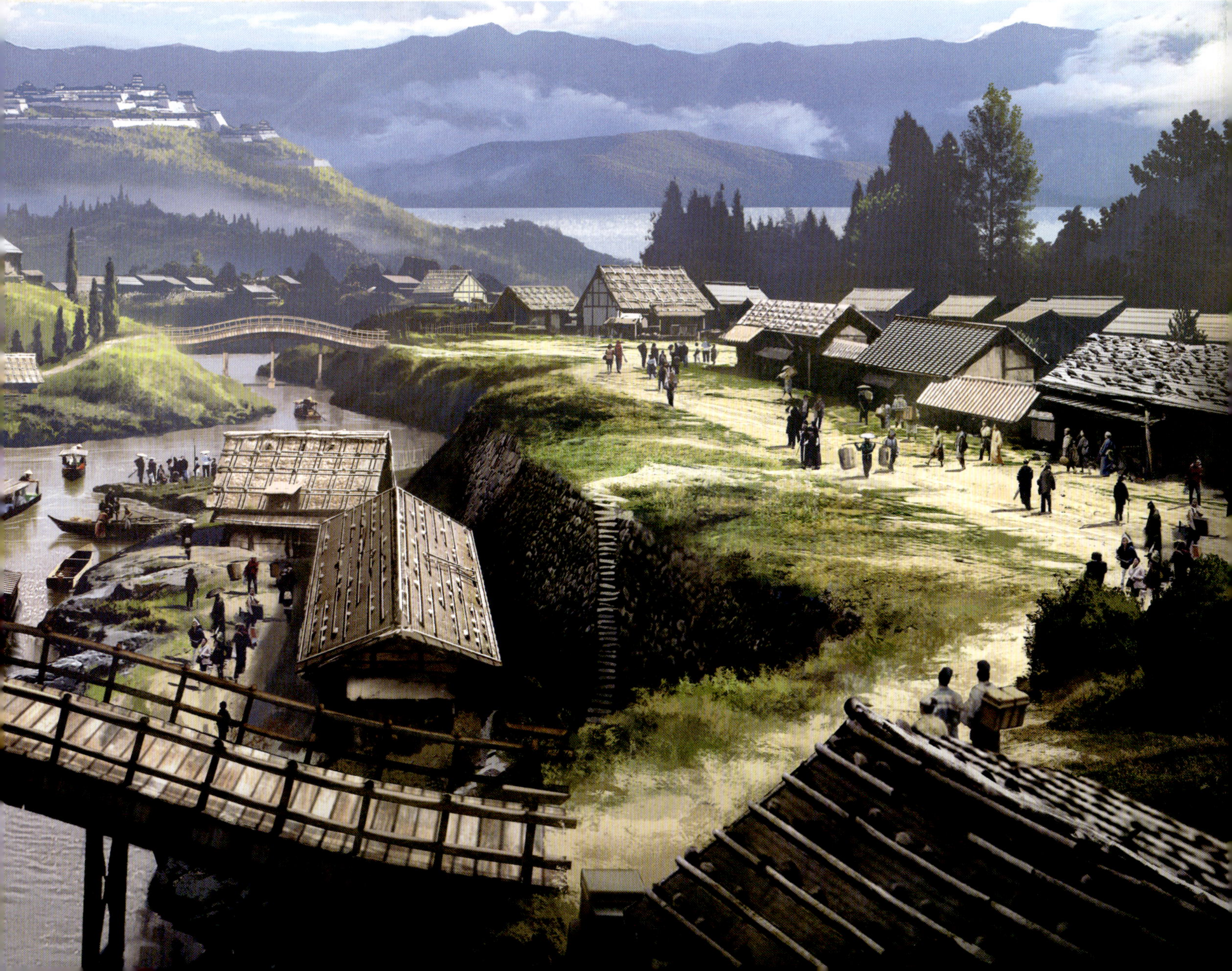

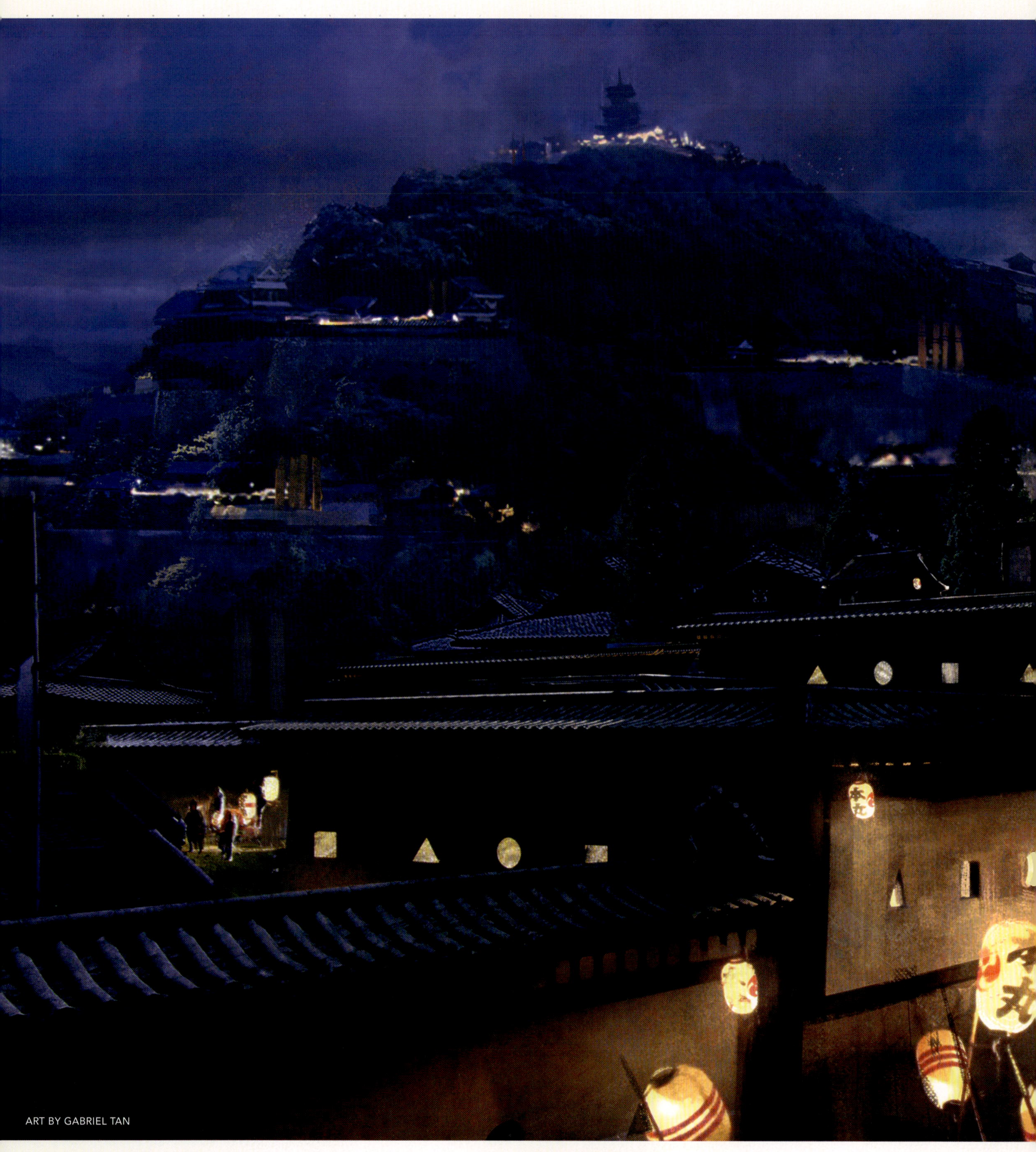
ART BY GABRIEL TAN

Oda Nobunaga was fond of lighting major thoroughfares at night with thousands of festive lanterns to impress visitors and create an iridescent aura of wealth and power.

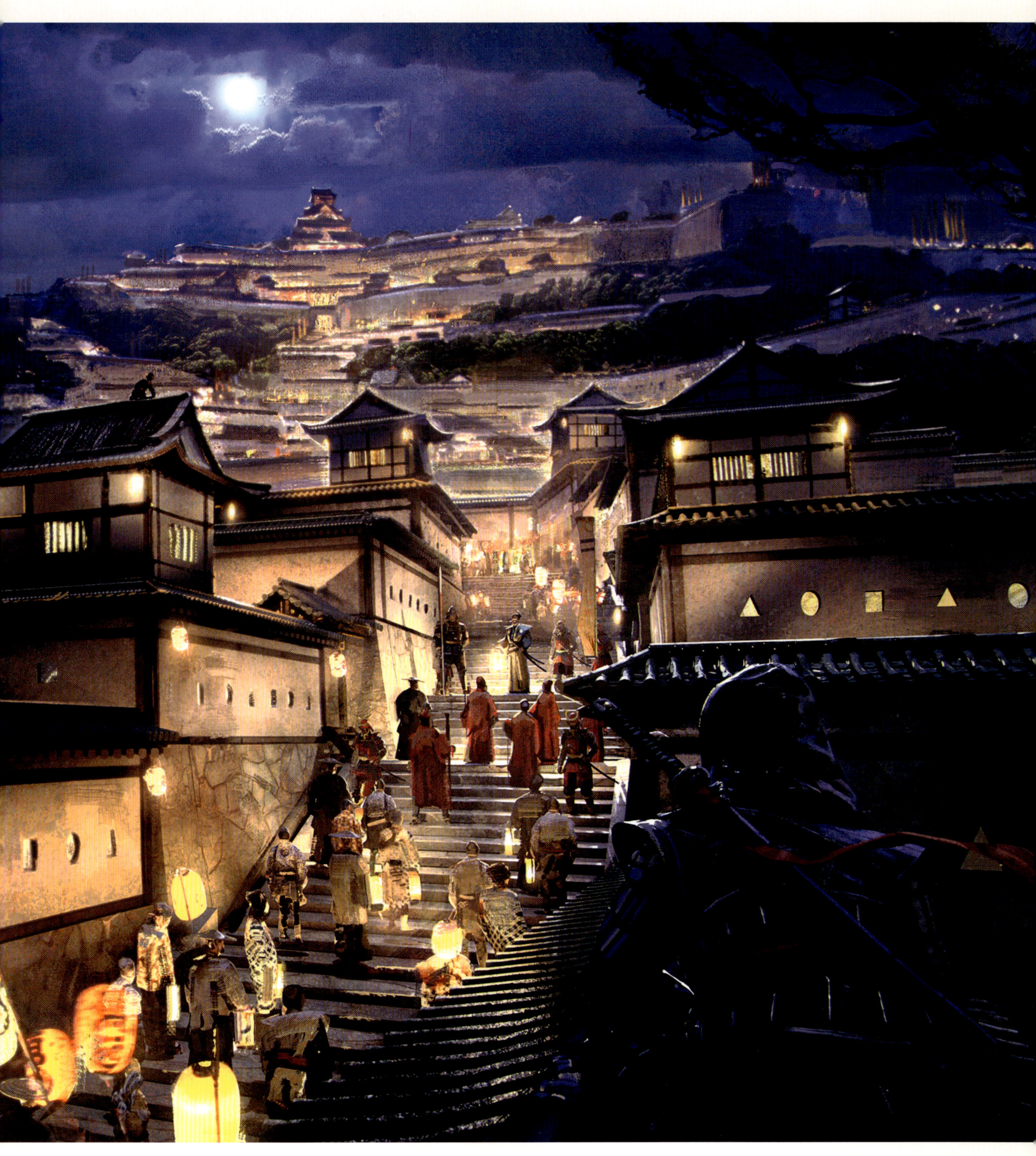

Here, Nobunaga and Yasuke lead a contingent of red-clad Jesuits up the brightly illuminated steps to Azuchi Castle at the top.

Sea trade with Asian and European partners was important to Oda Nobunaga's ascendancy as the "first uniter." He also controlled many important inland river checkpoints. This waterfront image of Azuchi Castle seen from the lake features a fortified island *(at left)* where Nobunaga stored many weapons. He deployed boats from this basin to trade silver for guns and other goods at international port cities in Wakasa and elsewhere.

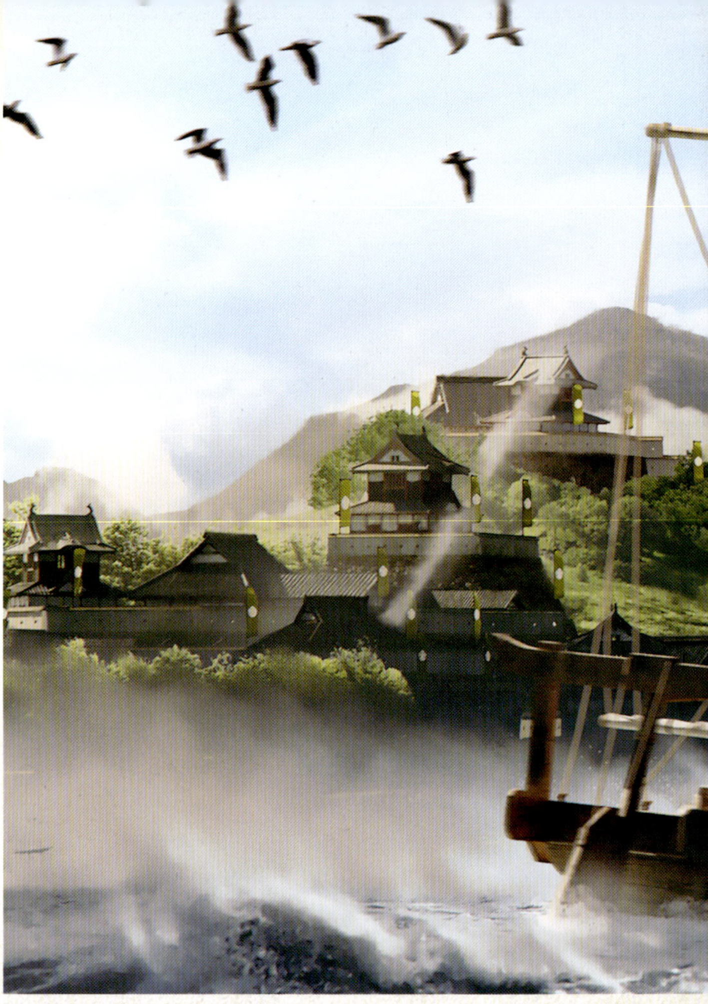

ART BY FRANCIS LAFLECHE

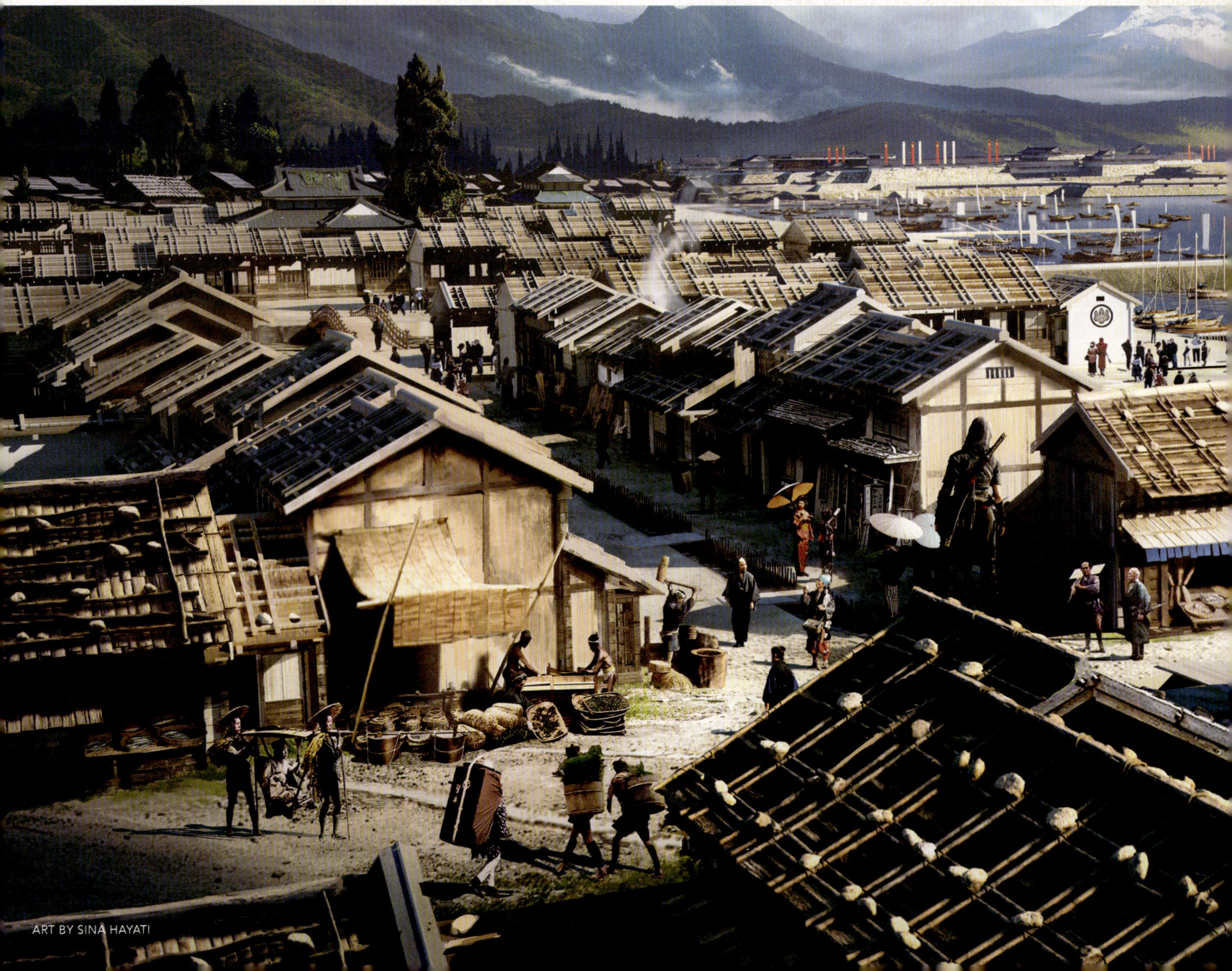

ART BY SINA HAYATI

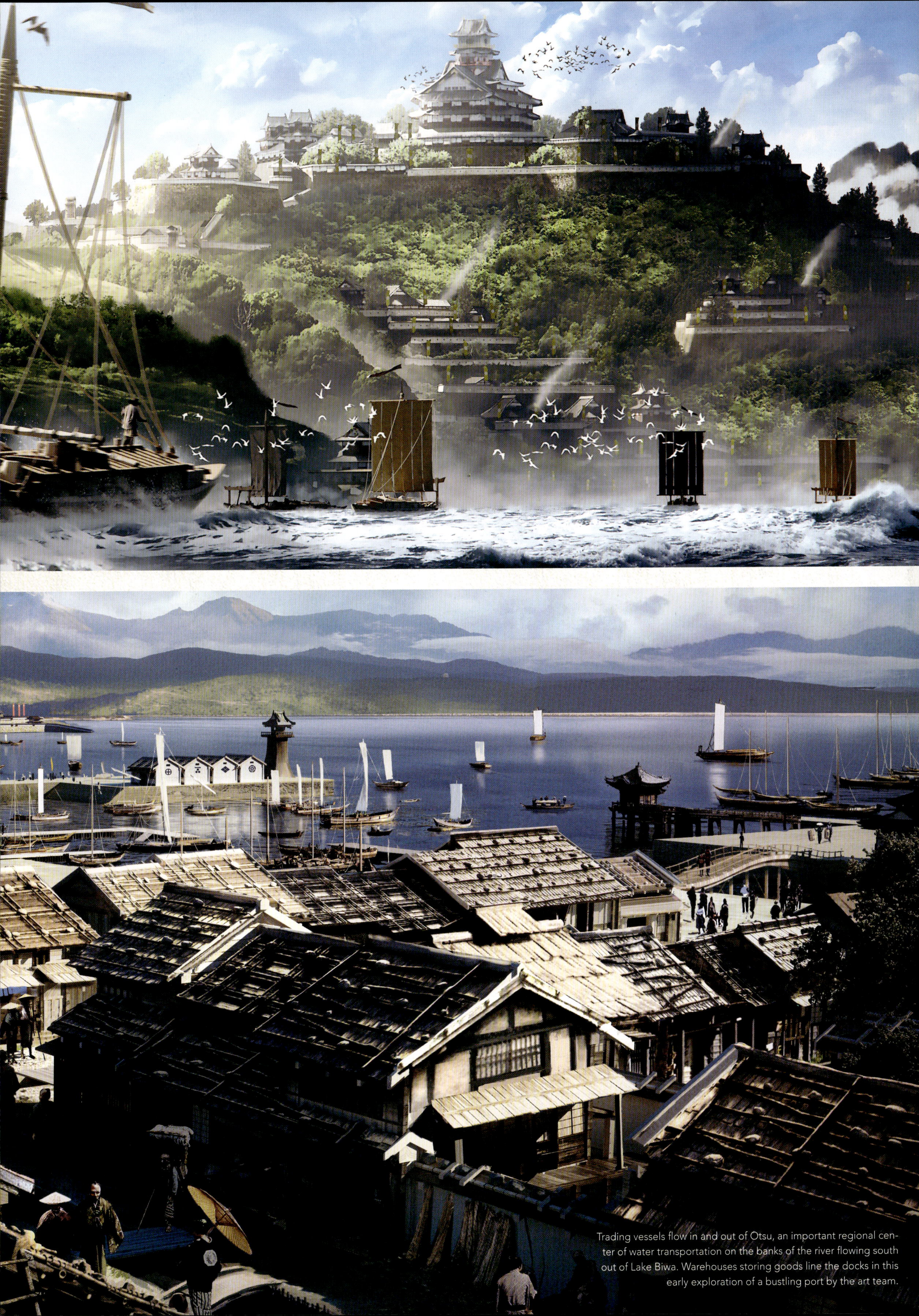

Trading vessels flow in and out of Otsu, an important regional center of water transportation on the banks of the river flowing south out of Lake Biwa. Warehouses storing goods line the docks in this early exploration of a bustling port by the art team.

ART BY SINA HAYATI

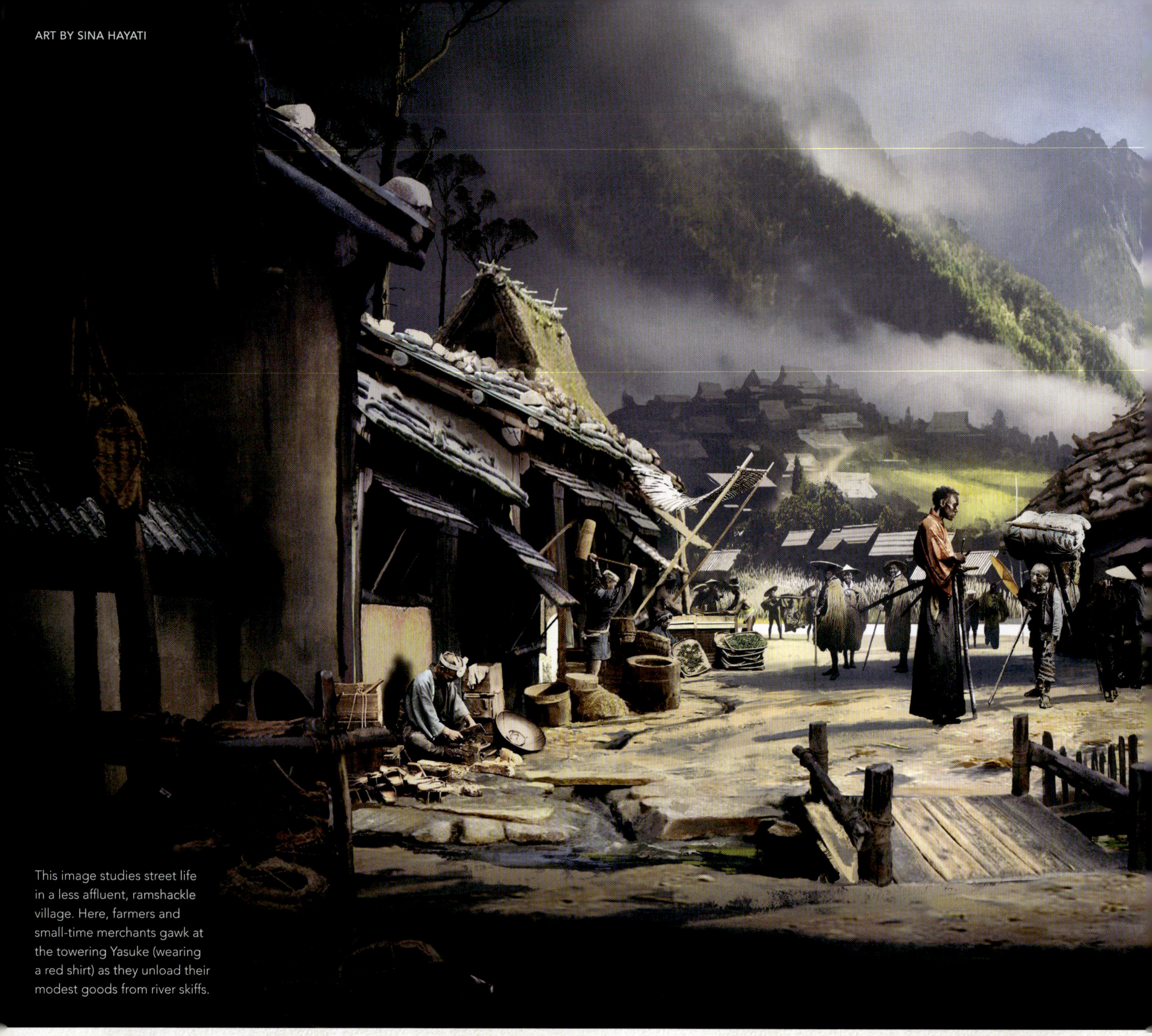

This image studies street life in a less affluent, ramshackle village. Here, farmers and small-time merchants gawk at the towering Yasuke (wearing a red shirt) as they unload their modest goods from river skiffs.

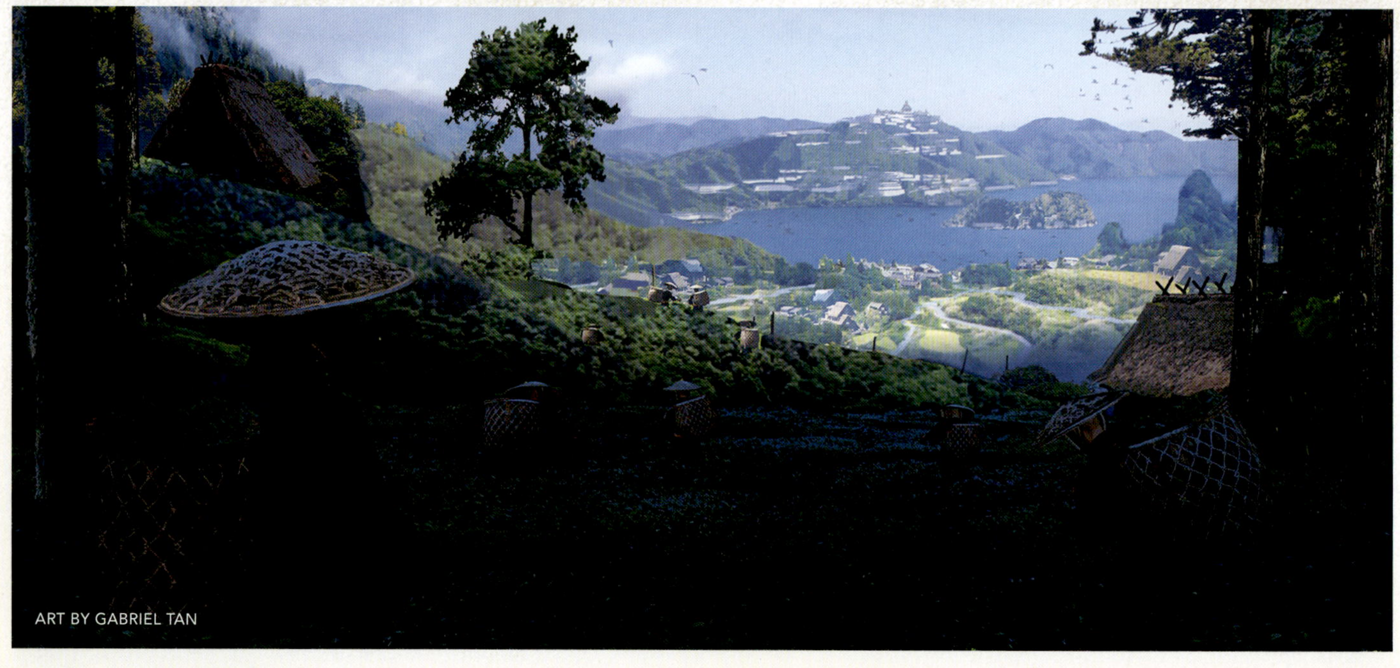

ART BY GABRIEL TAN

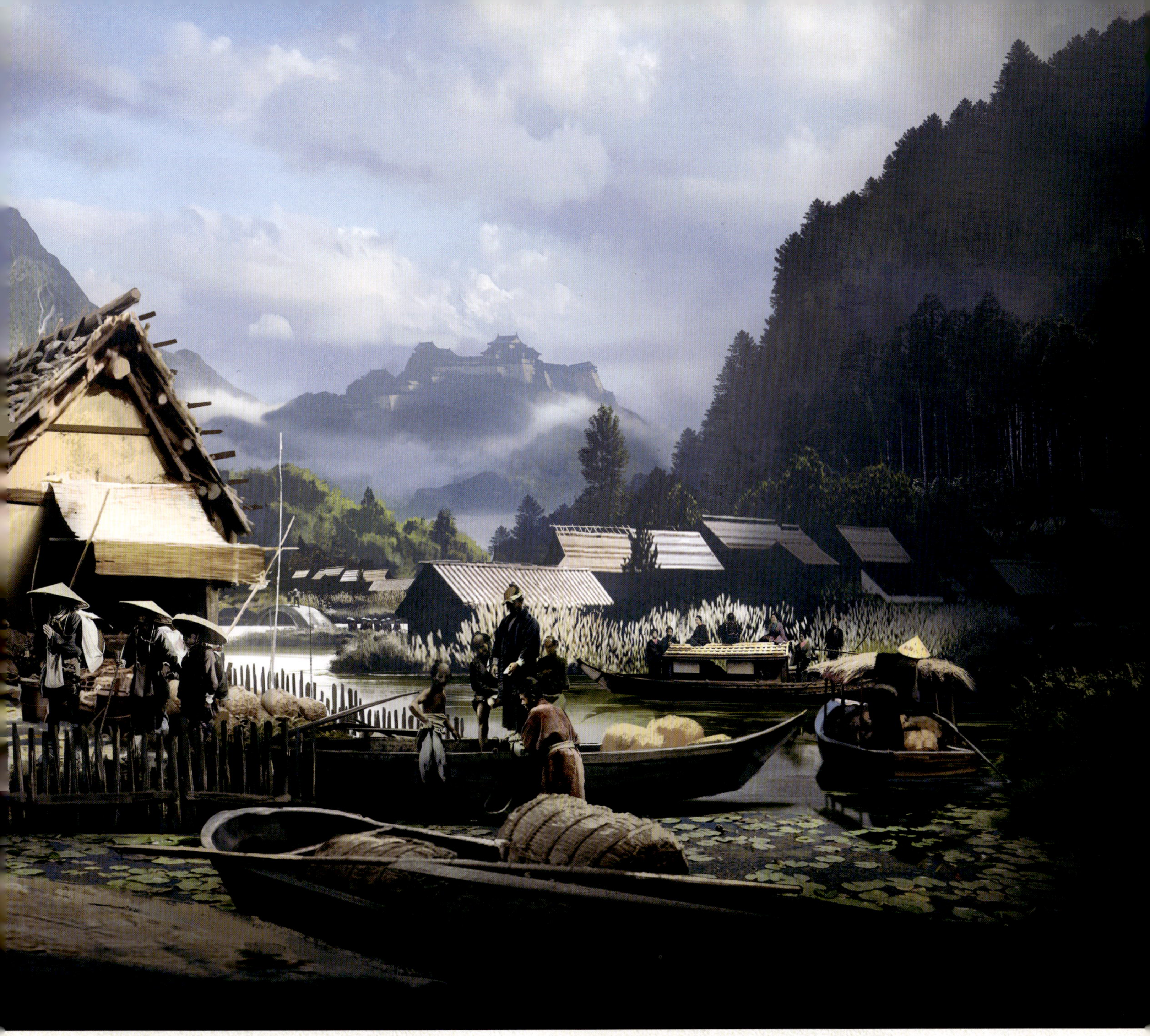

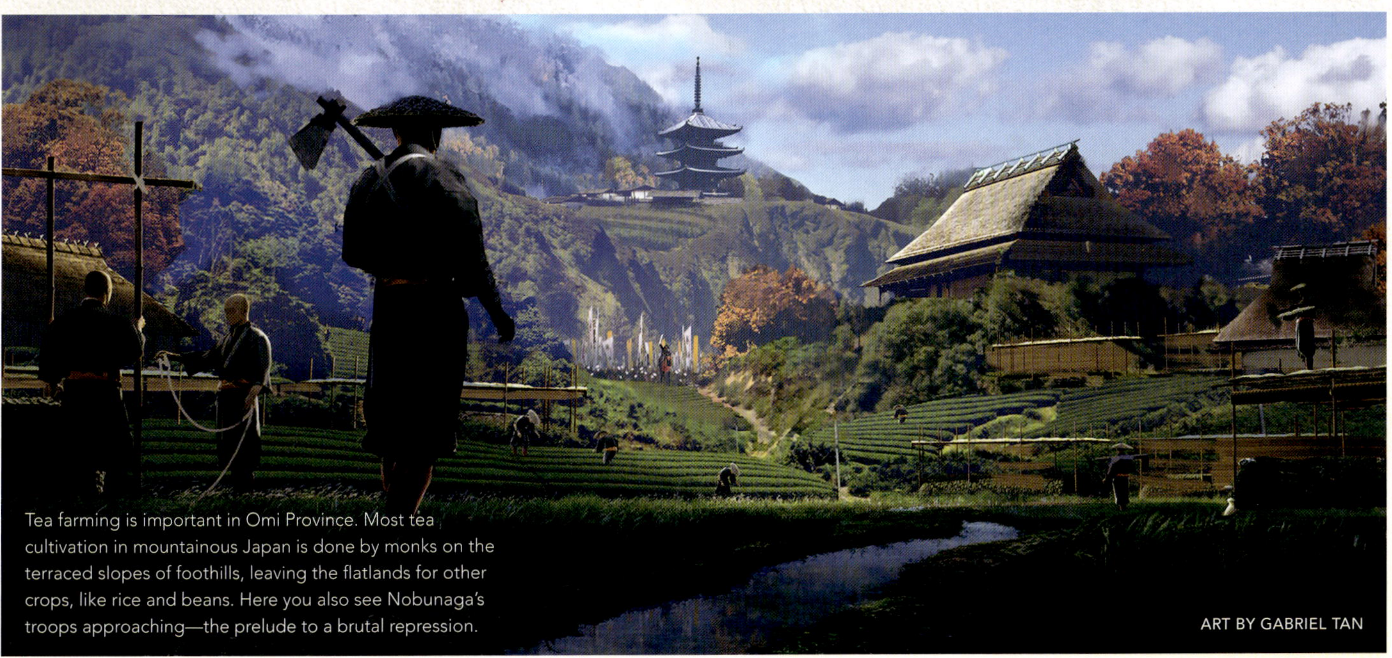

Tea farming is important in Omi Province. Most tea cultivation in mountainous Japan is done by monks on the terraced slopes of foothills, leaving the flatlands for other crops, like rice and beans. Here you also see Nobunaga's troops approaching—the prelude to a brutal repression.

ART BY GABRIEL TAN

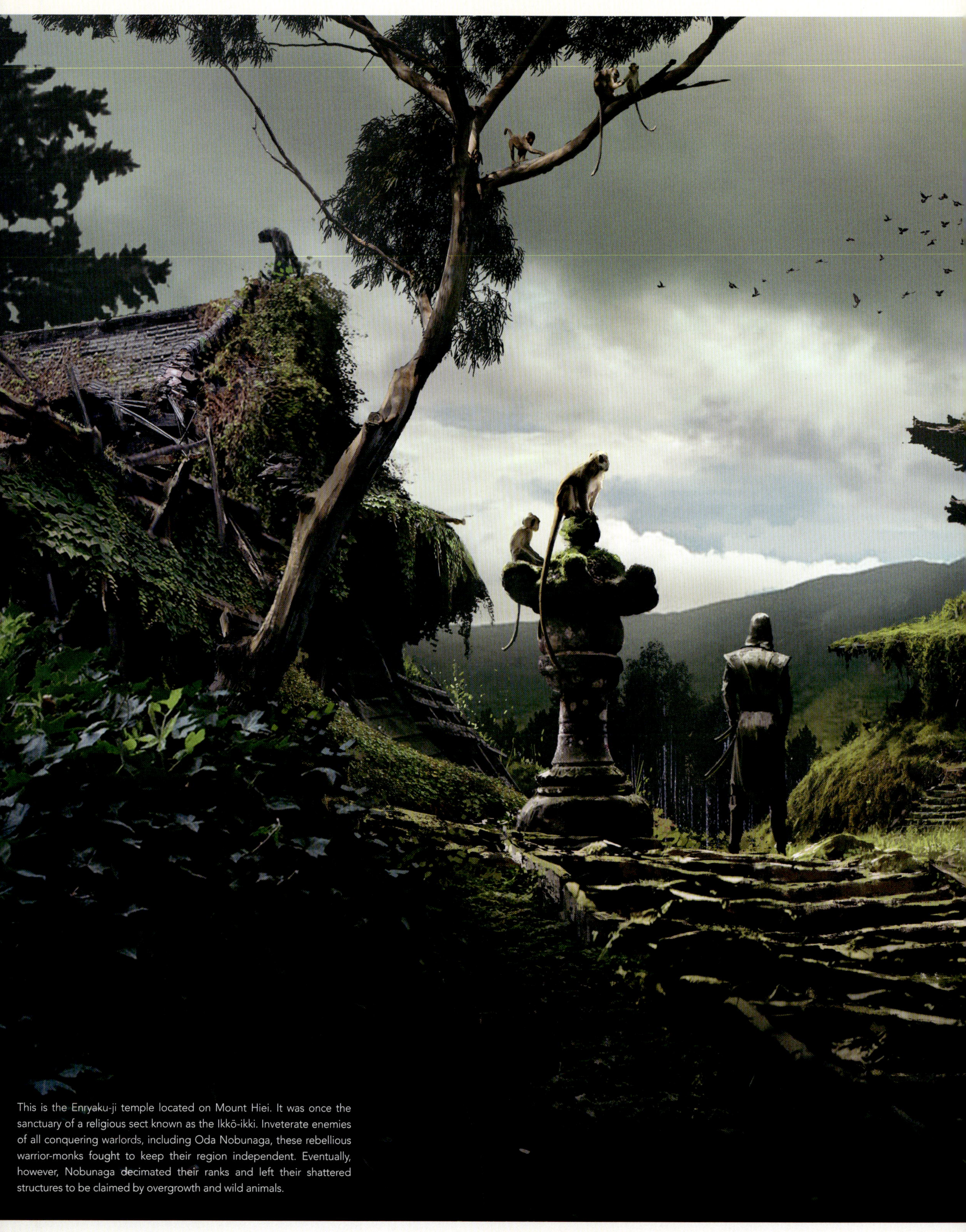

This is the Enryaku-ji temple located on Mount Hiei. It was once the sanctuary of a religious sect known as the Ikkō-ikki. Inveterate enemies of all conquering warlords, including Oda Nobunaga, these rebellious warrior-monks fought to keep their region independent. Eventually, however, Nobunaga decimated their ranks and left their shattered structures to be claimed by overgrowth and wild animals.

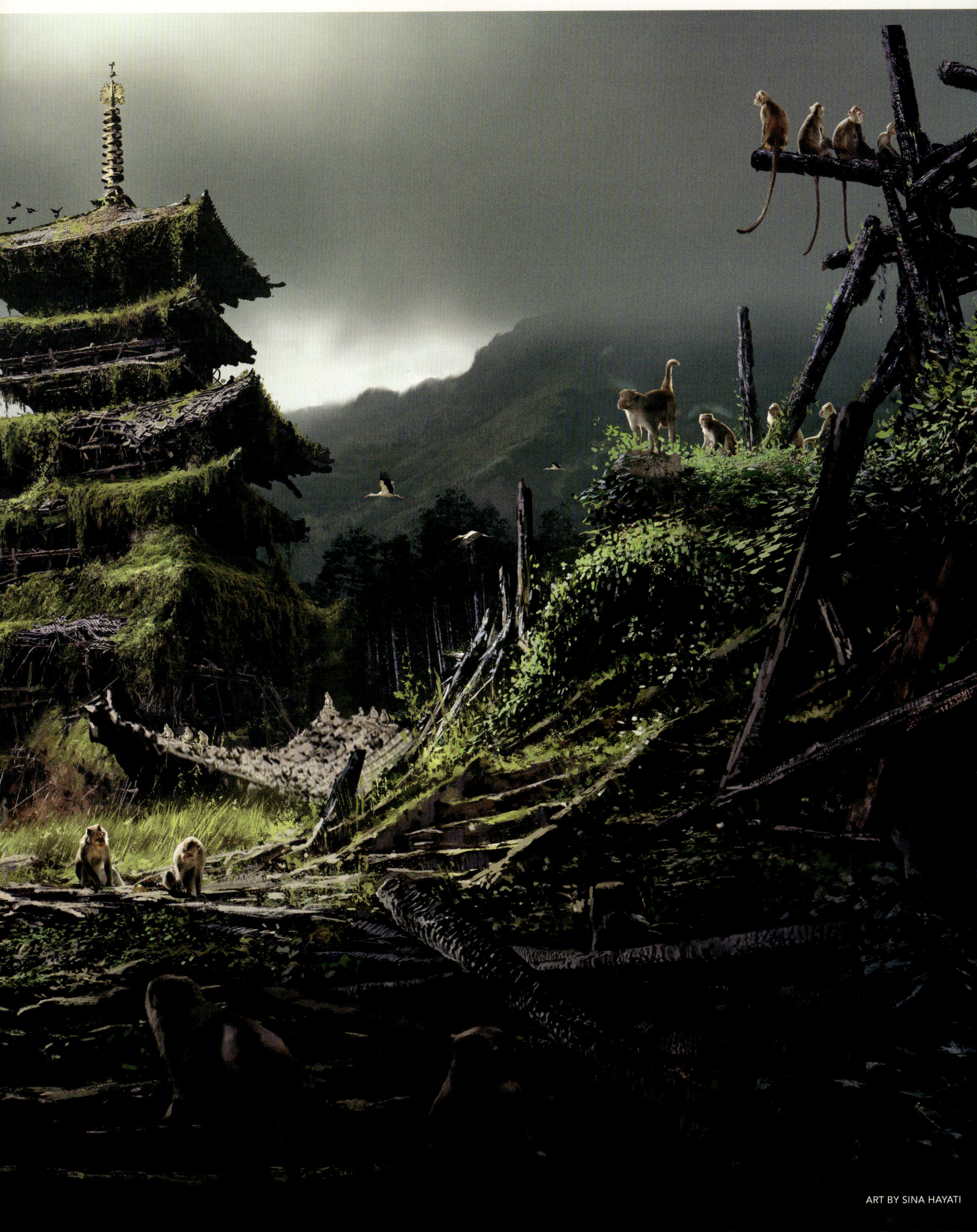

ART BY SINA HAYATI

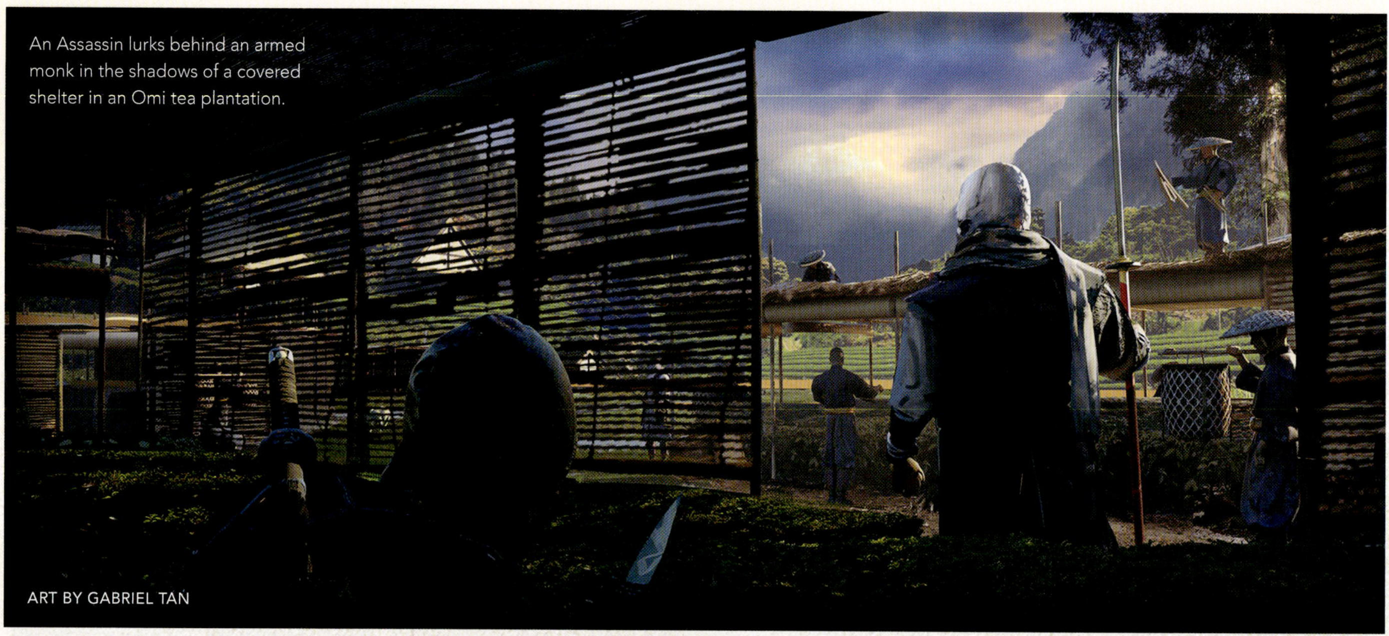

An Assassin lurks behind an armed monk in the shadows of a covered shelter in an Omi tea plantation.

ART BY GABRIEL TAN

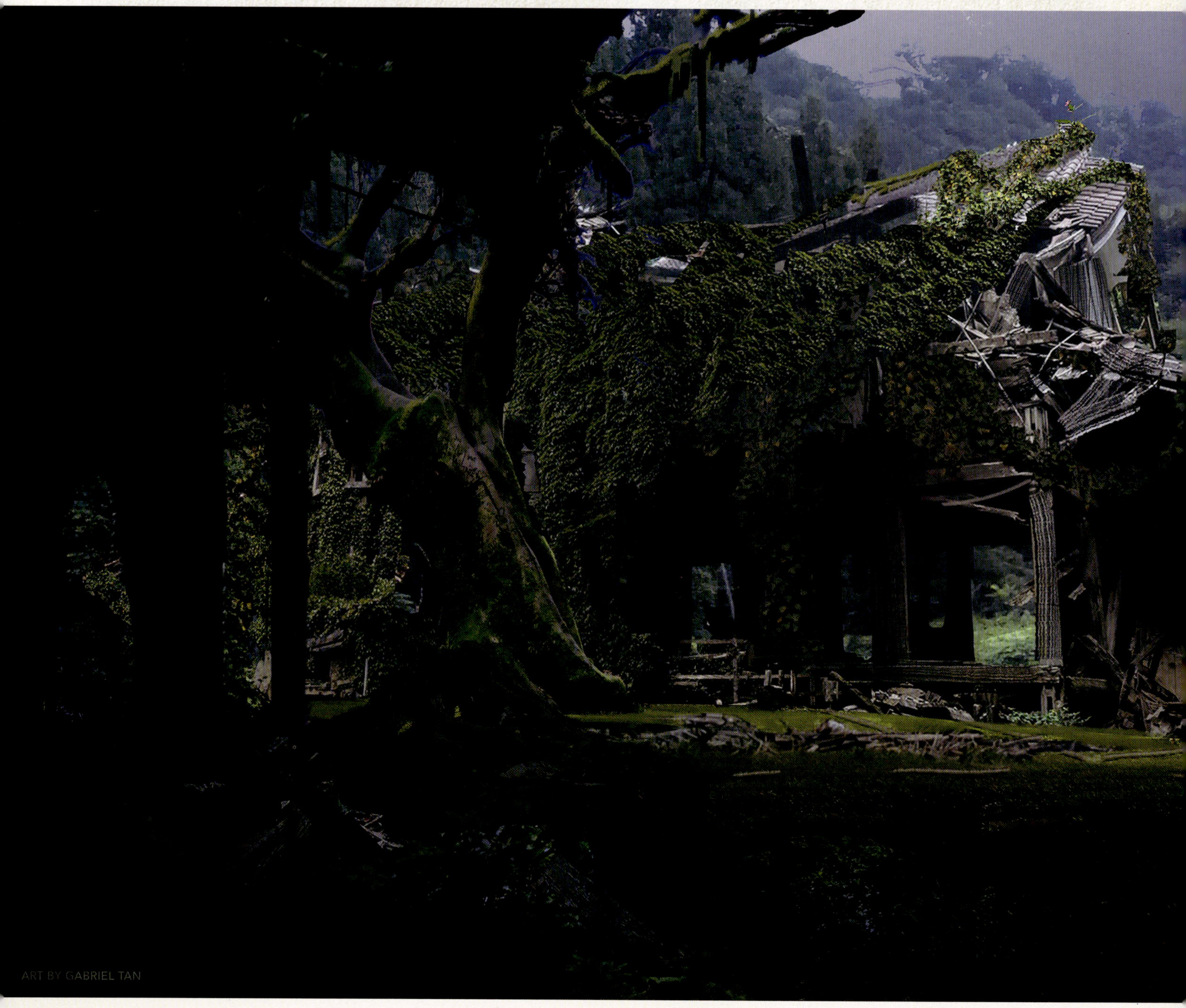

ART BY GABRIEL TAN

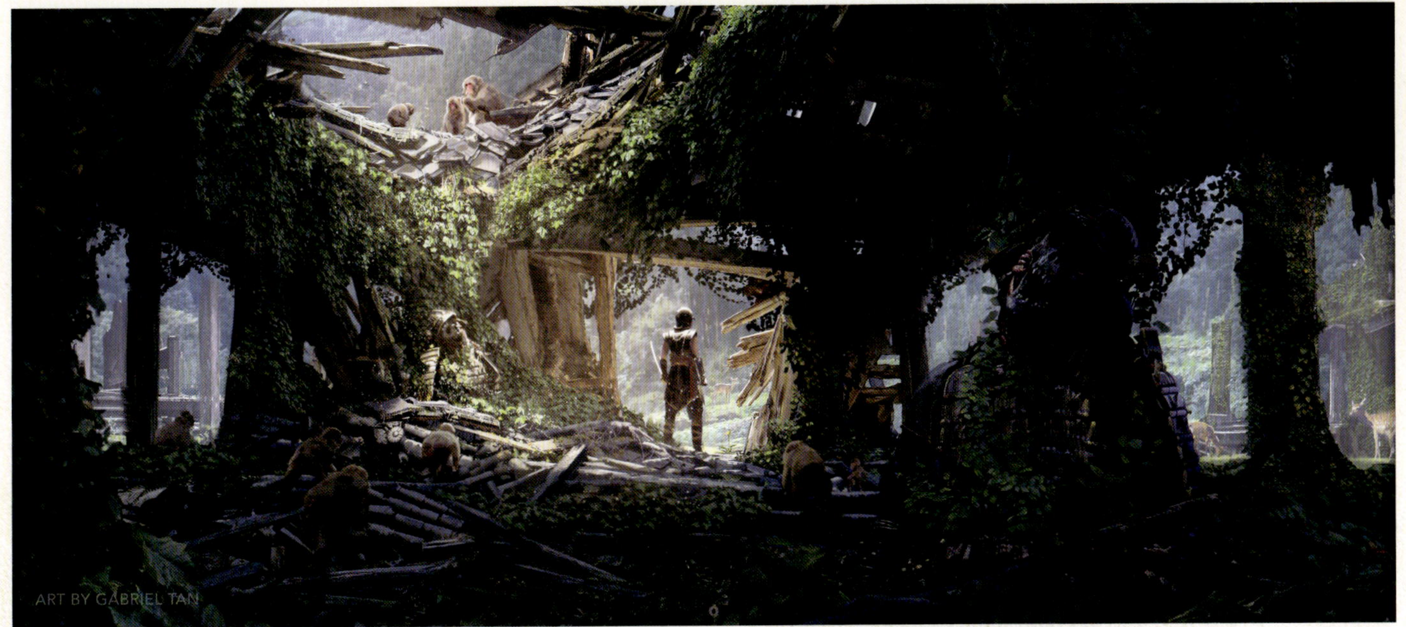
ART BY GABRIEL TAN

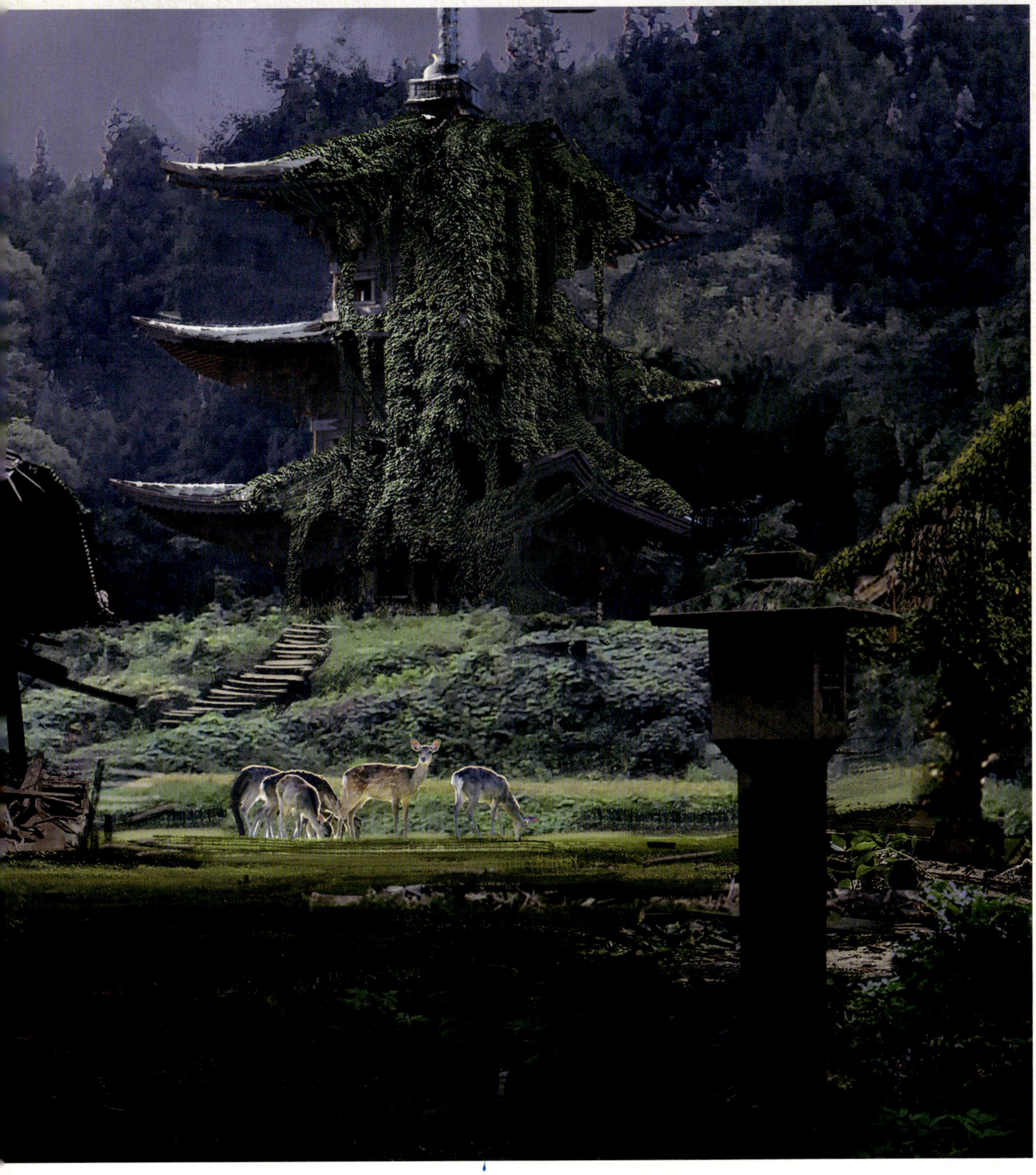

The concept art here further explores the idea of nature's inevitable reclamation of the shattered ruins wrought by man's wars. Note the fallen samurai against the wall in the interior image above, seemingly part of the architecture itself. "We wanted to portray the finality of war," says Tan. "Doesn't matter who or what you are, or which side you're on—Mother Nature wins in the end."

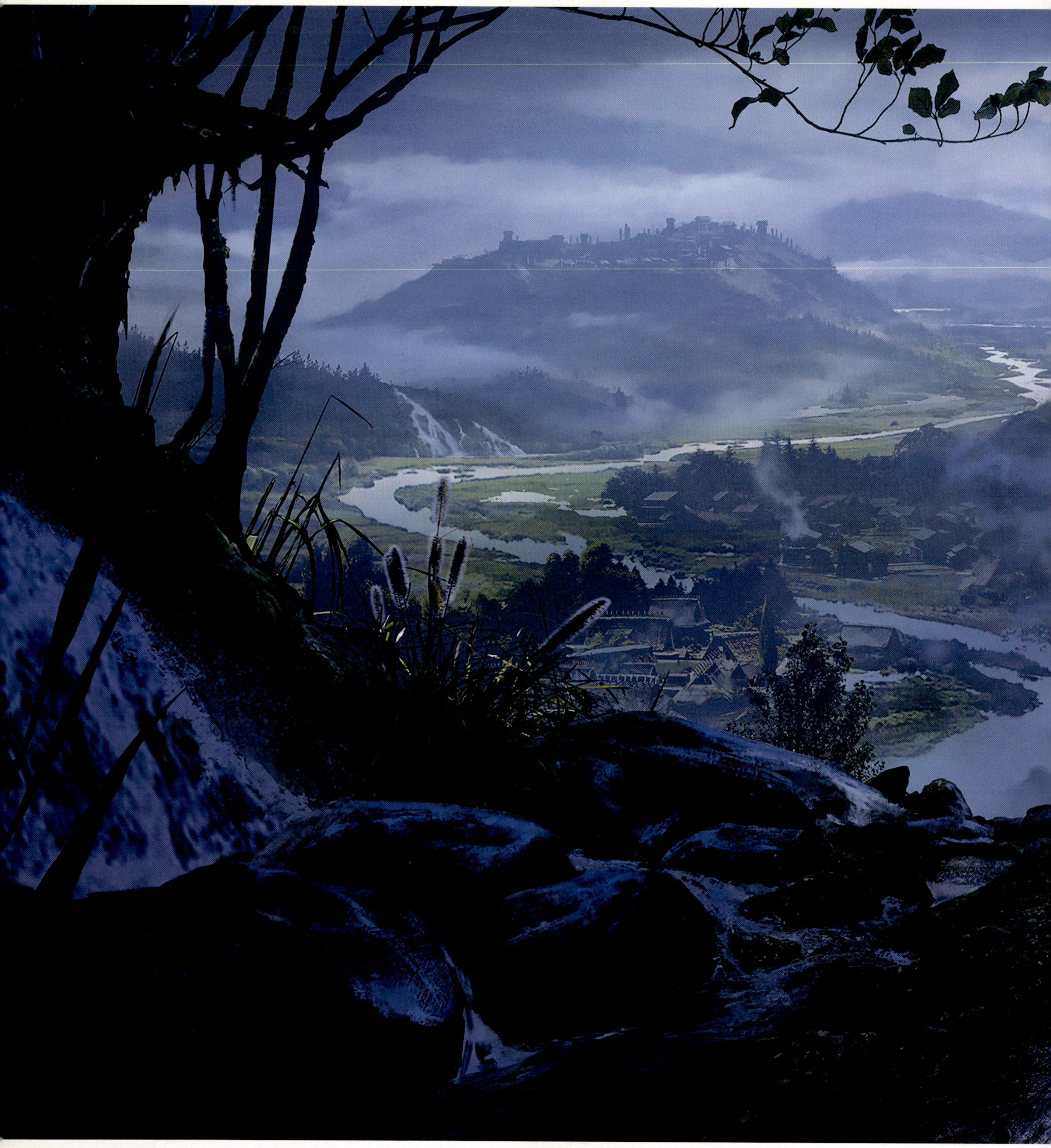

IGA *THE CRADLE OF THE* SHINOBI

Well hidden in a ring of rugged mountains, Iga Province is famous for its picturesque inaccessibility—craggy peaks wrapped in fog and thick, shadowy forests. As such, it is a natural birthplace for the *shinobi*, masters of shadow, stealth, and deception. Relatively small compared to surrounding provinces, Iga is crisscrossed by a web of treacherous roads winding through narrow alpine

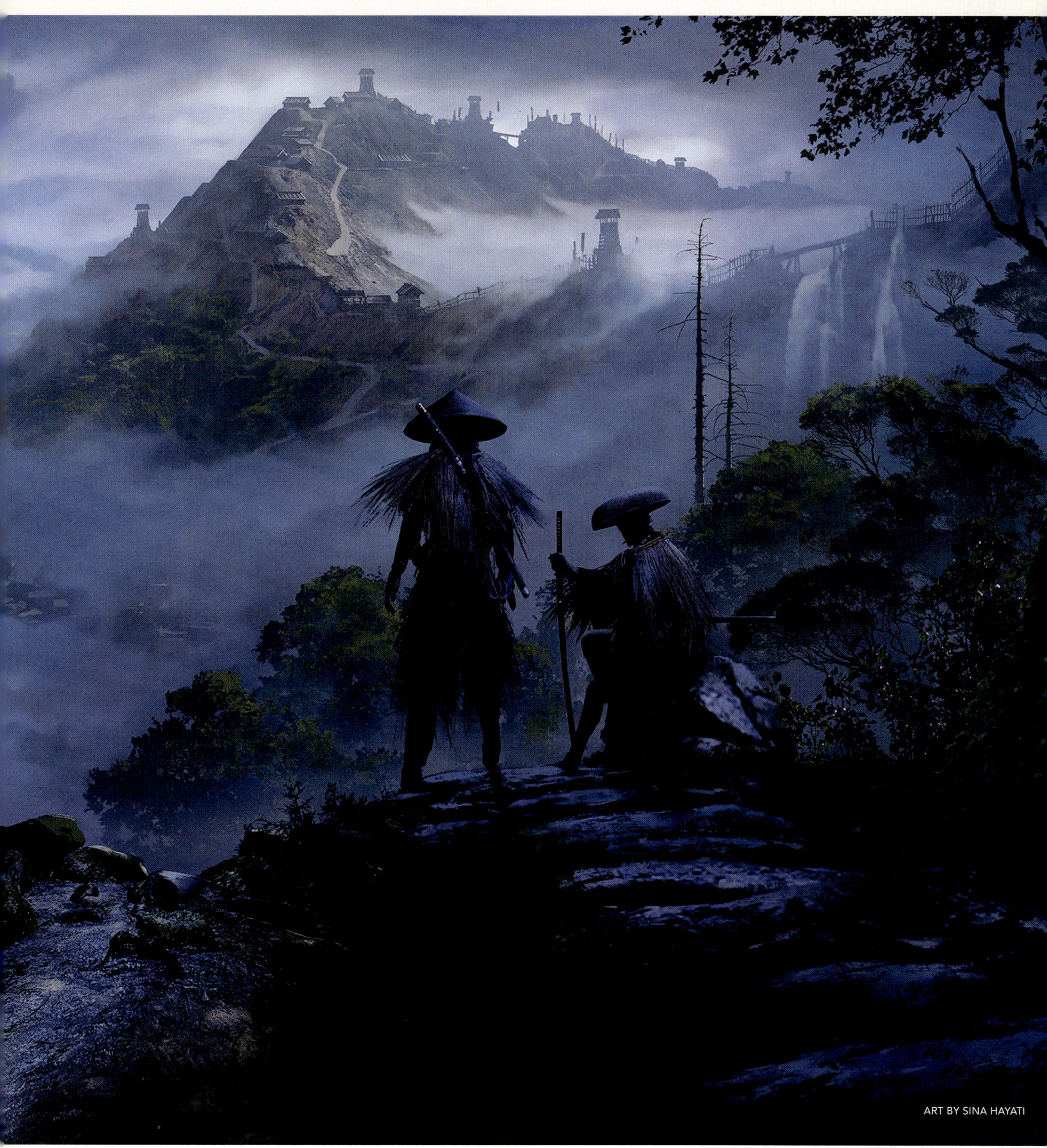

ART BY SINA HAYATI

passages, often unsafe to traverse. Its independent-minded inhabitants have formed a confederacy with their own terms of governance and an economy based on clay, coal, and ceramics.

Although Iga is bordered by four other provinces, its mountainous crossings and precarious access roads have fostered an autonomous and often rebellious spirit in its people. Armed incursions face a fierce resistance led by *shinobi* warriors. "We wanted images of ninja guerrilla tactics—dropping from trees, emerging from mist, pulling soldiers under bridges," says Tan. "Stalking their prey, and striking when you're at your weakest."

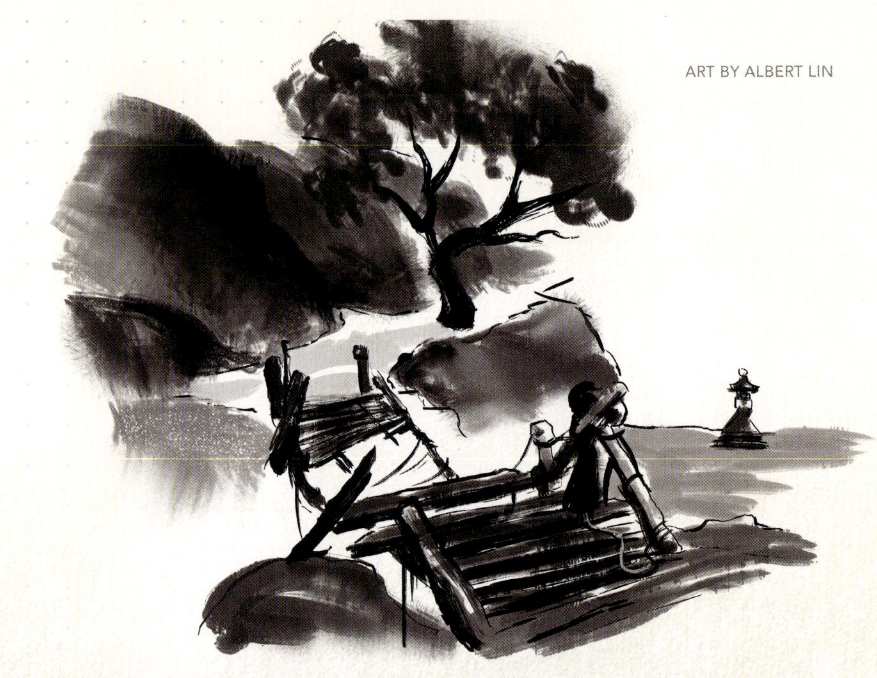

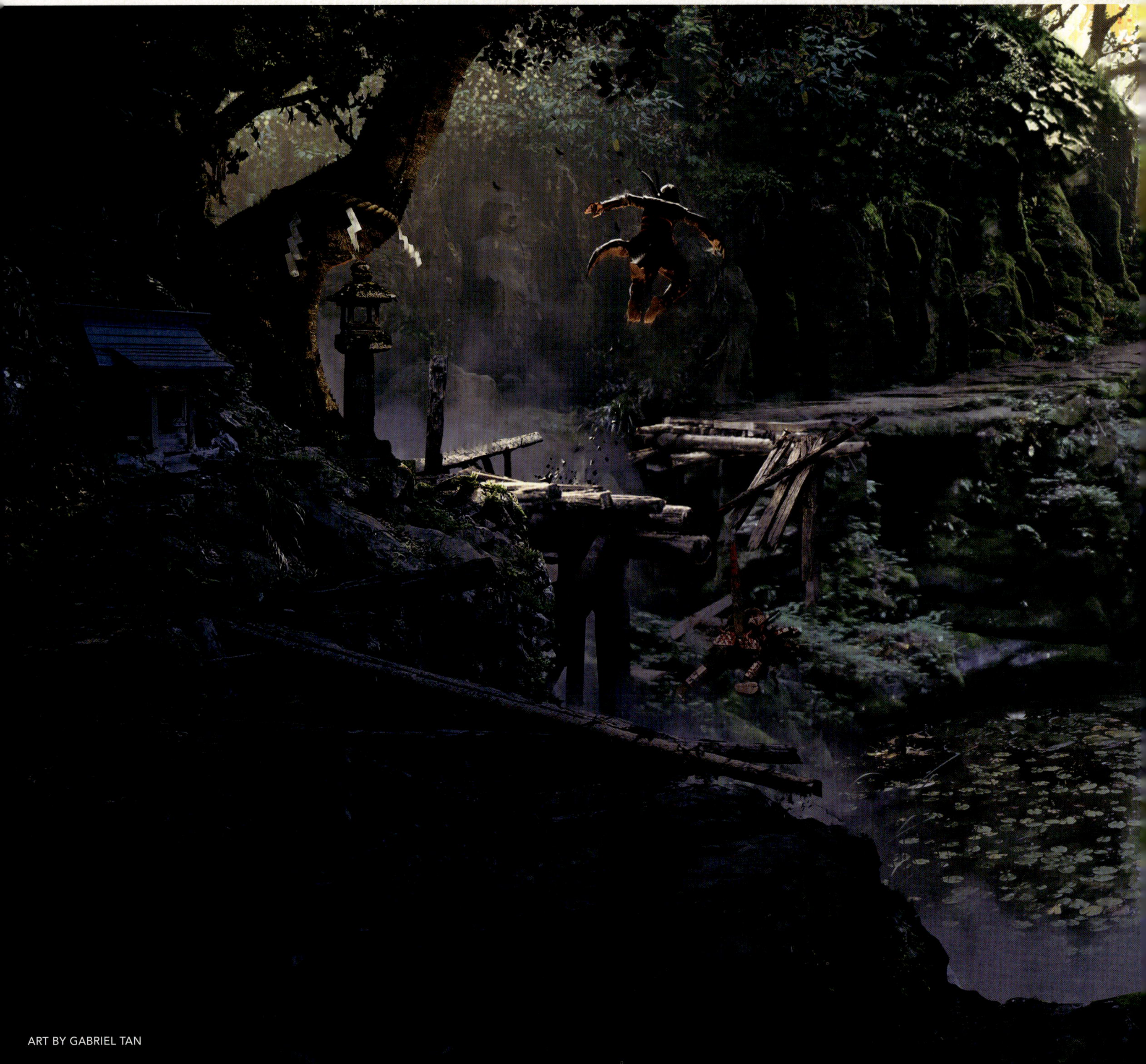

ART BY ALBERT LIN

ART BY GABRIEL TAN

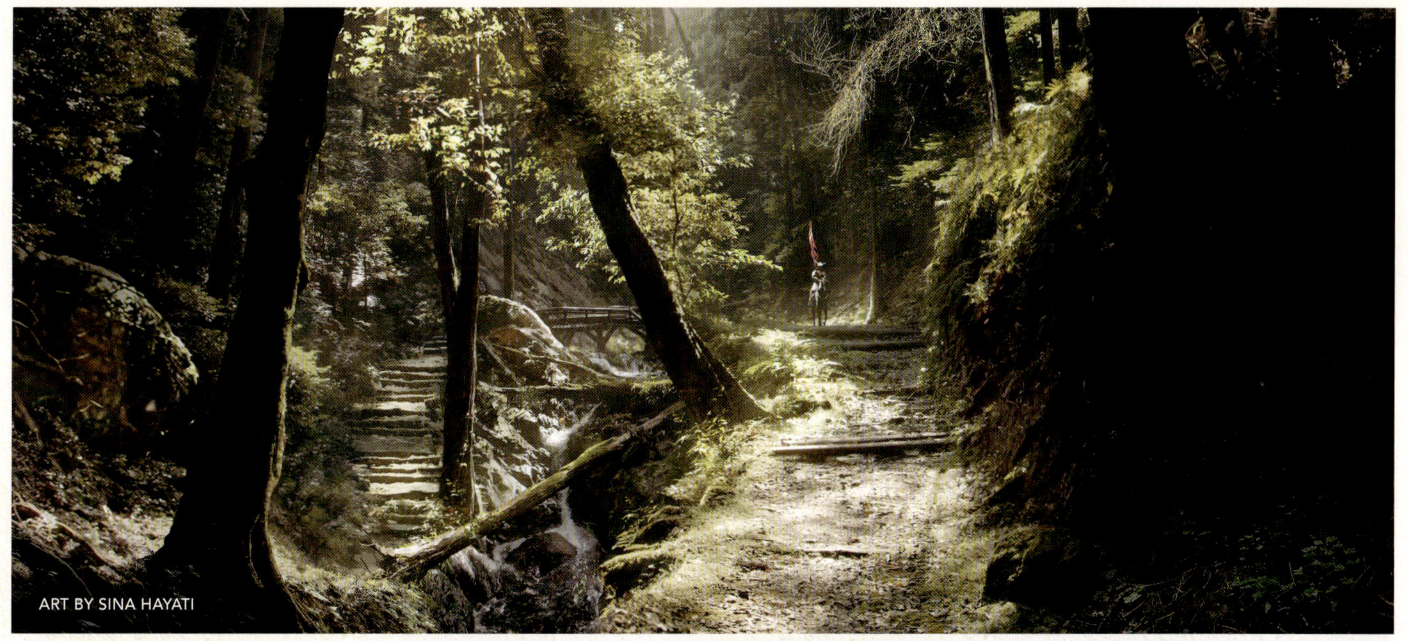

ART BY SINA HAYATI

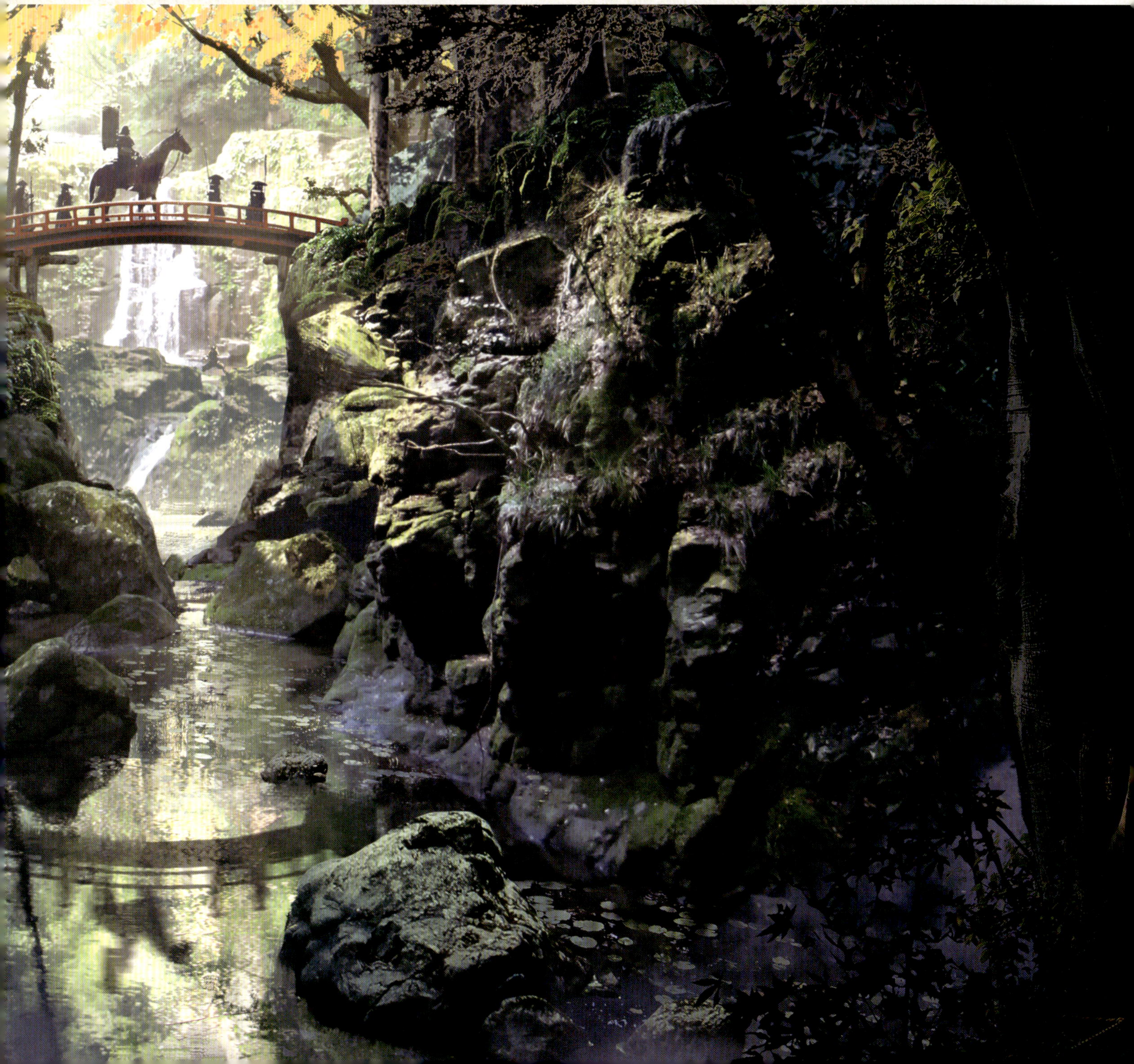

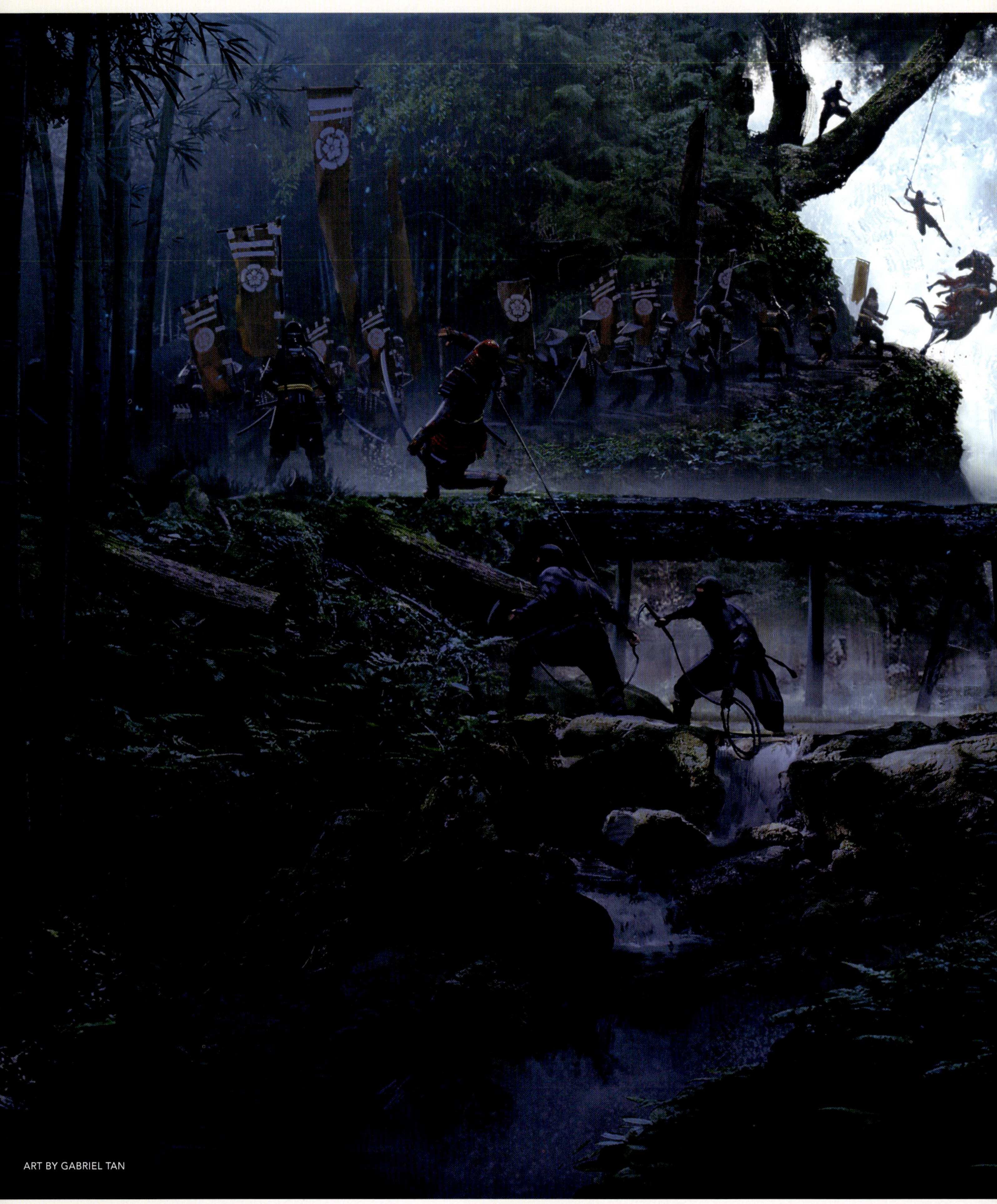
ART BY GABRIEL TAN

Mountainous and heavily wooded, Iga Province features an undulating topography where every path and line of sight is curved and often obscured.

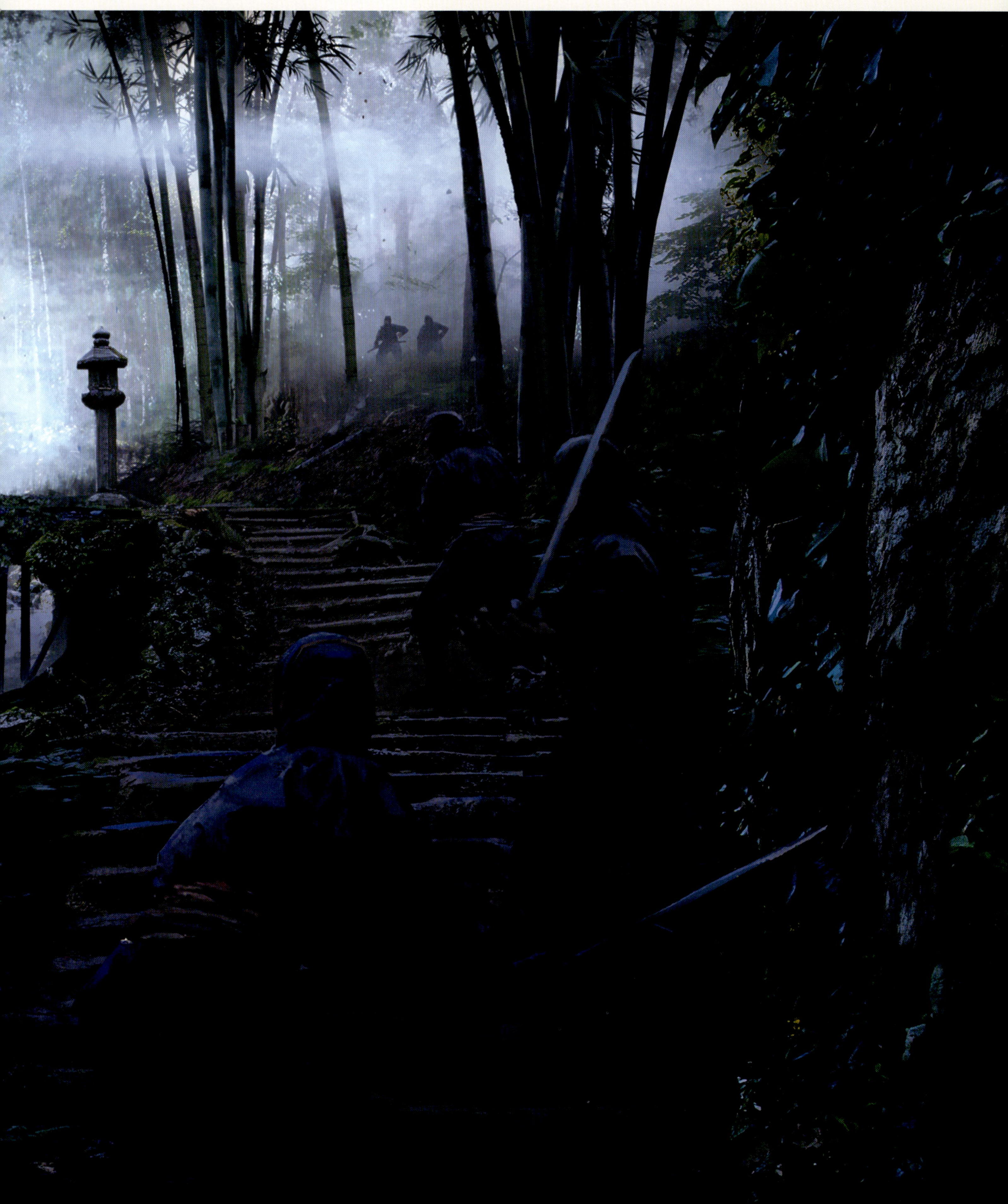

The dynamic weather system used in *Shadows* prompted the art team to depict a variety of overcast, windy, foggy, or misty landscapes with changing visibility. "High humidity and low clouds are a constant in Japanese weather patterns," says Tan, "so we modeled that in our concept art."

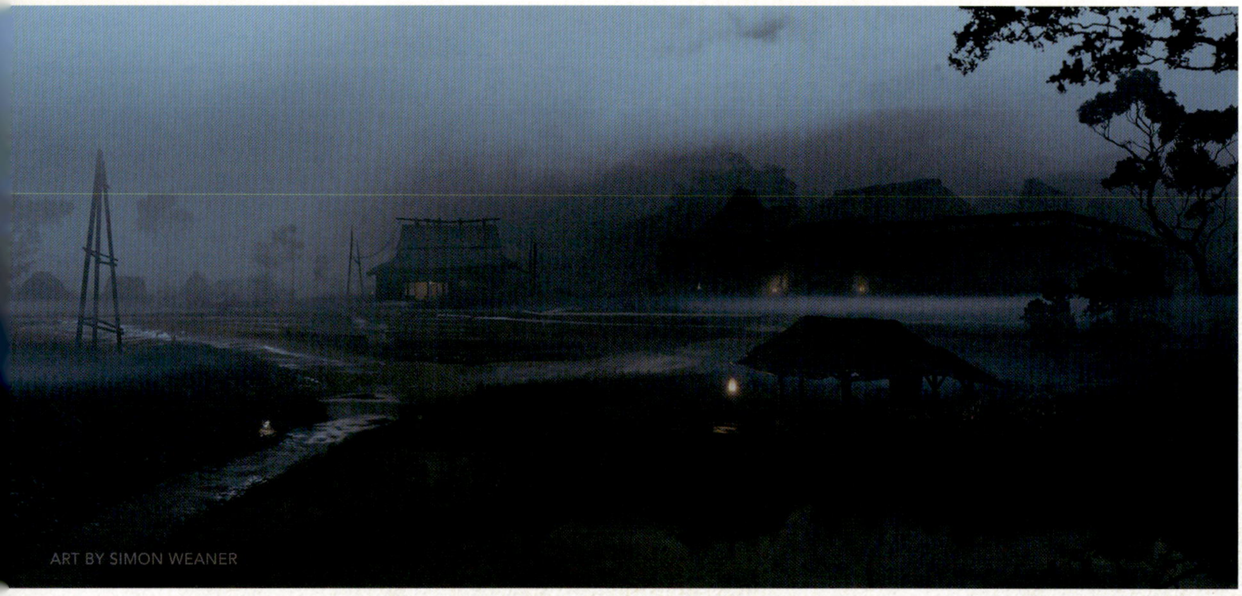

ART BY SIMON WEANER

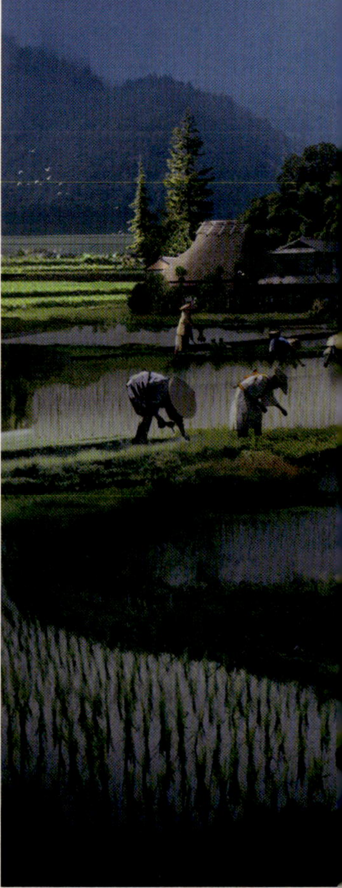

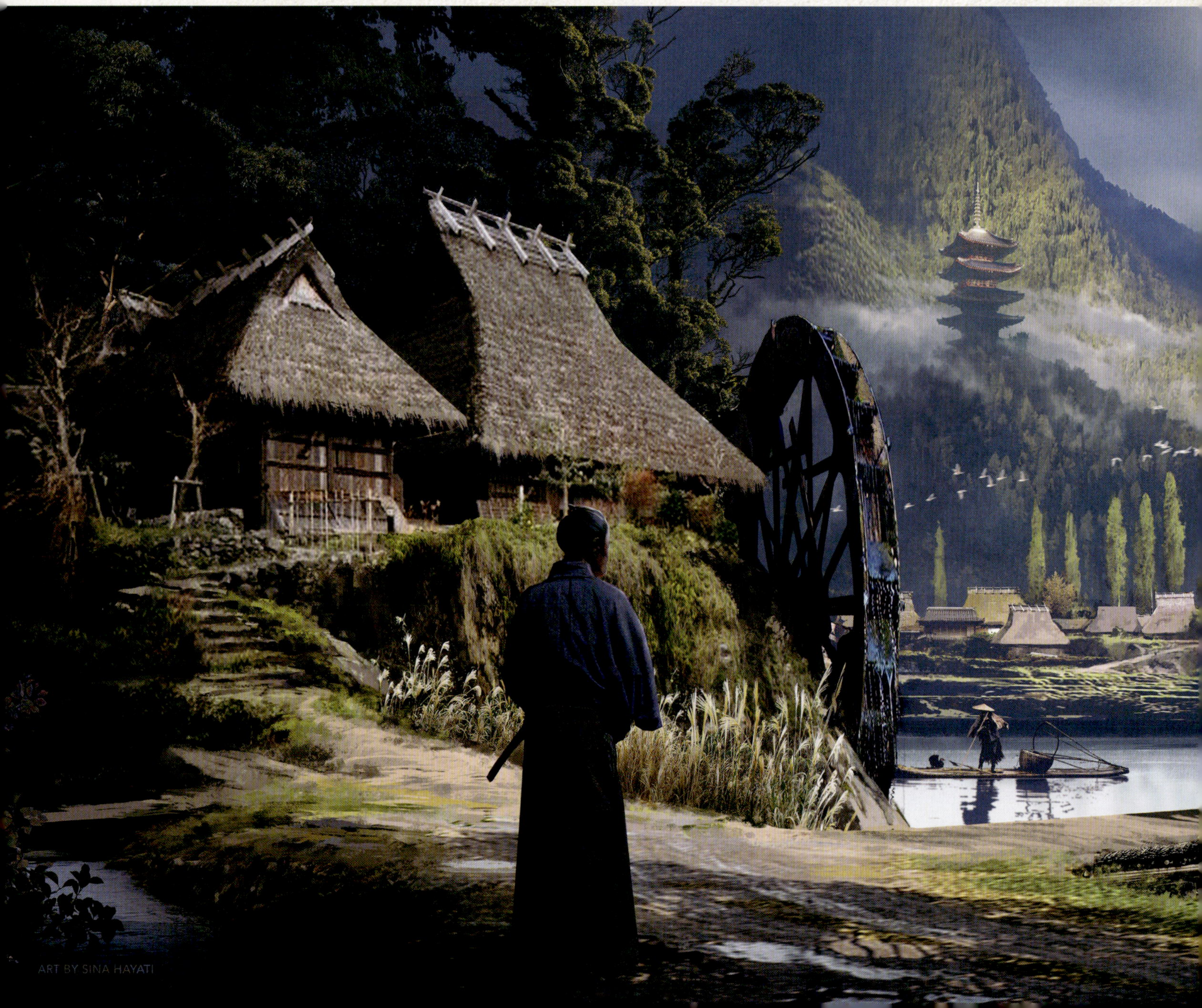

ART BY SINA HAYATI

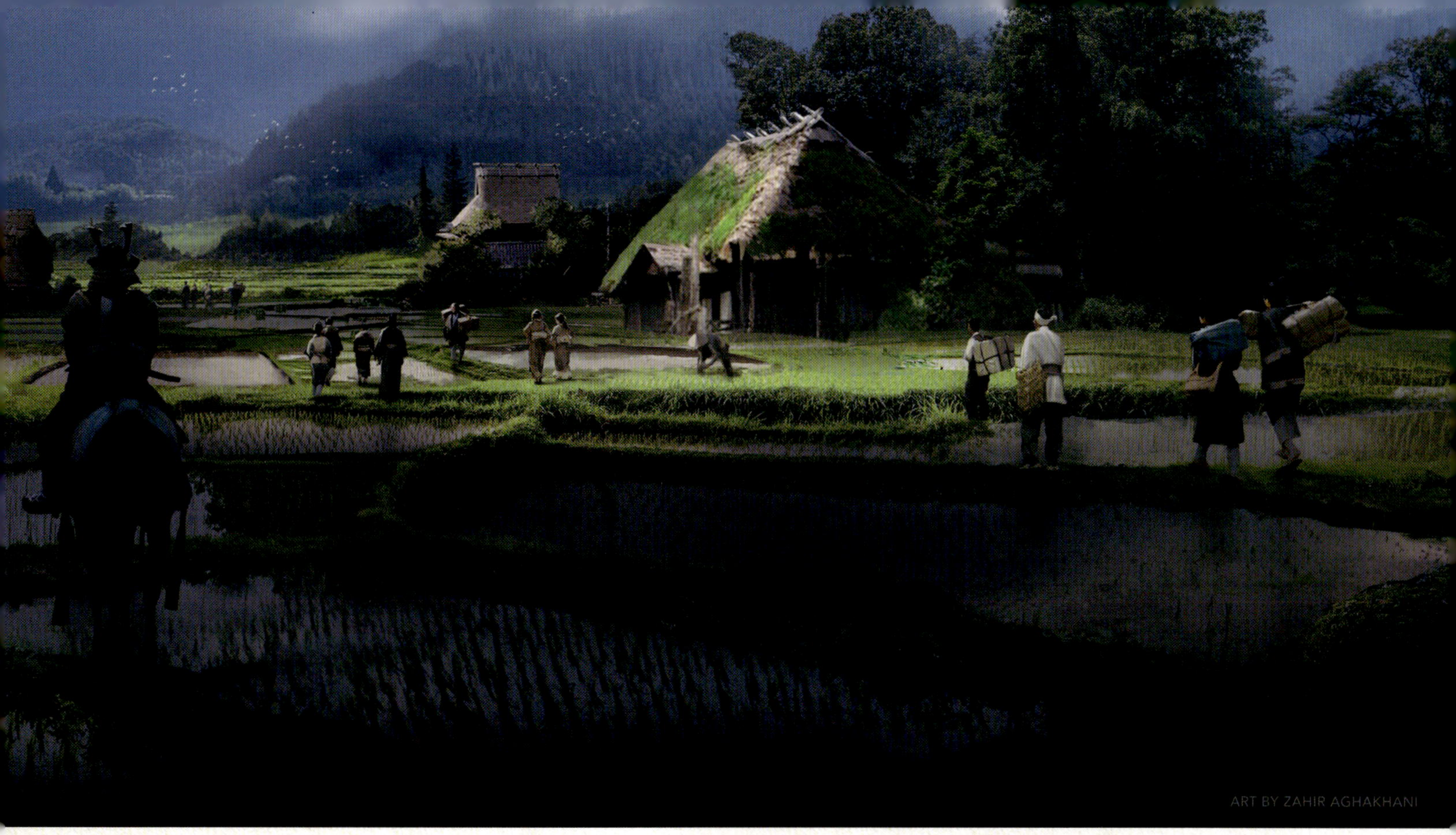

ART BY ZAHIR AGHAKHANI

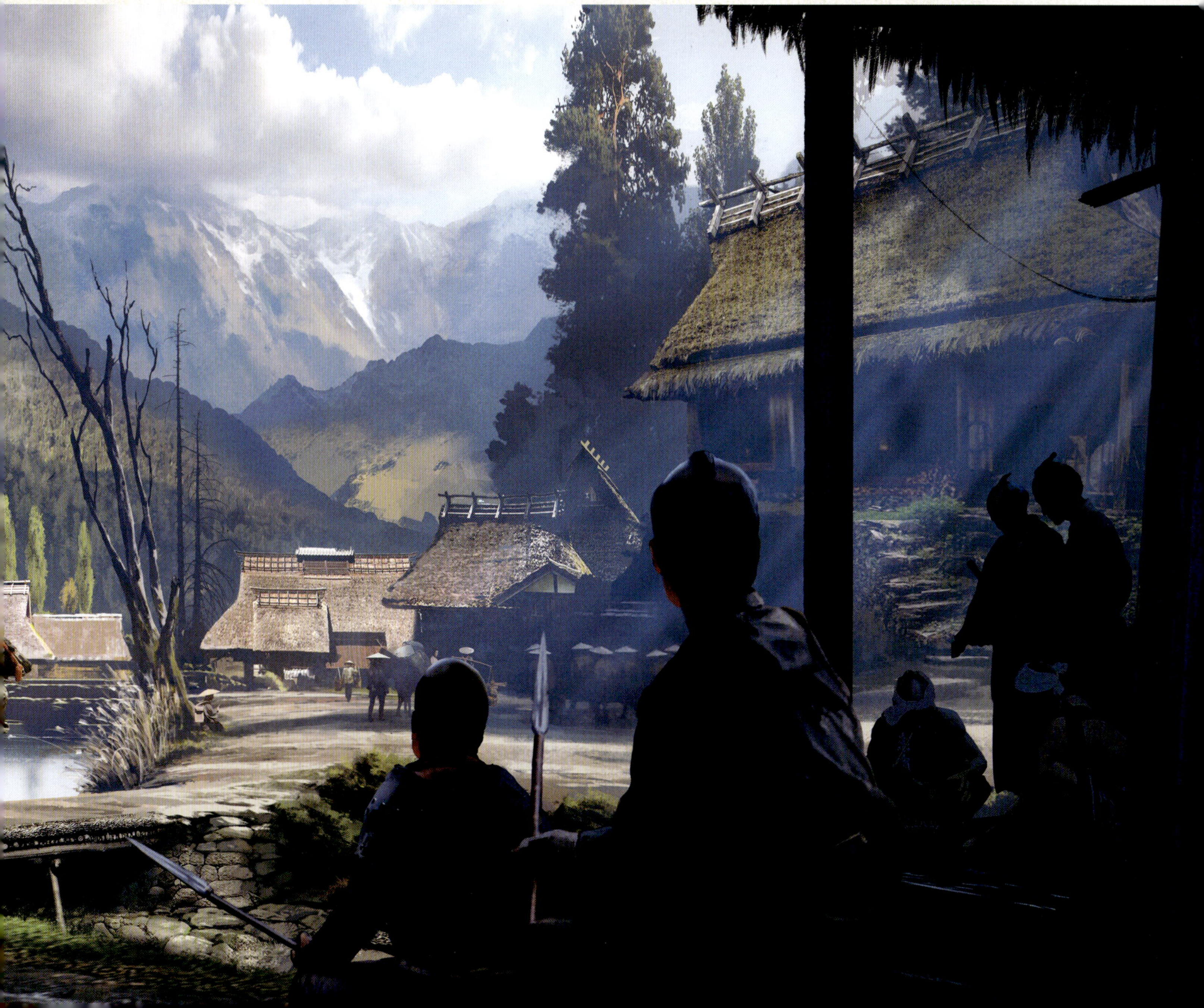

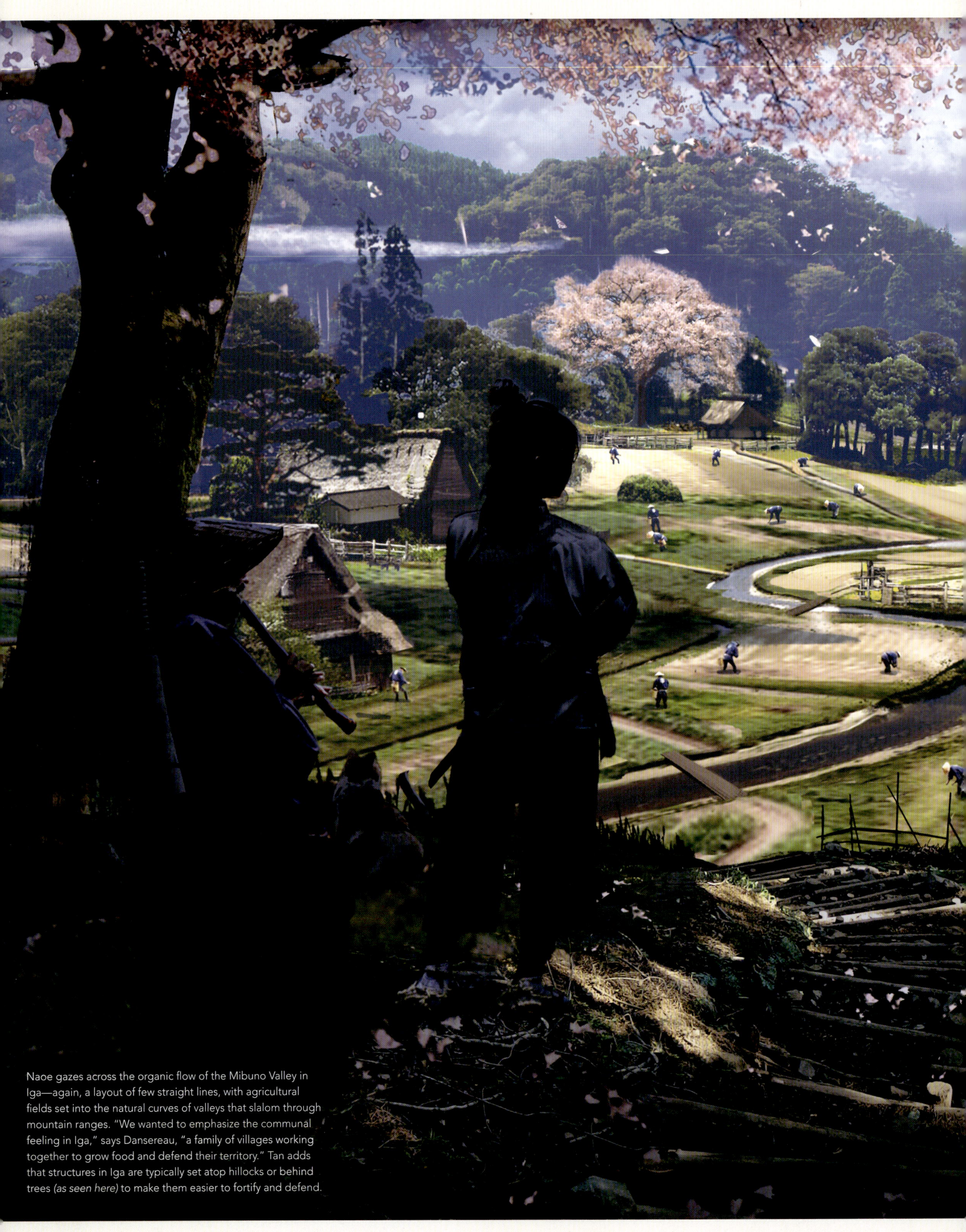

Naoe gazes across the organic flow of the Mibuno Valley in Iga—again, a layout of few straight lines, with agricultural fields set into the natural curves of valleys that slalom through mountain ranges. "We wanted to emphasize the communal feeling in Iga," says Dansereau, "a family of villages working together to grow food and defend their territory." Tan adds that structures in Iga are typically set atop hillocks or behind trees *(as seen here)* to make them easier to fortify and defend.

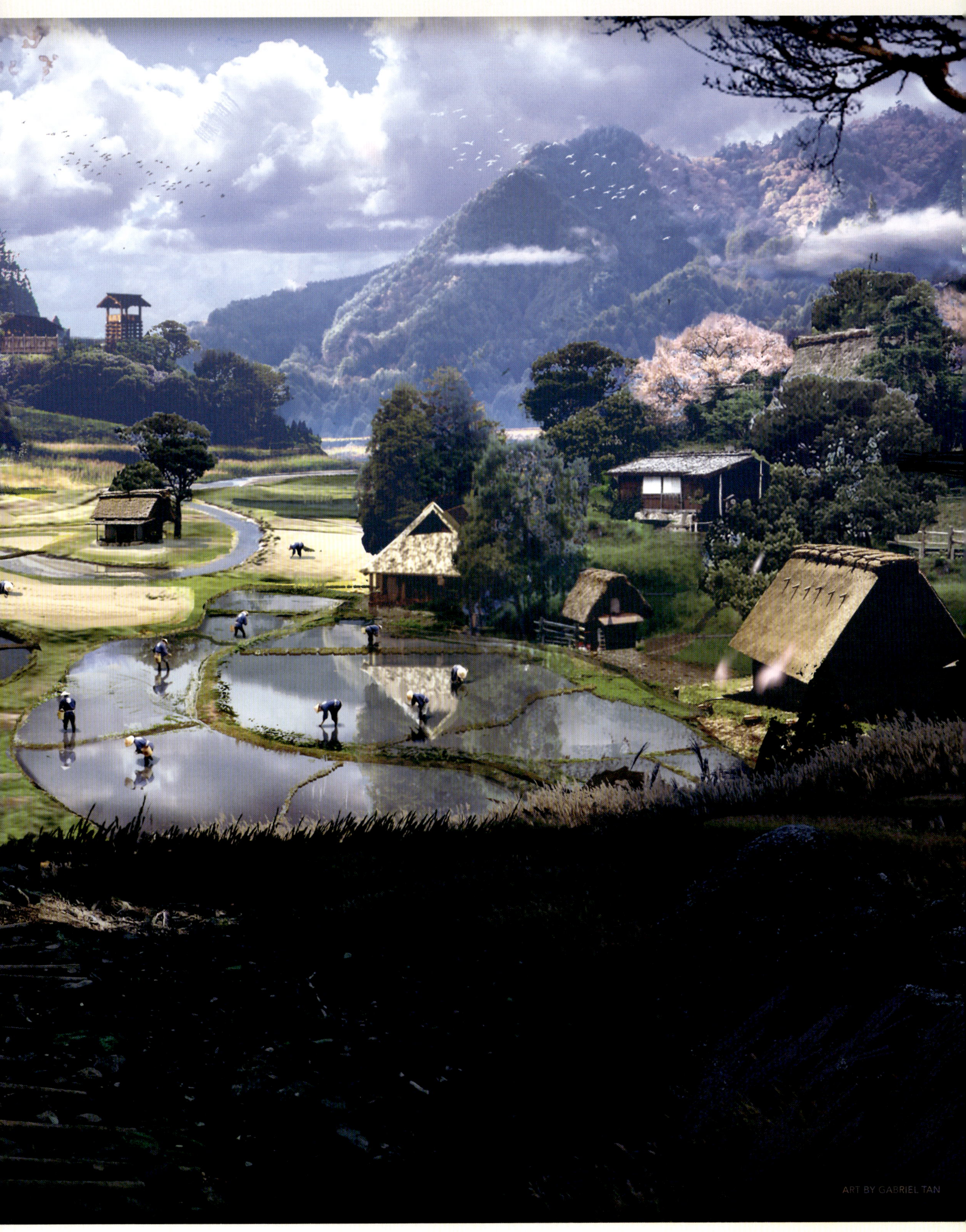
ART BY GABRIEL TAN

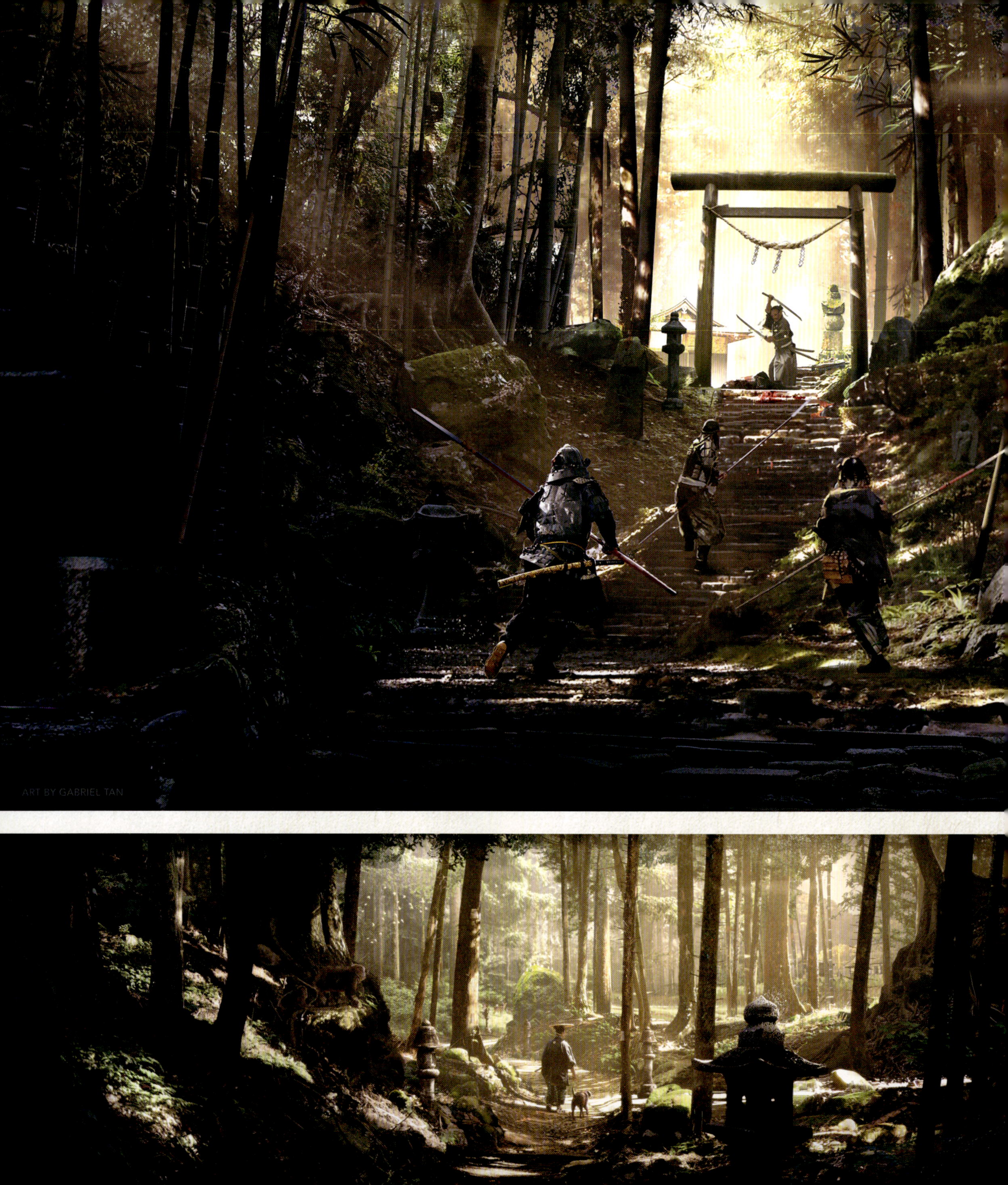

ART BY GABRIEL TAN

ART BY GABRIEL TAN

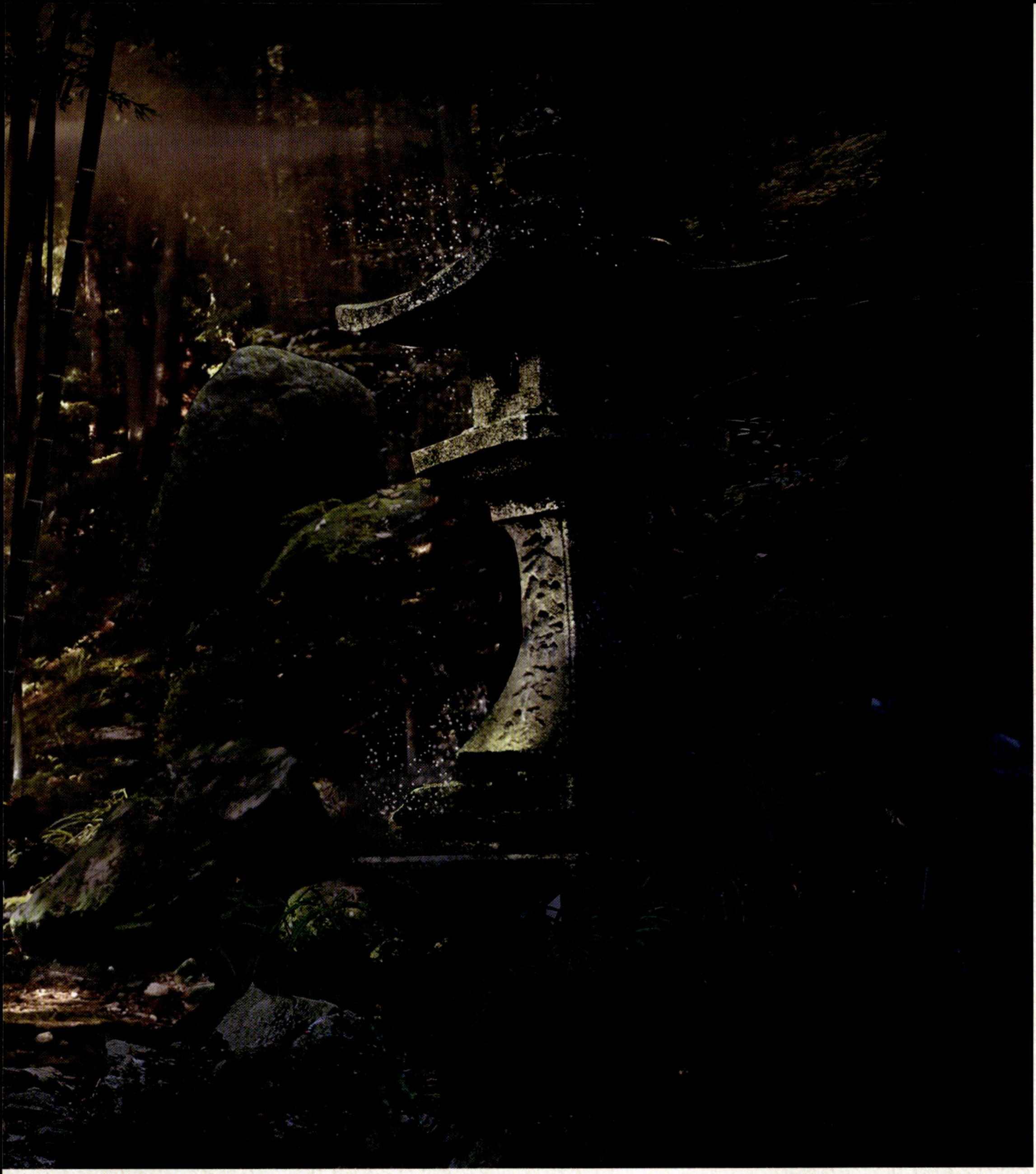

The Iga confederacy enjoyed early successes against predatory warlords, conducting masterful guerrilla operations in the province's dense, mountainous woodlands. In 1579, Iga's ninja clans decisively defeated a large force led by Oda Nobukatsu (Nobunaga's son), outmaneuvering the invaders in Iga's twisting forest passages. But two years later, Nobunaga himself led a massive invasion of more than forty thousand troops, attacking from six different directions and bringing Iga under his firm control.

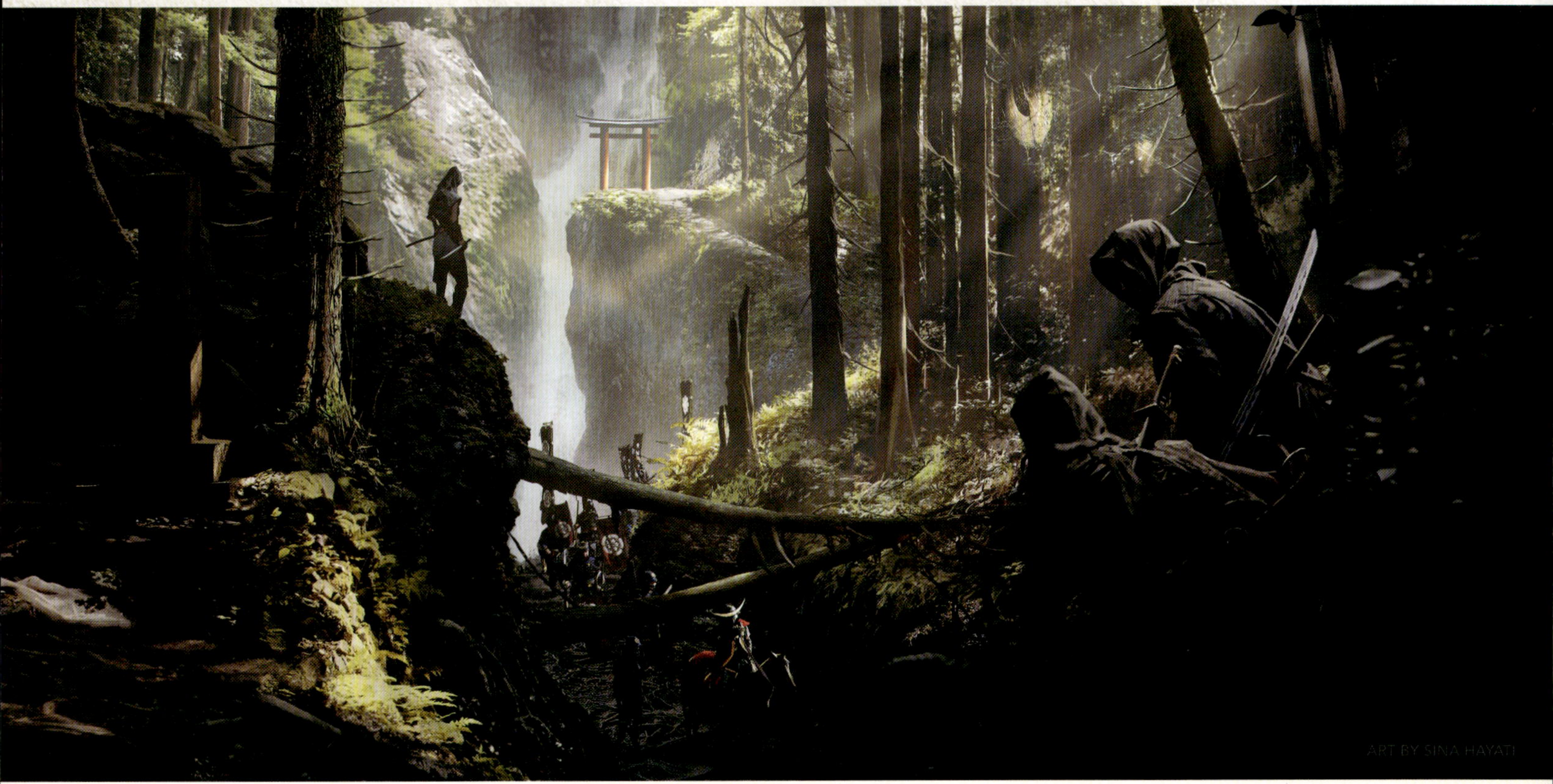

ART BY SINA HAYATI

Provinces in Japan's war-torn Sengoku period featured dozens of wooden hilltop fortresses and military compounds overlooking approach routes in valleys and passes.

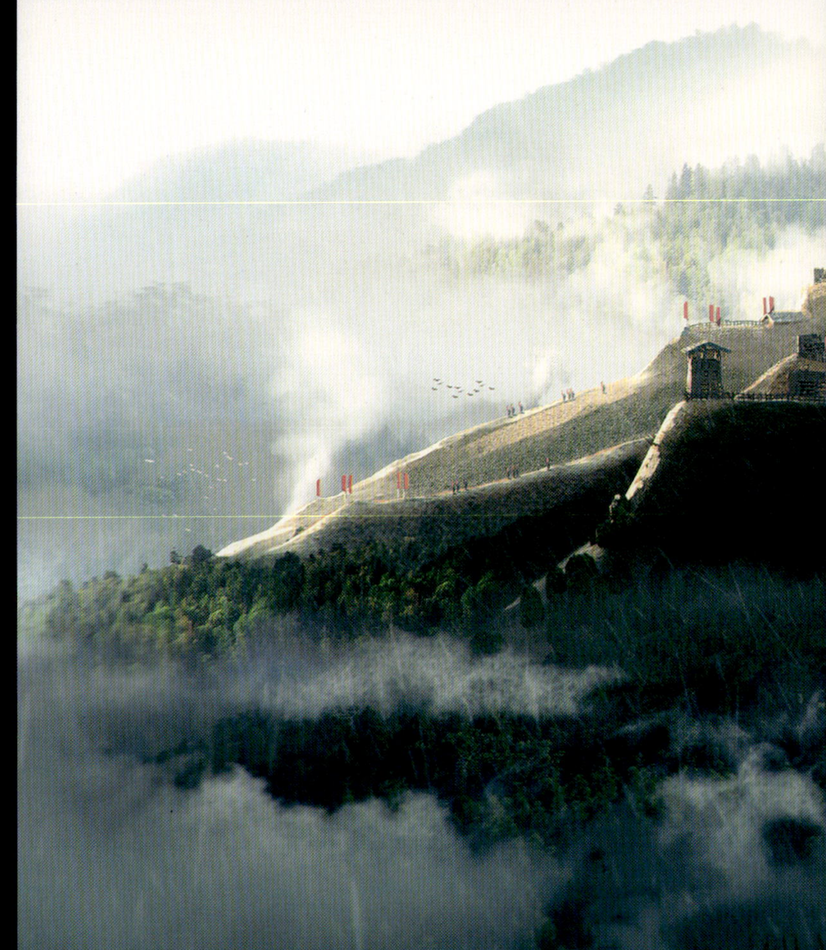

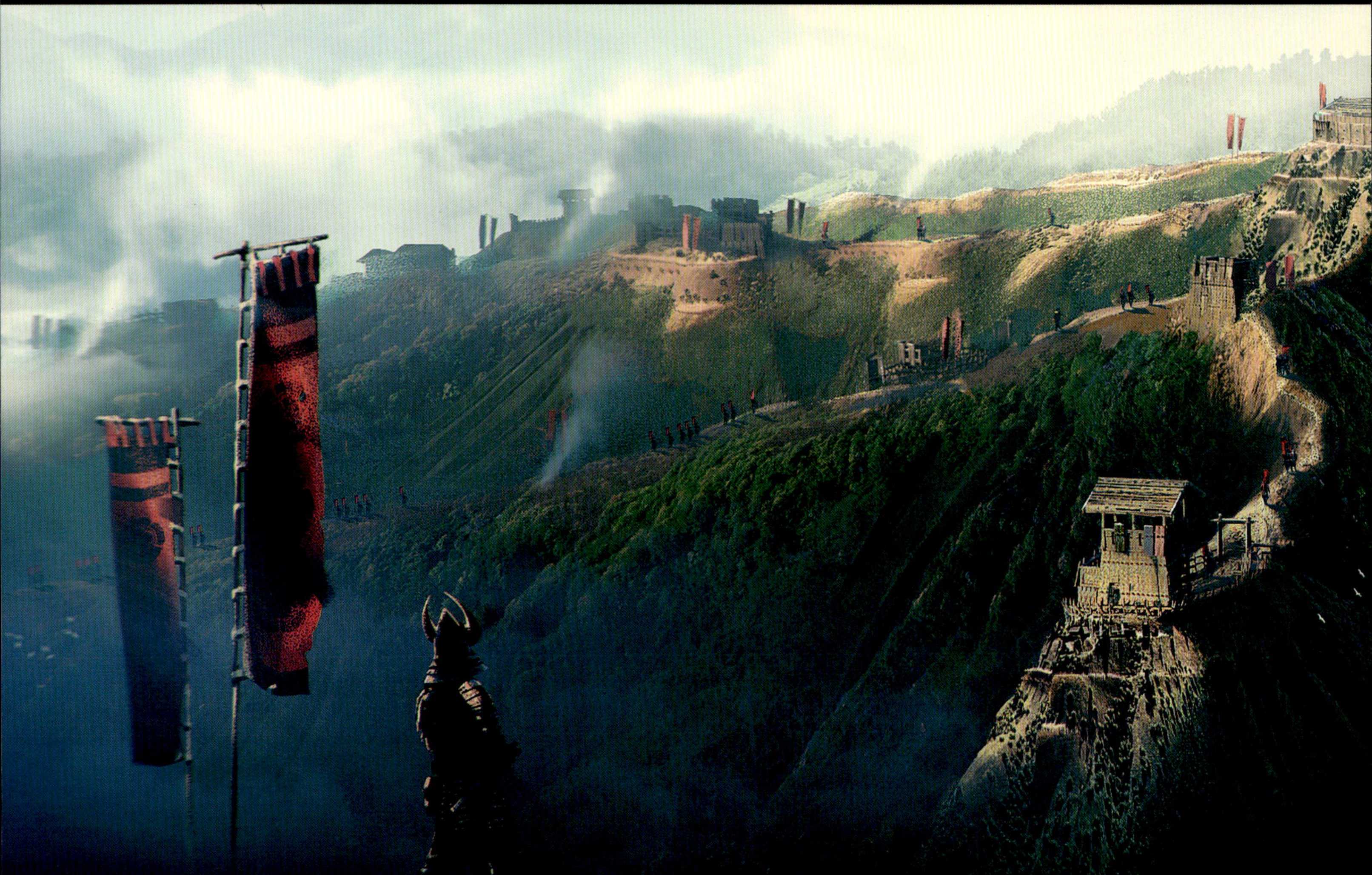

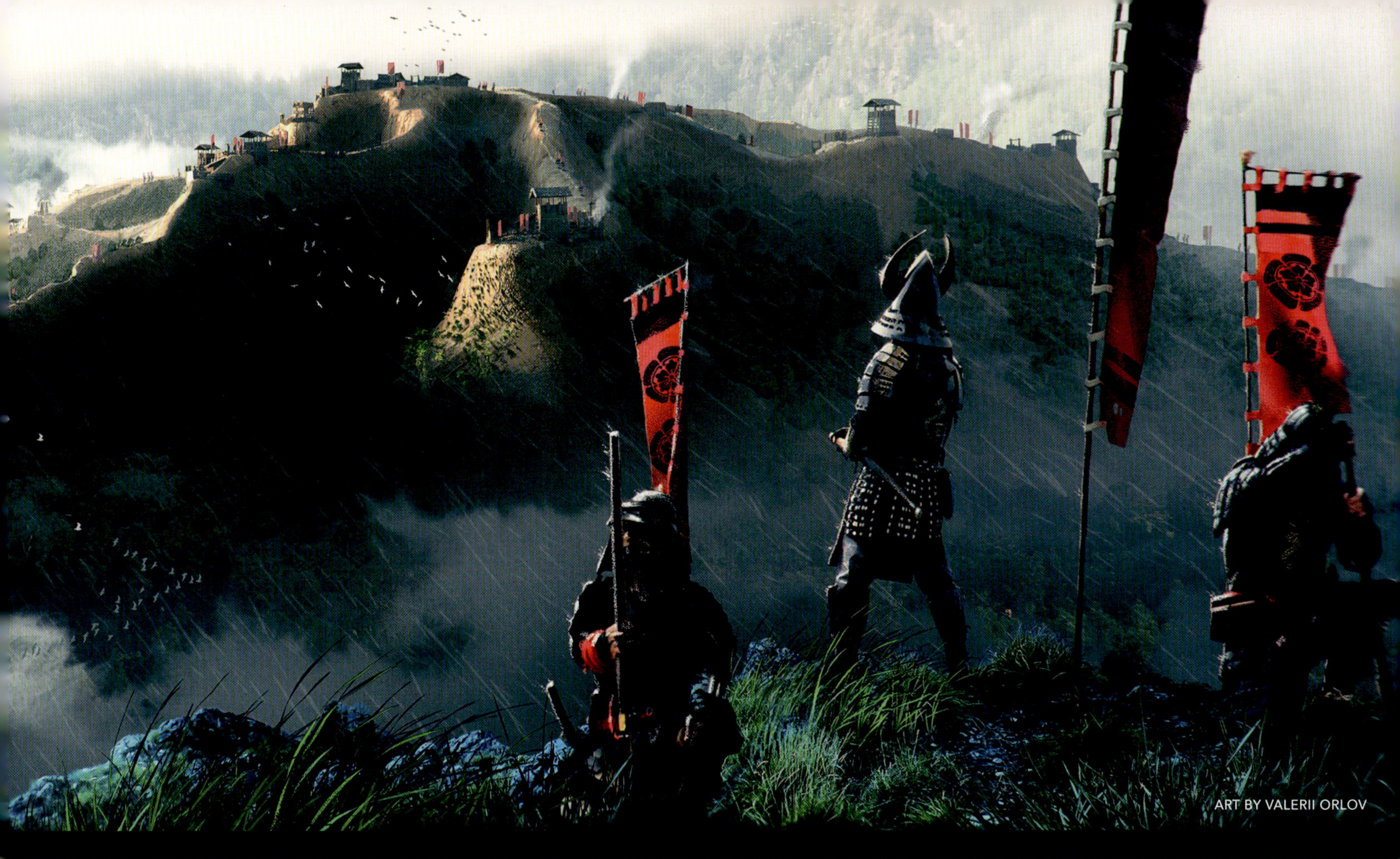

ART BY VALERII ORLOV

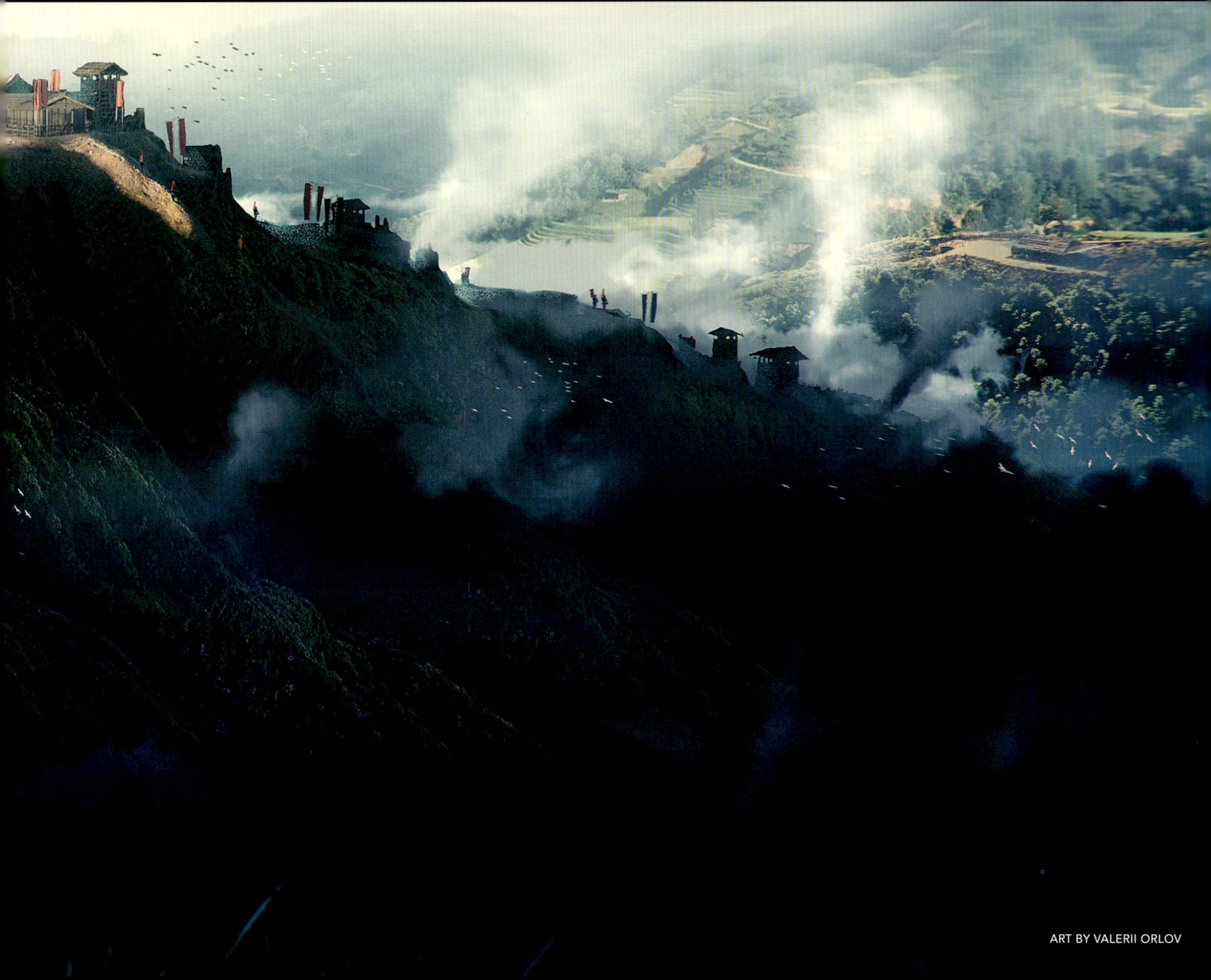

ART BY VALERII ORLOV

SETTSU *URBAN COMMERCIAL CENTER*

Settsu is the densest, most urban province of Japan, with a thriving cosmopolitan center featuring the great city of Osaka and the nearby seaport of Sakai, the primary hub of international trade in Japan. Settsu is a favorite destination of European merchants bringing precious goods (including matchlock firearms) to trade with the daimyos for silver, fine Japanese lacquerware, and other

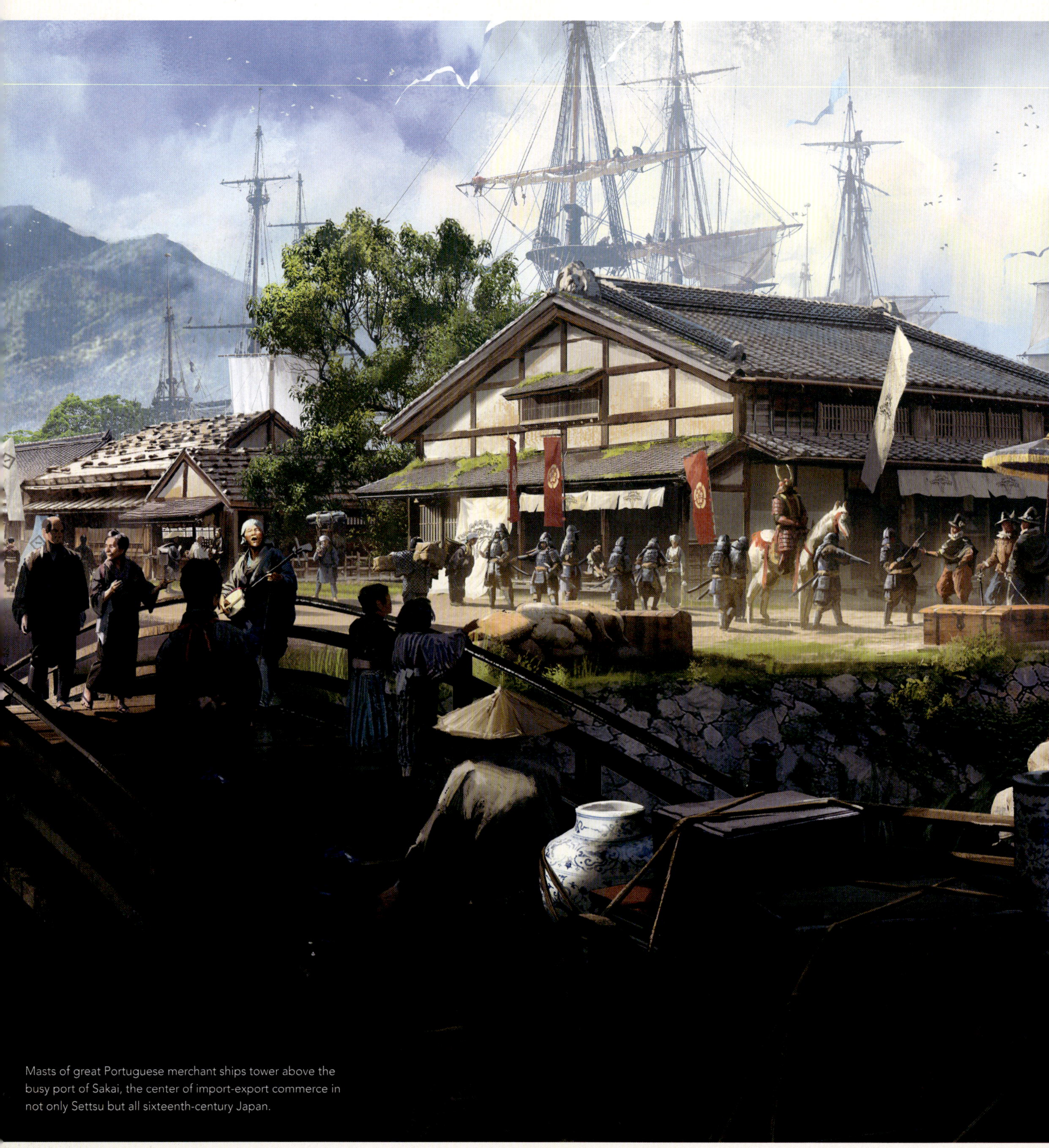

Masts of great Portuguese merchant ships tower above the busy port of Sakai, the center of import-export commerce in not only Settsu but all sixteenth-century Japan.

native exports. "The concept art team did a lot of research and explorations of Osaka's layout," says Dansereau. This spread presents a striking view of the market district of Sakai.

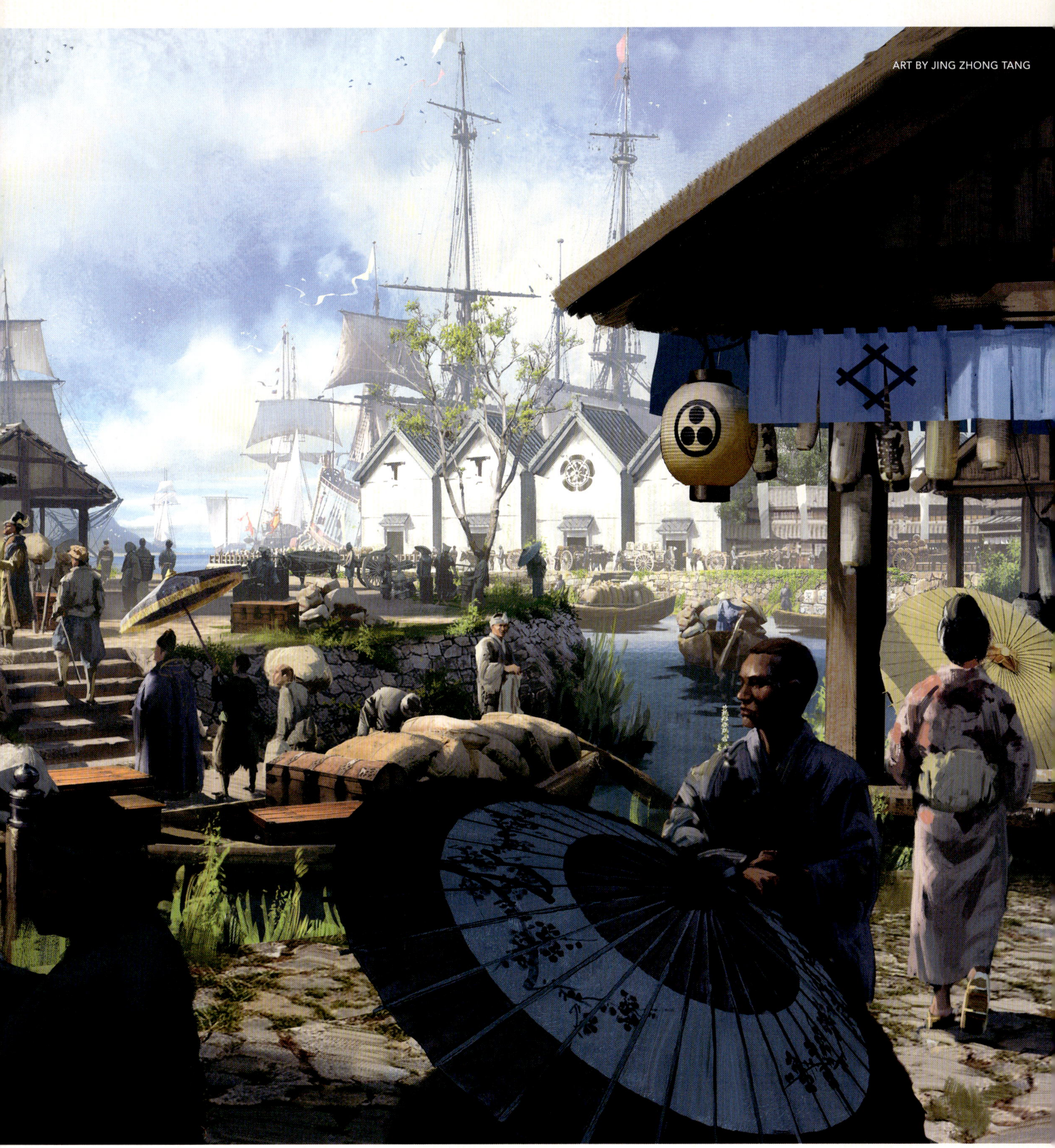

ART BY JING ZHONG TANG

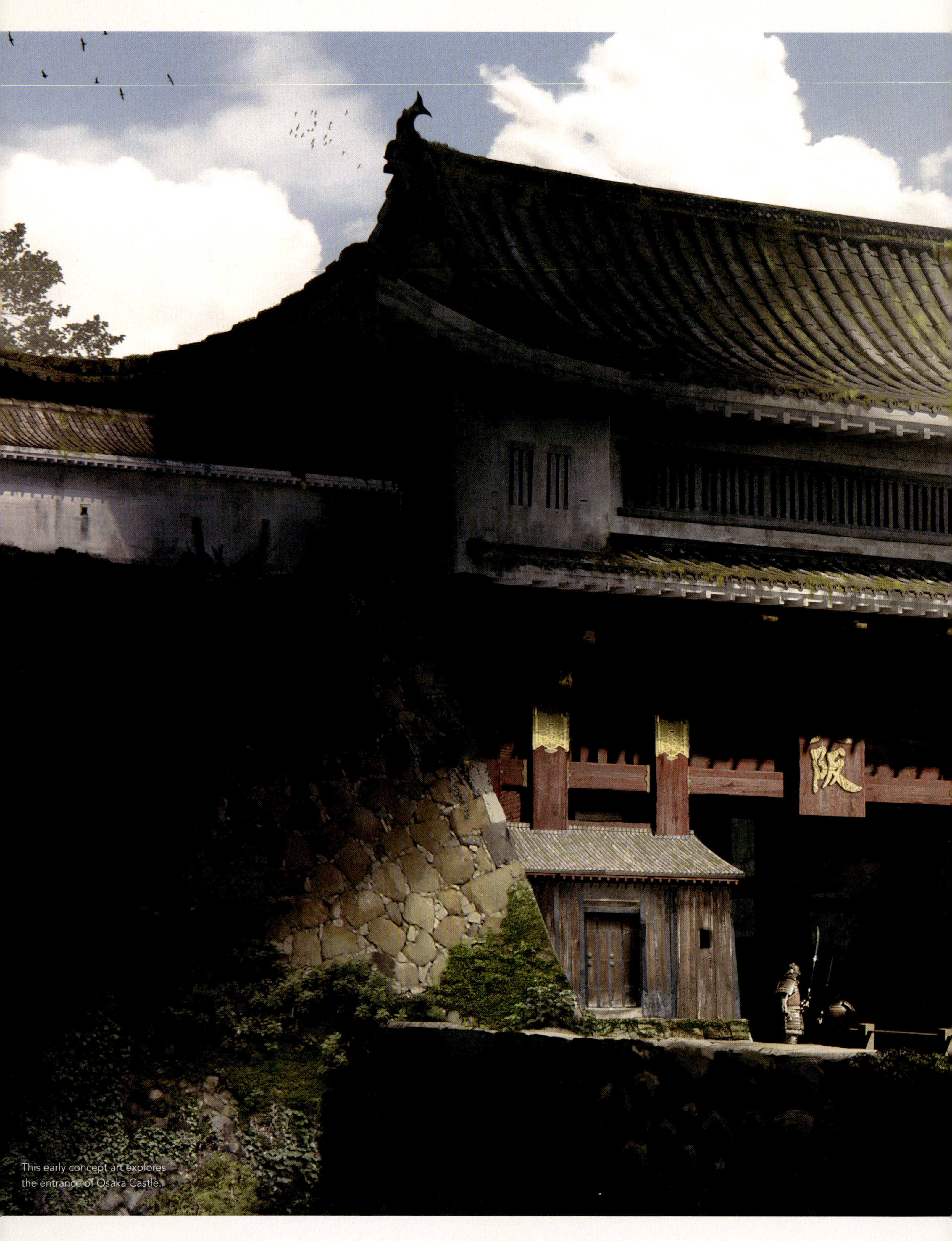

This early concept art explores the entrance of Osaka Castle.

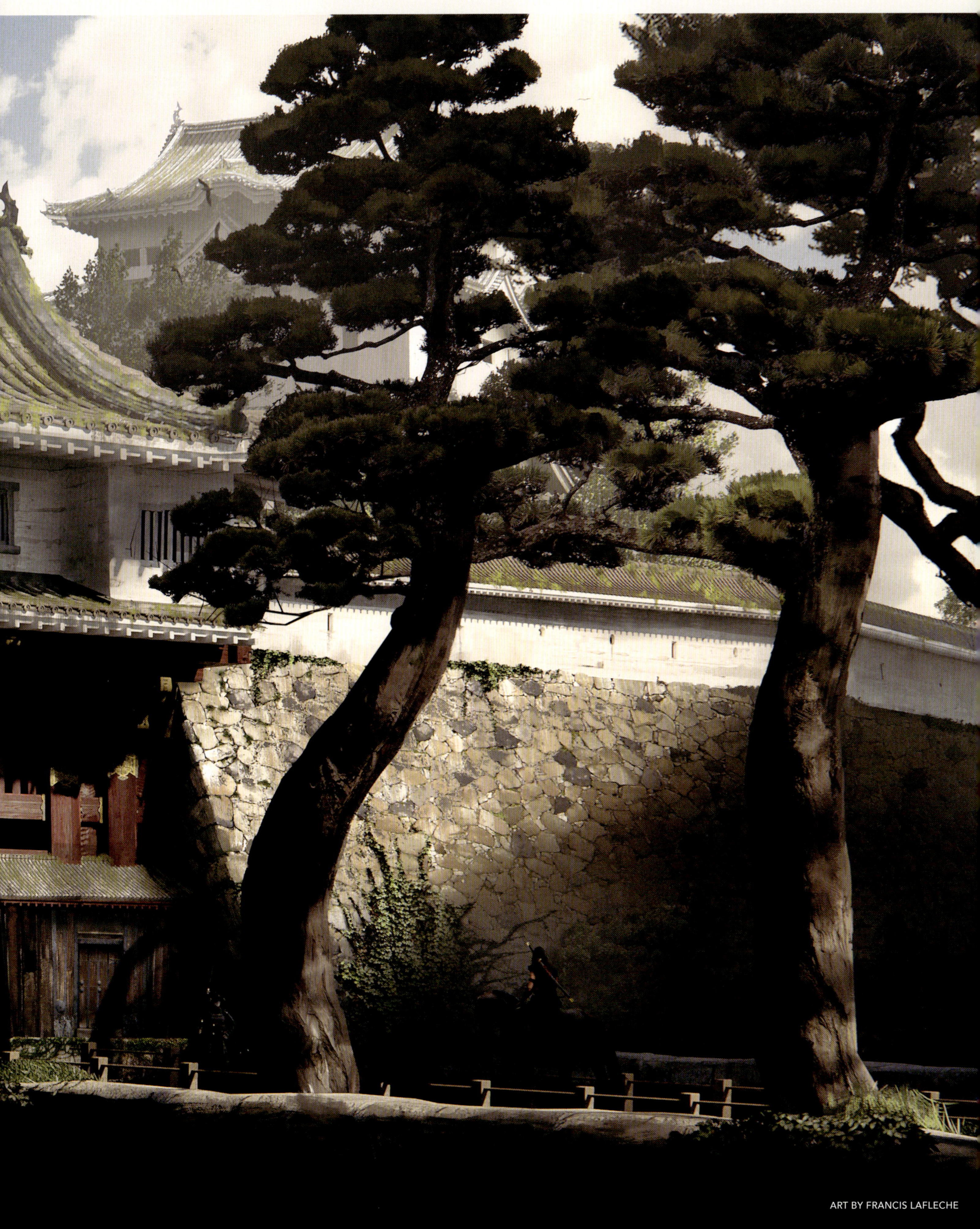

ART BY FRANCIS LAFLECHE

The arrival of Portuguese merchants and missionaries to Settsu ports brought new goods to the region. One of the most groundbreaking items—the harquebus—altered the balance of power in the civil wars raging across Japan at the end of the Sengoku period. Oda Nobunaga was an early adopter of occidental war techniques and technology; matchlock firearms let his troops defeat much larger forces.

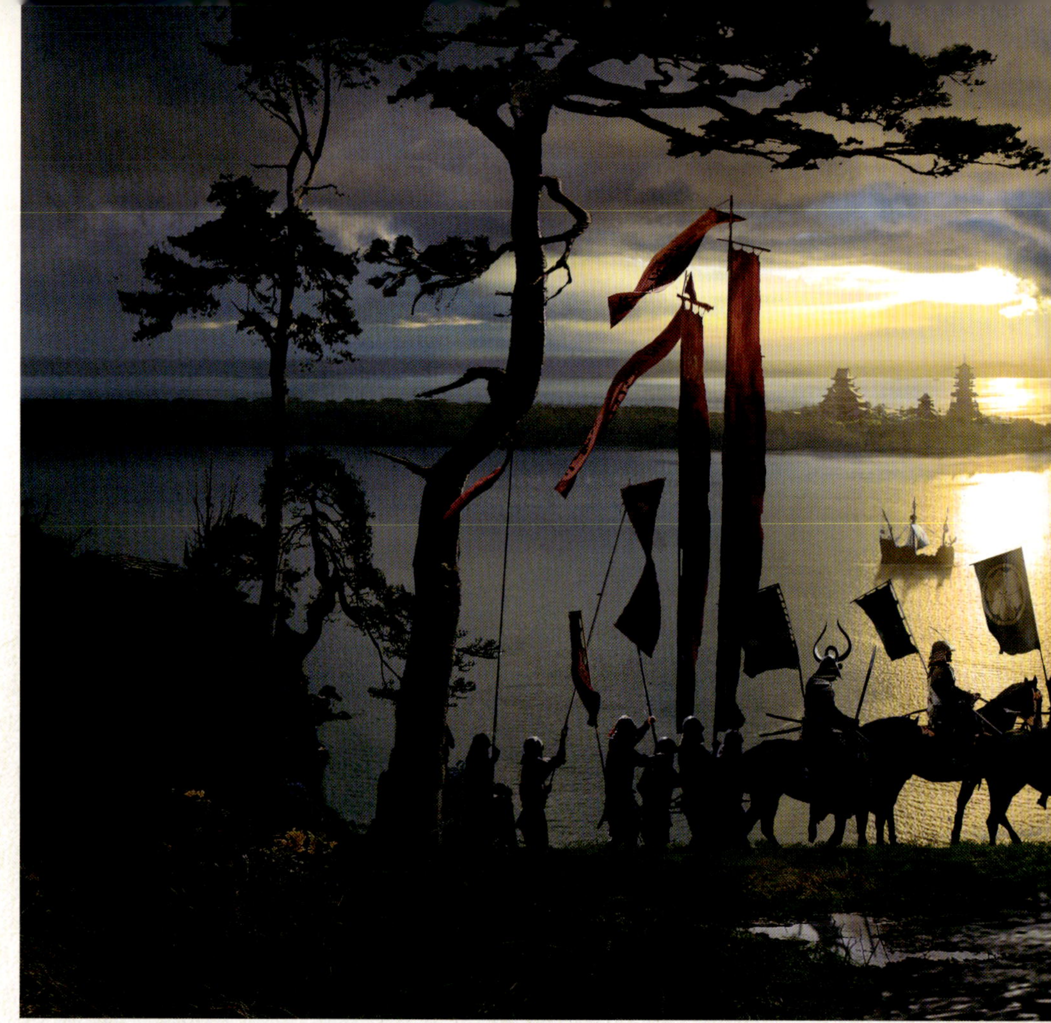

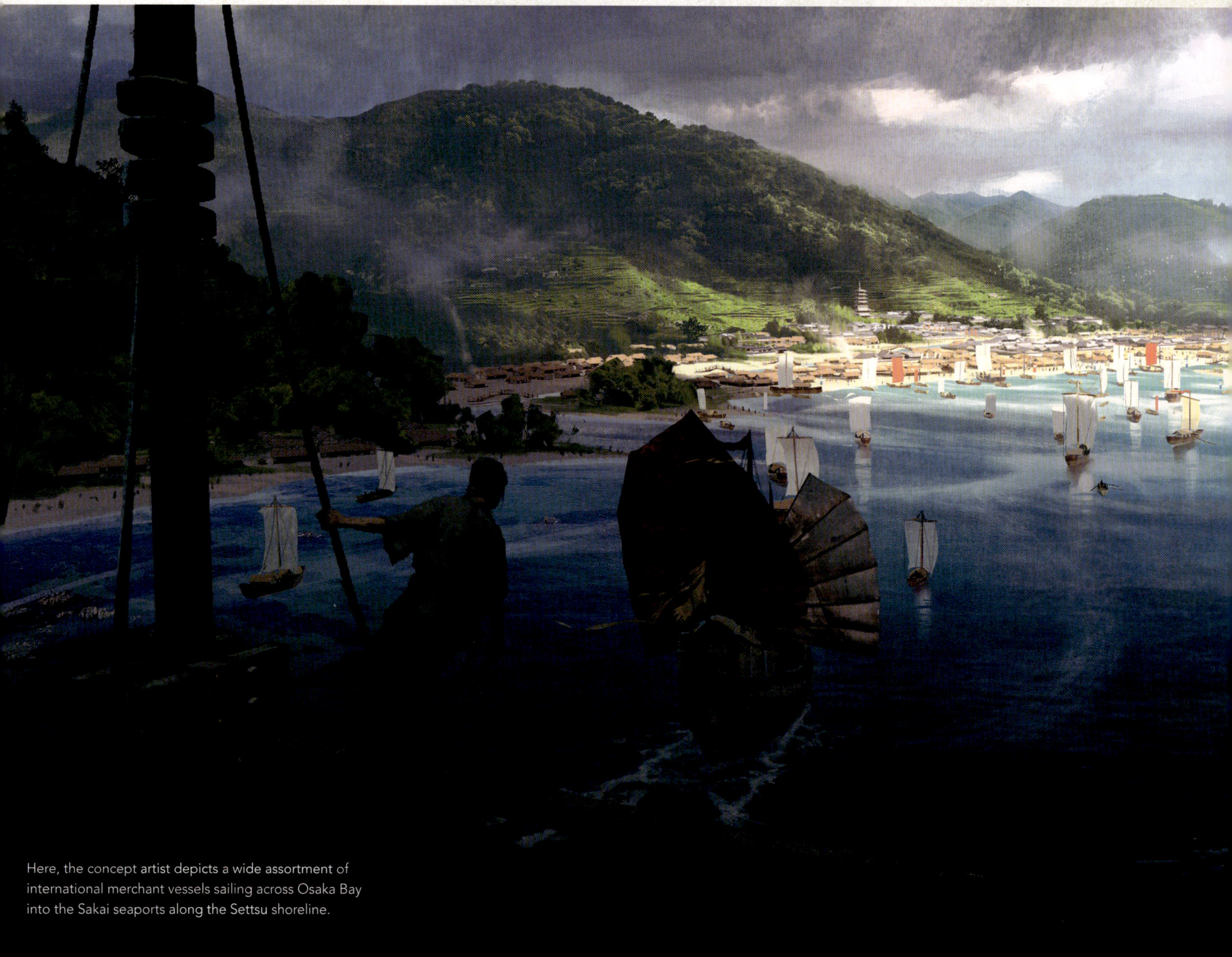

Here, the concept artist depicts a wide assortment of international merchant vessels sailing across Osaka Bay into the Sakai seaports along the Settsu shoreline.

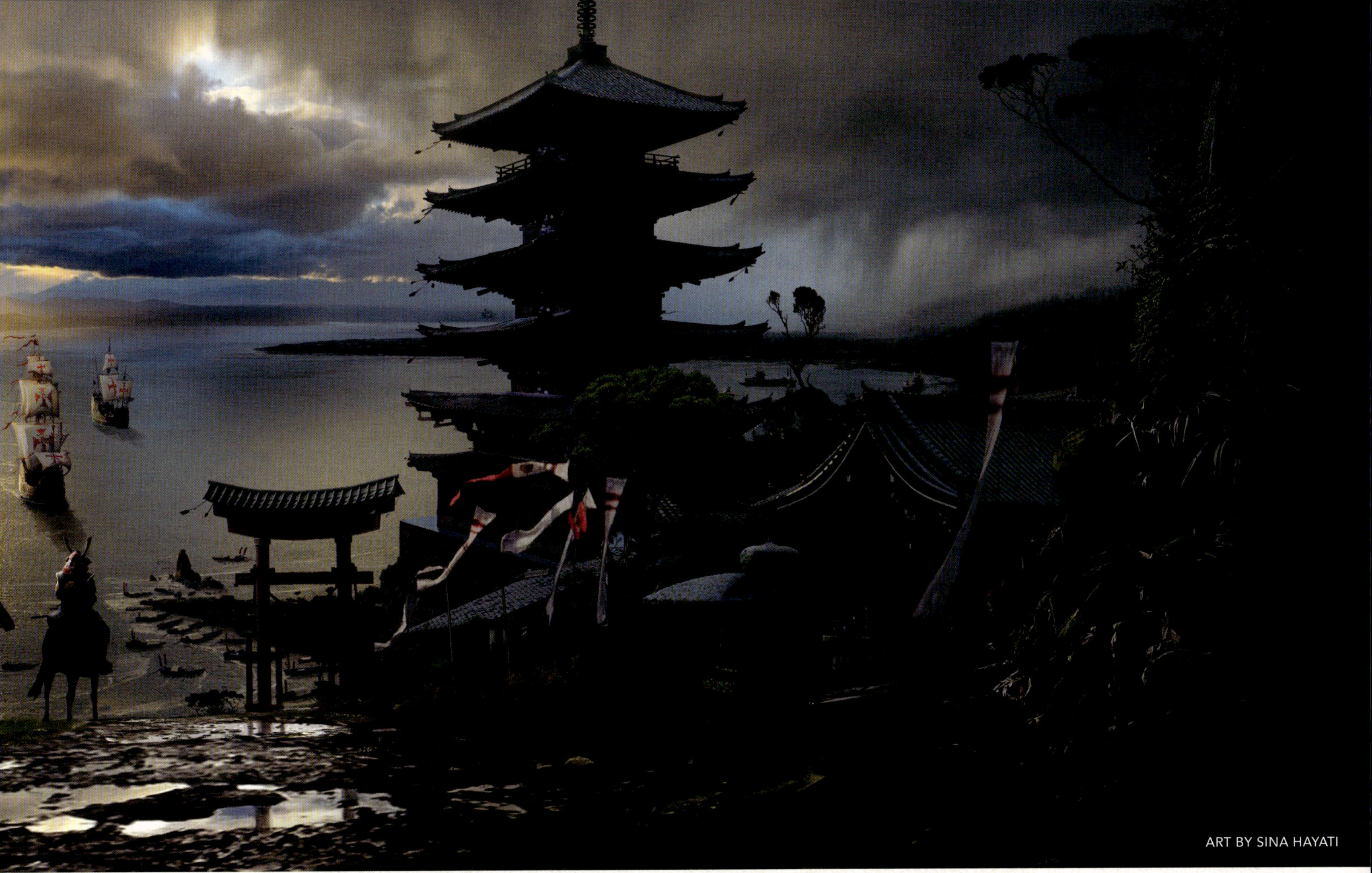

ART BY SINA HAYATI

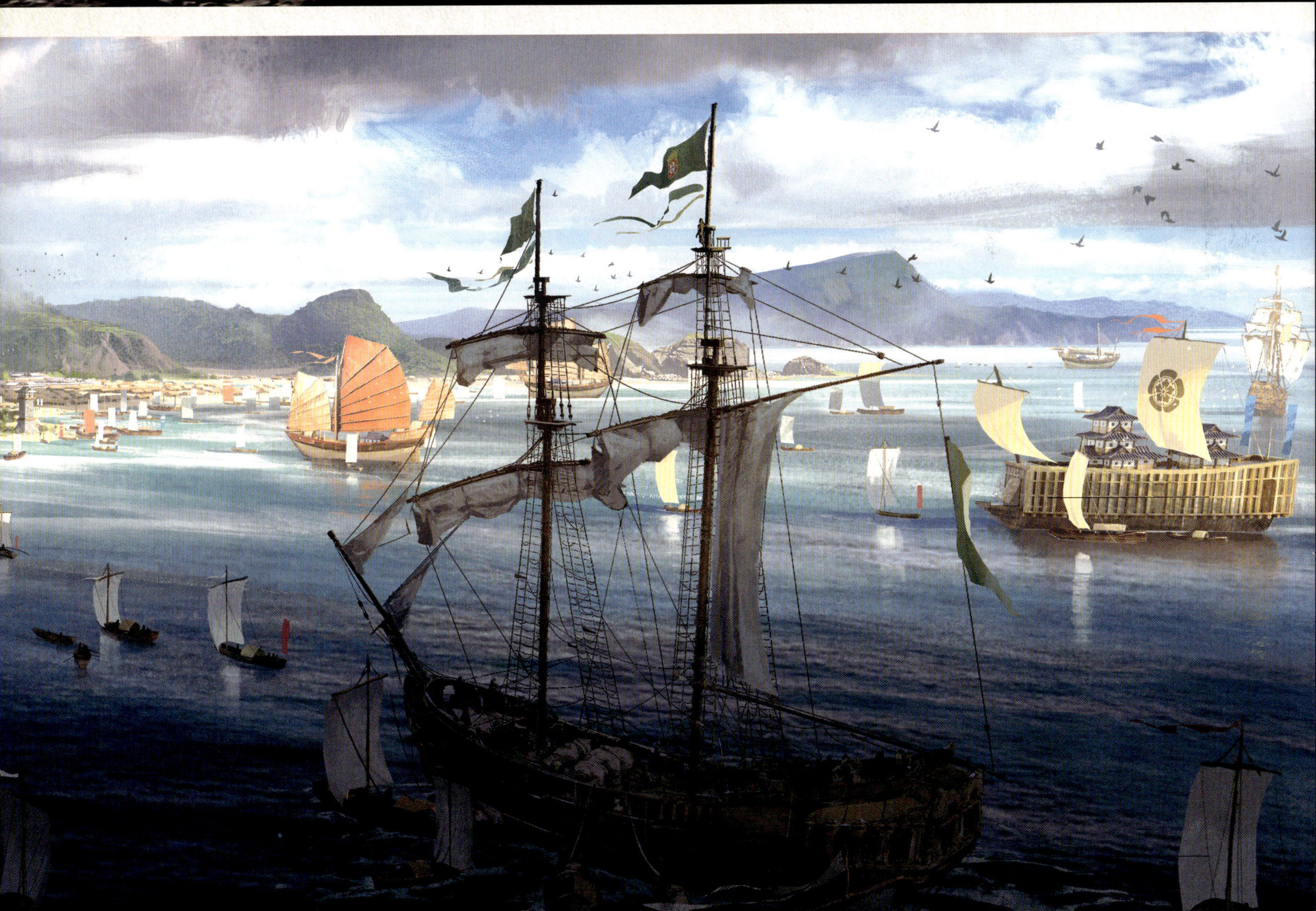

ART BY SINA HAYATI

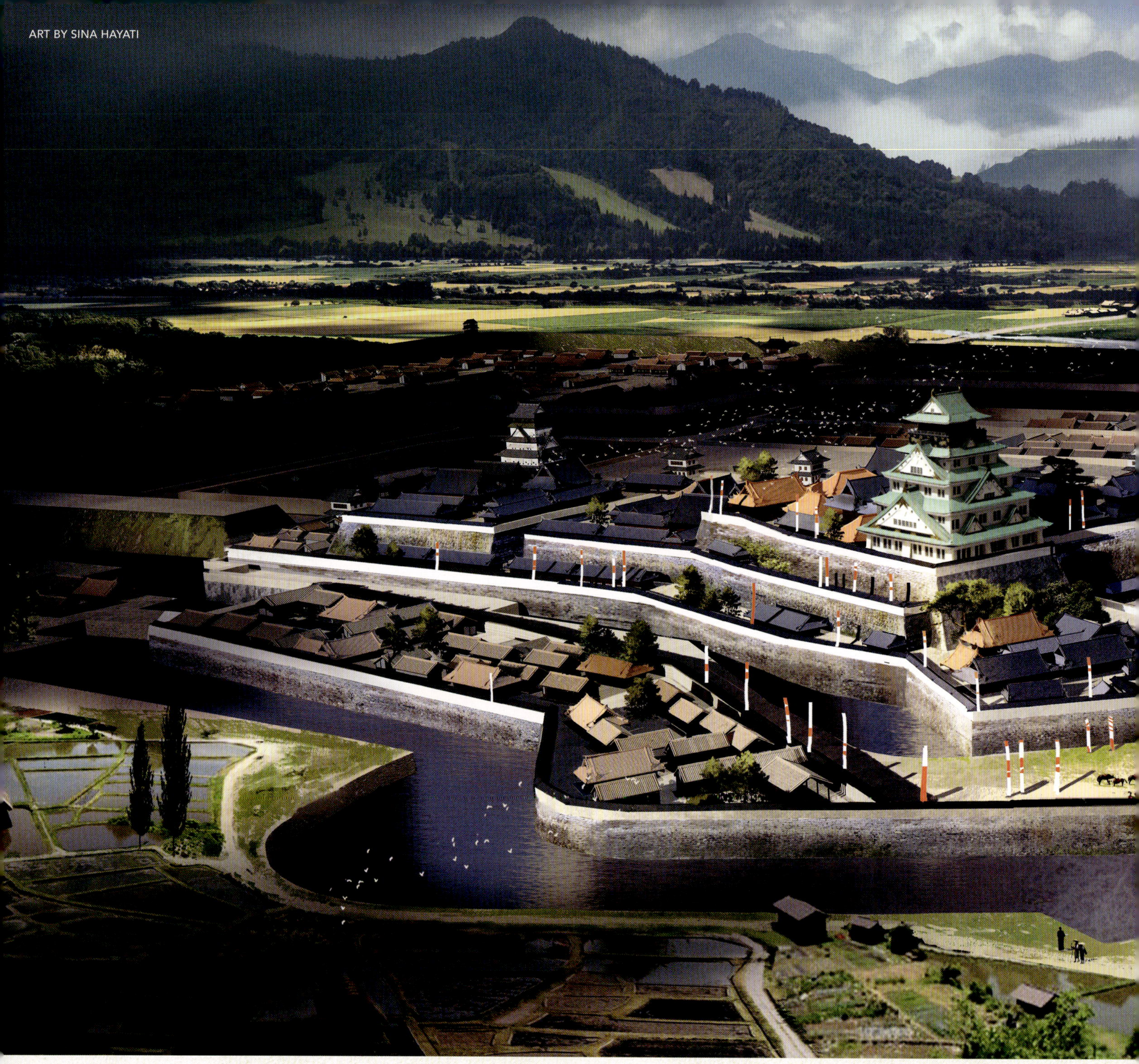

These ink sketches explore Settsu village huts, shrines, castles, and *kofun* of the Sengoku period. Feudal warlords had previously built their castles on high promontories, but the 1500s began to see more "castle towns" *(as seen above)* built on lowland plains—central strongholds surrounded by rings of samurai, merchant, and agricultural districts. "This arrangement helped towns develop a more centralized economy," says Dansereau.

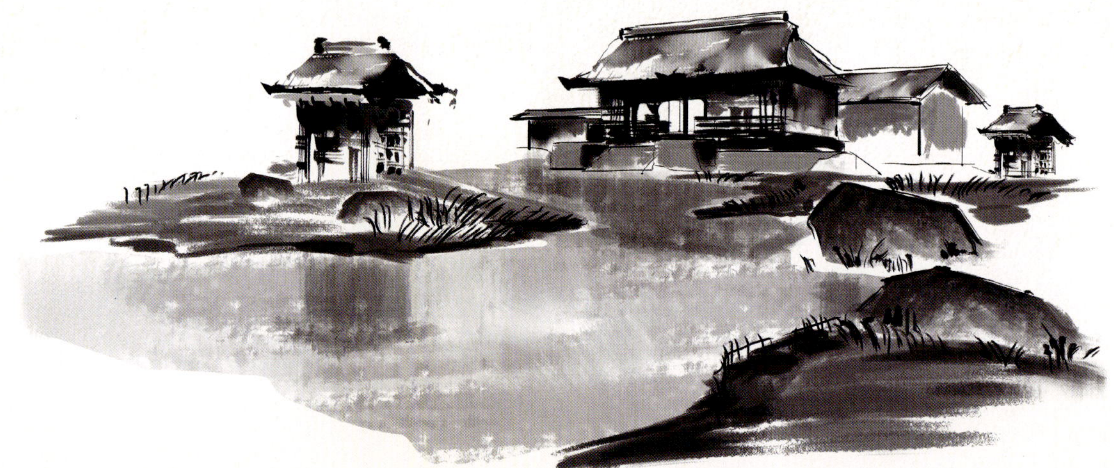

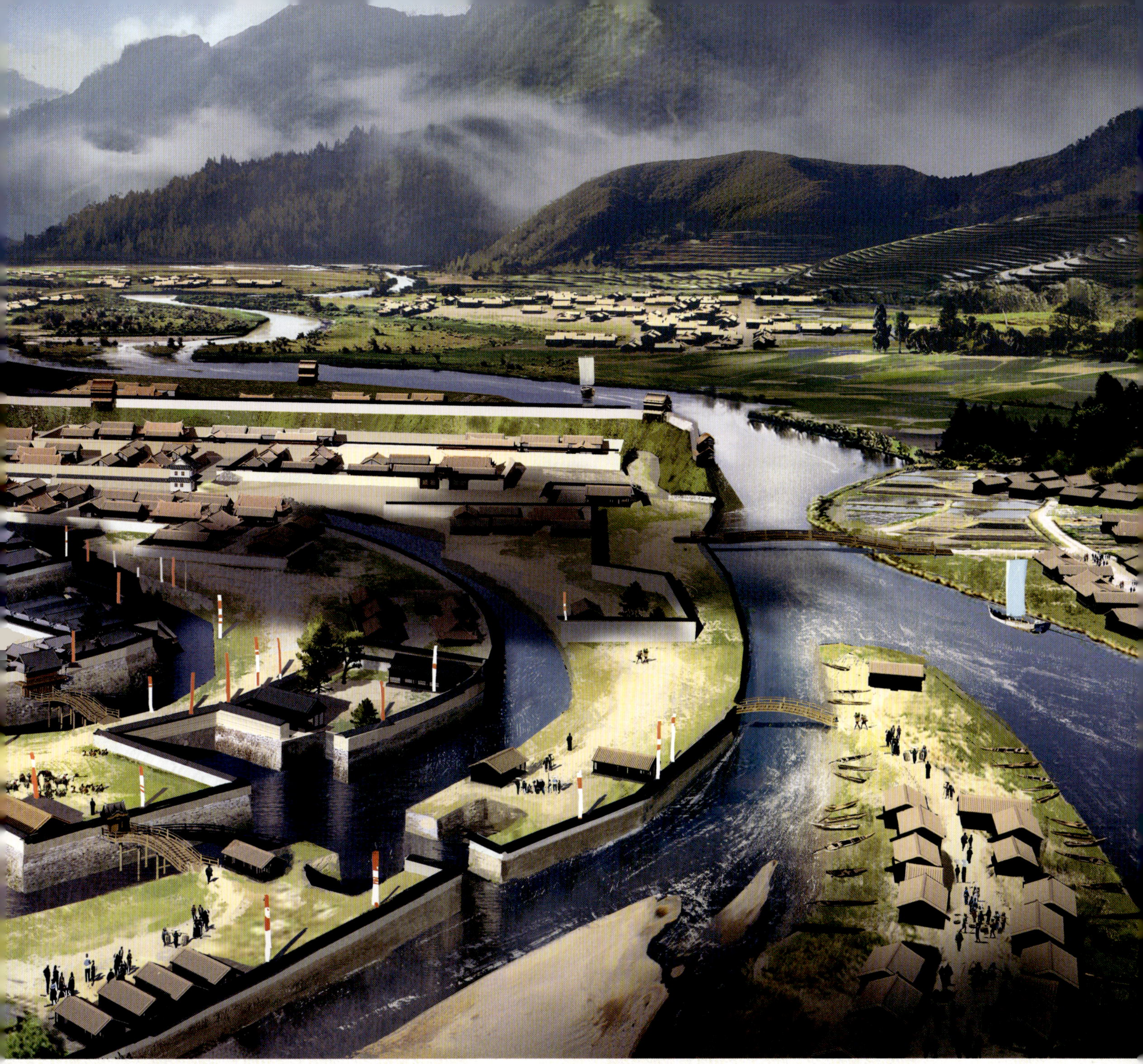

ART BY ALBERT LIN

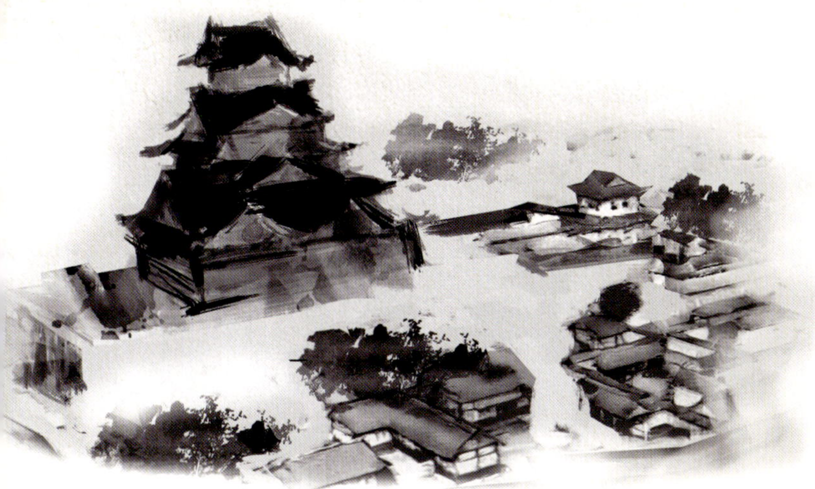

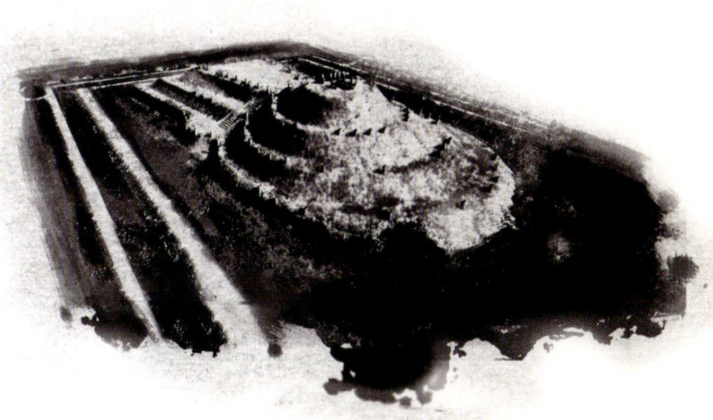

One of Settsu's most prominent structures is Osaka Castle, built atop the ruins of the Ishiyama Hongan-ji temple. The Buddhist monks of Hongan-ji had held out for ten years against a siege waged by Oda Nobunaga but finally surrendered in 1580. The temple was razed, and Nobunaga's successor, Toyotomi Hideyoshi, constructed his iconic fortress in its place. Osaka Castle served as Hideyoshi's base in the quest he inherited from Nobunaga—the unification of Japan.

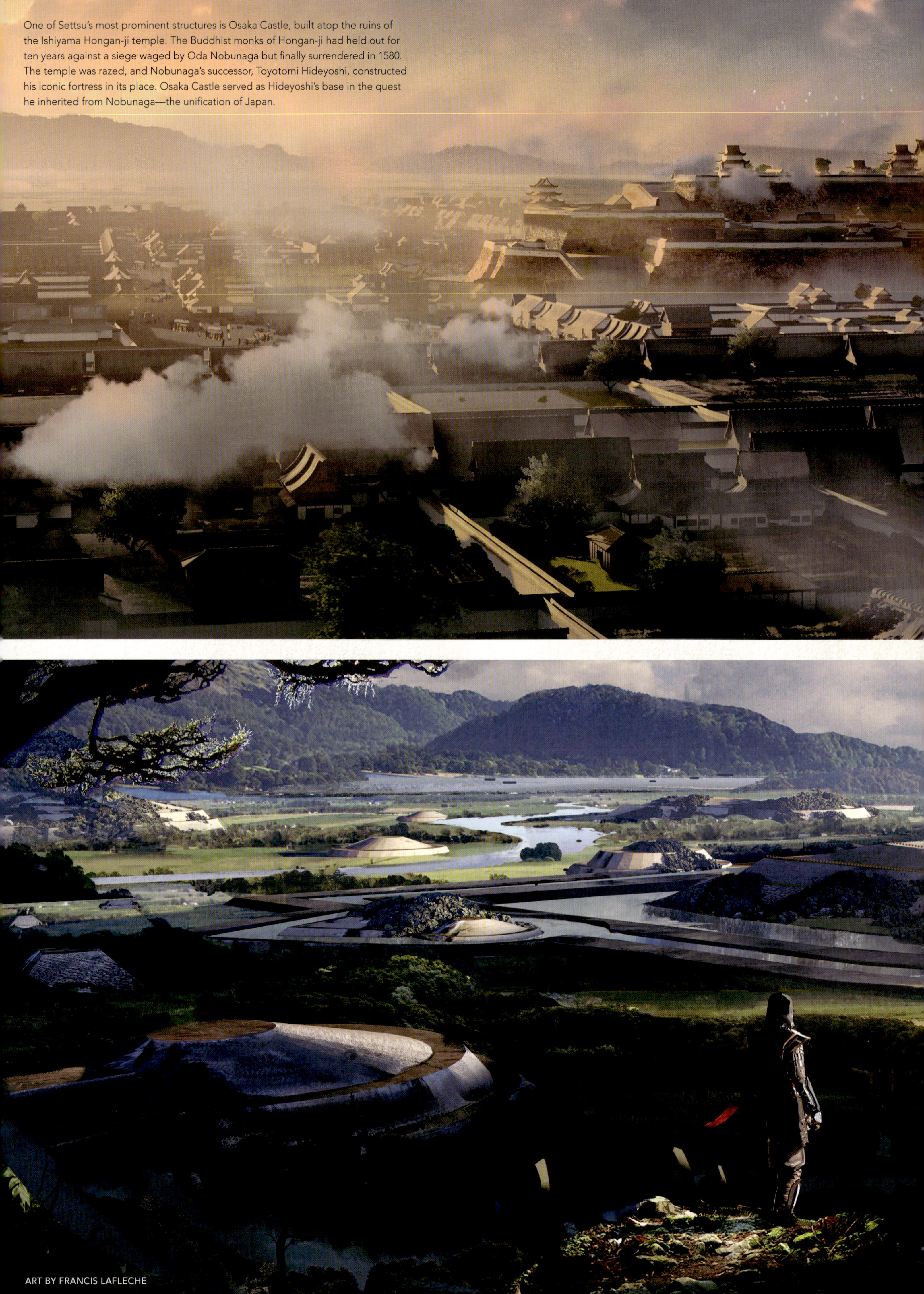

ART BY FRANCIS LAFLECHE

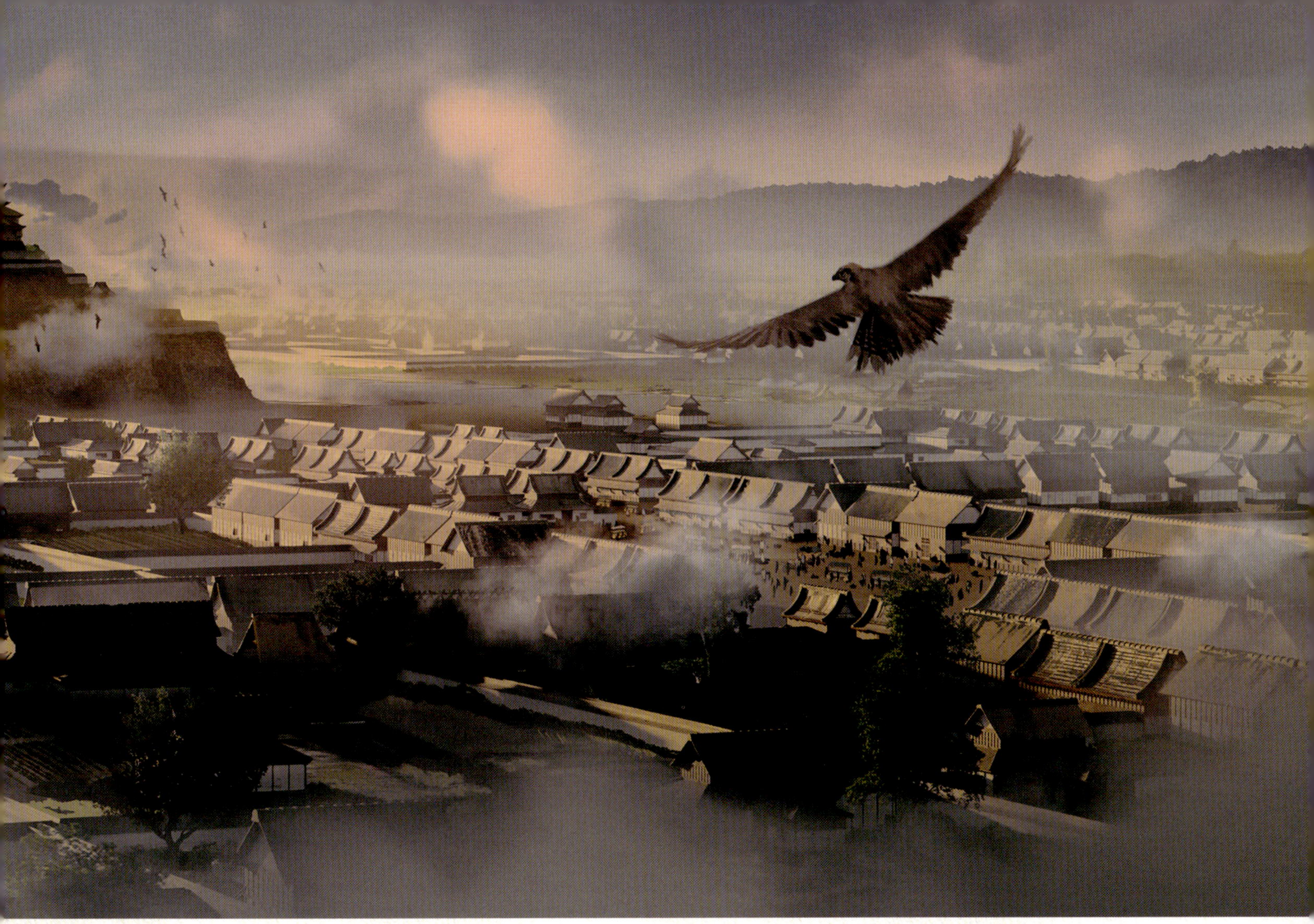

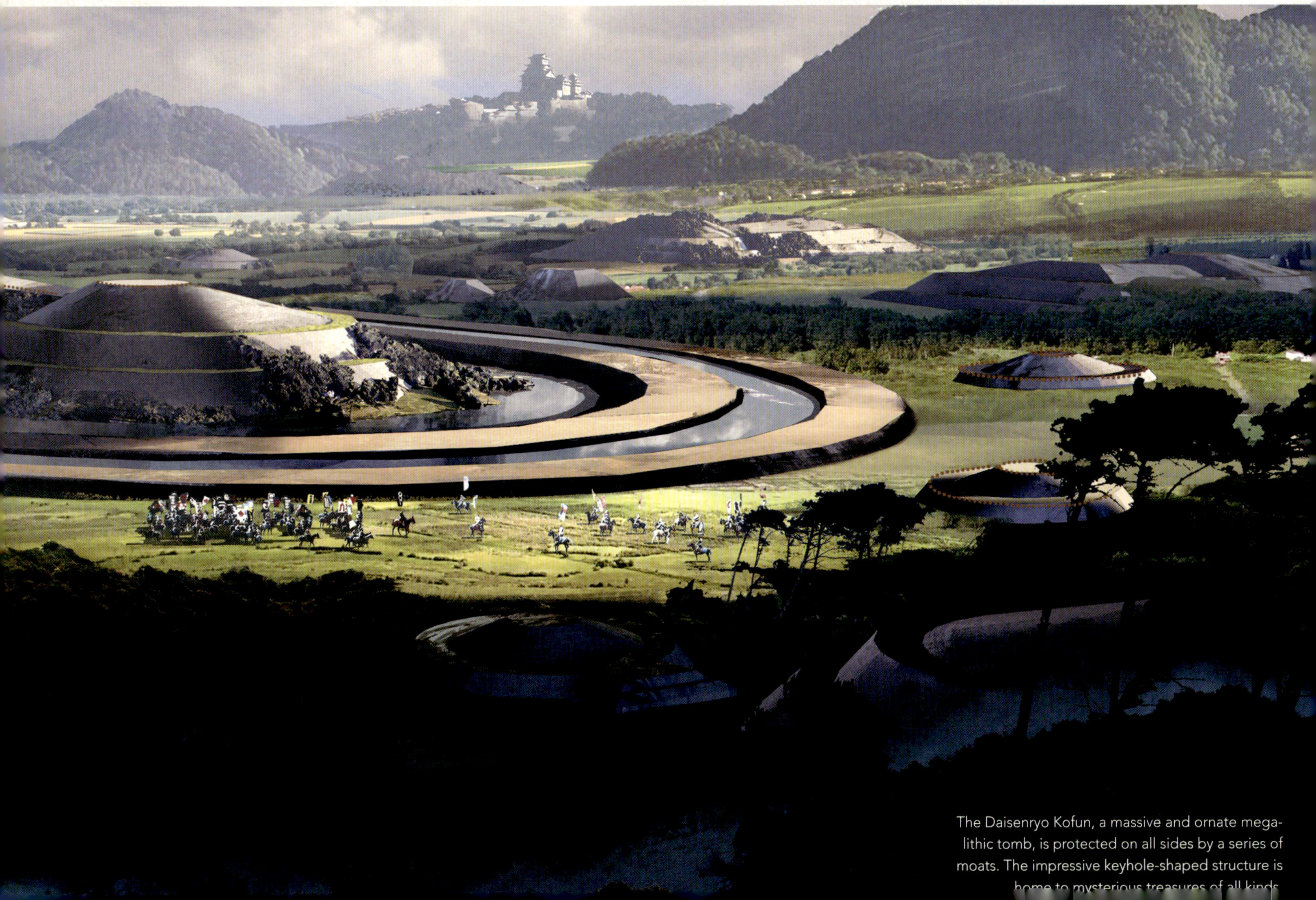

The Daisenryo Kofun, a massive and ornate megalithic tomb, is protected on all sides by a series of moats. The impressive keyhole-shaped structure is home to mysterious treasures of all kinds.

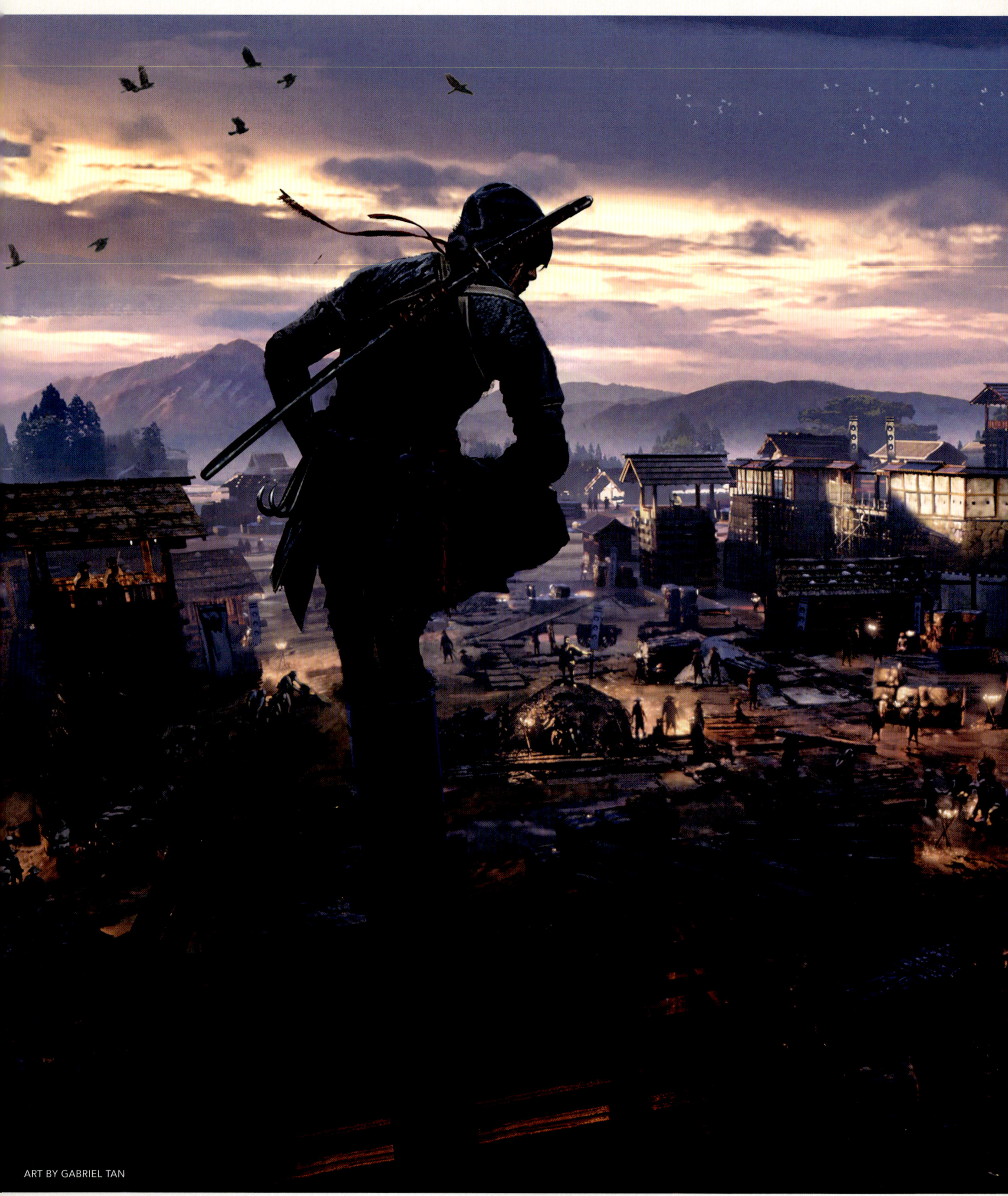
ART BY GABRIEL TAN

In this spectacular twilight panorama, Naoe perches on a vista point overlooking a section of Osaka Castle under construction, with its *tenshu* (the highest tower) rising at upper right. The concept image illustrates ways Naoe can use the construction chaos below to slip past guards and watchtowers to the next checkpoint. "It was a

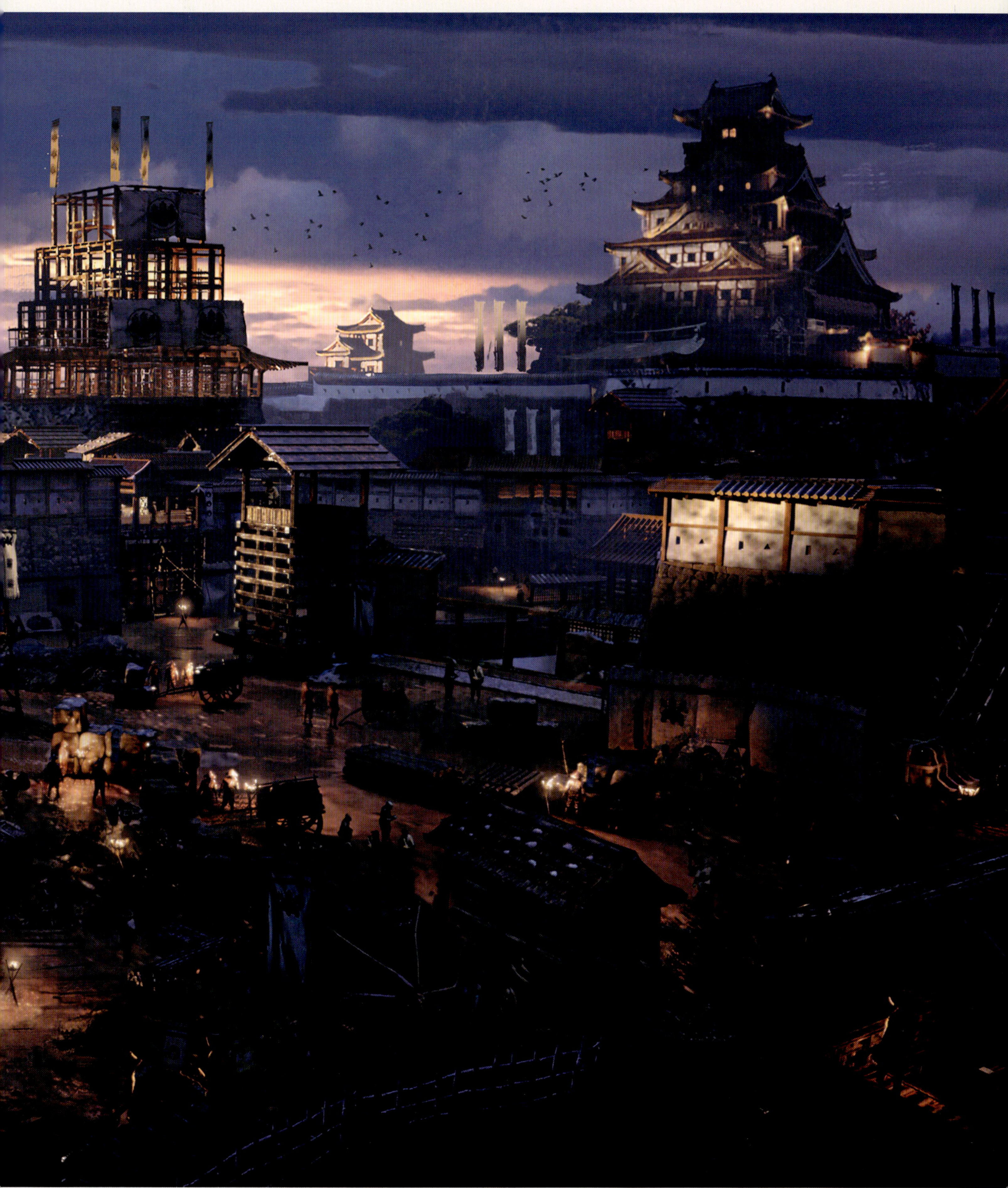

study to depict multiple points of entry for a standard *shinobi* mission," says Tan. "We always look to give Naoe wide leverage in crossing spaces." The piece also uses dramatic lighting to explore mood and atmosphere as the sun sets and torch lights blaze below.

YAMATO
THE OLD WORLD

Yamato, the birthplace of sumo, is the site of the ancient capital where centuries of emperors ruled and now lie entombed in mausoleums. It's known as a land where history and mystery are intertwined—for example, the province is home to the ancient "Asuka stones" *(below)*, a set of monolithic granite boulders carved with strange markings. Spiritual power also emanates from Yamato's famous temples and shrines. The Todai-ji temple complex *(right)* houses the world's largest bronze Buddha statue. Finally, Yamato is also where master smiths craft some of the finest Japanese katanas ever made.

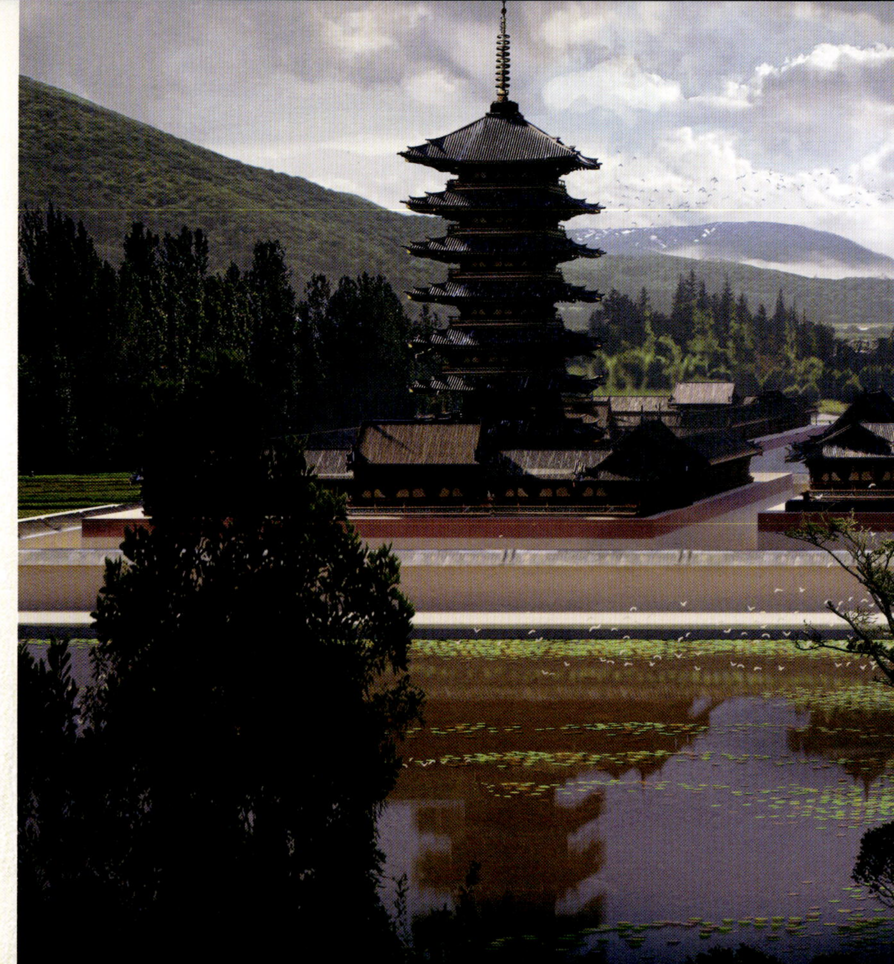

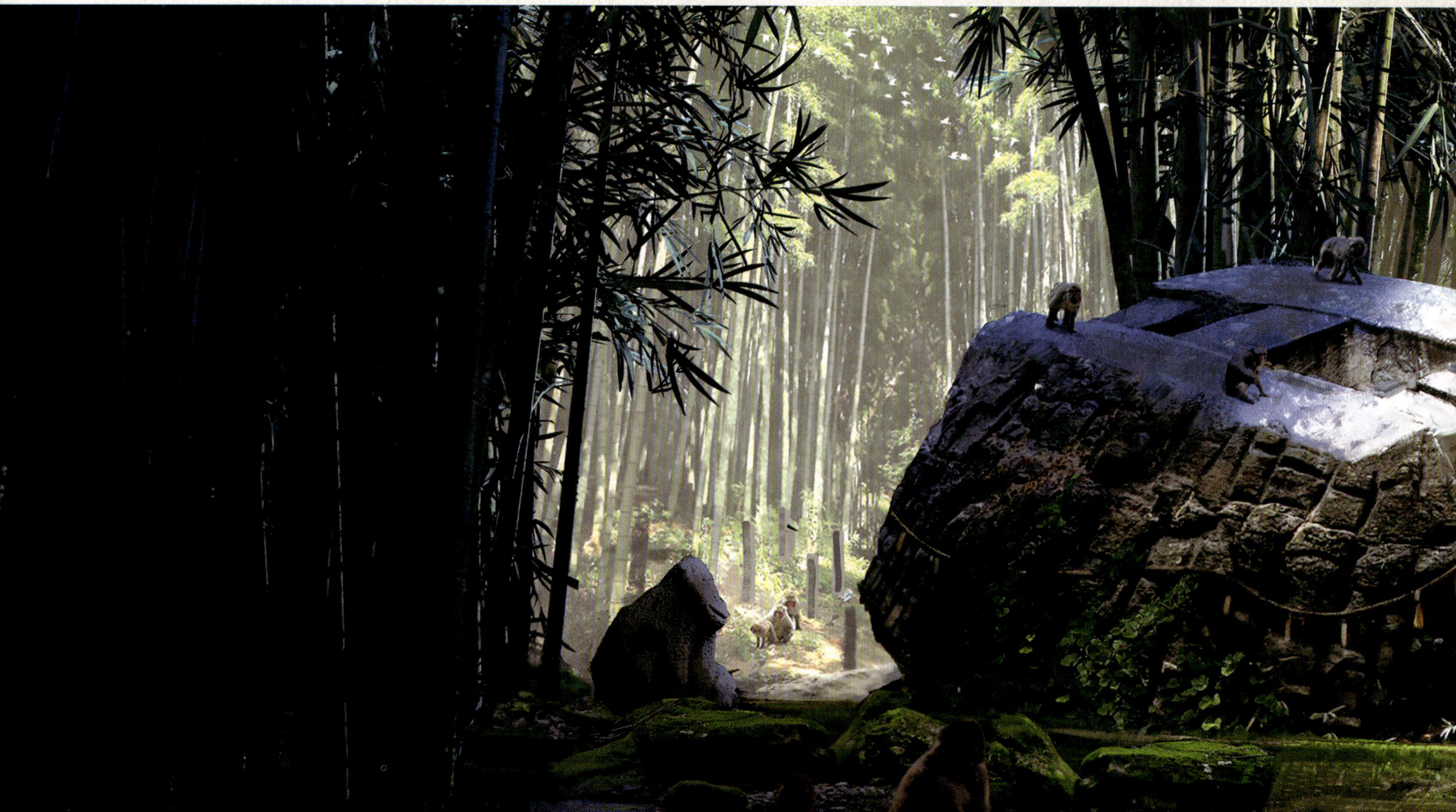

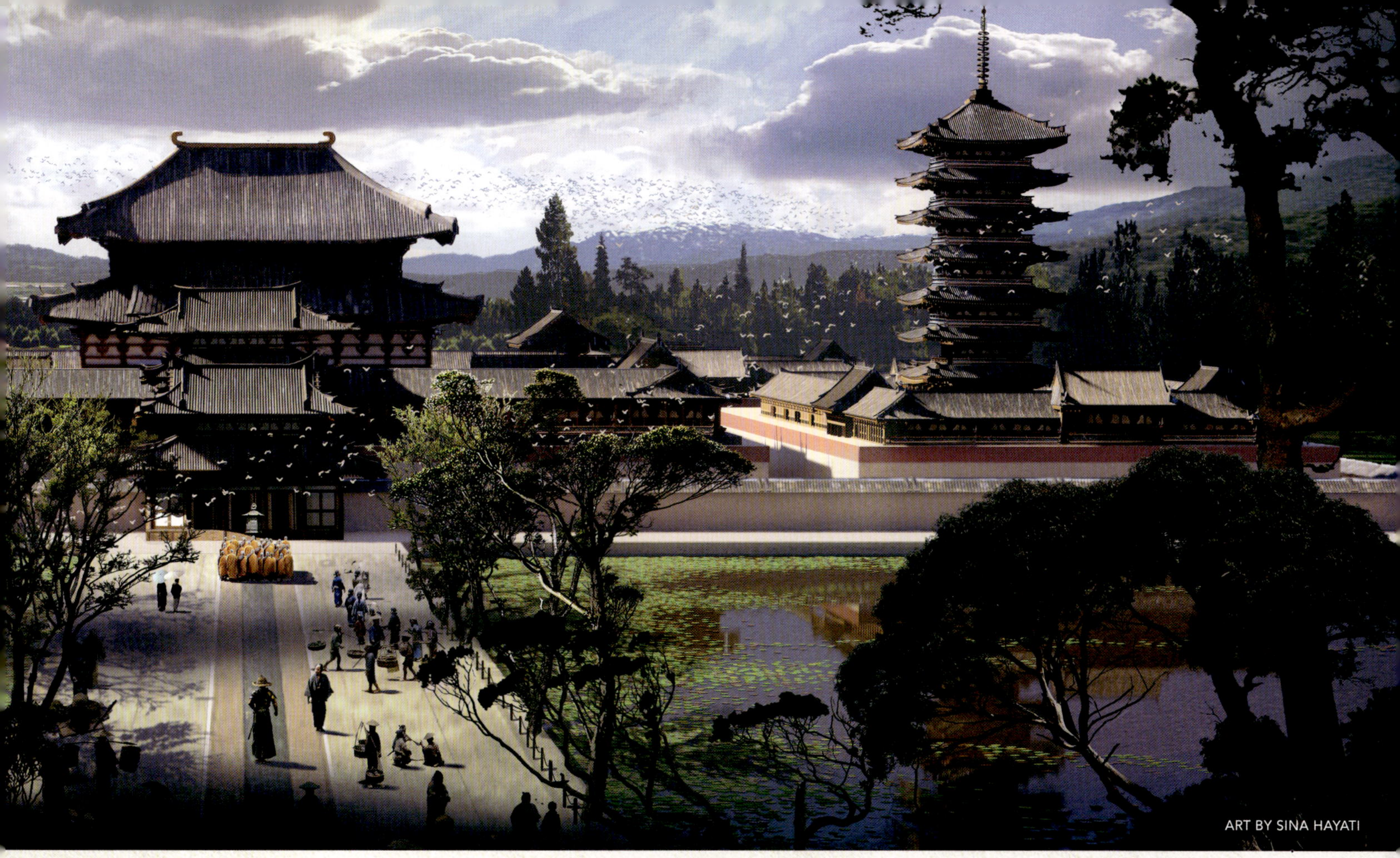

ART BY SINA HAYATI

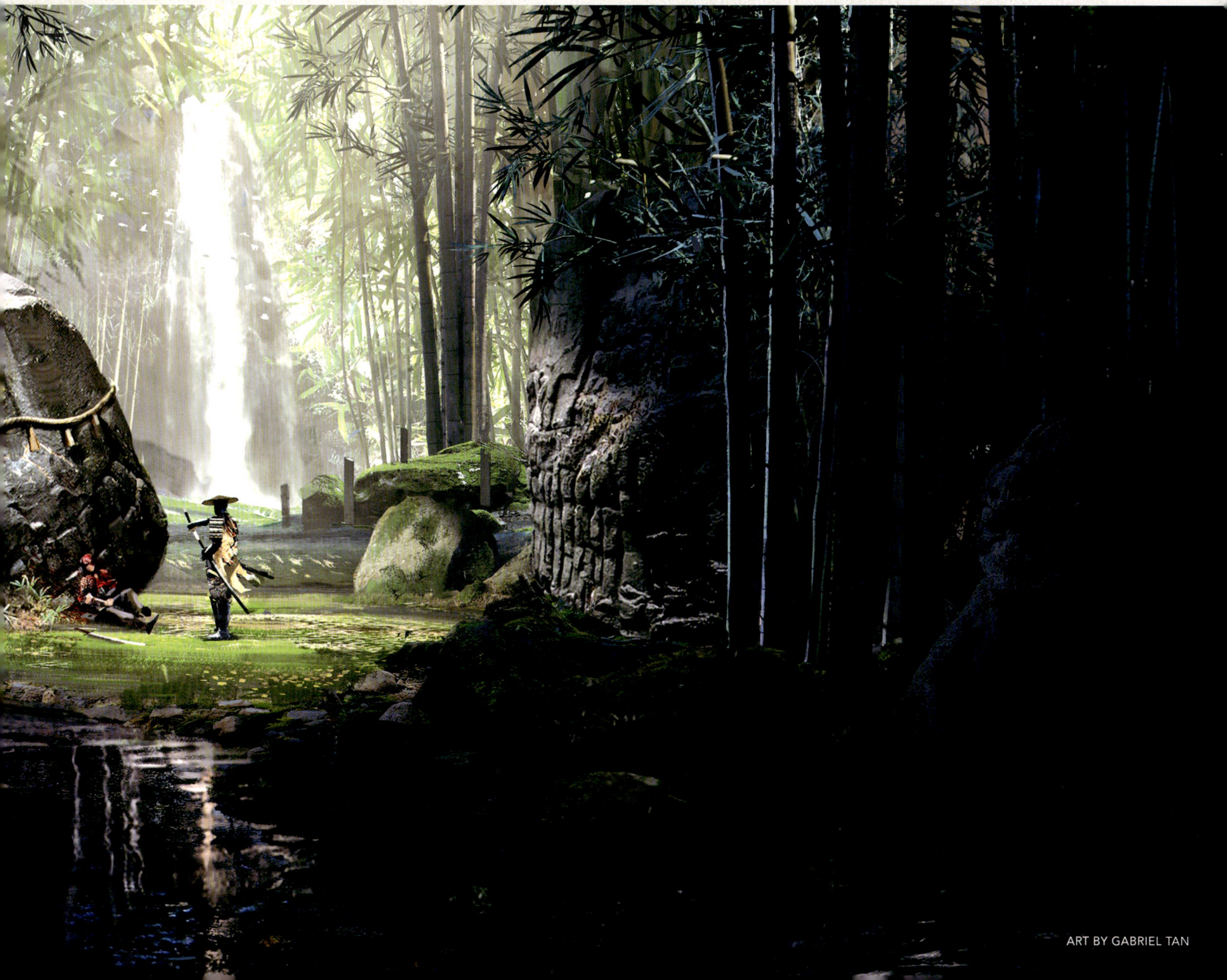

ART BY GABRIEL TAN

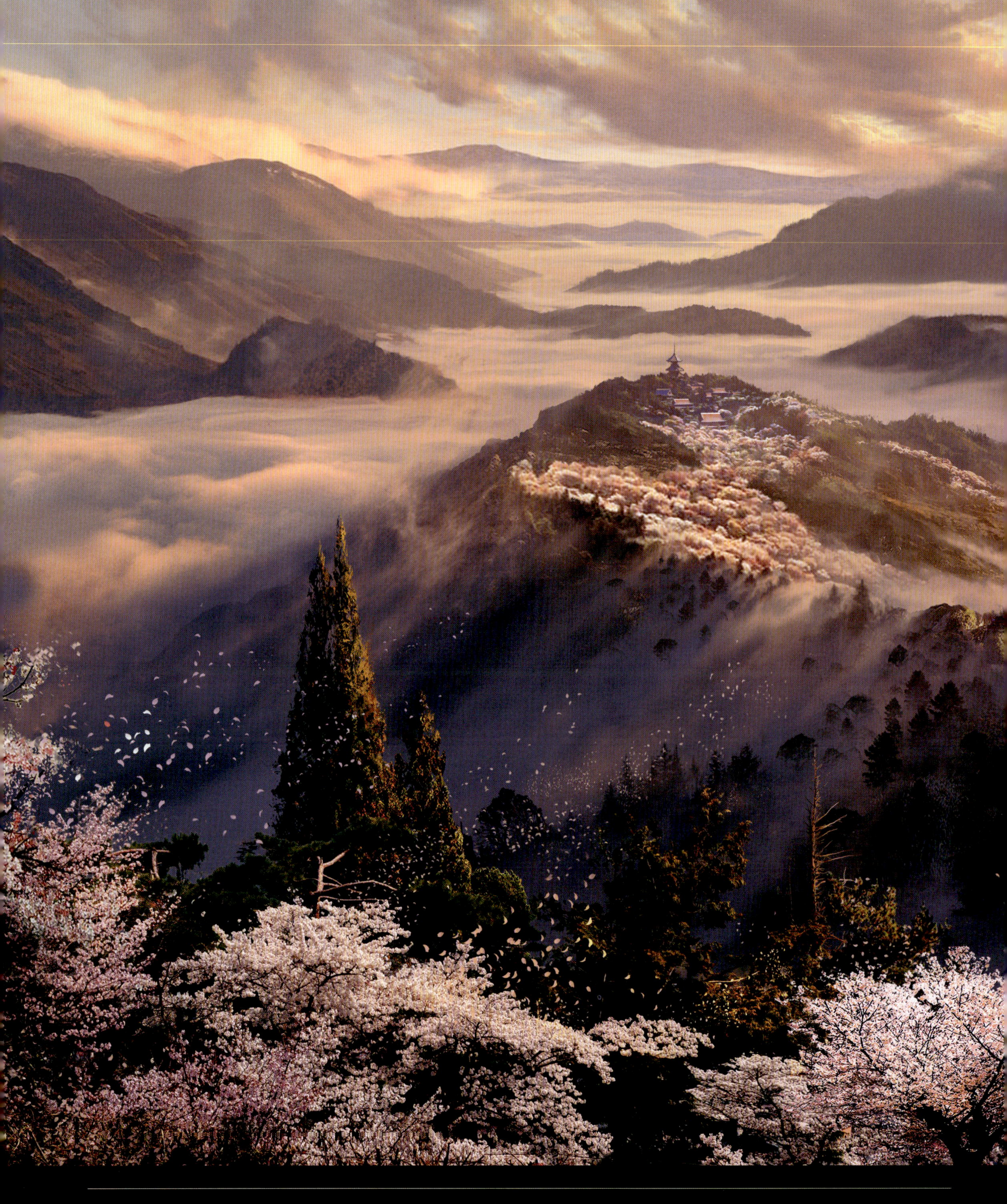

The art team sought to capture Yamato's mysterious beauty in this rendering of mist-shrouded mountaintops streaked with pink stands of blossoming cherry trees. "We also wanted to showcase our dynamic weather system with all those low clouds seeping over the ridges into the valleys," says Tan. Pathway markers called torii

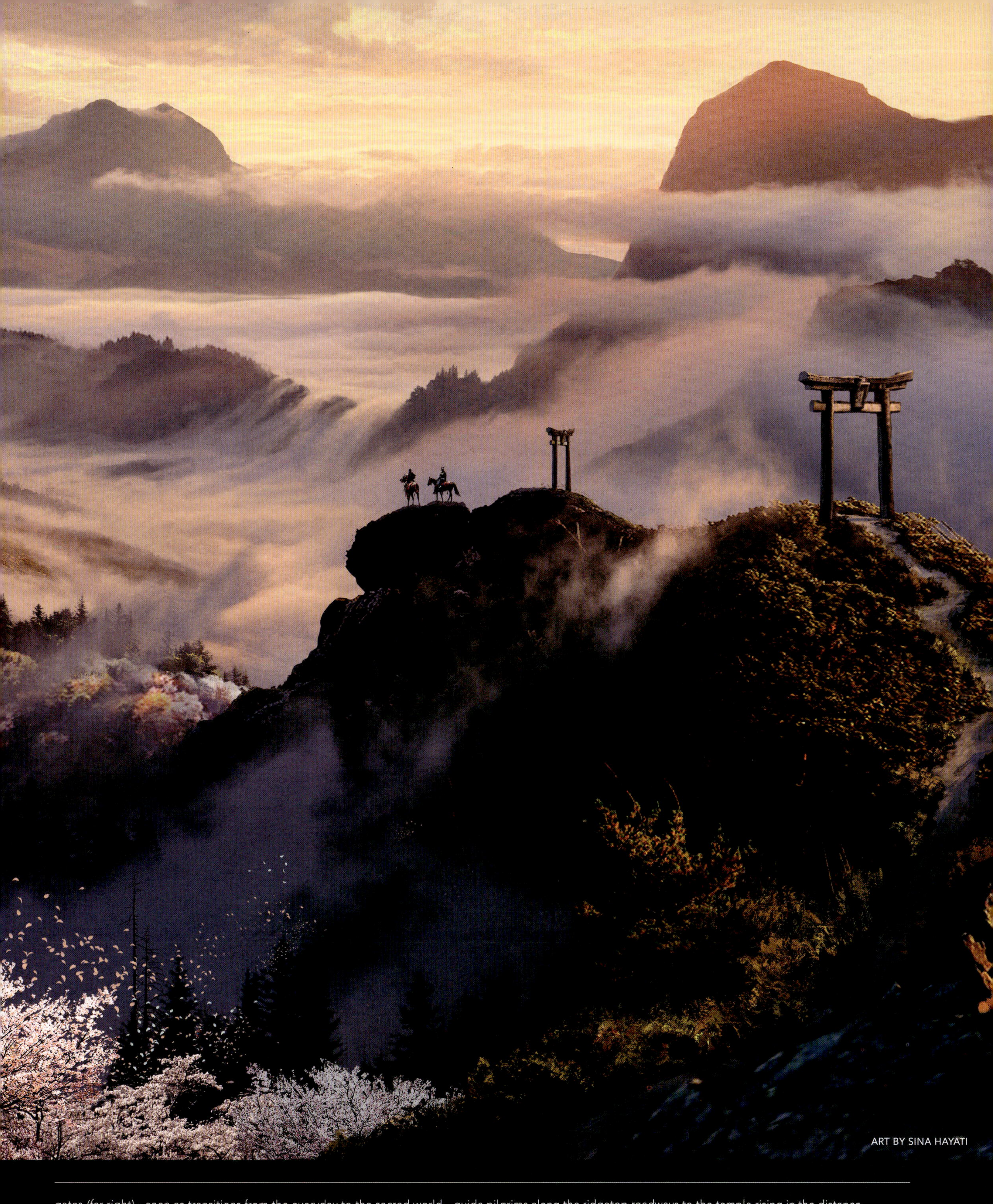

gates (*far right*)—seen as transitions from the everyday to the sacred world—guide pilgrims along the ridgetop roadways to the temple rising in the distance.

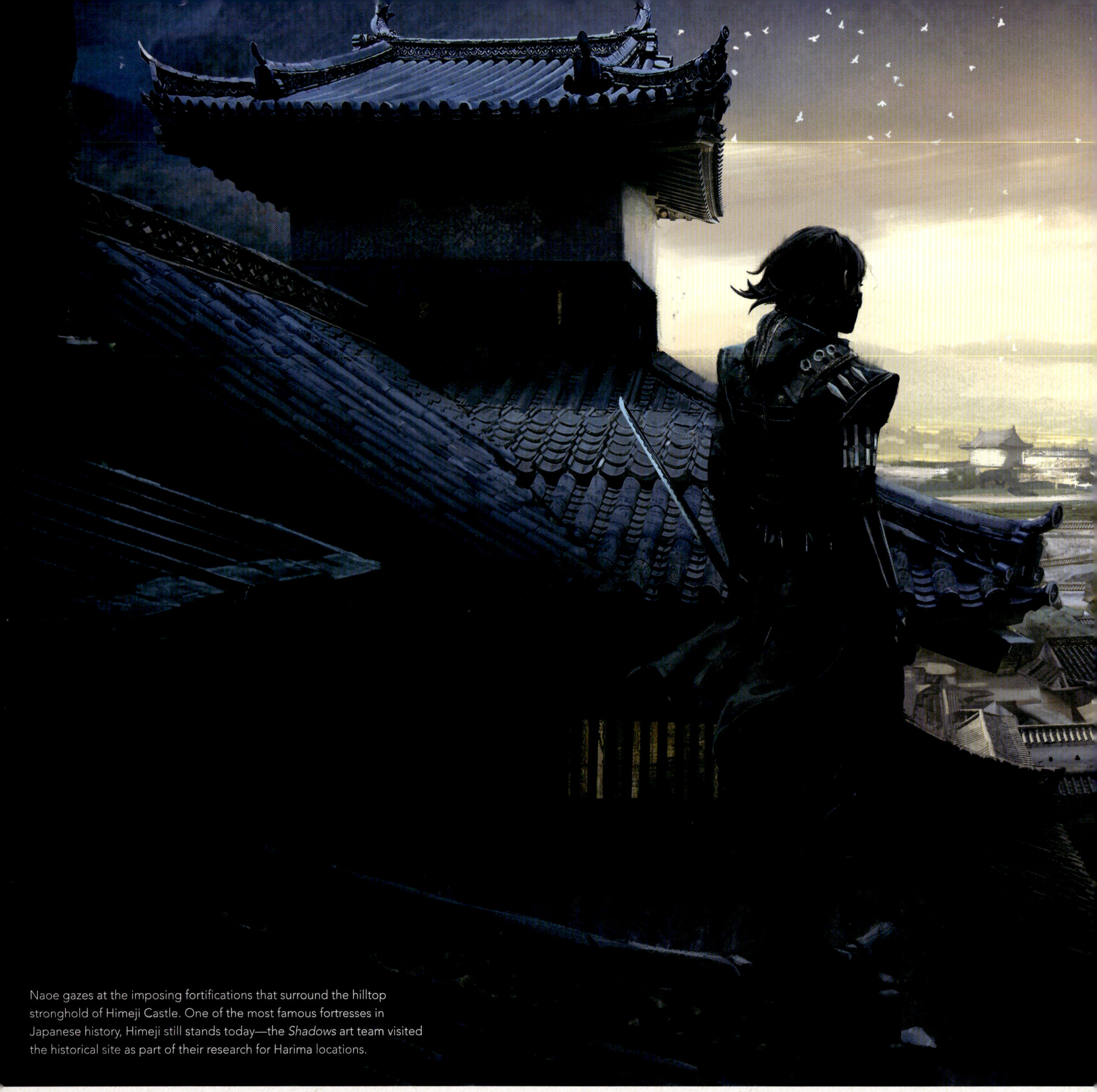

Naoe gazes at the imposing fortifications that surround the hilltop stronghold of Himeji Castle. One of the most famous fortresses in Japanese history, Himeji still stands today—the *Shadows* art team visited the historical site as part of their research for Harima locations.

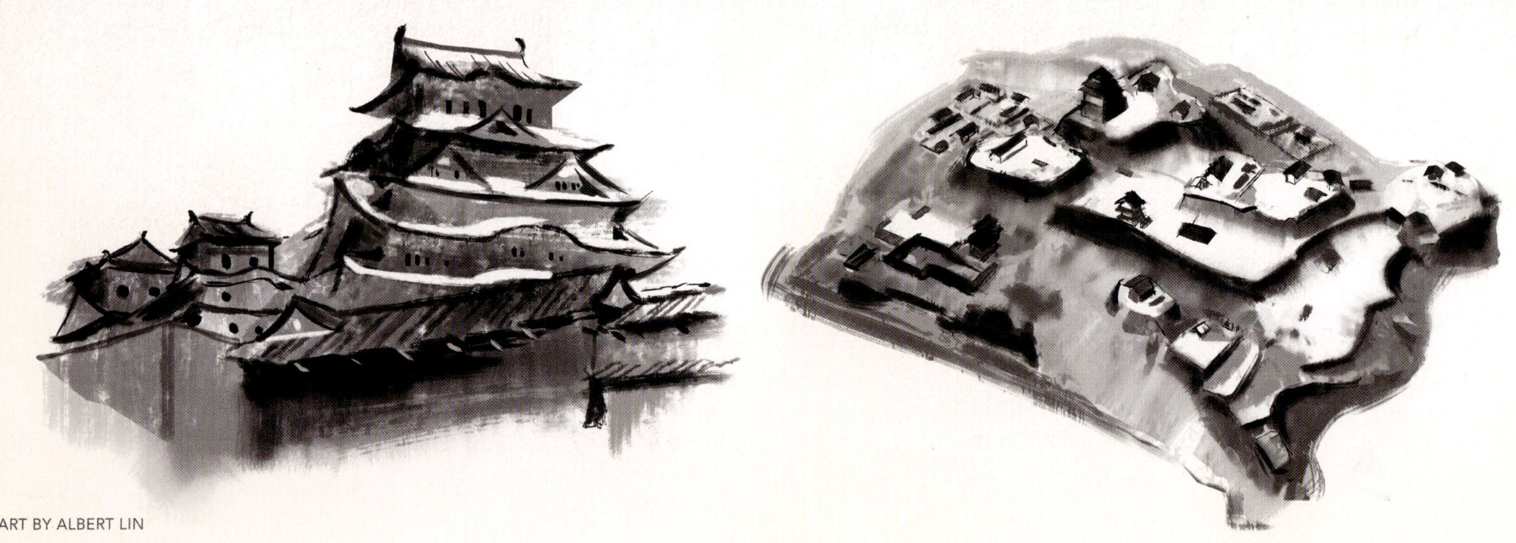

ART BY ALBERT LIN

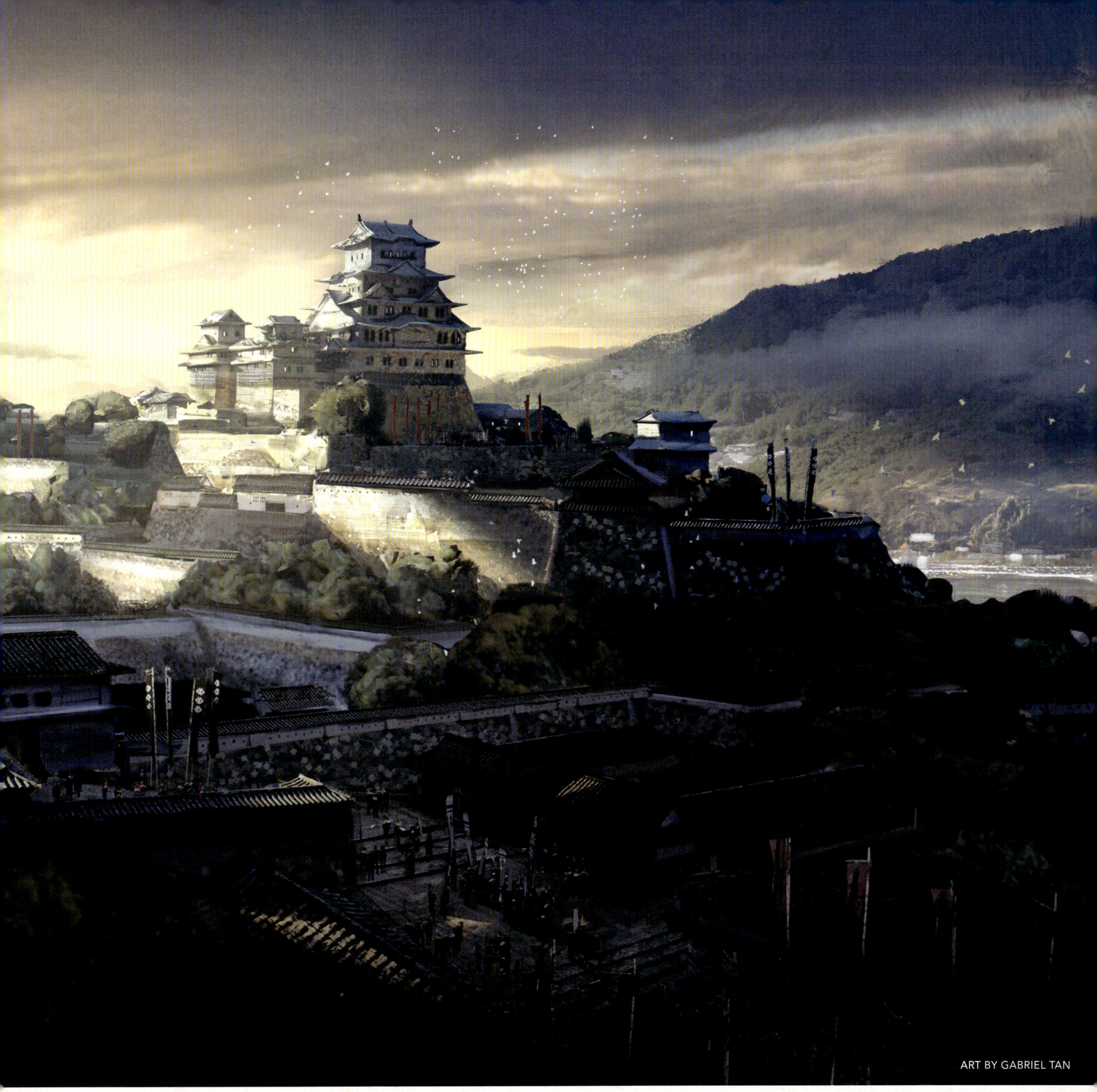

ART BY GABRIEL TAN

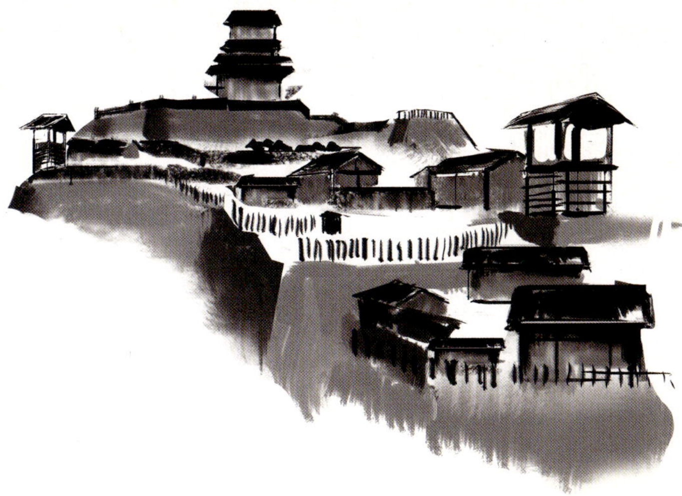

HARIMA

THE AFTERMATH OF WAR

At the end of the Sengoku period, Harima Province has been ravaged by military conflagration, including some of the deadliest wartime sieges in Japan's history. In *Assassin's Creed Shadows*, the Harima landscape is littered with the war's aftermath. Its former provincial rulers, the allied Bessho and Mori clans, have fallen to Oda Nobunaga's armies led by his two strongest generals: Toyotomi Hideyoshi, who laid siege to Himeji and Miki Castles, and Akechi Mitsuhide, who indiscriminately burned temples in the north.

ART BY JING ZHONG TANG

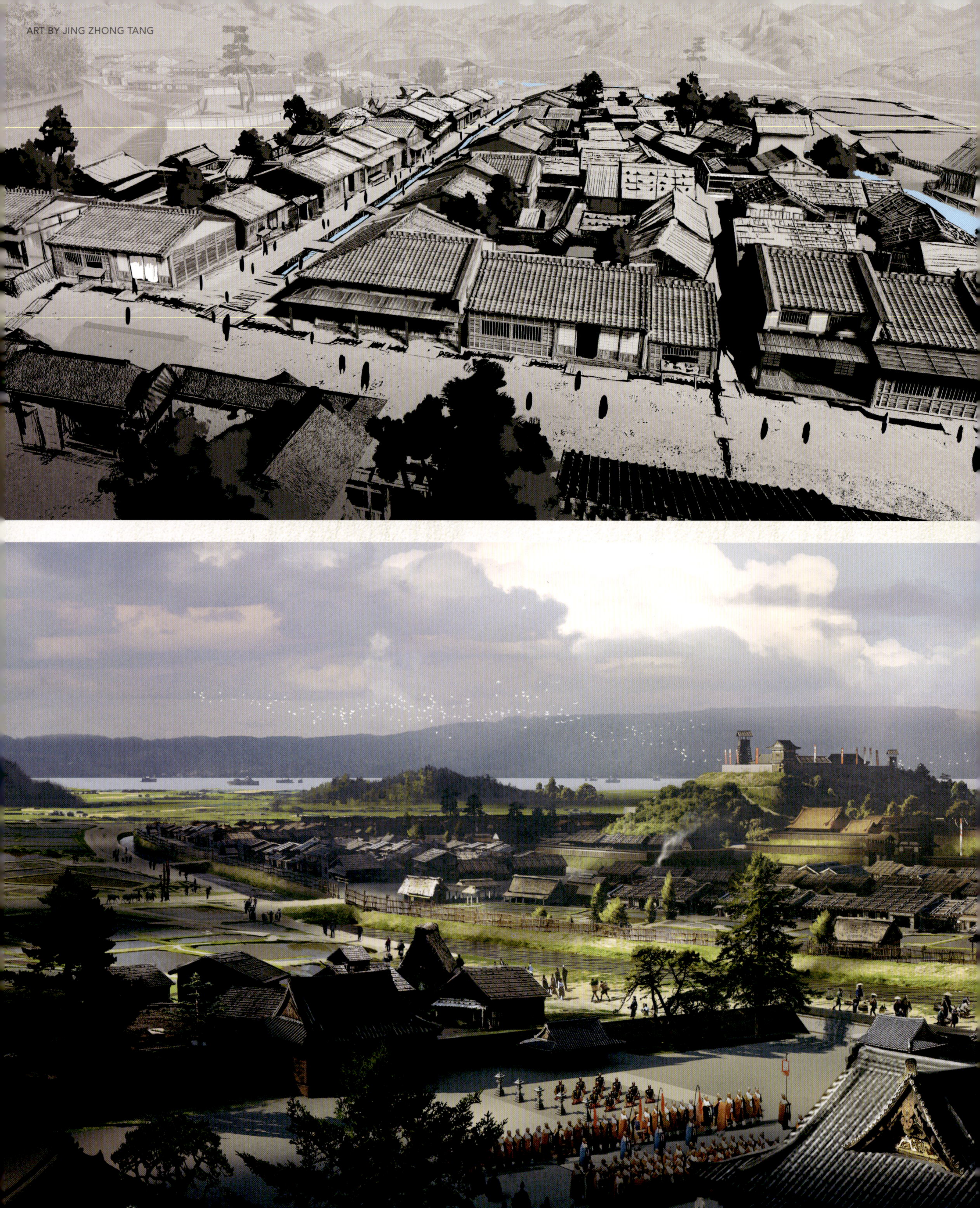

ART BY JING ZHONG TANG

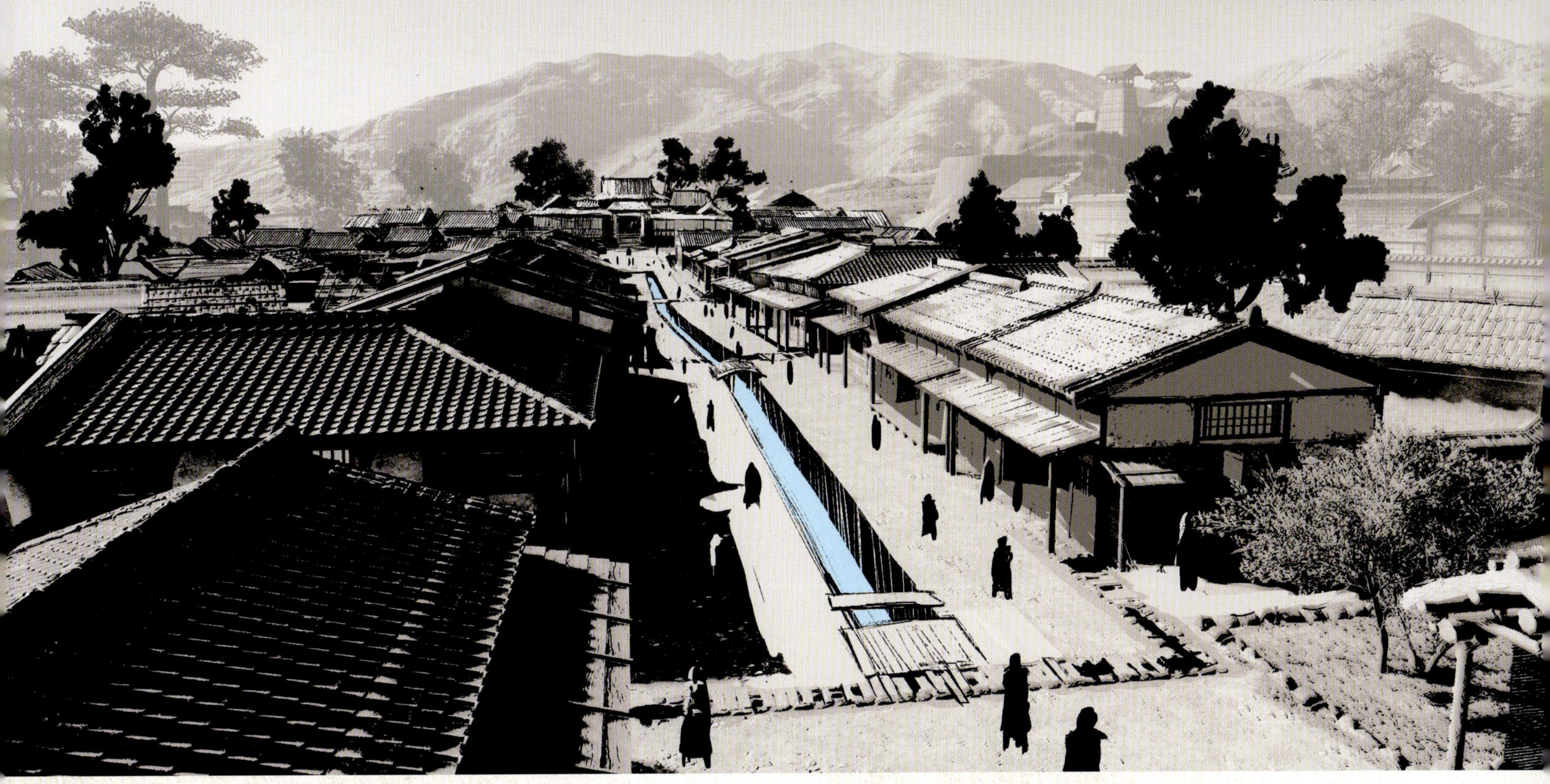

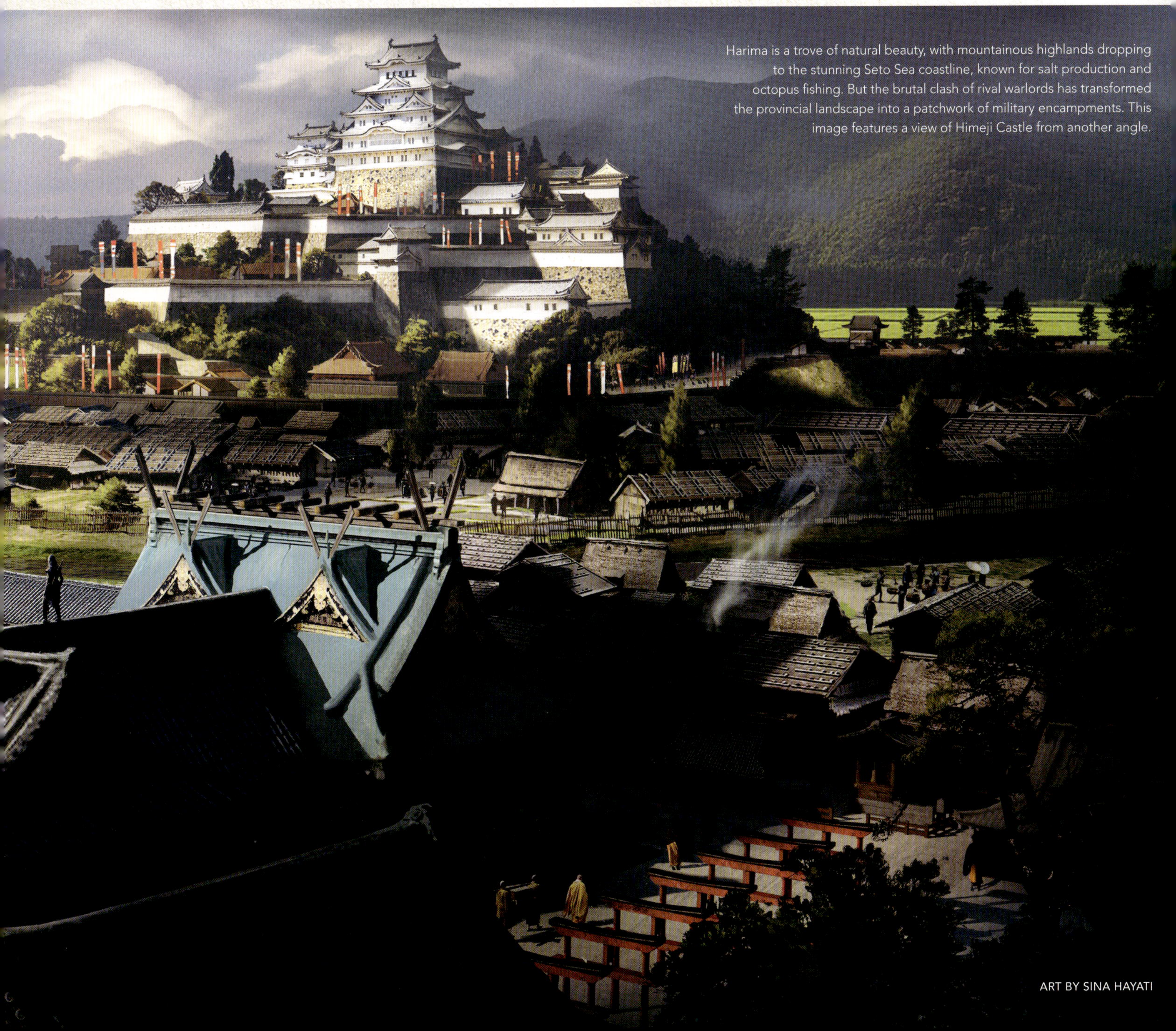

Harima is a trove of natural beauty, with mountainous highlands dropping to the stunning Seto Sea coastline, known for salt production and octopus fishing. But the brutal clash of rival warlords has transformed the provincial landscape into a patchwork of military encampments. This image features a view of Himeji Castle from another angle.

ART BY SINA HAYATI

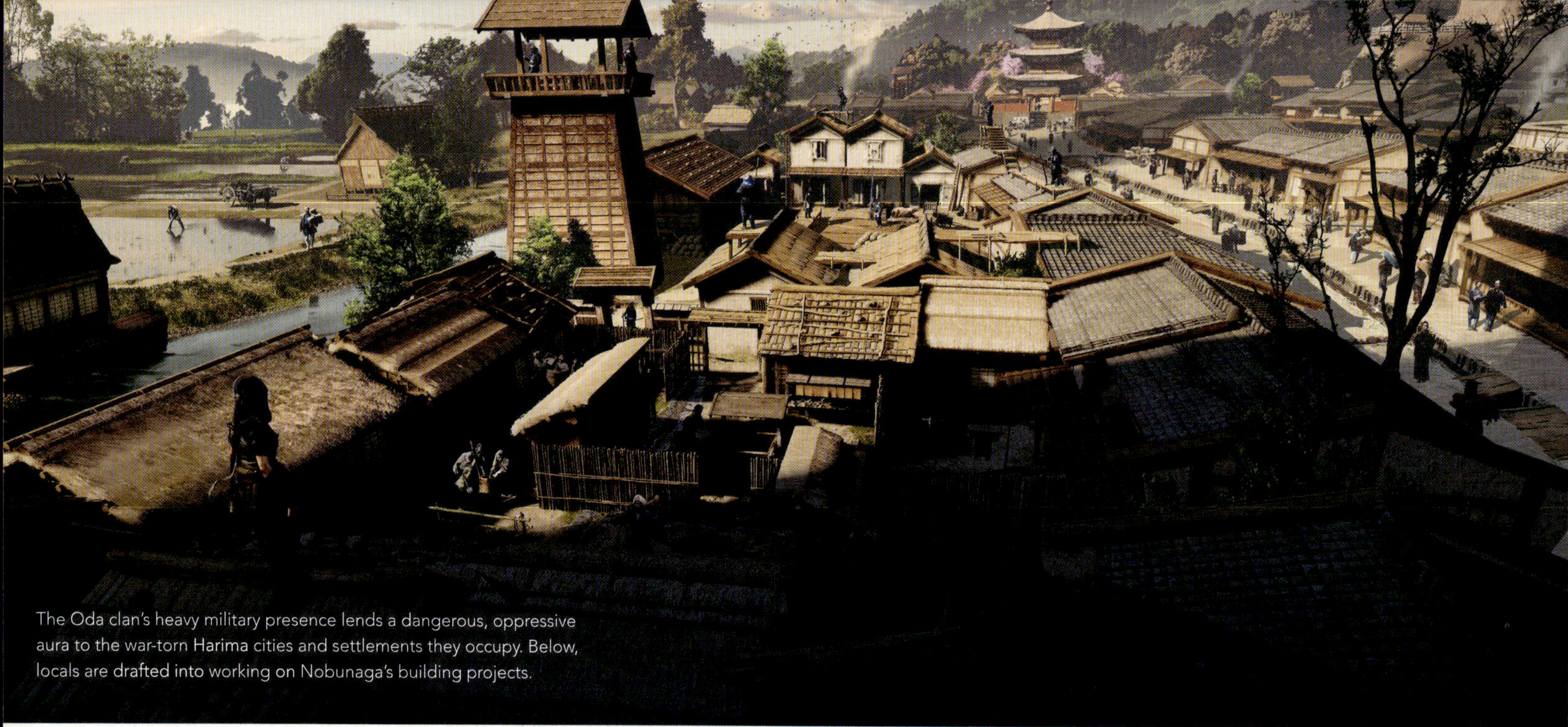

The Oda clan's heavy military presence lends a dangerous, oppressive aura to the war-torn Harima cities and settlements they occupy. Below, locals are drafted into working on Nobunaga's building projects.

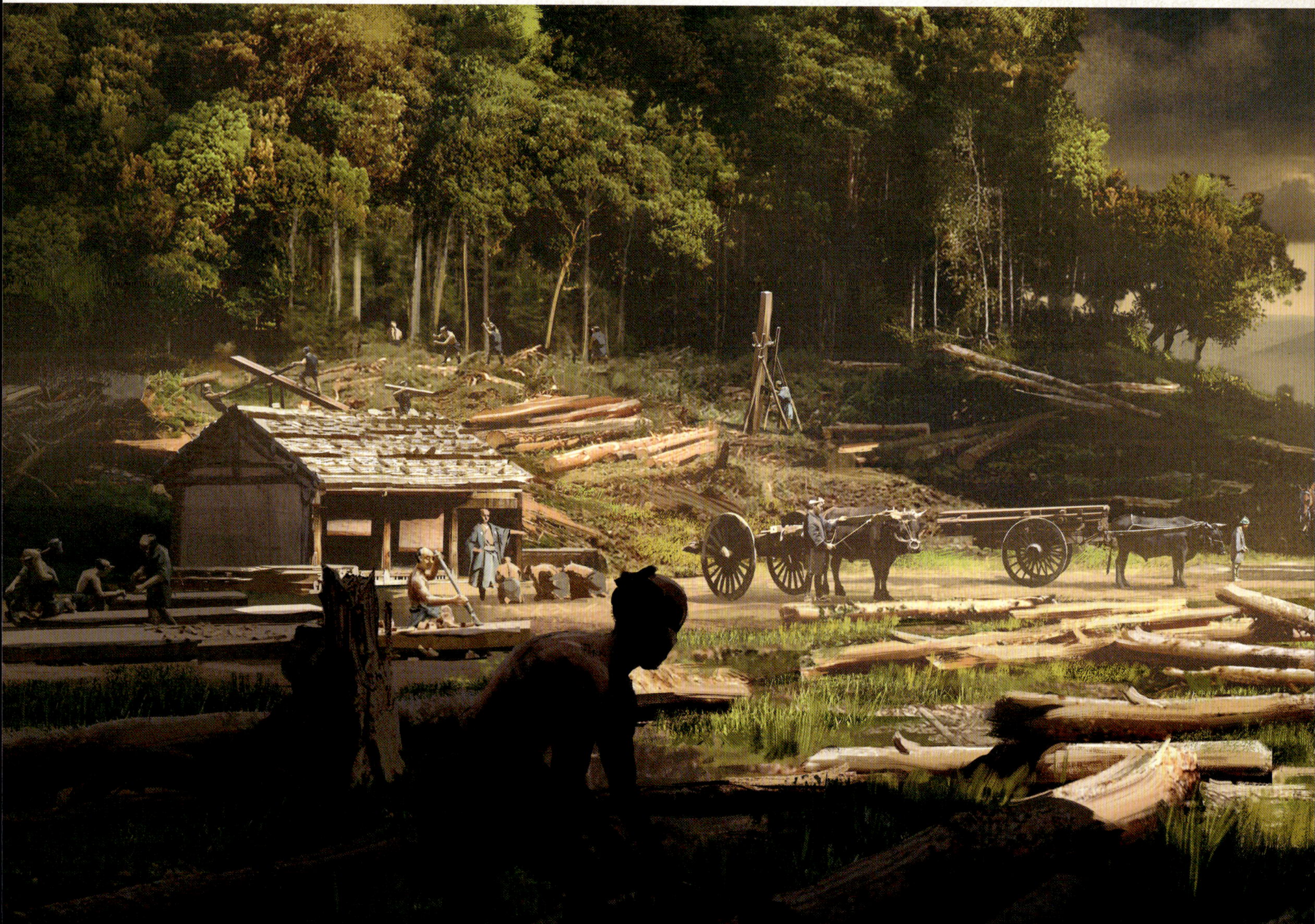

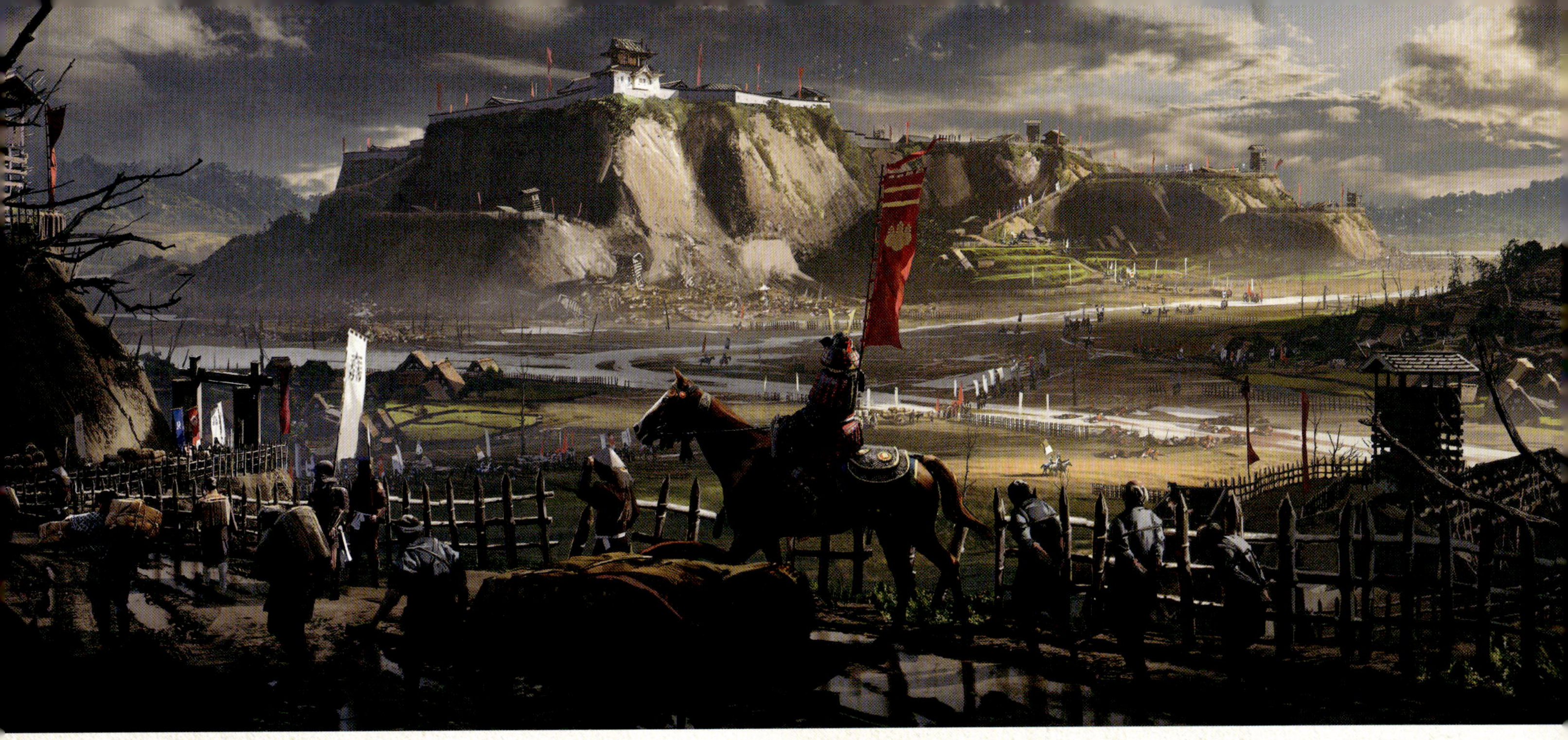

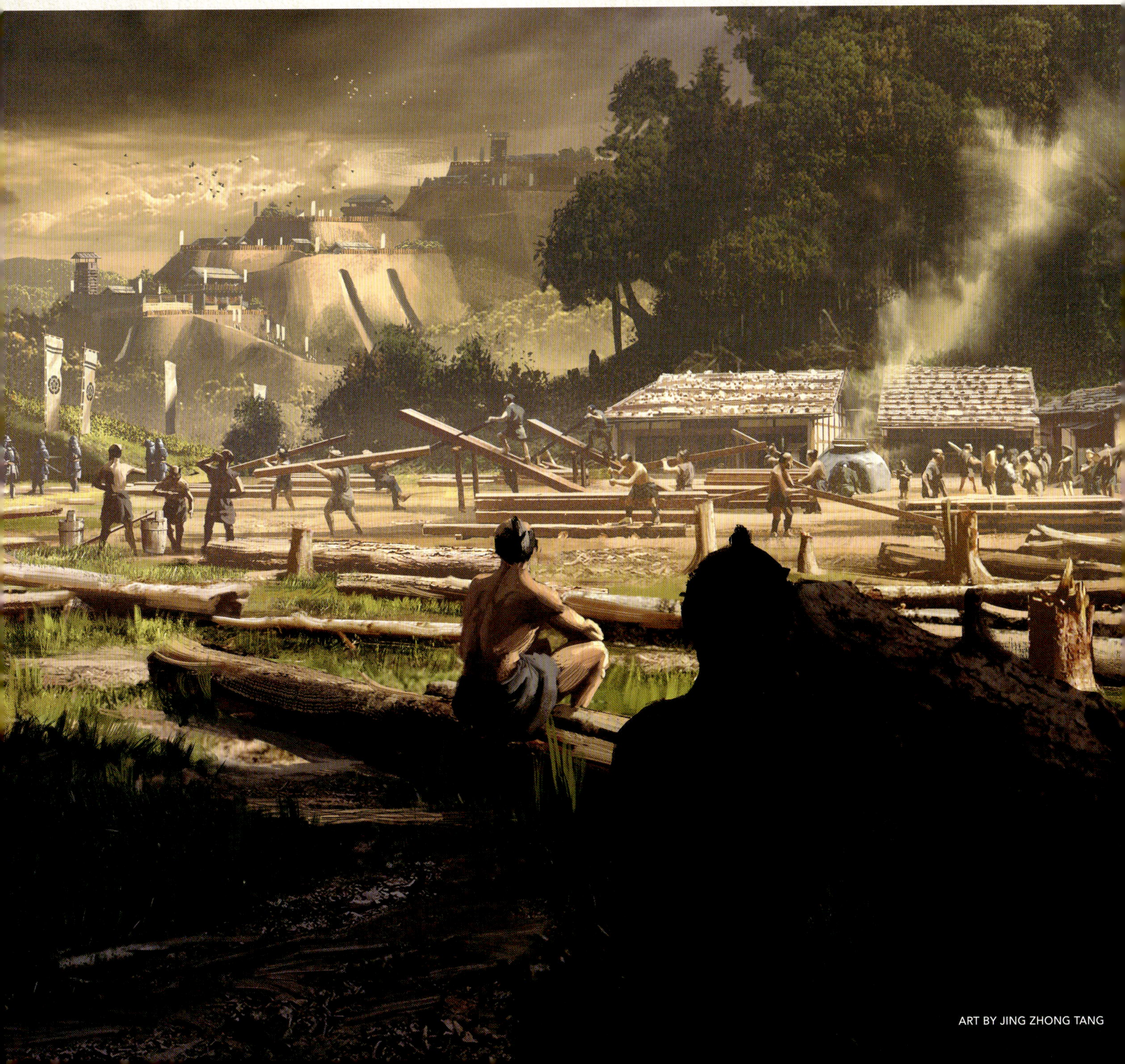

ART BY JING ZHONG TANG

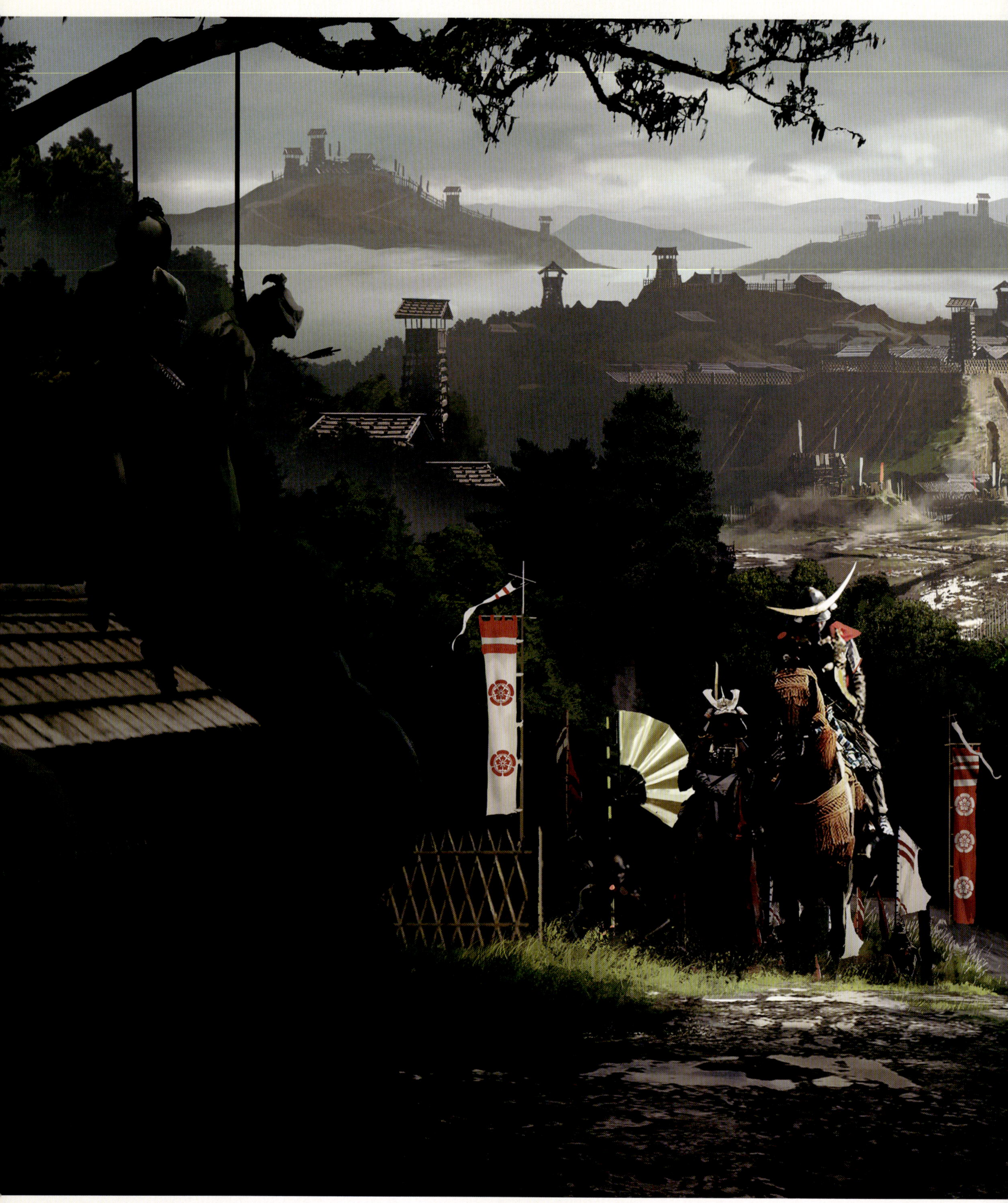

Stout military forts bristle on the hilltops of Harima Province, all connected by a web of well-guarded roads. Here, a network of camp towers surrounds the besieged Miki Castle, seen in the center of the image. Toyotomi Hideyoshi's army built more than forty of these forts to slowly choke off approach routes to the castle and starve out its

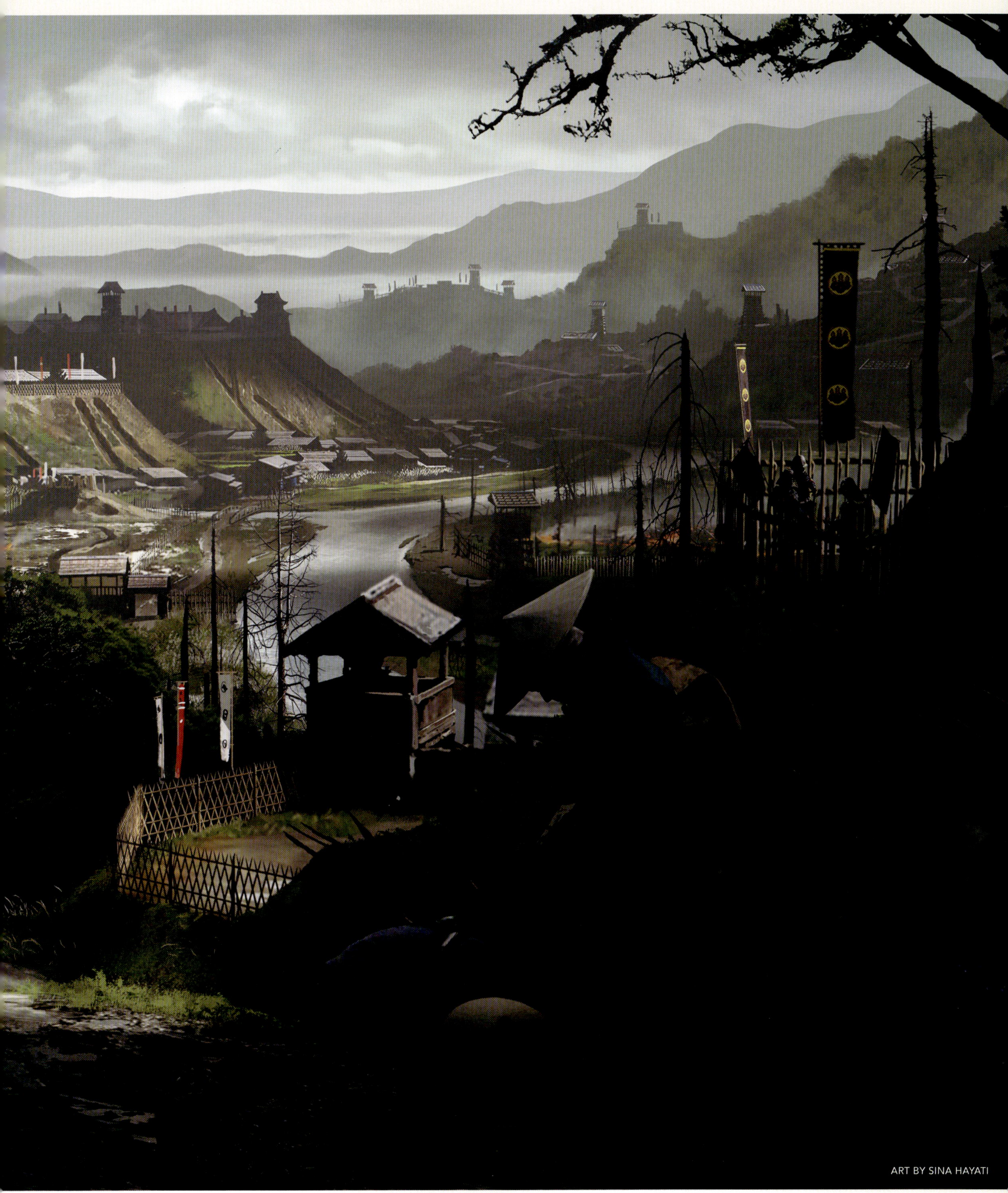
ART BY SINA HAYATI

garrison. "The siege was terrible. It lasted two years," says Tan. "We wanted to dramatize the brutality of the warlord's tightening grip." Captured resistance fighters and siege runners are seen imprisoned or worse at the outer edges of the image.

Oda Nobunaga's forces show no mercy in Harima, whether toward captured enemy soldiers or conscripted civilian survivors of the devastation. "Our concept art provides reference images to guide project teams in designing the physical details of settings—landscape treatments, construction materials, and so forth," says Dansereau. "But equally important is to create ambiance and visual context for the story."

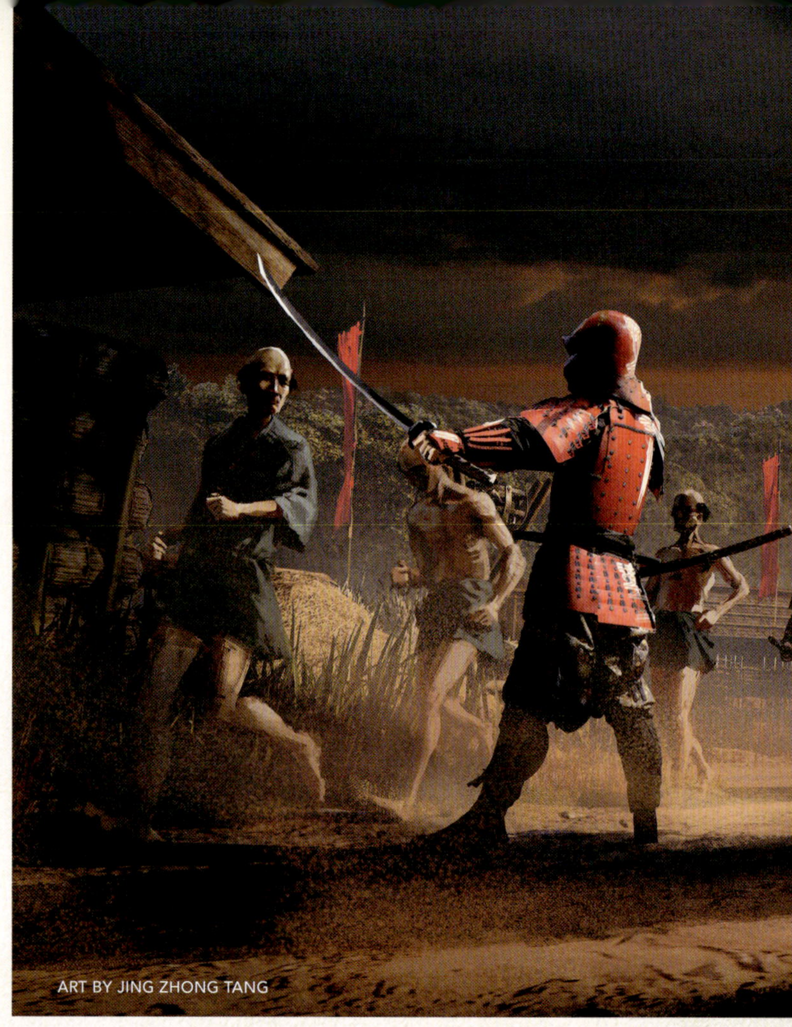

ART BY JING ZHONG TANG

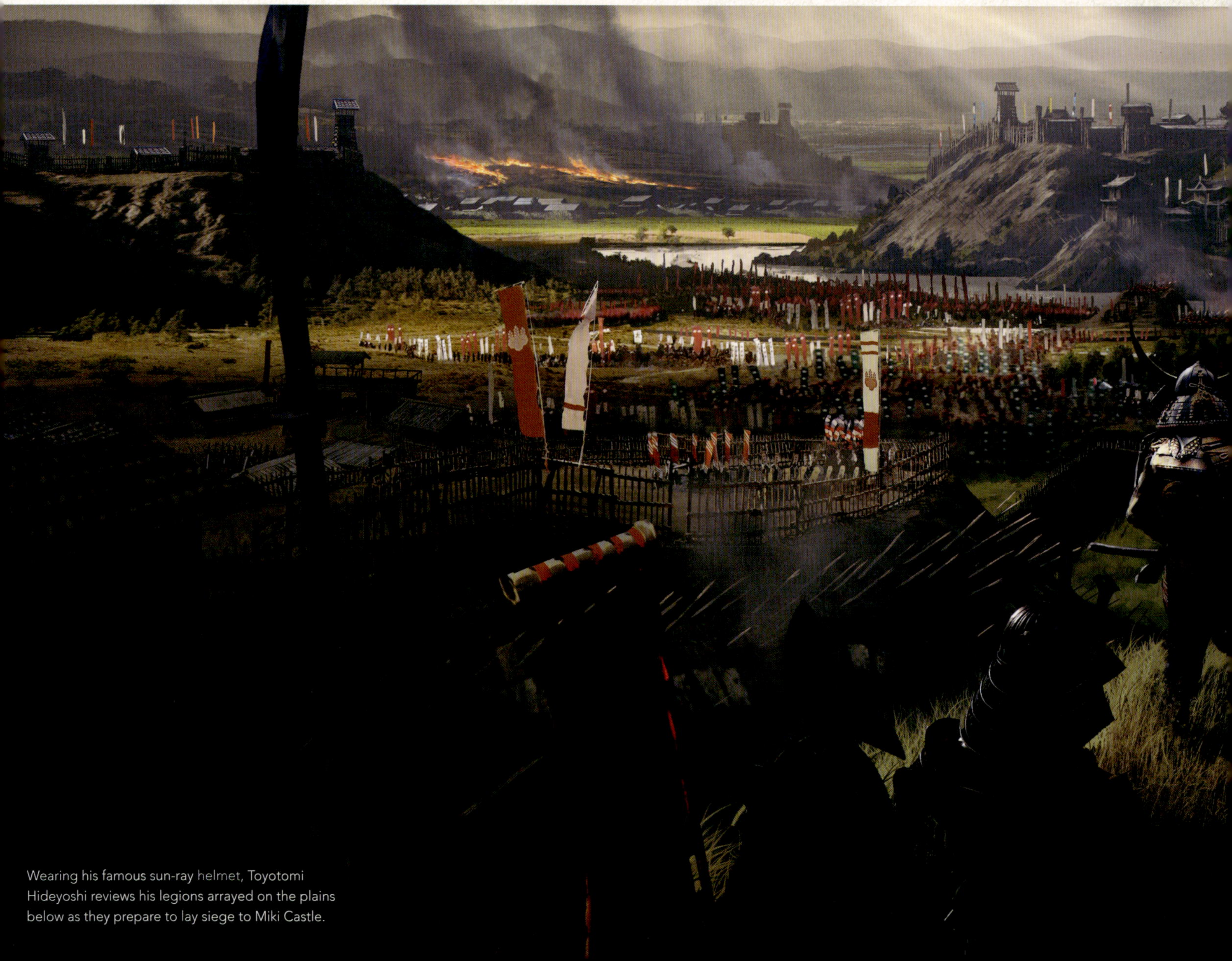

Wearing his famous sun-ray helmet, Toyotomi Hideyoshi reviews his legions arrayed on the plains below as they prepare to lay siege to Miki Castle.

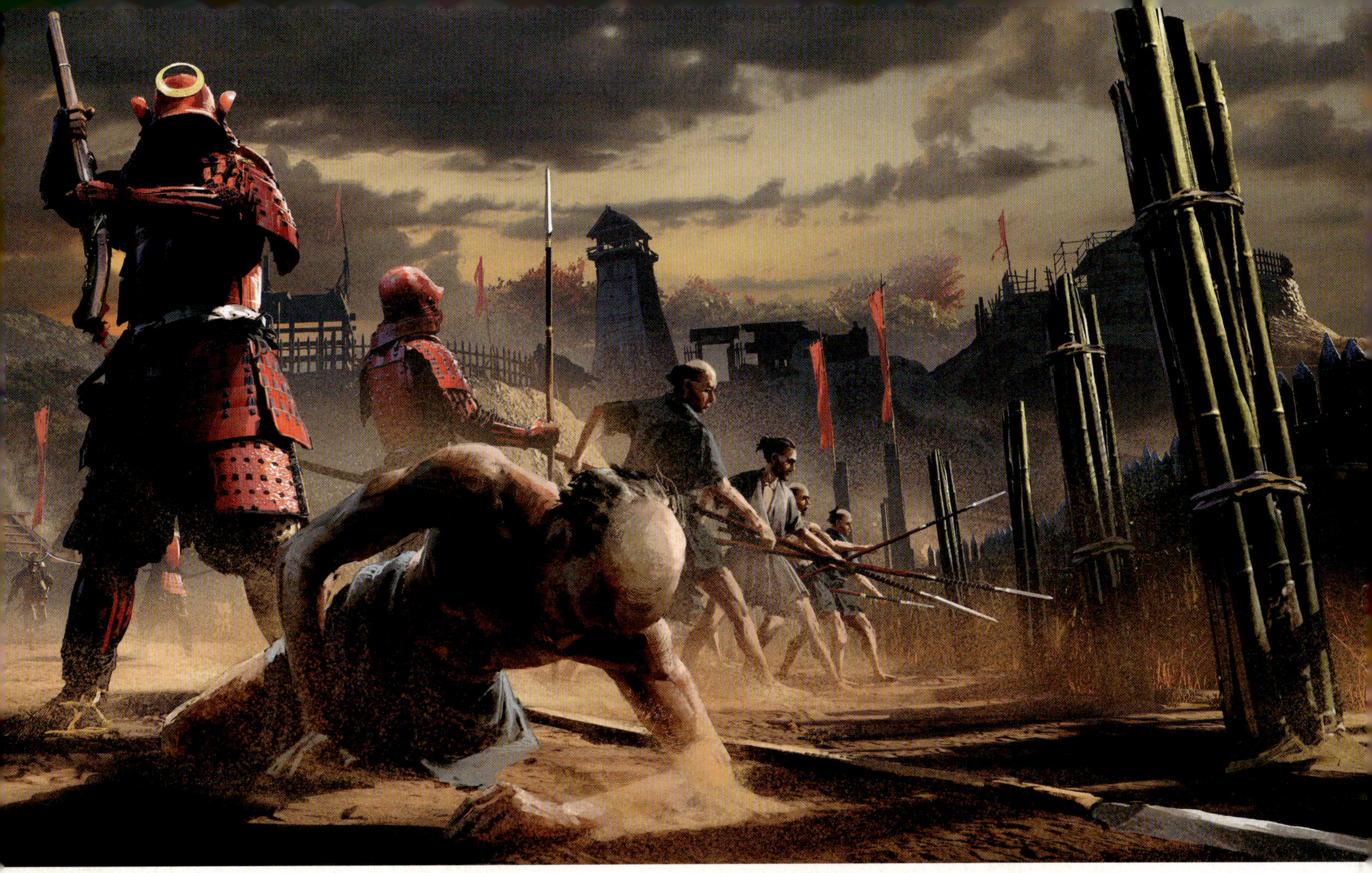

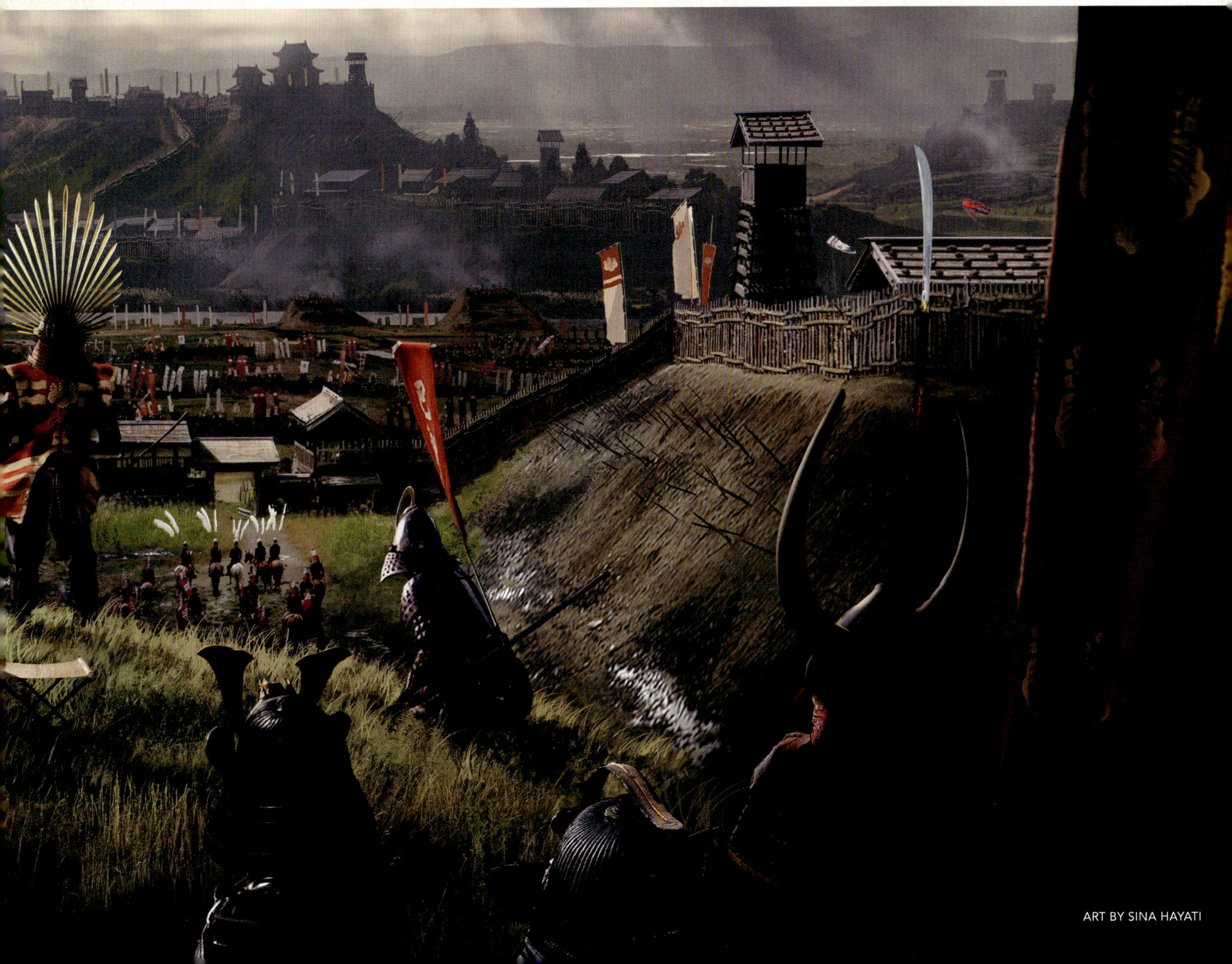

ART BY SINA HAYATI

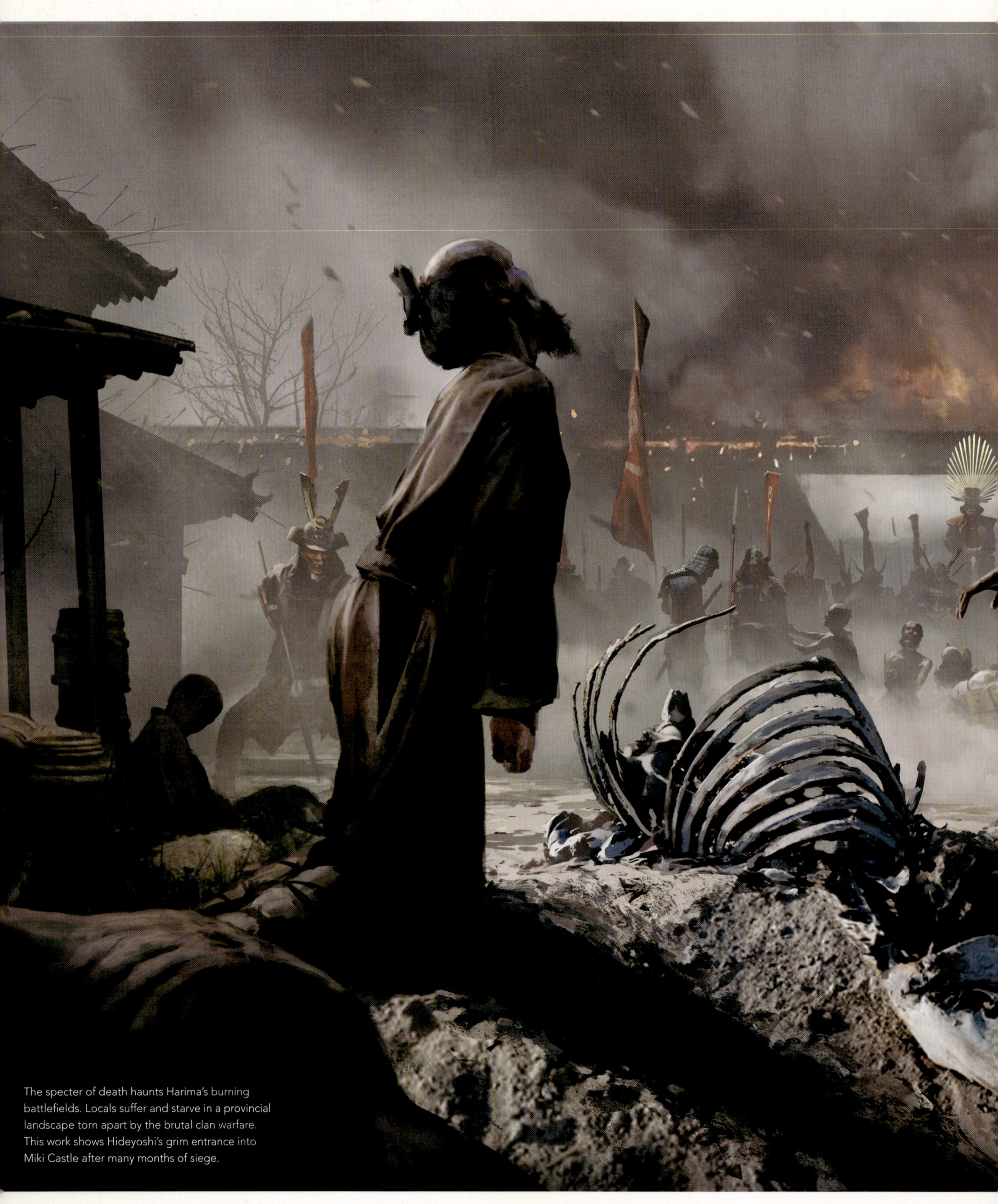

The specter of death haunts Harima's burning battlefields. Locals suffer and starve in a provincial landscape torn apart by the brutal clan warfare. This work shows Hideyoshi's grim entrance into Miki Castle after many months of siege.

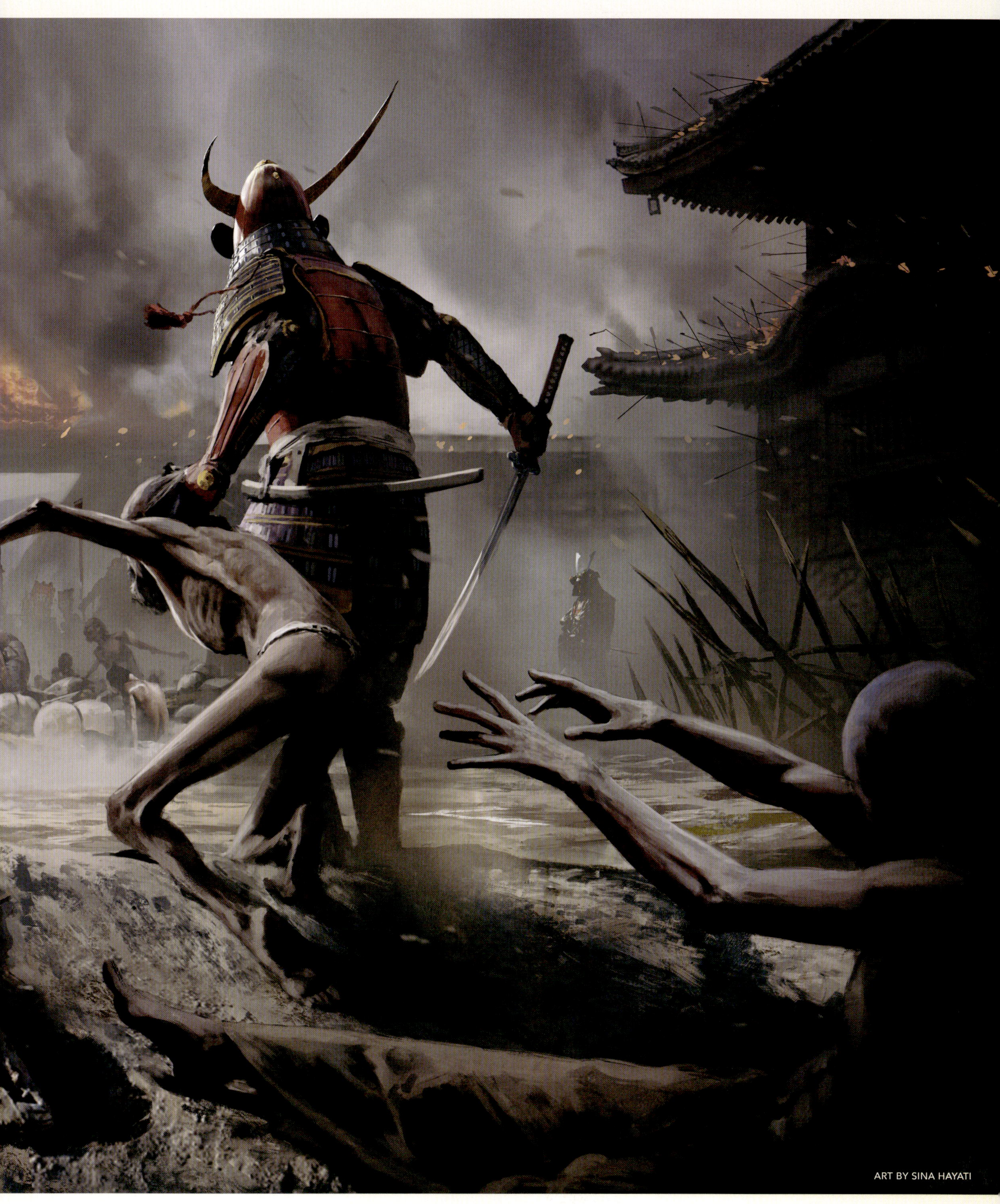
ART BY SINA HAYATI

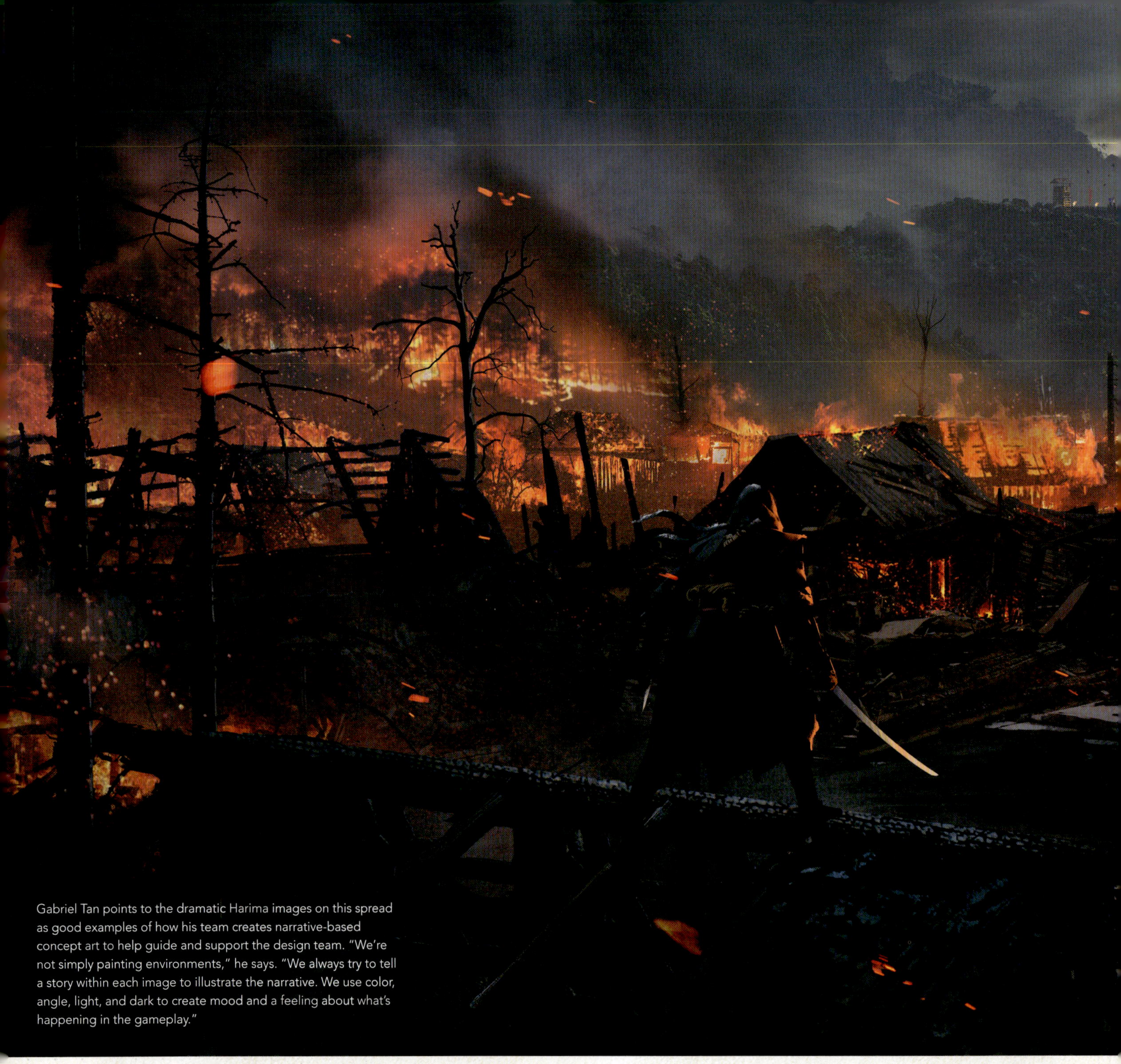

Gabriel Tan points to the dramatic Harima images on this spread as good examples of how his team creates narrative-based concept art to help guide and support the design team. "We're not simply painting environments," he says. "We always try to tell a story within each image to illustrate the narrative. We use color, angle, light, and dark to create mood and a feeling about what's happening in the gameplay."

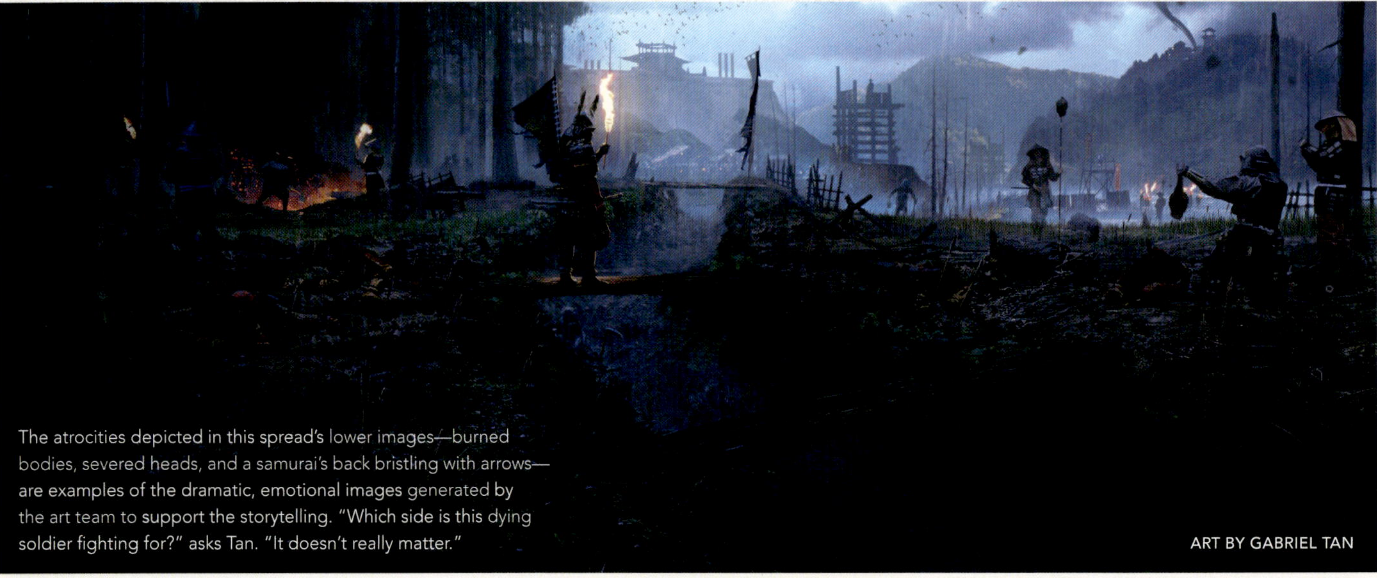

The atrocities depicted in this spread's lower images—burned bodies, severed heads, and a samurai's back bristling with arrows—are examples of the dramatic, emotional images generated by the art team to support the storytelling. "Which side is this dying soldier fighting for?" asks Tan. "It doesn't really matter."

ART BY GABRIEL TAN

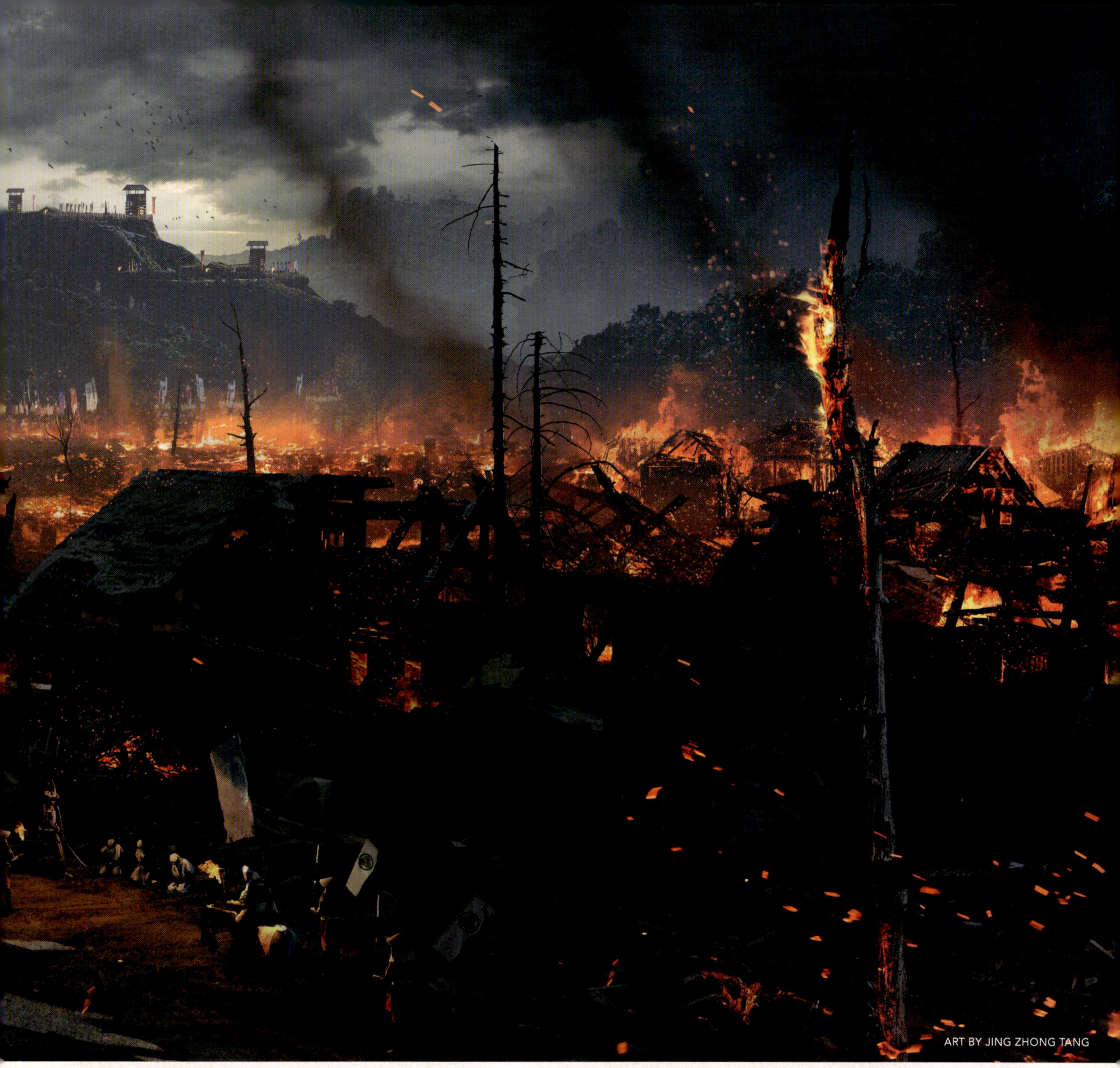

ART BY JING ZHONG TANG

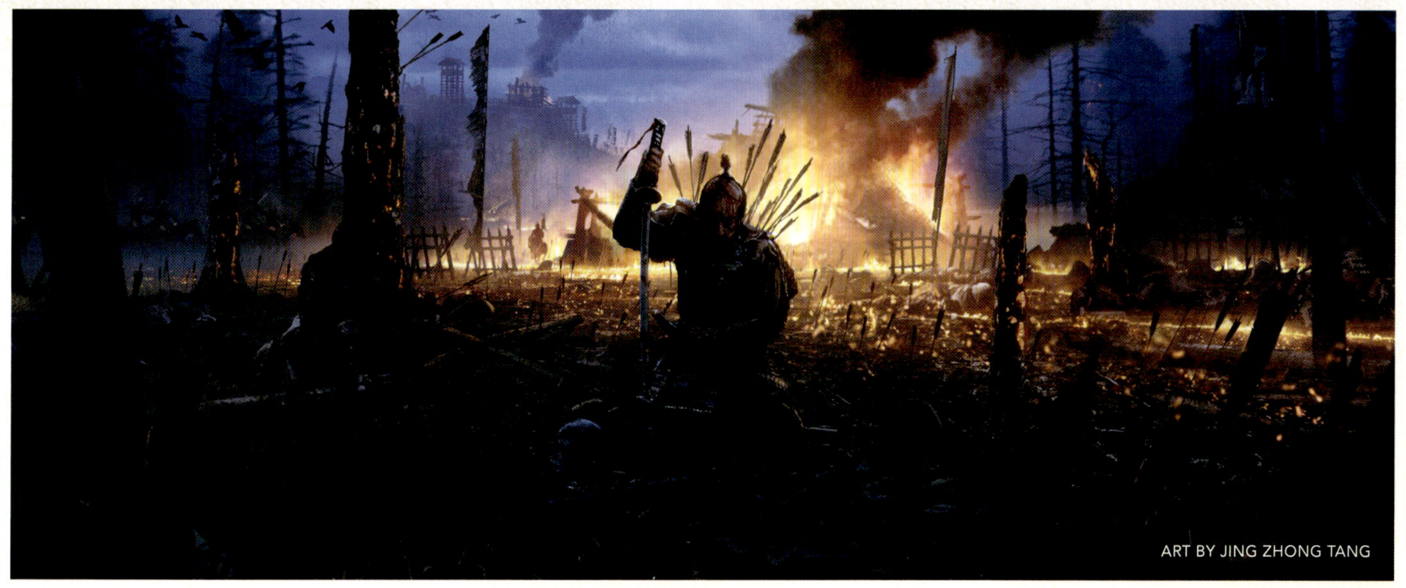

ART BY JING ZHONG TANG

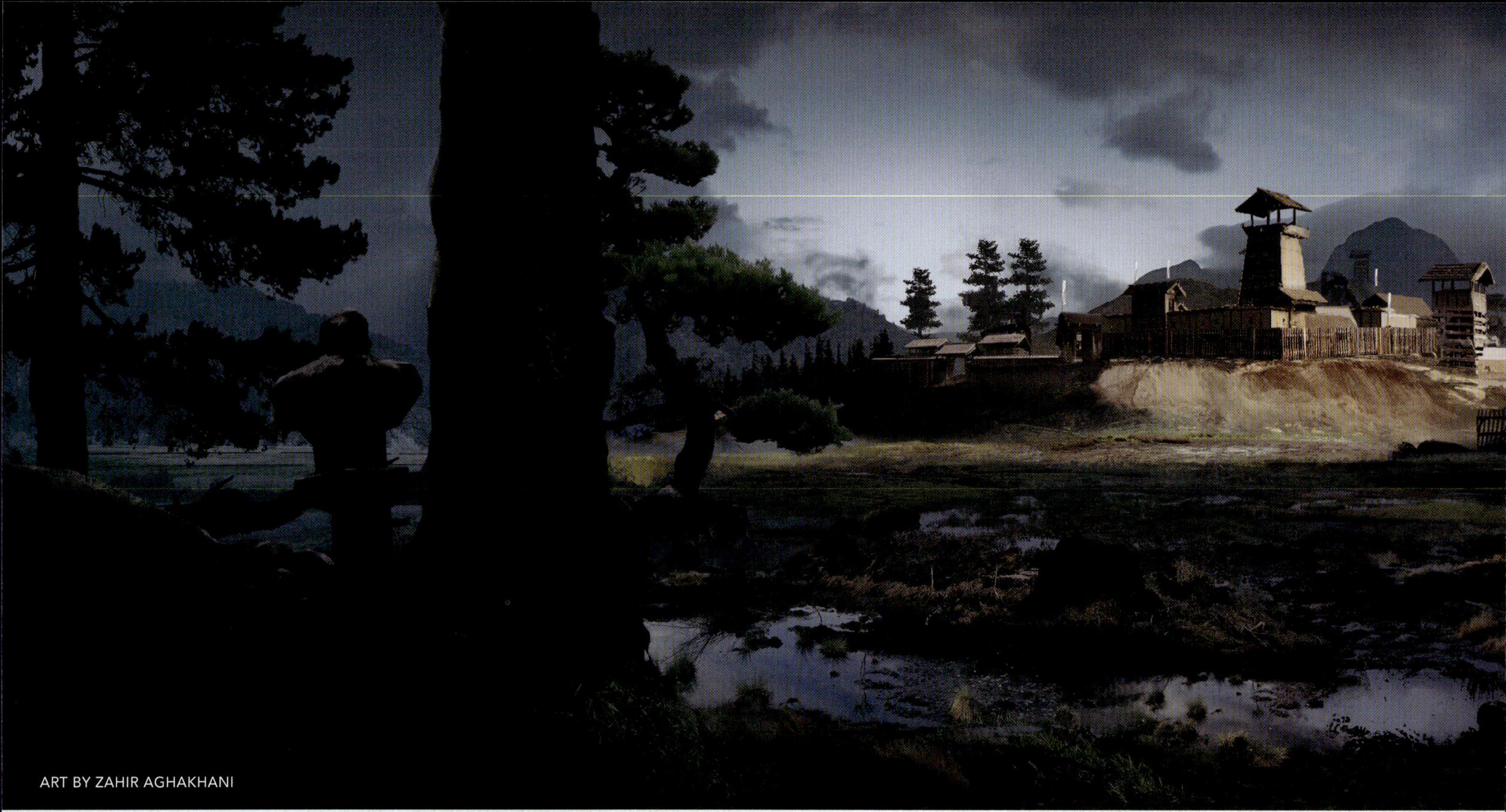

ART BY ZAHIR AGHAKHANI

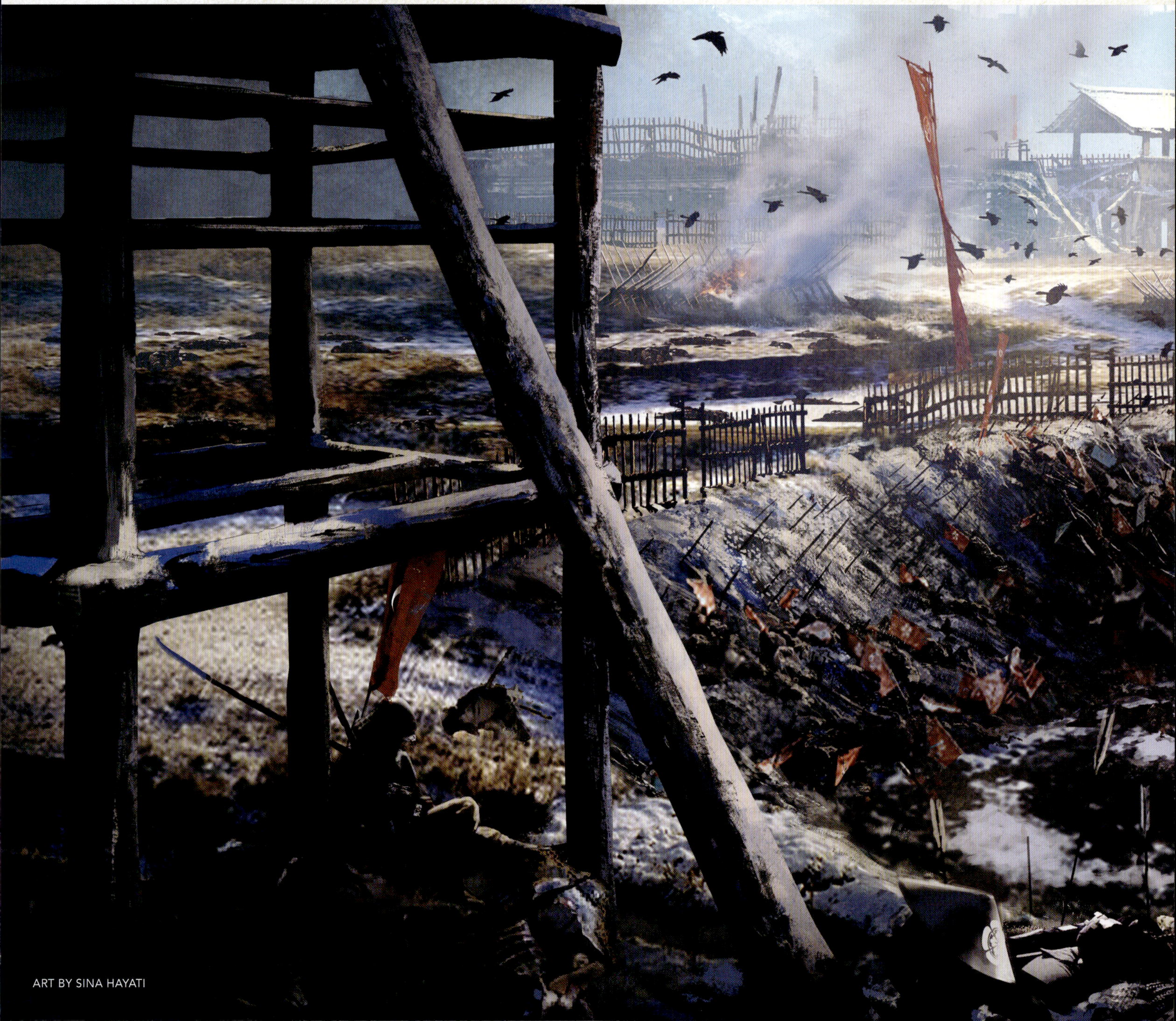

ART BY SINA HAYATI

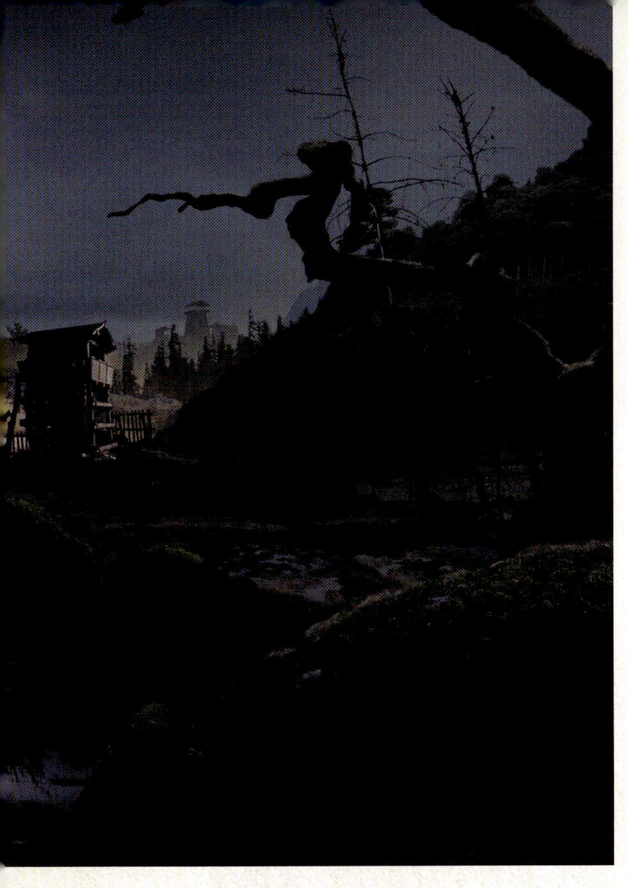

In the haunting image below, a lone horseman rides through a pit of death as a flock of crows descends upon the fallen in Harima. "Harima is the region where we really wanted to showcase the senseless devastation of war in this context," says Tan.

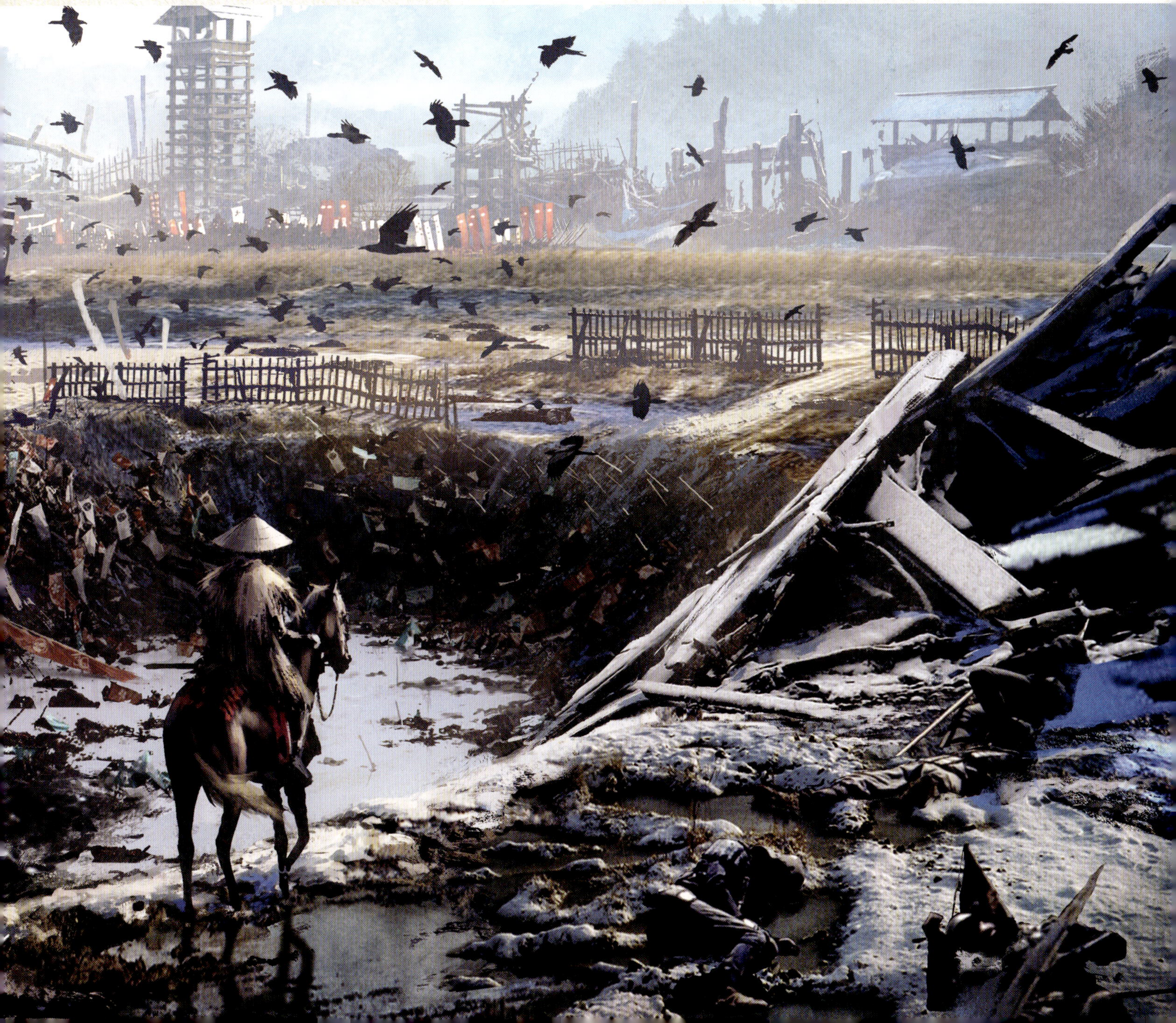

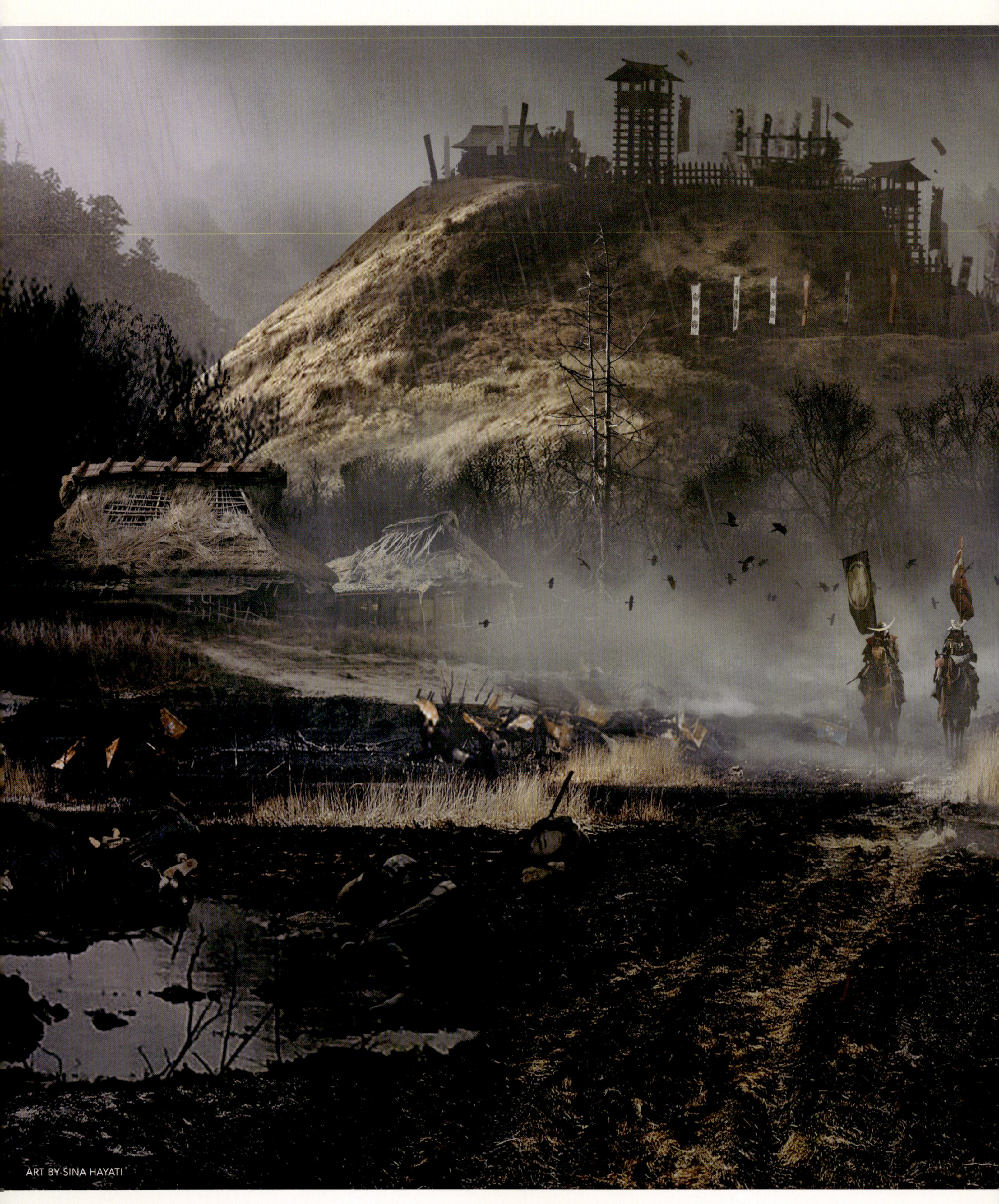
ART BY SINA HAYATI

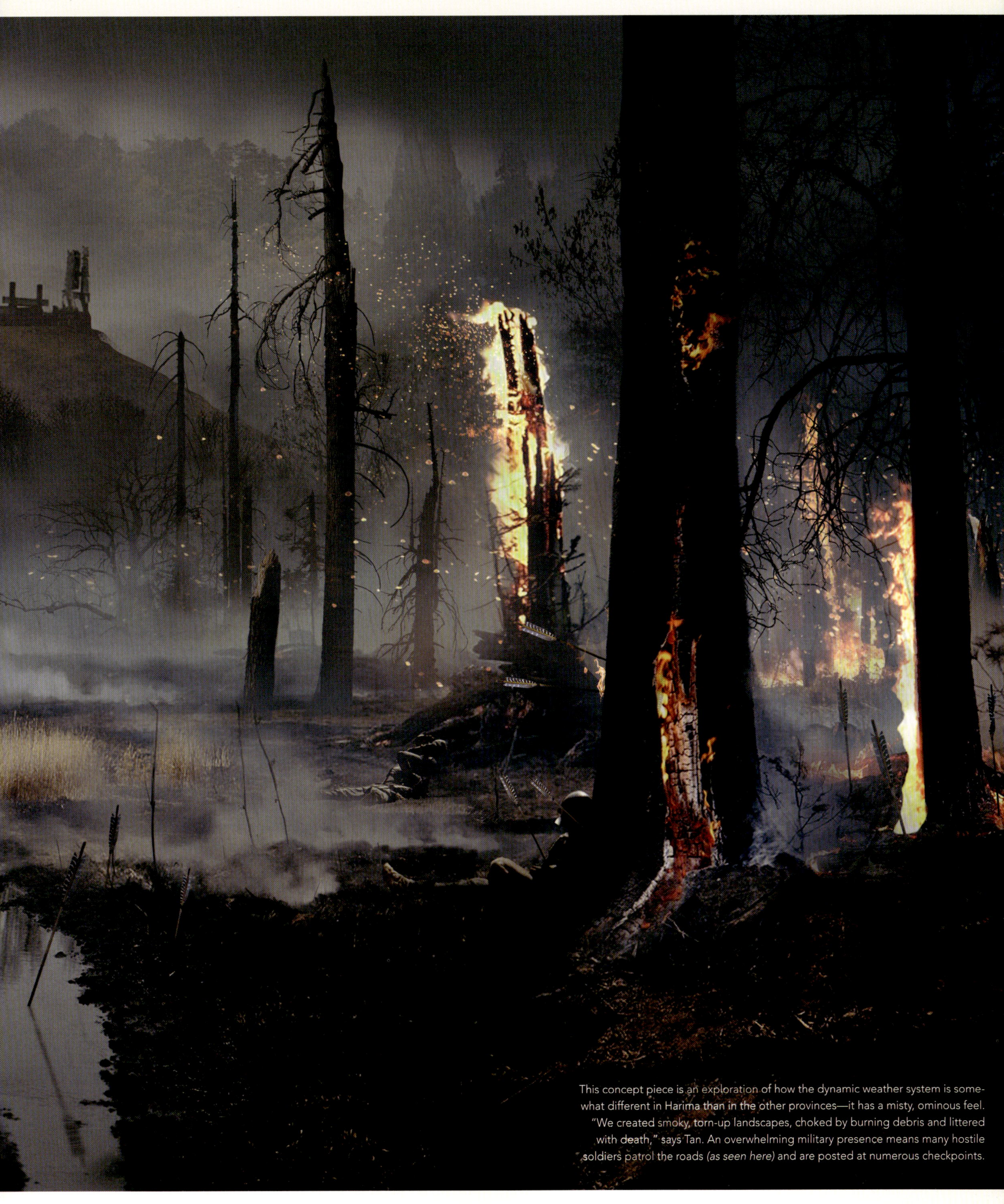

This concept piece is an exploration of how the dynamic weather system is somewhat different in Harima than in the other provinces—it has a misty, ominous feel. "We created smoky, torn-up landscapes, choked by burning debris and littered with death," says Tan. An overwhelming military presence means many hostile soldiers patrol the roads *(as seen here)* and are posted at numerous checkpoints.

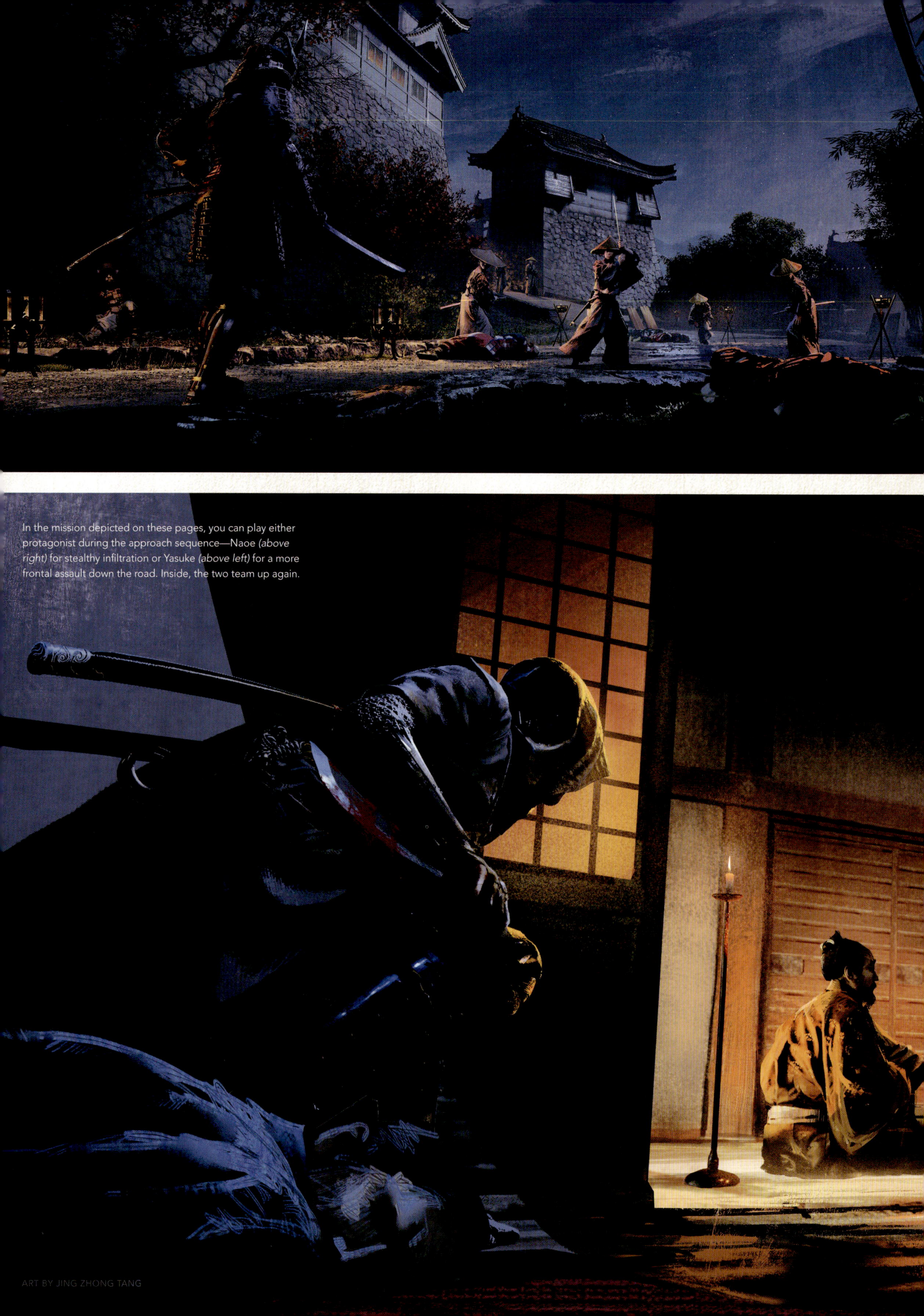

In the mission depicted on these pages, you can play either protagonist during the approach sequence—Naoe *(above right)* for stealthy infiltration or Yasuke *(above left)* for a more frontal assault down the road. Inside, the two team up again.

ART BY JING ZHONG TANG

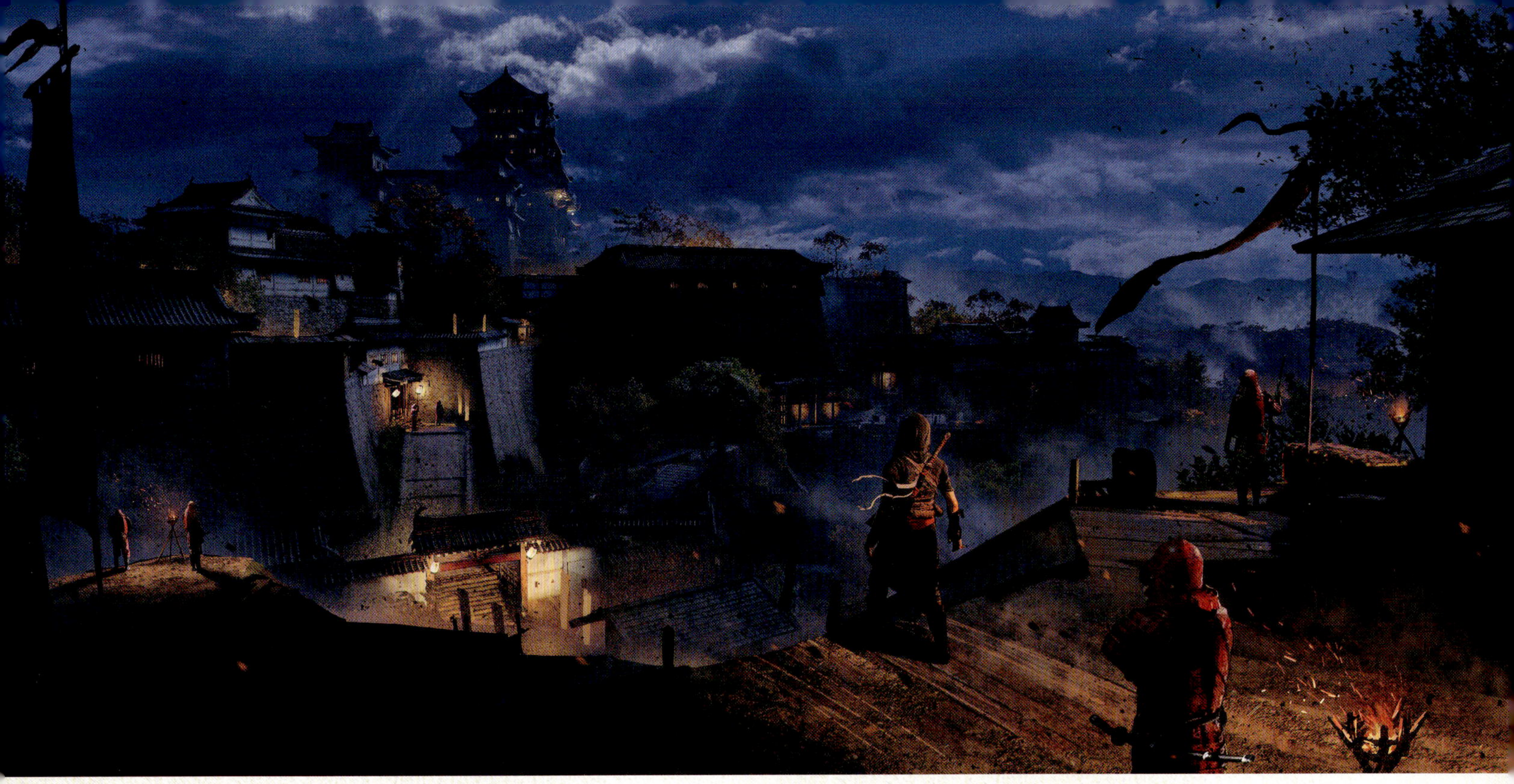

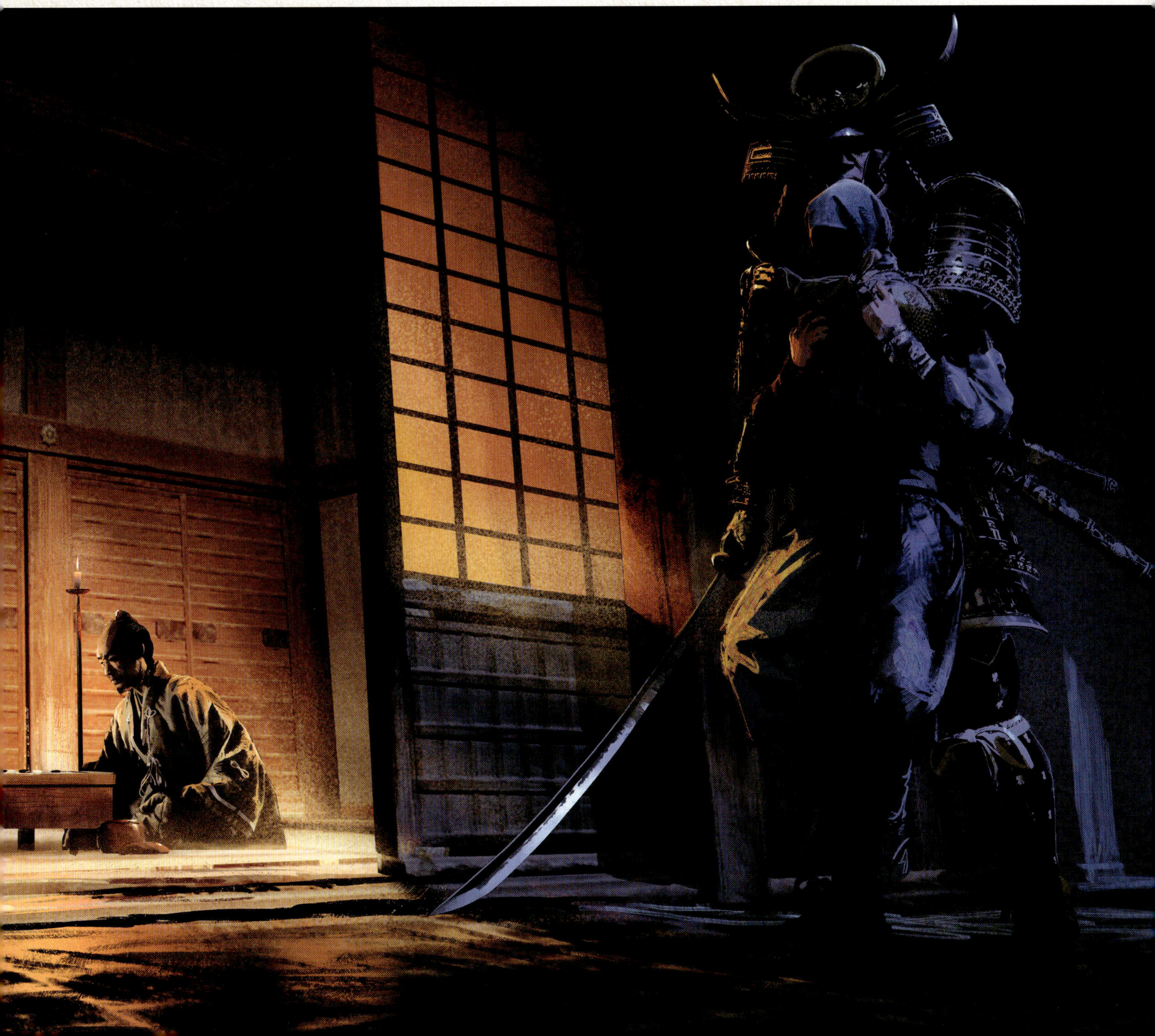

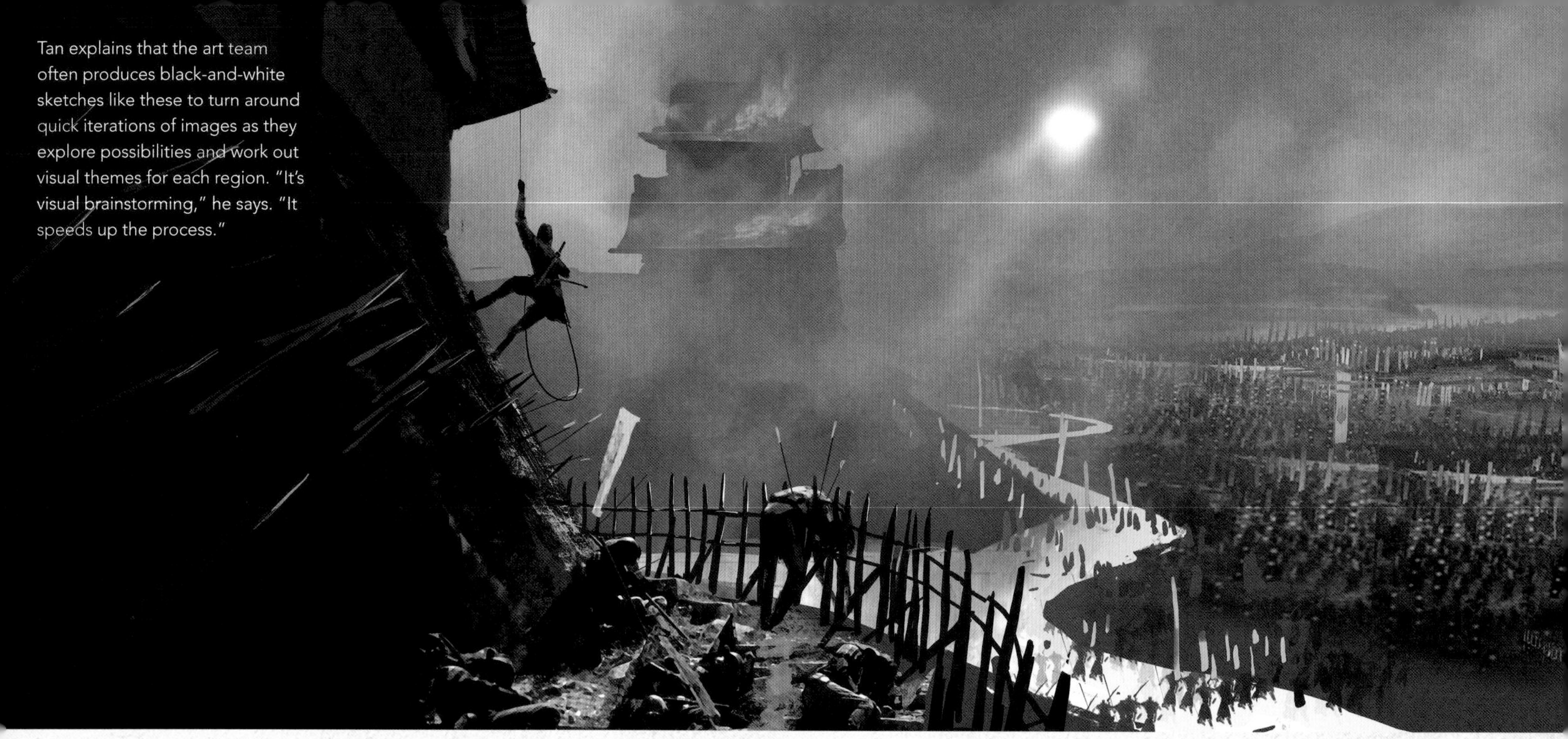

Tan explains that the art team often produces black-and-white sketches like these to turn around quick iterations of images as they explore possibilities and work out visual themes for each region. "It's visual brainstorming," he says. "It speeds up the process."

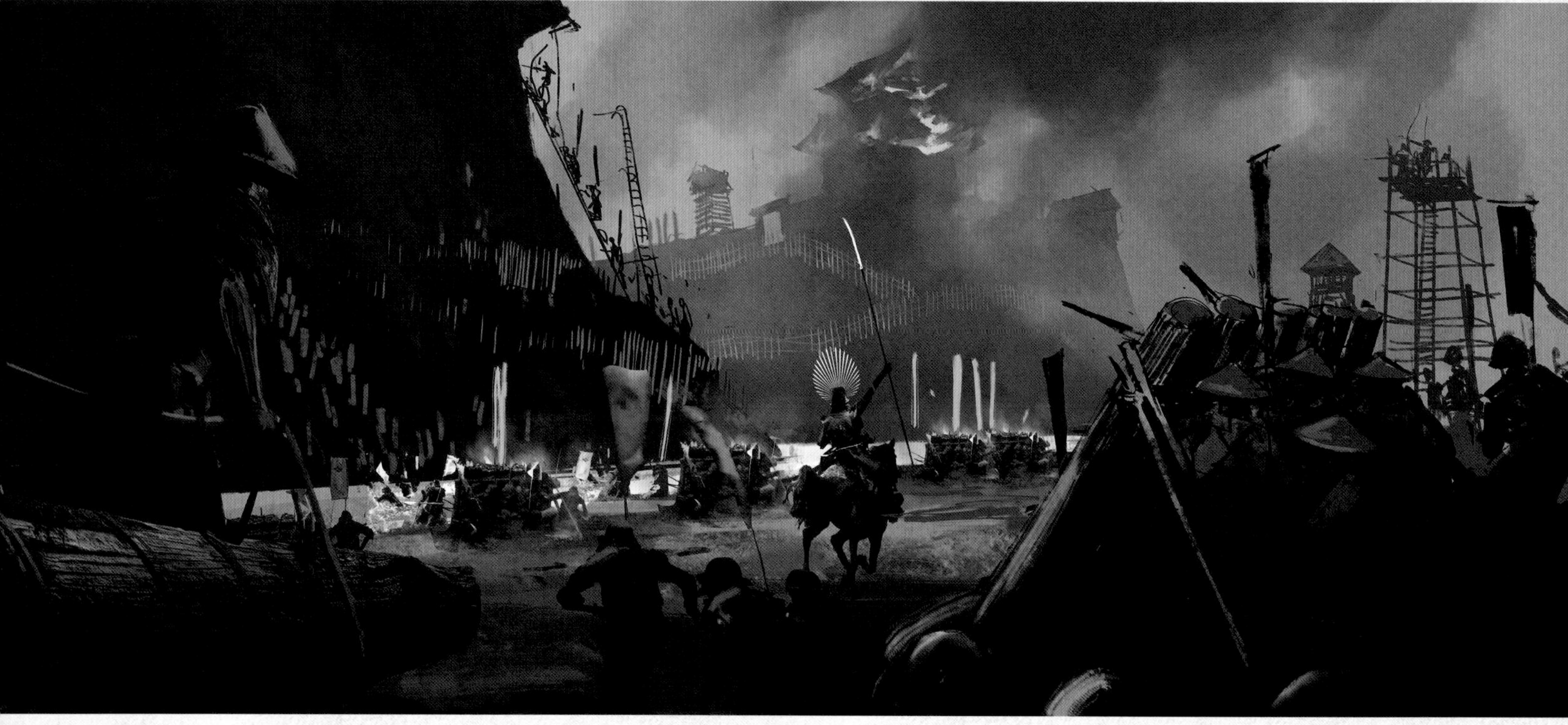

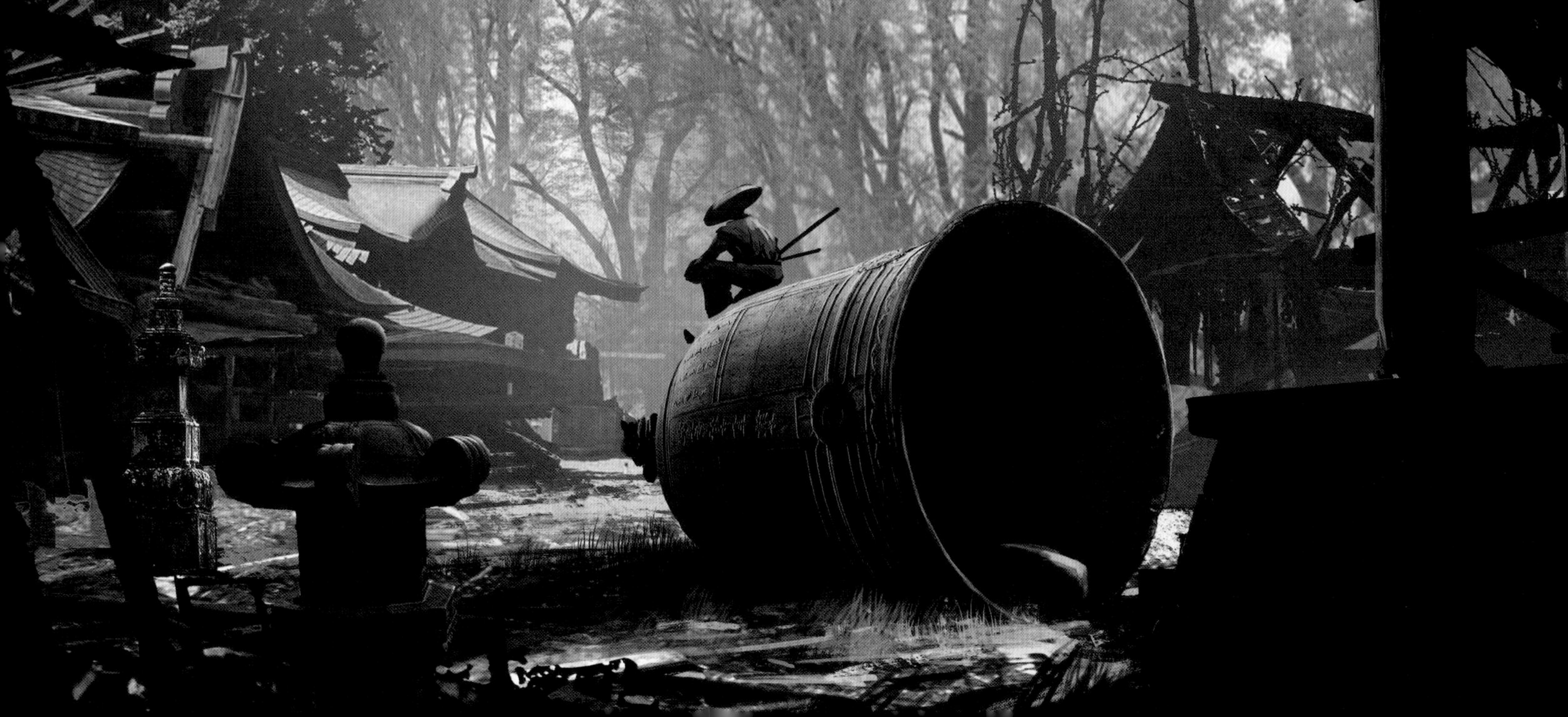

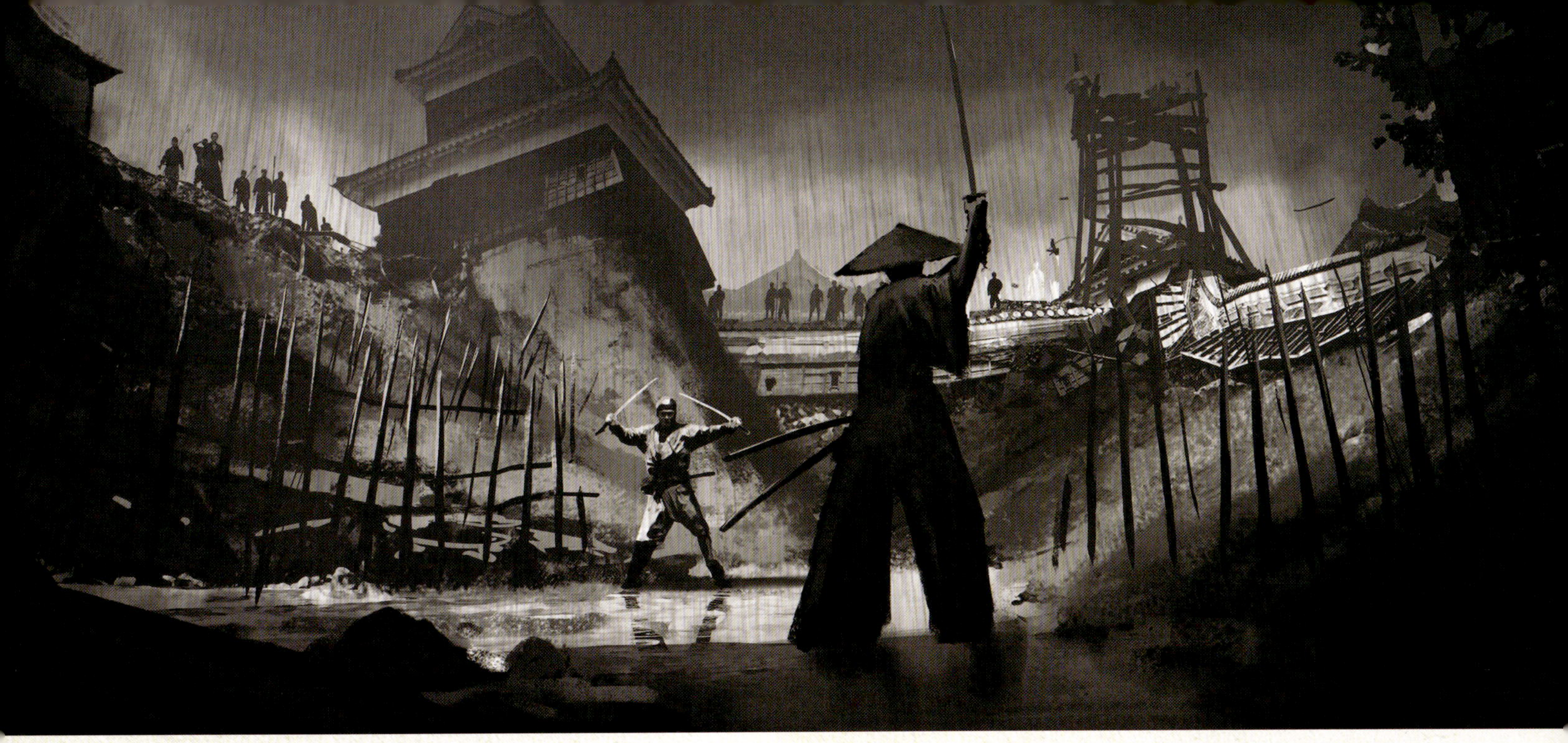

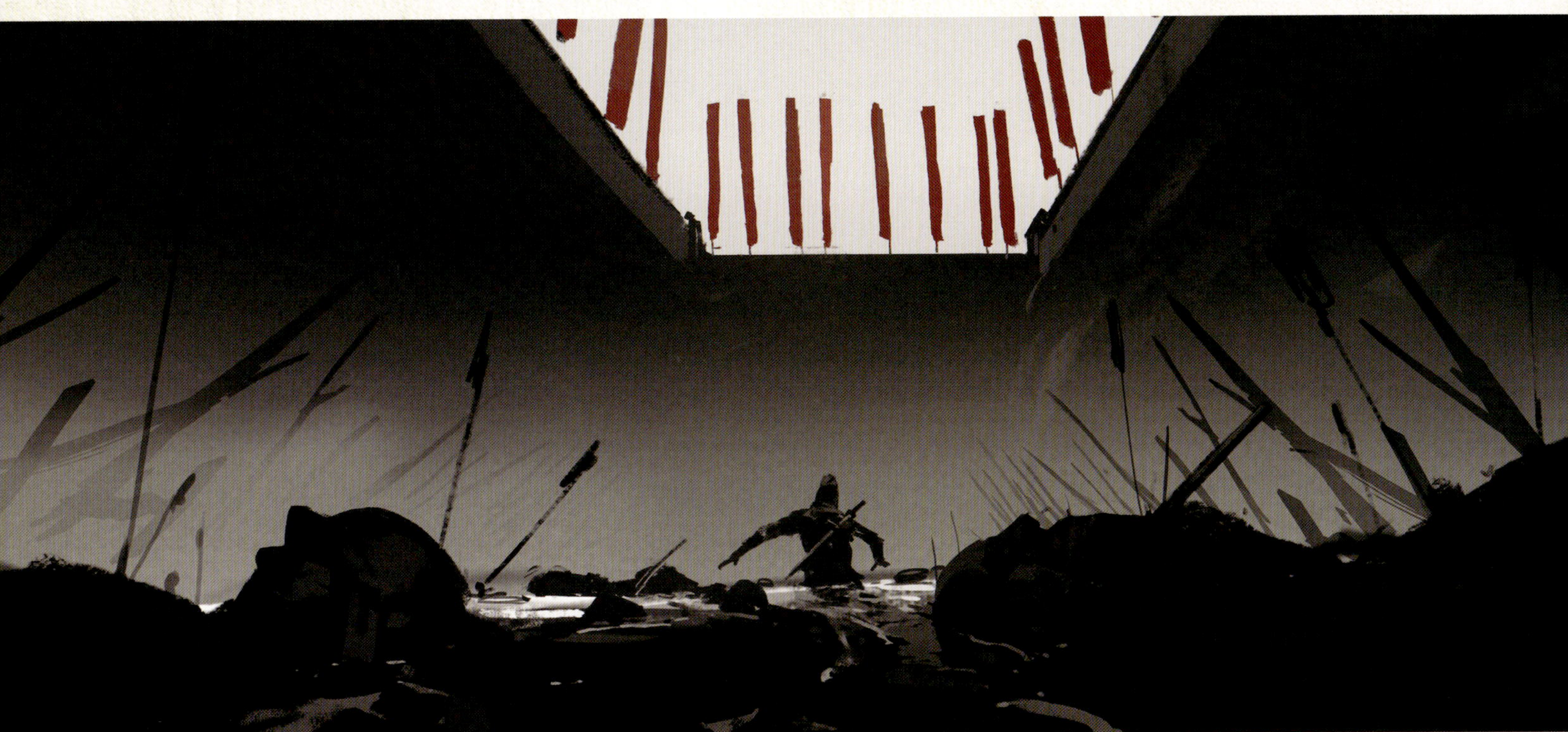

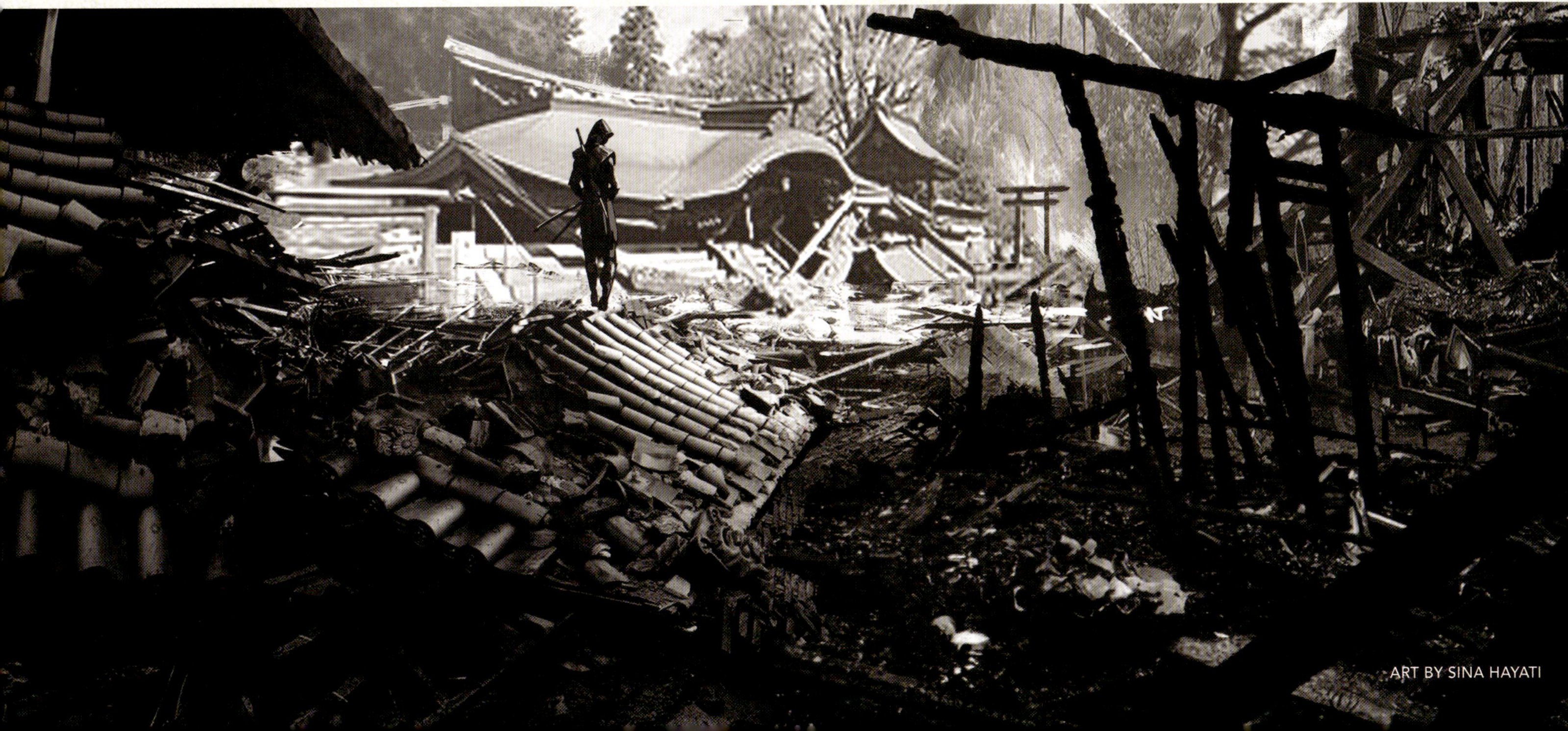

ART BY SINA HAYATI

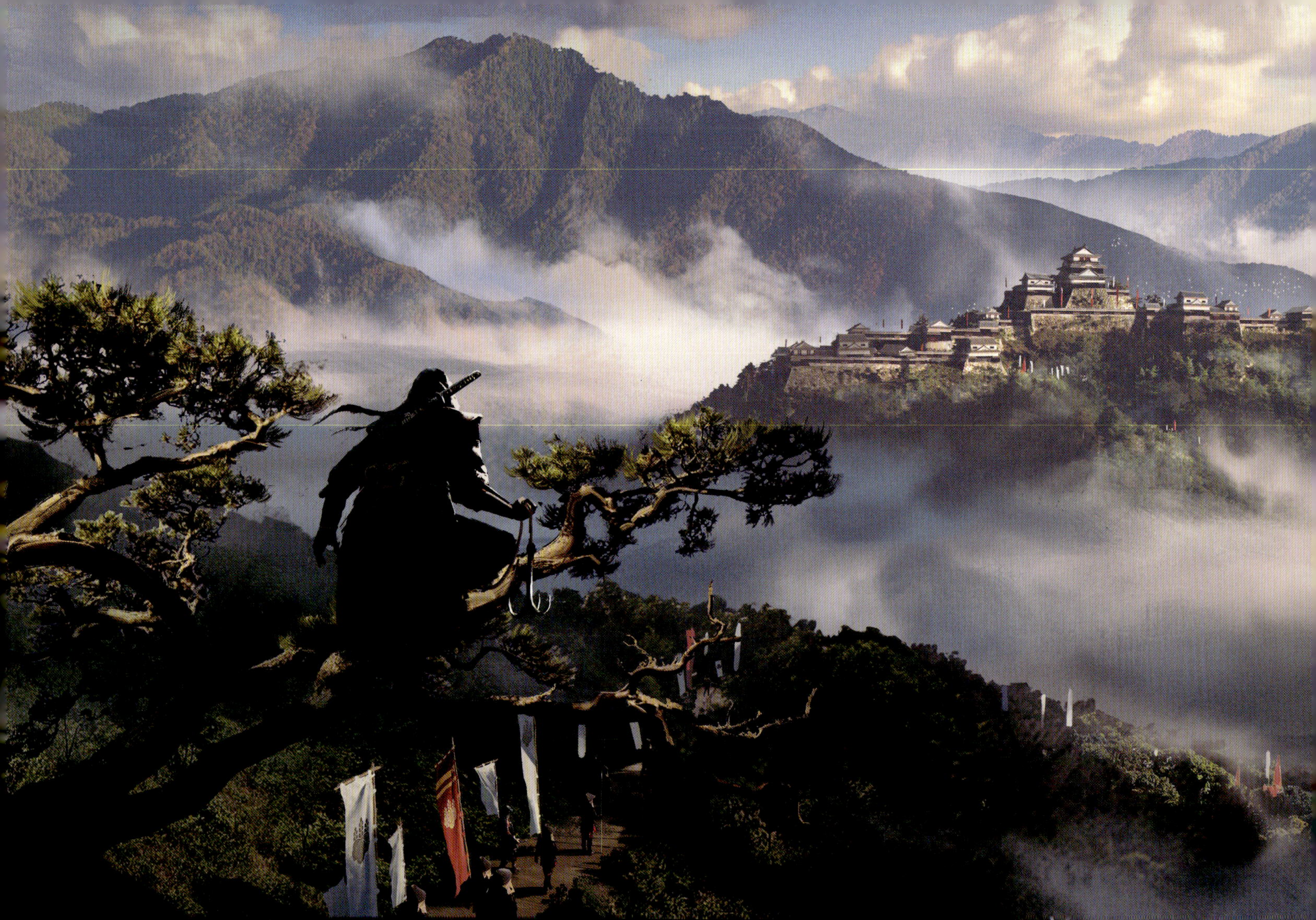

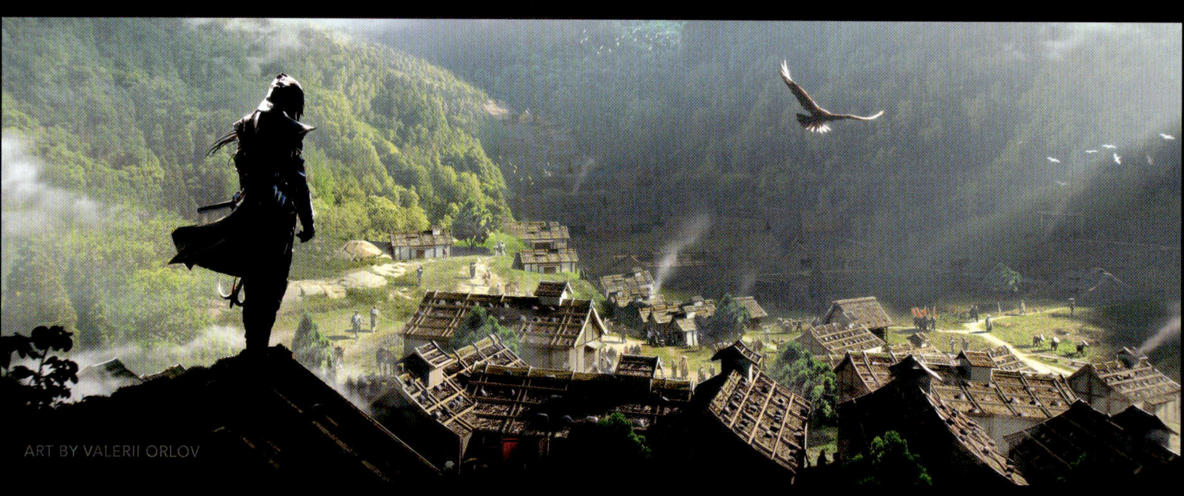

ART BY VALERII ORLOV

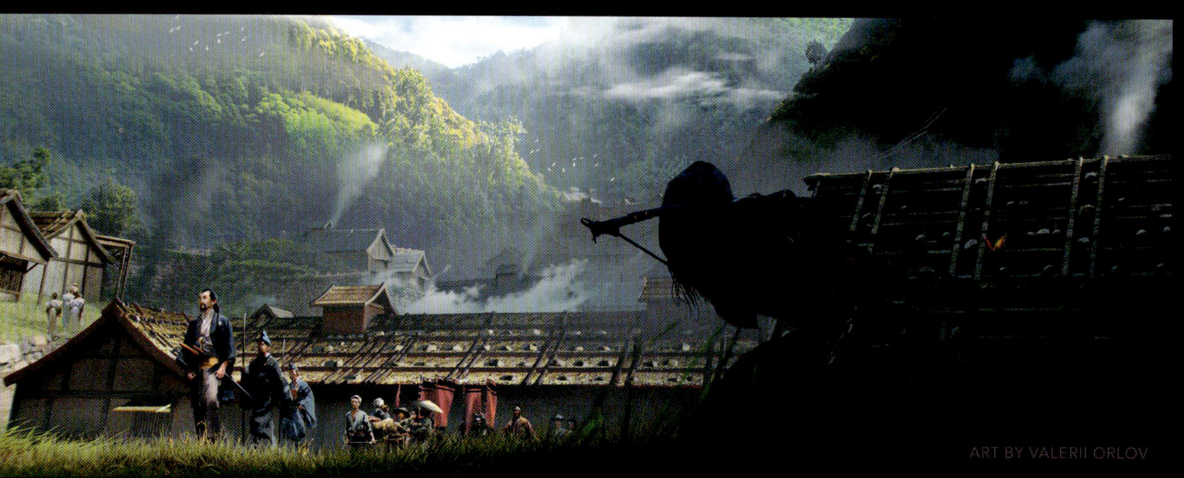

ART BY VALERII ORLOV

ART BY VALERII ORLOV

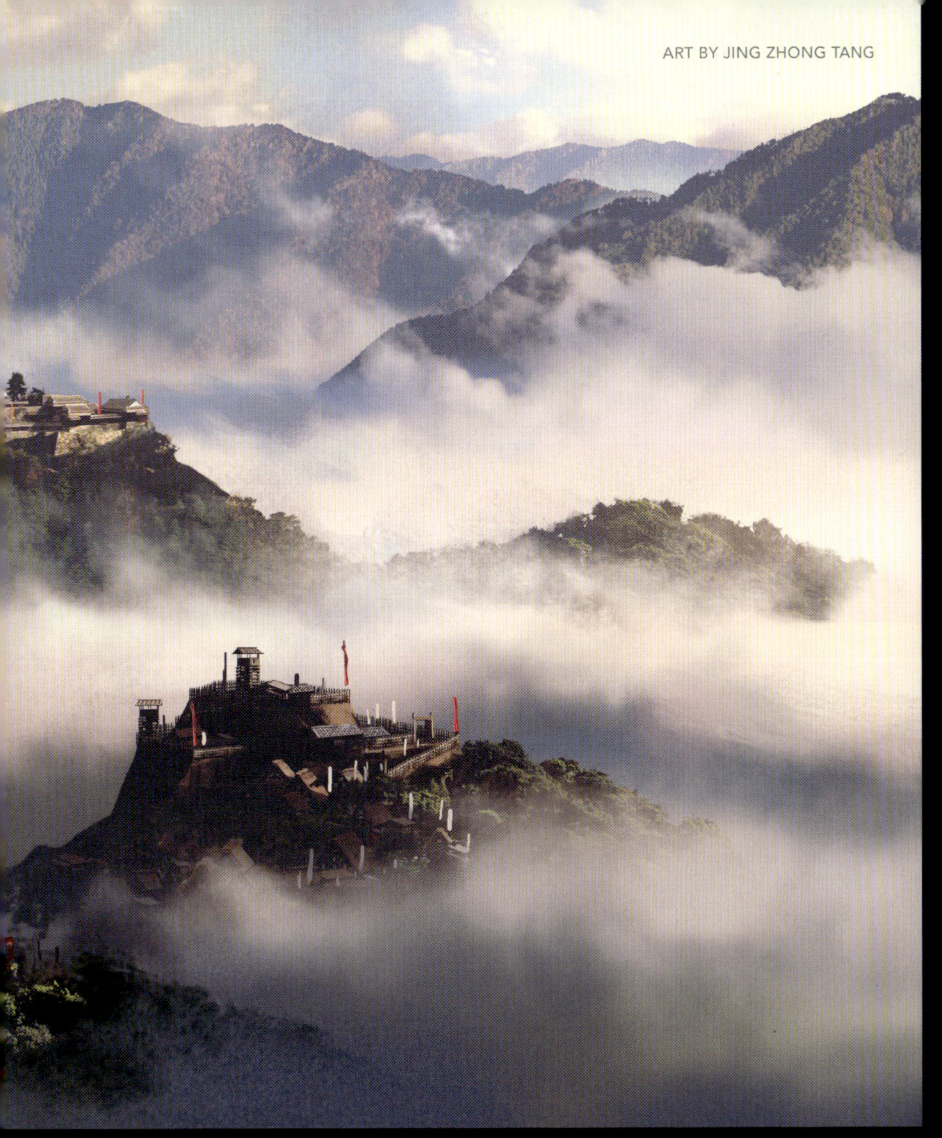

ART BY JING ZHONG TANG

TAMBA

LAND OF SILVER MINES

During the sixteenth century, Tamba Province's silver mines were a significant source of export leverage for Japan's trade with countries of East Asia and Europe. The mountainous region's mining towns produced the means for Japanese warlords to acquire the harquebus firearms and other advanced weaponry that had begun to tip the balance of power on the battlefield. Geographically, Tamba is also well known for its magnificent uplands and mountaintop vistas, one of which shelters a famous structure: Takeda Castle. On certain foggy mornings in autumn, the structure appears to float atop clouds hanging low in the basin below.

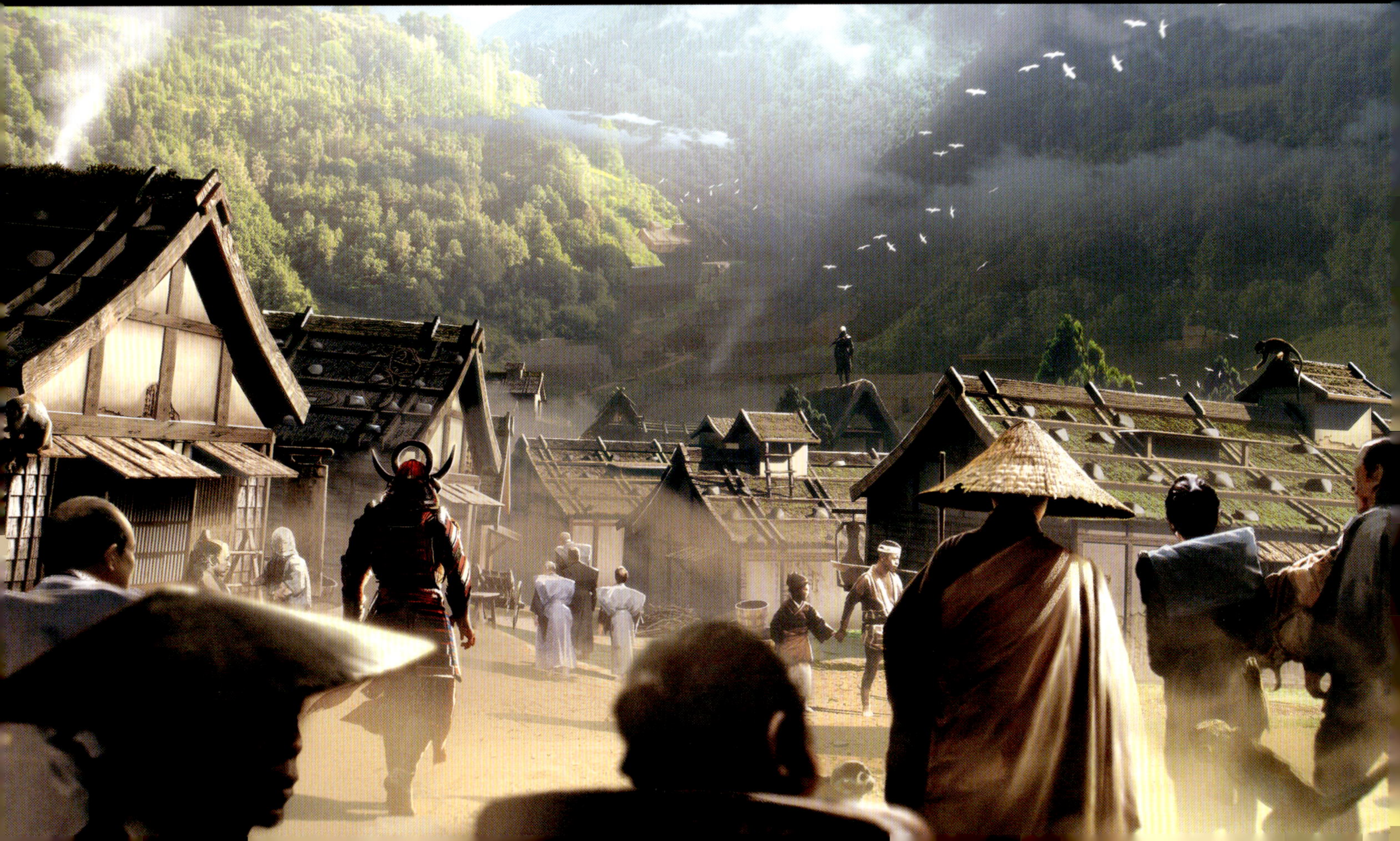

ART BY ALBERT LIN

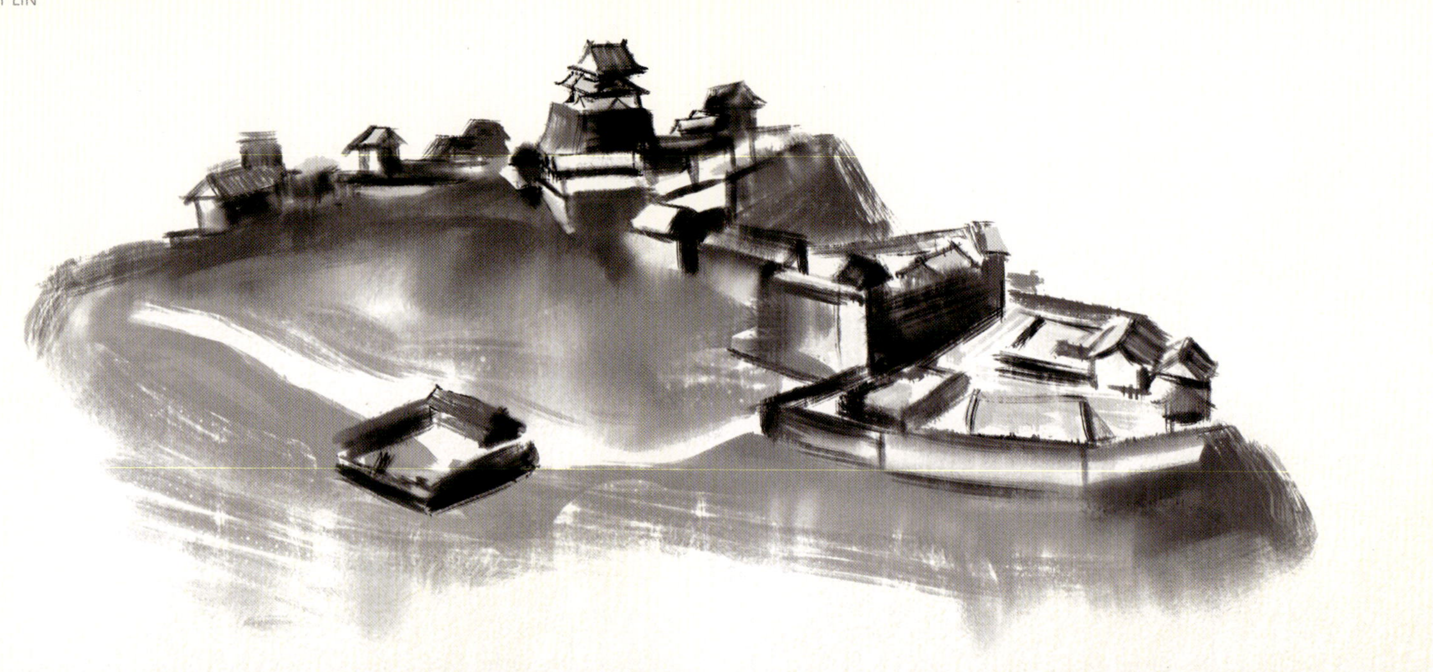

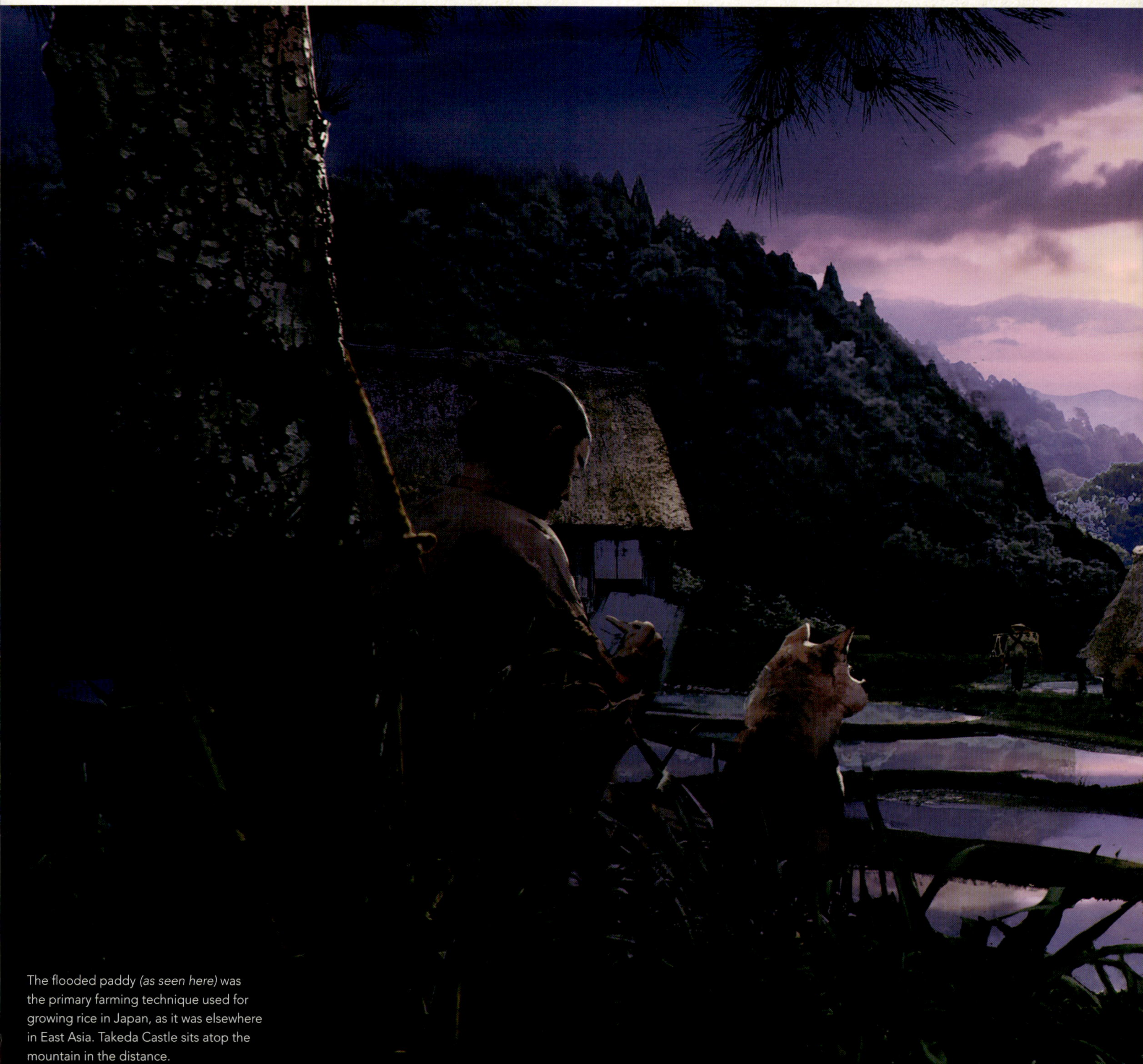

The flooded paddy *(as seen here)* was the primary farming technique used for growing rice in Japan, as it was elsewhere in East Asia. Takeda Castle sits atop the mountain in the distance.

More ink sketches explore visual concepts for the Takeda Castle mountaintop complex *(left)* and a typical silver-mining town *(right)* in the Tamba region. "Silver is such a precious resource for the ruling elite in Japan at this time," says Tan—after all, Tamba's mines create the wealth that lets warlords build an imposing castle like Takeda.

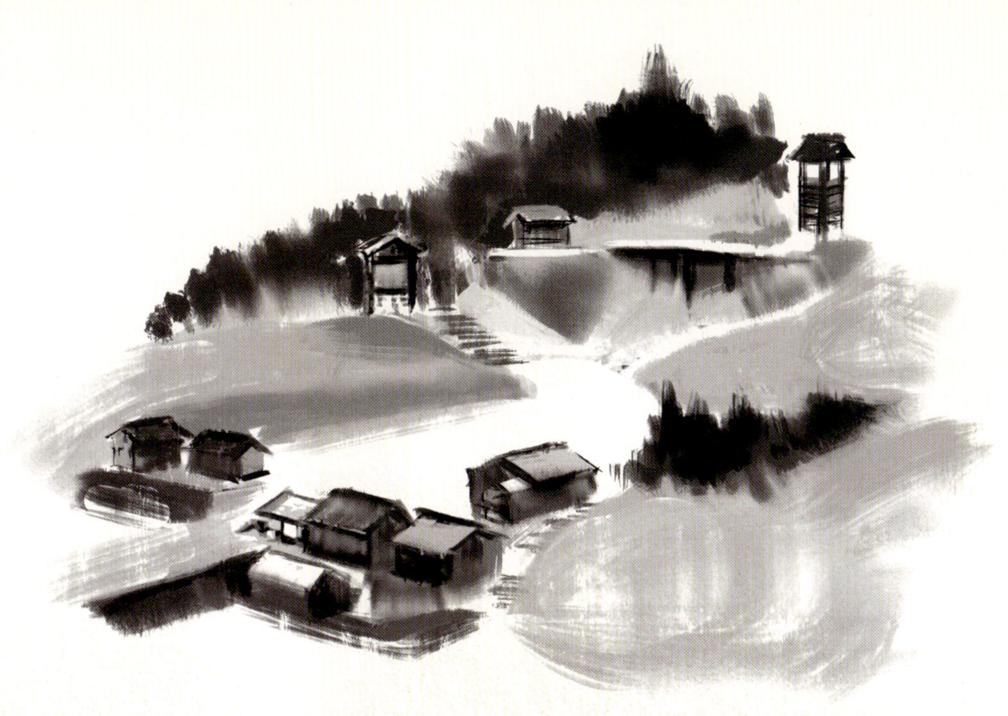

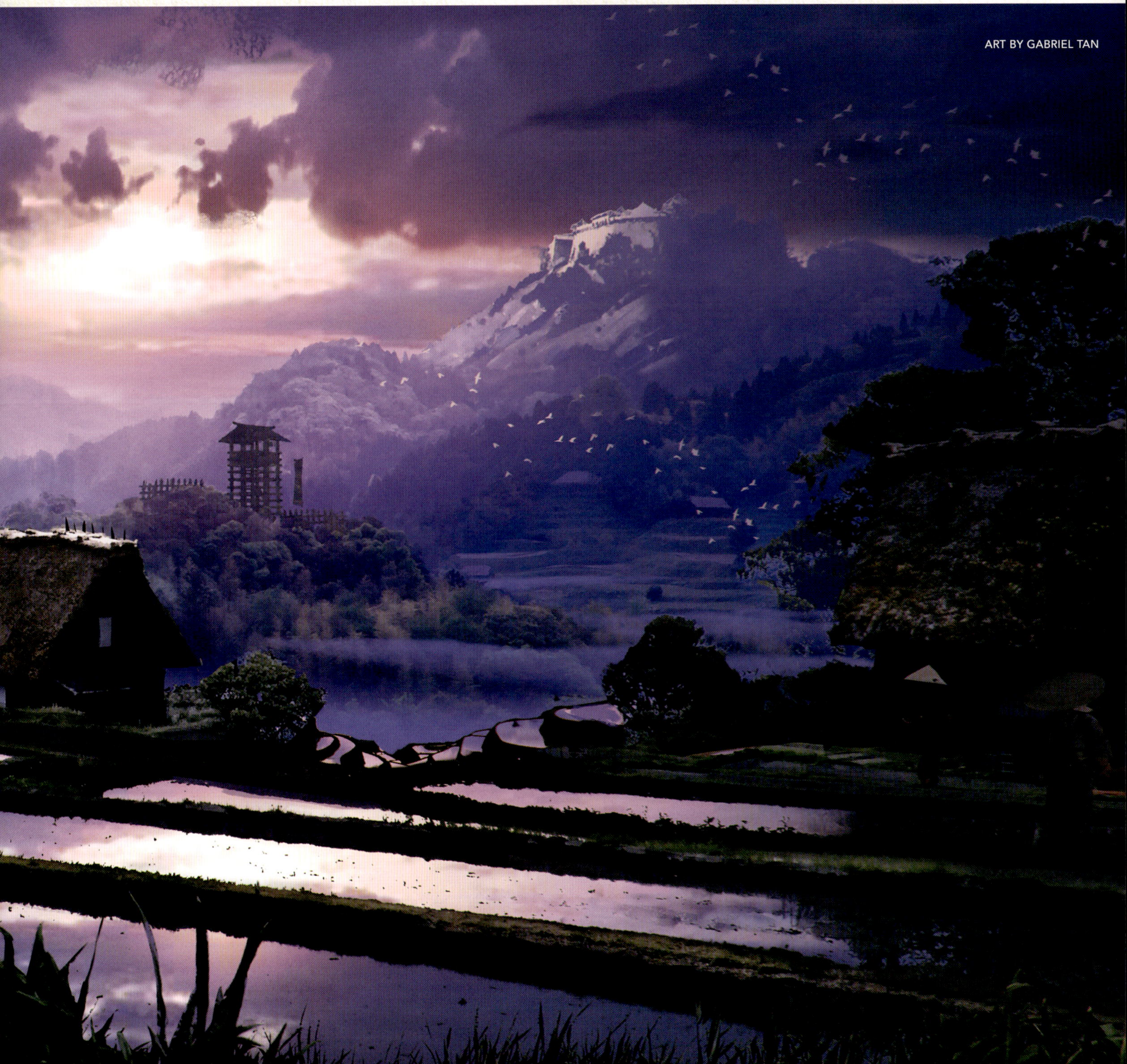

ART BY GABRIEL TAN

Before a design team starts building a location in-game, concept artists typically work up line drawings like these to help nail down the look and layout of the environment. "We work out where things go—temples, castles, commercial neighborhoods, military spaces," says Tan. "We want to make sure it's all historically accurate as well as workable for gameplay purposes." The drawing at lower right is a detailed study for a Tamba silver-mining town.

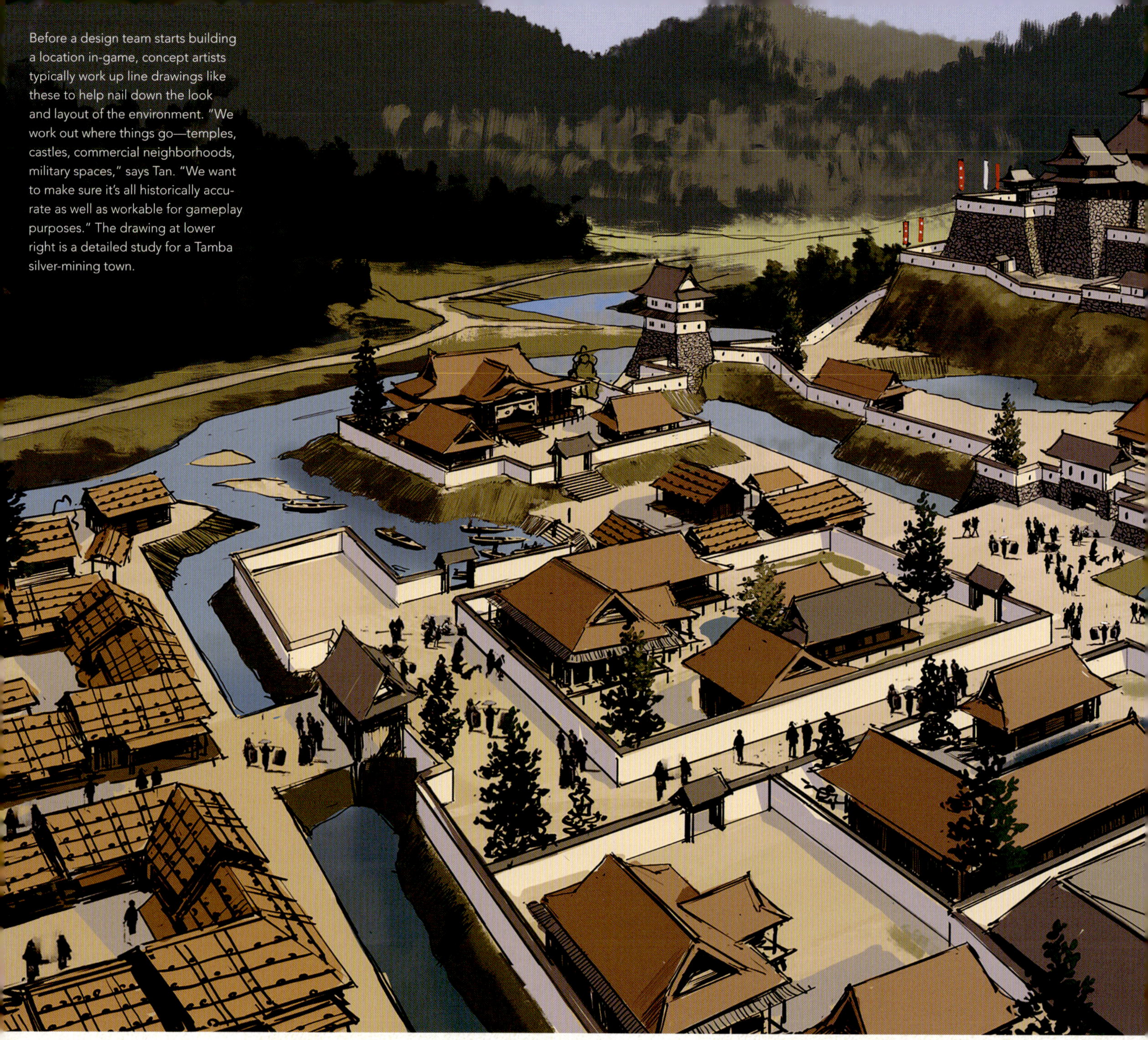

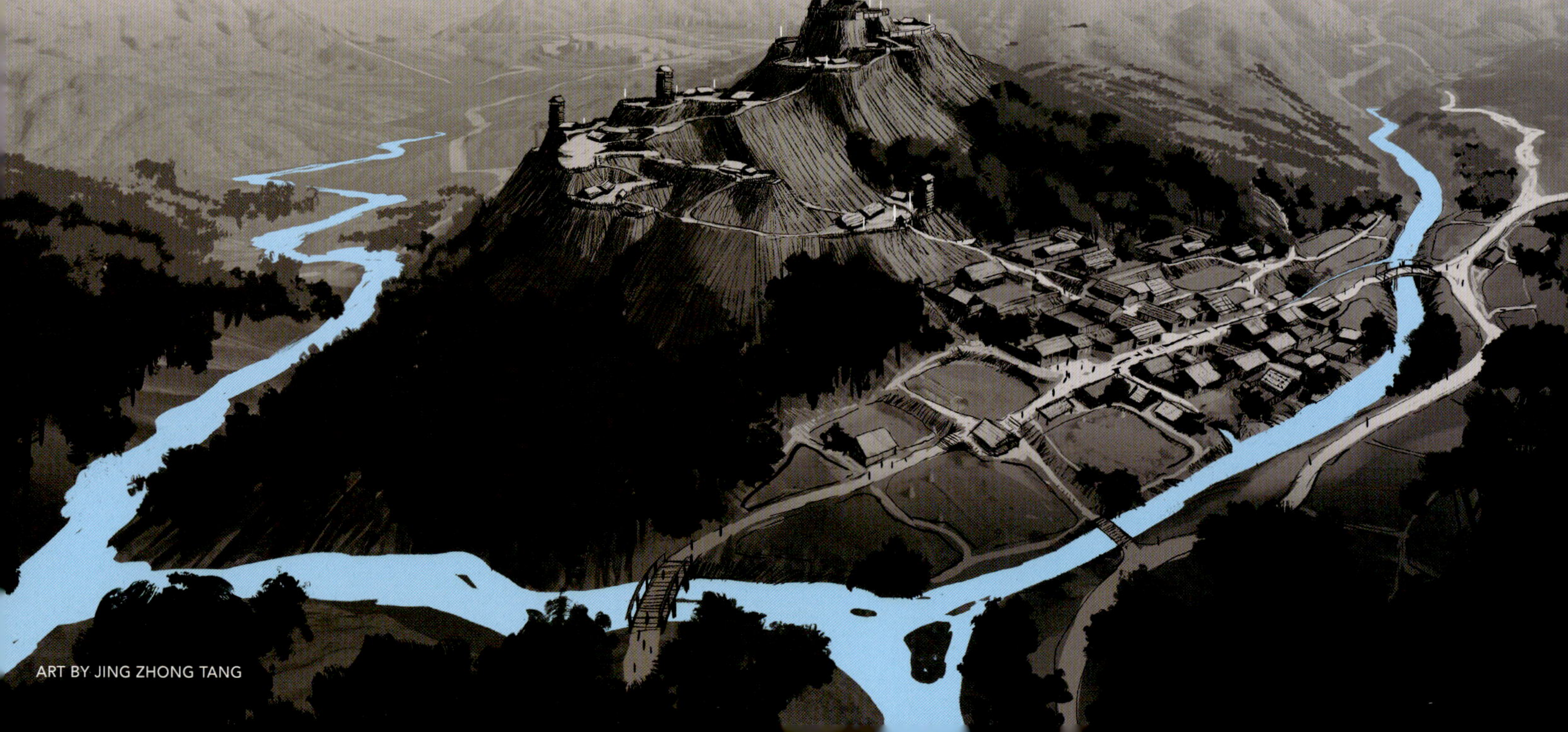

ART BY JING ZHONG TANG

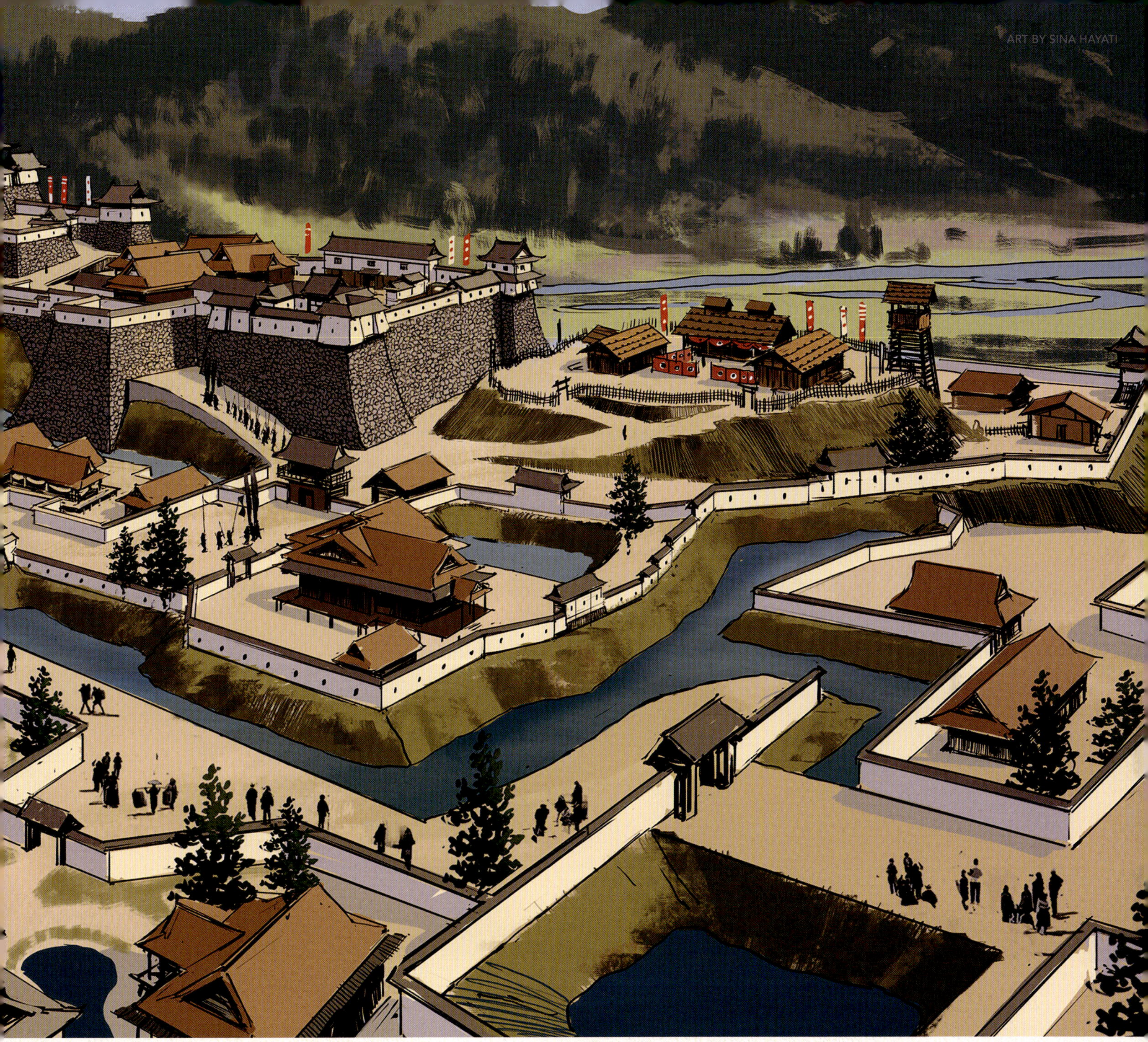

ART BY SINA HAYATI

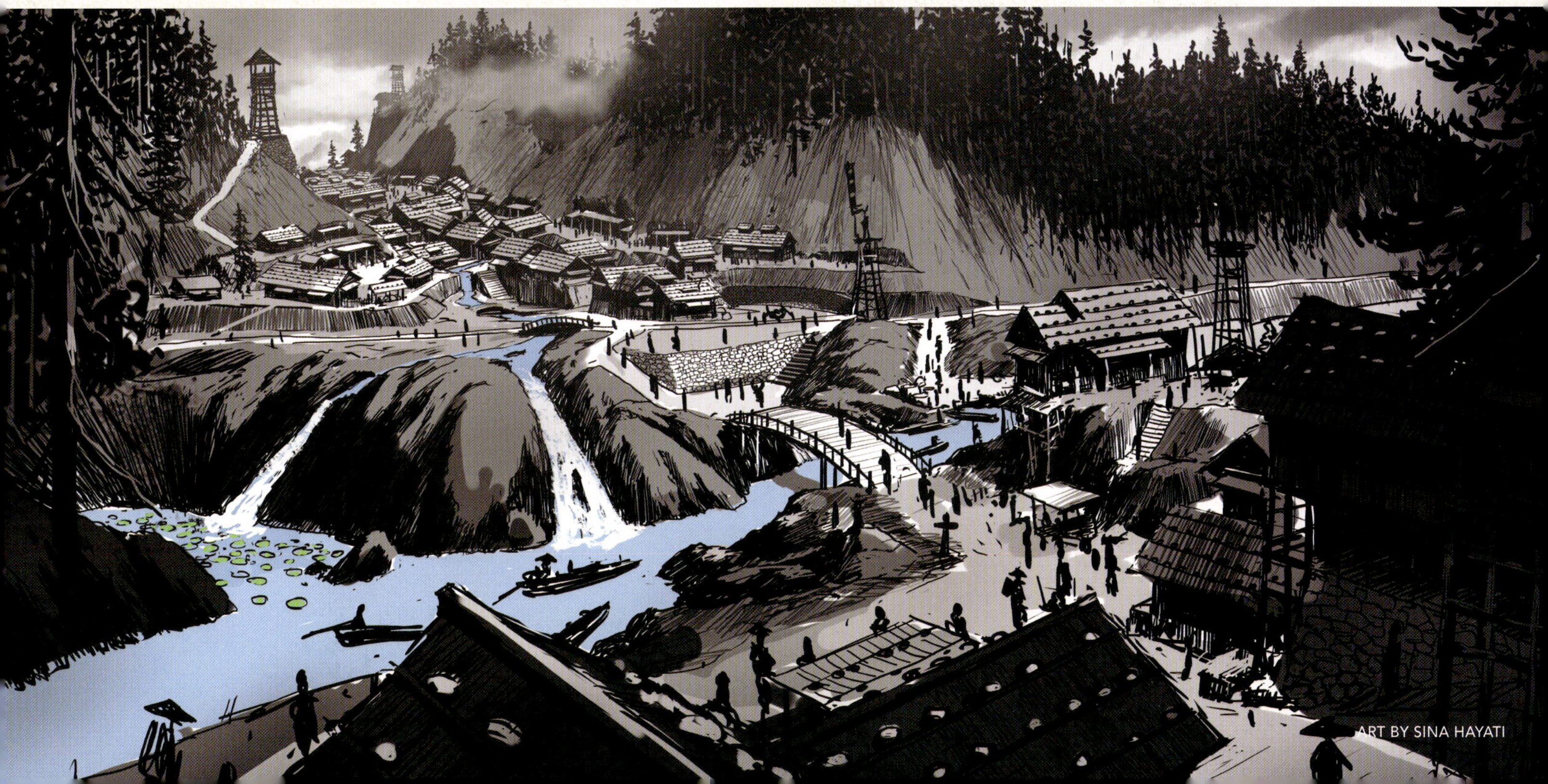

ART BY SINA HAYATI

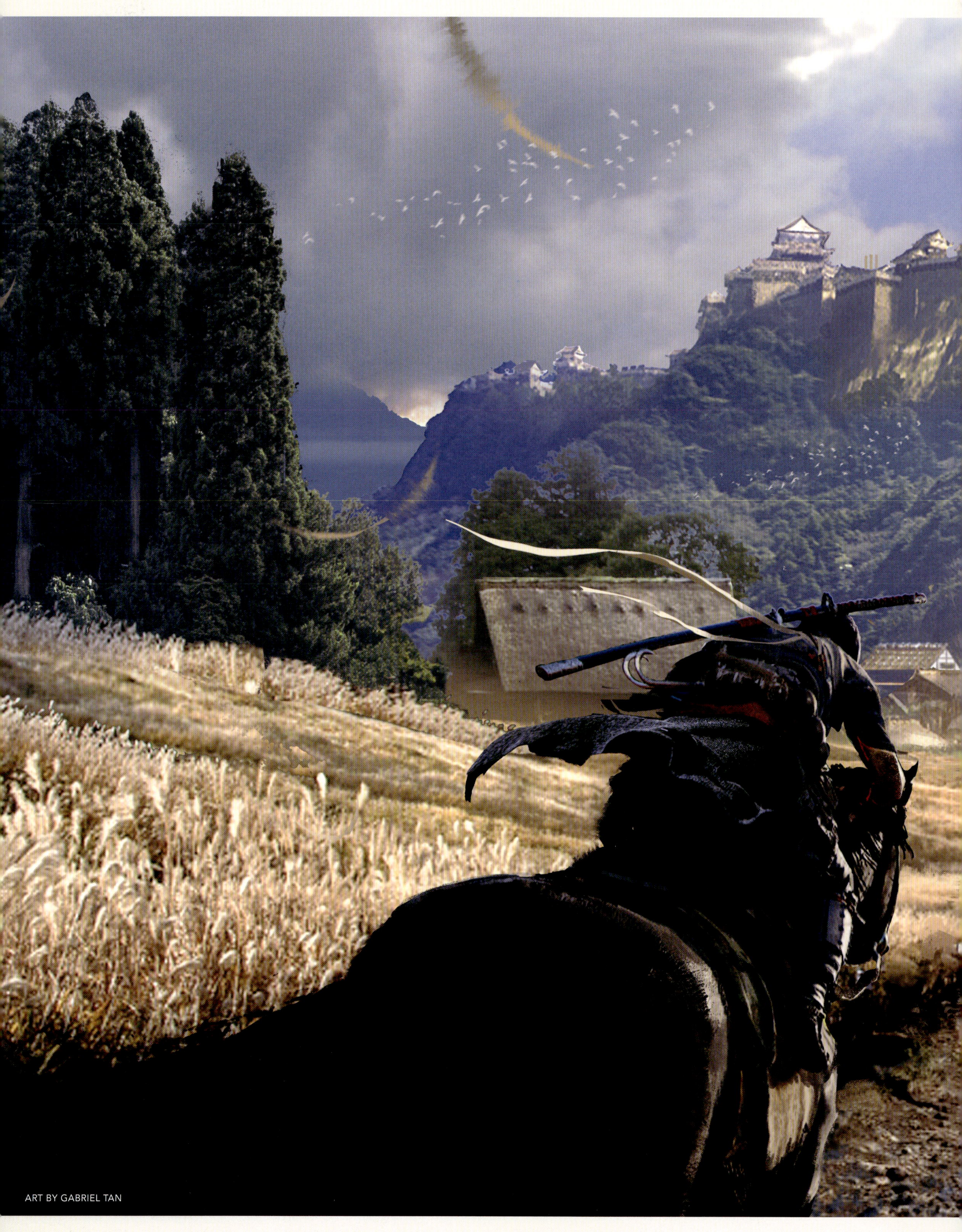

ART BY GABRIEL TAN

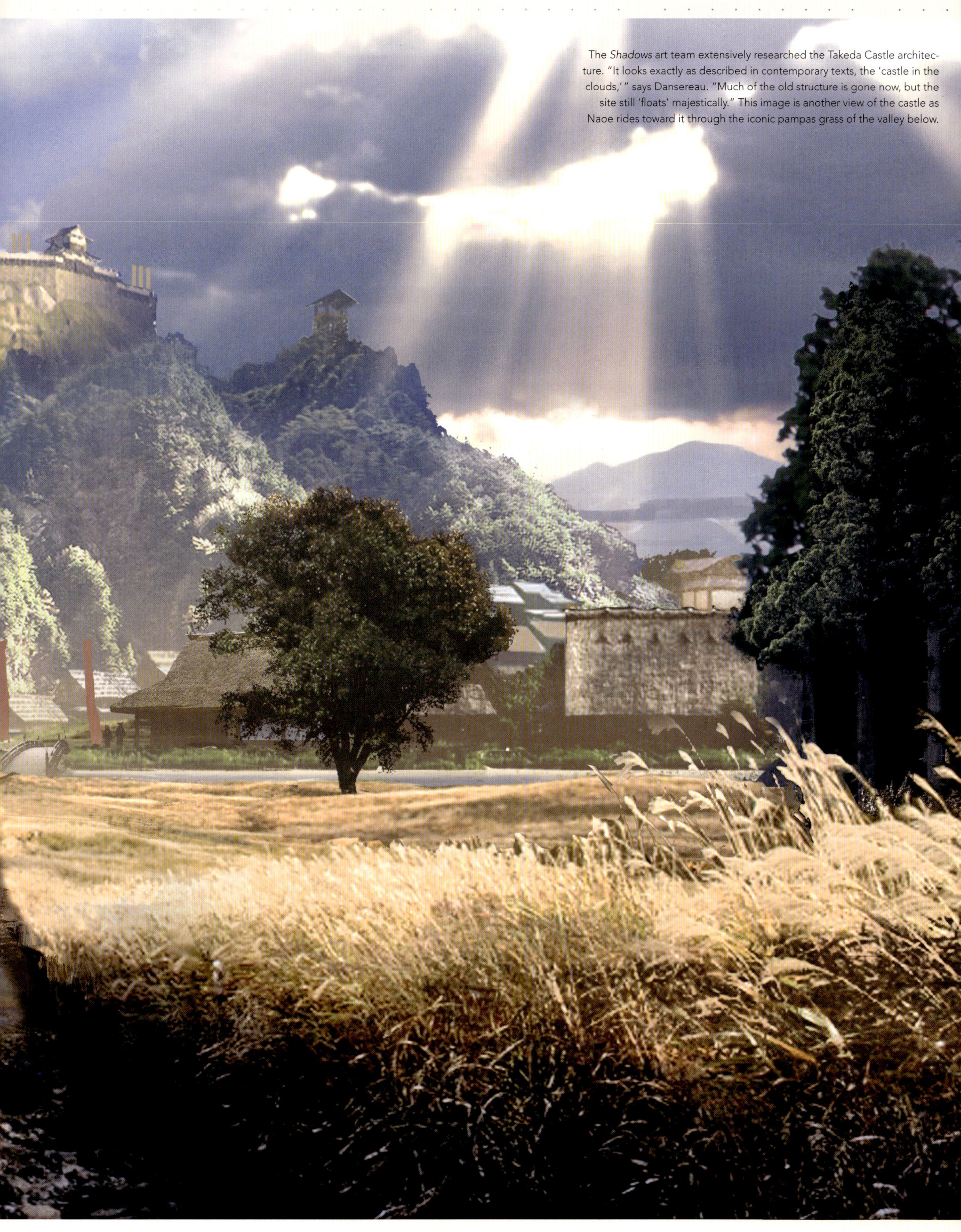

The *Shadows* art team extensively researched the Takeda Castle architecture. "It looks exactly as described in contemporary texts, the 'castle in the clouds,'" says Dansereau. "Much of the old structure is gone now, but the site still 'floats' majestically." This image is another view of the castle as Naoe rides toward it through the iconic pampas grass of the valley below.

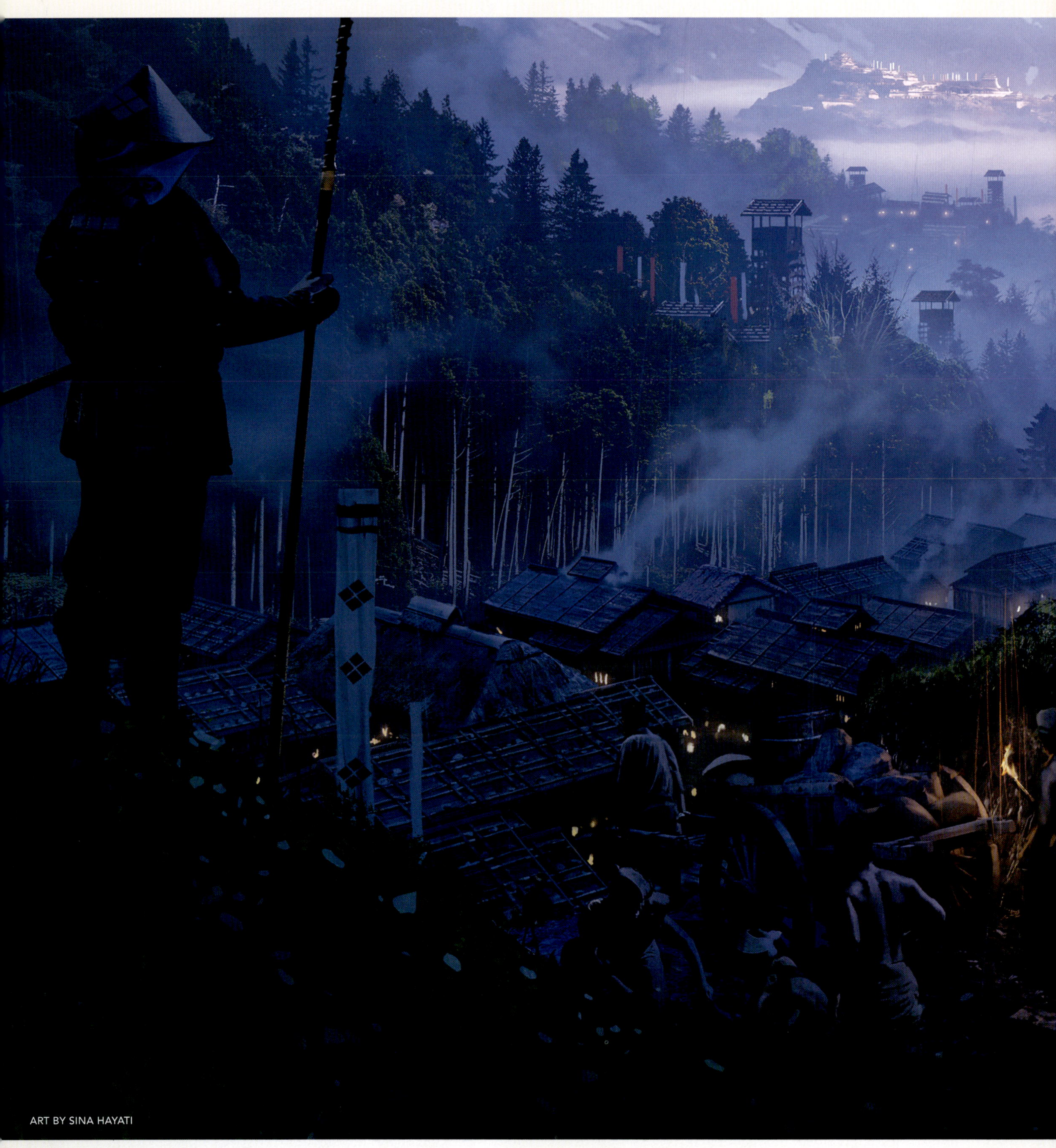

ART BY SINA HAYATI

This concept work is another attempt to create a historically accurate image of Tamba silver-mining operations—no intricate tunneling, just miners digging out square caves and hauling cartloads of ore for processing back in town. "We know the miners were paid laborers, not forced labor or slaves," says Gabriel Tan. "But the ore was immensely

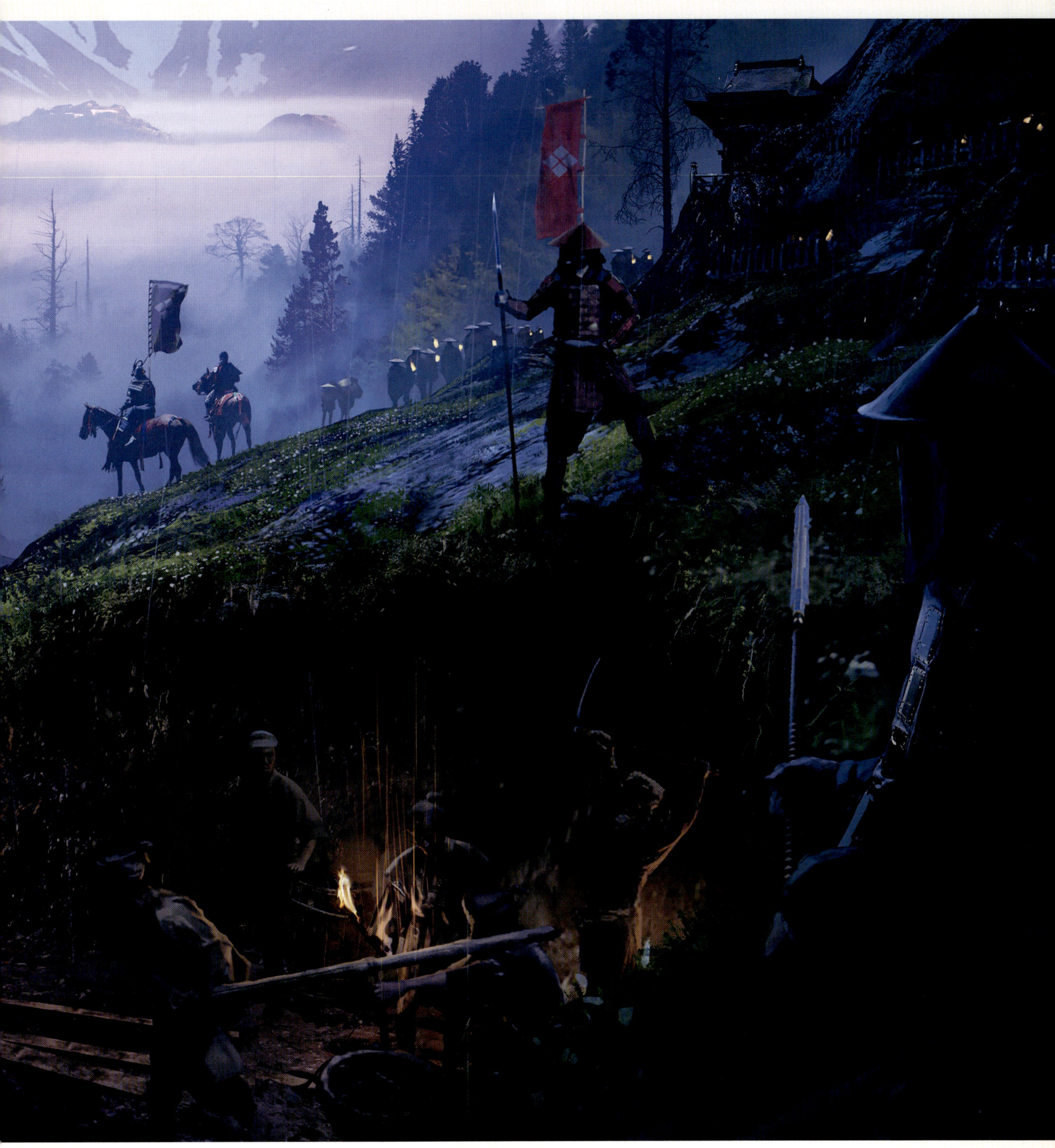

valuable"—so valuable that the controlling daimyo would keep a strong contingent of troops onsite to oversee and guard the activity. "We also wanted to depict Tamba's climate," adds Tan. "It's a humid, foggy region, lots of low clouds swirling through mountain passes." Note Takeda Castle at the top of the image, floating on clouds in the distance.

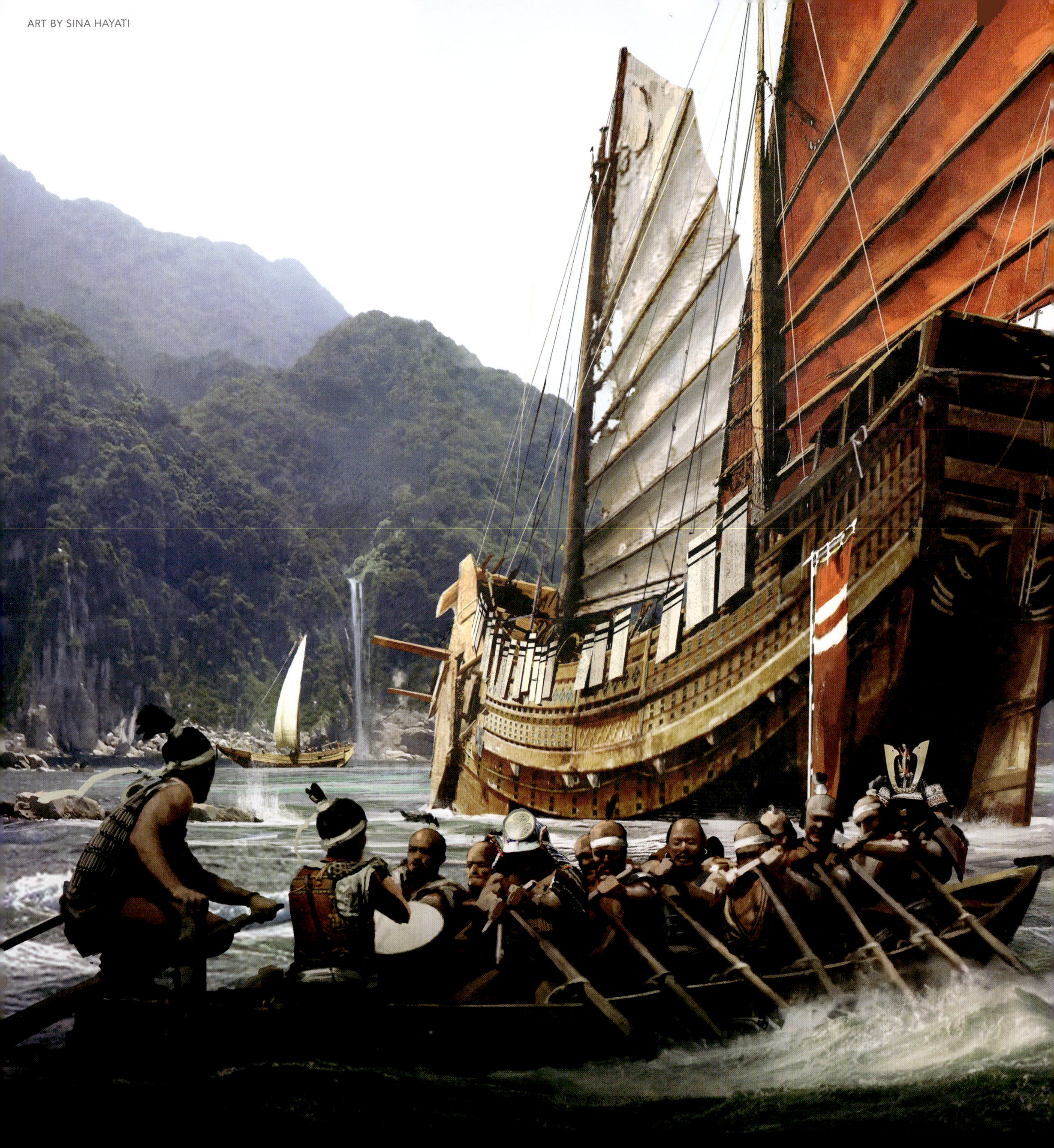

ART BY SINA HAYATI

WAKASA *ASIAN IMPORT-EXPORT CENTER*

Known for its extensive commercial connections to the Asian mainland at the eastern end of the Silk Road, Wakasa Province is a primary departure point for shipments of rice and other goods, especially to China and Korea. The province is famous for its sea trade, its remarkable fisheries . . . and its pirates (*as seen above*). Wakasa-based shipping attracted its share of

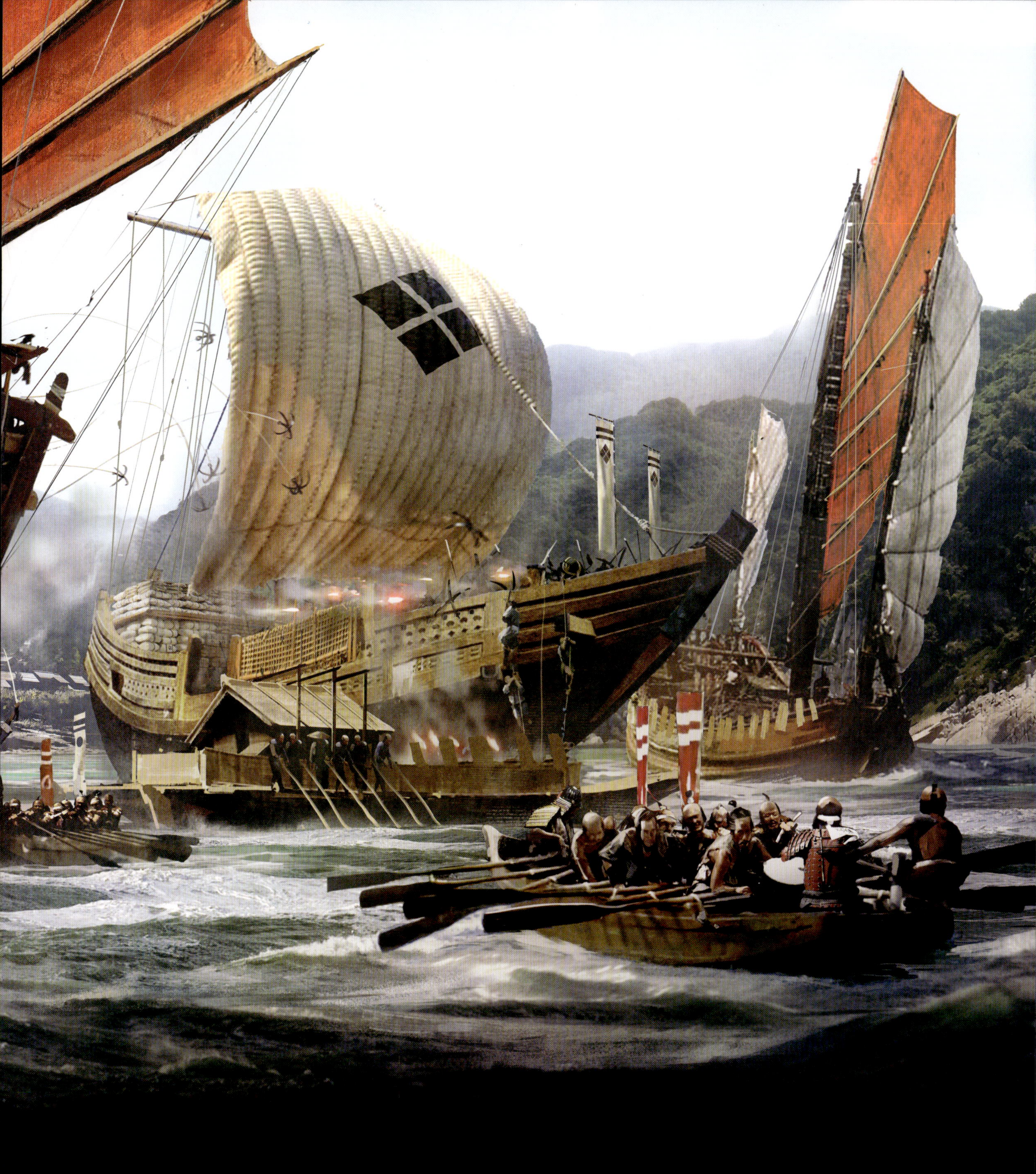

malevolent seafarers. Steep coastal cliffs and secluded coves and inlets made for perfect pirate hideouts. This stirring image shows crews of raiders rowing out to commandeer the huge red-sailed Chinese junks filled with trade cargo. While there's no naval fight in the game, this concept helped to set the tone for the province.

ART BY ALBERT LIN

Ink sketches at right explore the province's northern highlands and steep coastal cliffs. The image below depicts Wakasa pirates hauling ill-gotten Chinese goods ashore to a makeshift hideout—note the crude watchtower at far left.

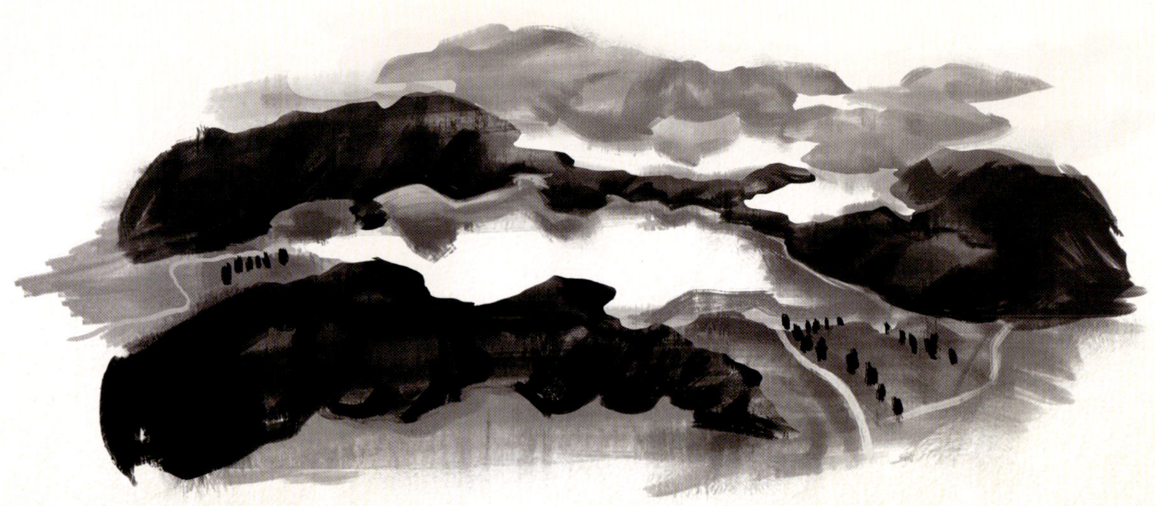

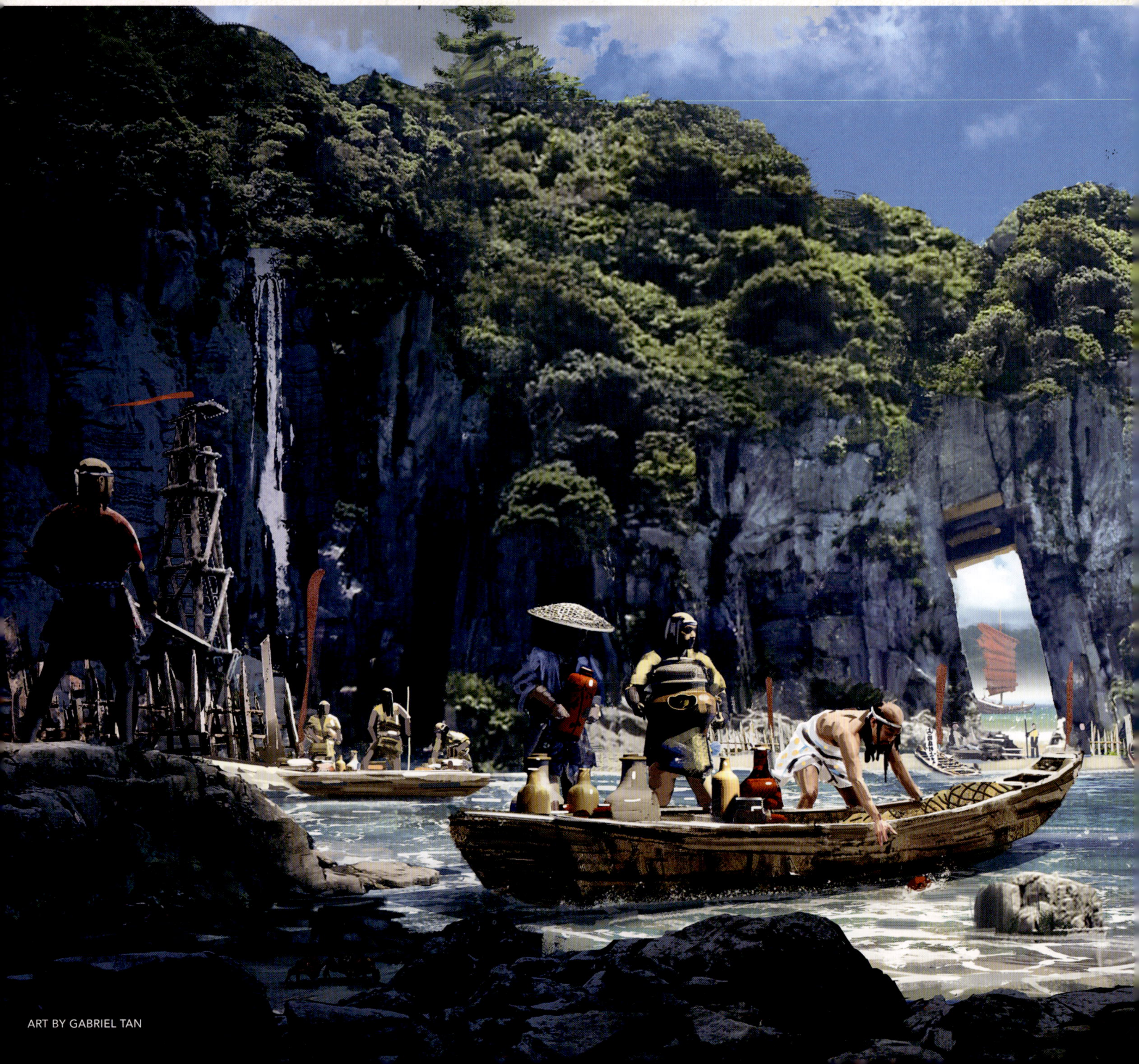

ART BY GABRIEL TAN

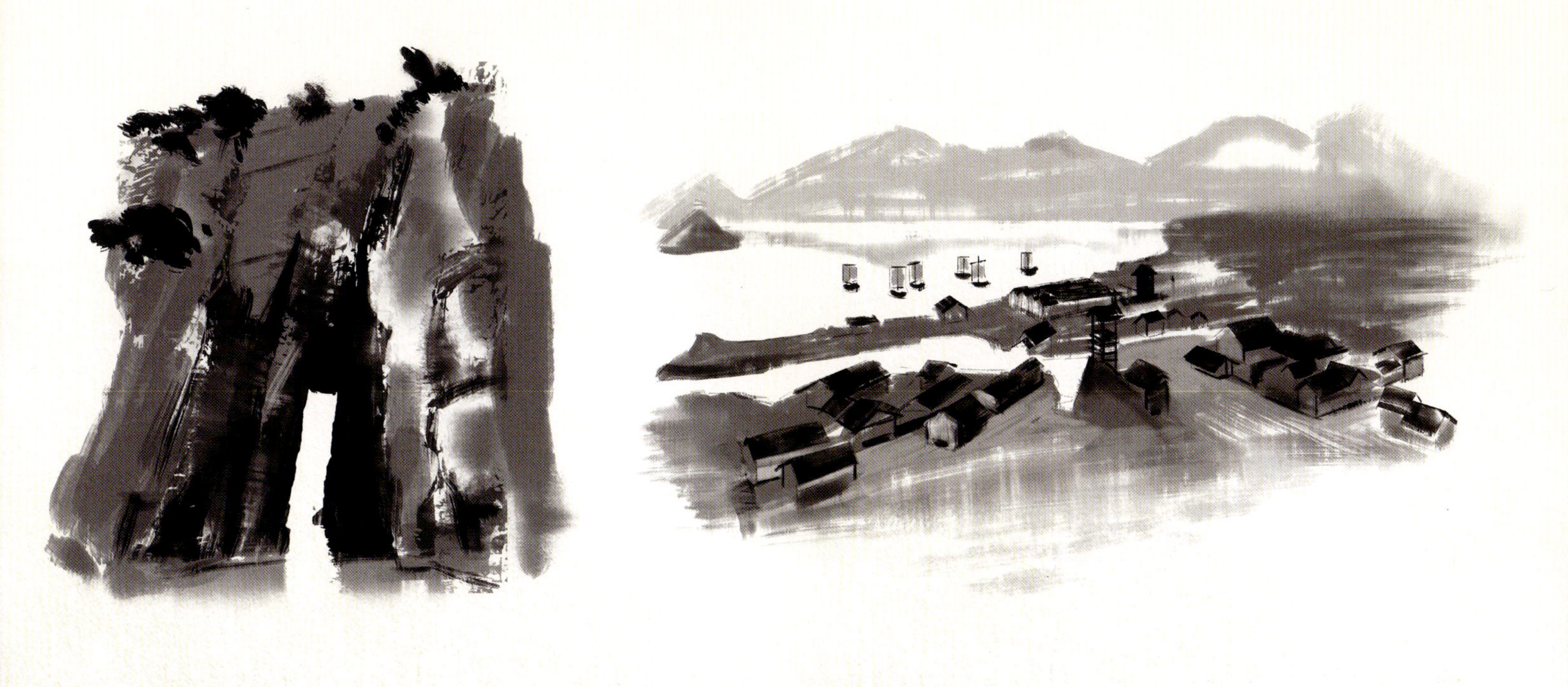

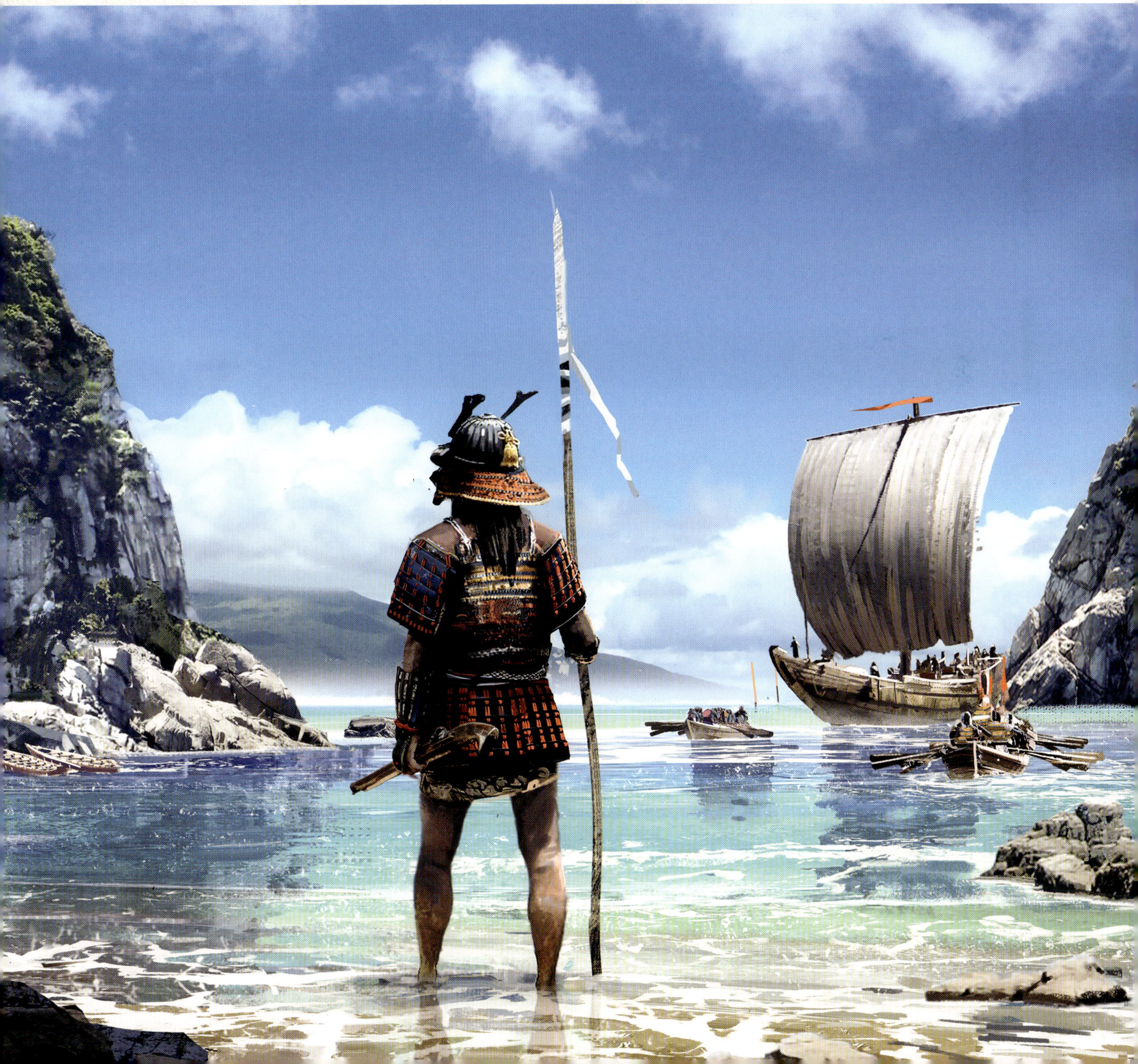

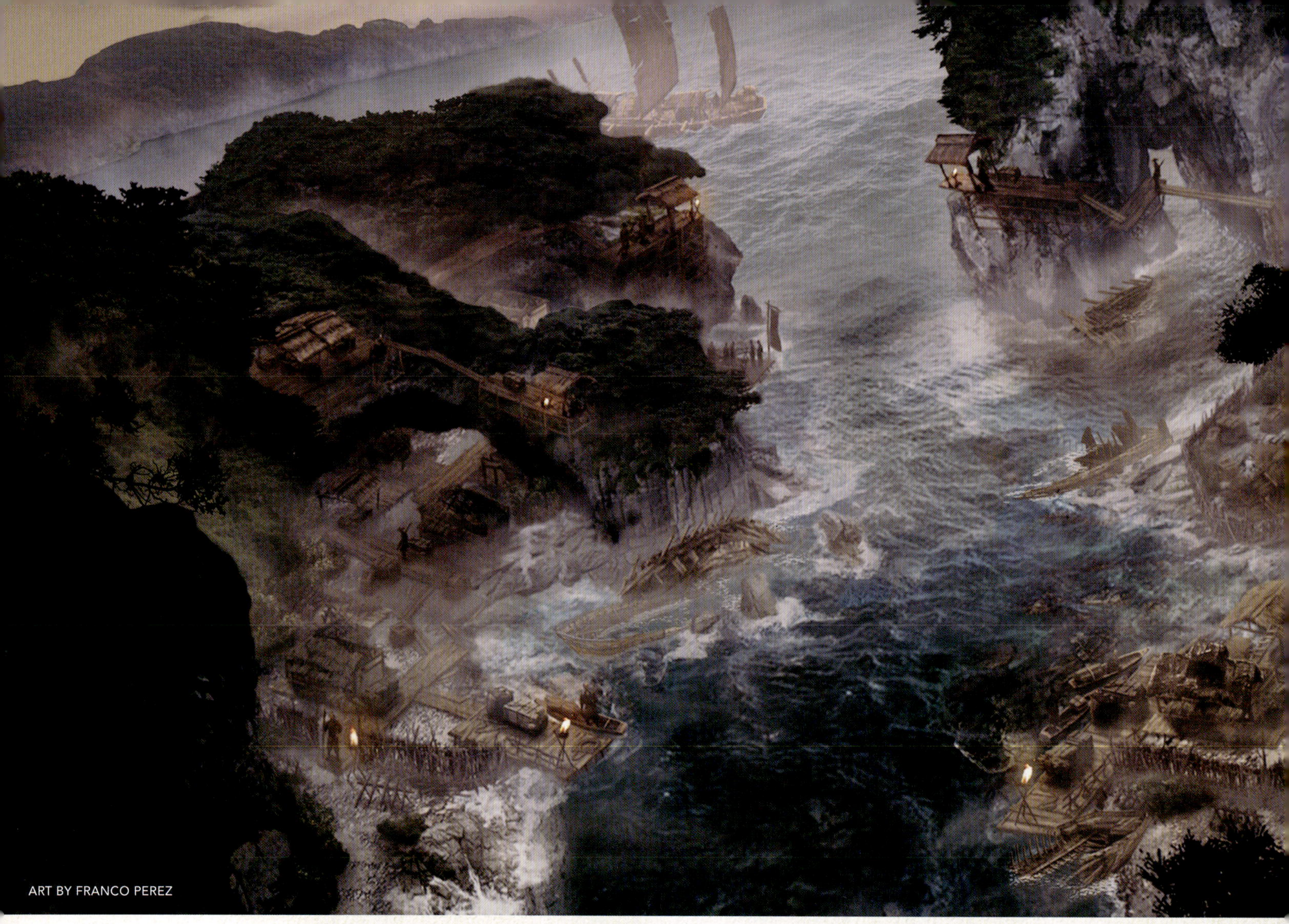

ART BY FRANCO PEREZ

This nighttime image is a concept overview of Obama, an important international seaport on the Wakasa coast. "Regional trade with China was so important that ports typically featured a Chinatown section," says Tan. Here, you can see the bright, lantern-lit main street of Obama's Chinatown, a warm glow in the blue darkness.

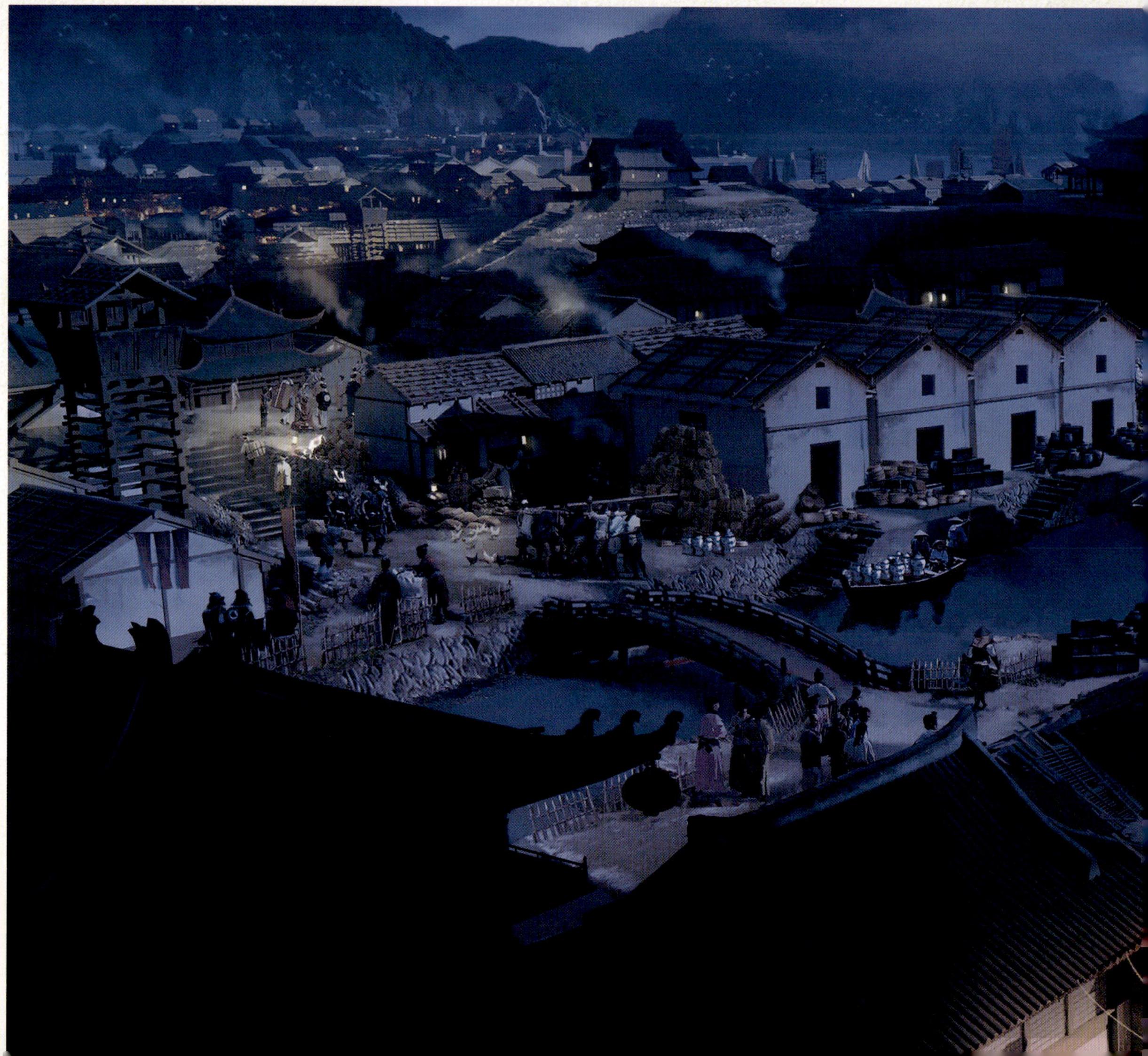

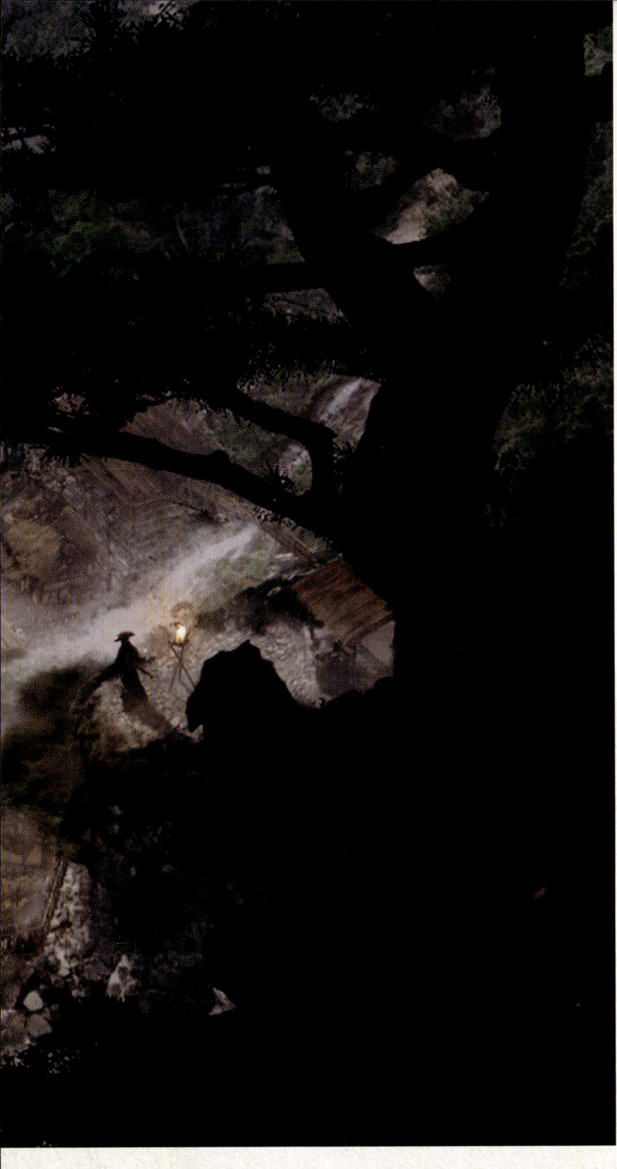

This concept piece is an overhead view of a hideout cove, a place largely hidden from the eyes of naval warships trolling the coastline for pirate lairs. Unfortunately, when the waters get rough, it can wreak havoc in the cove. Here, you can see wrecked boats and shattered waterfront structures.

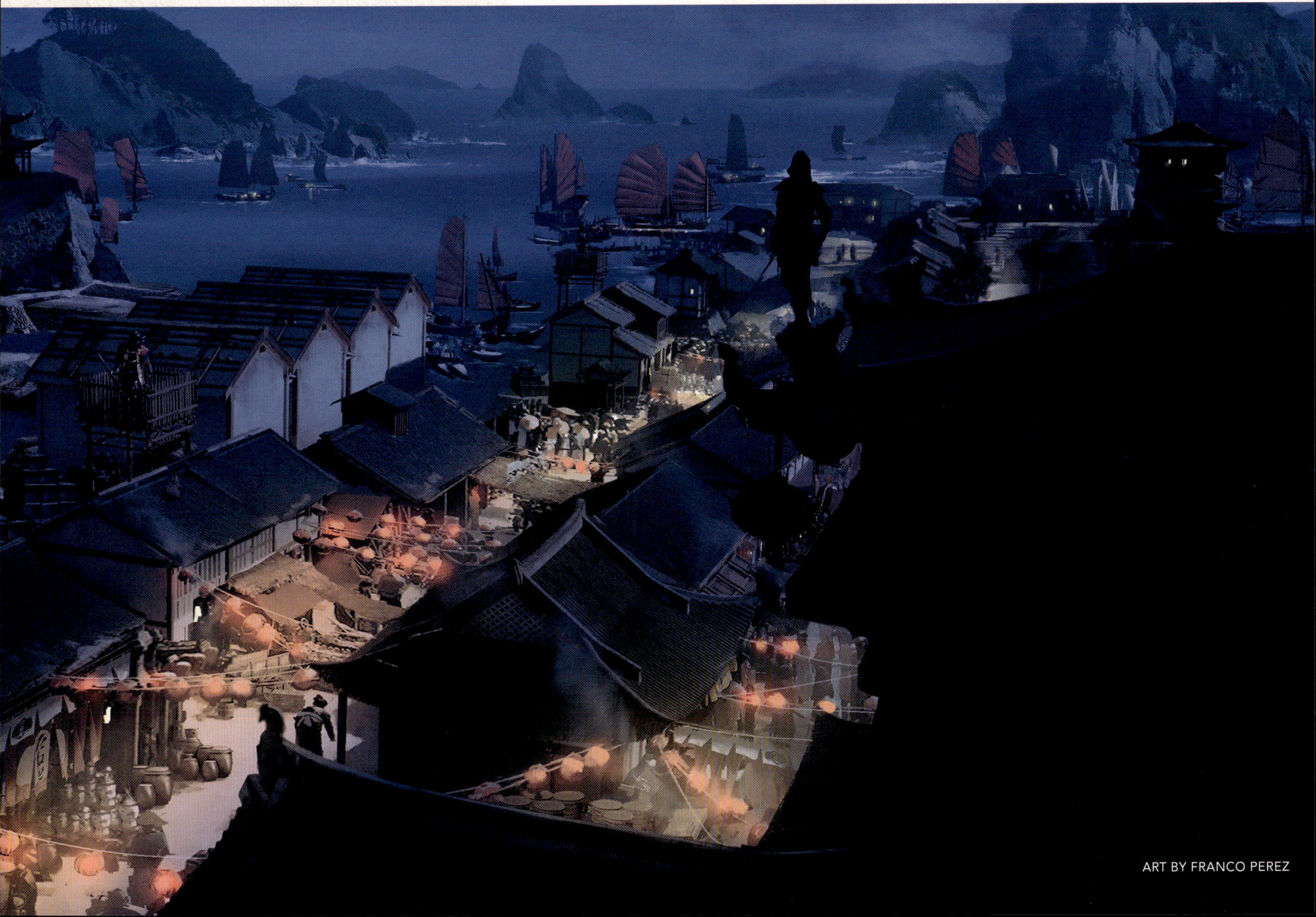

ART BY FRANCO PEREZ

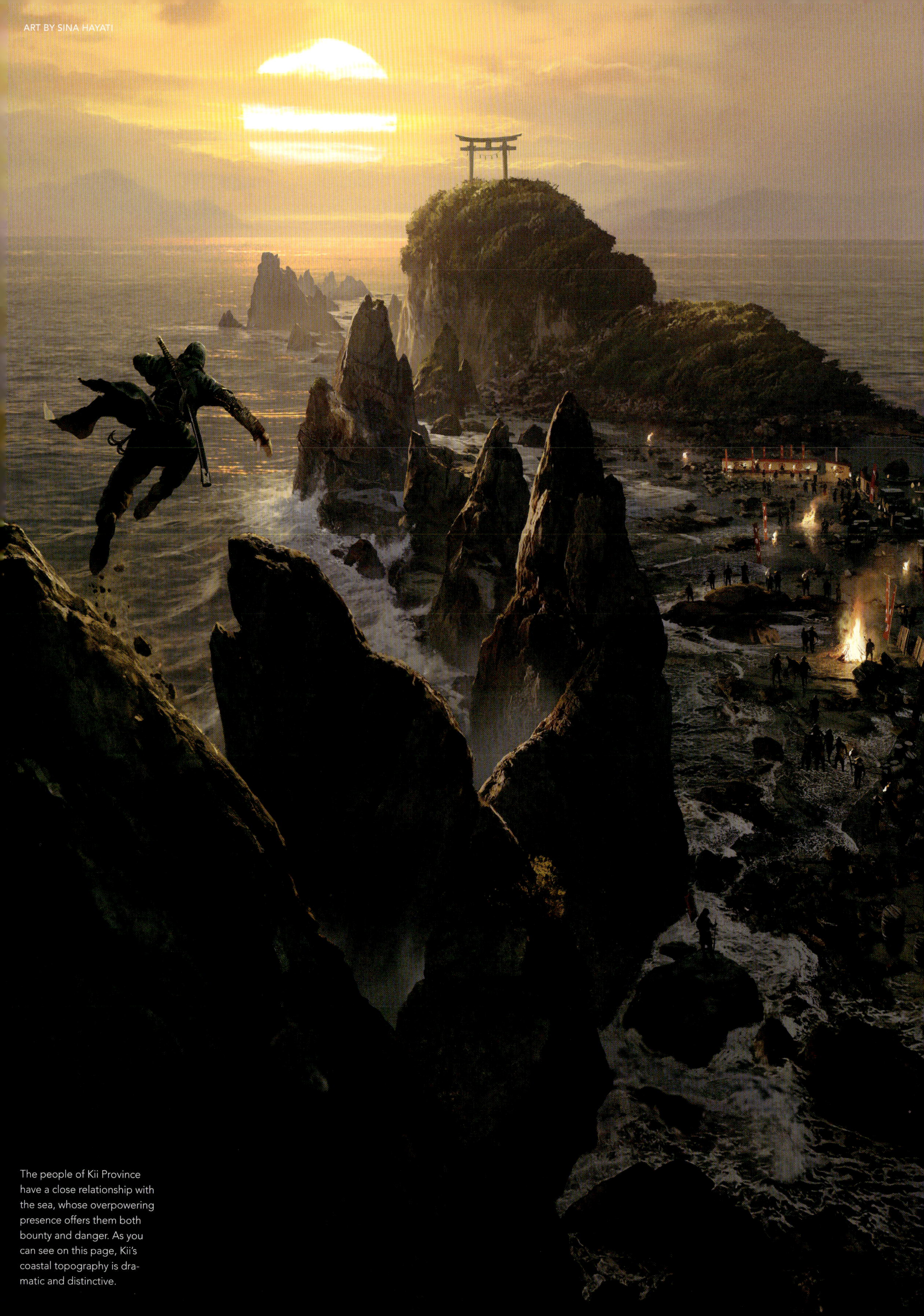

ART BY SINA HAYATI

The people of Kii Province have a close relationship with the sea, whose overpowering presence offers them both bounty and danger. As you can see on this page, Kii's coastal topography is dramatic and distinctive.

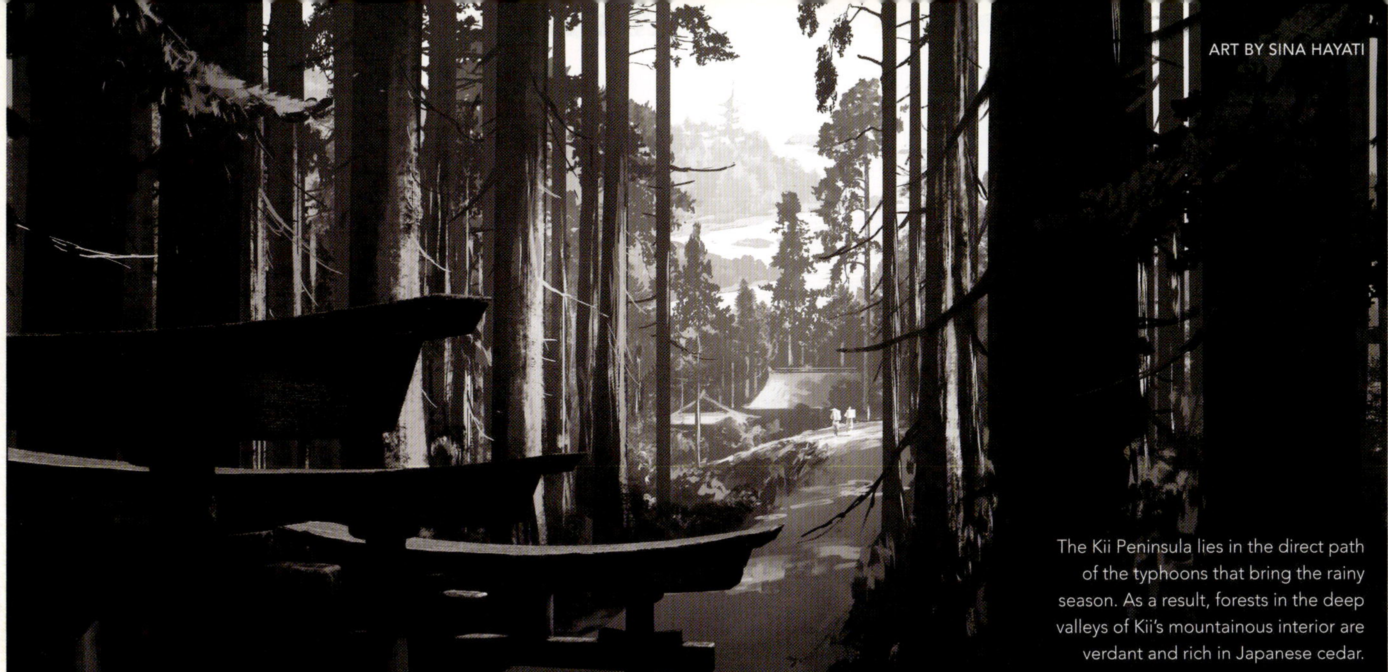

The Kii Peninsula lies in the direct path of the typhoons that bring the rainy season. As a result, forests in the deep valleys of Kii's mountainous interior are verdant and rich in Japanese cedar.

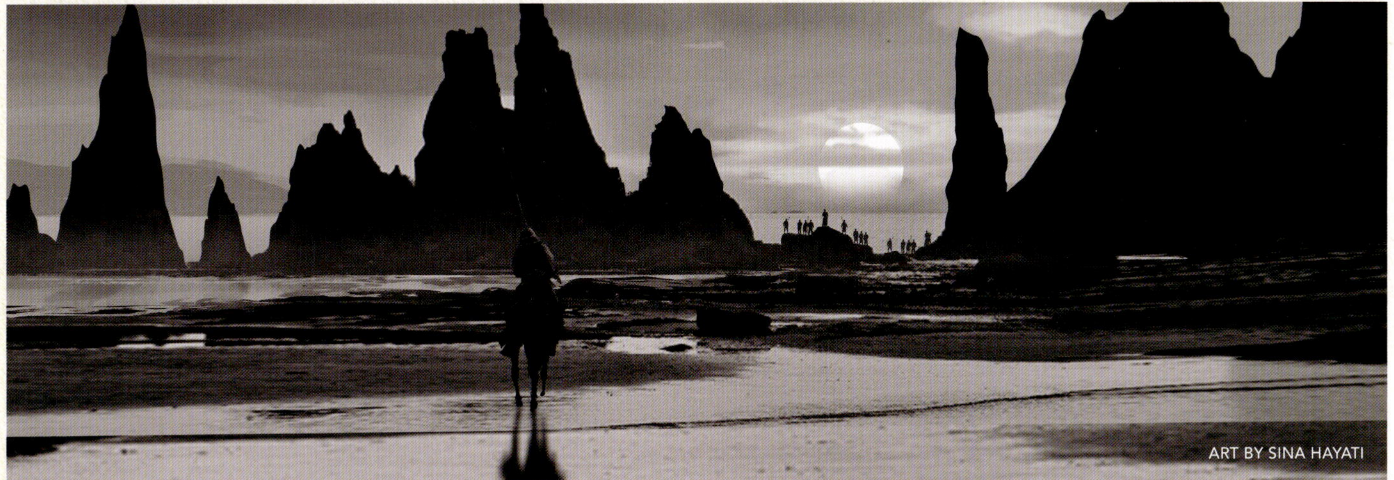

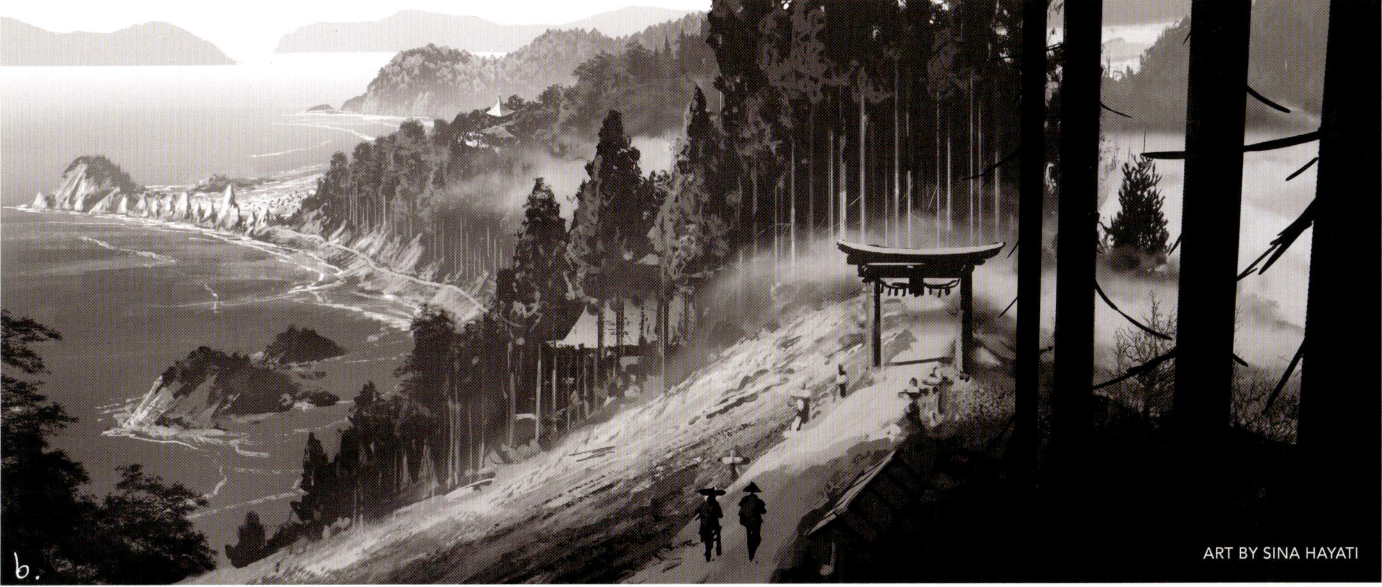

KII *THE SPIRITUAL JOURNEY*

Despite the turmoil of war, the people of Japan often seek spiritual enlightenment in pilgrimage. In Kii Province, a region filled with shrines and temples, a strong collective of religious believers—warriors, peasants, and sailors—fight to preserve Kii's political autonomy against Oda Nobunaga's unification campaign. The province is well known for its remarkable artists and craftspeople, producing distinct goods such as lacquerware, woodcuts, and exquisite fan and umbrella designs.

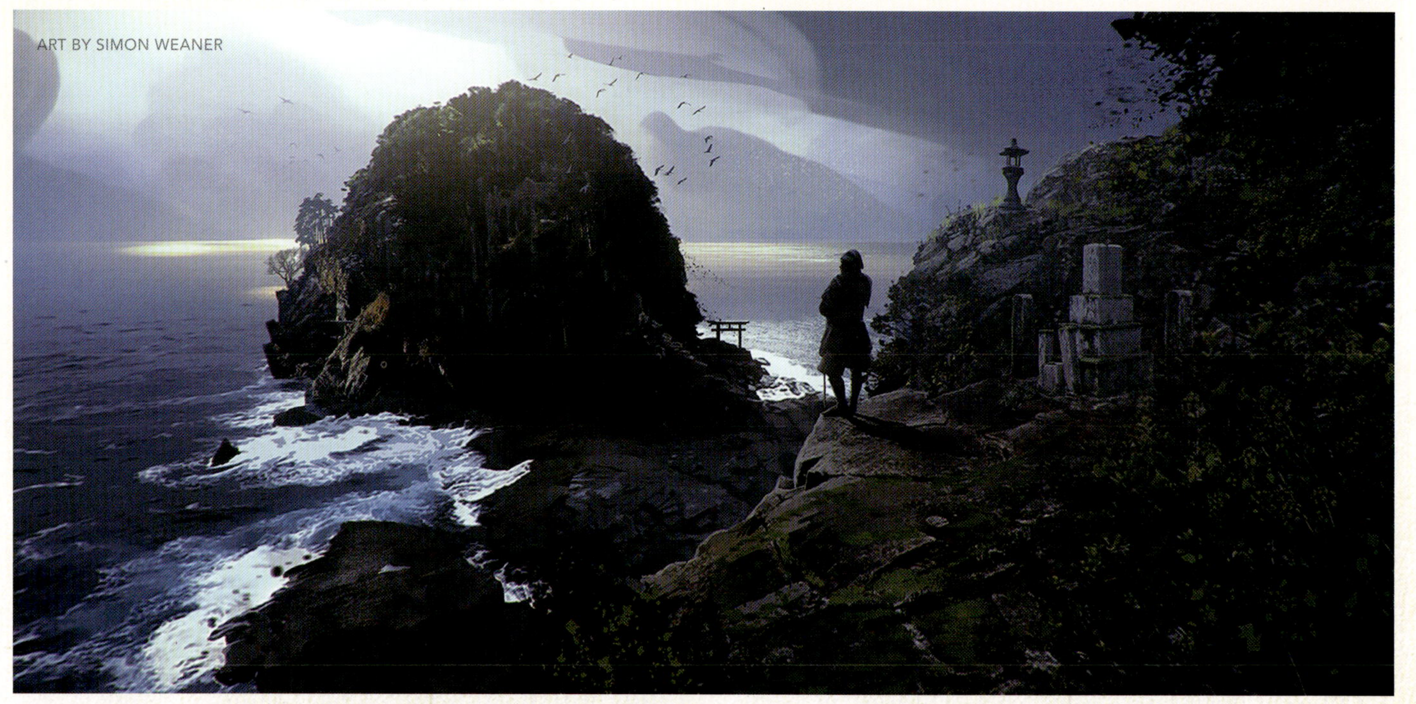

ART BY SIMON WEANER

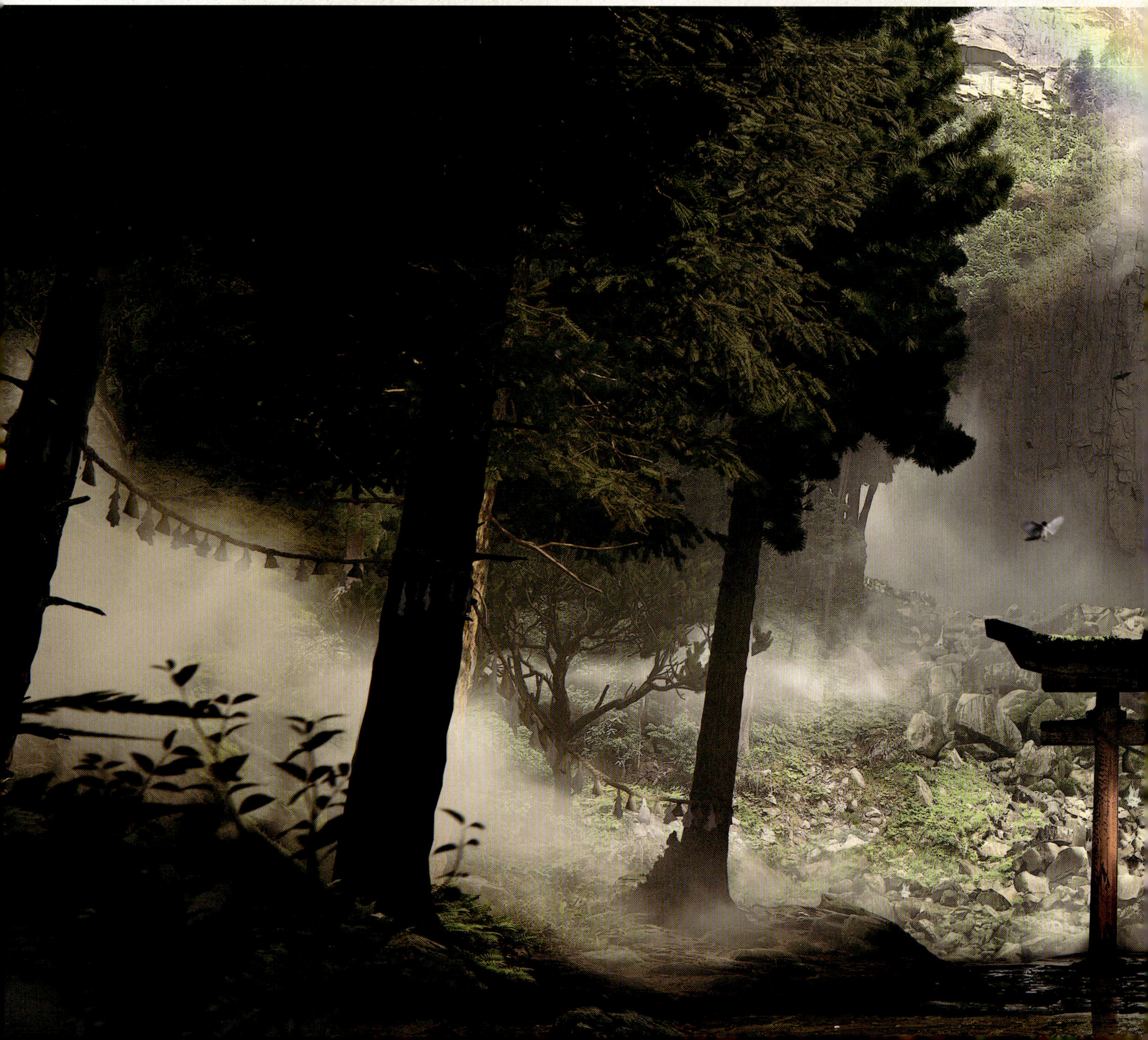

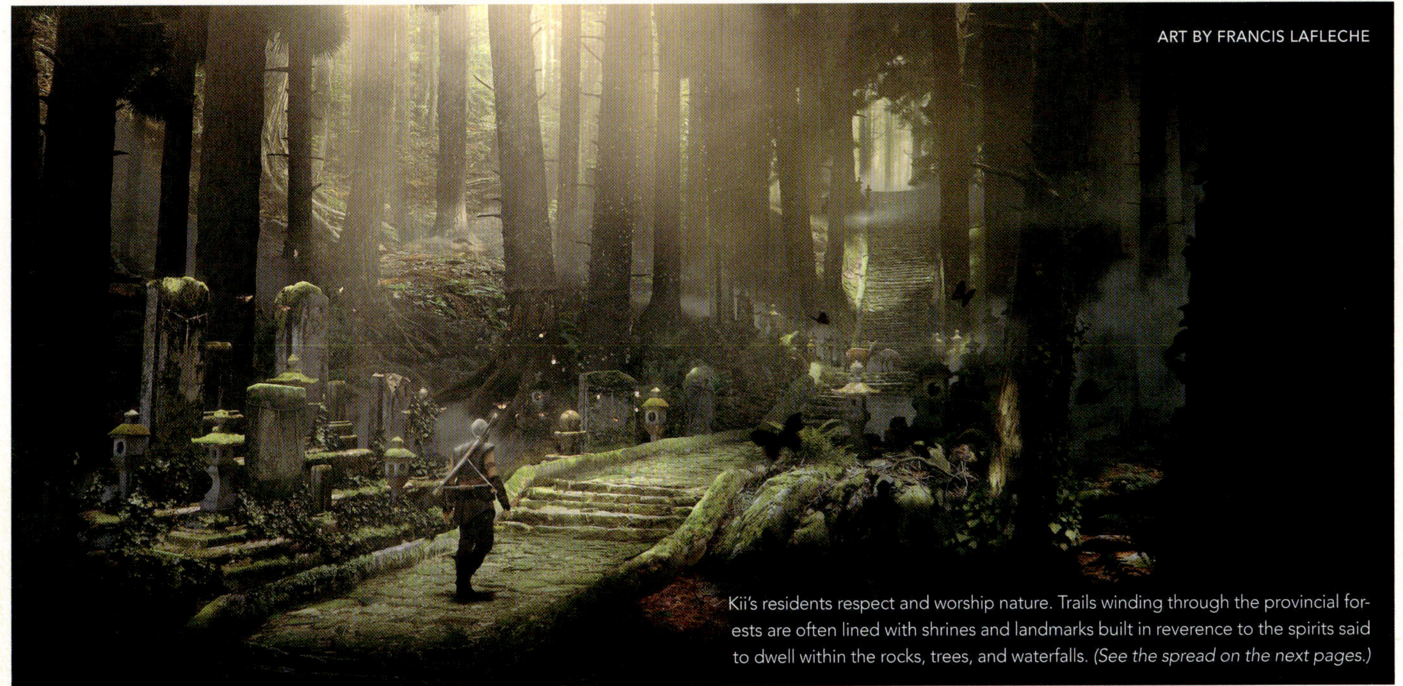

ART BY FRANCIS LAFLECHE

Kii's residents respect and worship nature. Trails winding through the provincial forests are often lined with shrines and landmarks built in reverence to the spirits said to dwell within the rocks, trees, and waterfalls. *(See the spread on the next pages.)*

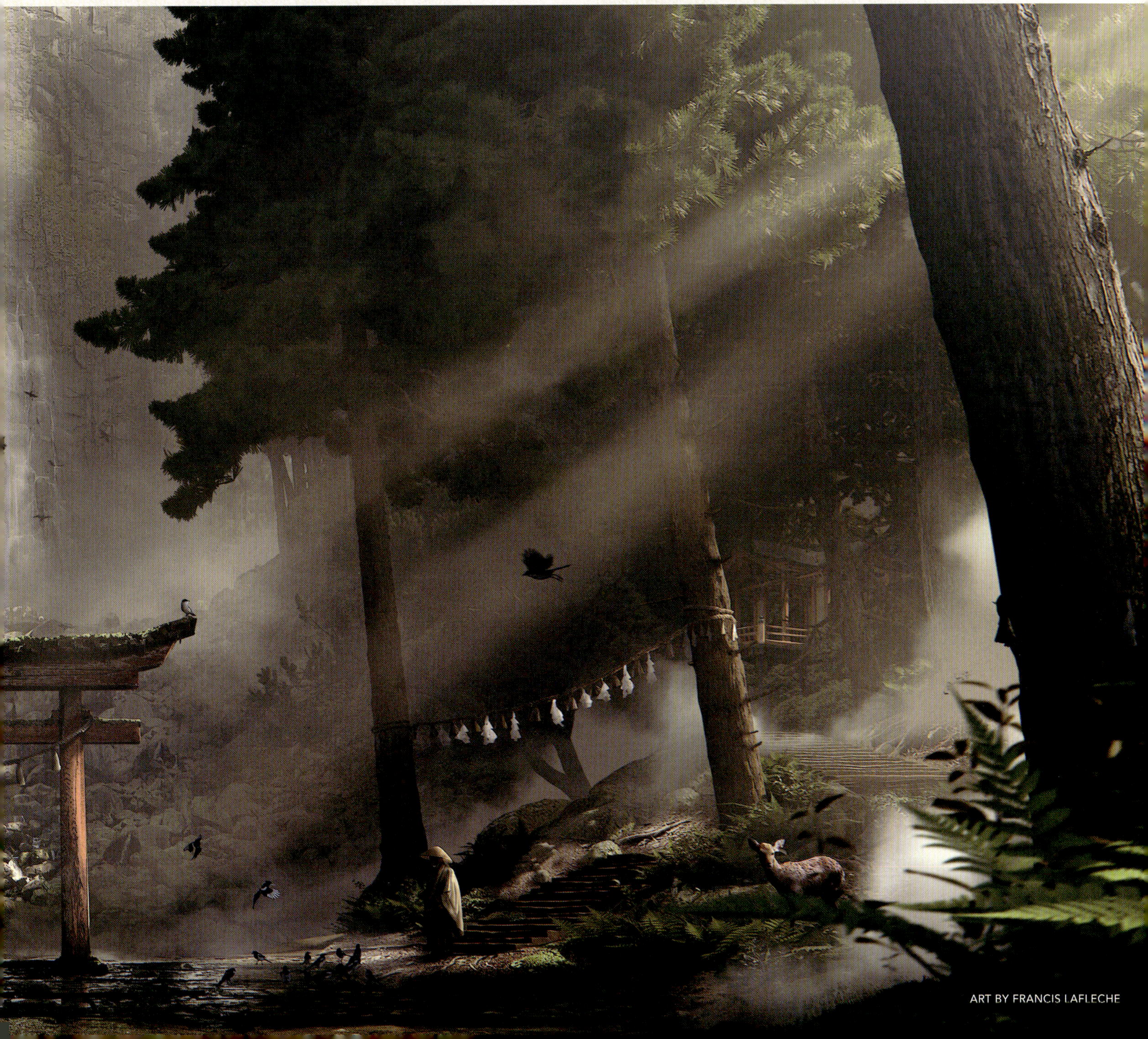

ART BY FRANCIS LAFLECHE

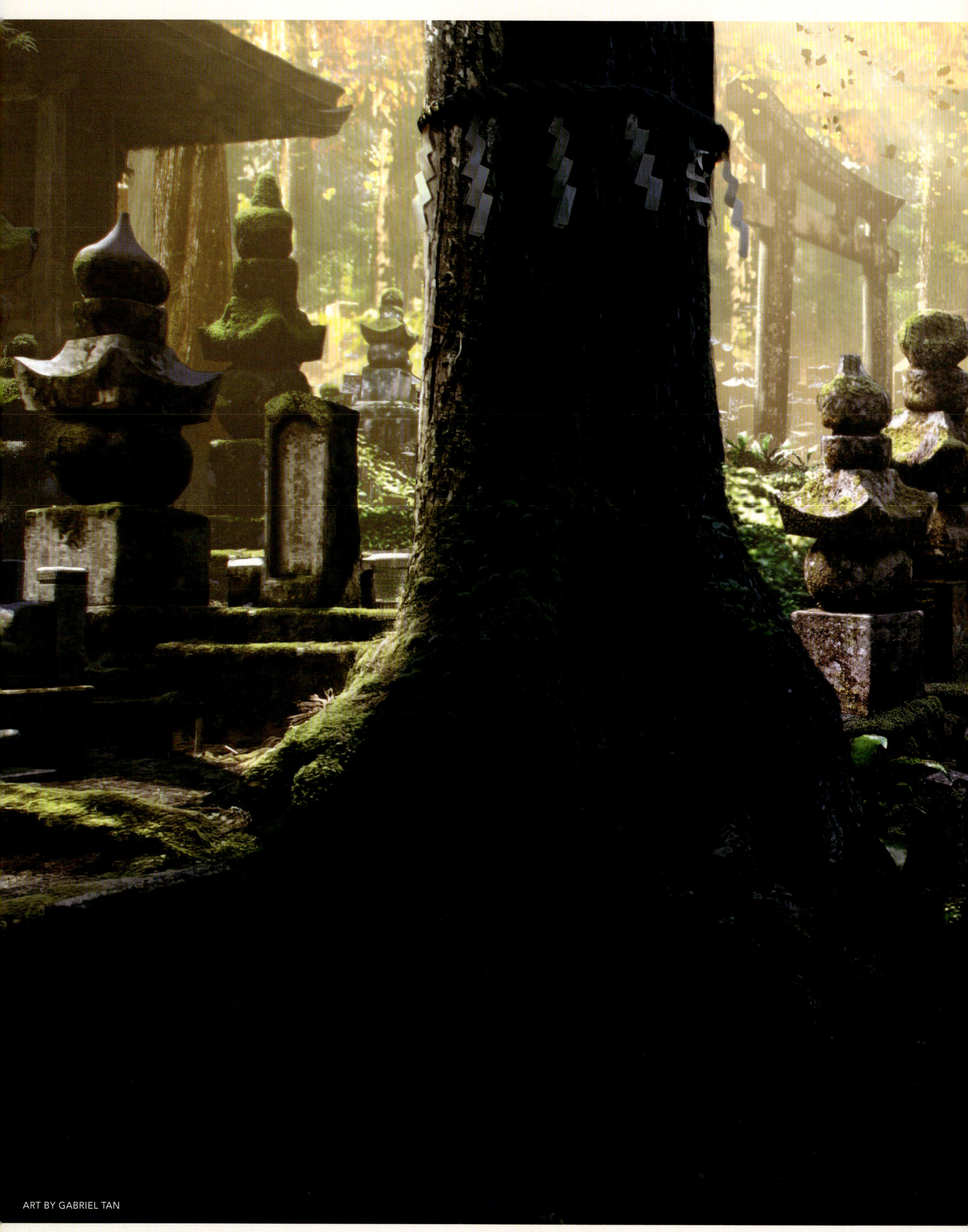

ART BY GABRIEL TAN

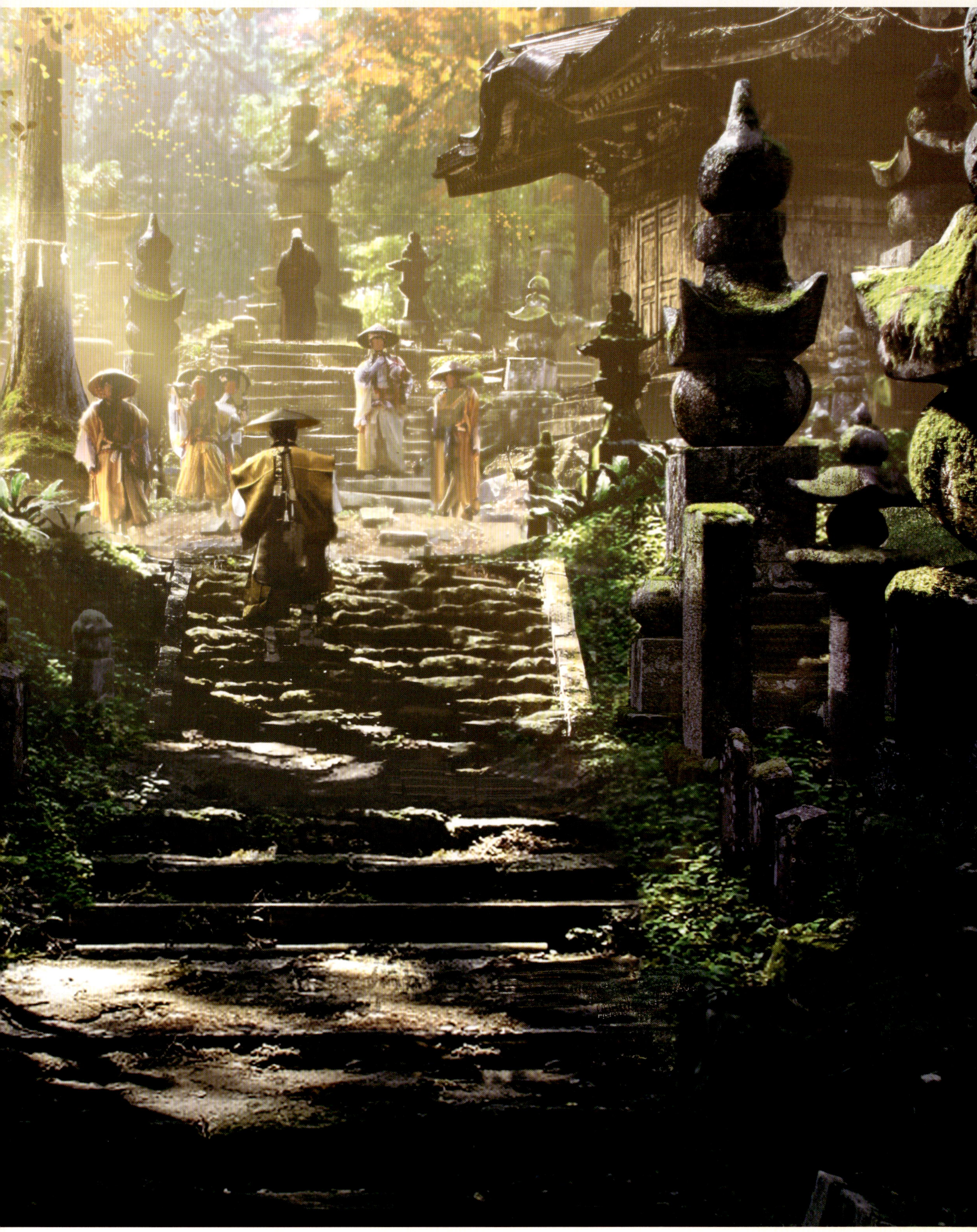

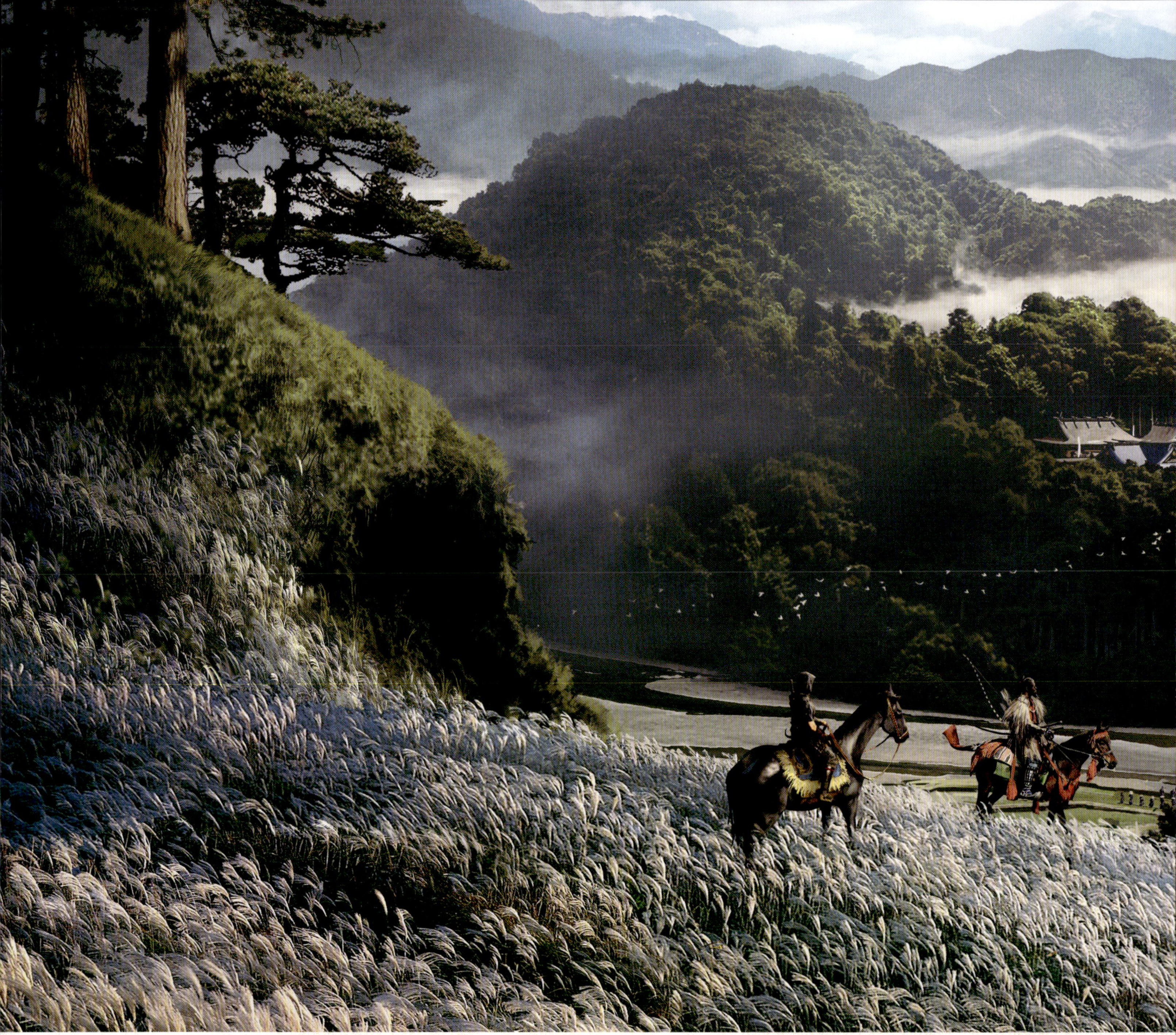

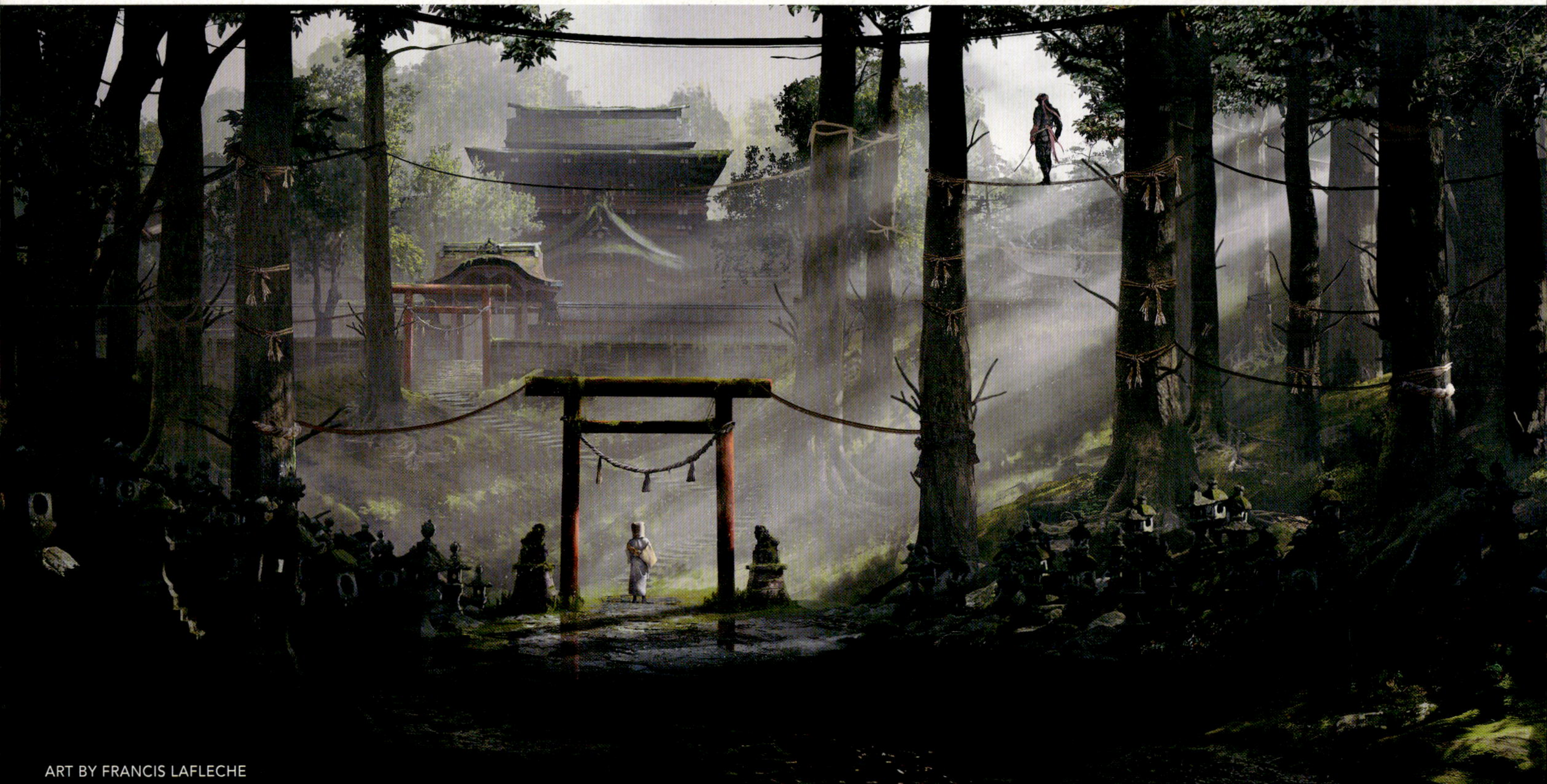

ART BY FRANCIS LAFLECHE

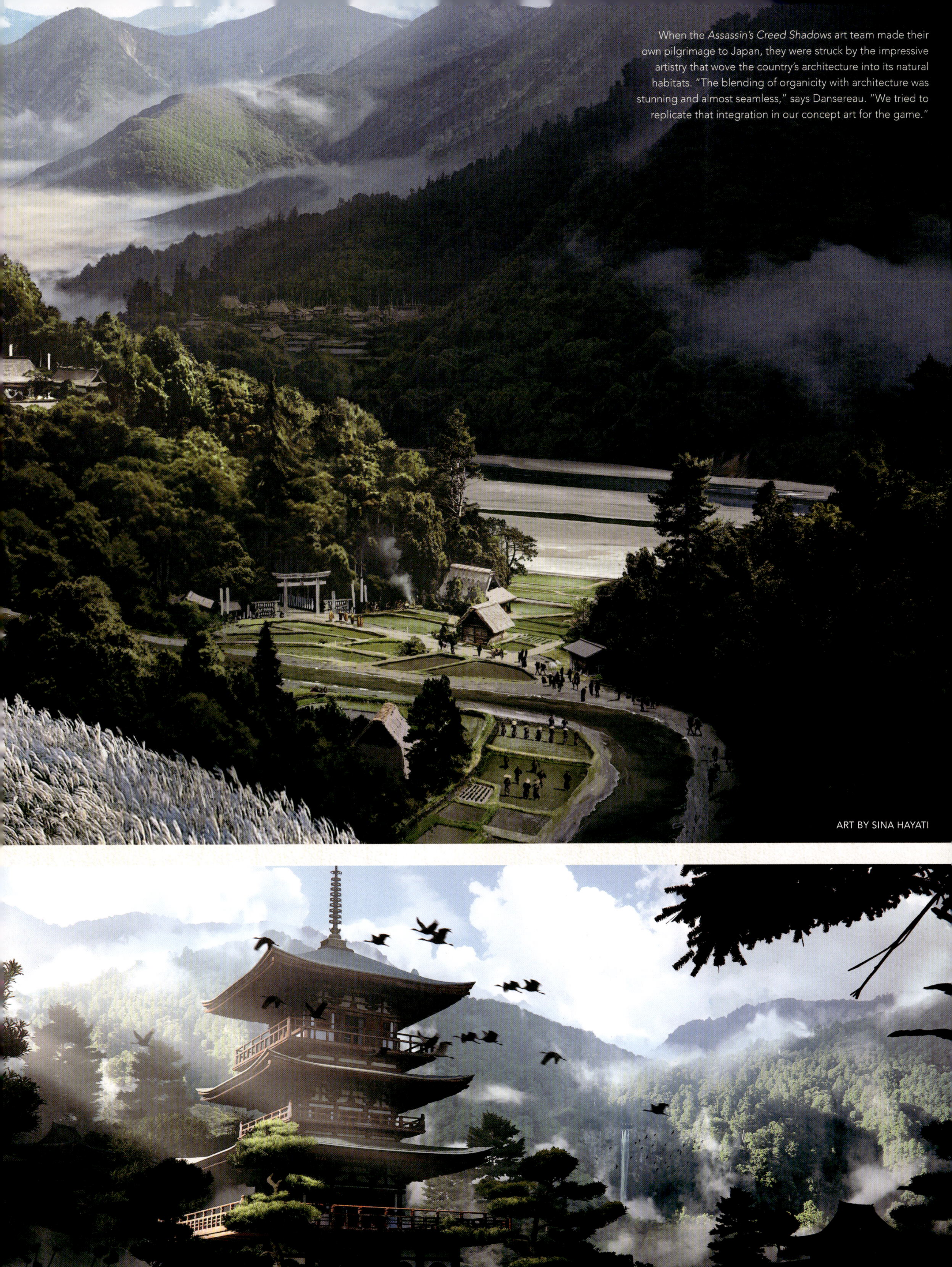

When the *Assassin's Creed Shadows* art team made their own pilgrimage to Japan, they were struck by the impressive artistry that wove the country's architecture into its natural habitats. "The blending of organicity with architecture was stunning and almost seamless," says Dansereau. "We tried to replicate that integration in our concept art for the game."

ART BY SINA HAYATI

ART BY FRANCIS LAFLECHE

NATURE OF JAPAN

The *Assassin's Creed* series is known for crafting hyper-realistic biomes that are as meticulously researched as a master's thesis in natural science. "It's true, every game is back to school for us," says Vincent Lamontagne, associate art director and head of the biomes team. Indeed, the art team's research for *Assassin's Creed Shadows* took Lamontagne on an educational scouting trip to Japan to survey some of the most stunning natural beauty on the planet. "A reverence for nature is deeply embedded in Japanese culture," he says, "and we really wanted to honor that."

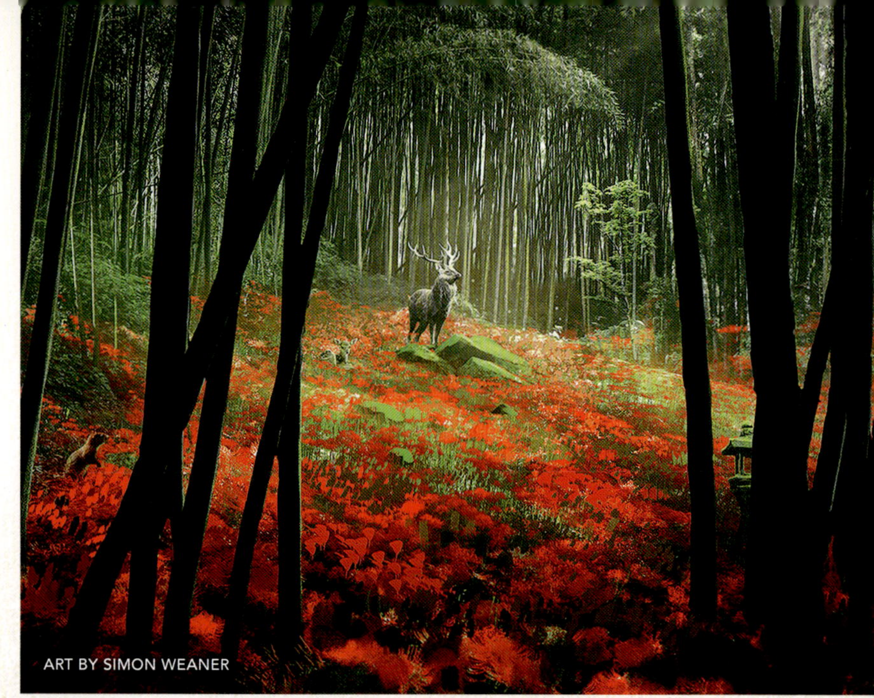

ART BY SIMON WEANER

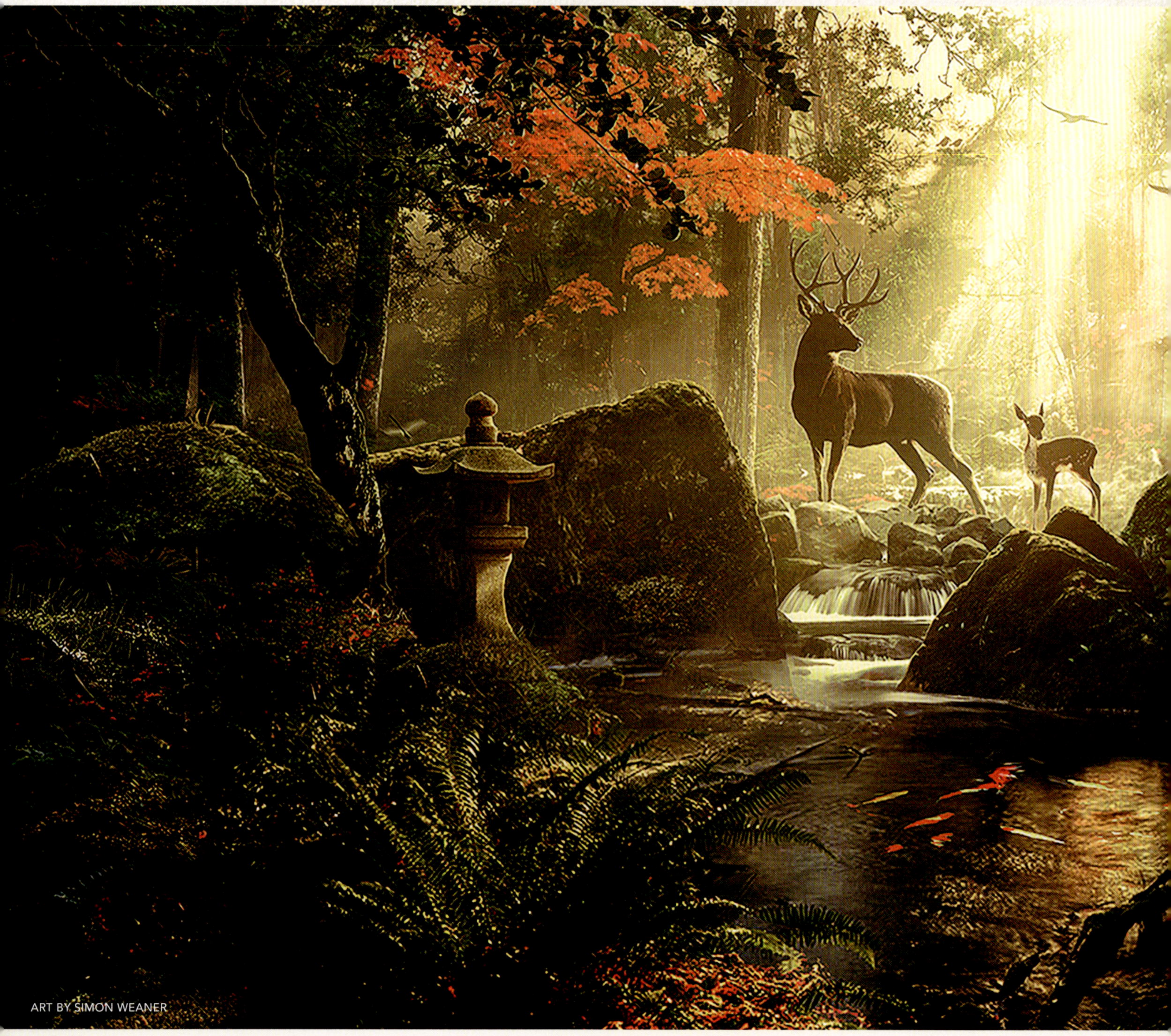

ART BY SIMON WEANER

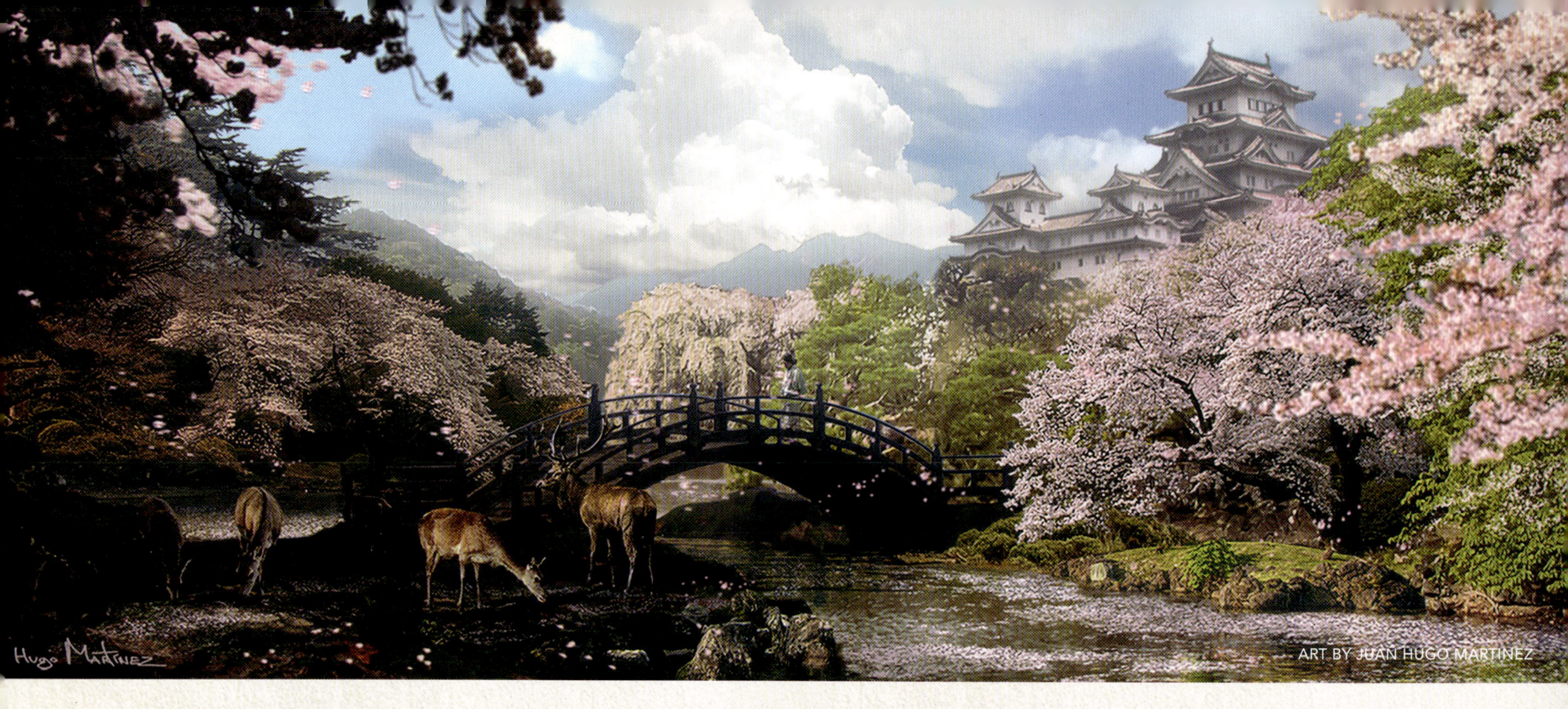

ART BY JUAN HUGO MARTINEZ

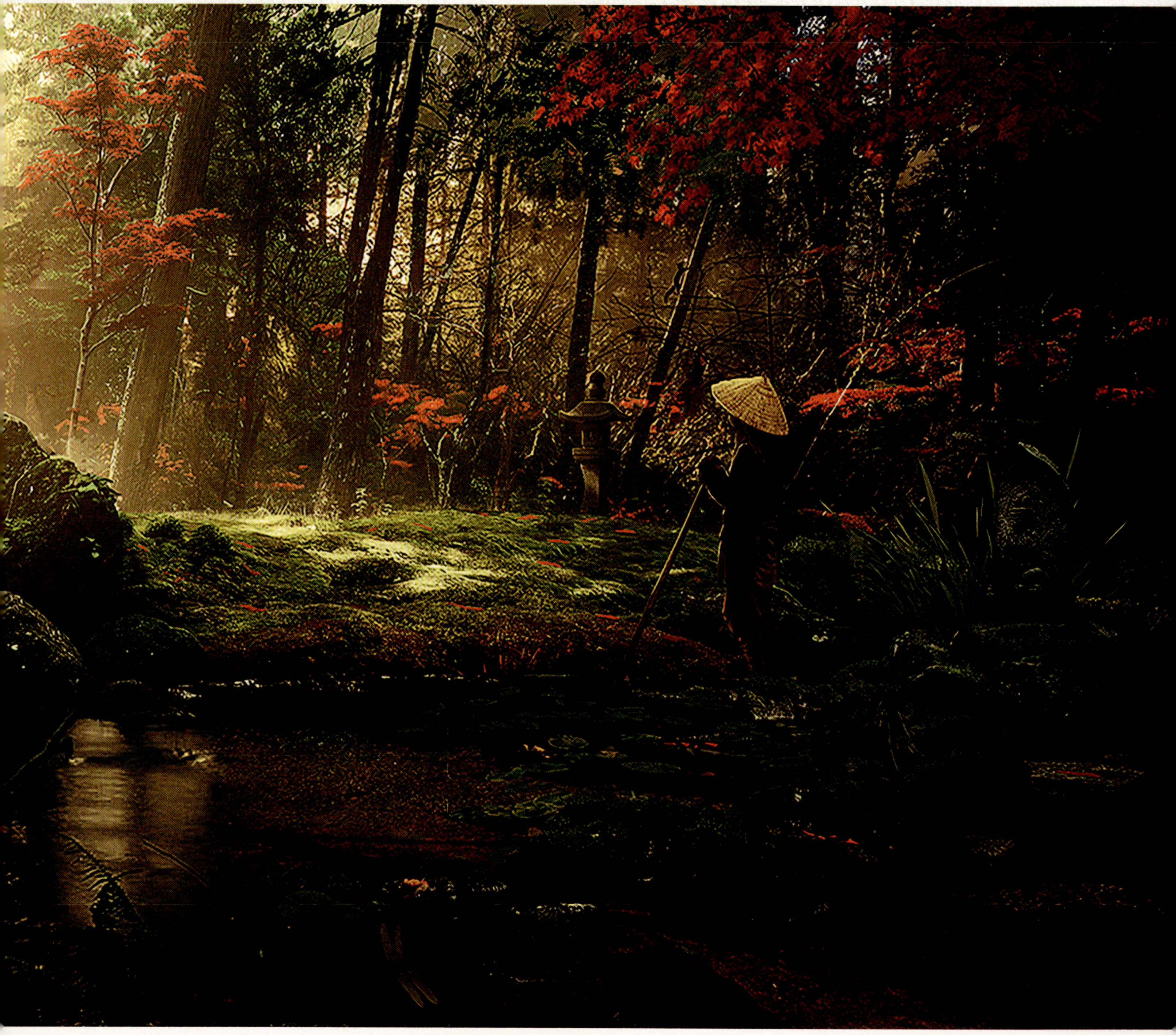

Shadows' new and innovative "dynamic seasons" technology posed a major test for Lamontagne's team—biomes in each region had to be re-created for all four seasons! "We had to render different states of the same place," he says. "But we thought the challenge was very cool; it got us fired up." *Below:* Concept art for spring and fall.

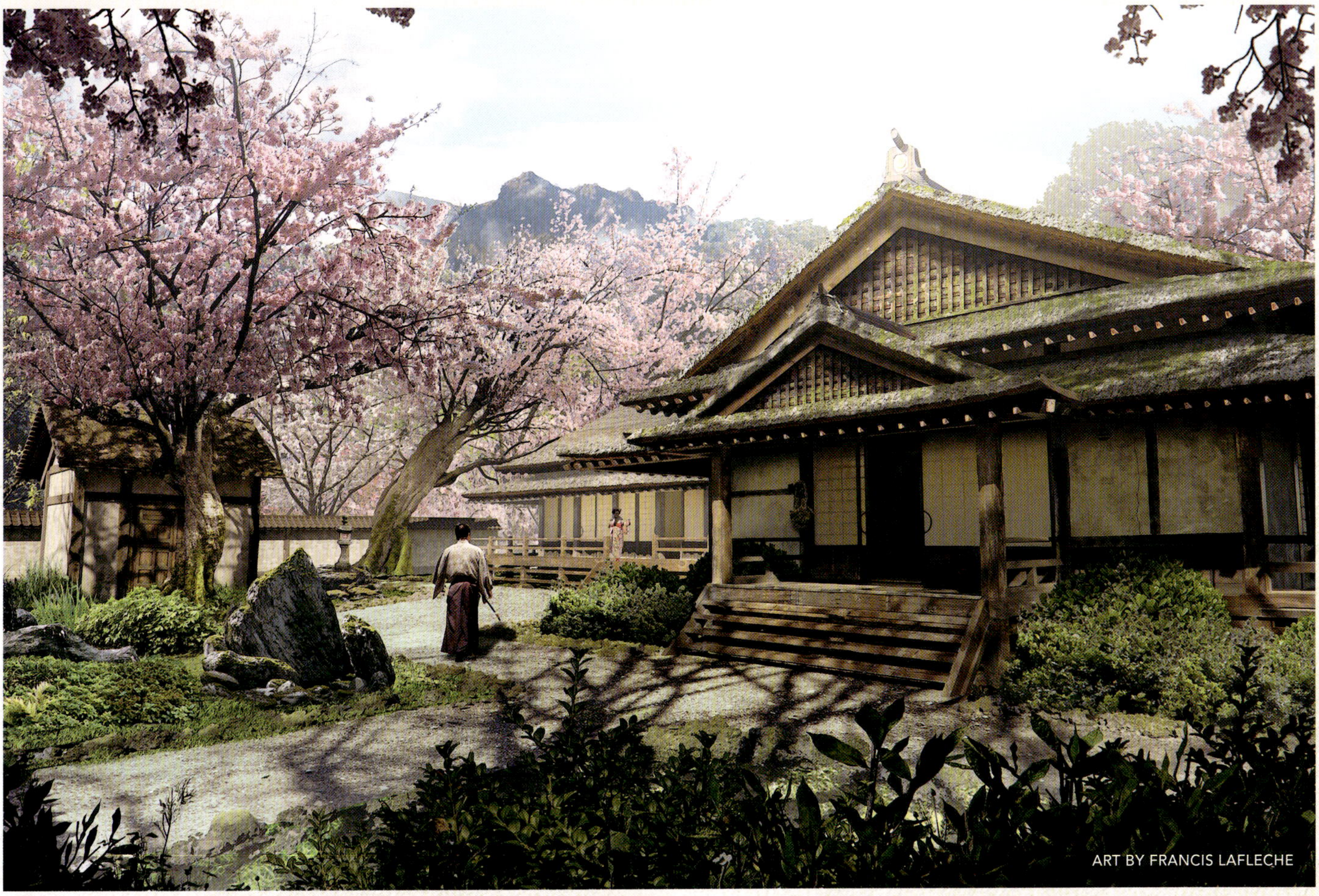

ART BY FRANCIS LAFLECHE

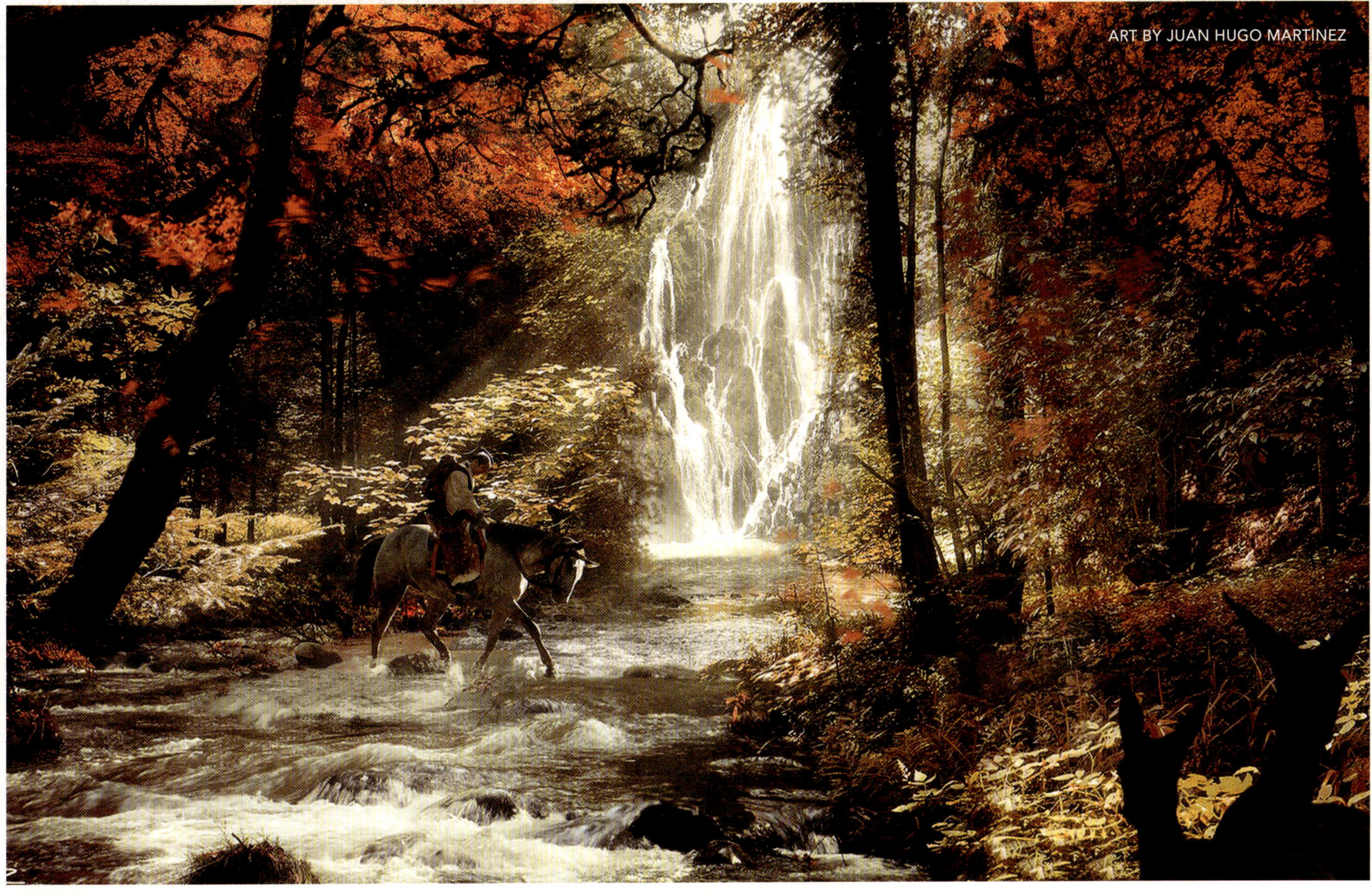

ART BY JUAN HUGO MARTINEZ

Diversity and dynamism were key pillars of the *Assassin's Creed Shadows* design philosophy and thus became a driving force behind the art direction. In the new weather system, the movements of nature—wind, rain, fog, smoke, snow—bring an ever-changing gameplay impact. *Below:* Concept art for the rainy summer season and winter.

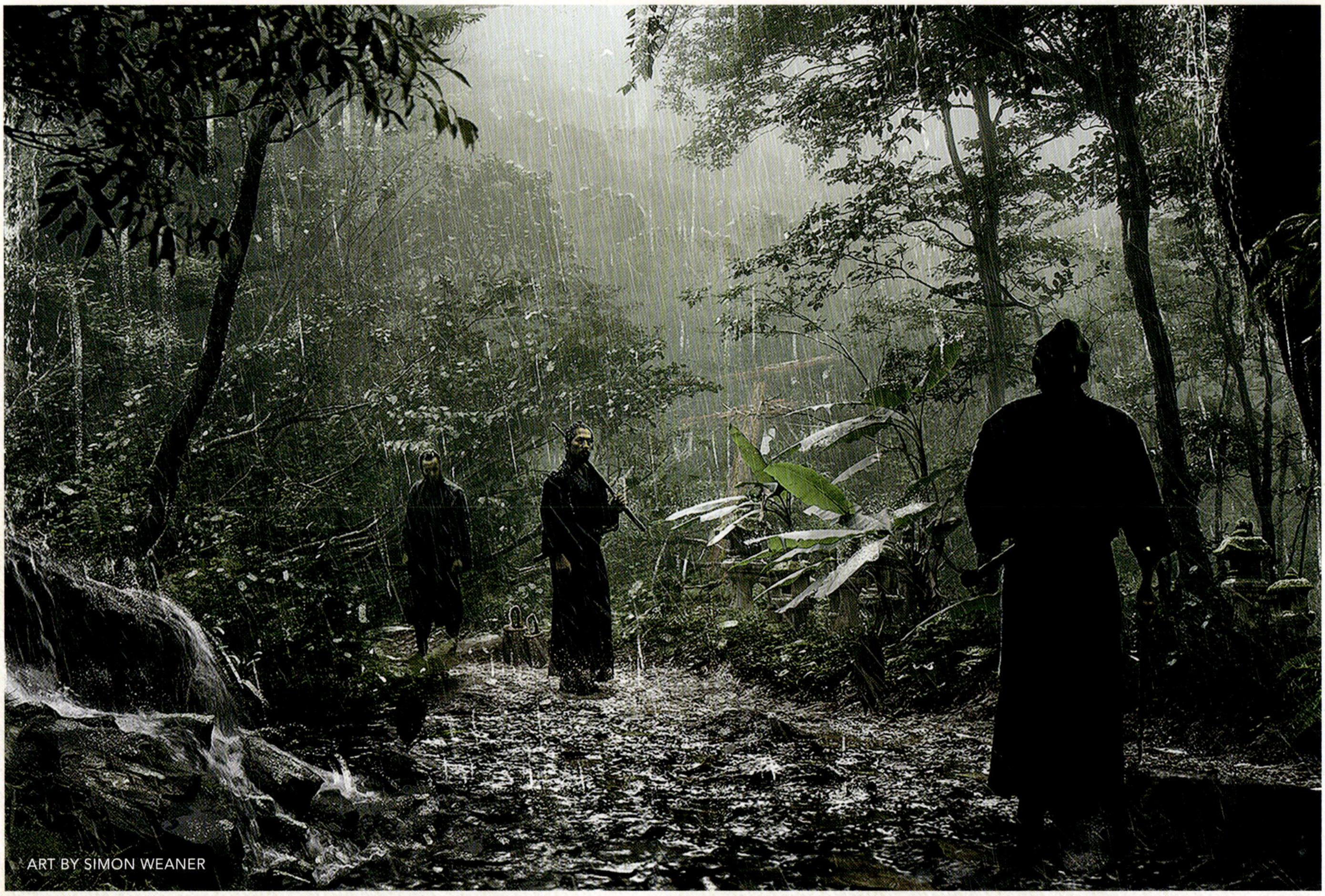

ART BY SIMON WEANER

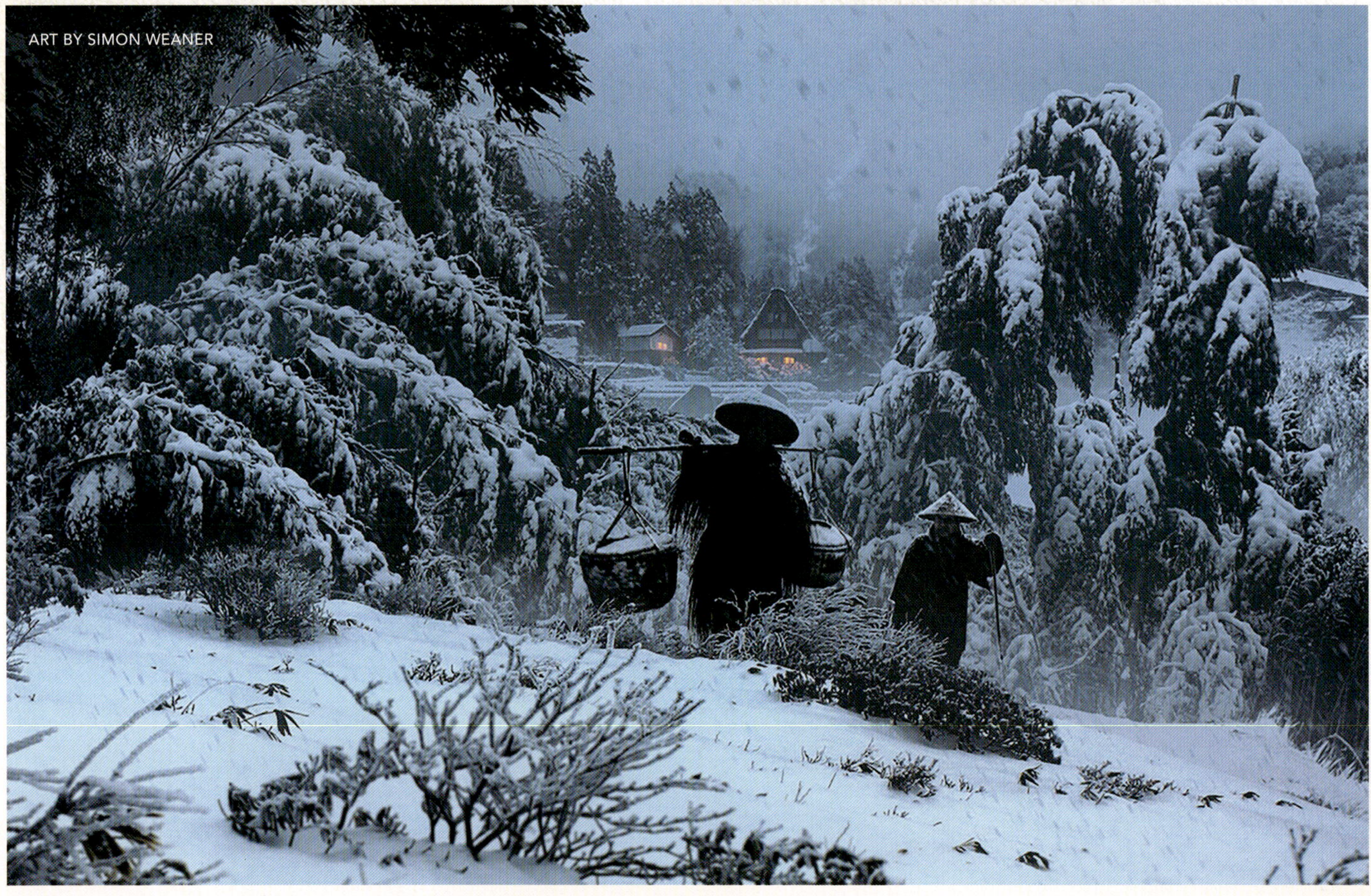

ART BY SIMON WEANER

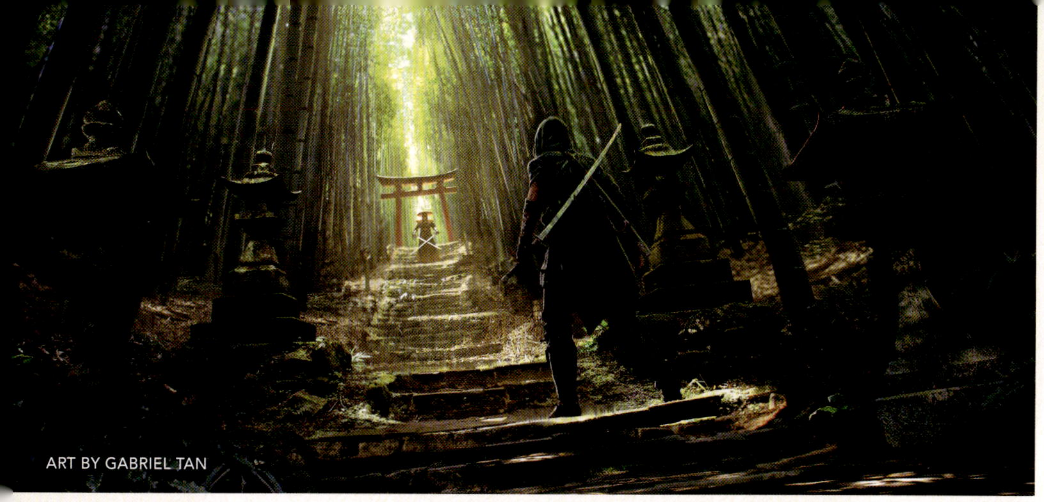

ART BY GABRIEL TAN

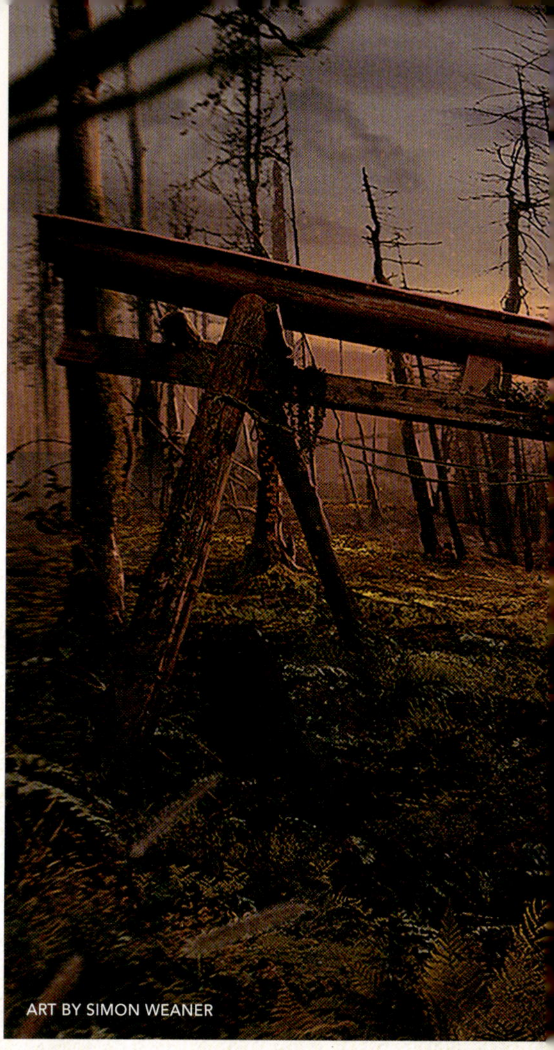

ART BY SIMON WEANER

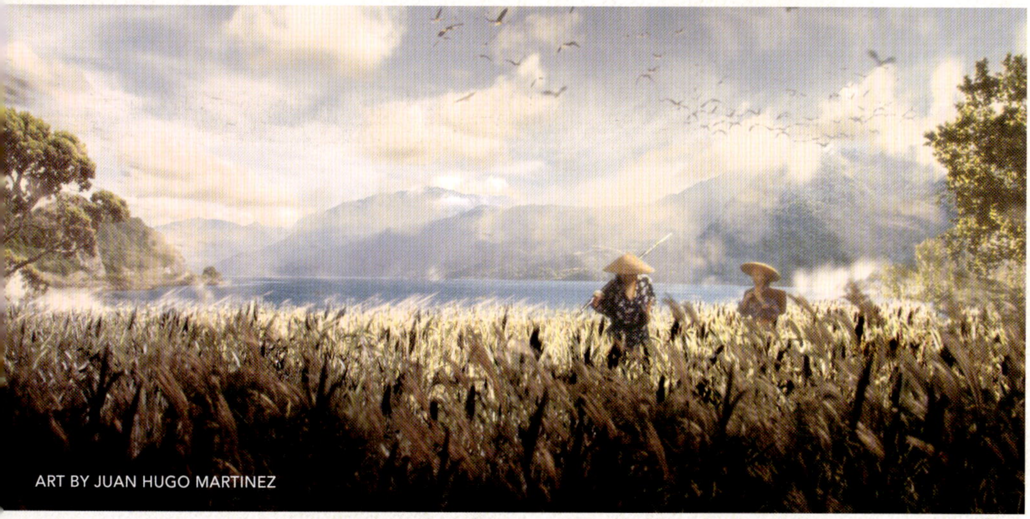

ART BY JUAN HUGO MARTINEZ

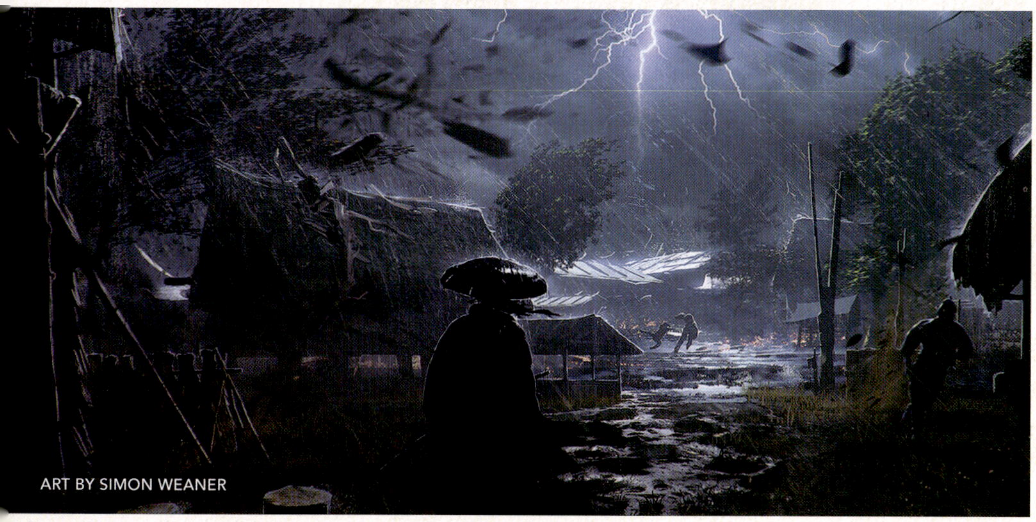

ART BY SIMON WEANER

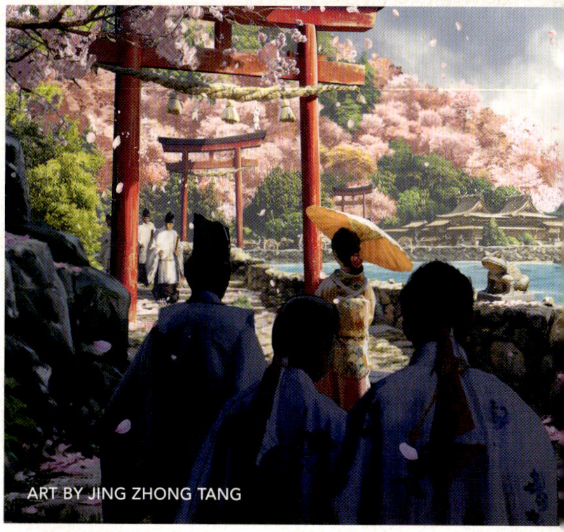

ART BY JING ZHONG TANG

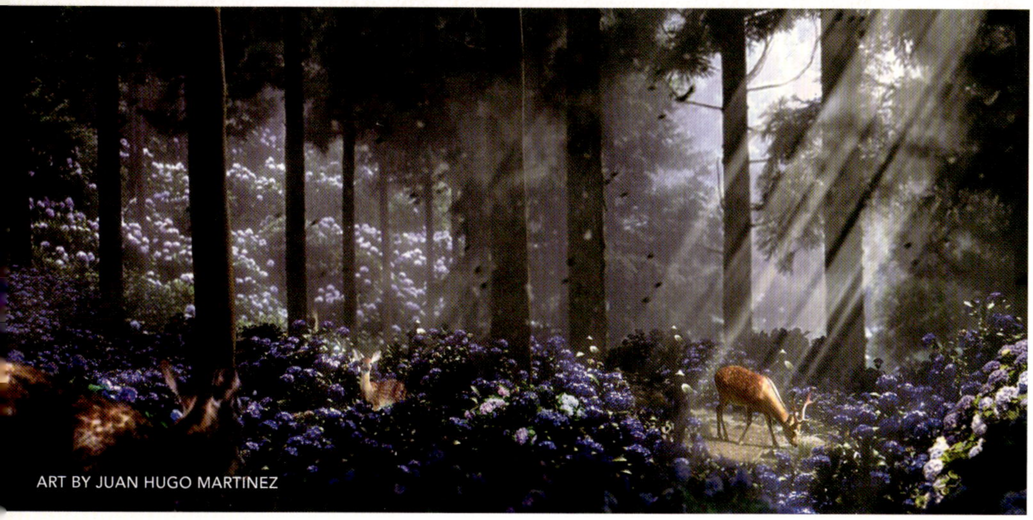

ART BY JUAN HUGO MARTINEZ

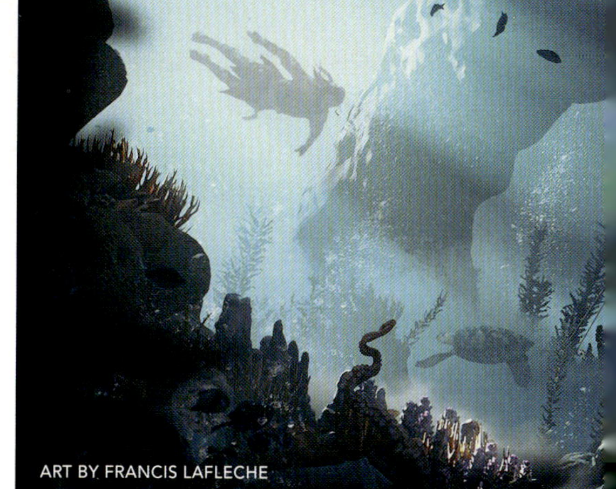

ART BY FRANCIS LAFLECHE

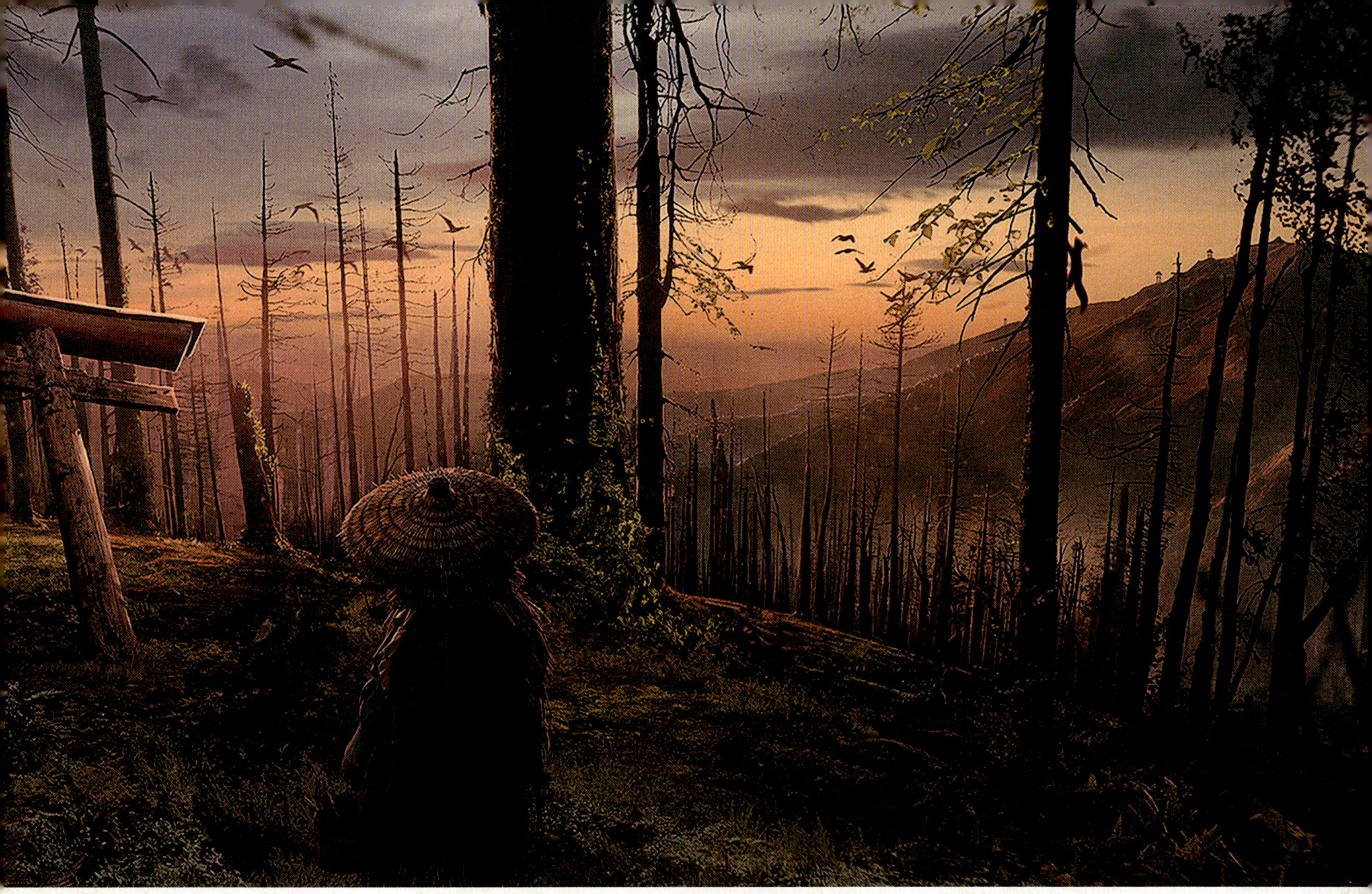

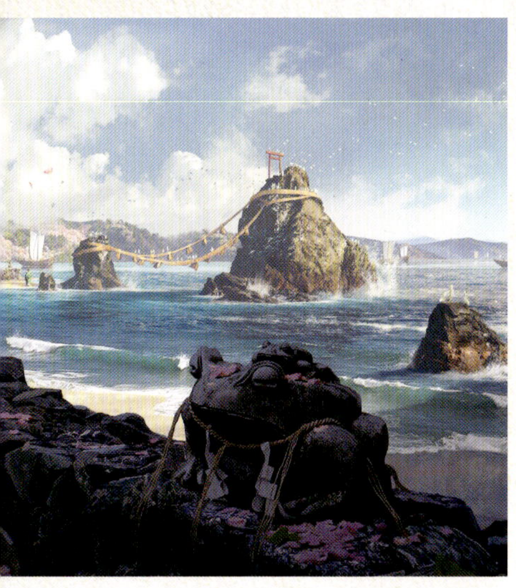

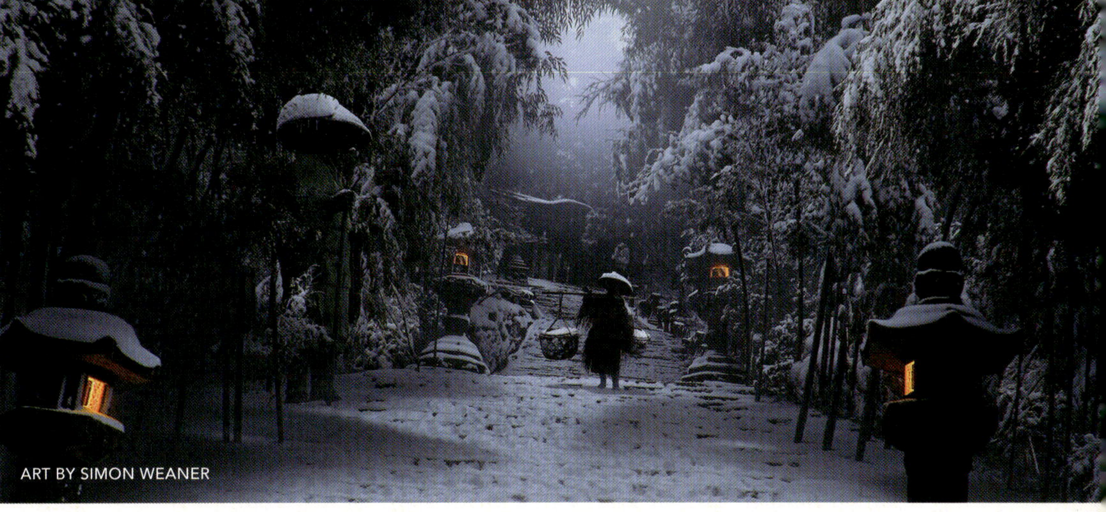

ART BY SIMON WEANER

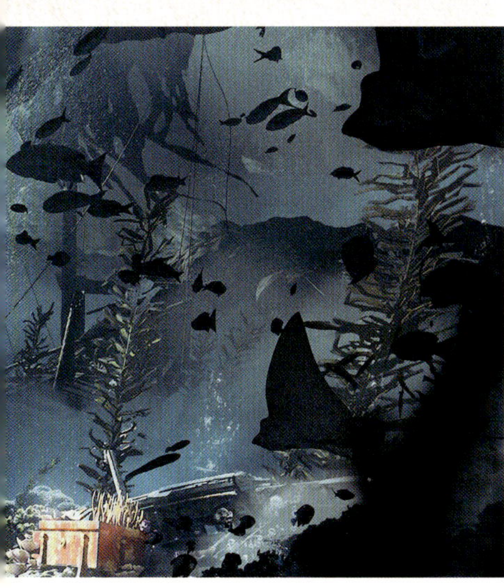

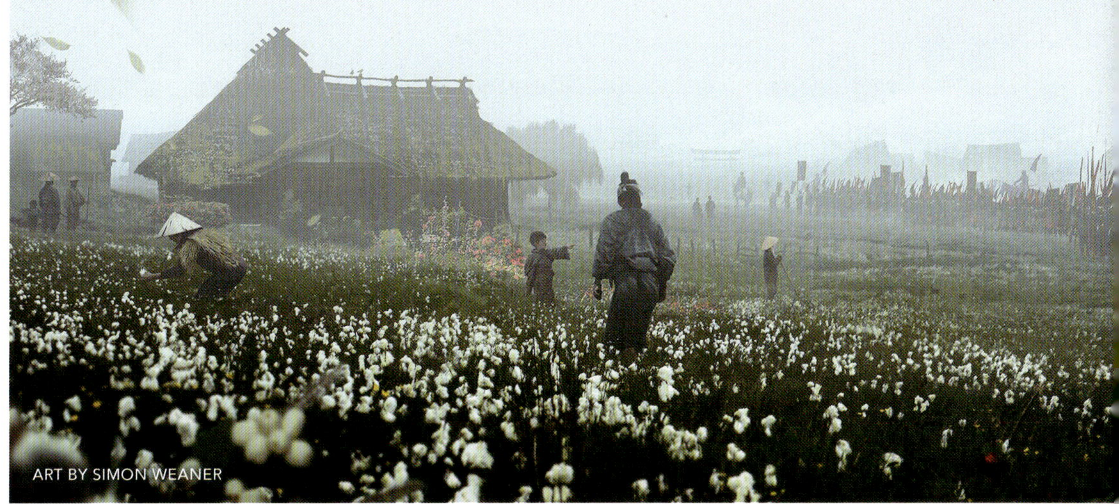

ART BY SIMON WEANER

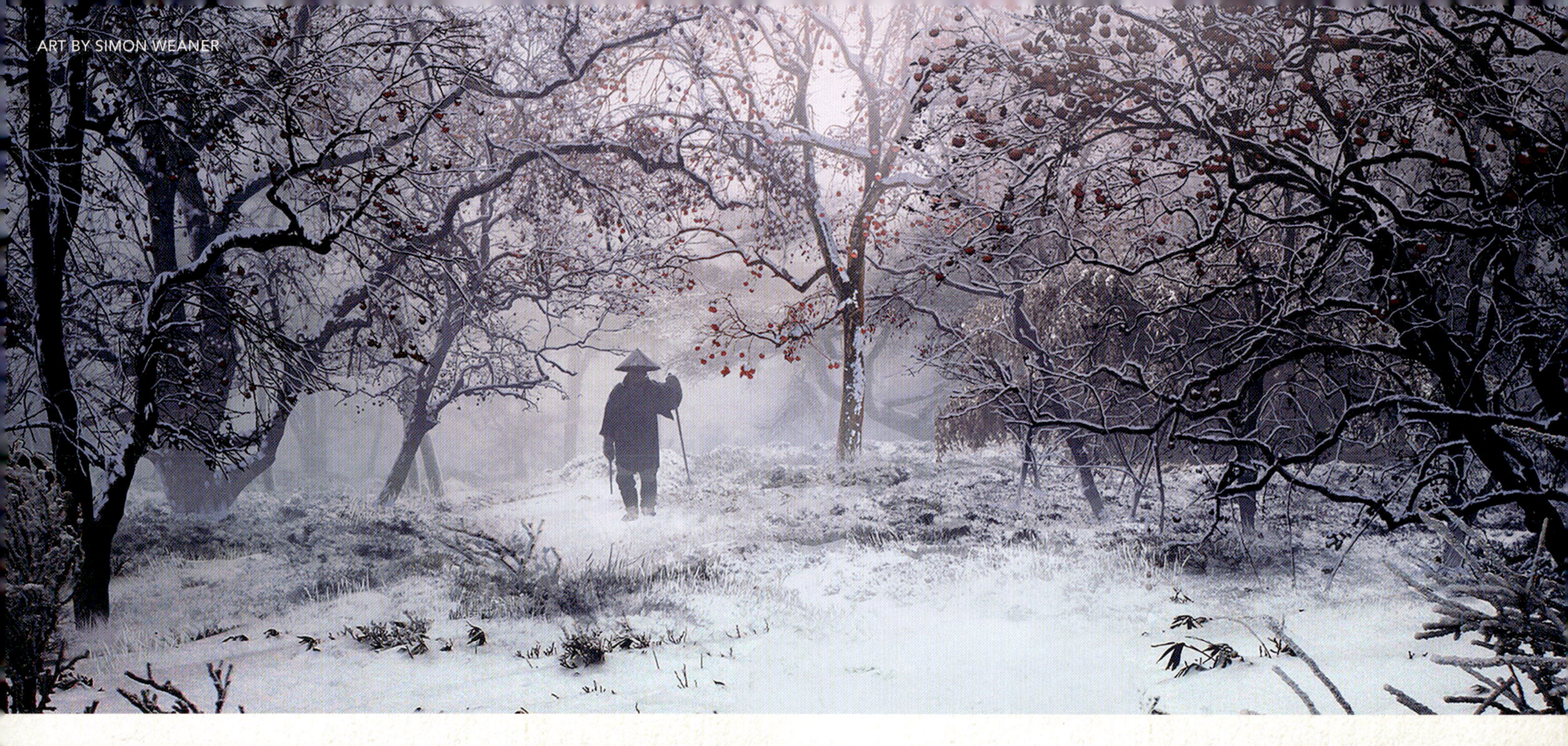
ART BY SIMON WEANER

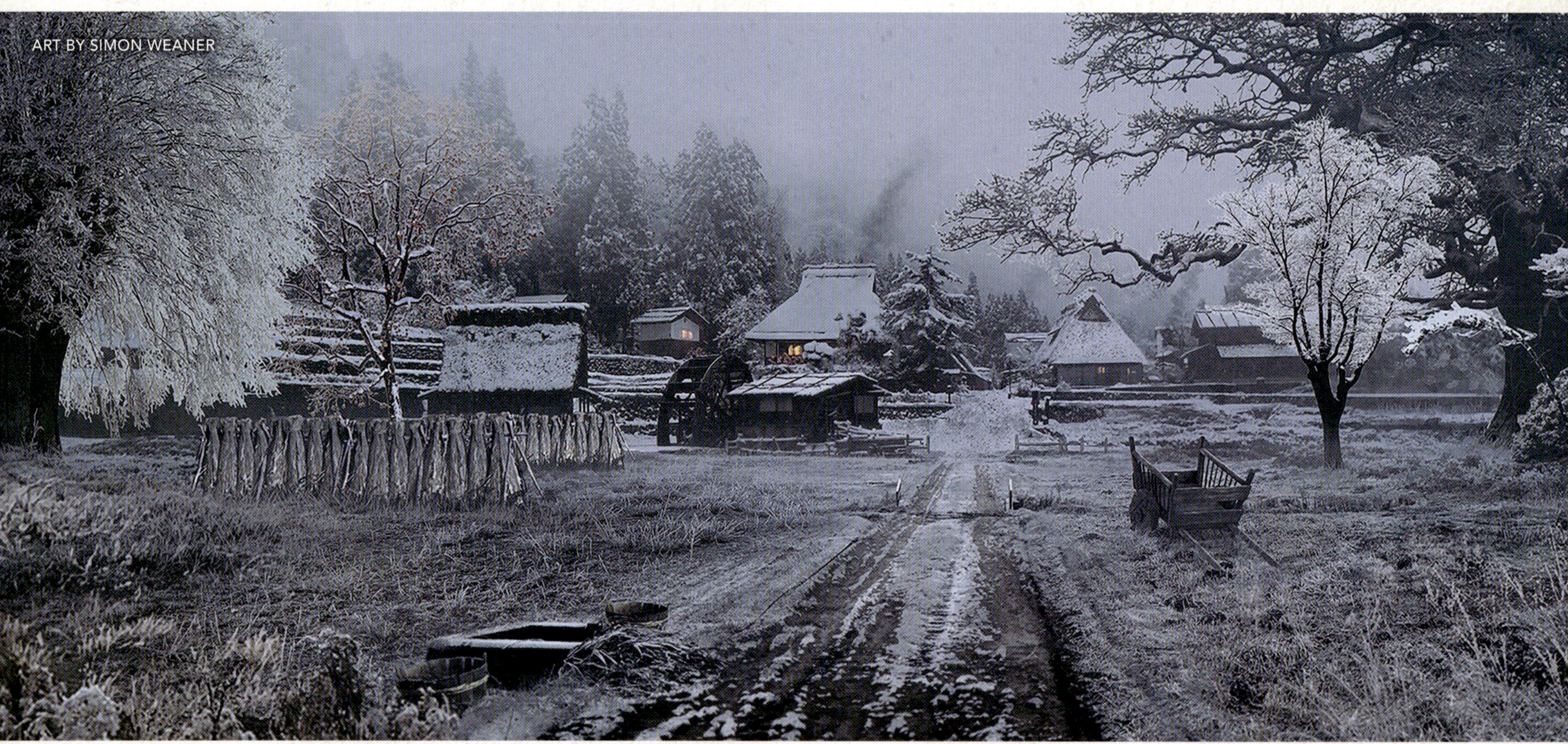
ART BY SIMON WEANER

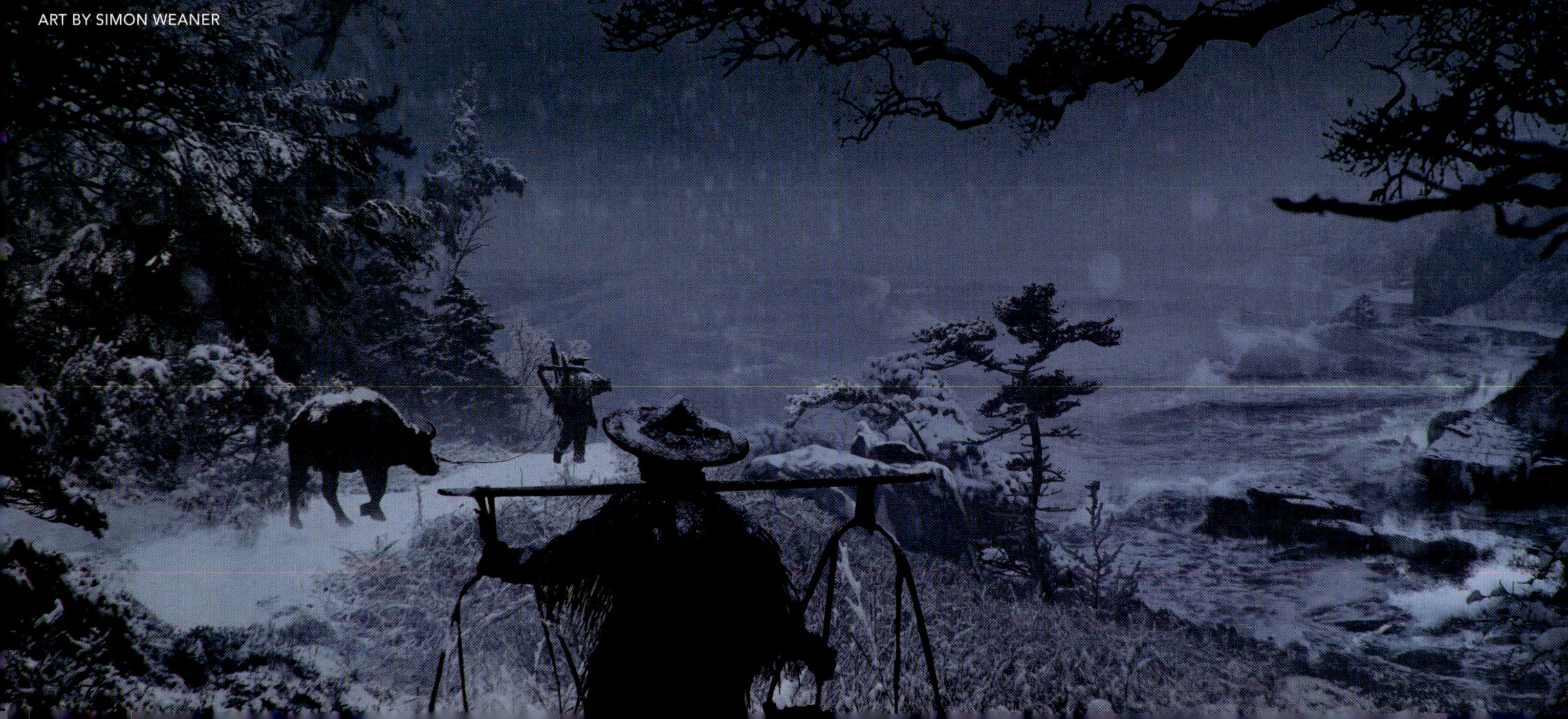
ART BY SIMON WEANER

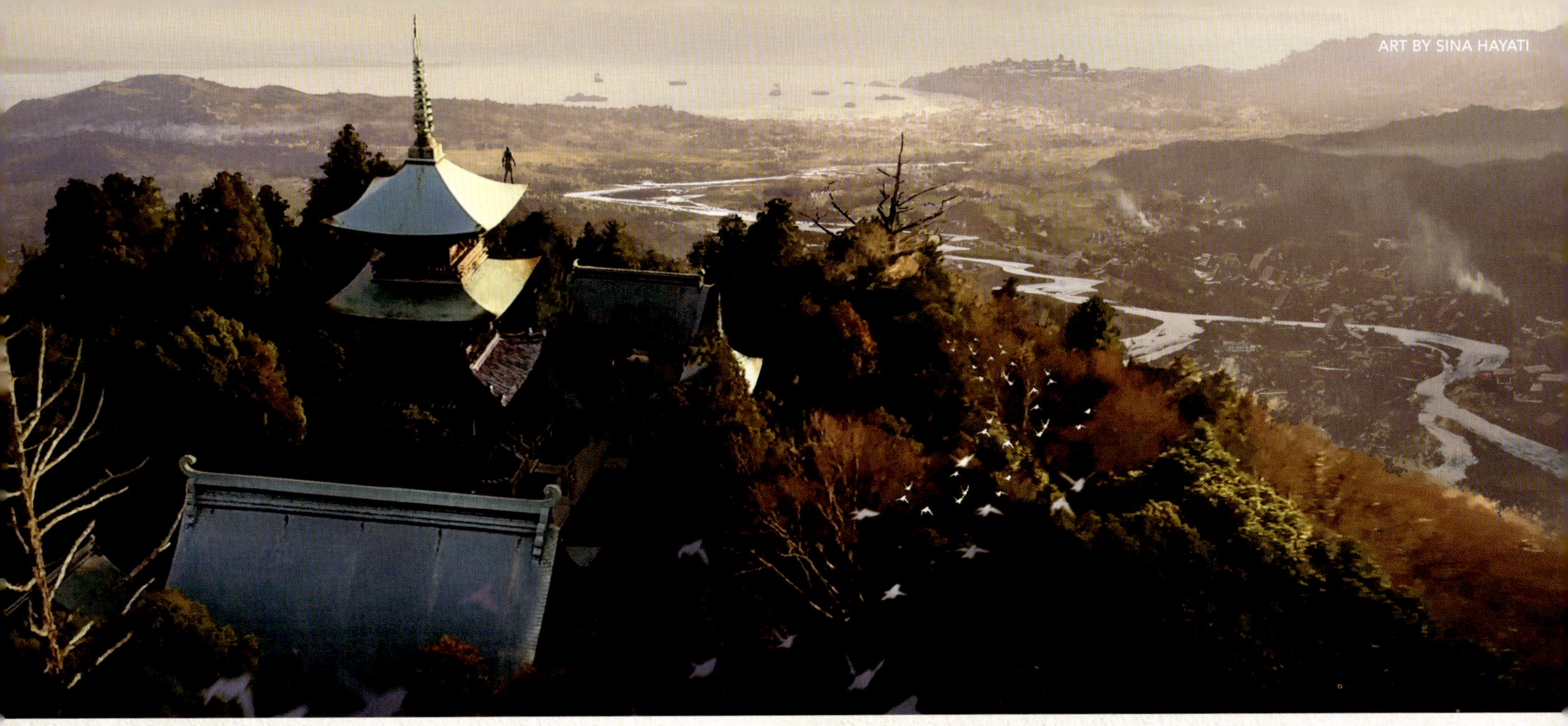

ART BY SINA HAYATI

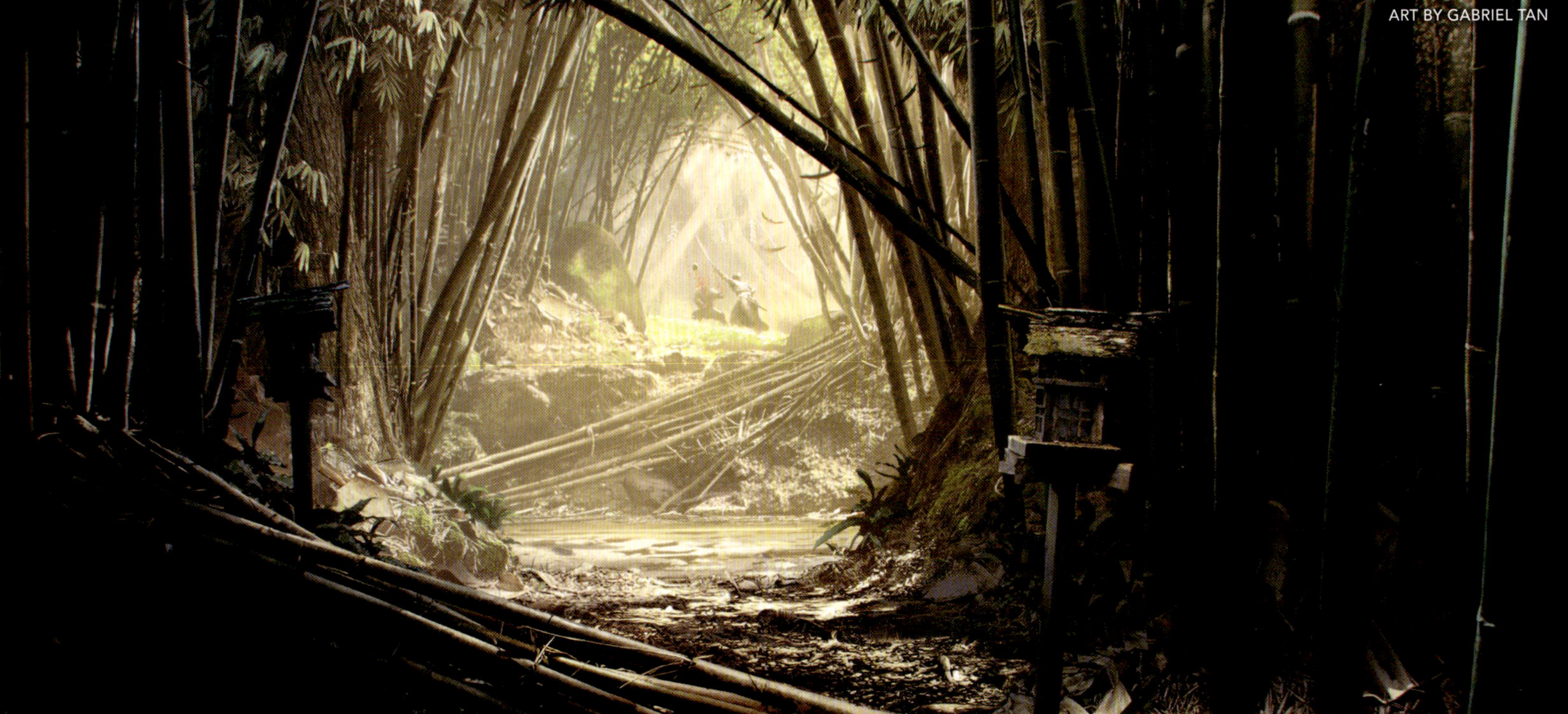

ART BY GABRIEL TAN

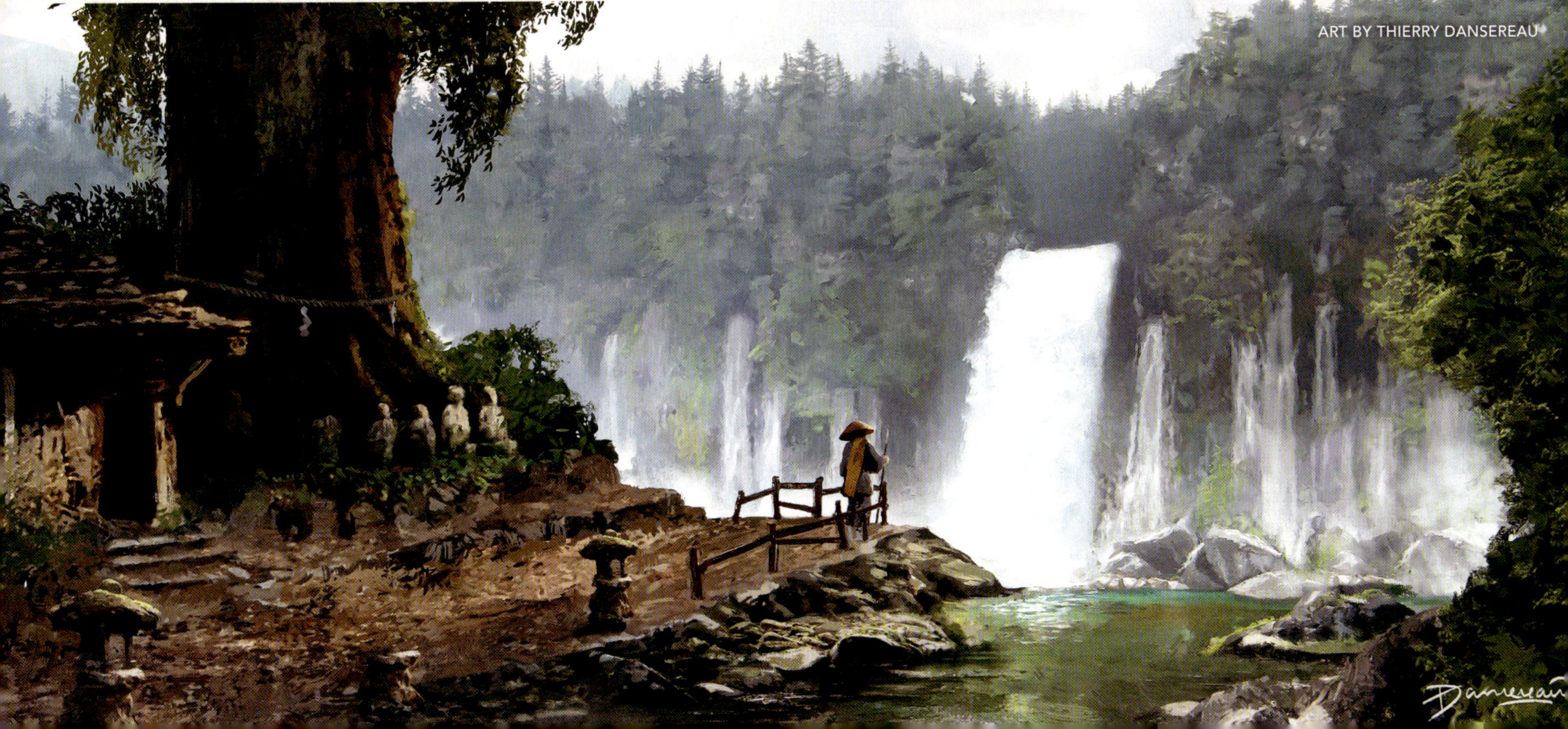

ART BY THIERRY DANSEREAU

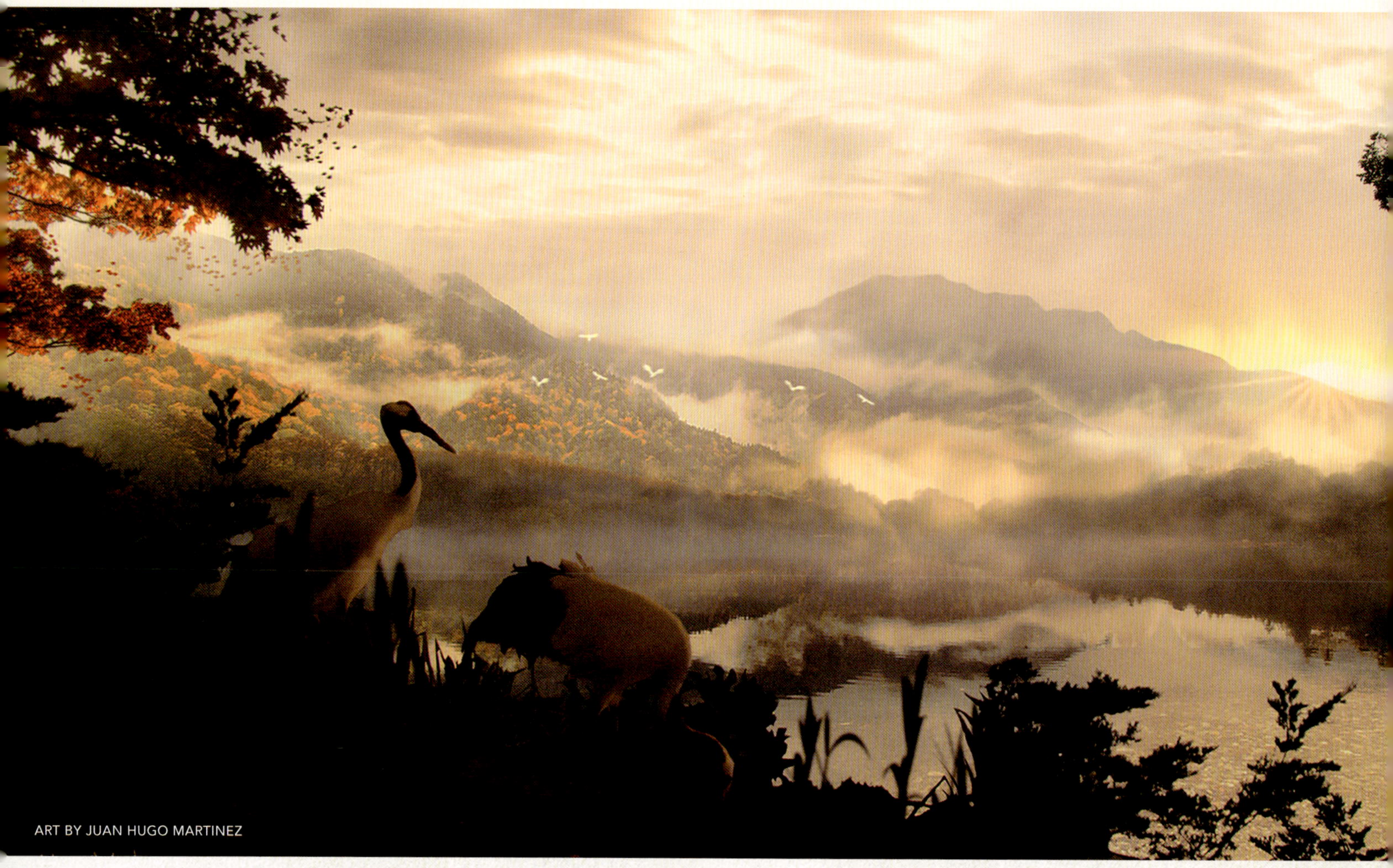

ART BY JUAN HUGO MARTINEZ

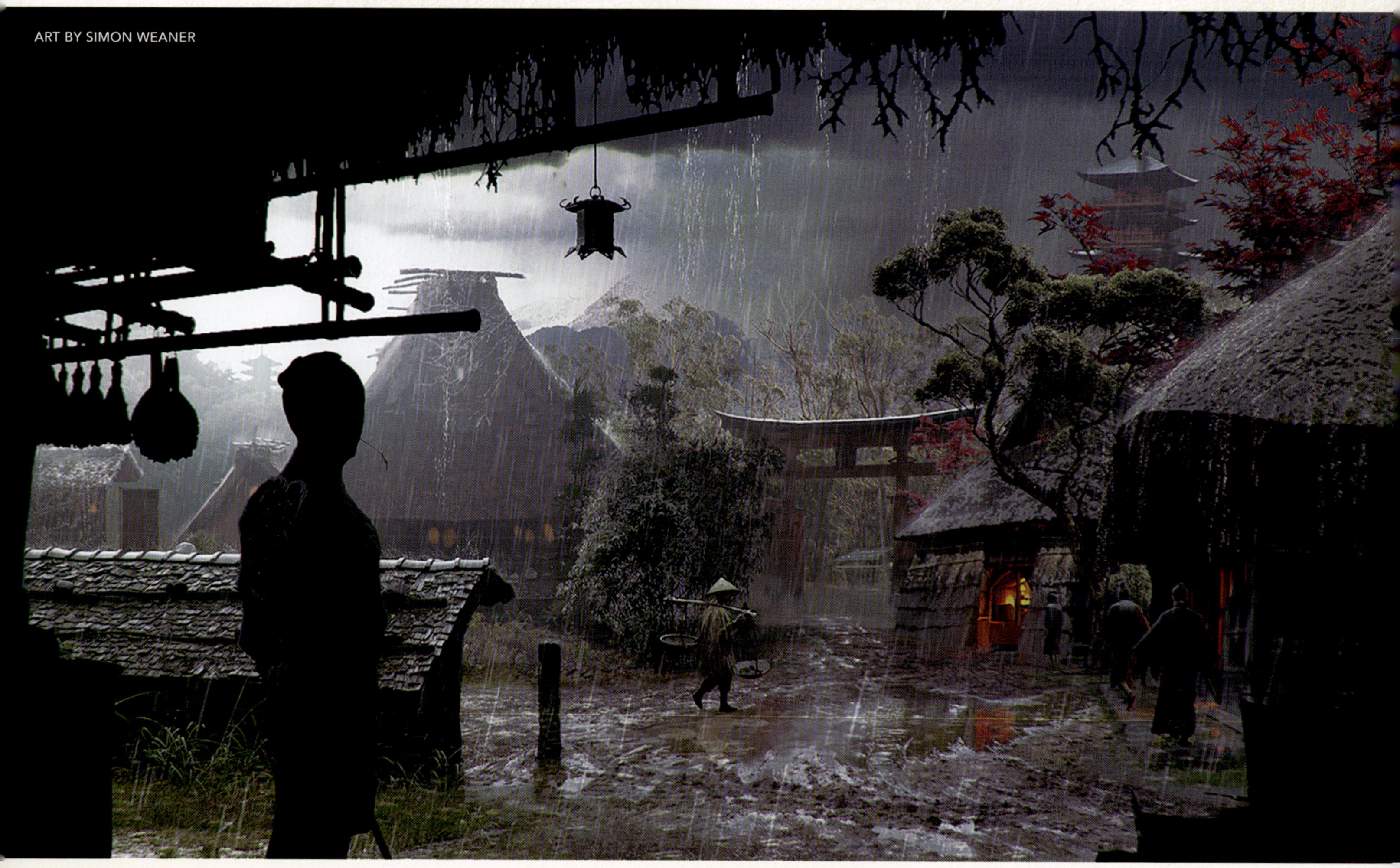

ART BY SIMON WEANER

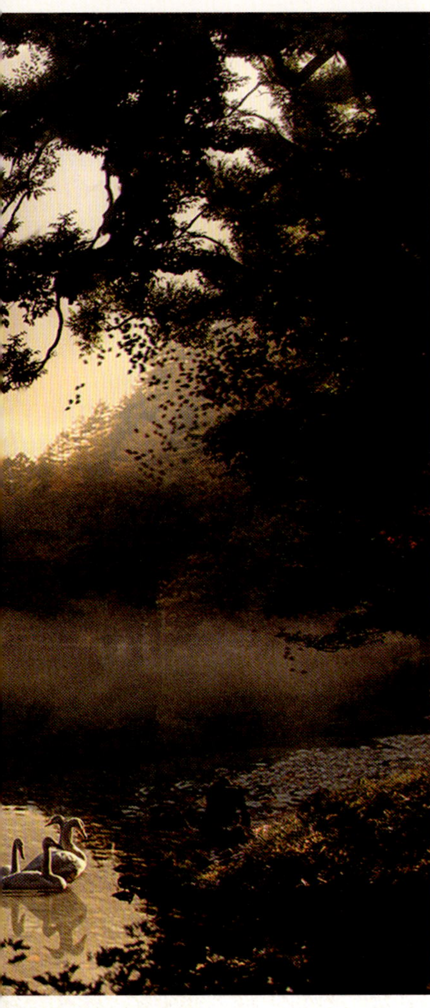

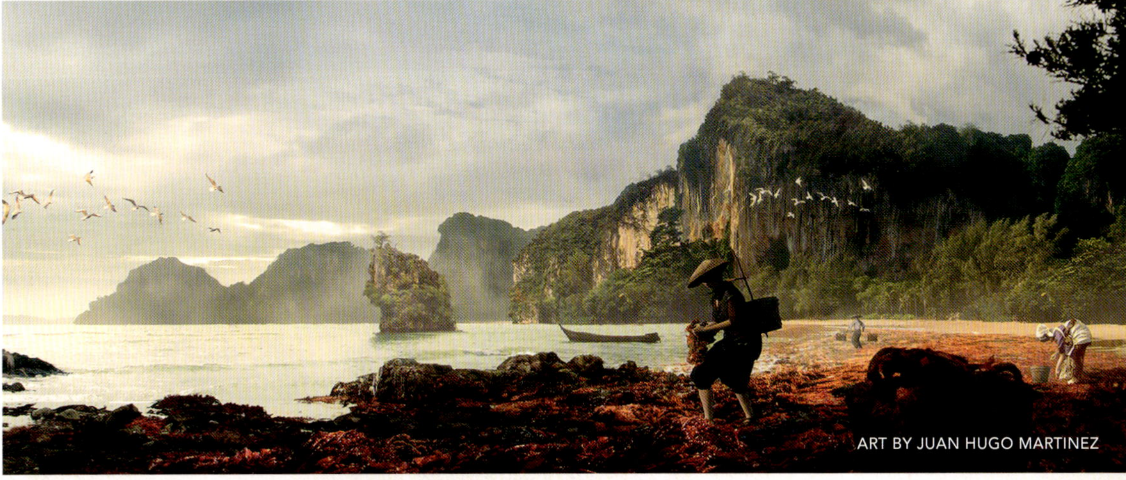

ART BY JUAN HUGO MARTINEZ

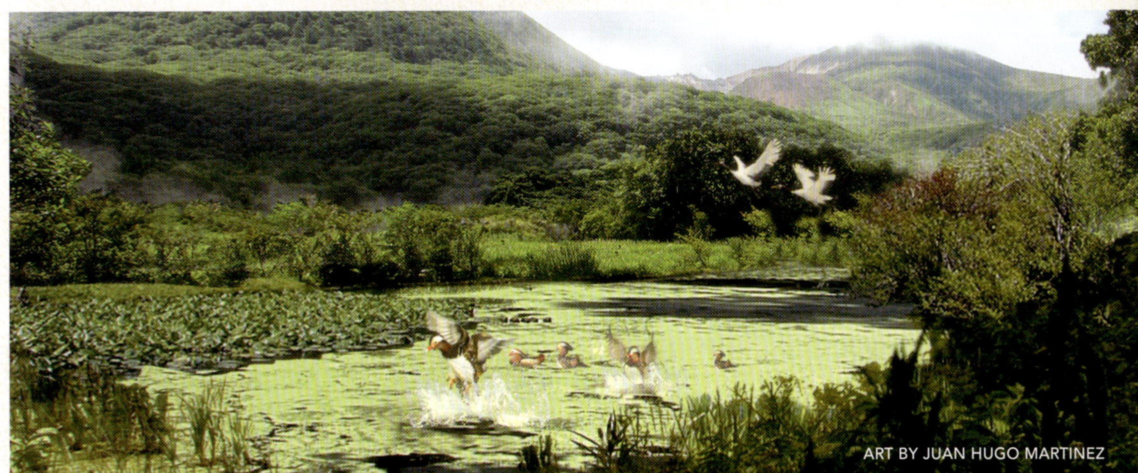

ART BY JUAN HUGO MARTINEZ

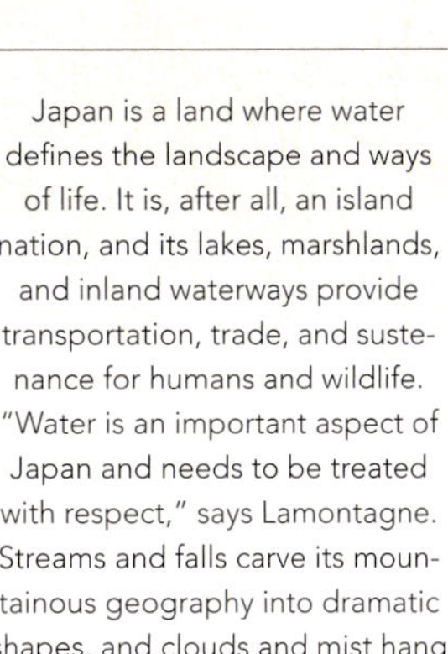

Japan is a land where water defines the landscape and ways of life. It is, after all, an island nation, and its lakes, marshlands, and inland waterways provide transportation, trade, and sustenance for humans and wildlife. "Water is an important aspect of Japan and needs to be treated with respect," says Lamontagne. Streams and falls carve its mountainous geography into dramatic shapes, and clouds and mist hang low over the valleys.

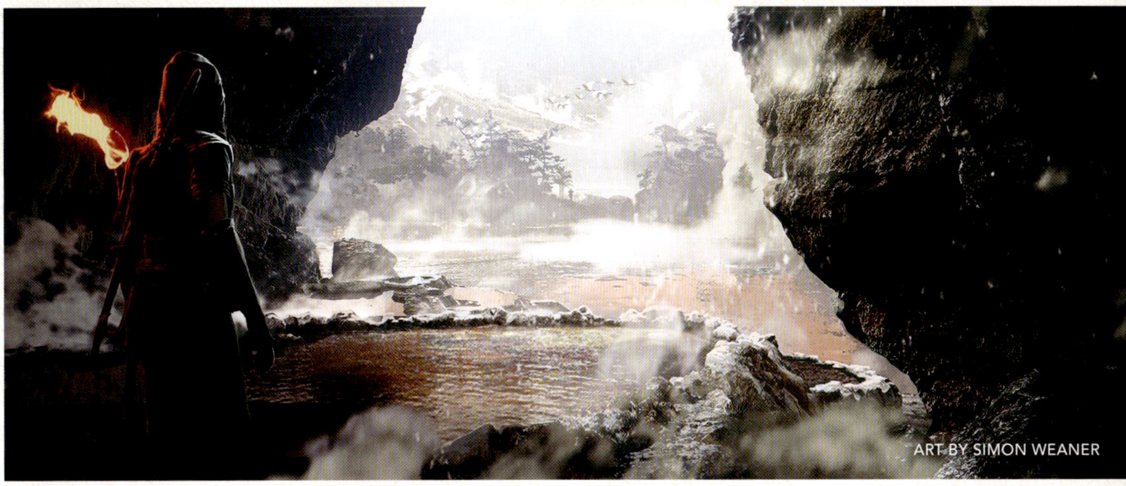

ART BY SIMON WEANER

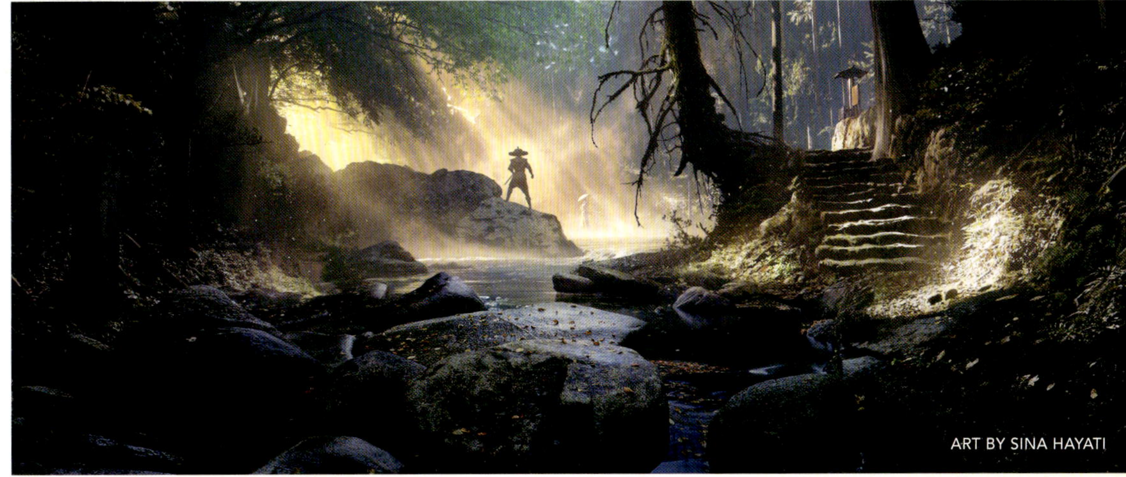

ART BY SINA HAYATI

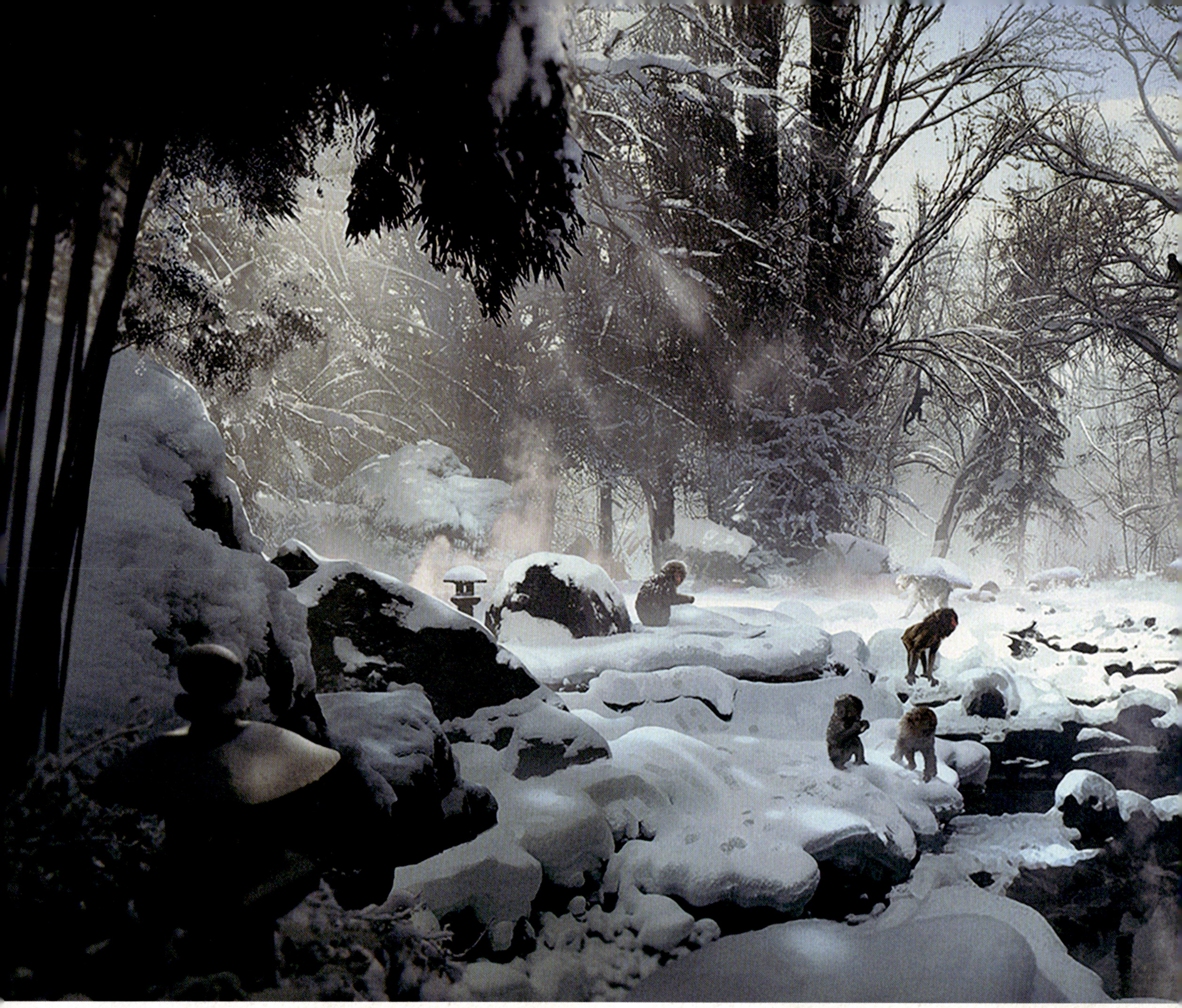

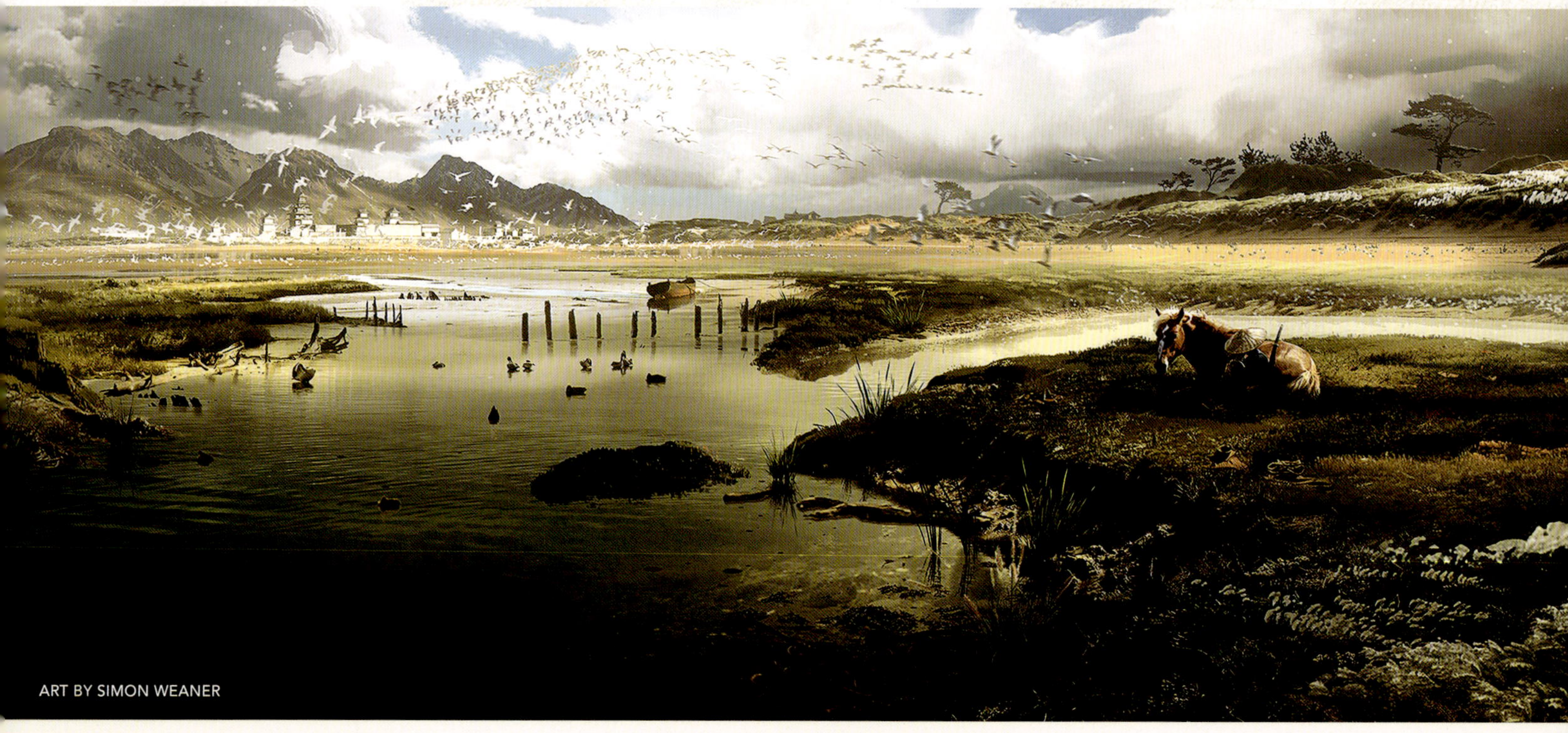

ART BY SIMON WEANER

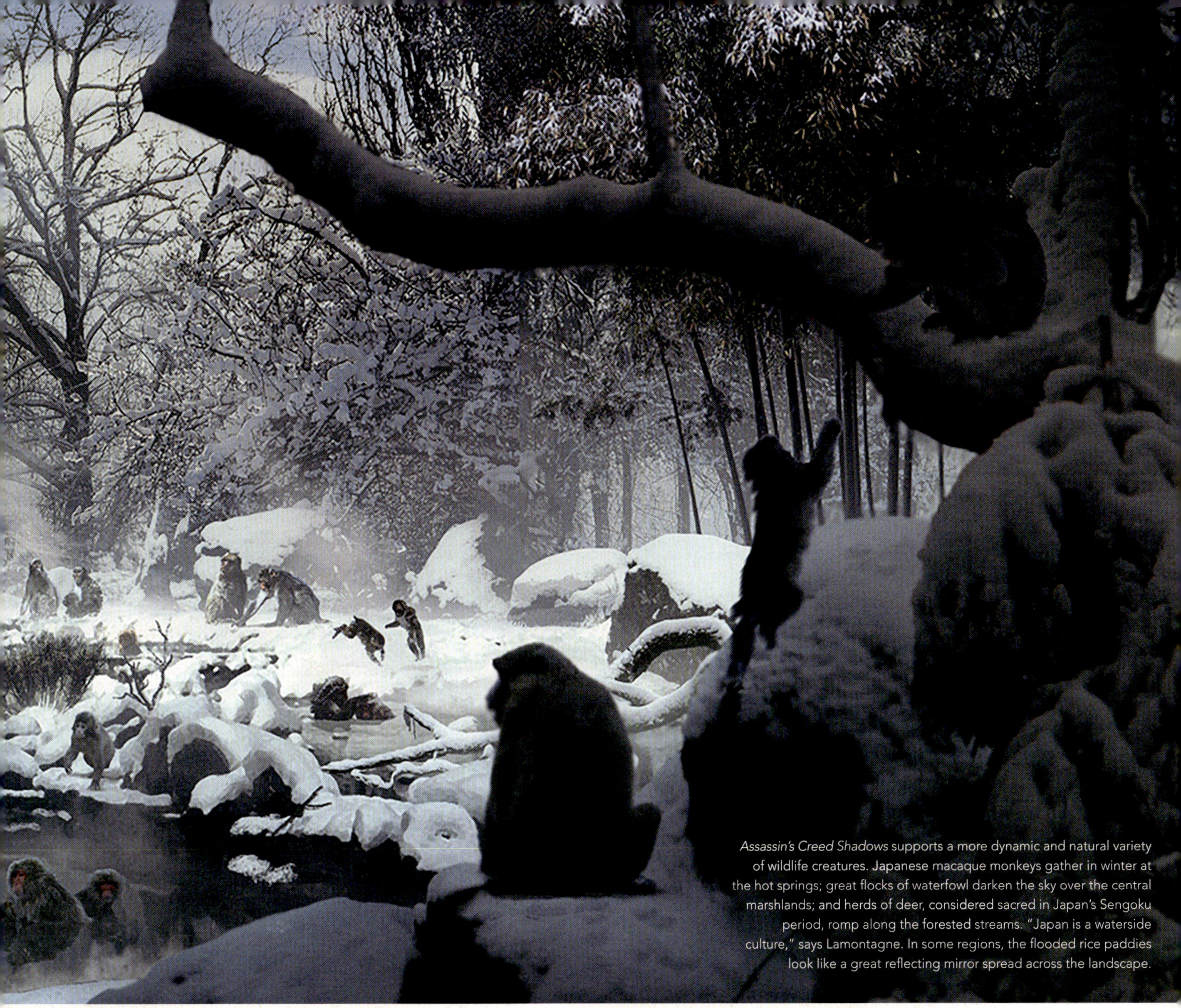

Assassin's Creed Shadows supports a more dynamic and natural variety of wildlife creatures. Japanese macaque monkeys gather in winter at the hot springs; great flocks of waterfowl darken the sky over the central marshlands; and herds of deer, considered sacred in Japan's Sengoku period, romp along the forested streams. "Japan is a waterside culture," says Lamontagne. In some regions, the flooded rice paddies look like a great reflecting mirror spread across the landscape.

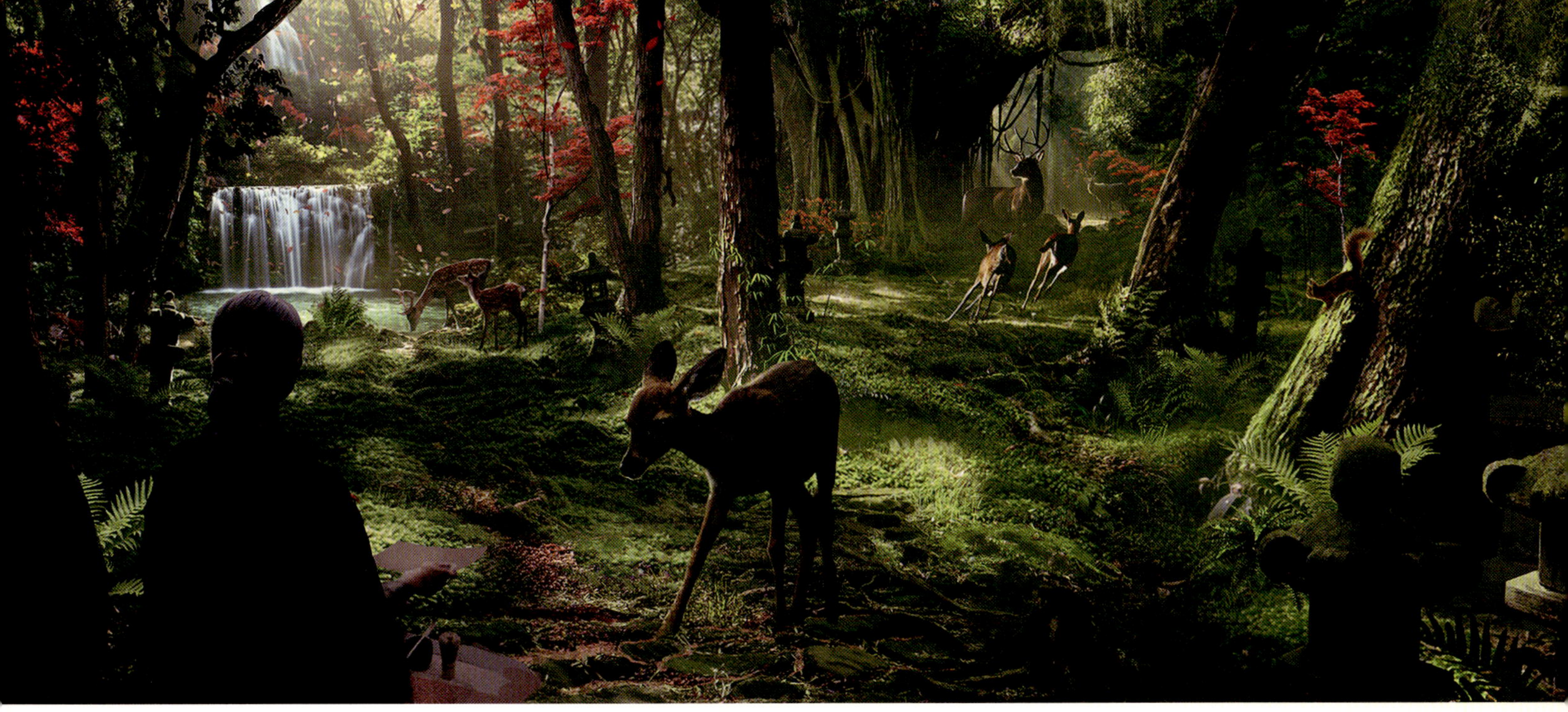

WILDLIFE

Wildlife creation and placement in the game world came under the purview of the biome team during the making of *Assassin's Creed Shadows*. "This was at our request," says Lamontagne. "We wanted to treat our biomes like true ecosystems." The idea was to distribute creatures in more natural ways across landscapes—near bodies of water, for example—and to give them more natural behaviors and awareness systems.

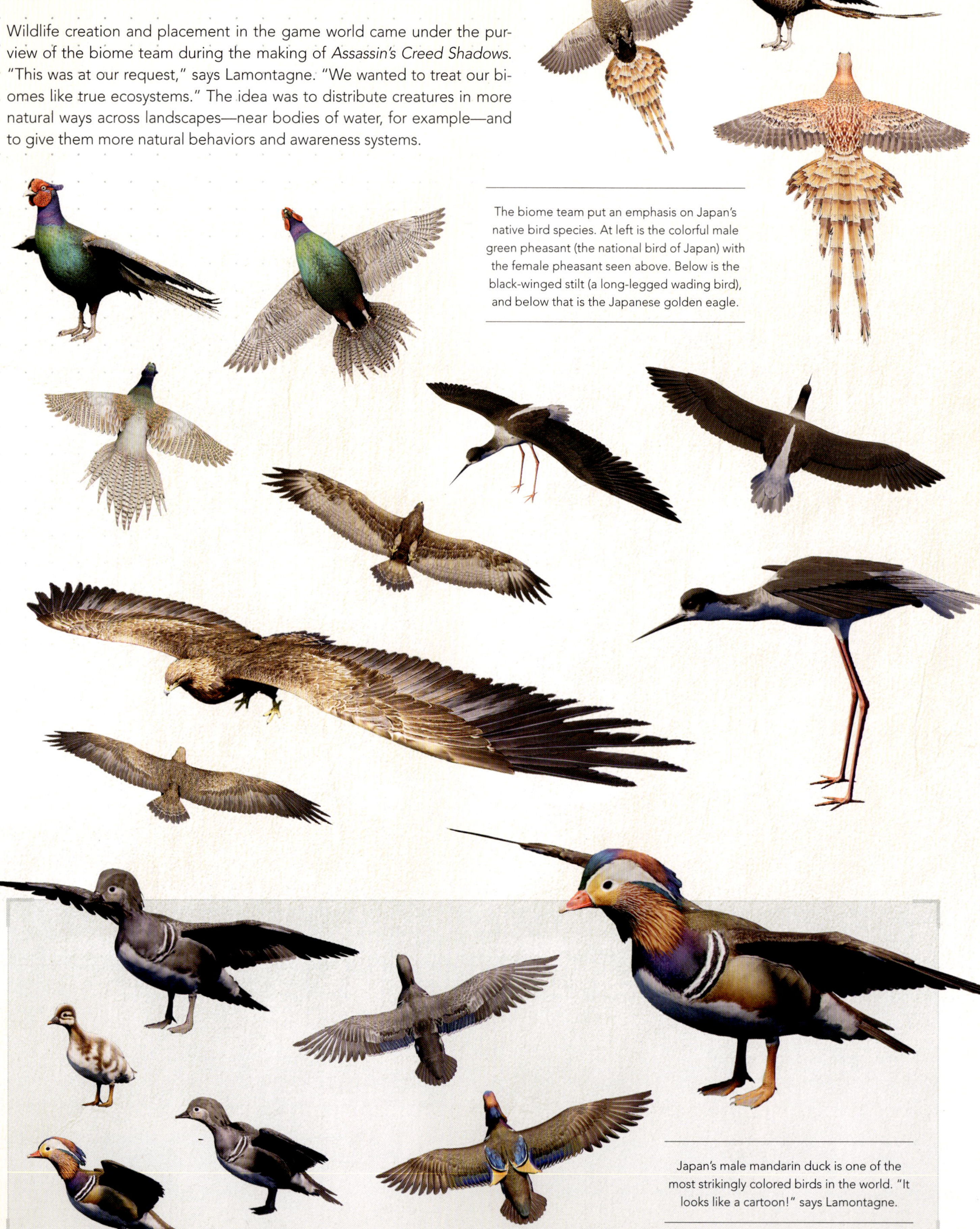

The biome team put an emphasis on Japan's native bird species. At left is the colorful male green pheasant (the national bird of Japan) with the female pheasant seen above. Below is the black-winged stilt (a long-legged wading bird), and below that is the Japanese golden eagle.

Japan's male mandarin duck is one of the most strikingly colored birds in the world. "It looks like a cartoon!" says Lamontagne.

ART BY XU XIAO TING, YE WEN XIANG, AND CHEN QIAN

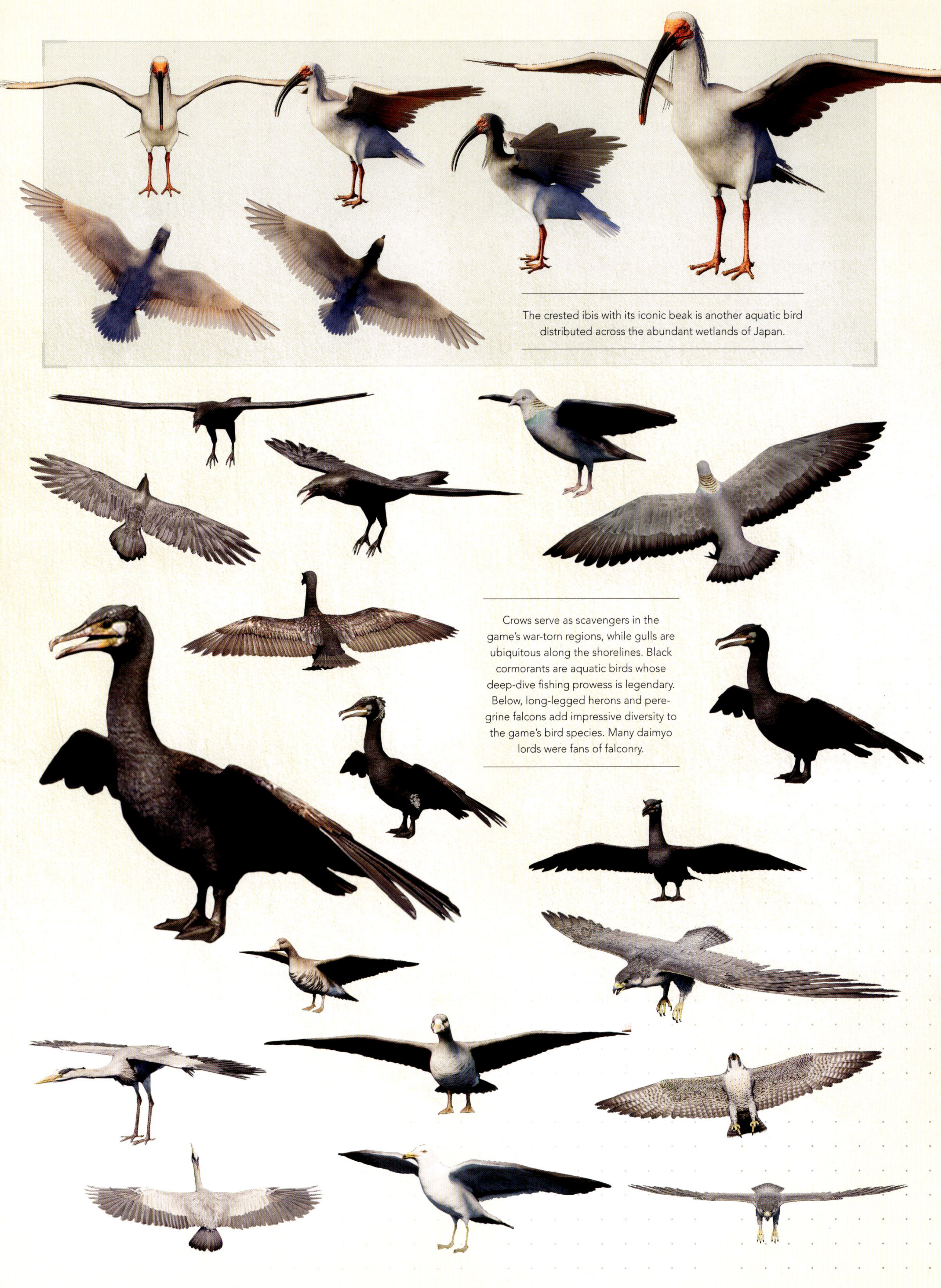

The crested ibis with its iconic beak is another aquatic bird distributed across the abundant wetlands of Japan.

Crows serve as scavengers in the game's war-torn regions, while gulls are ubiquitous along the shorelines. Black cormorants are aquatic birds whose deep-dive fishing prowess is legendary. Below, long-legged herons and peregrine falcons add impressive diversity to the game's bird species. Many daimyo lords were fans of falconry.

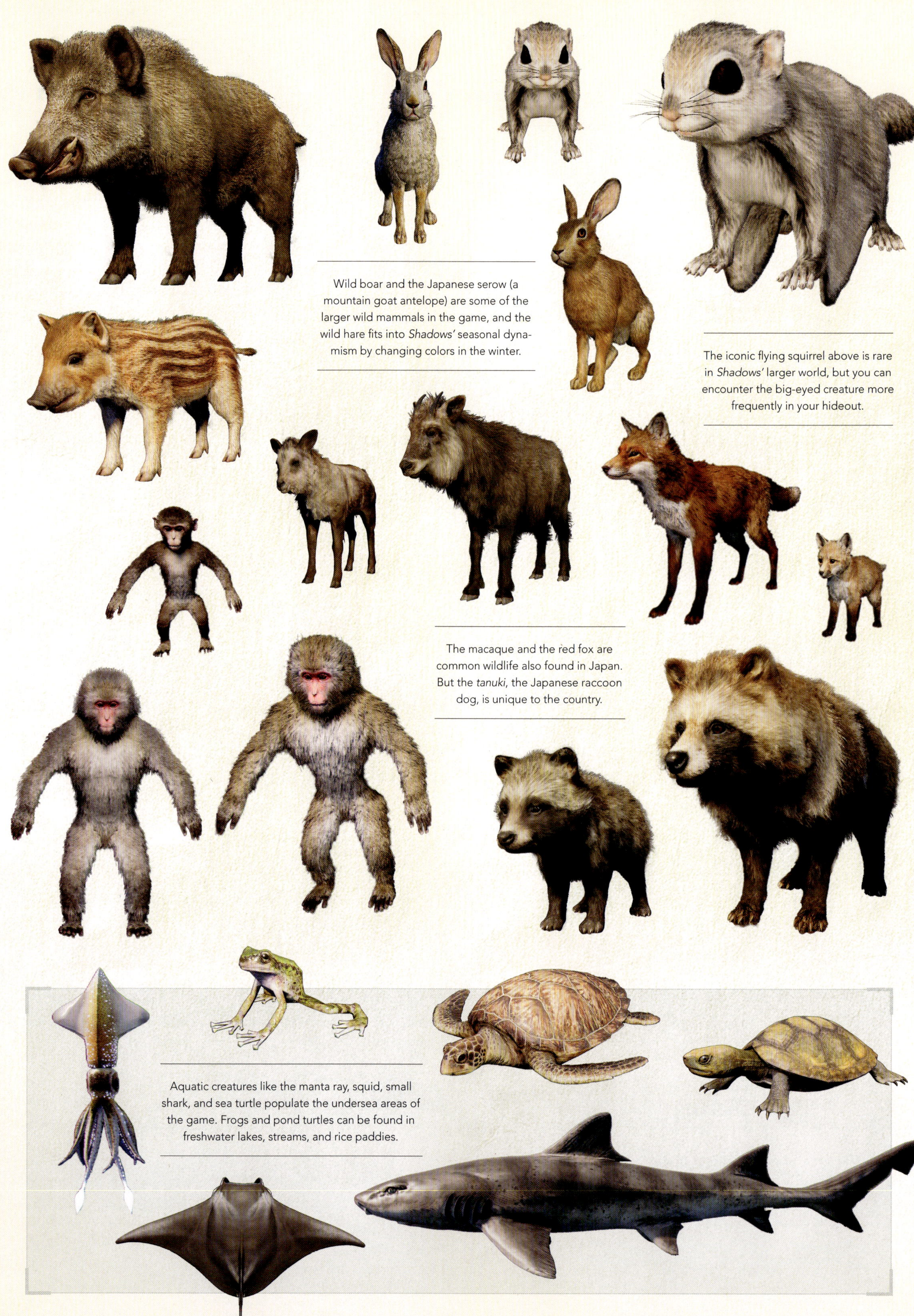

Wild boar and the Japanese serow (a mountain goat antelope) are some of the larger wild mammals in the game, and the wild hare fits into *Shadows'* seasonal dynamism by changing colors in the winter.

The iconic flying squirrel above is rare in *Shadows'* larger world, but you can encounter the big-eyed creature more frequently in your hideout.

The macaque and the red fox are common wildlife also found in Japan. But the *tanuki*, the Japanese raccoon dog, is unique to the country.

Aquatic creatures like the manta ray, squid, small shark, and sea turtle populate the undersea areas of the game. Frogs and pond turtles can be found in freshwater lakes, streams, and rice paddies.

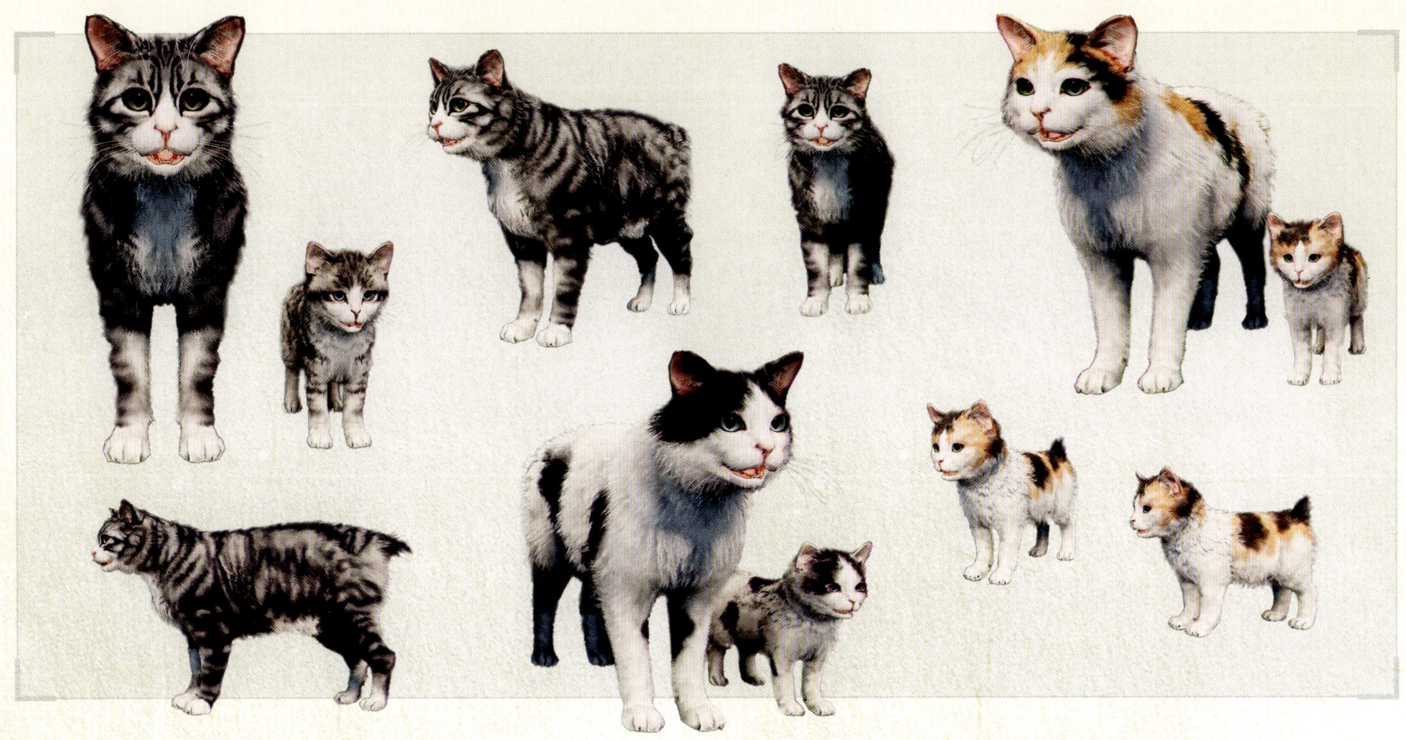

DOMESTIC ANIMALS

Domestication of animals was not common in sixteenth-century Japan. The biome team learned that whereas crop farming, particularly of rice, was extensive and widespread, animal farms were almost nonexistent. "At that time most Japanese relied on fishing for their meat," says Lamontagne. On the farm, oxen served as labor for cultivating the fields, but beef and poultry production was scarce.

Dogs were the primary domestic animal found in Japanese culture, particularly the Akita breed, which originated in the mountains of northern Japan. *Shadows* also features the Japanese bobtail cat, a short-tailed breed of domestic feline.

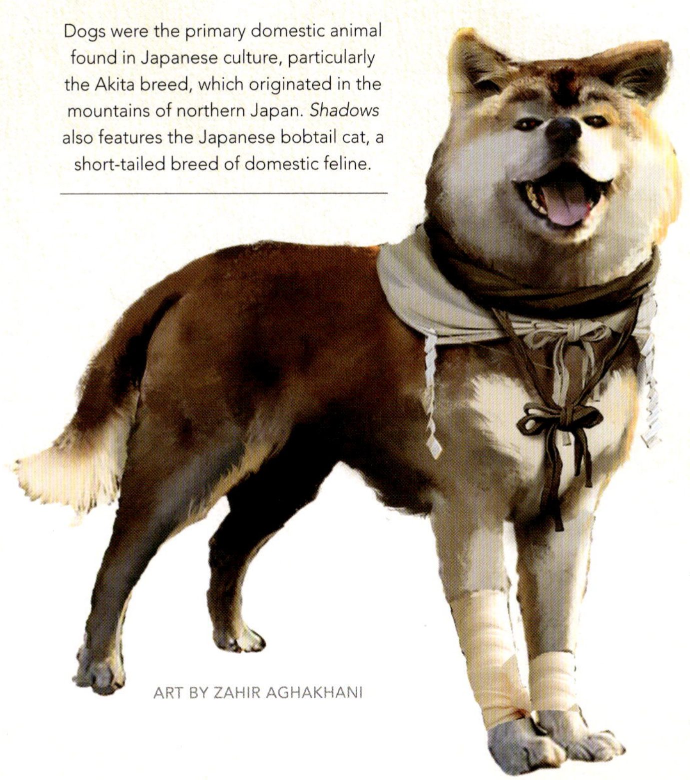

ART BY ZAHIR AGHAKHANI

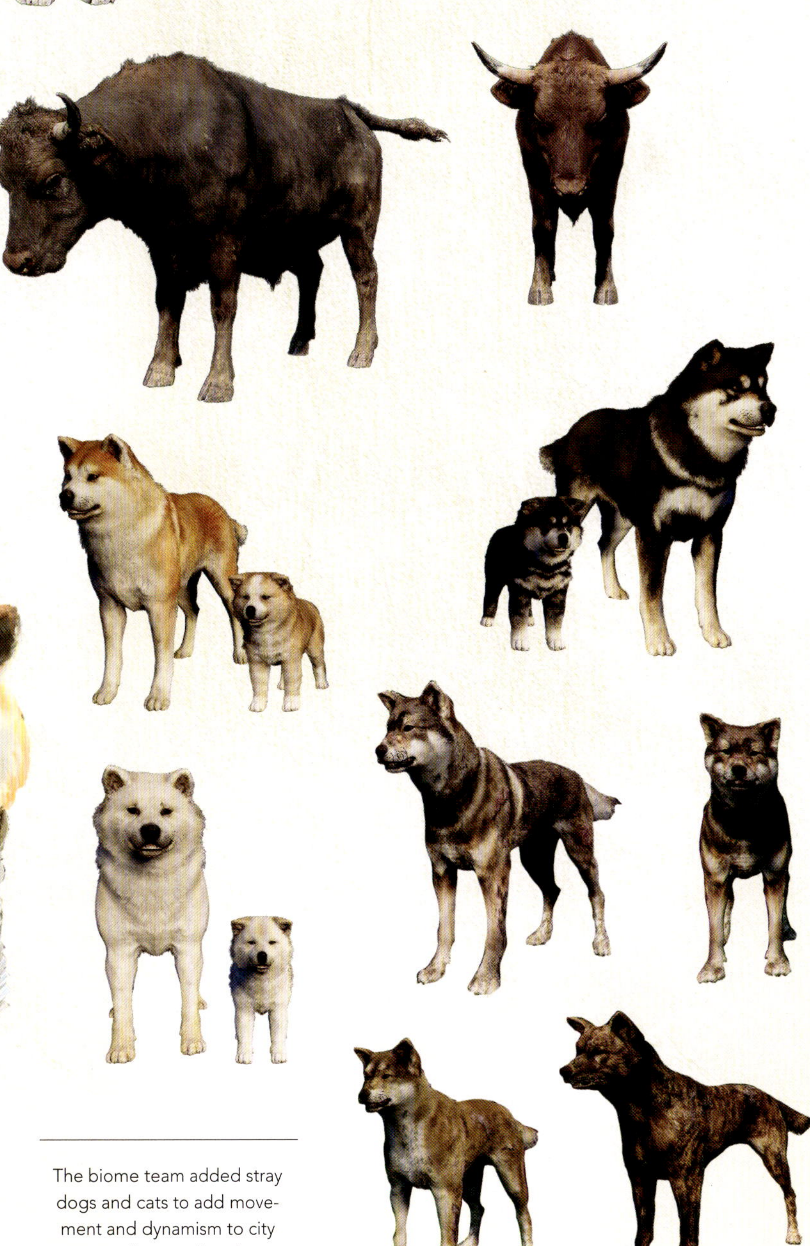

The biome team added stray dogs and cats to add movement and dynamism to city streets, alleys, and rooftops.

ART BY XU XIAO TING, YE WEN XIANG, AND CHEN QIAN

LEGENDARY ANIMALS

The *Shadows* biome team worked with game design to introduce several iconic creatures linked to Japanese folklore. "You see a lot of shape-shifter animals in those legends," says Vincent Lamontagne. "Gods and forest spirits and other supernatural beings, appearing in the form of fantastic animals." At right, the *kitsune*, a three-tailed silver fox, was said to be a spirit who could be many things—a trickster, a messenger for deities, a faithful guardian, or even a friend or lover.

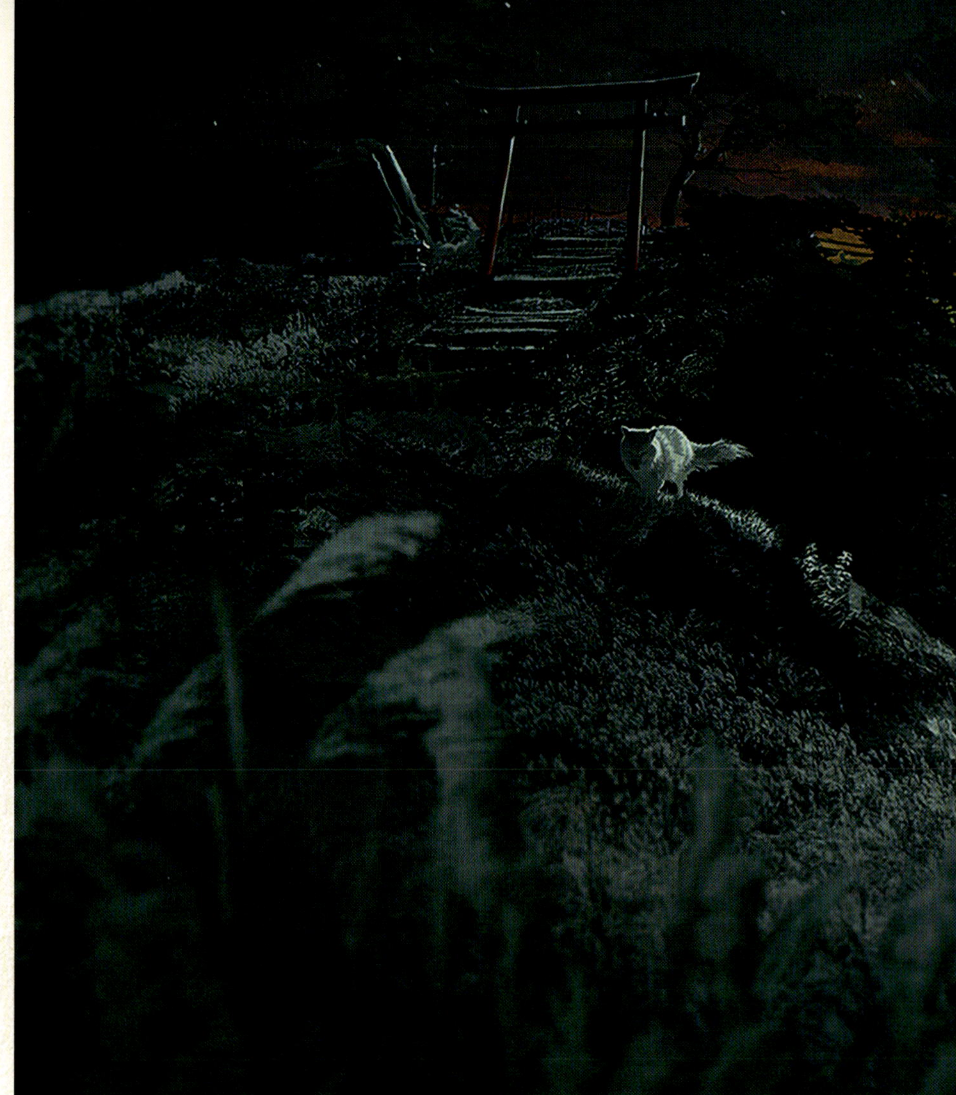

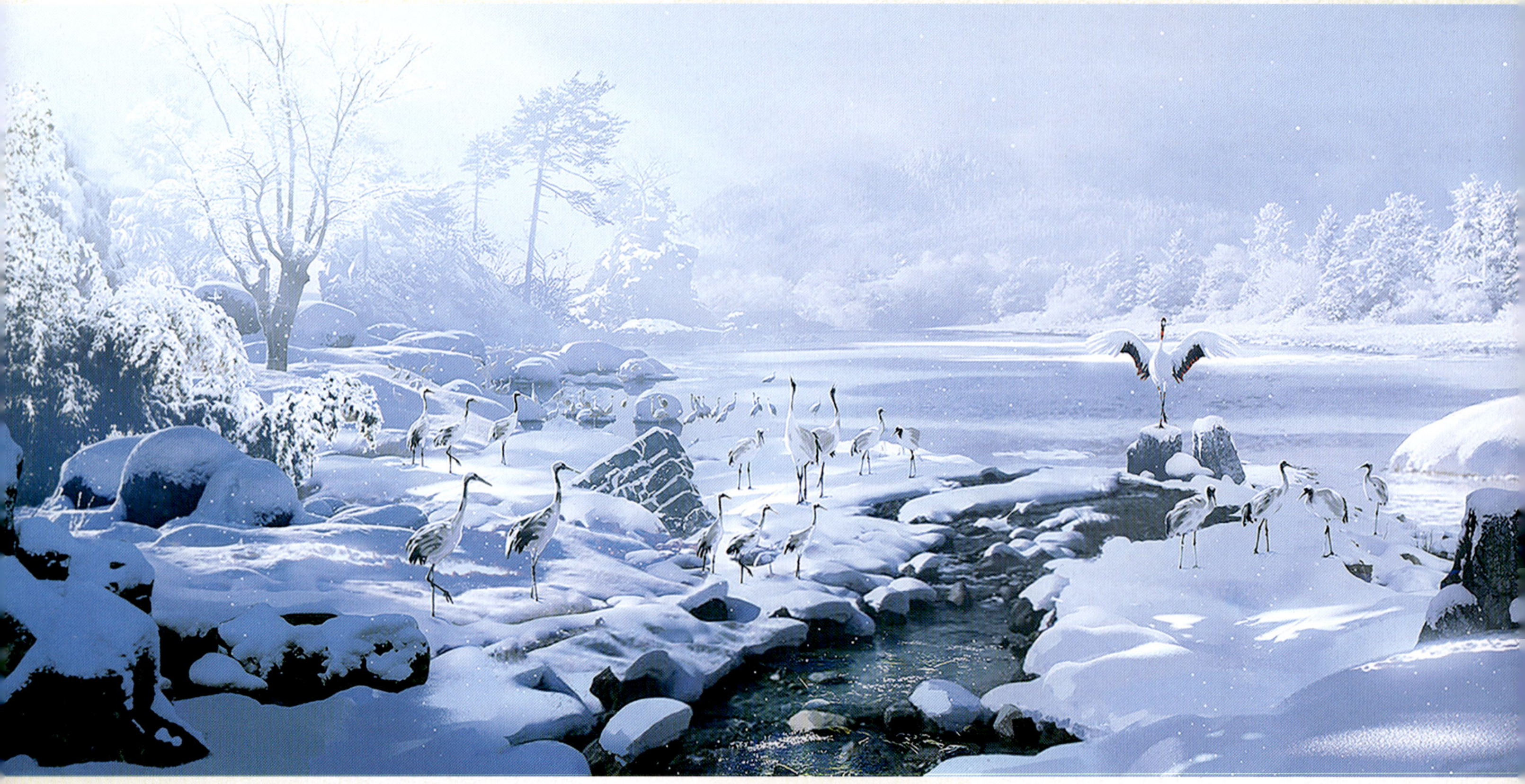

Two other creatures found in Japanese folklore: Above, the rare red-crowned crane is seen as a symbol of luck, longevity, and fidelity. His remarkable dance is renowned for its grace and intricacy—in the game, this crane lives among flocks of herons. The white stag *(right)* sports great antlers festooned with cherry blossoms that are said to bring life back to nature in the spring.

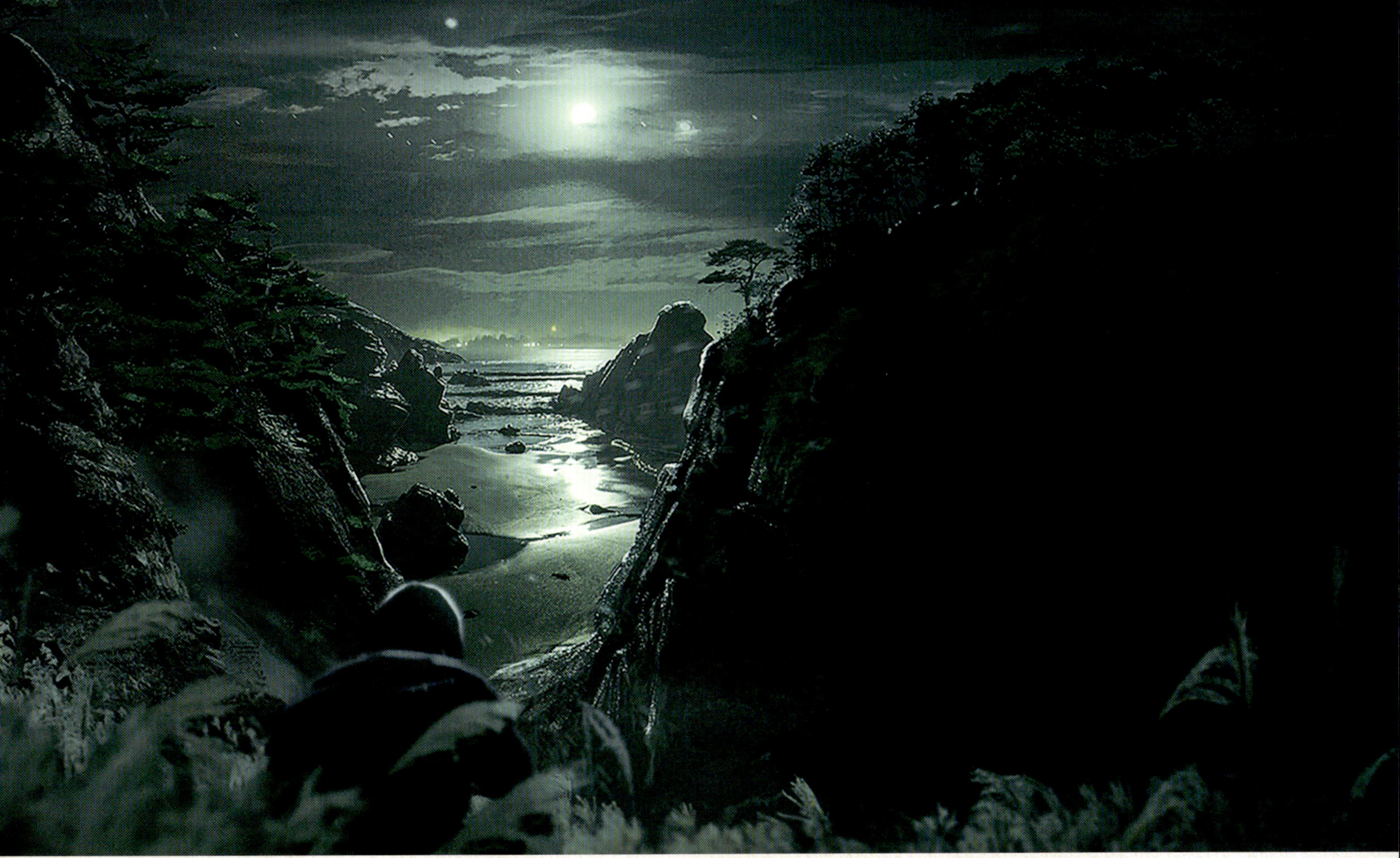

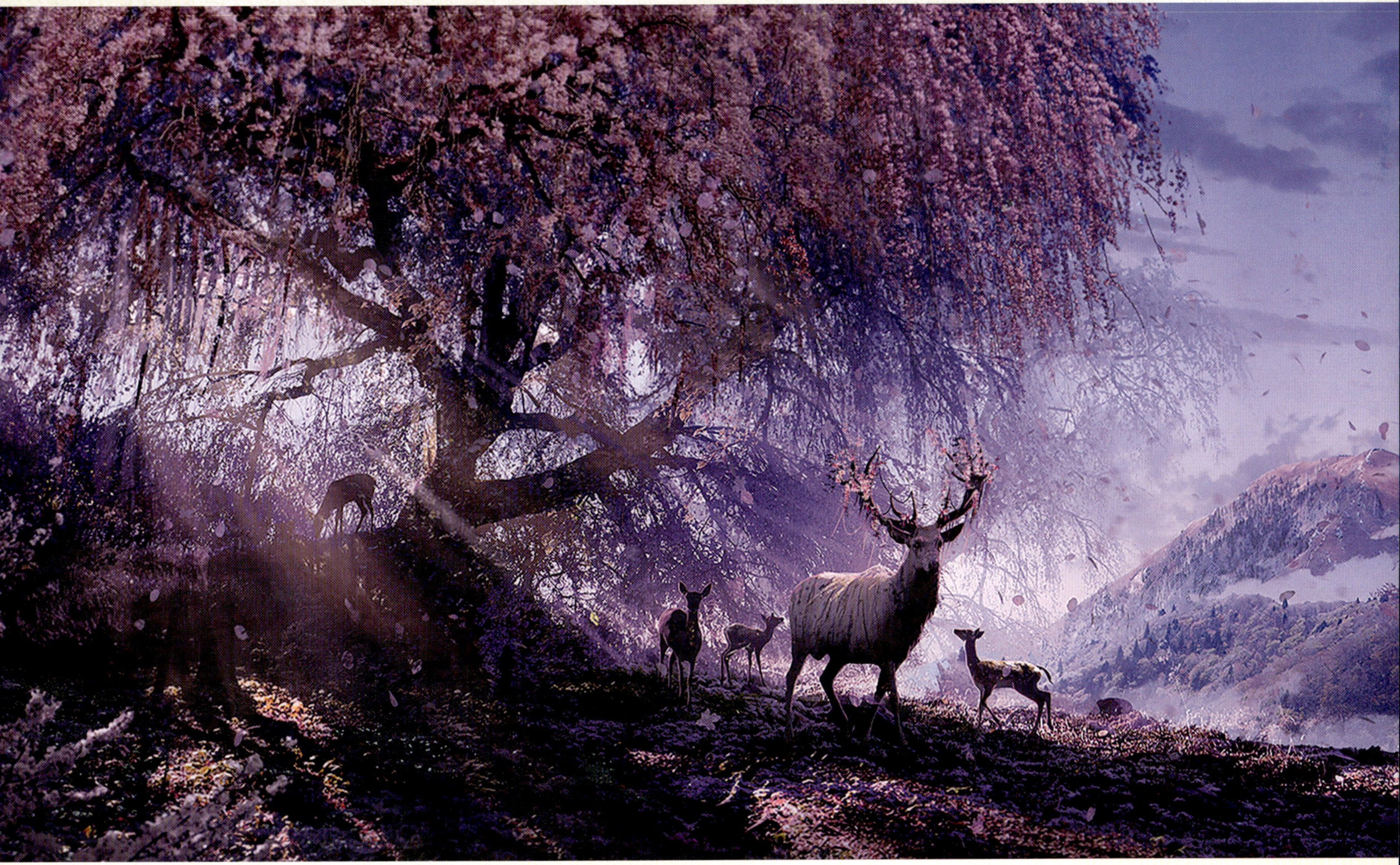

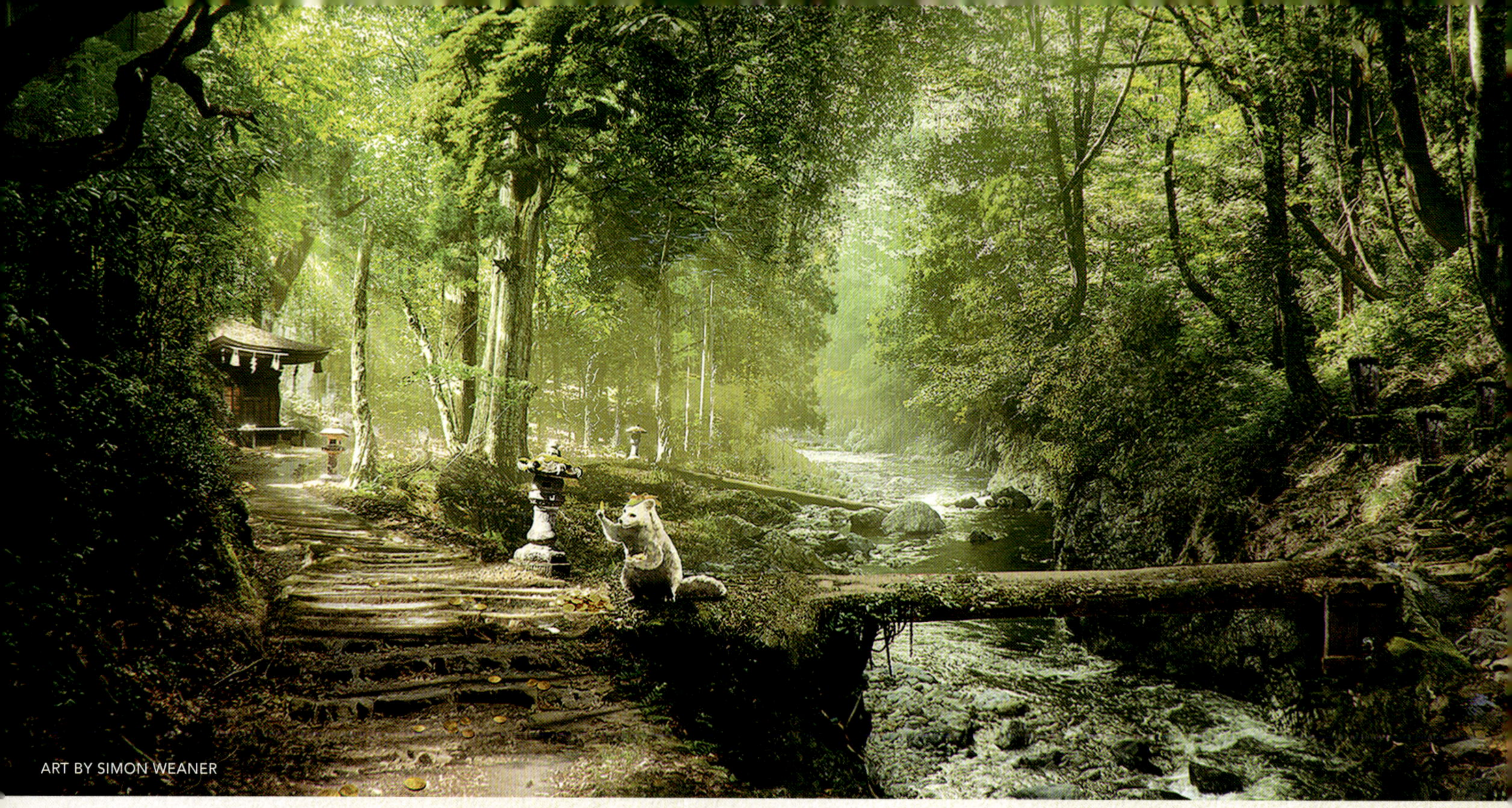

ART BY SIMON WEANER

ART BY ALBERT LIN

This white *tanuki* (the Japanese raccoon dog) is extremely rare and seen as an omen of good luck in Japan. It was a natural choice as a legendary animal in the game. In traditional Japanese folk art, the white *tanuki* is depicted with a leaf on its forehead, symbolizing nature, its source of spiritual power.

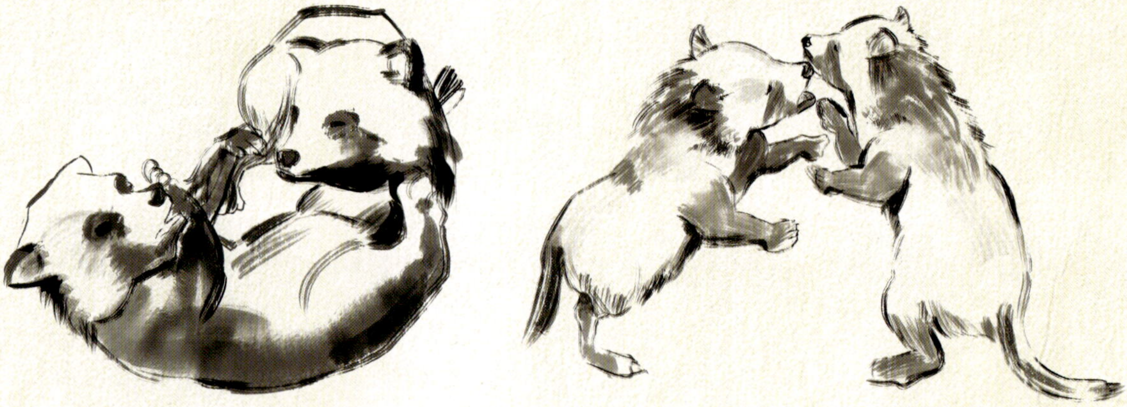

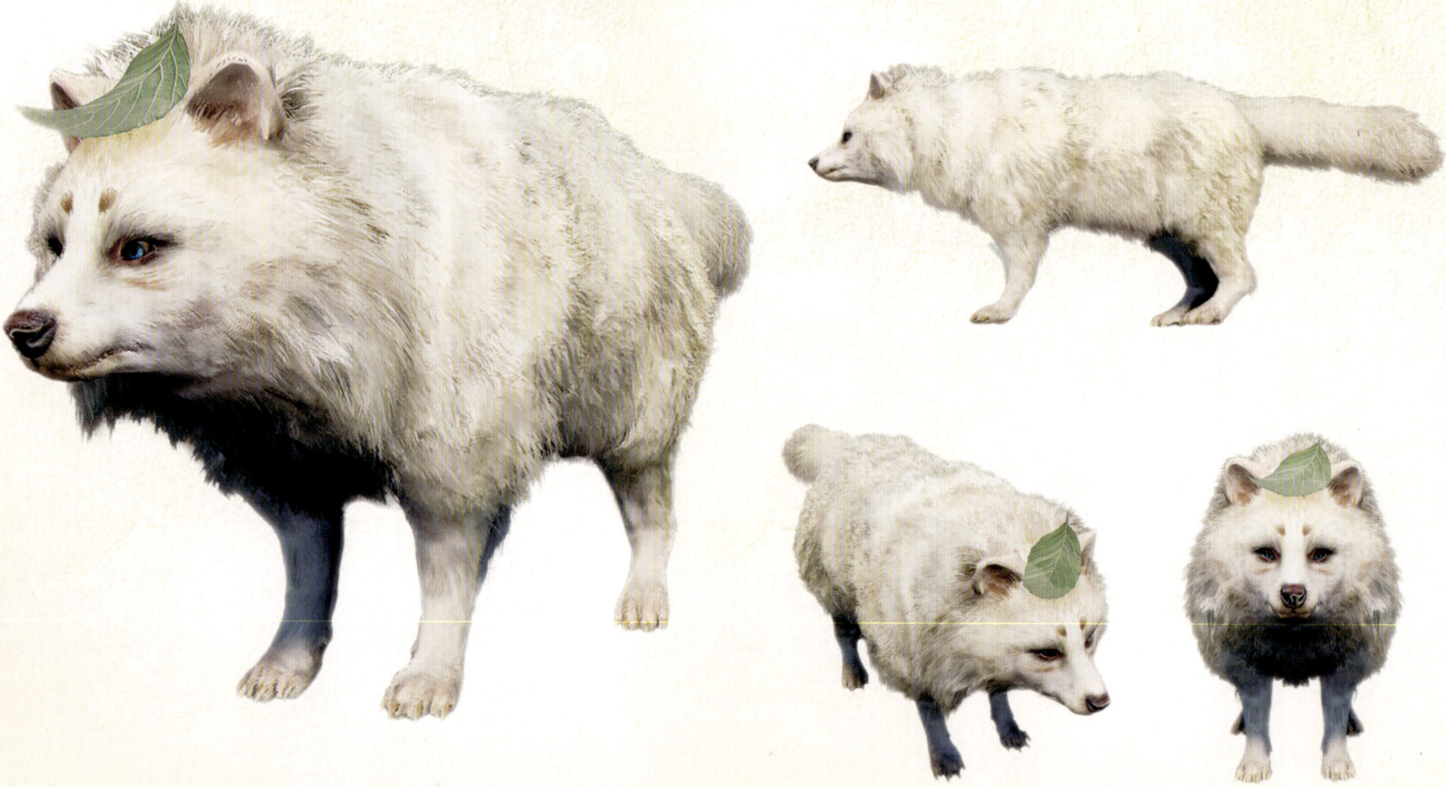

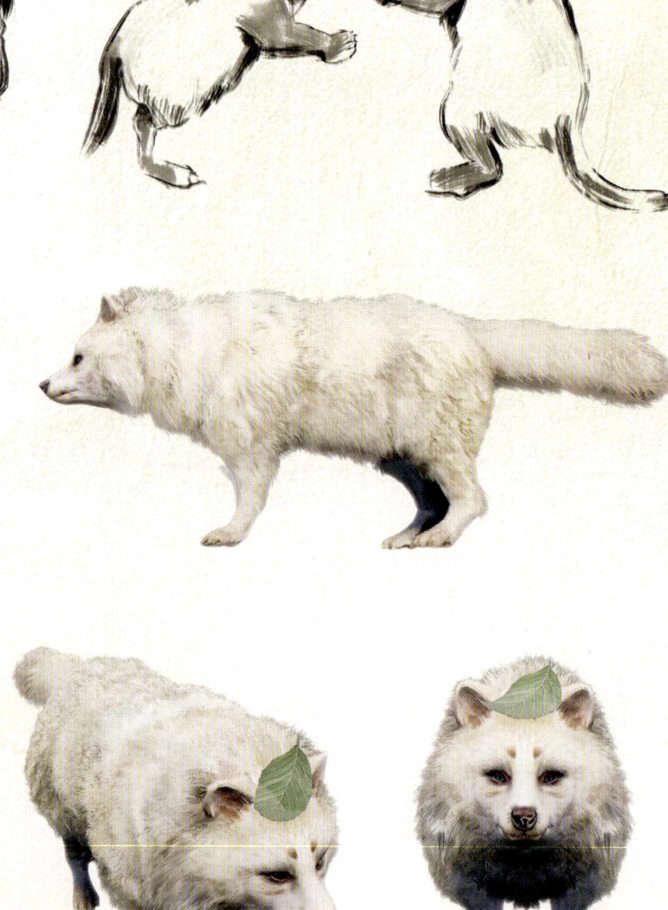

ART BY XU XIAO TING, YE WEN XIANG, AND CHEN QIAN

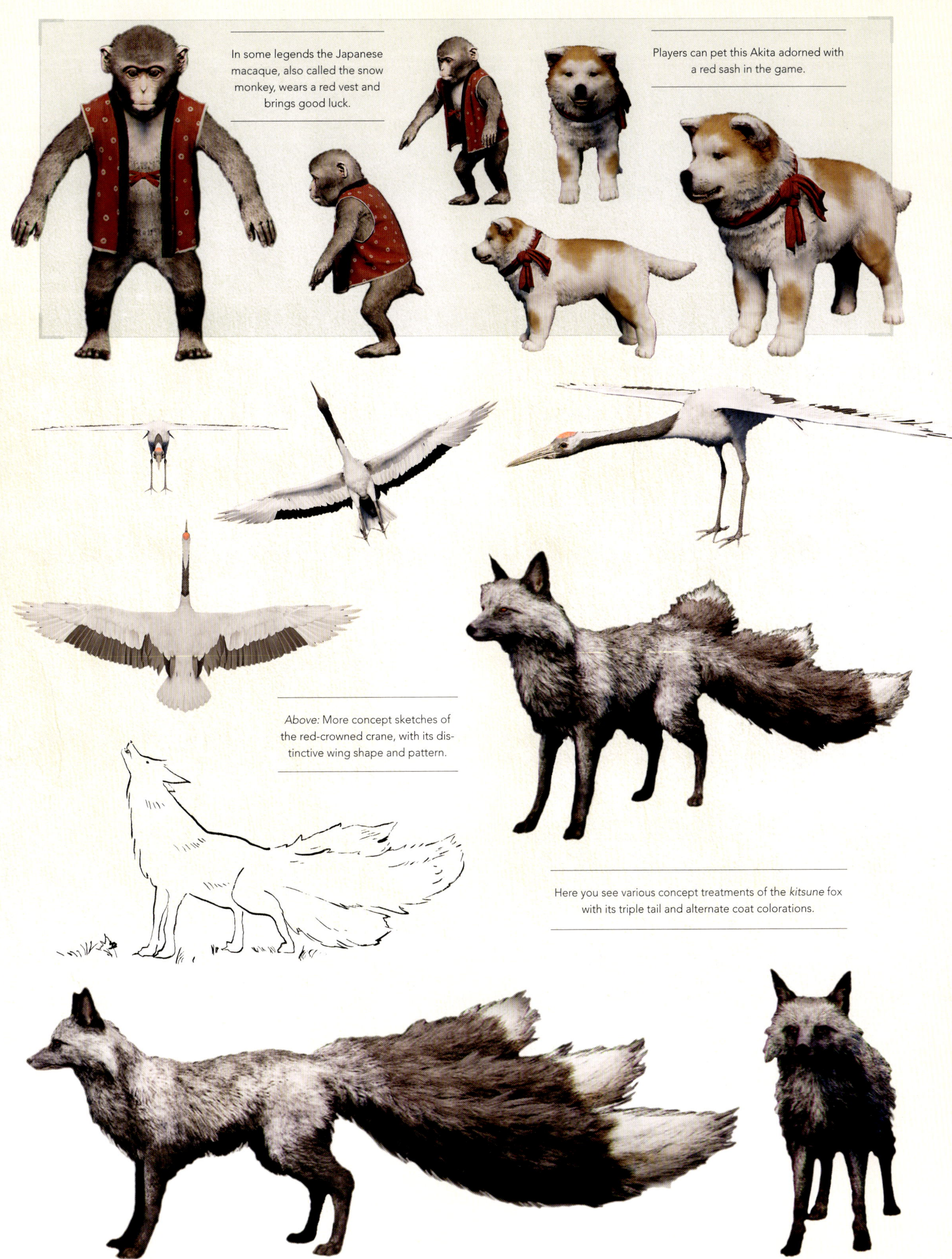

In some legends the Japanese macaque, also called the snow monkey, wears a red vest and brings good luck.

Players can pet this Akita adorned with a red sash in the game.

Above: More concept sketches of the red-crowned crane, with its distinctive wing shape and pattern.

Here you see various concept treatments of the *kitsune* fox with its triple tail and alternate coat colorations.

ARCHITECTURE

The *Assassin's Creed Shadows* architecture team, led by Dominic Gladu-Despatis, created a series of construction "kits" full of modular 3D structural components and materials. These kits allowed level designers to mix and match elements to build a wide array of structures that maintain thematic continuity between exterior and interior spaces. The kits are divided into four major categories: castles, sanctuaries (Shinto and Buddhist temples), upscale dwellings (daimyo mansions), and a range of "regular" housing modules for middle- and lower-class residents, such as merchants, farmers, fishermen, and peasants. The last category includes components for military camps and outposts.

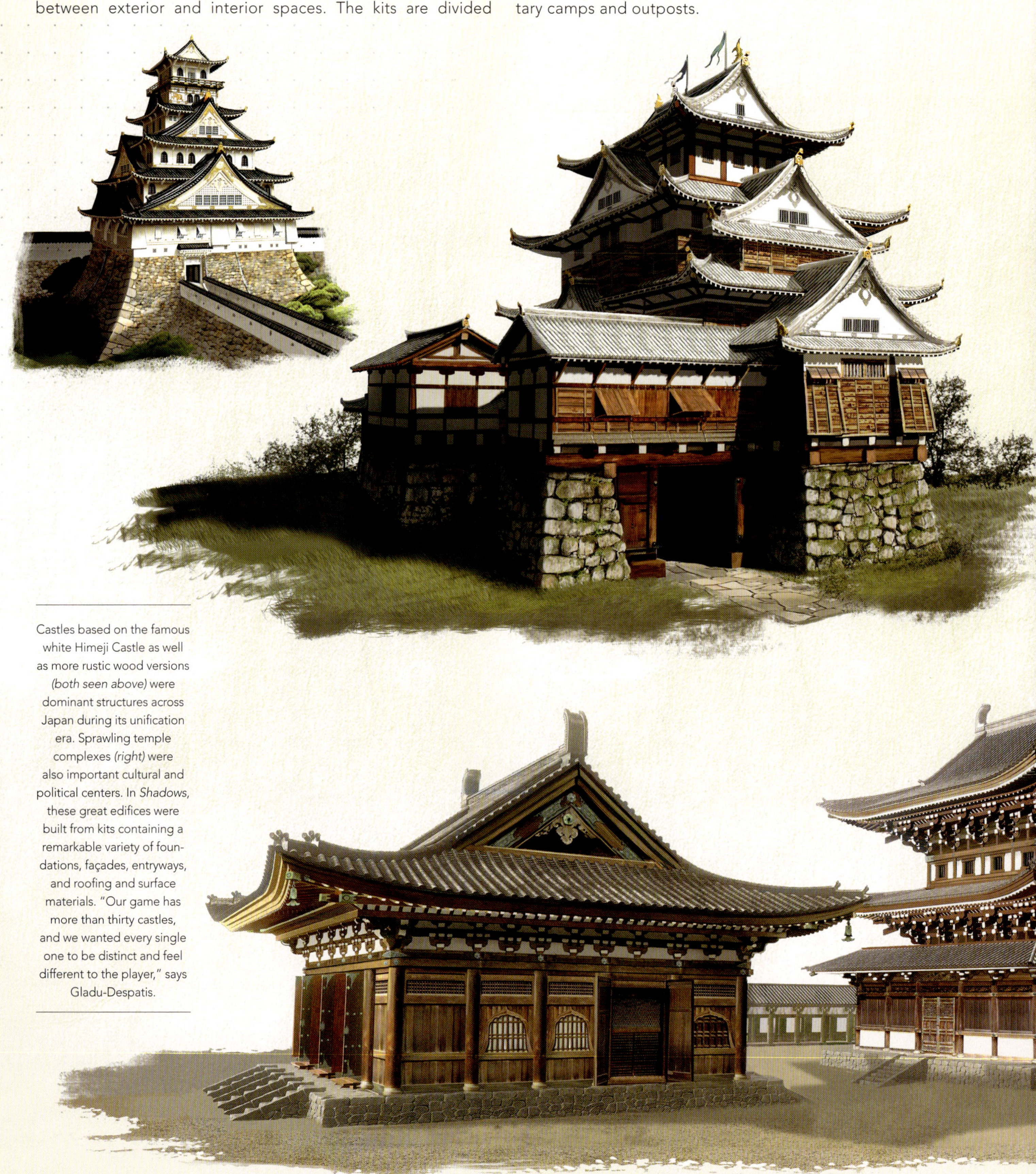

Castles based on the famous white Himeji Castle as well as more rustic wood versions *(both seen above)* were dominant structures across Japan during its unification era. Sprawling temple complexes *(right)* were also important cultural and political centers. In *Shadows*, these great edifices were built from kits containing a remarkable variety of foundations, façades, entryways, and roofing and surface materials. "Our game has more than thirty castles, and we wanted every single one to be distinct and feel different to the player," says Gladu-Despatis.

ART BY CAROLINE SOUCY

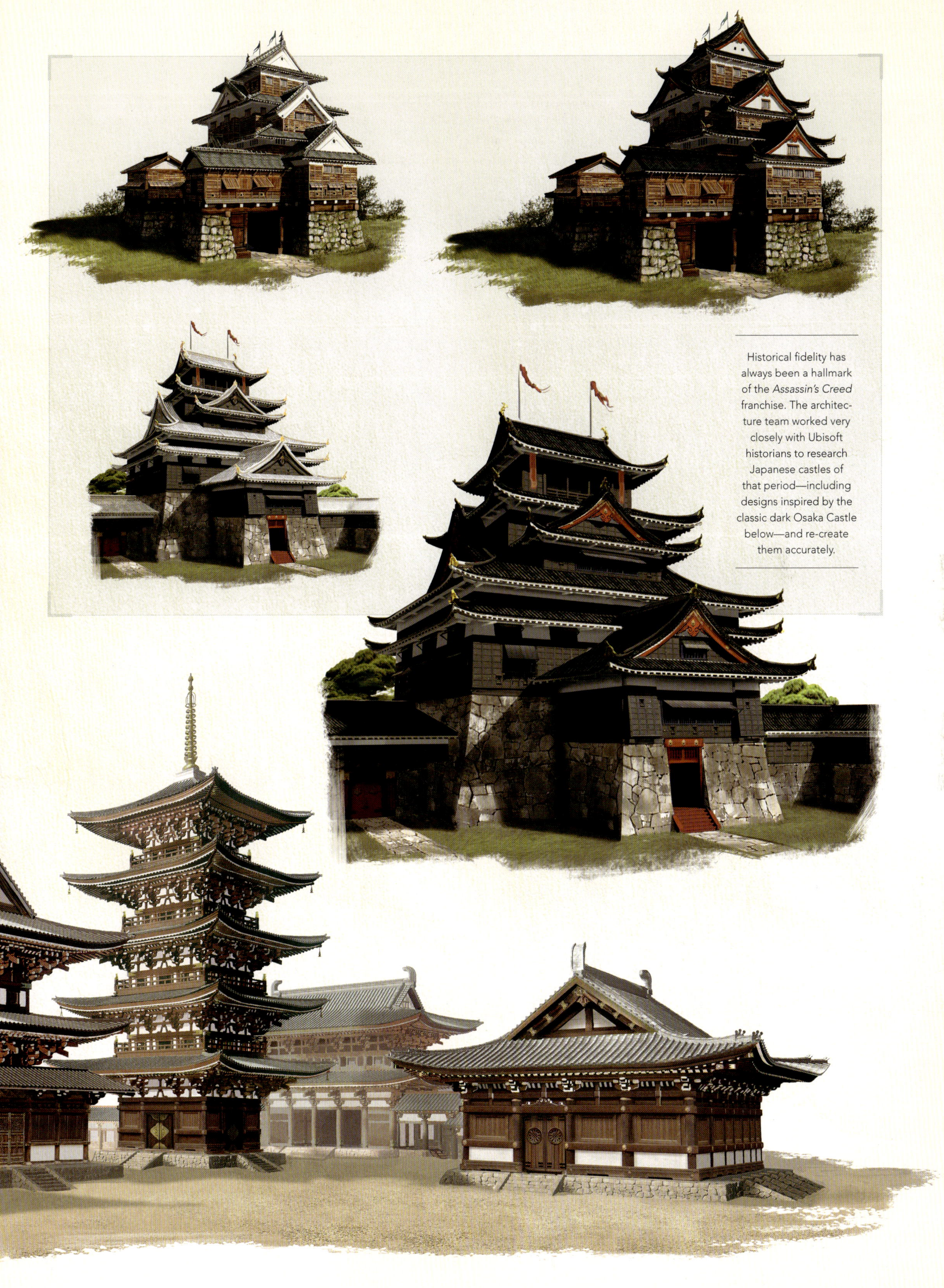

Historical fidelity has always been a hallmark of the *Assassin's Creed* franchise. The architecture team worked very closely with Ubisoft historians to research Japanese castles of that period—including designs inspired by the classic dark Osaka Castle below—and re-create them accurately.

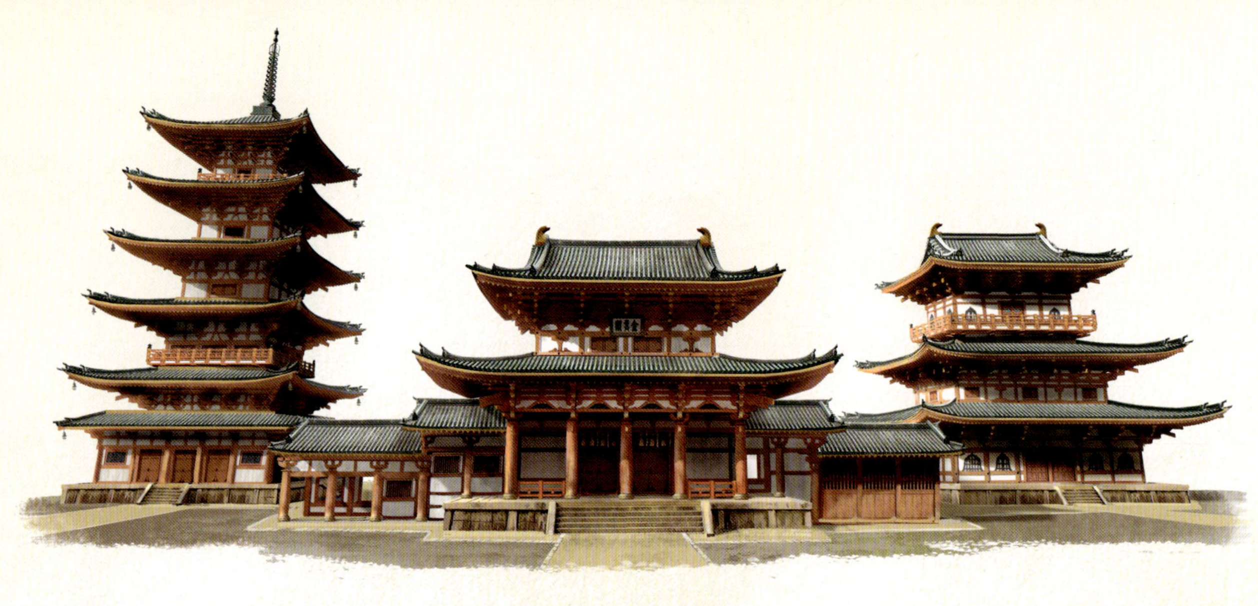

The game's sanctuary architecture (like the Buddhist temple at left) characteristically features a main hall in the center of the layout with an iconic multitiered pagoda nearby. Below, a military outpost constructed from the team's military kit is studded with barracks and watchtowers.

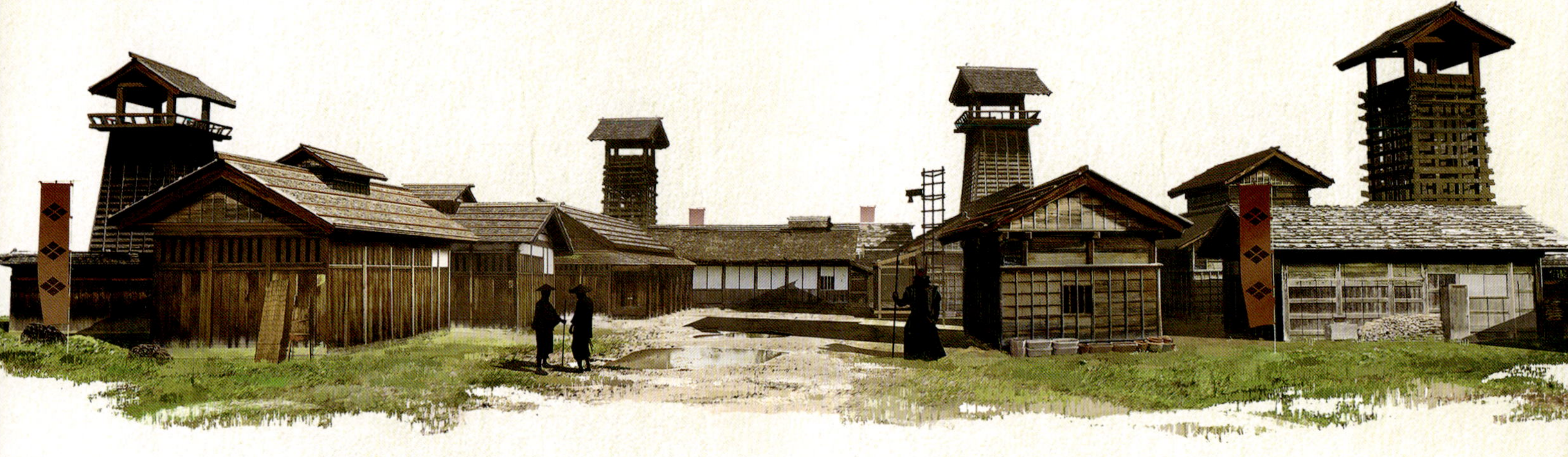

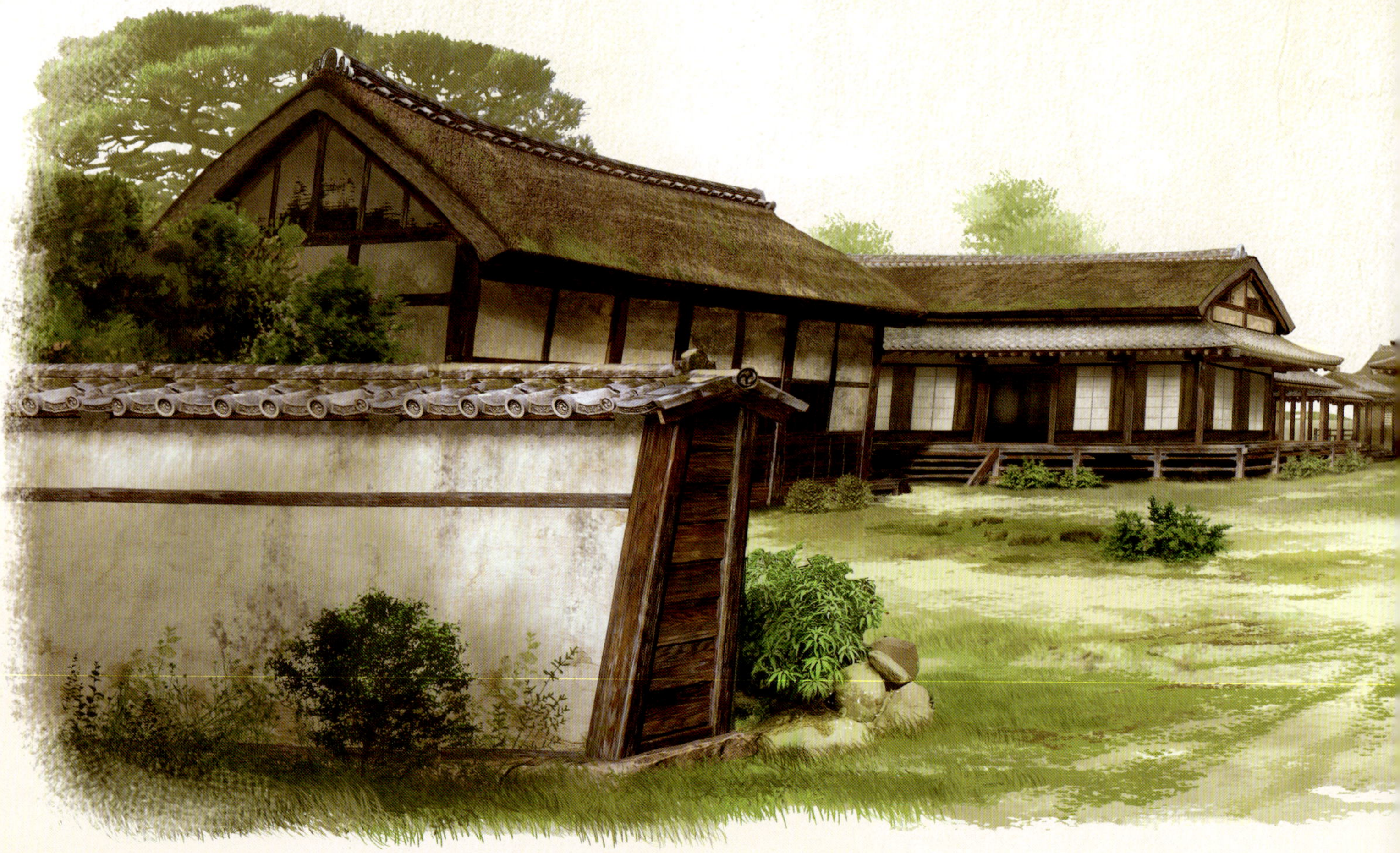

ART BY CAROLINE SOUCY

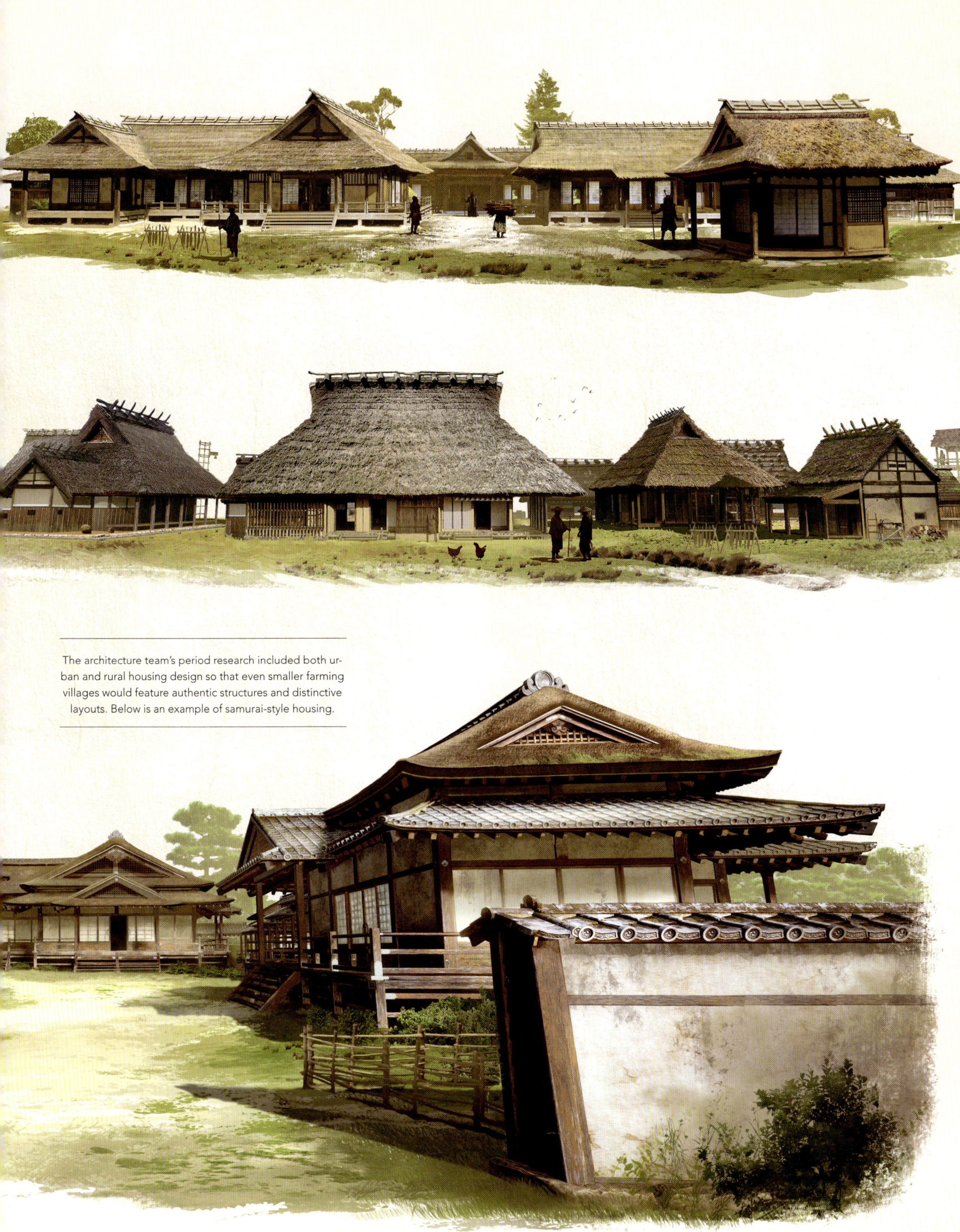

The architecture team's period research included both urban and rural housing design so that even smaller farming villages would feature authentic structures and distinctive layouts. Below is an example of samurai-style housing.

Directly below you see a spread of Japanese residential and commercial structures for towns and cities. The construction materials range from refined to rundown, letting designers build distinct neighborhoods based on economic status. For example, the two middle images on this page are lower-class main streets, whereas the upscale daimyo home at bottom is built from the mansion kit.

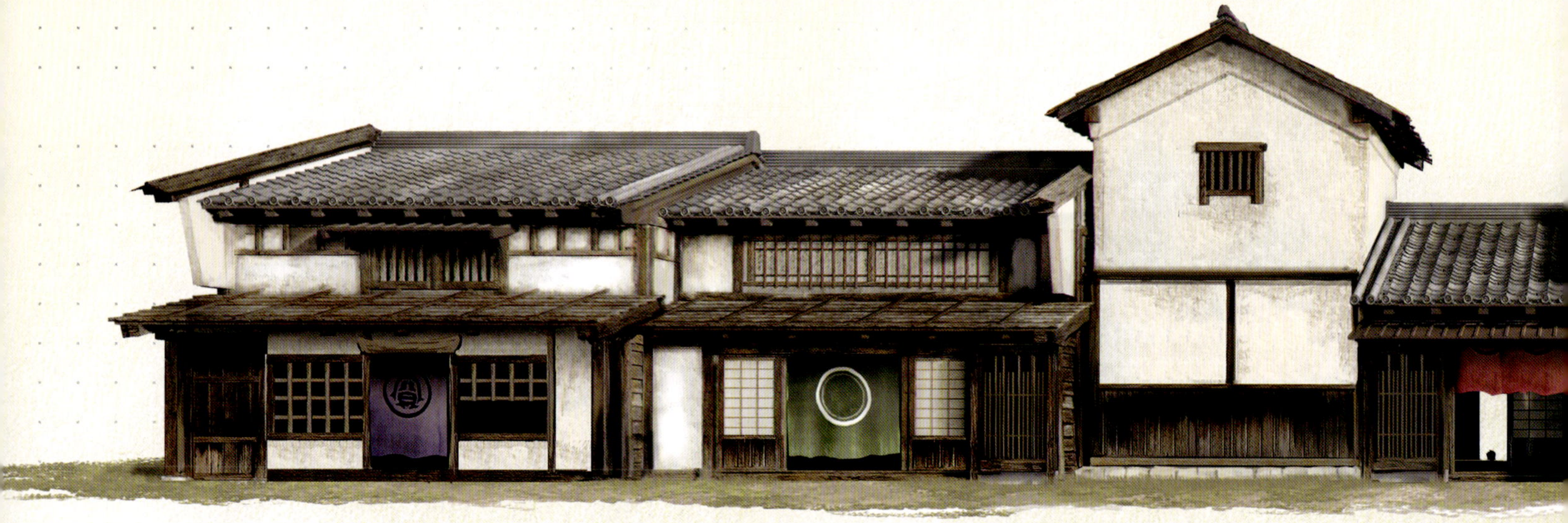

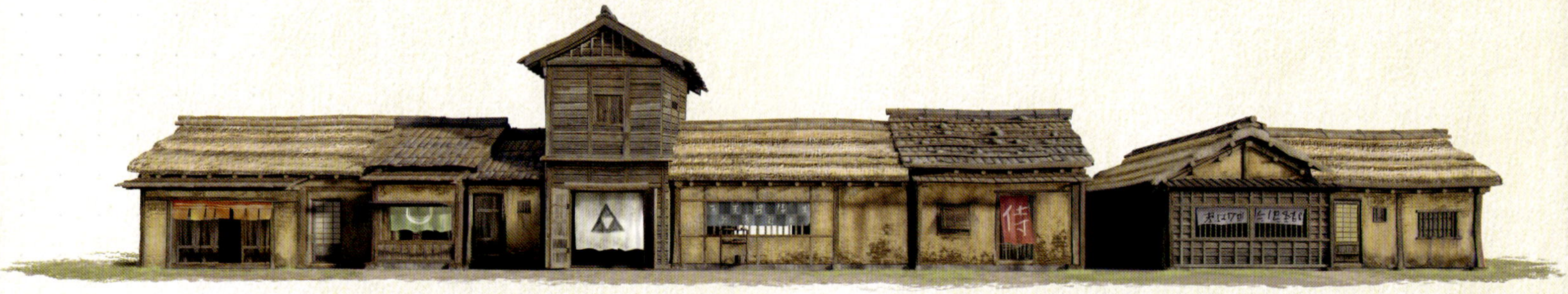

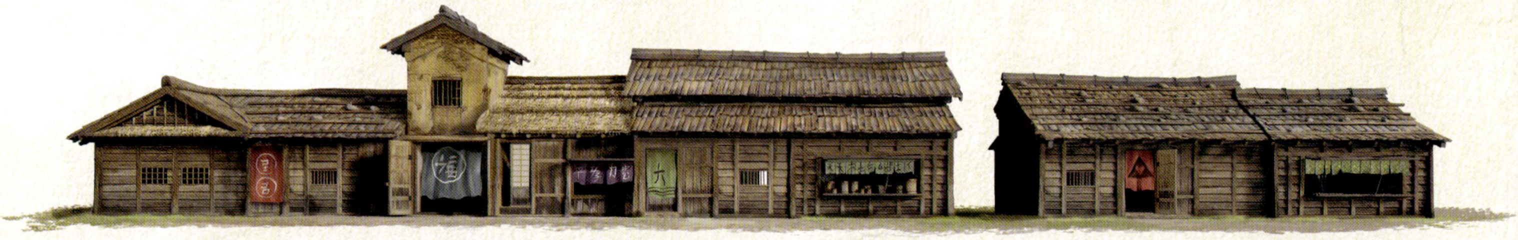

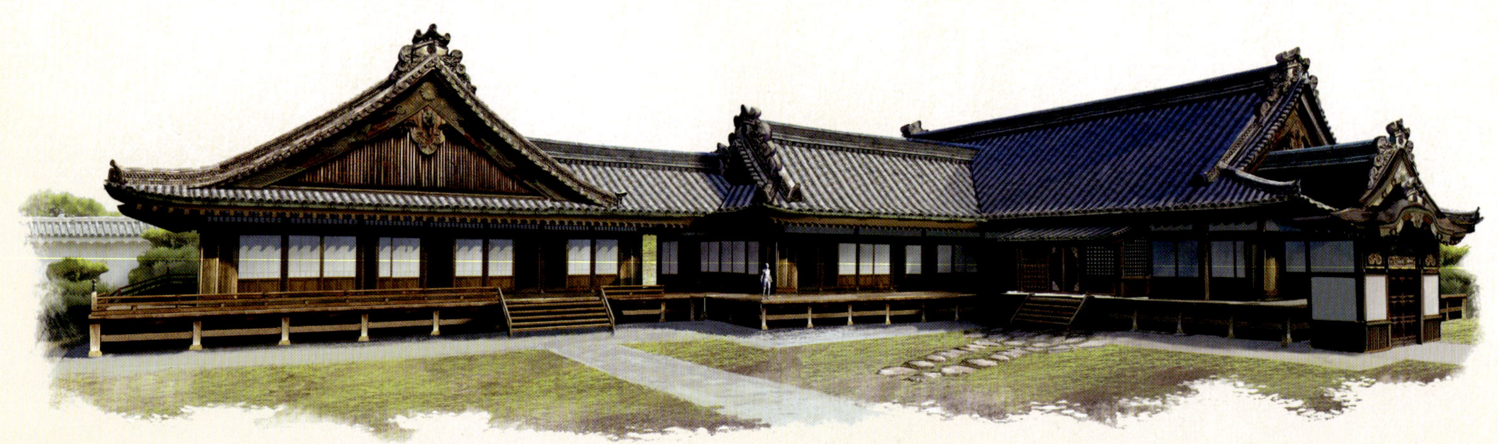

ART BY CAROLINE SOUCY

Housing rows let players navigate stealthily across rooftops; the two middle images here depict midlevel housing that is easily traversable. The kits also include sanctuary sets that differentiate between the game's religious sects—for example, at the bottom of the page you see a traditional torii gate in the foreground that marks this temple complex as Shinto.

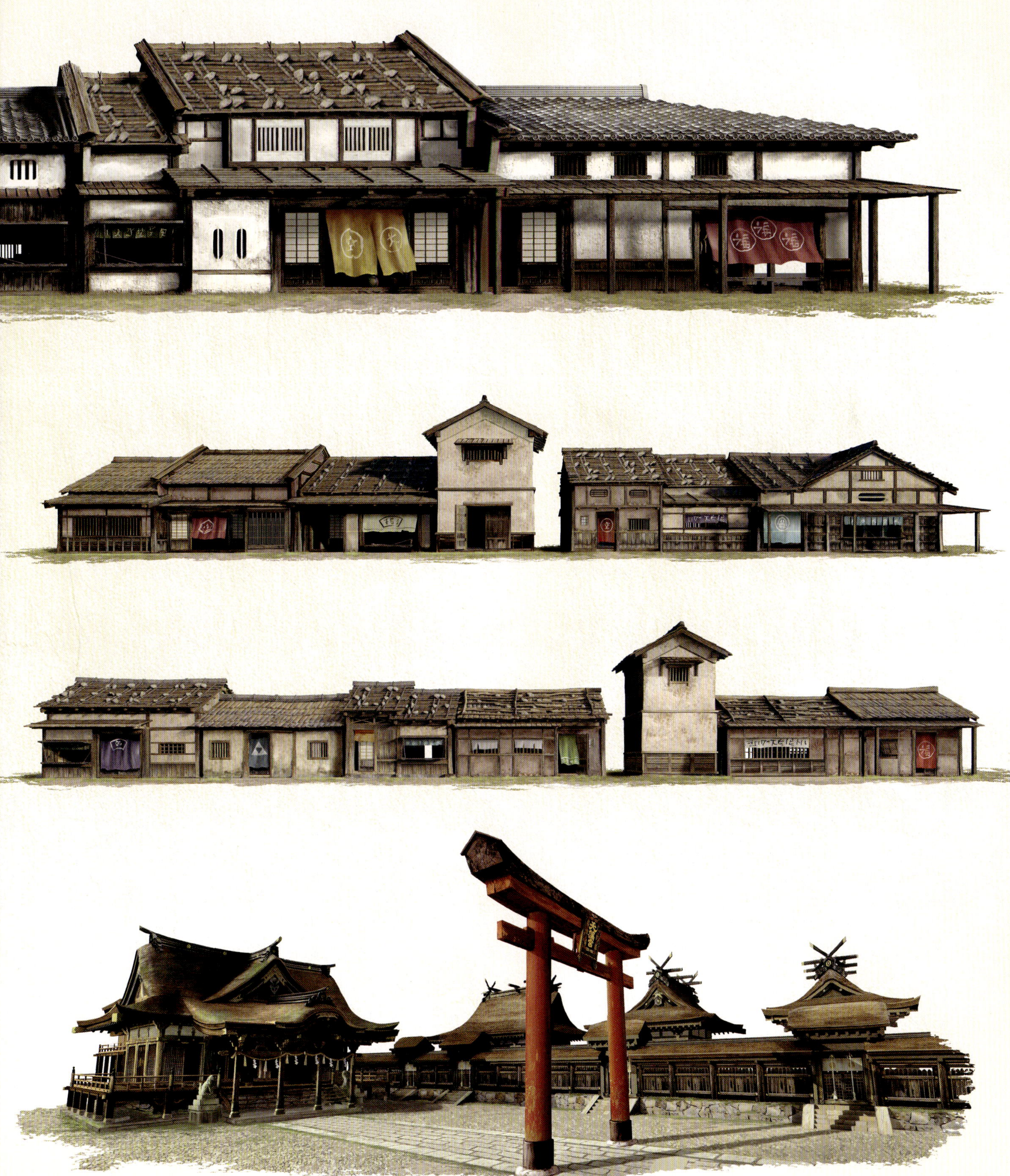

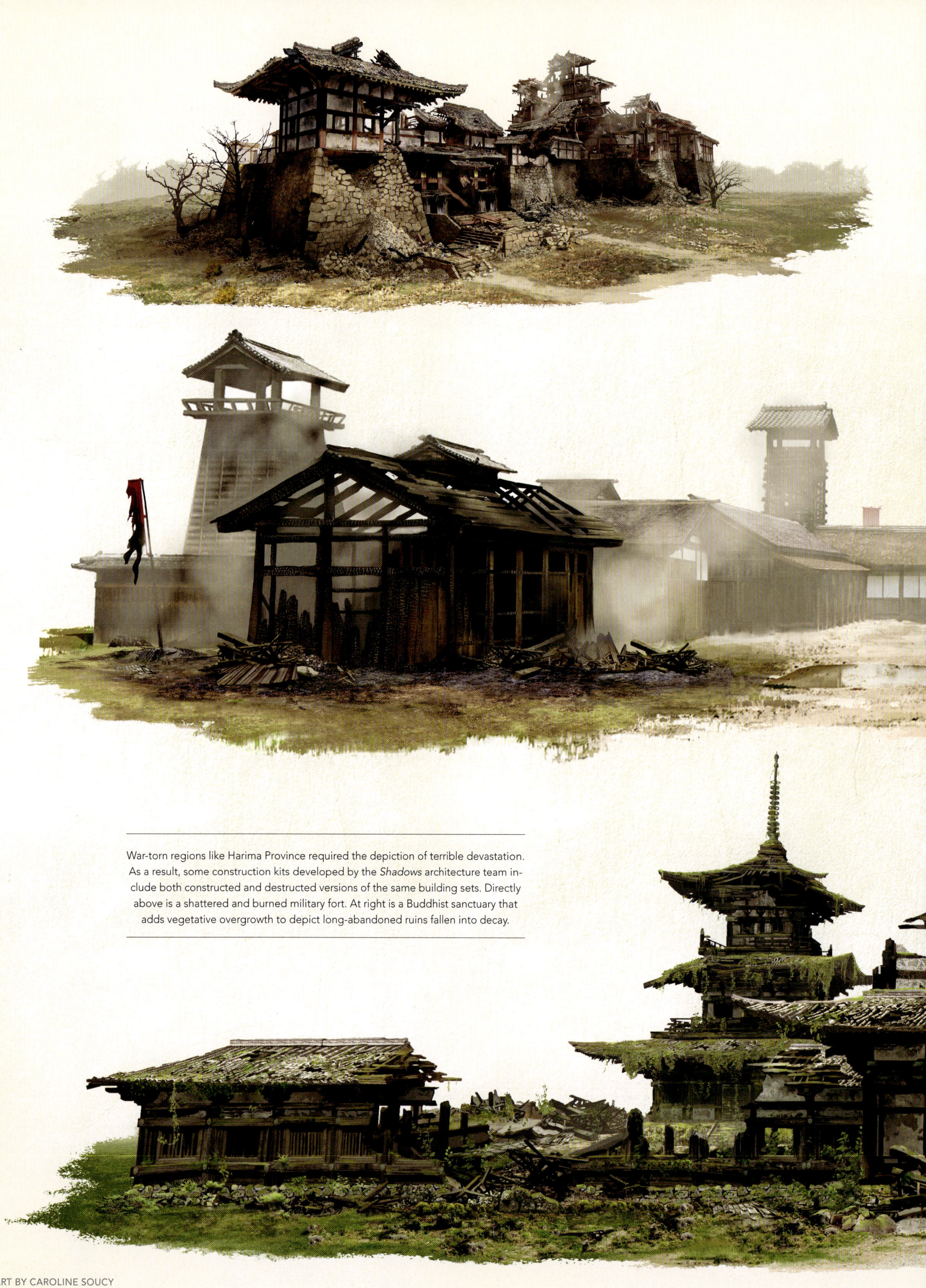

War-torn regions like Harima Province required the depiction of terrible devastation. As a result, some construction kits developed by the *Shadows* architecture team include both constructed and destructed versions of the same building sets. Directly above is a shattered and burned military fort. At right is a Buddhist sanctuary that adds vegetative overgrowth to depict long-abandoned ruins fallen into decay.

ART BY CAROLINE SOUCY

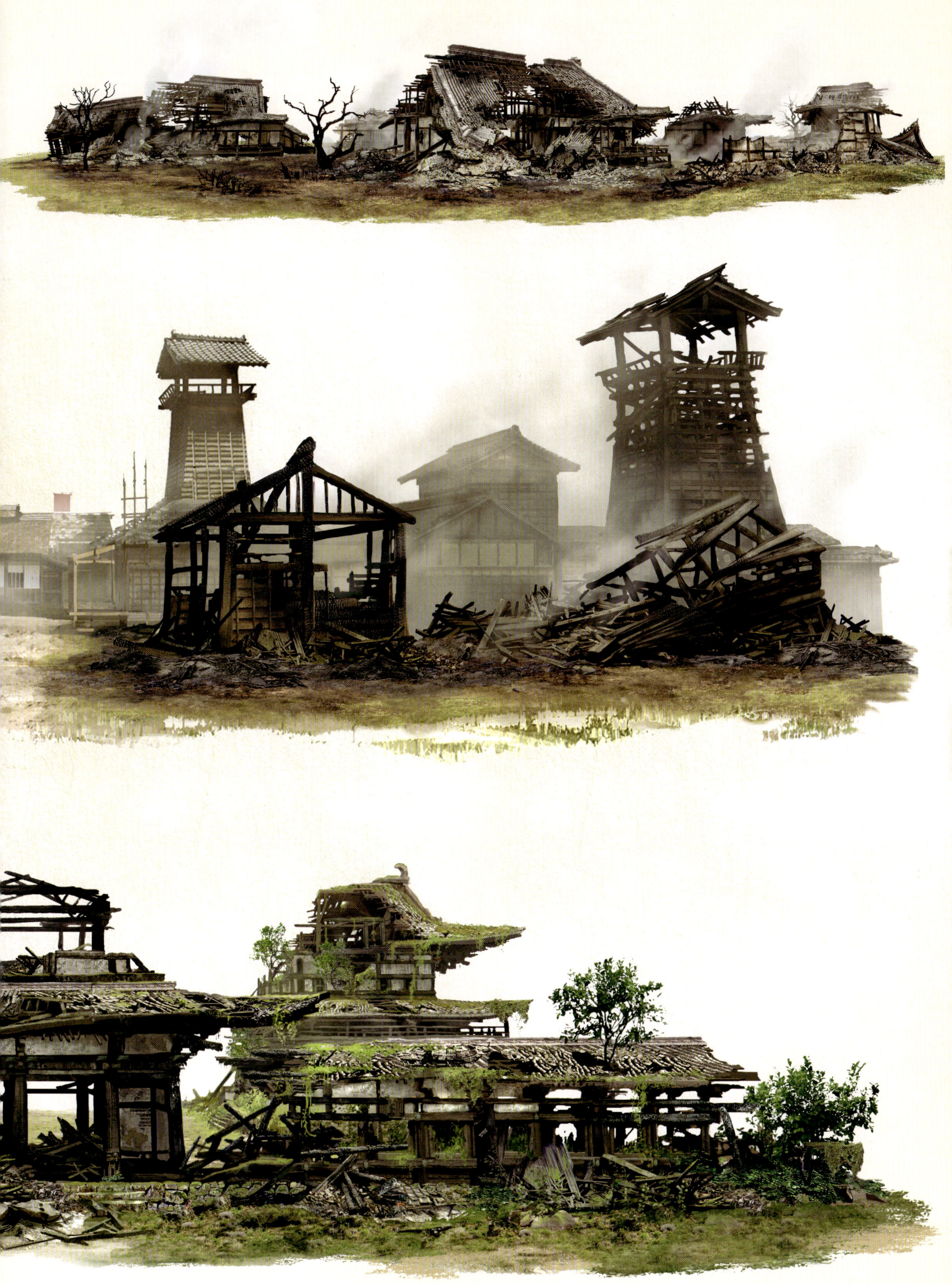

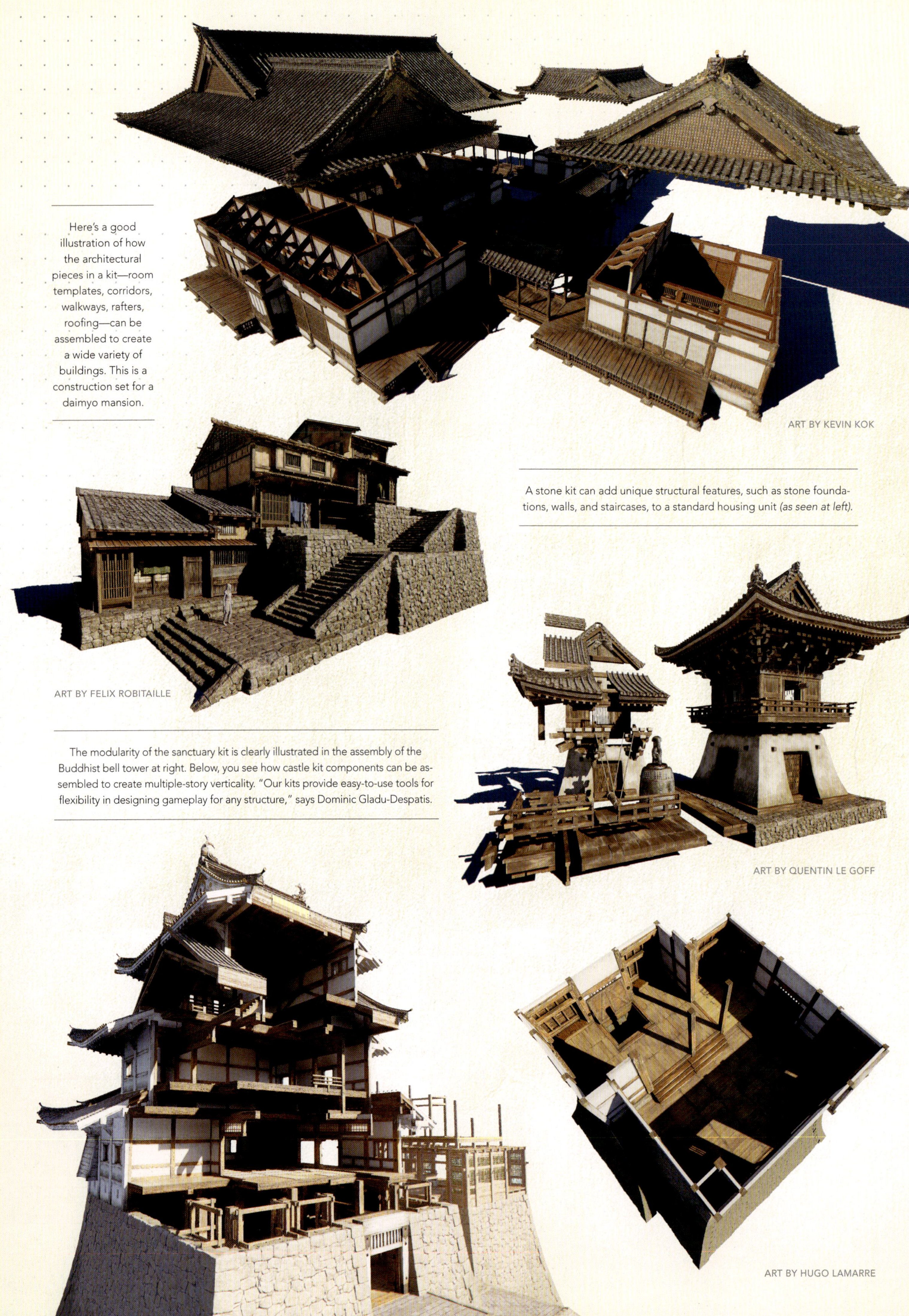

Here's a good illustration of how the architectural pieces in a kit—room templates, corridors, walkways, rafters, roofing—can be assembled to create a wide variety of buildings. This is a construction set for a daimyo mansion.

ART BY KEVIN KOK

A stone kit can add unique structural features, such as stone foundations, walls, and staircases, to a standard housing unit *(as seen at left)*.

ART BY FELIX ROBITAILLE

The modularity of the sanctuary kit is clearly illustrated in the assembly of the Buddhist bell tower at right. Below, you see how castle kit components can be assembled to create multiple-story verticality. "Our kits provide easy-to-use tools for flexibility in designing gameplay for any structure," says Dominic Gladu-Despatis.

ART BY QUENTIN LE GOFF

ART BY HUGO LAMARRE

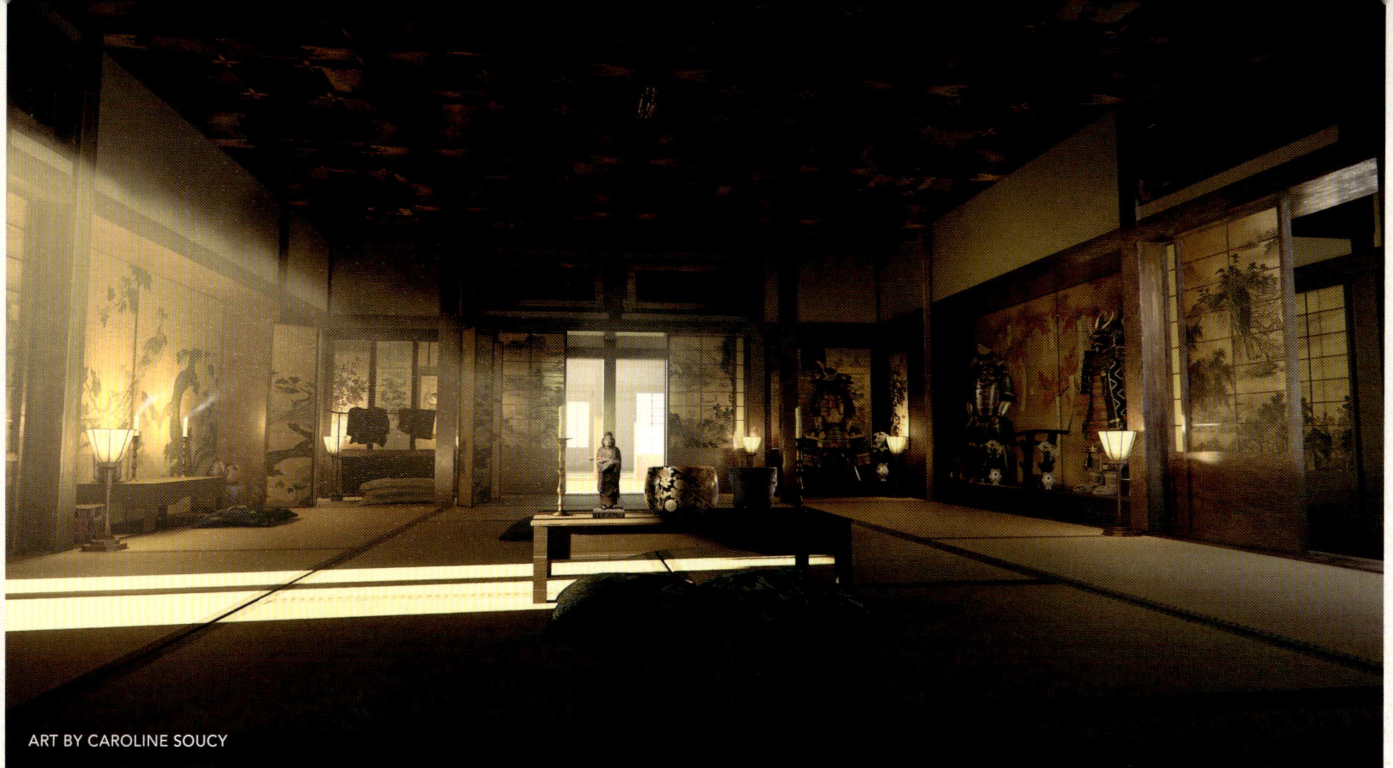
ART BY CAROLINE SOUCY

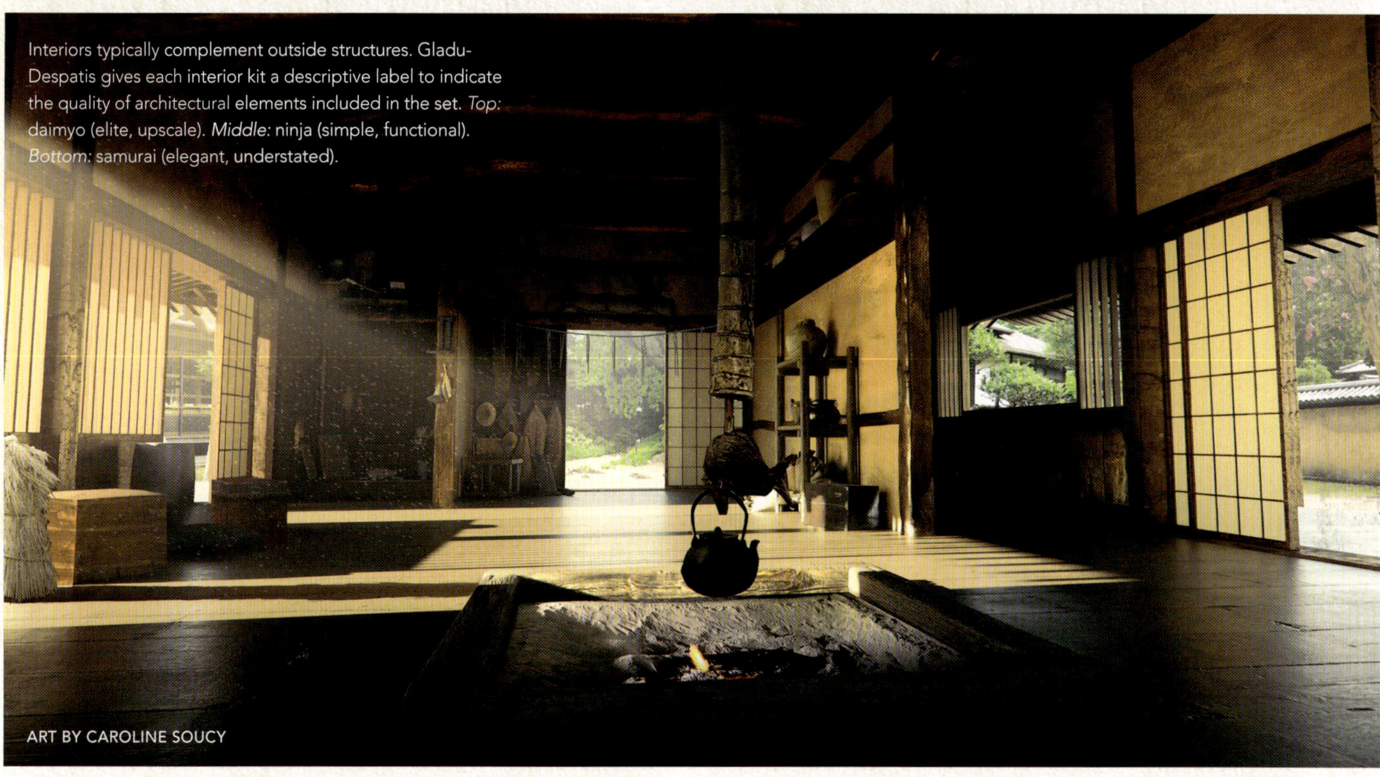
Interiors typically complement outside structures. Gladu-Despatis gives each interior kit a descriptive label to indicate the quality of architectural elements included in the set. *Top:* daimyo (elite, upscale). *Middle:* ninja (simple, functional). *Bottom:* samurai (elegant, understated).

ART BY CAROLINE SOUCY

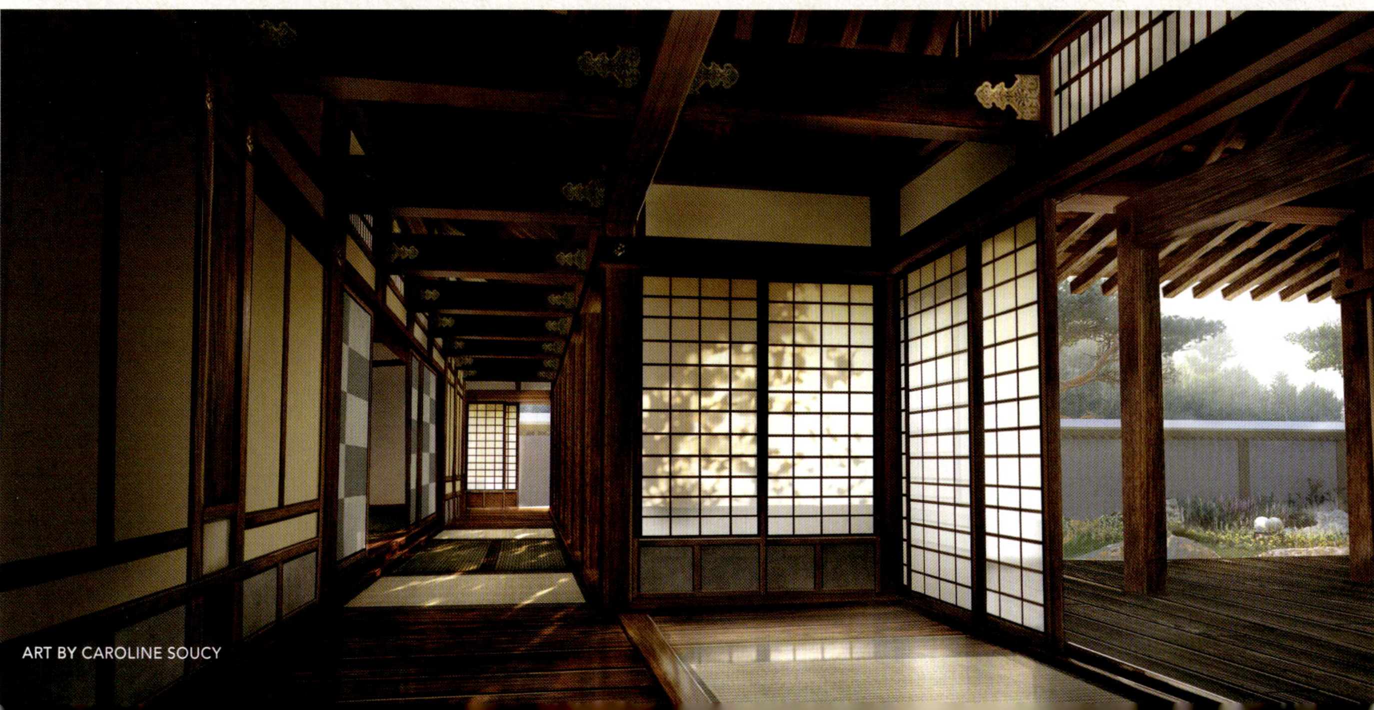
ART BY CAROLINE SOUCY

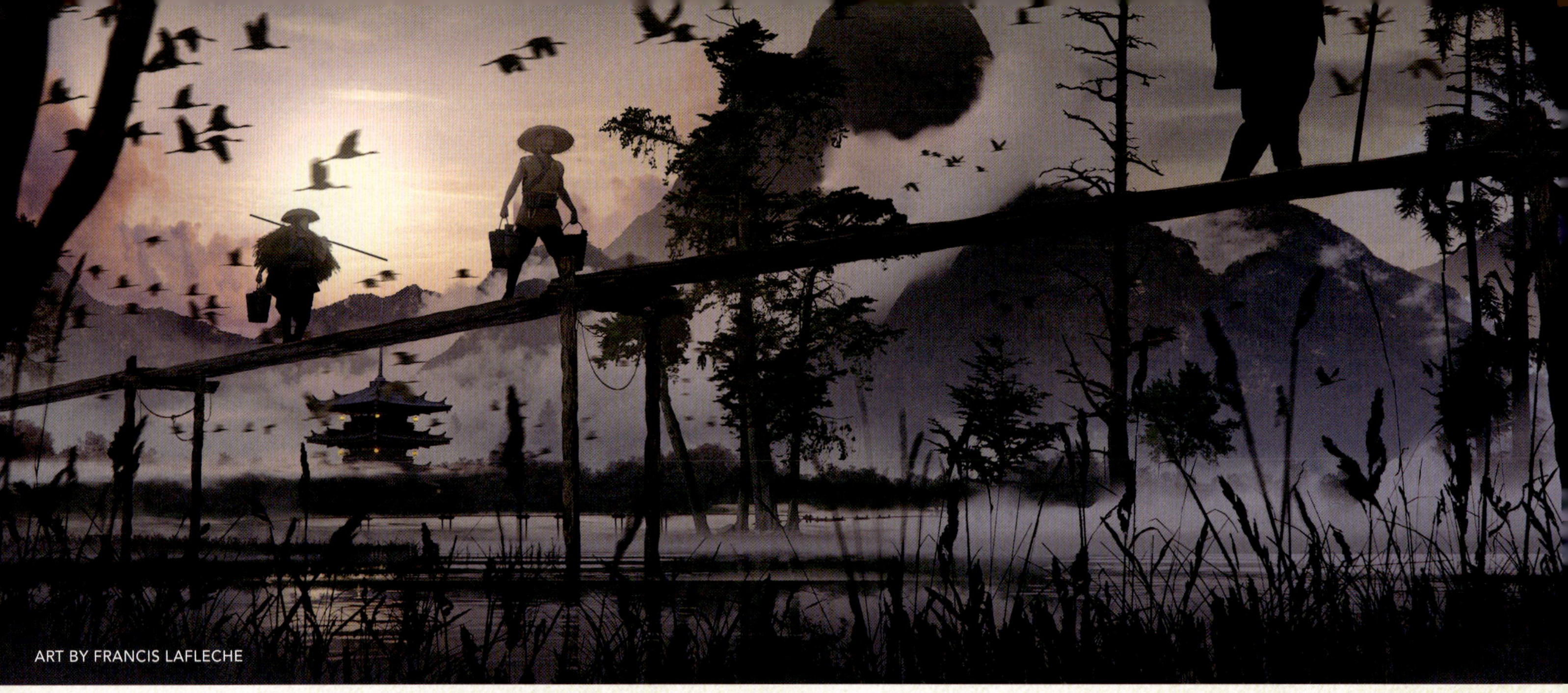

ART BY FRANCIS LAFLECHE

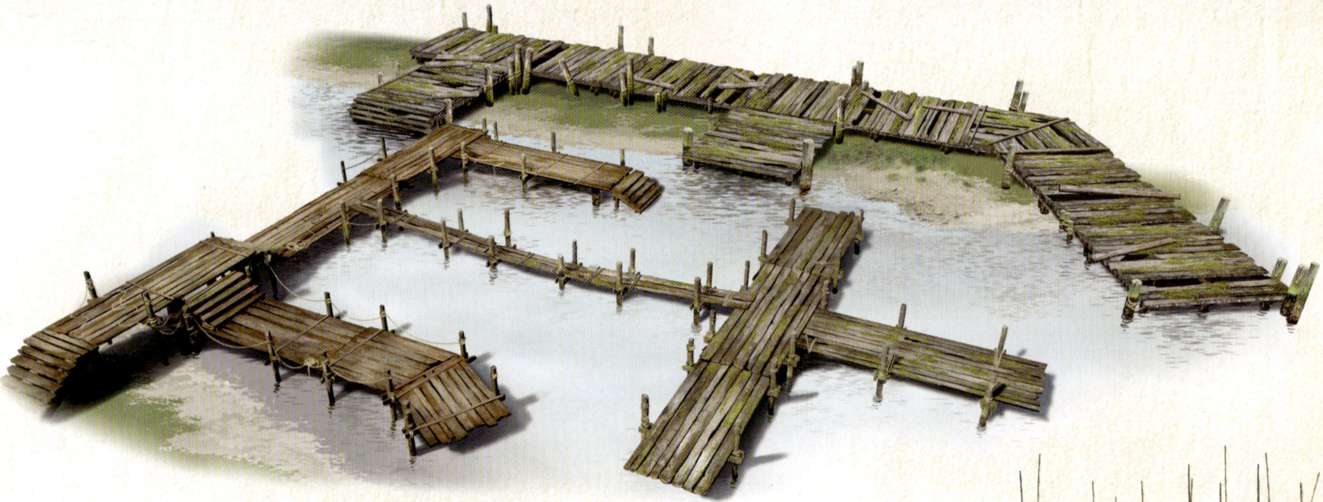

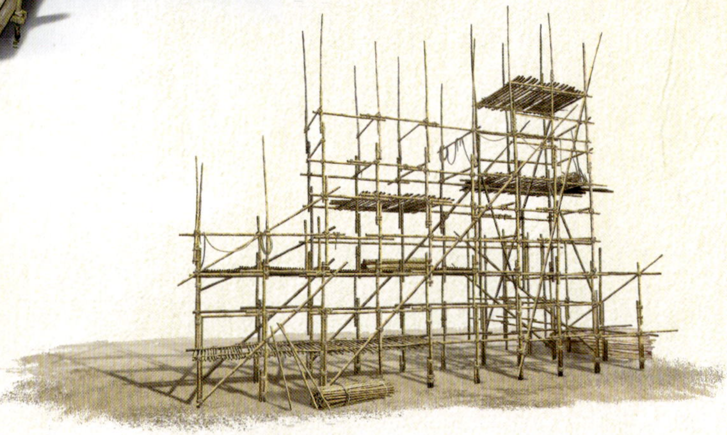

Along with the intact and the destroyed or ruined versions of each architecture kit, the team also created an "in-progress" kit—i.e., skeleton sections of buildings that are clearly under construction, with open frames and no walls. This kit includes generic scaffolding that can be placed around any structure to indicate states of construction or repair. "This was particularly useful in Osaka, where the aft section of the main castle was being built during our time period," says Gladu-Despatis.

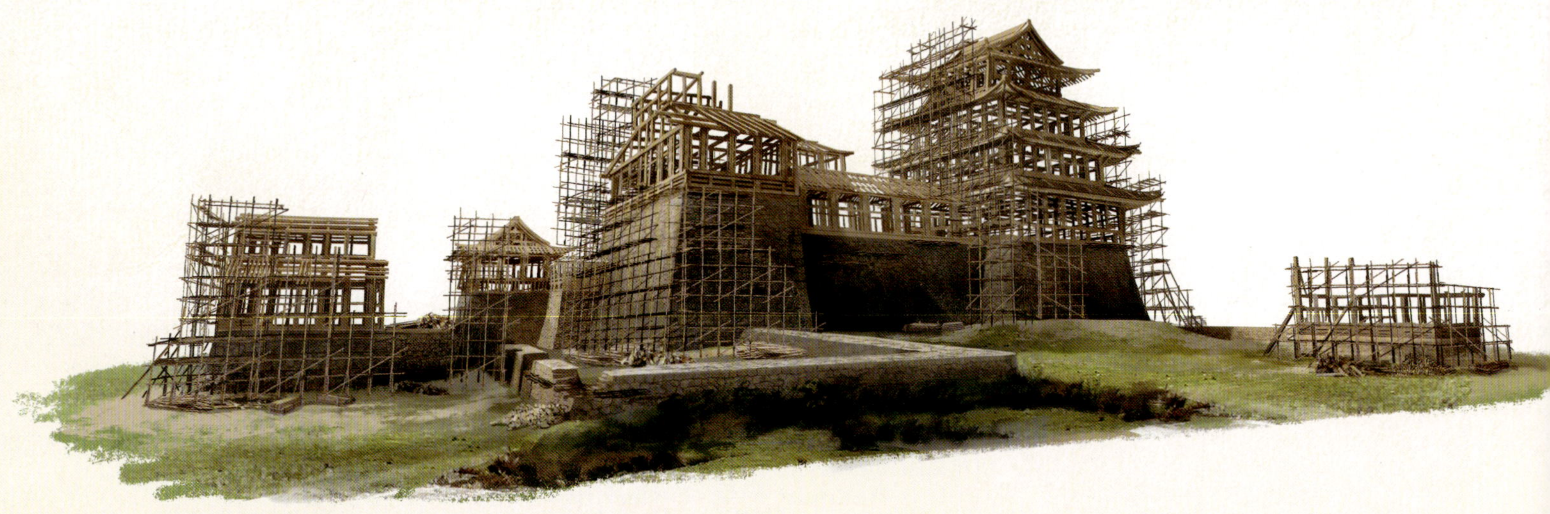

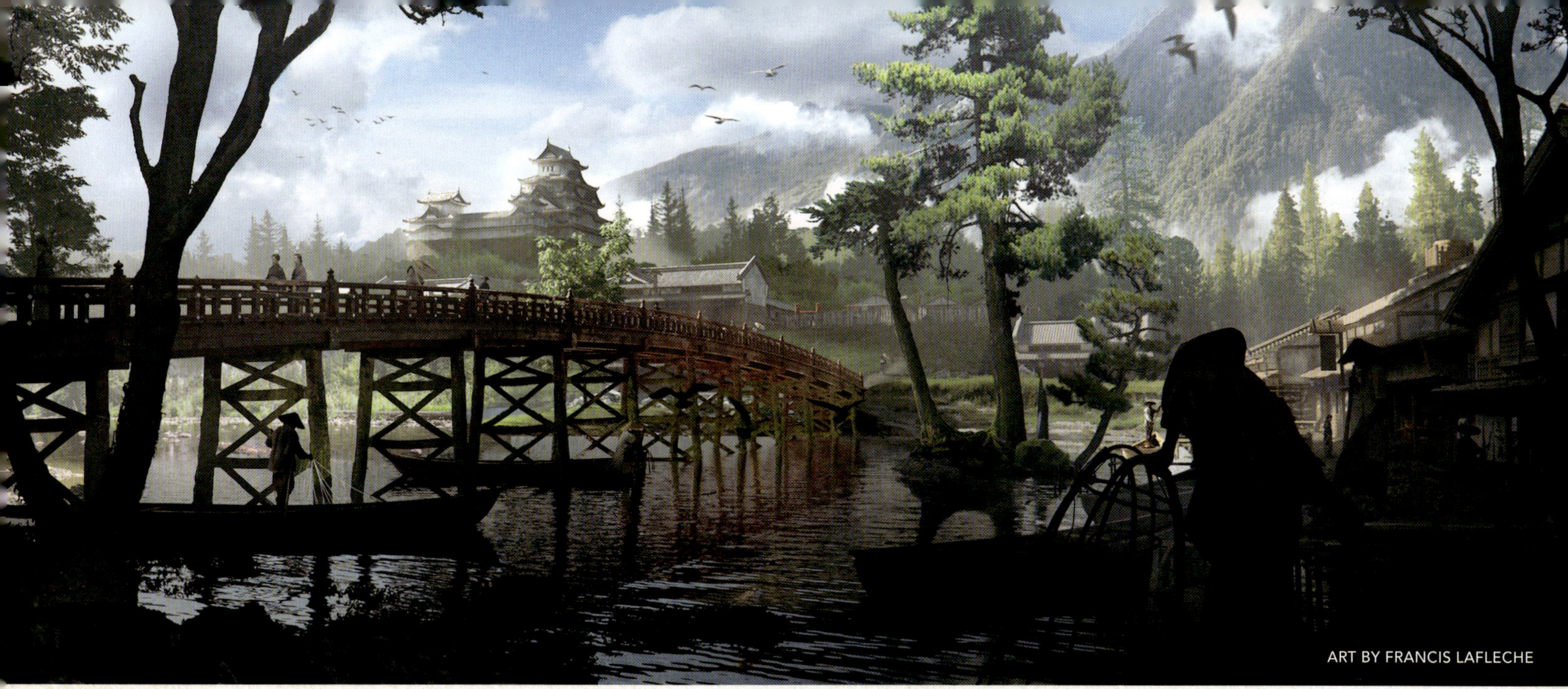

ART BY FRANCIS LAFLECHE

Japan's topography features abundant water features, such as seacoasts, rivers, canals, and other waterways, plus plenty of flooded rice paddies. This called for a variety of bridge, pier, and walkway components to allow for traversal and other gameplay elements.

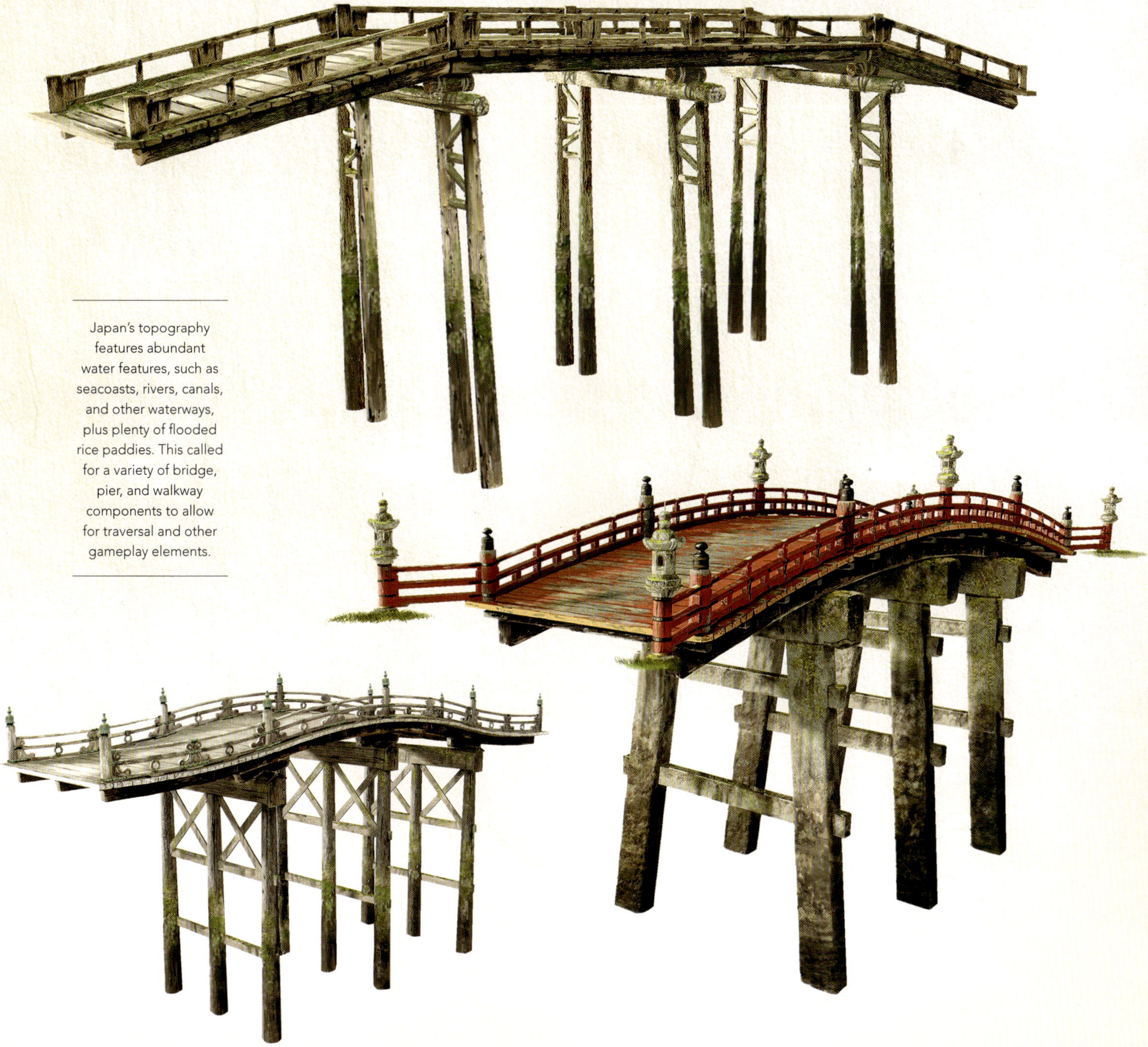

ART BY CAROLINE SOUCY

MATERIALS

Texture research for *Assassin's Creed Shadows* included a deep dive into the types of materials commonly used for exteriors and interiors in sixteenth-century Japanese architecture. It also included a survey of the natural textures of ground surfaces and rockfaces in each region. According to lead materials artist Dimitri Alexis, the team learned about Japanese construction and crafting techniques, such as plaster making, ceramic tiling, material tinting, and wood-preservation methods. "We used that research to create our 'recipes' of texture blending for surface detail, taking into account processes like aging and discoloration as well," says Alexis.

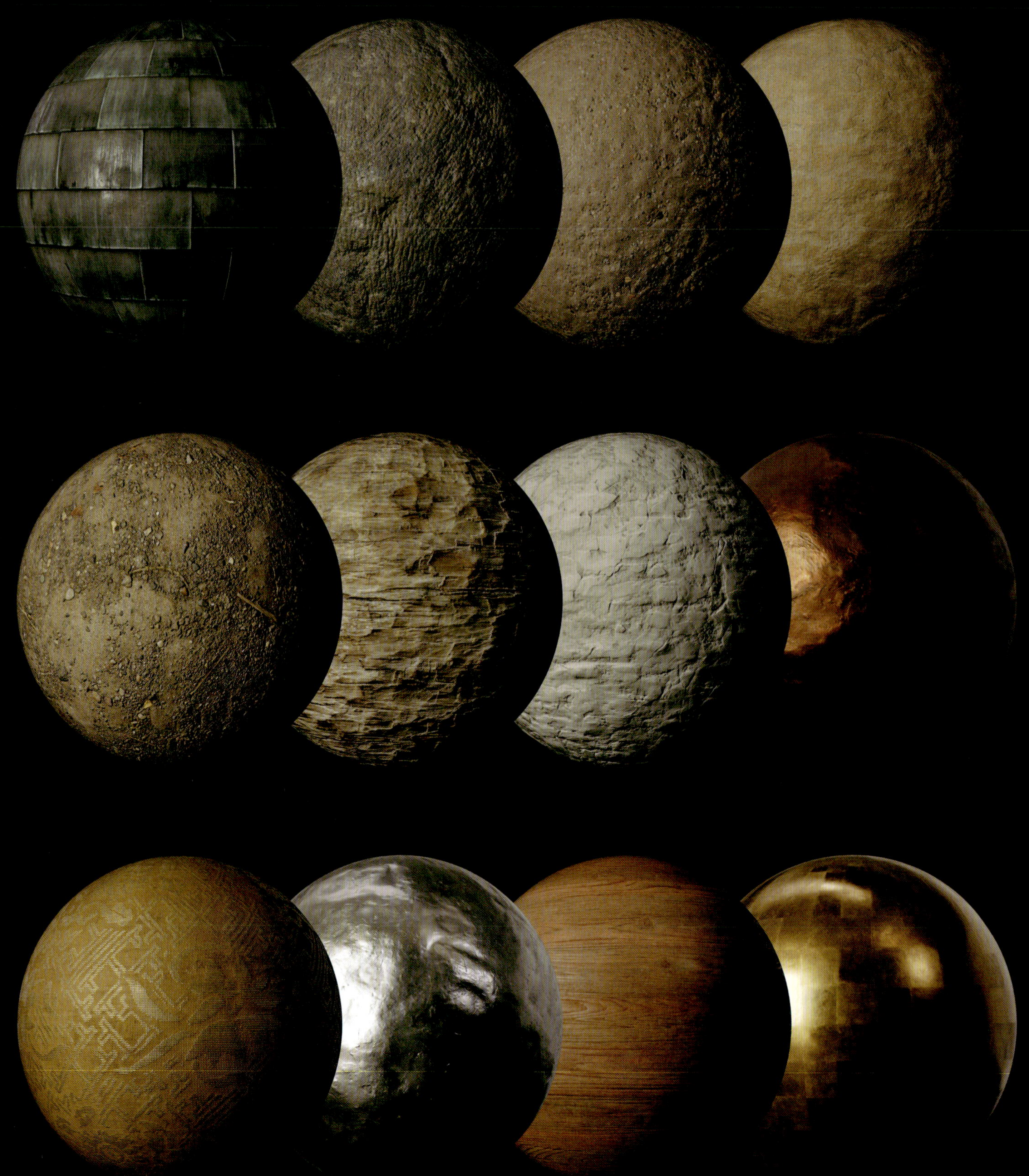

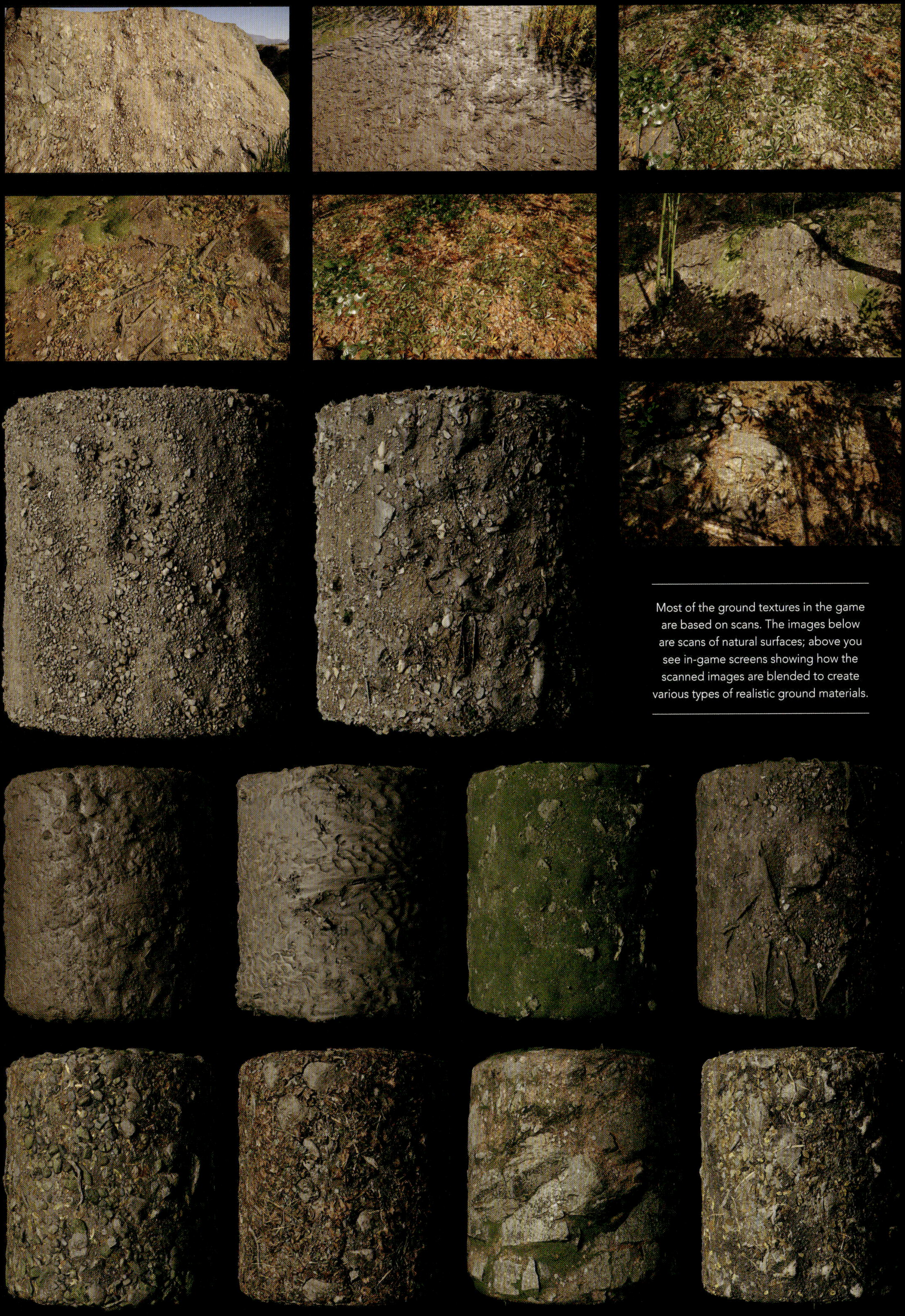

Most of the ground textures in the game are based on scans. The images below are scans of natural surfaces; above you see in-game screens showing how the scanned images are blended to create various types of realistic ground materials.

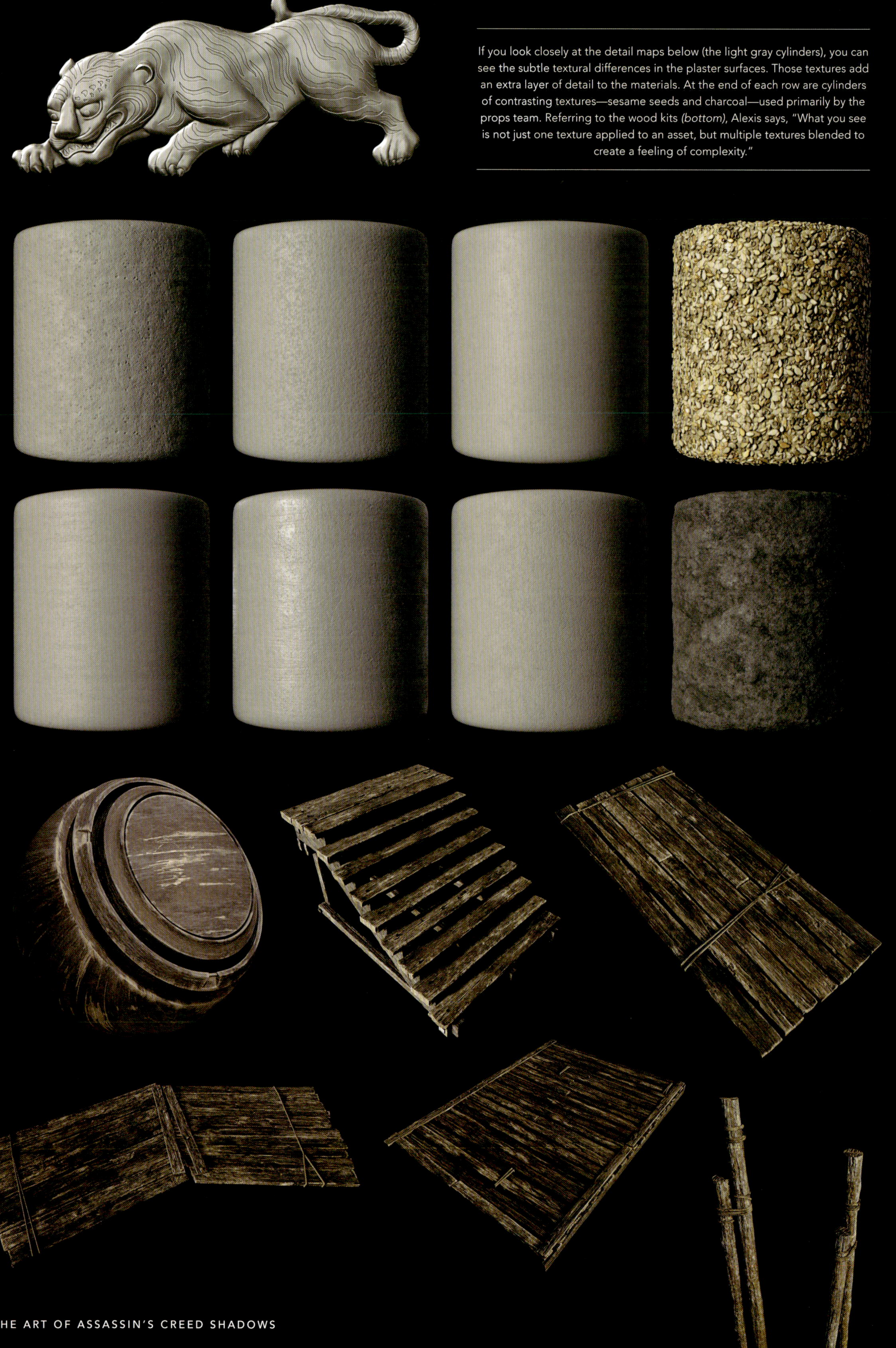

If you look closely at the detail maps below (the light gray cylinders), you can see the subtle textural differences in the plaster surfaces. Those textures add an extra layer of detail to the materials. At the end of each row are cylinders of contrasting textures—sesame seeds and charcoal—used primarily by the props team. Referring to the wood kits *(bottom)*, Alexis says, "What you see is not just one texture applied to an asset, but multiple textures blended to create a feeling of complexity."

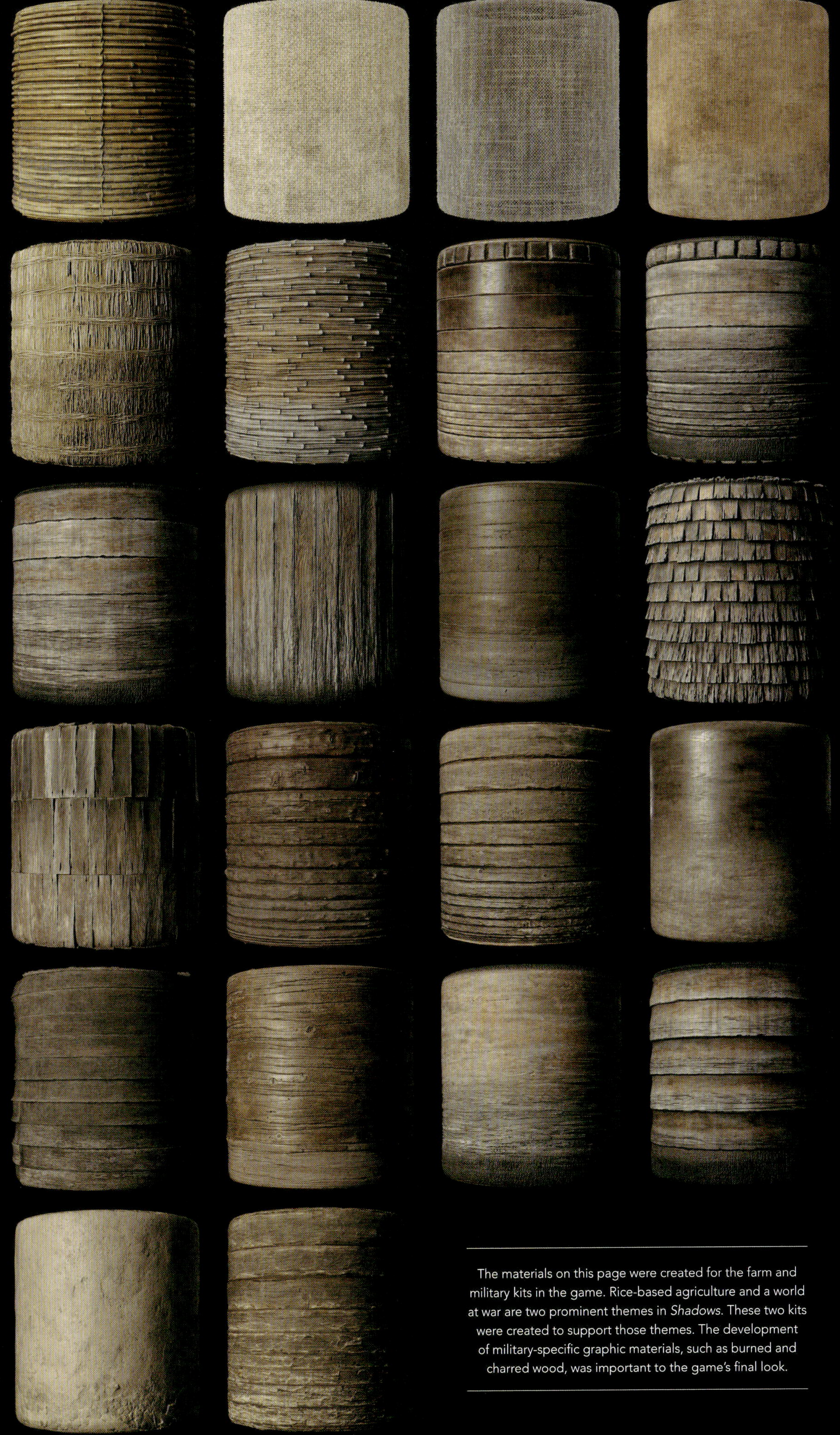

The materials on this page were created for the farm and military kits in the game. Rice-based agriculture and a world at war are two prominent themes in *Shadows*. These two kits were created to support those themes. The development of military-specific graphic materials, such as burned and charred wood, was important to the game's final look.

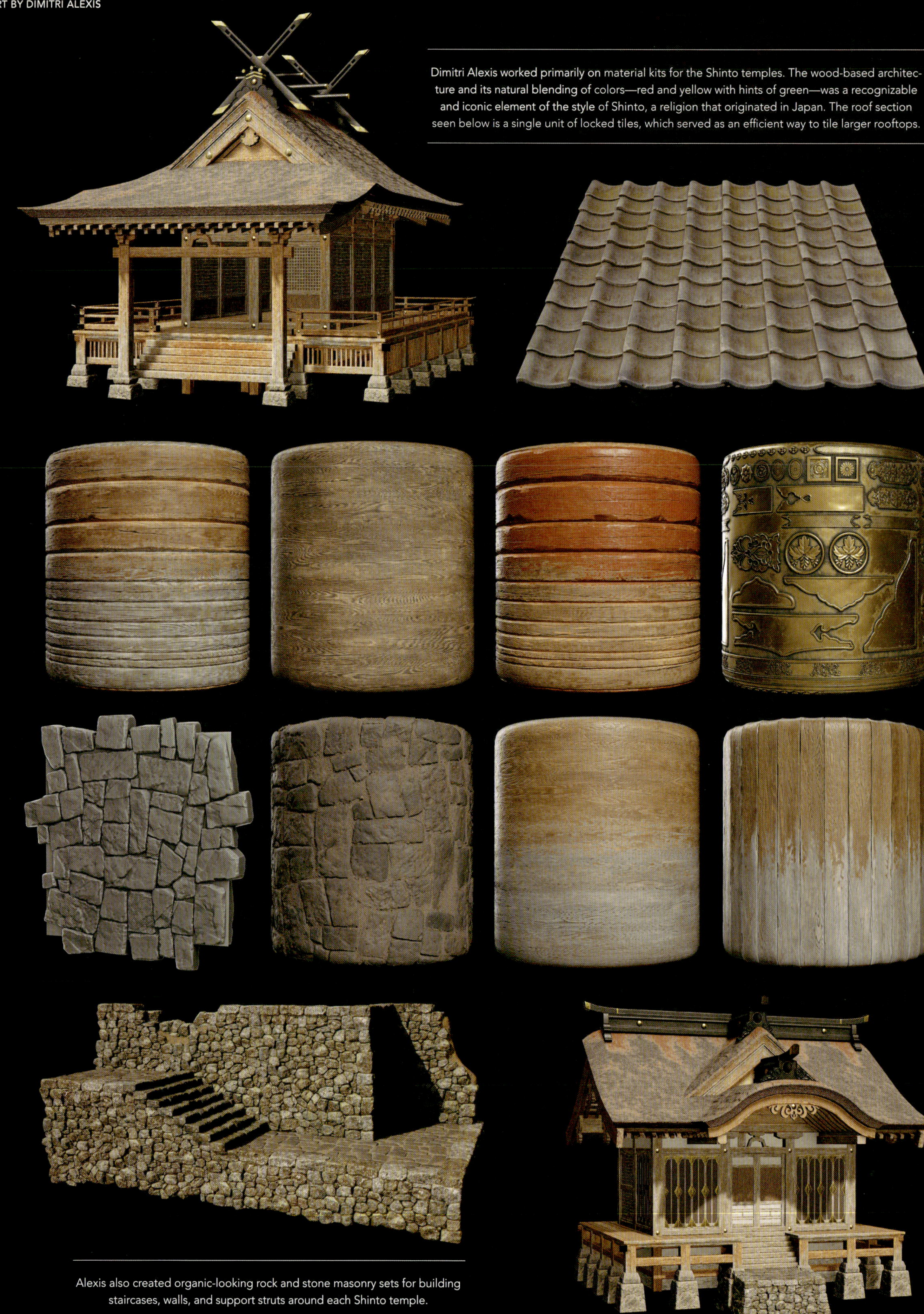

Dimitri Alexis worked primarily on material kits for the Shinto temples. The wood-based architecture and its natural blending of colors—red and yellow with hints of green—was a recognizable and iconic element of the style of Shinto, a religion that originated in Japan. The roof section seen below is a single unit of locked tiles, which served as an efficient way to tile larger rooftops.

Alexis also created organic-looking rock and stone masonry sets for building staircases, walls, and support struts around each Shinto temple.

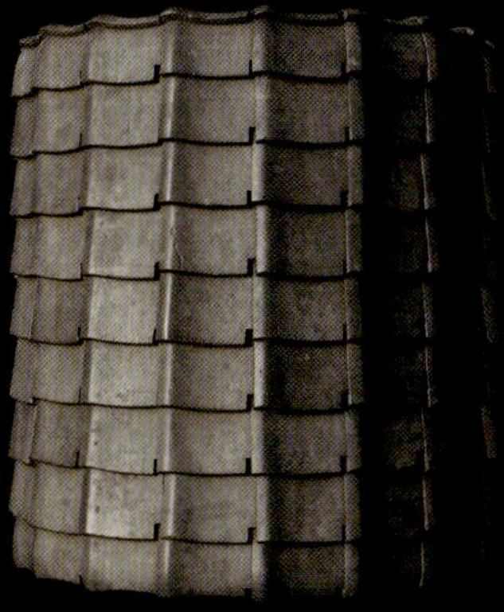

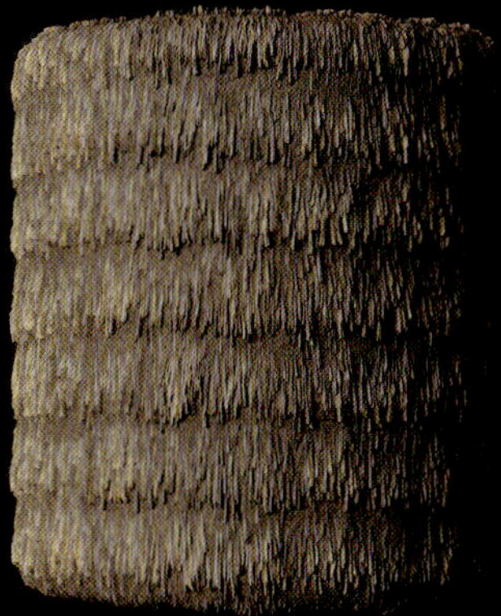

The assets here are a combination of tiled and thatched straw materials to re-create the classic roofing style *(below)* of samurai residences.

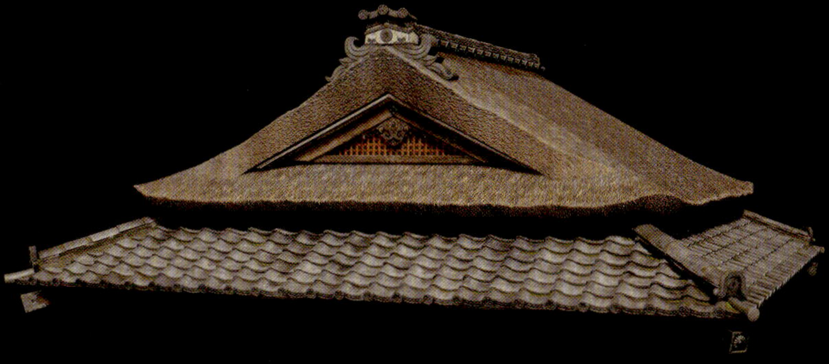

Below is an array of plaster and wood materials specifically created for rural housing kits; an example house is seen at bottom left. For smaller or more intricately shaped roofs, artists could work with individual roofing tiles like those in the pile seen here.

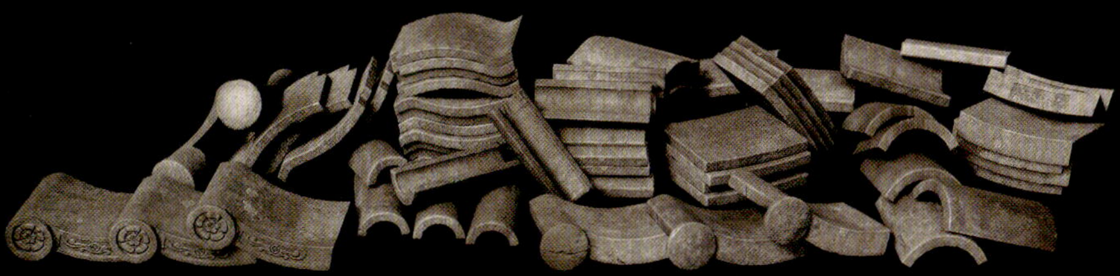

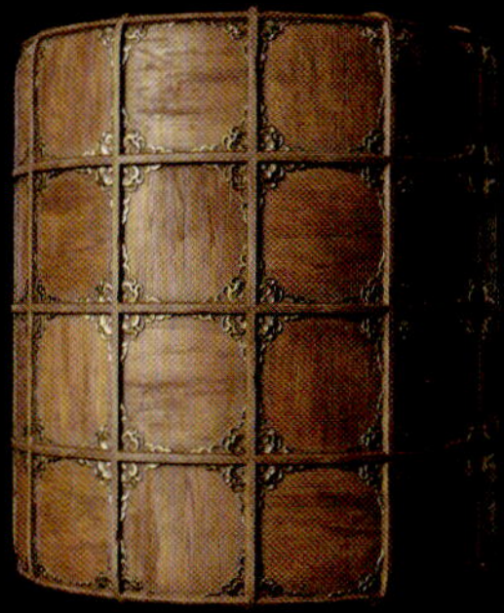

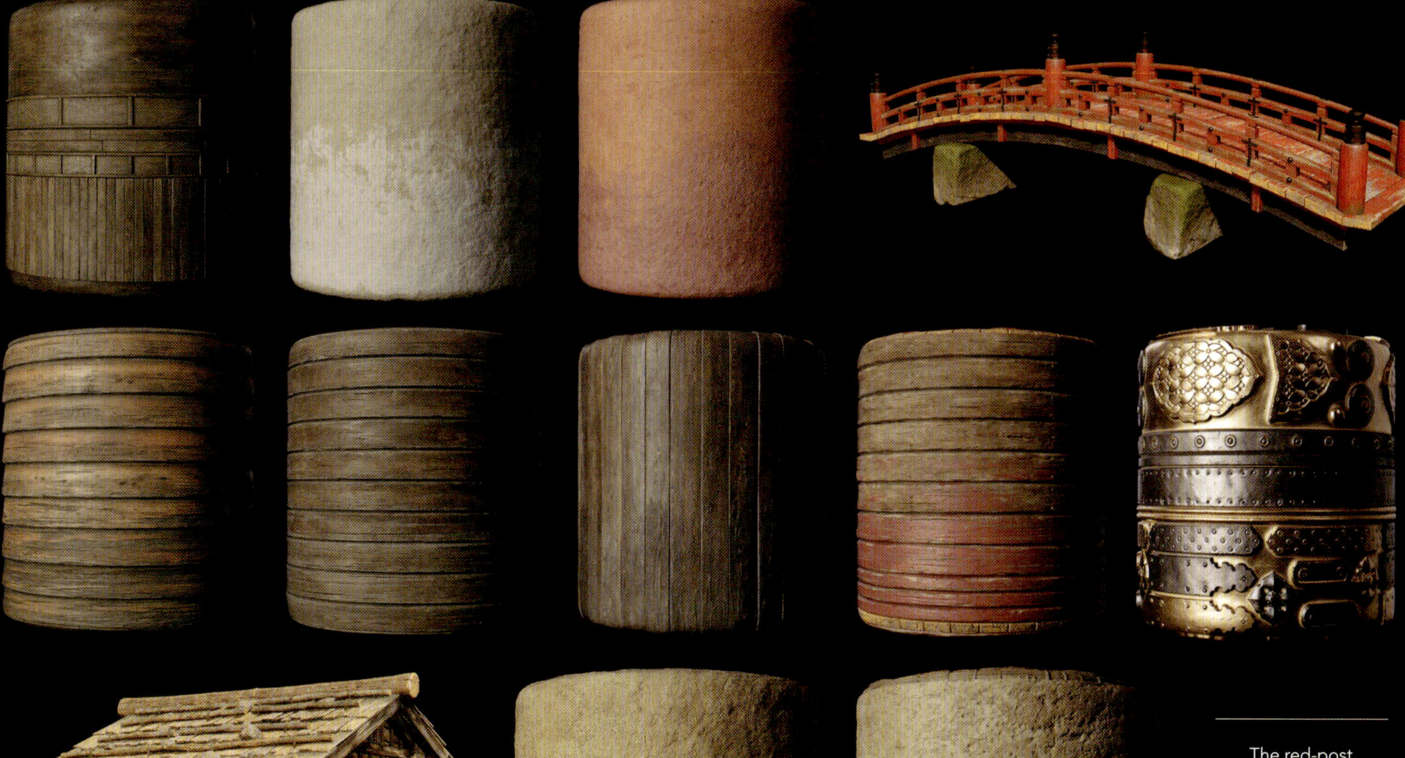

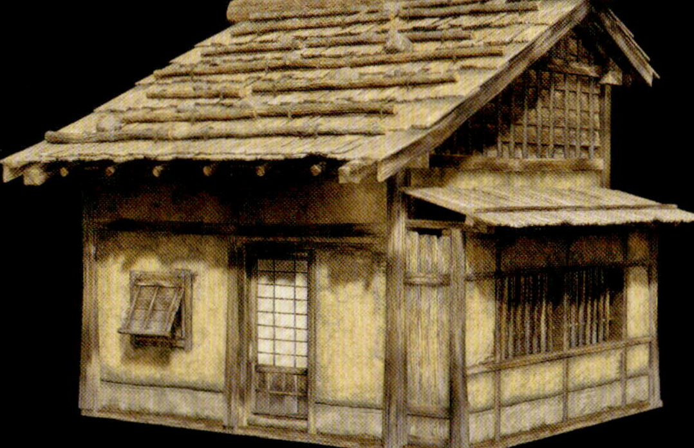

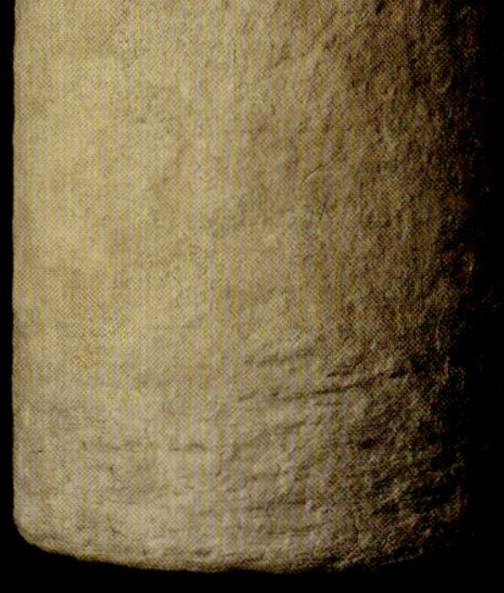

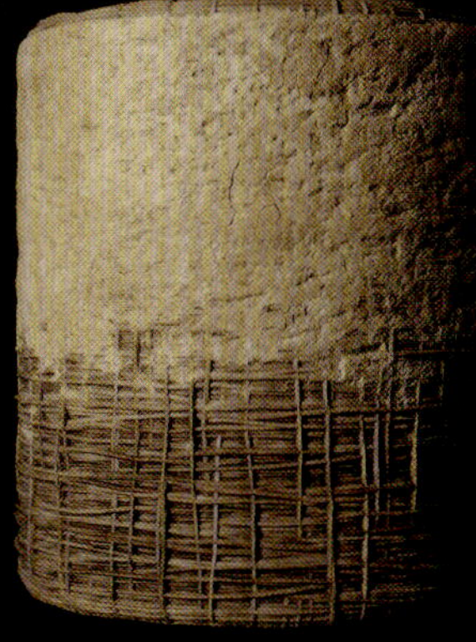

The red-post bridge seen above is another iconic Japanese sight—its color, shape, and lacquered wood were often associated with samurai tradition in Japan's culture.

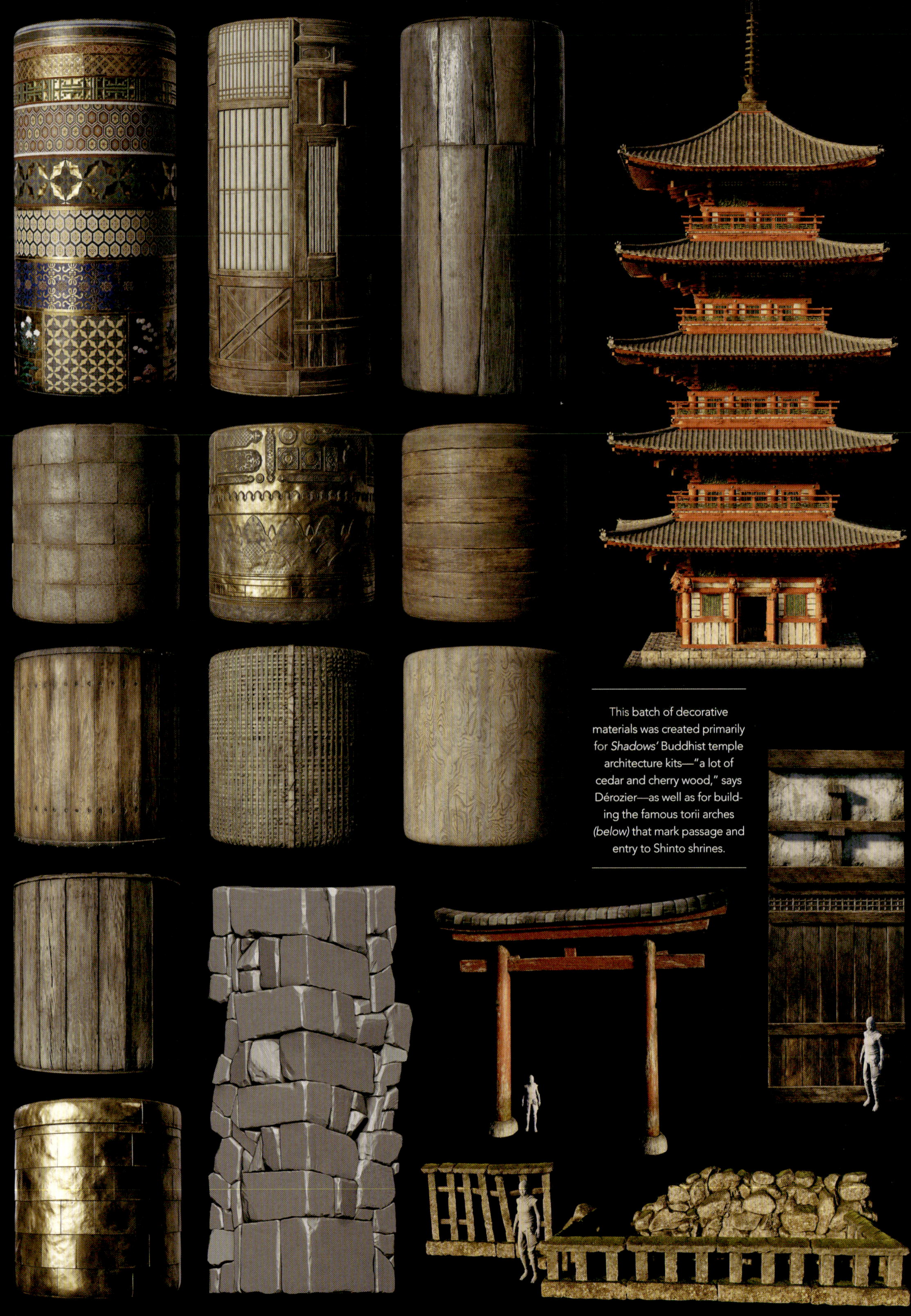

This batch of decorative materials was created primarily for *Shadows'* Buddhist temple architecture kits—"a lot of cedar and cherry wood," says Dérozier—as well as for building the famous torii arches *(below)* that mark passage and entry to Shinto shrines.

Vincent Dérozier developed these elegant materials for use in the construction kits for the richly decorated mansions of the wealthy daimyo lords in the game. "The inspiration for many of the patterns came from those found in temples," notes Dérozier. The last cylinder of rough stone at bottom right is a material used for fortifications around the great houses and castles.

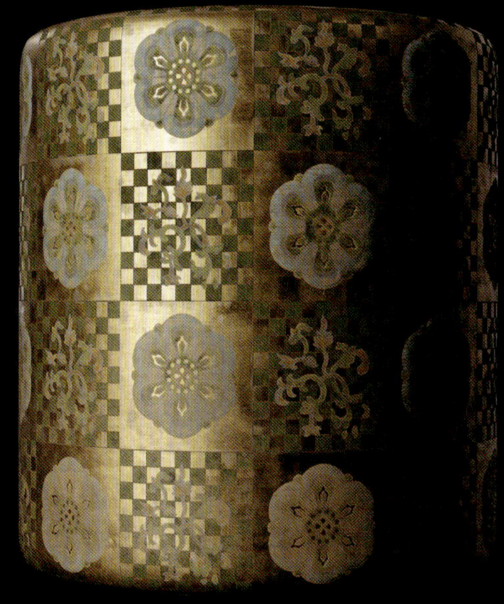

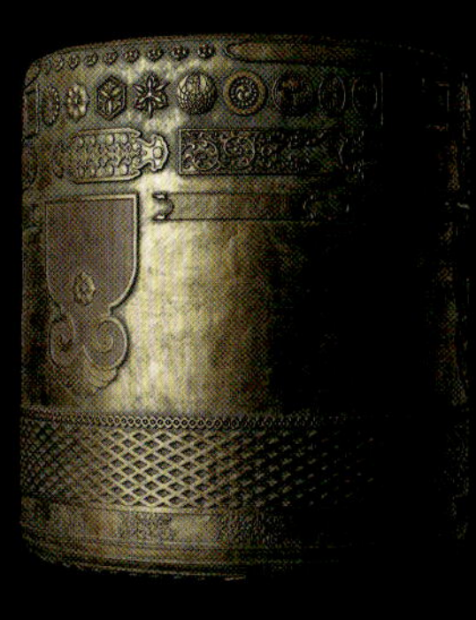

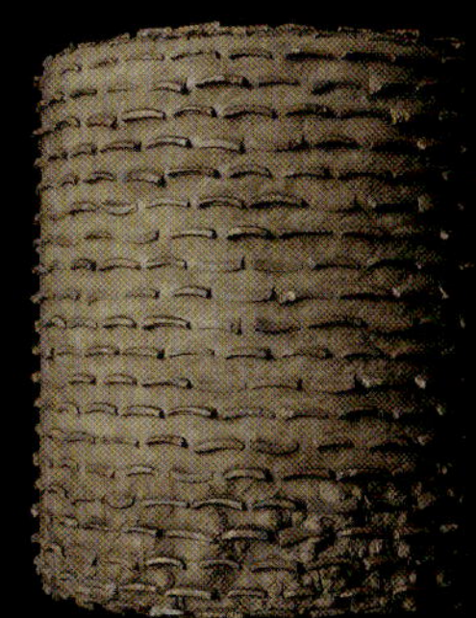

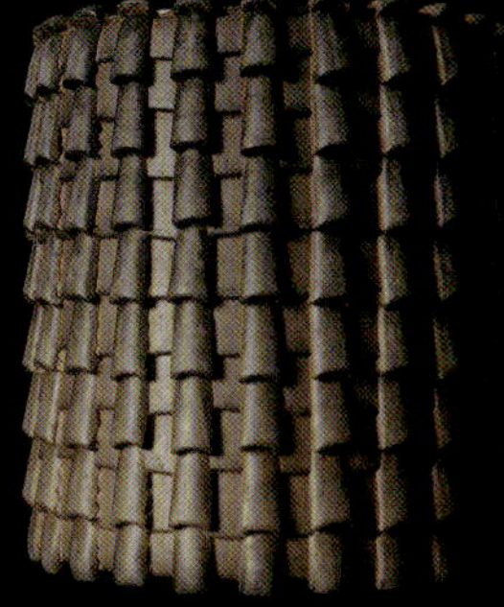

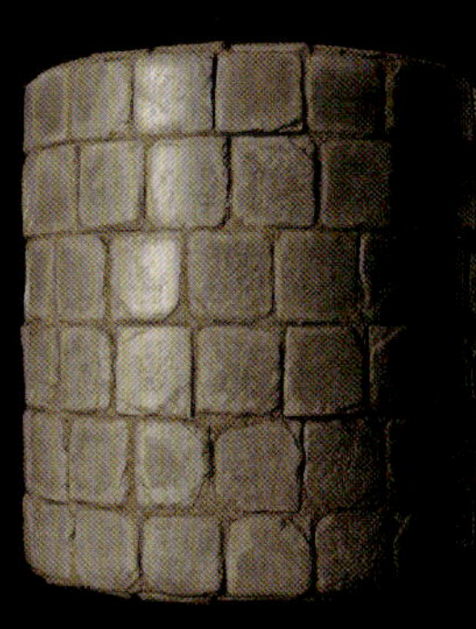

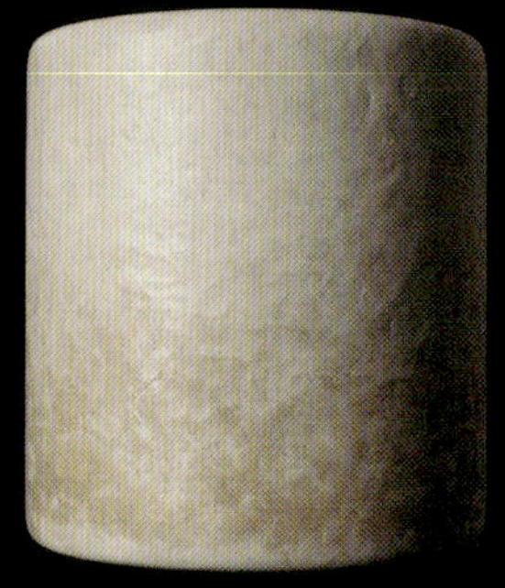

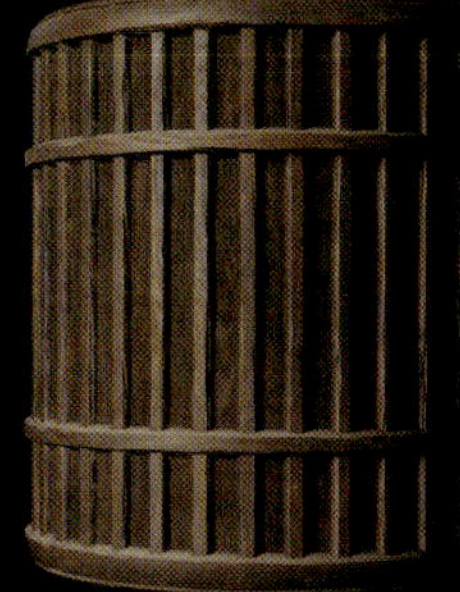

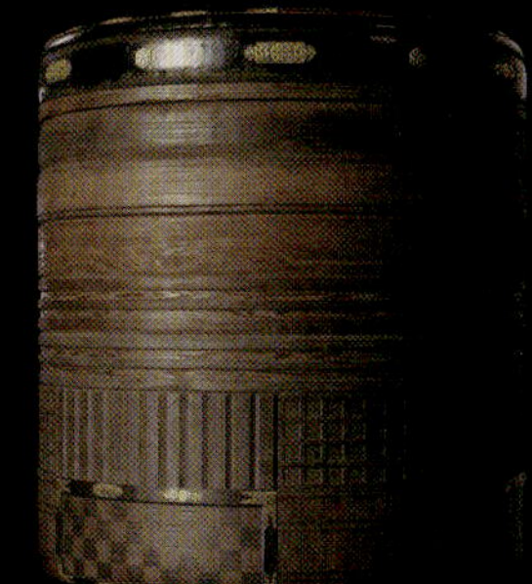

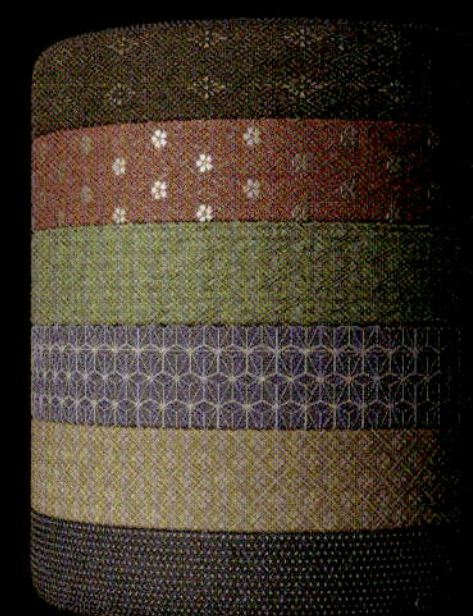

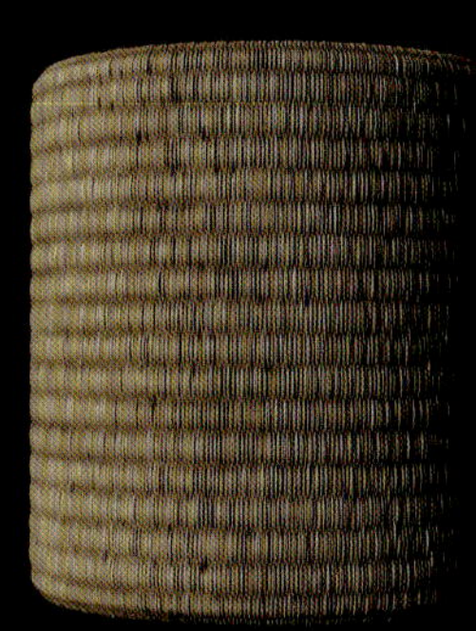

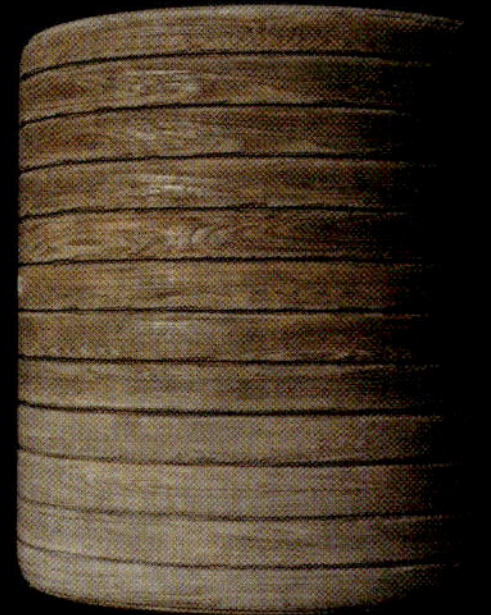

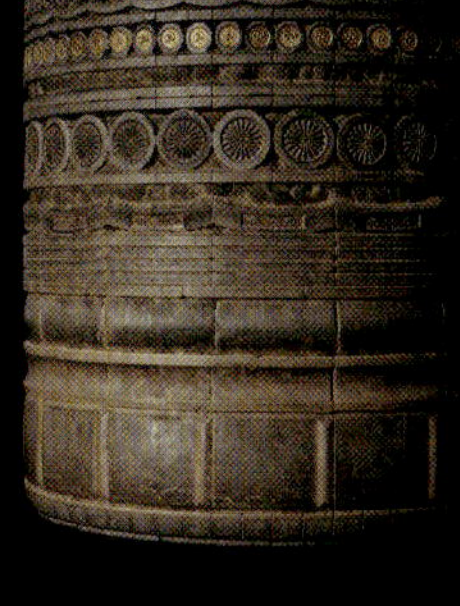

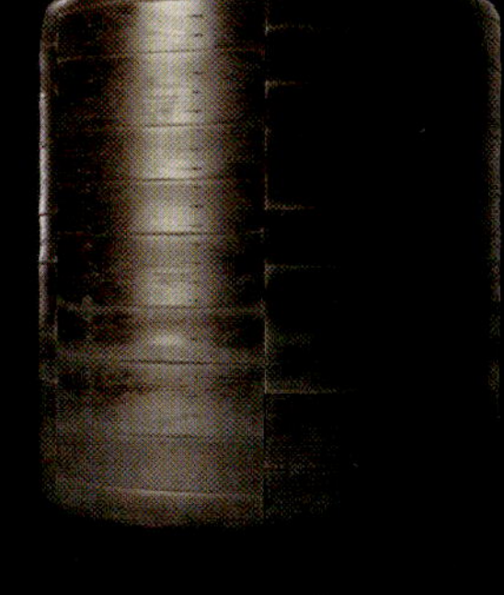

The "daimyo/mansion" kit includes modular structural components and materials for floors and tatami mats, ceilings, interior and exterior walls, roofs, and roofing tiles—anything that's an architectural surface. 3D artists would use the kit to construct a house and then layer the custom materials onto its surfaces.

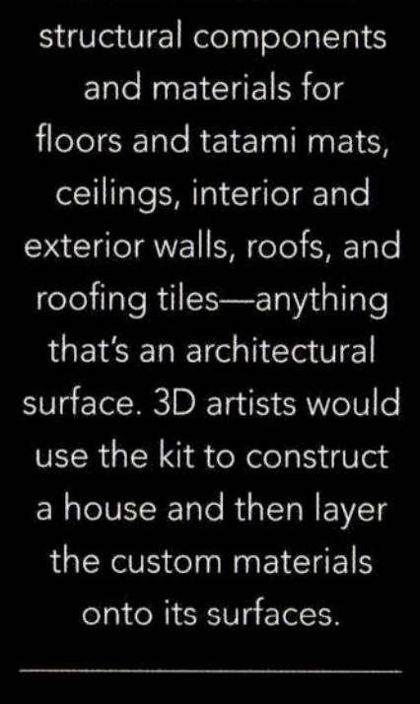

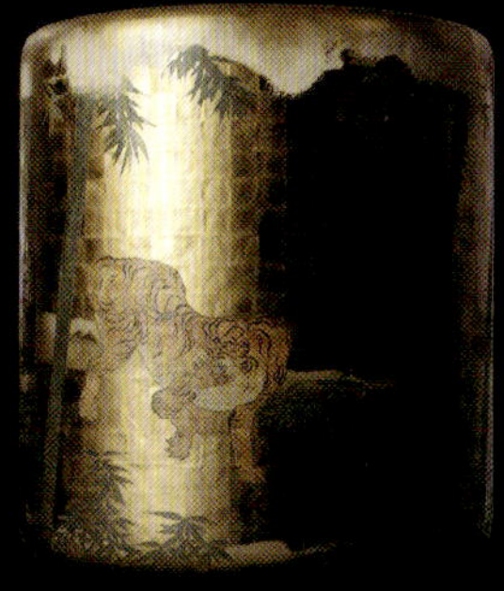

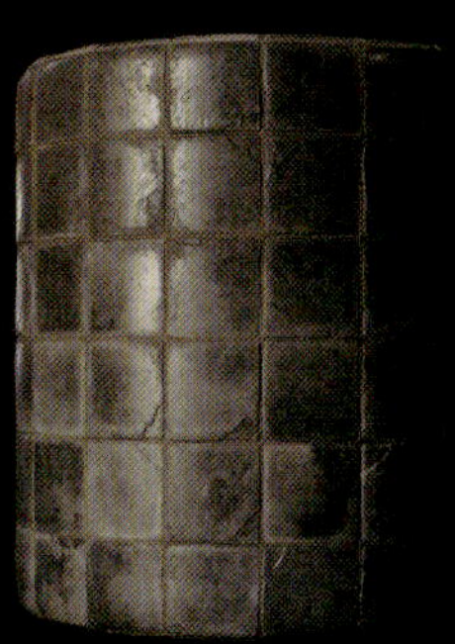

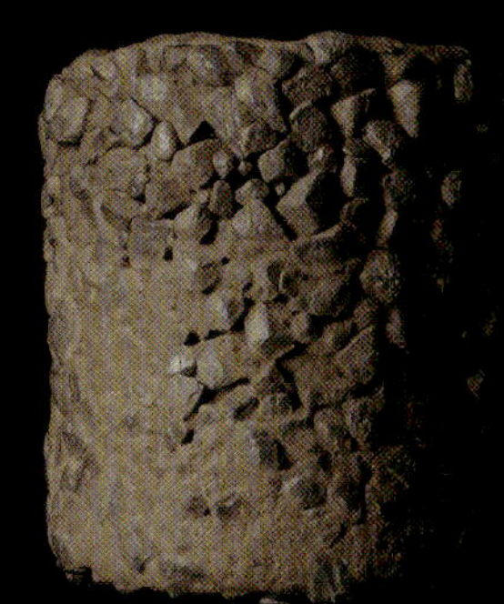

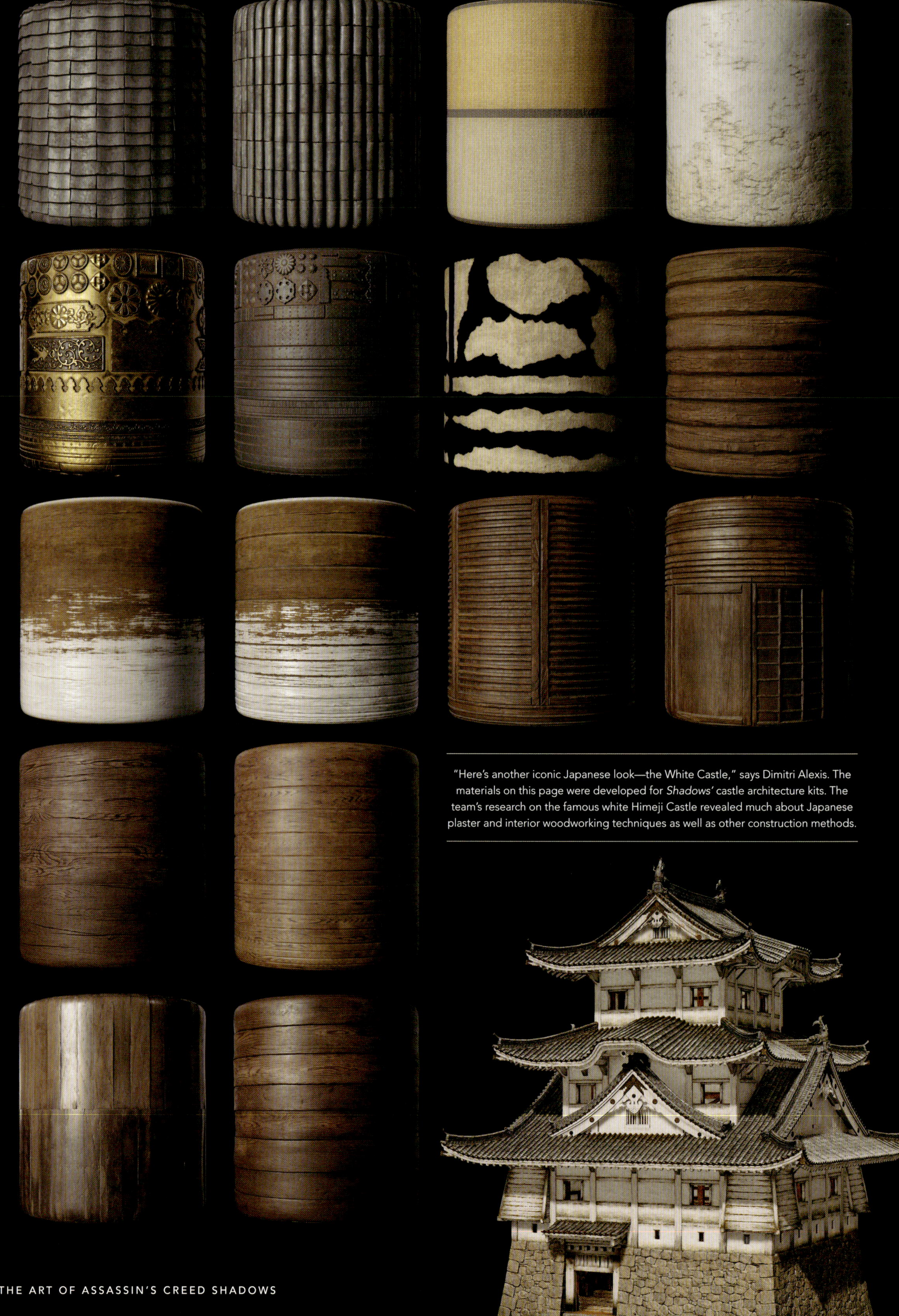

"Here's another iconic Japanese look—the White Castle," says Dimitri Alexis. The materials on this page were developed for *Shadows'* castle architecture kits. The team's research on the famous white Himeji Castle revealed much about Japanese plaster and interior woodworking techniques as well as other construction methods.

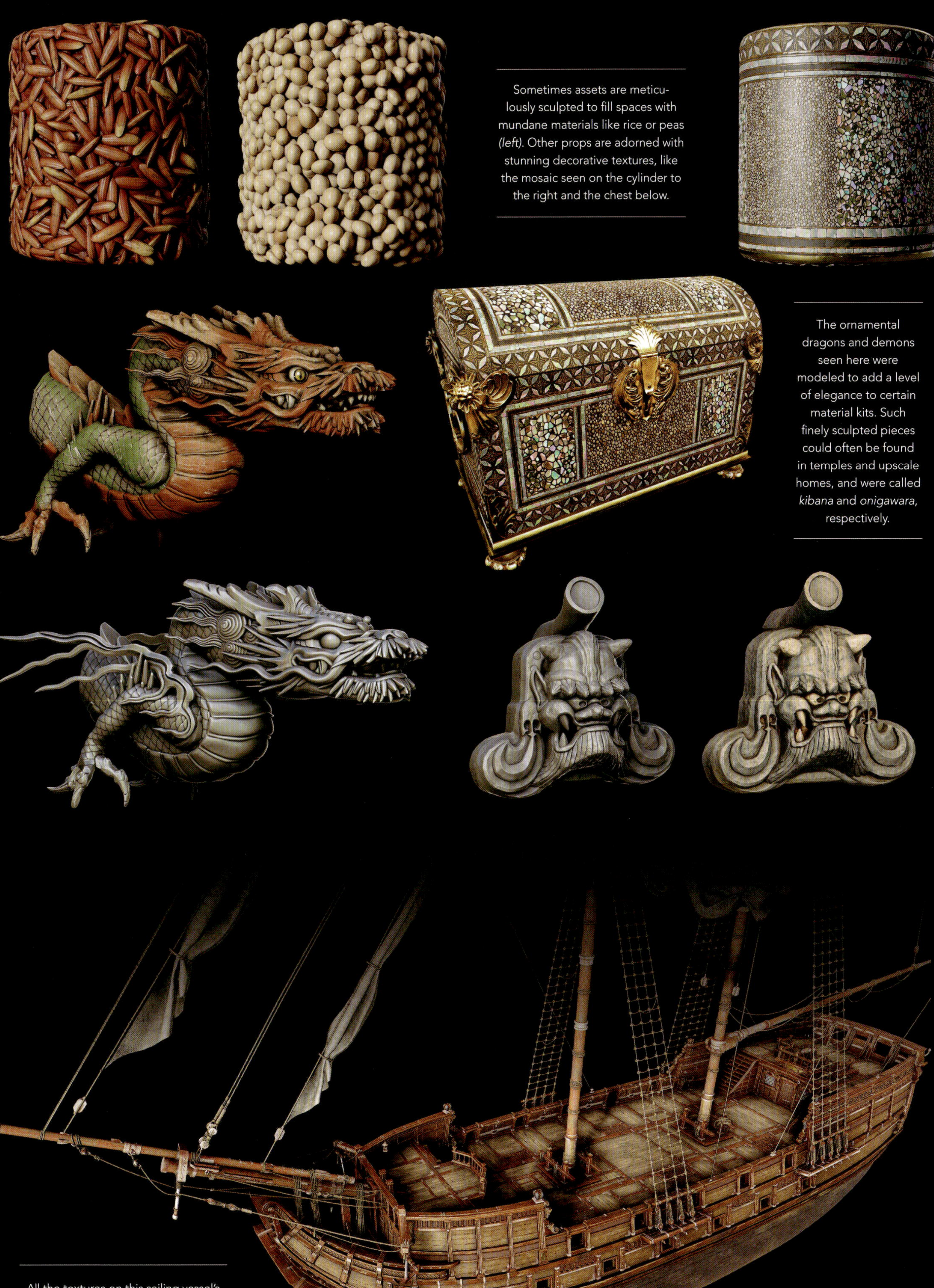

Sometimes assets are meticulously sculpted to fill spaces with mundane materials like rice or peas *(left)*. Other props are adorned with stunning decorative textures, like the mosaic seen on the cylinder to the right and the chest below.

The ornamental dragons and demons seen here were modeled to add a level of elegance to certain material kits. Such finely sculpted pieces could often be found in temples and upscale homes, and were called *kibana* and *onigawara*, respectively.

All the textures on this sailing vessel's structural surfaces were handcrafted and painstakingly applied.

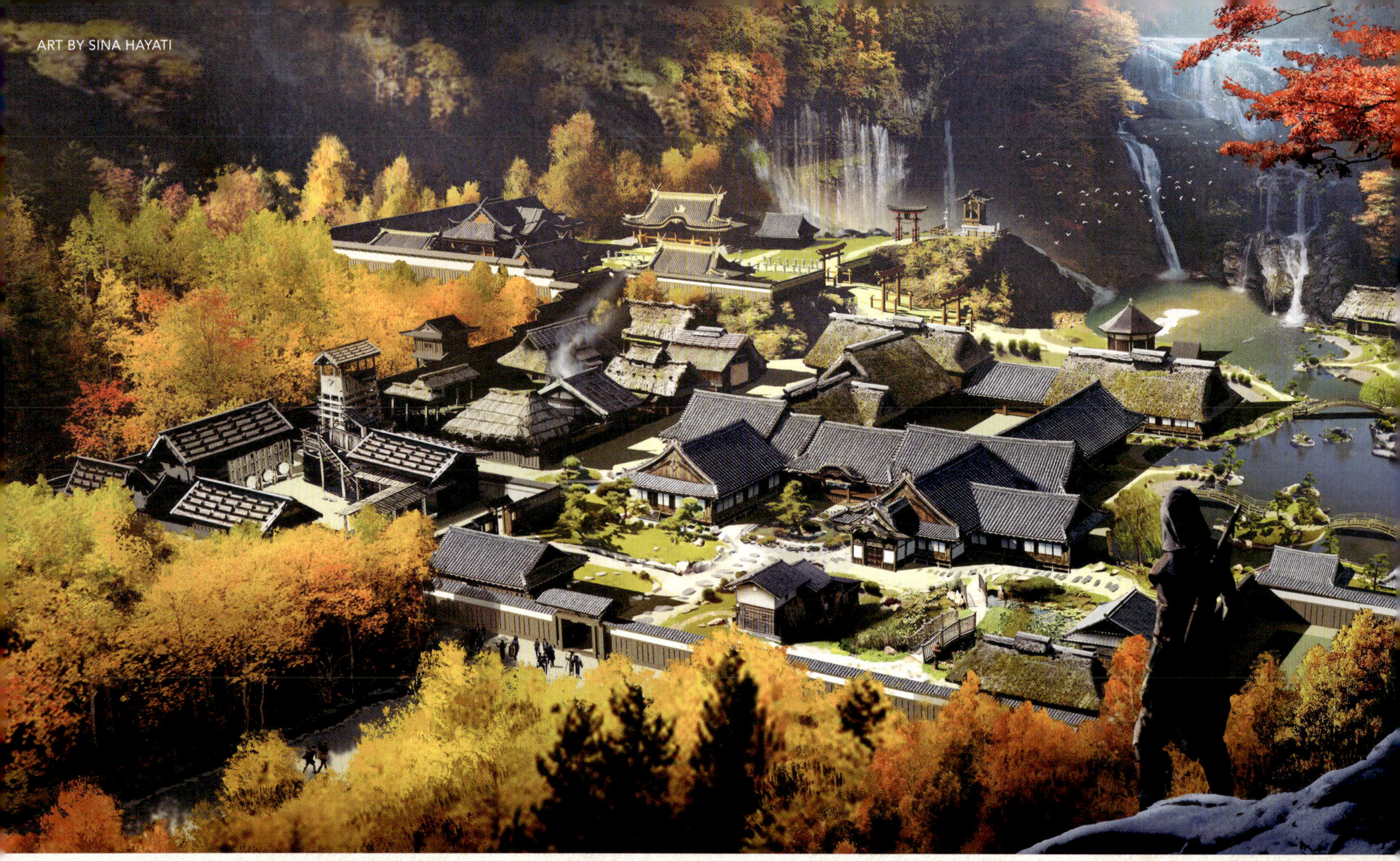

ART BY SINA HAYATI

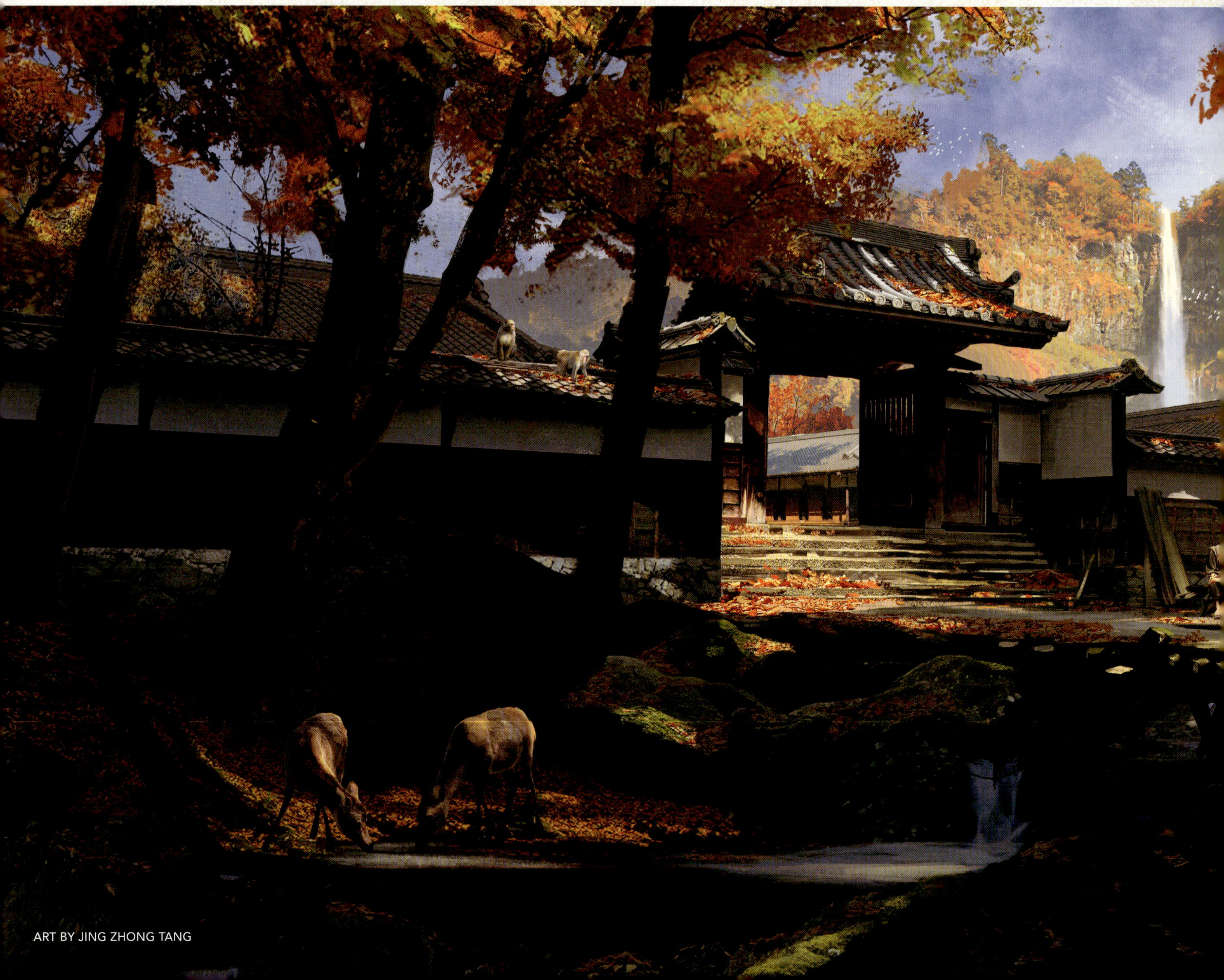

ART BY JING ZHONG TANG

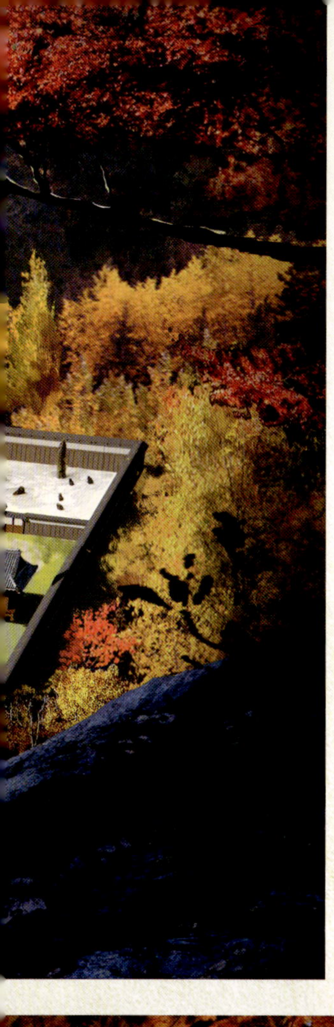

HIDEOUT

One of the great features of *Assassin's Creed Shadows* is the ability to design your own personal sanctuary: the hideout. The game gives players easy-to-use construction kits and tools like the ones employed by the level design teams. As you accumulate more wealth, you can upgrade your hideout facilities and structures. "Eventually, you can build quite an impressive refuge," says *Shadows* art director Thierry Dansereau. "We wanted customization to be a cool aspect of your lair."

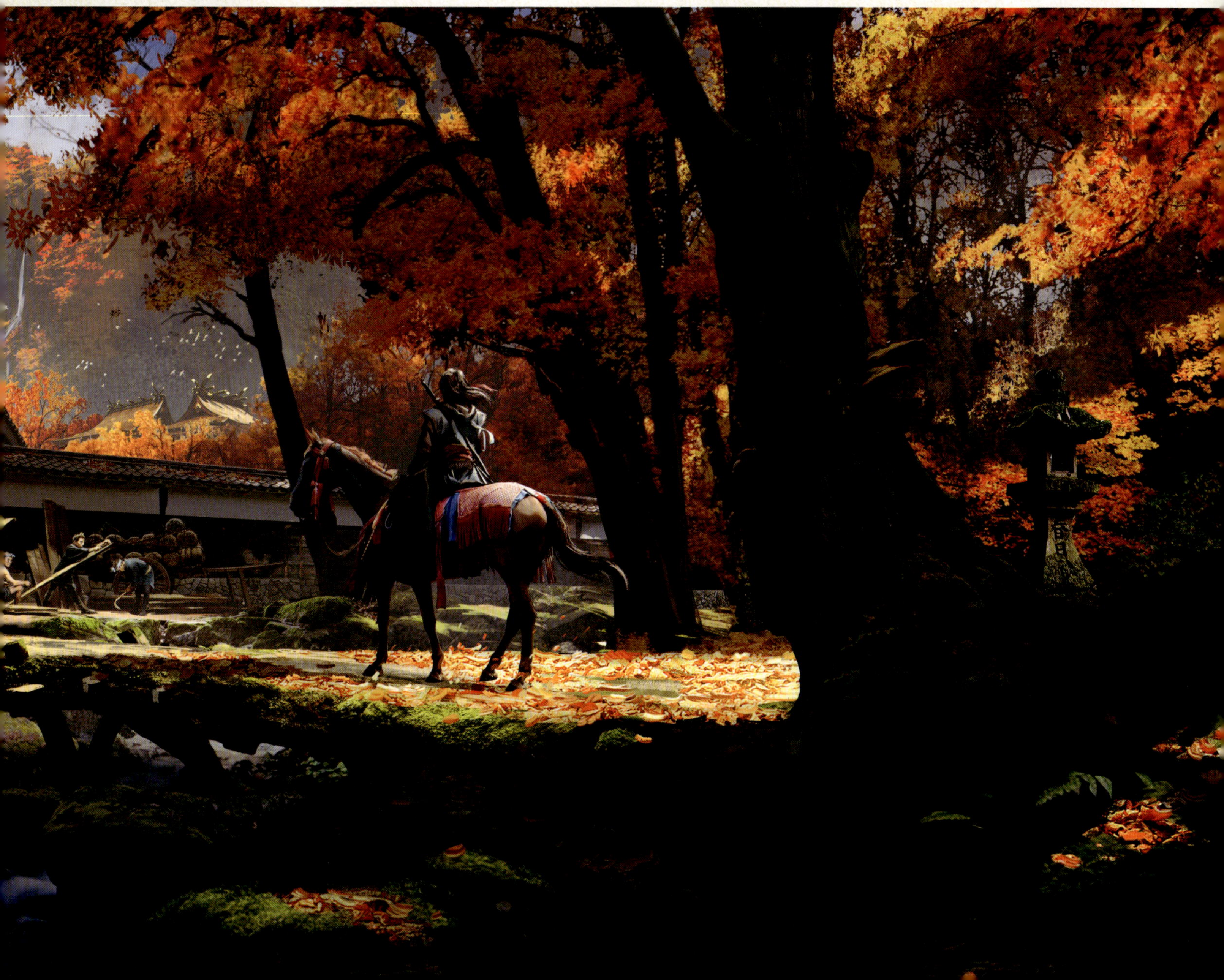

WEAPONS

The team's goal for the weapons was to create a broad spectrum of unique equipment styles, each serving as a testament to the exceptional craftsmanship of the weapon makers in feudal Japan.

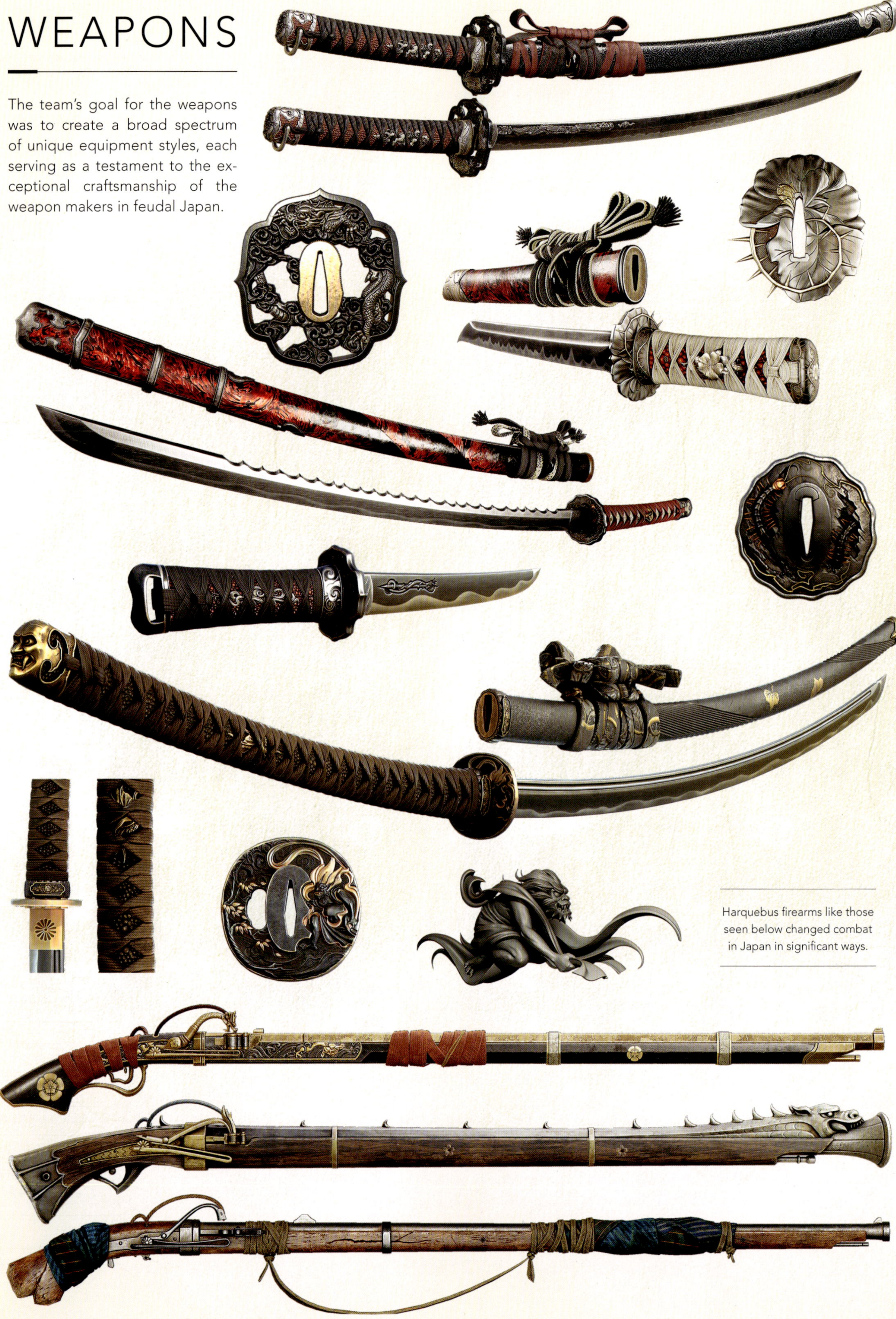

Harquebus firearms like those seen below changed combat in Japan in significant ways.

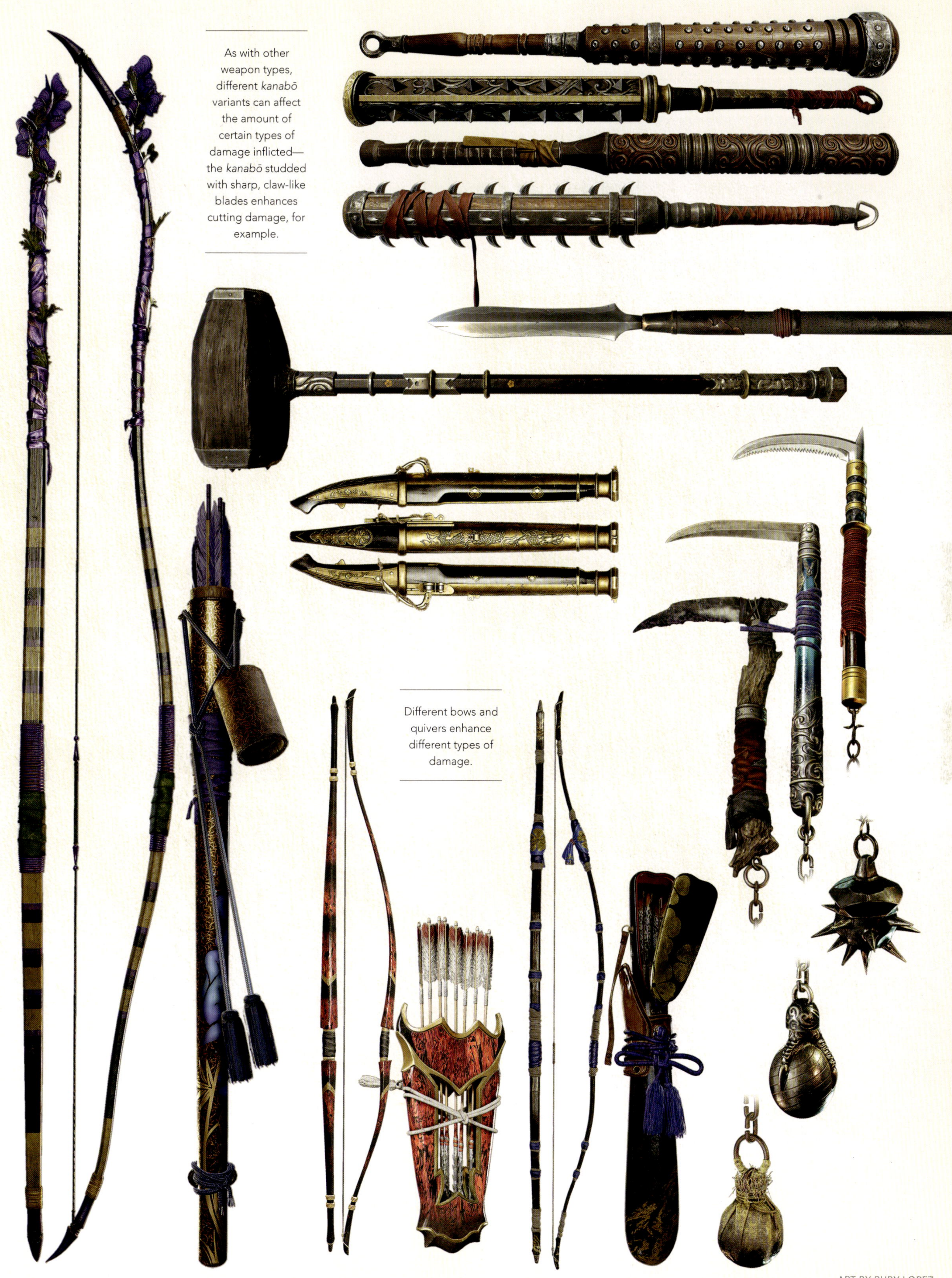

As with other weapon types, different *kanabō* variants can affect the amount of certain types of damage inflicted—the *kanabō* studded with sharp, claw-like blades enhances cutting damage, for example.

Different bows and quivers enhance different types of damage.

ART BY RUBY LOPEZ AND JOSHUA PEDRON

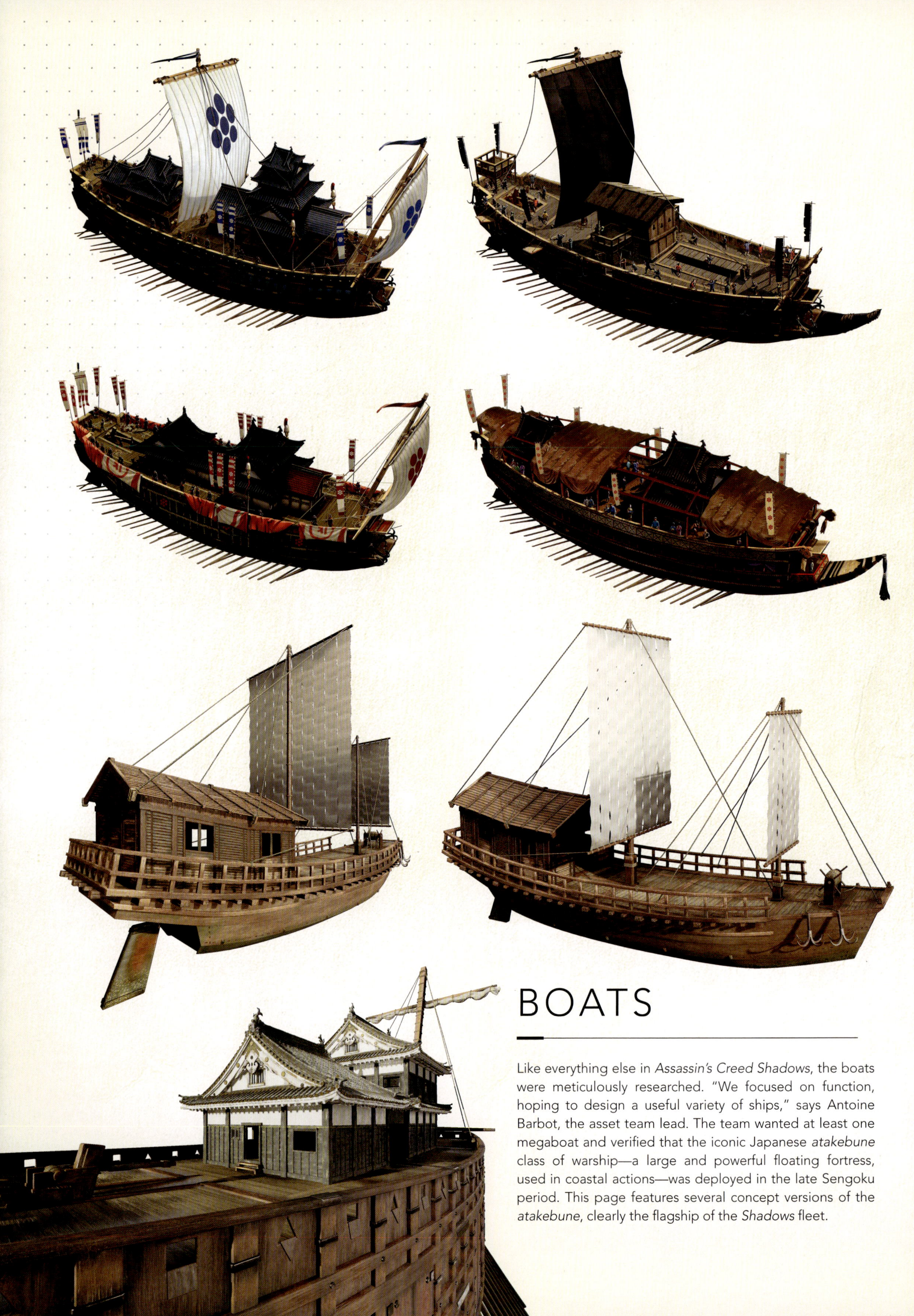

BOATS

Like everything else in *Assassin's Creed Shadows*, the boats were meticulously researched. "We focused on function, hoping to design a useful variety of ships," says Antoine Barbot, the asset team lead. The team wanted at least one megaboat and verified that the iconic Japanese *atakebune* class of warship—a large and powerful floating fortress, used in coastal actions—was deployed in the late Sengoku period. This page features several concept versions of the *atakebune*, clearly the flagship of the *Shadows* fleet.

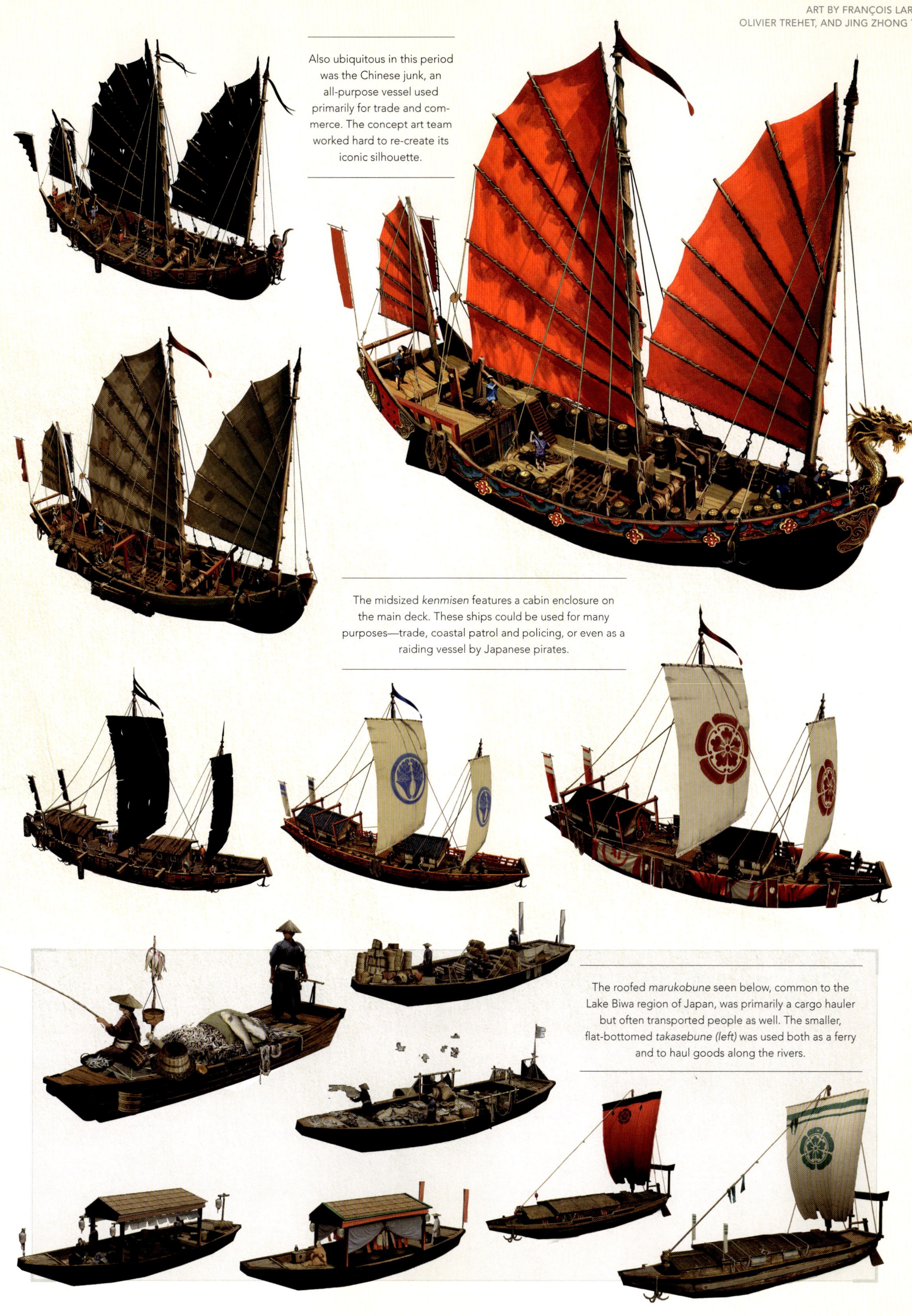

Also ubiquitous in this period was the Chinese junk, an all-purpose vessel used primarily for trade and commerce. The concept art team worked hard to re-create its iconic silhouette.

The midsized *kenmisen* features a cabin enclosure on the main deck. These ships could be used for many purposes—trade, coastal patrol and policing, or even as a raiding vessel by Japanese pirates.

The roofed *marukobune* seen below, common to the Lake Biwa region of Japan, was primarily a cargo hauler but often transported people as well. The smaller, flat-bottomed *takasebune (left)* was used both as a ferry and to haul goods along the rivers.

PROPS

Japan is particularly good at preserving its history and artifacts, and so the assets team had access to extensive resources, according to Antoine Barbot. But he also points out that if they'd adhered too closely to historical accuracy, a large percentage of the in-game prop kits in *Shadows* would be brown wooden items, "not very interesting visually." To create colorful props, the team had to focus more on the kinds of assets found in wealthier neighborhoods. For example, the tea sets seen here are very authentic but somewhat more upscale than you'd find in most households of the period.

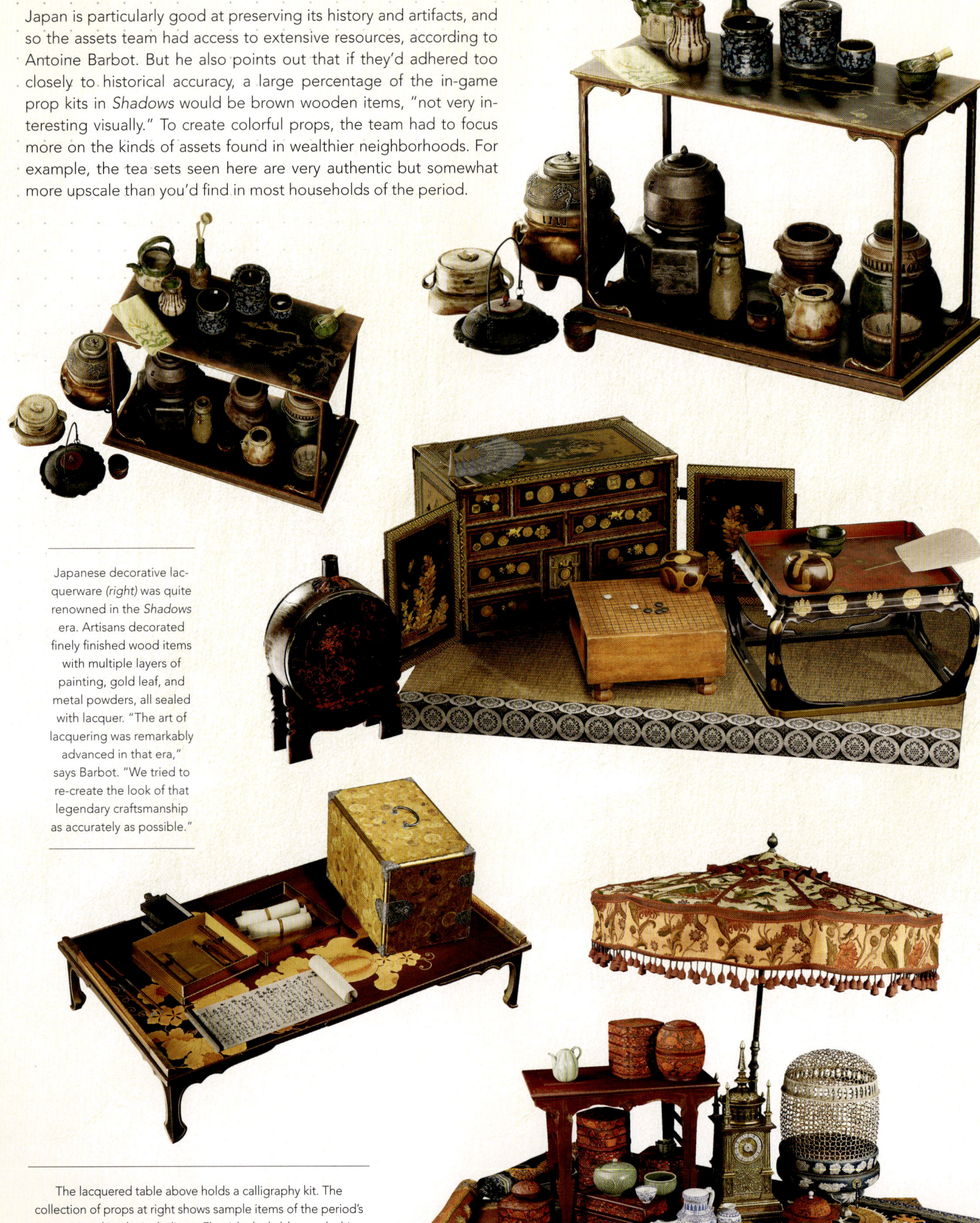

Japanese decorative lacquerware *(right)* was quite renowned in the *Shadows* era. Artisans decorated finely finished wood items with multiple layers of painting, gold leaf, and metal powders, all sealed with lacquer. "The art of lacquering was remarkably advanced in that era," says Barbot. "We tried to re-create the look of that legendary craftsmanship as accurately as possible."

The lacquered table above holds a calligraphy kit. The collection of props at right shows sample items of the period's international trade, including a Flemish clock, blue-and-white Chinese porcelain, green Korean ceramics, and a unique gilded cage from Europe for transporting exotic insects or birds.

ART BY JULIEN MANON, LAKSHYA, FRANÇOIS LARRIEU, JUSTIN VAILLANCOURT, DMYTRO MOTUZ, AND DAVID THERRIEN

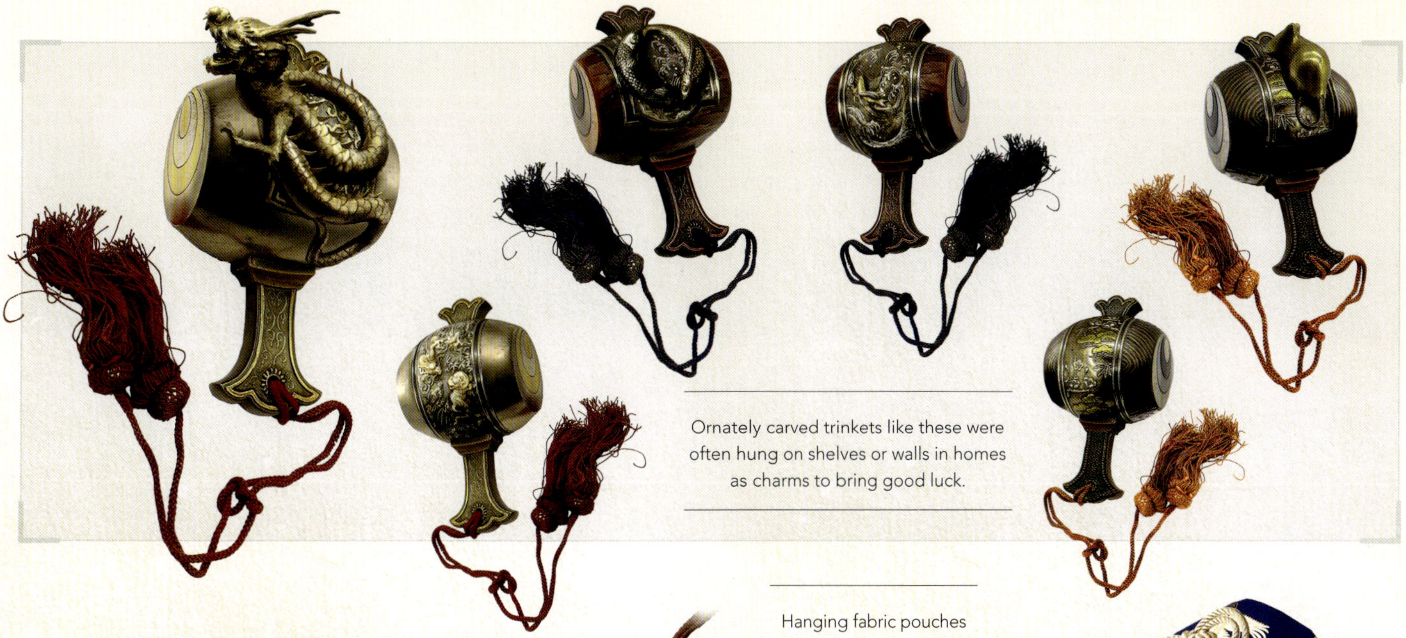

Ornately carved trinkets like these were often hung on shelves or walls in homes as charms to bring good luck.

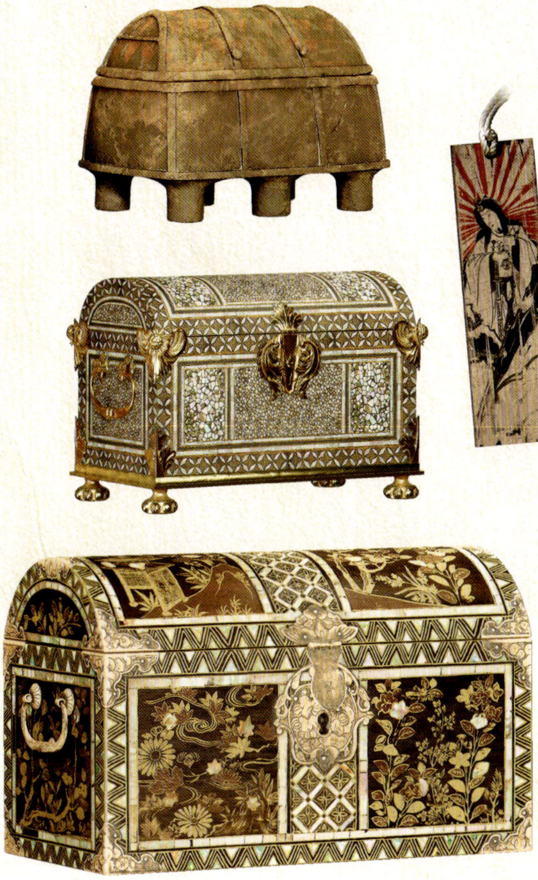

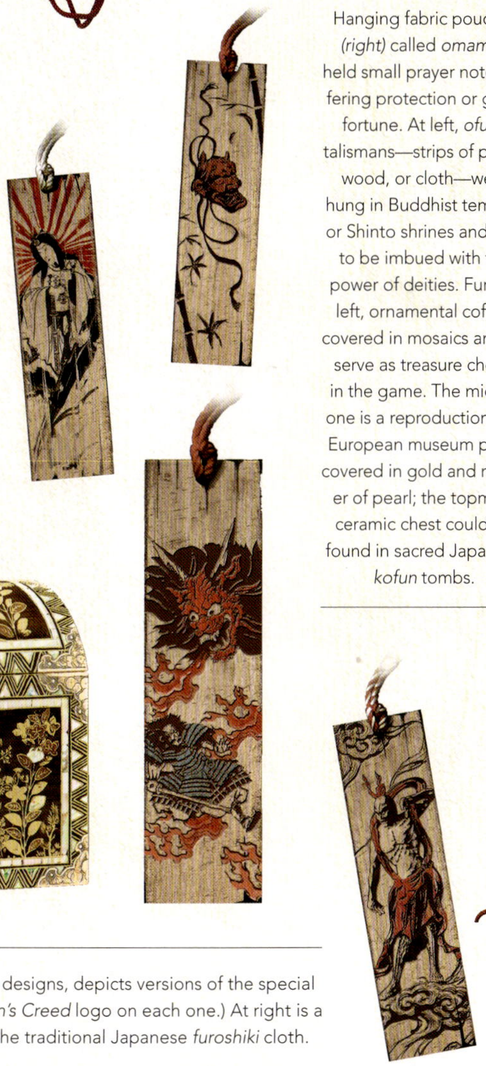

Hanging fabric pouches *(right)* called *omamori* held small prayer notes offering protection or good fortune. At left, *ofuda* talismans—strips of paper, wood, or cloth—were hung in Buddhist temples or Shinto shrines and said to be imbued with the power of deities. Further left, ornamental coffers covered in mosaics and art serve as treasure chests in the game. The middle one is a reproduction of a European museum piece covered in gold and mother of pearl; the topmost ceramic chest could be found in sacred Japanese *kofun* tombs.

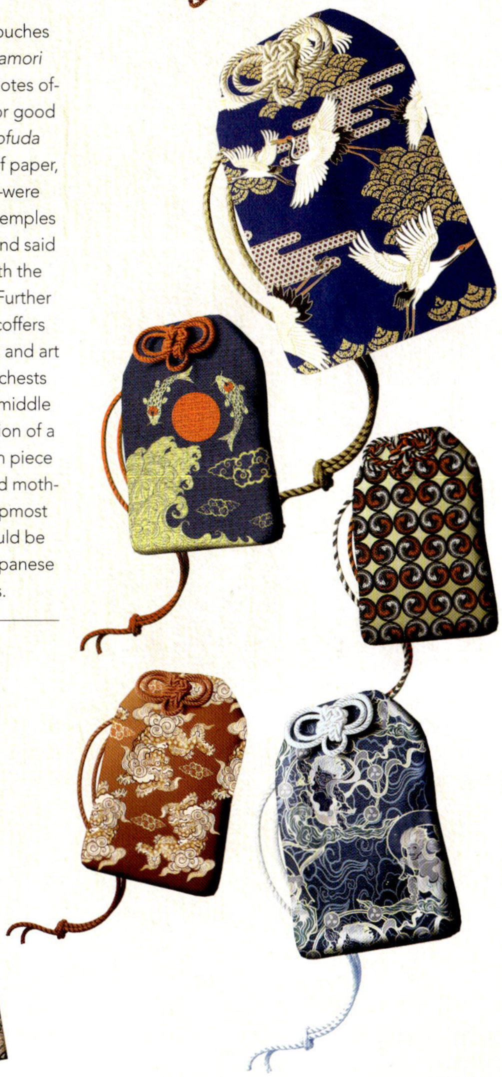

The concept art below, inspired by various Japanese designs, depicts versions of the special chests found in the *Shadows* world. (Note the *Assassin's Creed* logo on each one.) At right is a box wrapped in a knotted piece of fabric based on the traditional Japanese *furoshiki* cloth.

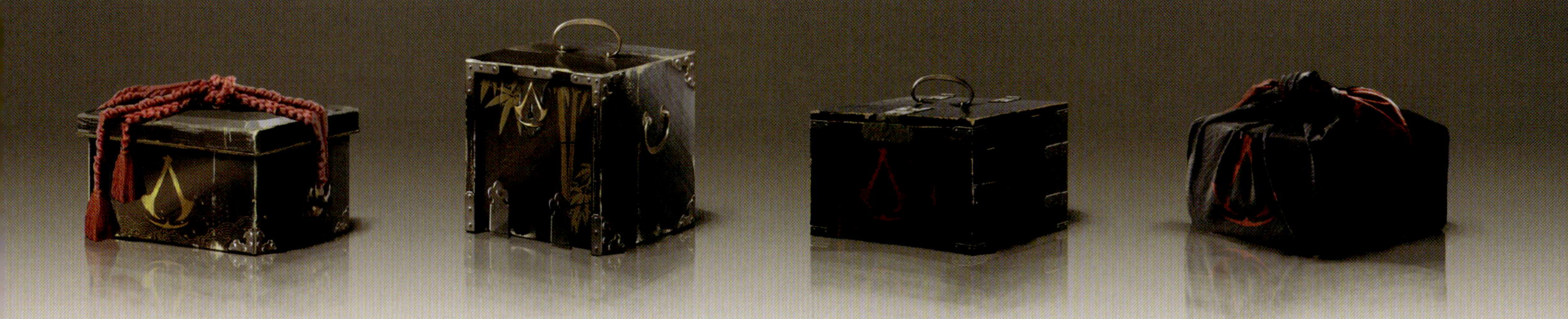

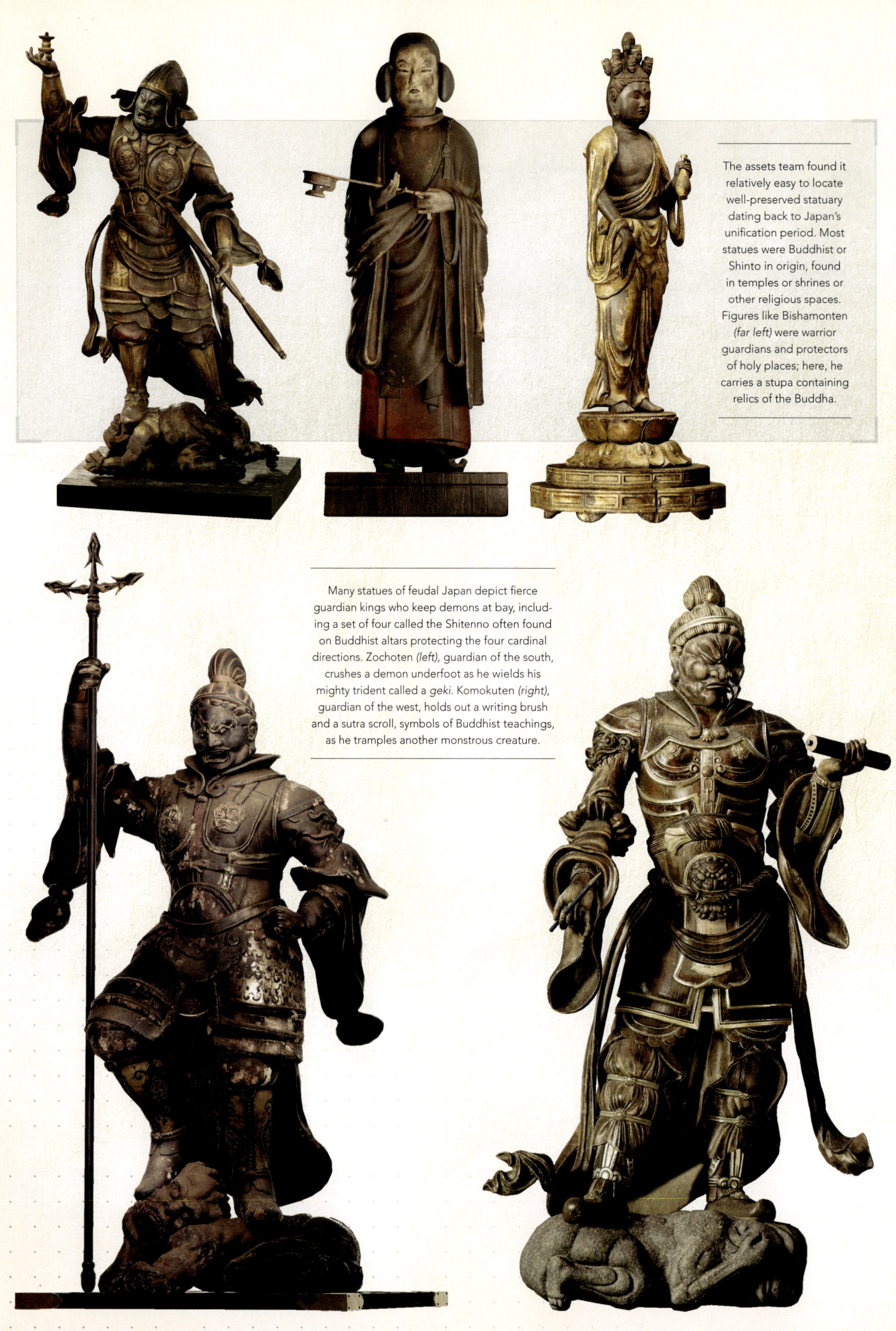

The assets team found it relatively easy to locate well-preserved statuary dating back to Japan's unification period. Most statues were Buddhist or Shinto in origin, found in temples or shrines or other religious spaces. Figures like Bishamonten *(far left)* were warrior guardians and protectors of holy places; here, he carries a stupa containing relics of the Buddha.

Many statues of feudal Japan depict fierce guardian kings who keep demons at bay, including a set of four called the Shitenno often found on Buddhist altars protecting the four cardinal directions. Zochoten *(left)*, guardian of the south, crushes a demon underfoot as he wields his mighty trident called a *geki*. Komokuten *(right)*, guardian of the west, holds out a writing brush and a sutra scroll, symbols of Buddhist teachings, as he trample another monstrous creature.

ART BY JULIEN MANON, LAKSHYA, FRANÇOIS LARRIEU, JUSTIN VAILLANCOURT, AND EDUARD GODLACH

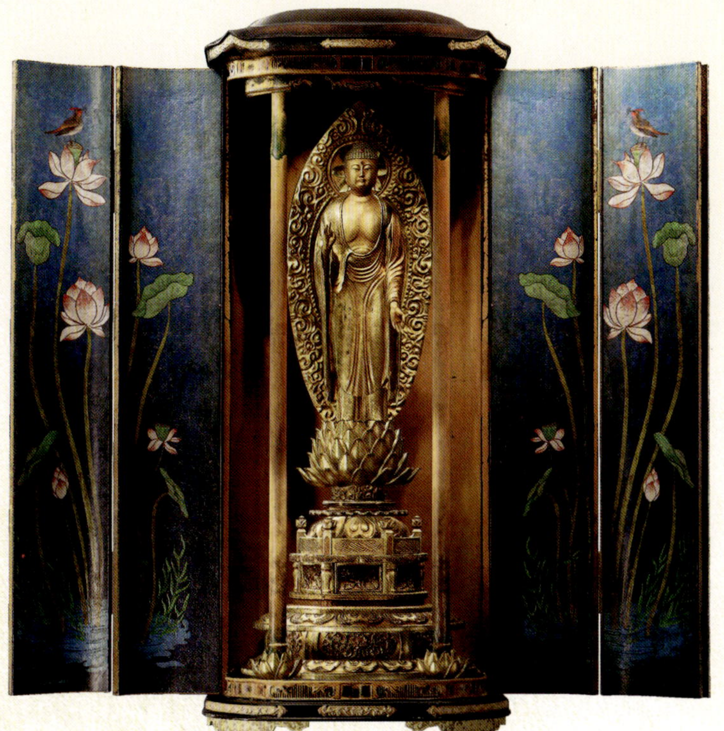

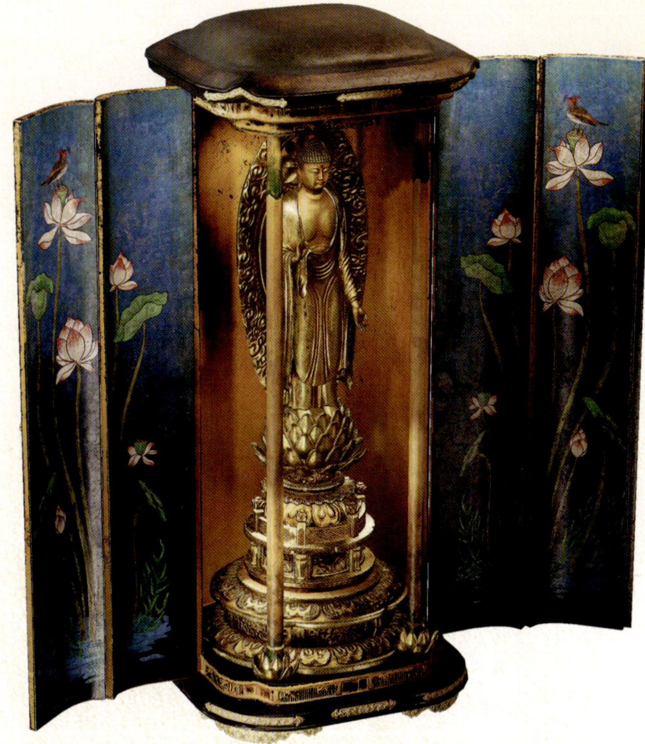

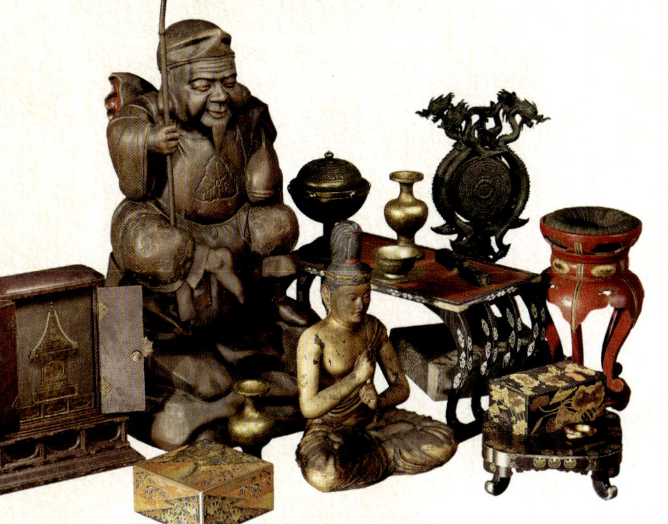

Above, these beautifully textured altars in closable cabinets can be found in Buddhist temples. At left you see an array of sanctuary items, such as incense bowls, urns, Buddha statues, and a black dragon gong on the table. Below, moss-covered stone sculptures grace outdoor Shinto shrines and cemeteries where visitors can place fruit offerings on the altars.

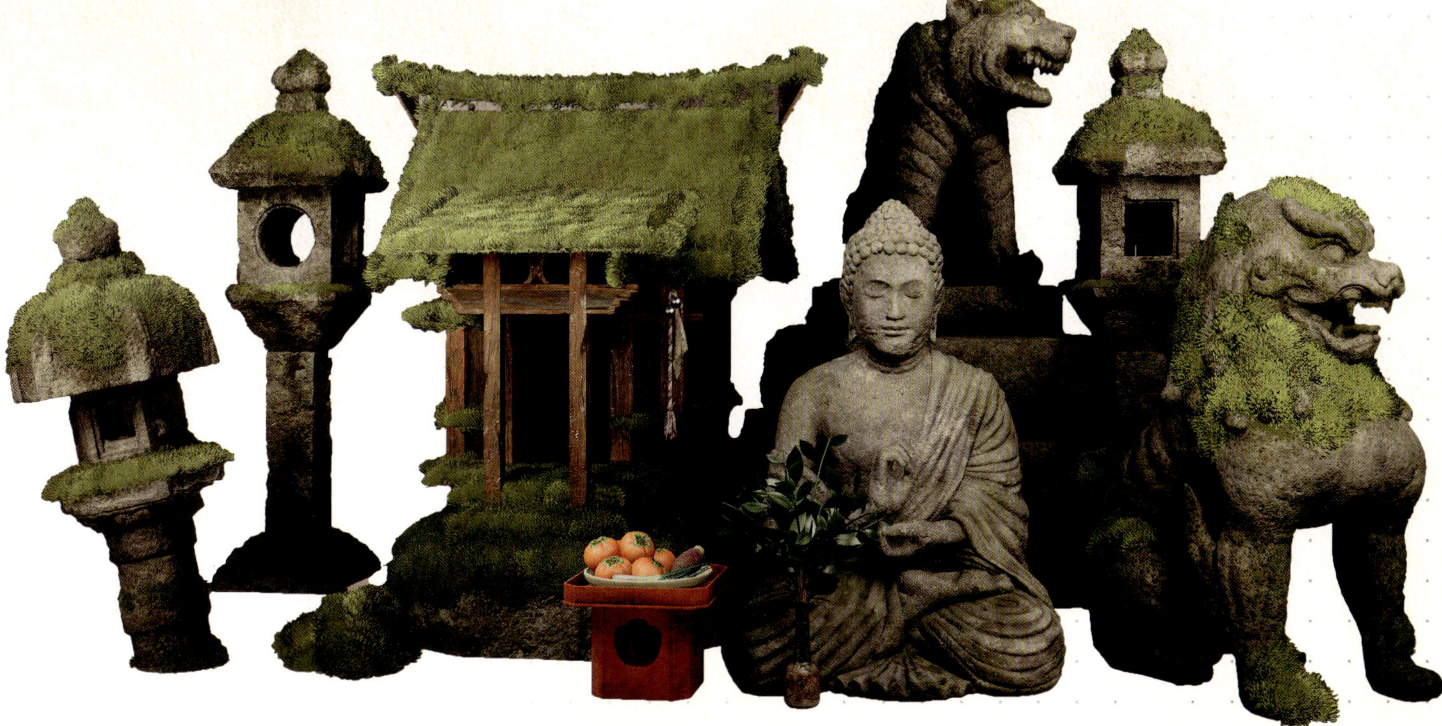

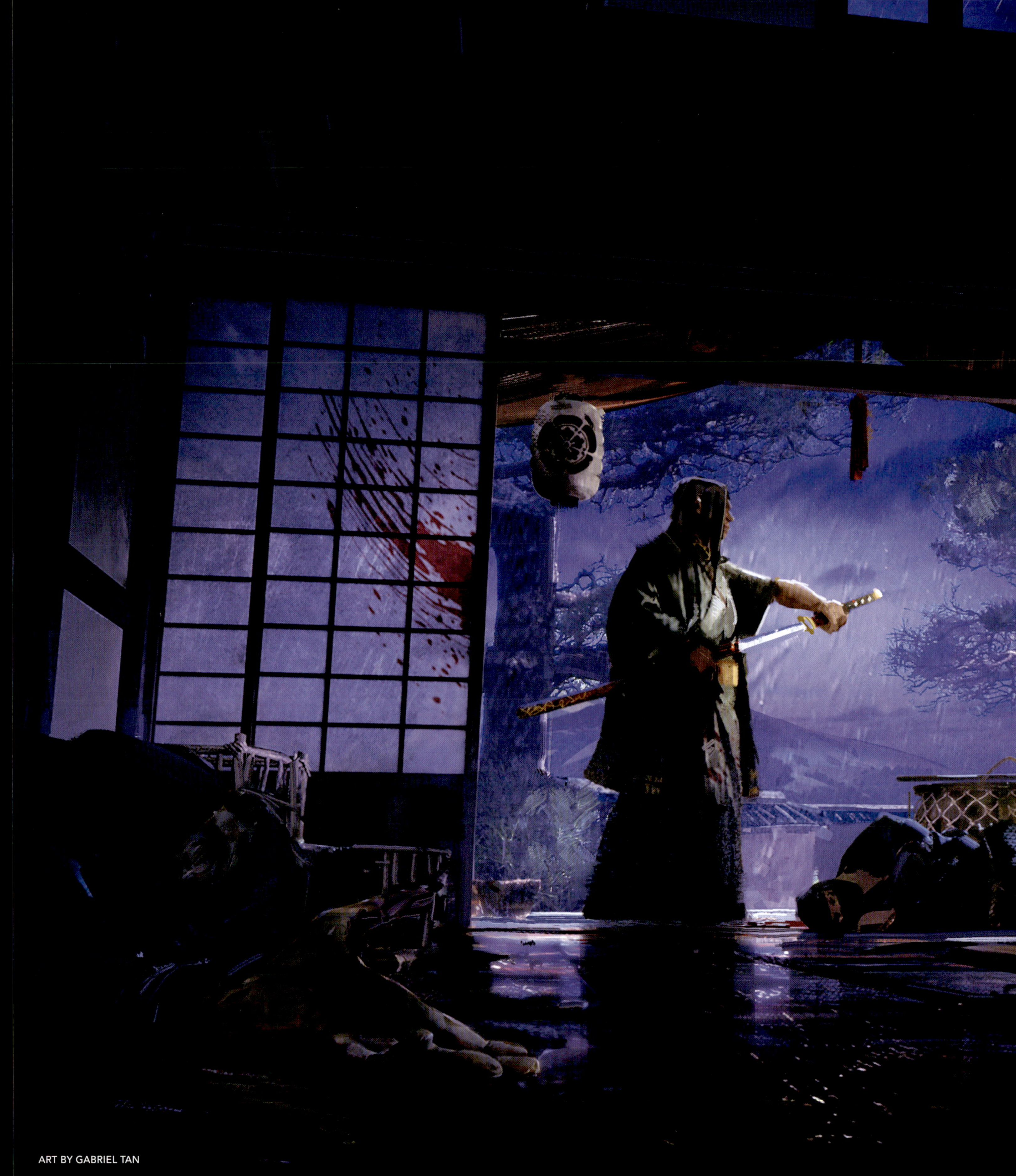

ART BY GABRIEL TAN

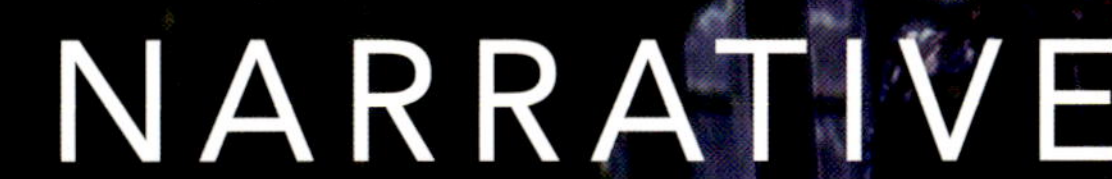

NARRATIVE

CHAPTER THREE

Concept art plays an important role in the overall game design process. The *Assassin's Creed Shadows* art team worked closely with the narrative team to flesh out the look of the game's protagonists, Naoe and Yasuke, as well as all of the other major characters and bosses in the game. Artists also helped conceive and sculpt the enemy archetypes and throngs of neutral crowd characters (like peasants, merchants, farmers, fishermen, and townsfolk) who populate the cities, towns, and countryside of feudal Japan in *Shadows*.

But aside from creating physical details of character and world building, the *Shadows* art team also helped the narrative department tell the *Shadows* story. As you'll see later in this chapter, the artists used their tools—color, lighting, angle, and perspective—to create the visual tone of specific scenes, adding mood, atmosphere, and emotional punch to key story sequences. "Narrative concept art enhances thematic development and provides key visual reference points for our storytellers throughout the process," says art director Thierry Dansereau.

ART BY FRED RAMBAUD

ODA NOBUNAGA

As the *Shadows* timeline begins, Nobunaga is crushing regional rivals in central Japan (including Naoe's province of Iga) in brutal fashion . . . and then instituting progressive reforms, leaving the newly unified regions better off than before. A mercurial personality, the head of the Oda clan inspires both fierce loyalty and bitter resentment. Impressed by Yasuke's stature and presence, he brings the towering servant of Jesuit missionaries into his own service and elevates him to the rank of samurai. His daimyo outfit seen here features embroidered silk and striking *shibori*-like patterns, evoking the classic Japanese technique for dyeing textiles.

ART BY VINCENT GAIGNEUX

AKECHI MITSUHIDE

Once the favored general of Oda Nobunaga, Mitsuhide has become in recent years a target of the ruling daimyo's ridicule and abuse. He maintains a stoic loyalty until Nobunaga orders an execution that violates the terms of a peace agreement Mitsuhide negotiated with the Hatano clan—a violation that results in the Hatanos' retaliatory murder of Mitsuhide's mother. This leads to his own cunning revenge plot against his lord. He's seen here clad in classic, high-quality red armor befitting a general.

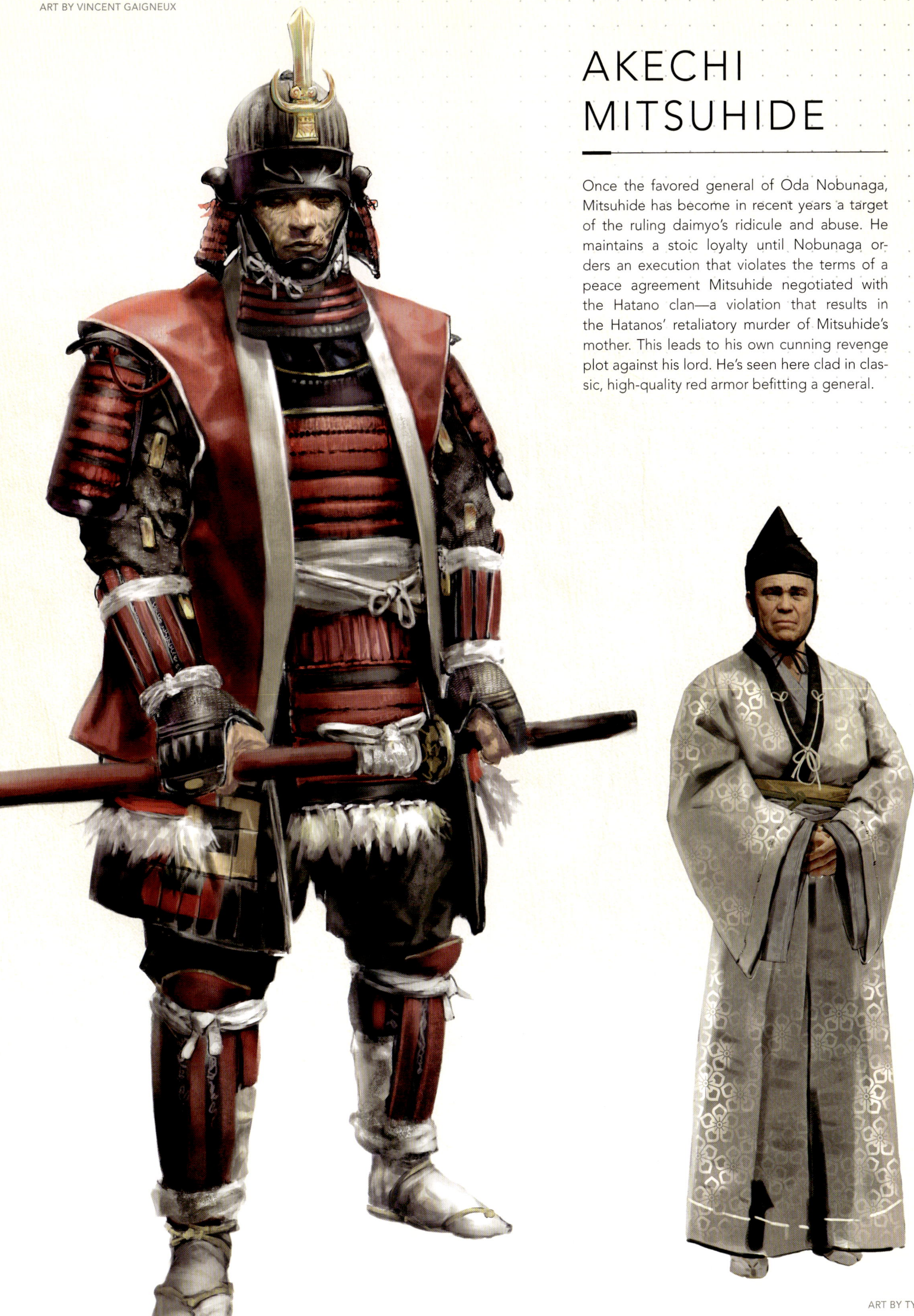

ART BY TYLER RYAN

ASHIKAGA YOSHIAKI

Yoshiaki is the last in an aristocratic line with a claim on the shogunate. Living in the shadow of his clan's glory, he yearns to reclaim his status. A master in the art of manipulation, he plots with his partners to regain control over Japan. Here he wears a luxurious gold-embroidered kimono, exuding confidence.

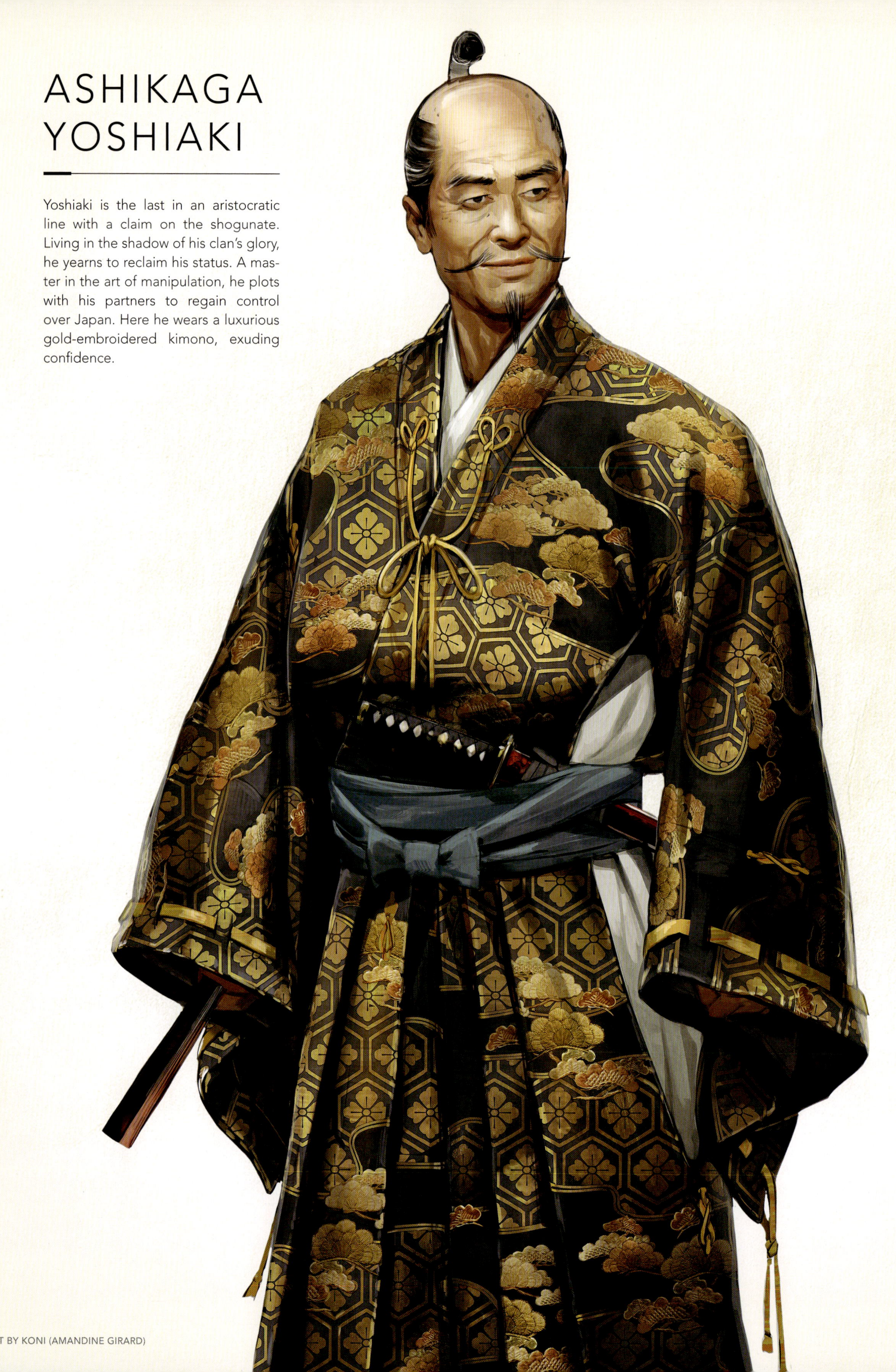

ART BY KONI (AMANDINE GIRARD)

ART BY VINCENT GAIGNEUX

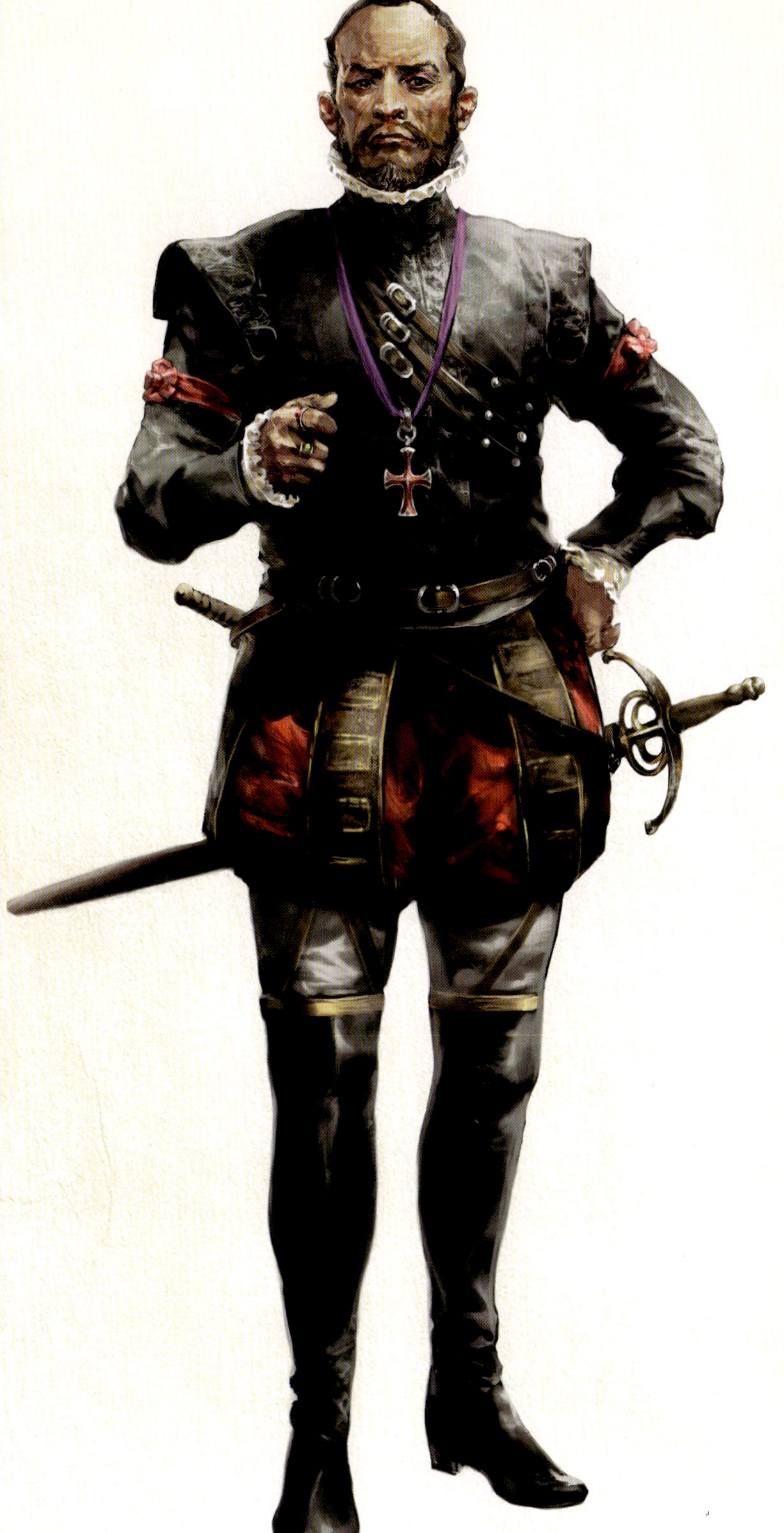

NUNO CARO

This Portuguese Templar has spent twenty years immersing himself in Japanese culture in a nefarious attempt to establish Western power in the Far East and extend his order's influence across Japan's warring provinces. The concept art portrays Nuno clad in a classic Portuguese nobleman's outfit and wearing the Templar cross. Nuno also seeks to plunder ancient Japanese treasures and artifacts—in particular, the Imperial Regalia, said to be of immeasurable worth. He's pitiless, aloof, methodical . . . and an incident on a slave ship has made him the target of Yasuke's hatred.

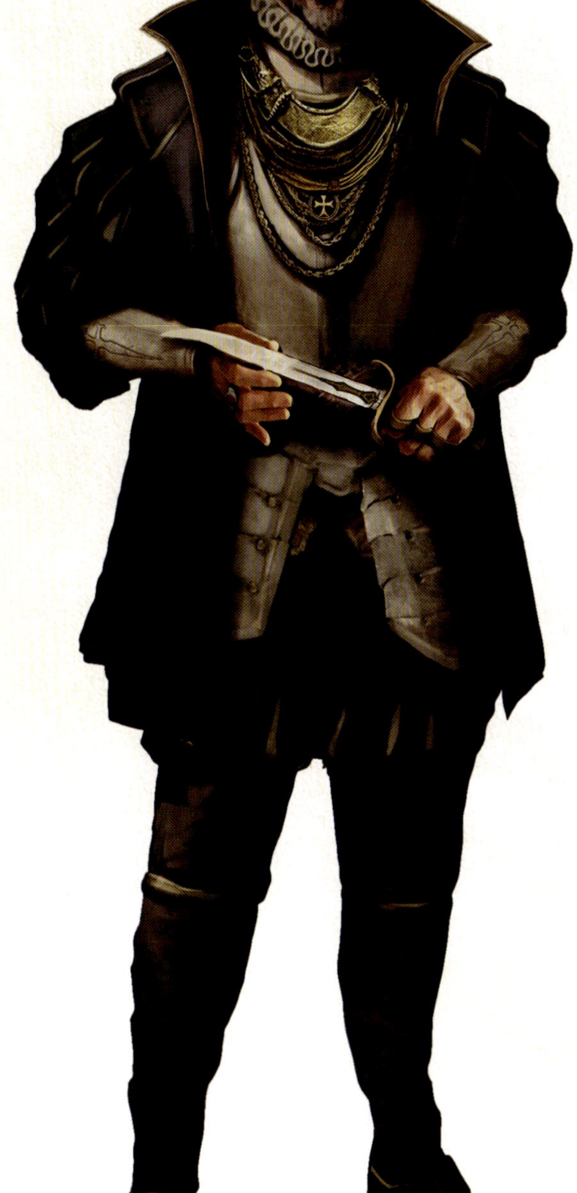

DUARTE DE MELO

This merciless and wealthy Portuguese trader is engaged in the brutal industry of slave trade. He will be forced to face the wrath and vengeance of *Shadows'* protagonists.

ART BY KATE CRUZ

ART BY VINCENT GAIGNEUX

KAMIIZUMI NOBUTSUNA

Yasuke's katana master and trainer, old Nobutsuna is a legend among the samurai sword bearers in Japan. Formerly a greatly respected military general, he sees combat as both art and choreography, and thus he founded his renowned center of Shinkage-ryu (New Shadow School) to train protégés in martial mastery. The art team researched an older, classic armor set for Nobutsuna *(seen below)* to reinforce his "old-school" dedication to the timeless values of ancient Japan.

LADY OICHI

One of the most famous and iconic noblewomen of Japan's unification period, Lady Oichi is Oda Nobunaga's beloved younger sister and a calming presence in his Azuchi Castle. Indeed, her honorable influence in his court has helped bring a sense of stability to the entire region. After meeting Yasuke, she becomes a champion and adviser of the towering African samurai. Her unique haircut is a historically accurate style that was codified for noblewomen of the era. Here, she wears a highly formal Japanese *uchikake* robe, a lavishly designed kimono.

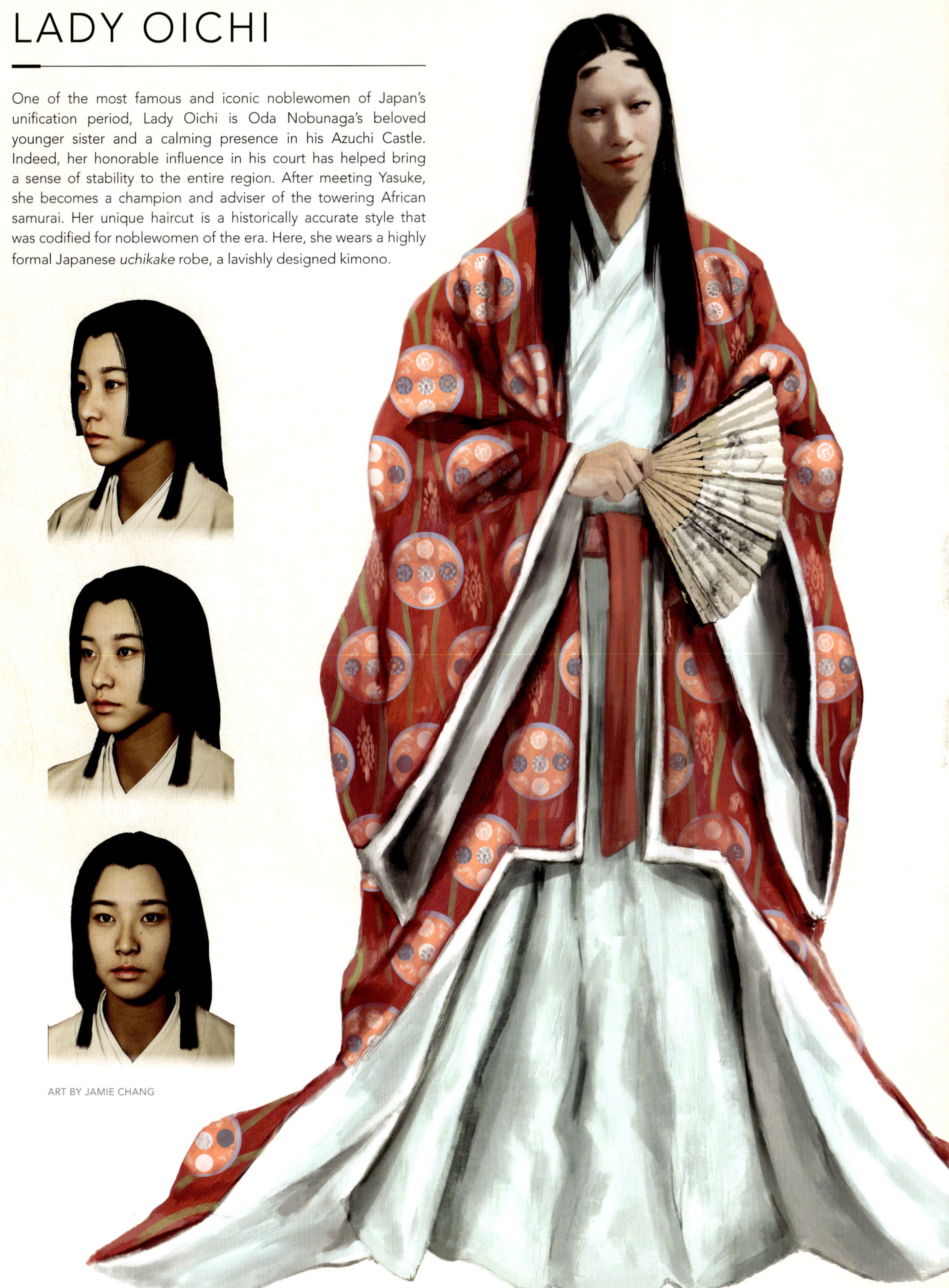

ART BY JAMIE CHANG

ART BY VINCENT GAIGNEUX

TOYOTOMI (HASHIBA) HIDEYOSHI

Hideyoshi rose from humble peasant roots to become Oda Nobunaga's most loyal and trusted lieutenant and a powerful daimyo in his own right—his conquests earned him the ceremonial surname "Hashiba." This distinguished samurai general, troubled by a growing Western influence across the provinces, seeks to fulfill Nobunaga's vision of uniting Japan's warring factions into a single, strong, independent nation. Hideyoshi's famous armor was topped by his legendary sun-ray helmet, a sight that galvanized his troops and struck terror into his foes.

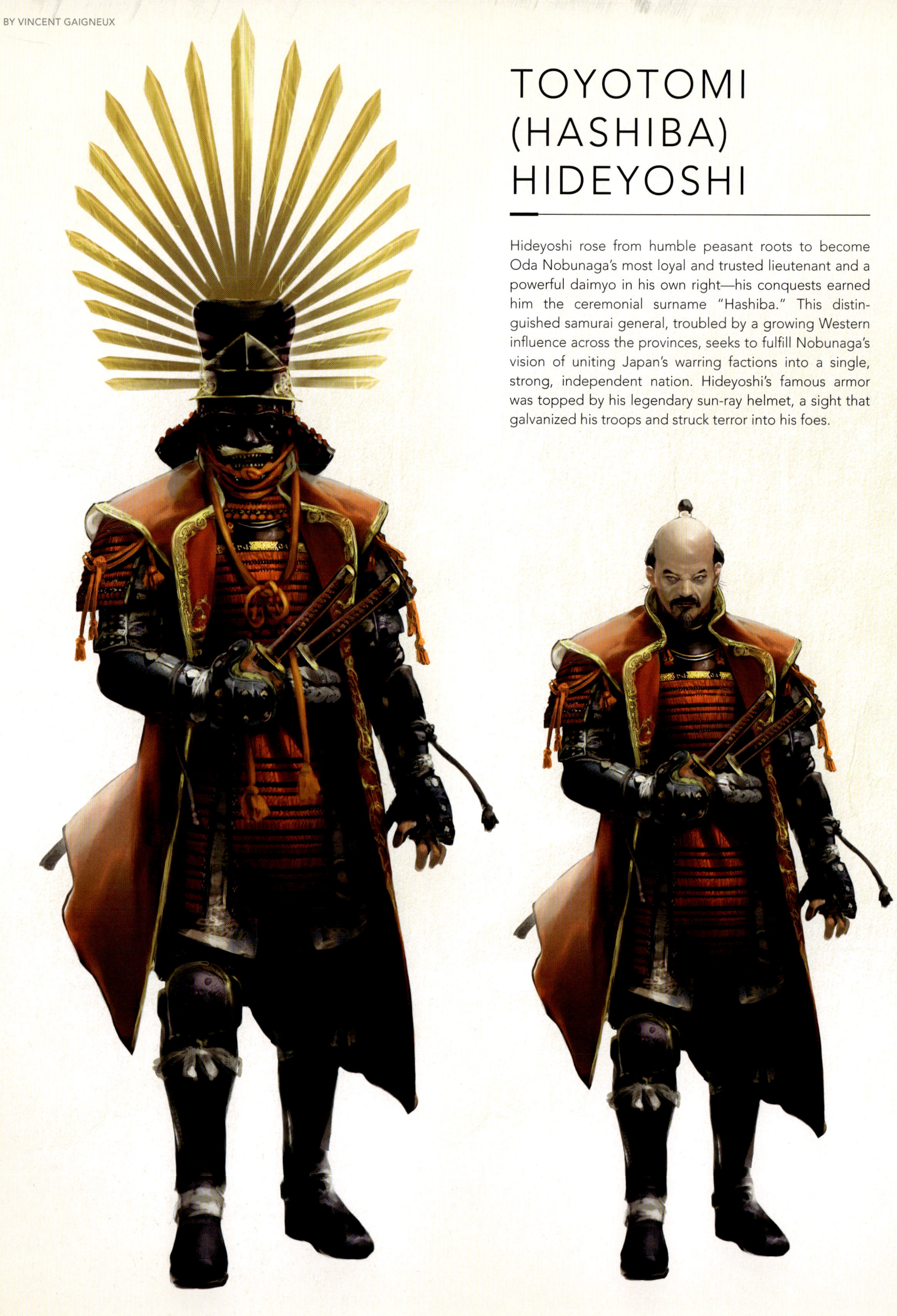

LADY NENE

The wife of Toyotomi Hideyoshi was a political powerhouse, holding as much diplomatic sway as anyone in Japan during this era. She was so trusted that Oda Nobunaga himself would send her correspondence with his official seal, a mark typically reserved for classified military documents. His stamp of approval made her a trusted ally to many in the upper echelon of society. She became one of her husband's closest aides and confidantes, often advising him on matters of governance. Here, Lady Nene wears a delicately embroidered *uchikake* kimono designed to form a perfect arc on the ground behind her.

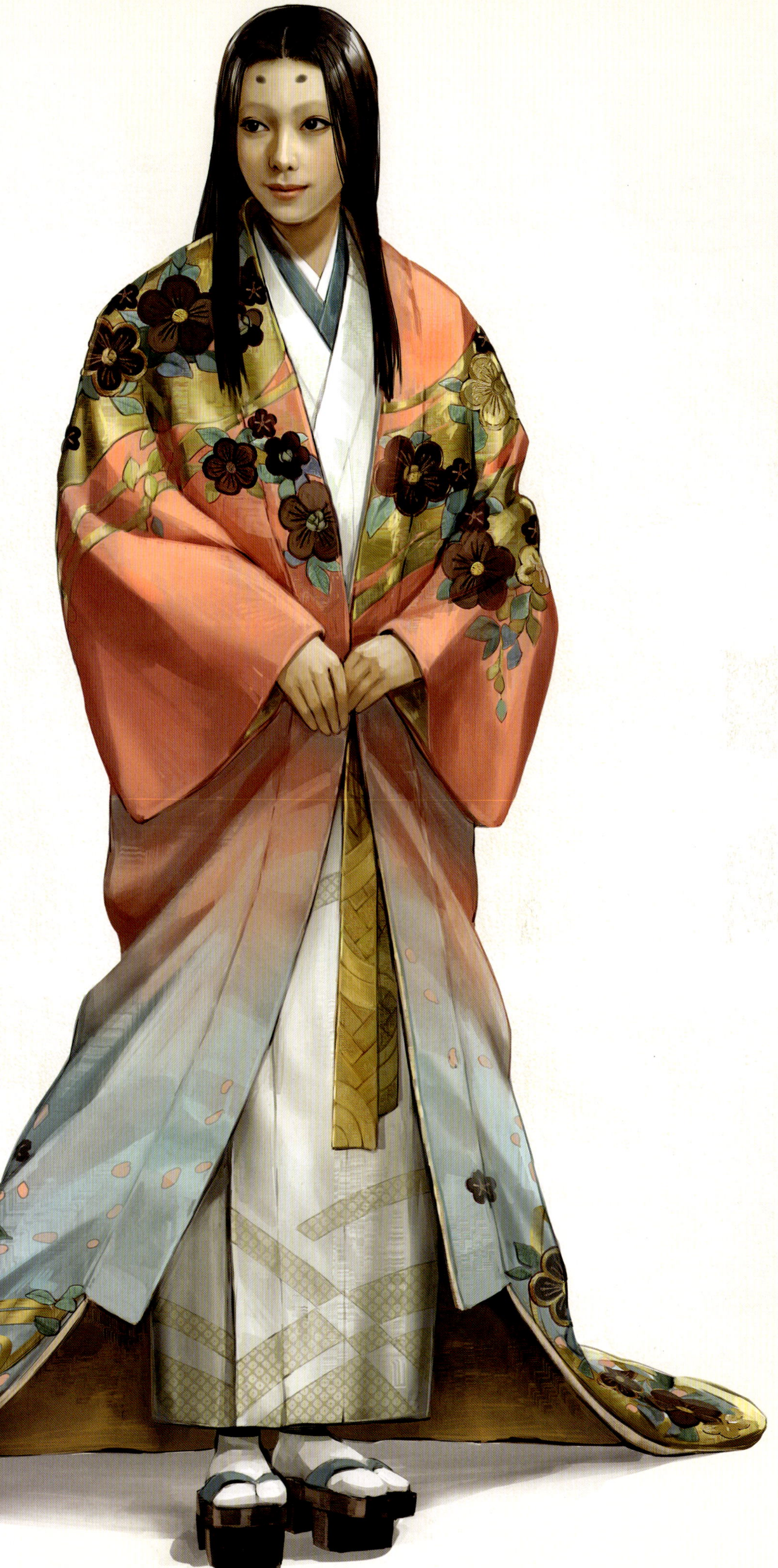

HATTORI HANZO

Hanzo, one of the most renowned warriors in Japanese history, was known for his daring nighttime raids. As pragmatic as he was fearless in combat, he could be ruthless in political matters—for example, after years of committed leadership of the Iga *shinobi* clans in their struggle for independent self-rule, he ultimately lent his sword to the unification efforts of Tokugawa Ieyasu. His black combat armor was designed to have a distinctive ninja look.

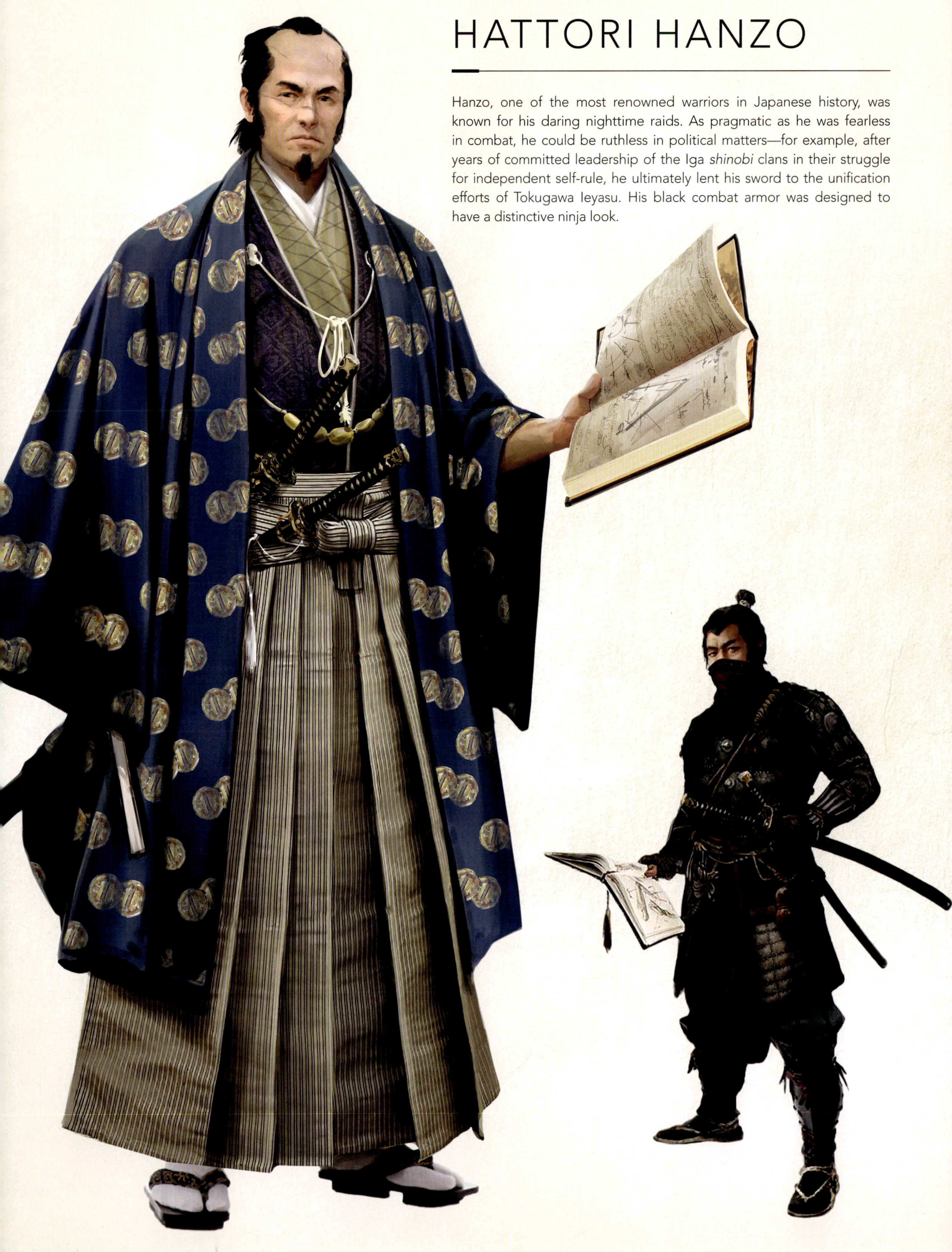

JUNJIRO

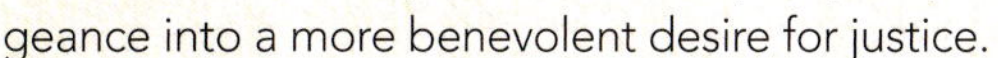

Junjiro is an eight-year-old bundle of relentless positivity who lives in a crumbling old temple with his guardian, the aged monk Sorin. After he finds Naoe near death, they nurse her back to health, and Junjiro becomes the mascot of Naoe and Yasuke's league of allies. Despite losing his father (a member of the notorious Shinbakufu) to Naoe's sword, the boy finds a well of forgiveness and eventually sees her as a sister. His optimism and empathy help Naoe turn her own hunger for vengeance into a more benevolent desire for justice.

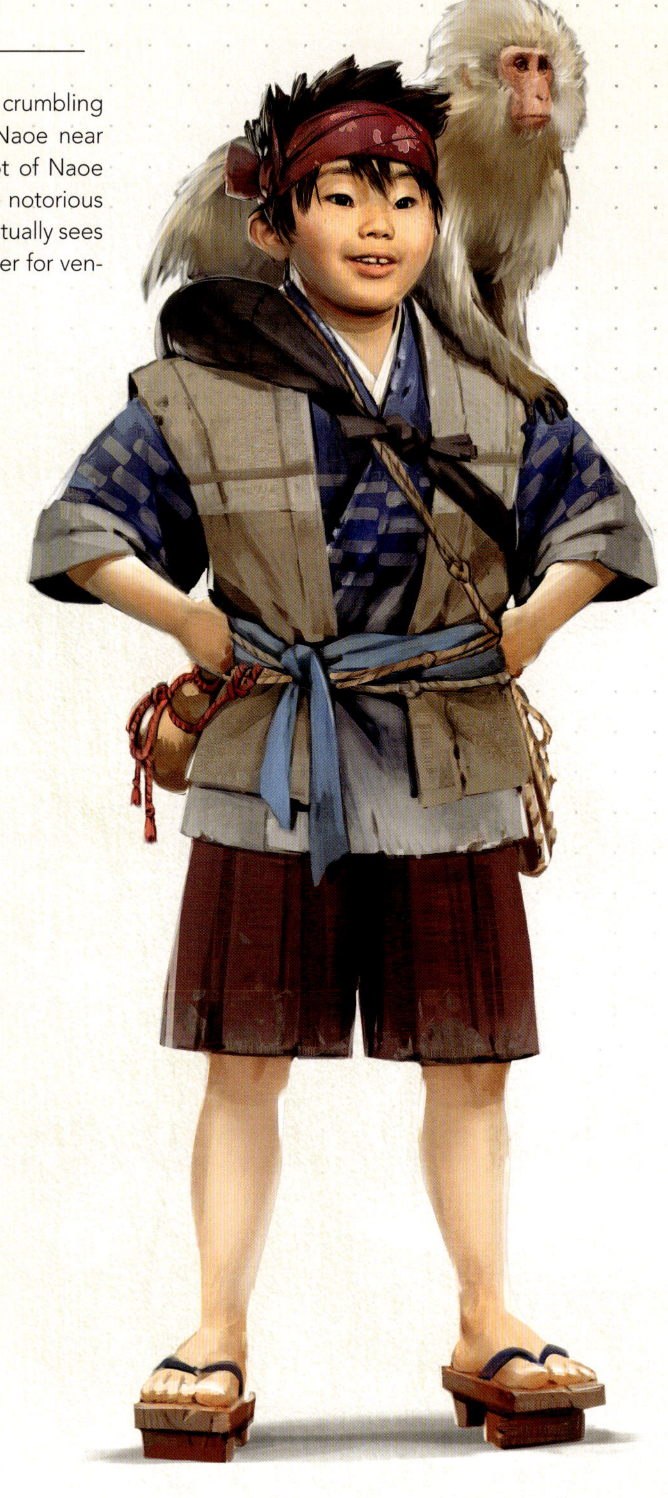

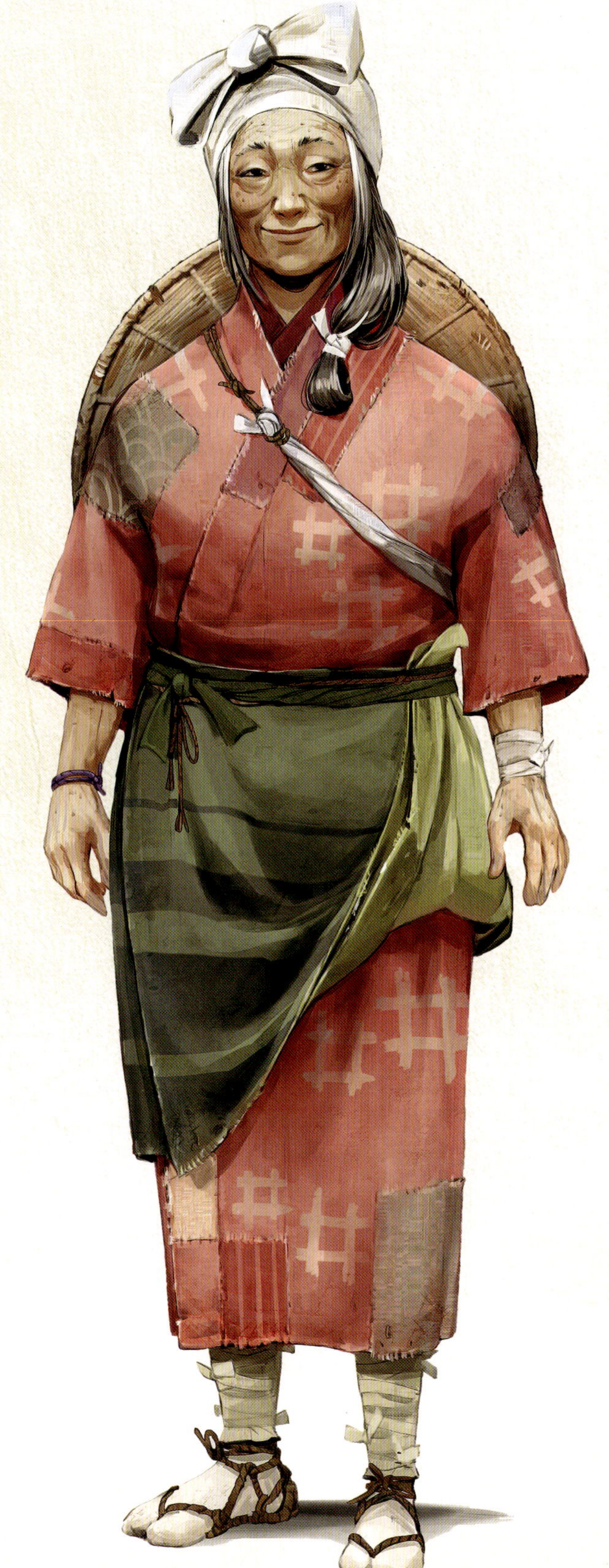

MATSU

A respected Iga elder, Matsu was once a fearless *shinobi* herself, navigating rooftops and ropes with wild abandon. Now she embraces each new day as a blessing, grateful for life's simplicity. Beneath her calm grandmotherly exterior, glimpses of her ninja skills emerge as she chops vegetables with a flourish.

ART BY VINCENT GAIGNEUX AND TYLER RYAN

FUJIBAYASHI NAGATO

Naoe's father is a great warrior of unparalleled skill and a leader of the confederation of ninja clans in Iga Province. Fierce and lethal, he fights furiously against the onslaught of regional daimyos seeking to overrun Iga's rugged terrain. But despite his deadly talents, Nagato is also renowned for empathy and wisdom—key *shinobi* traits that he seeks to pass on to Naoe. He will also pass on his Hidden Blade, the Assassins' iconic weapon.

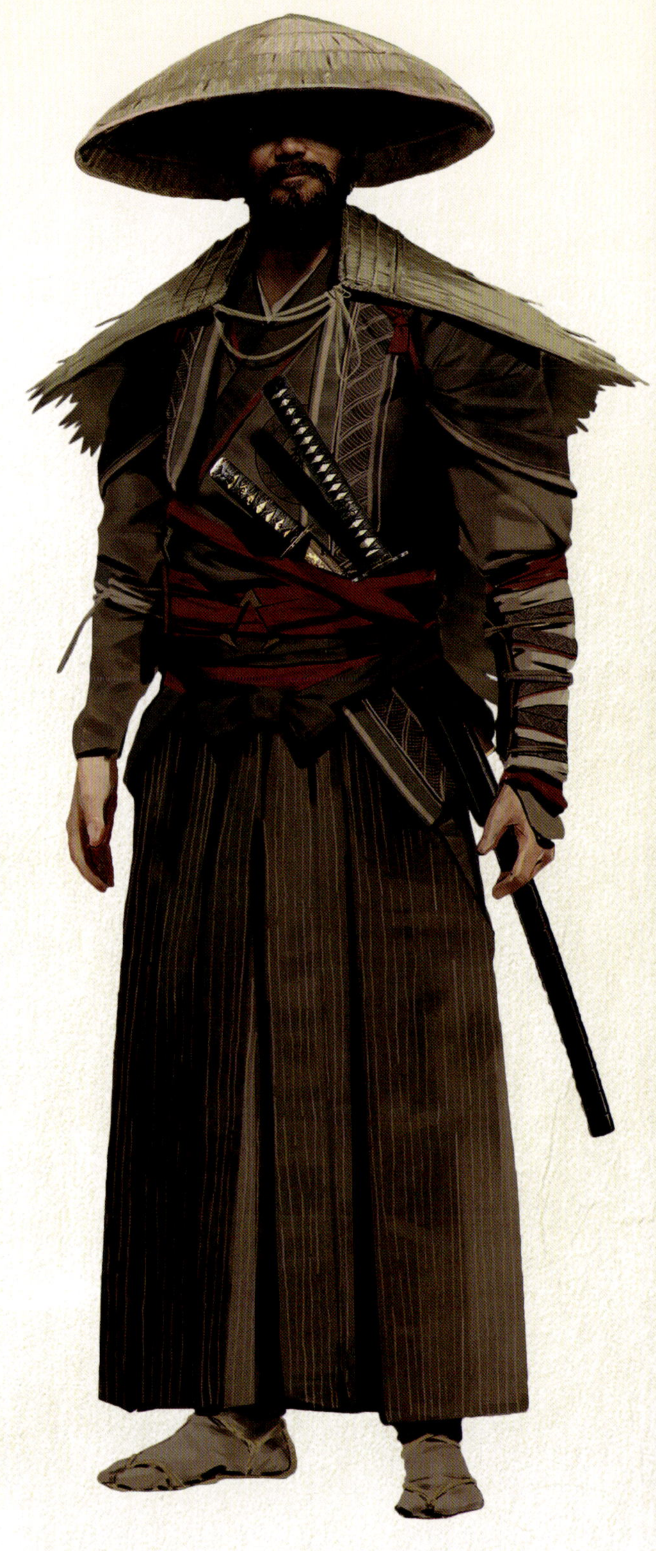

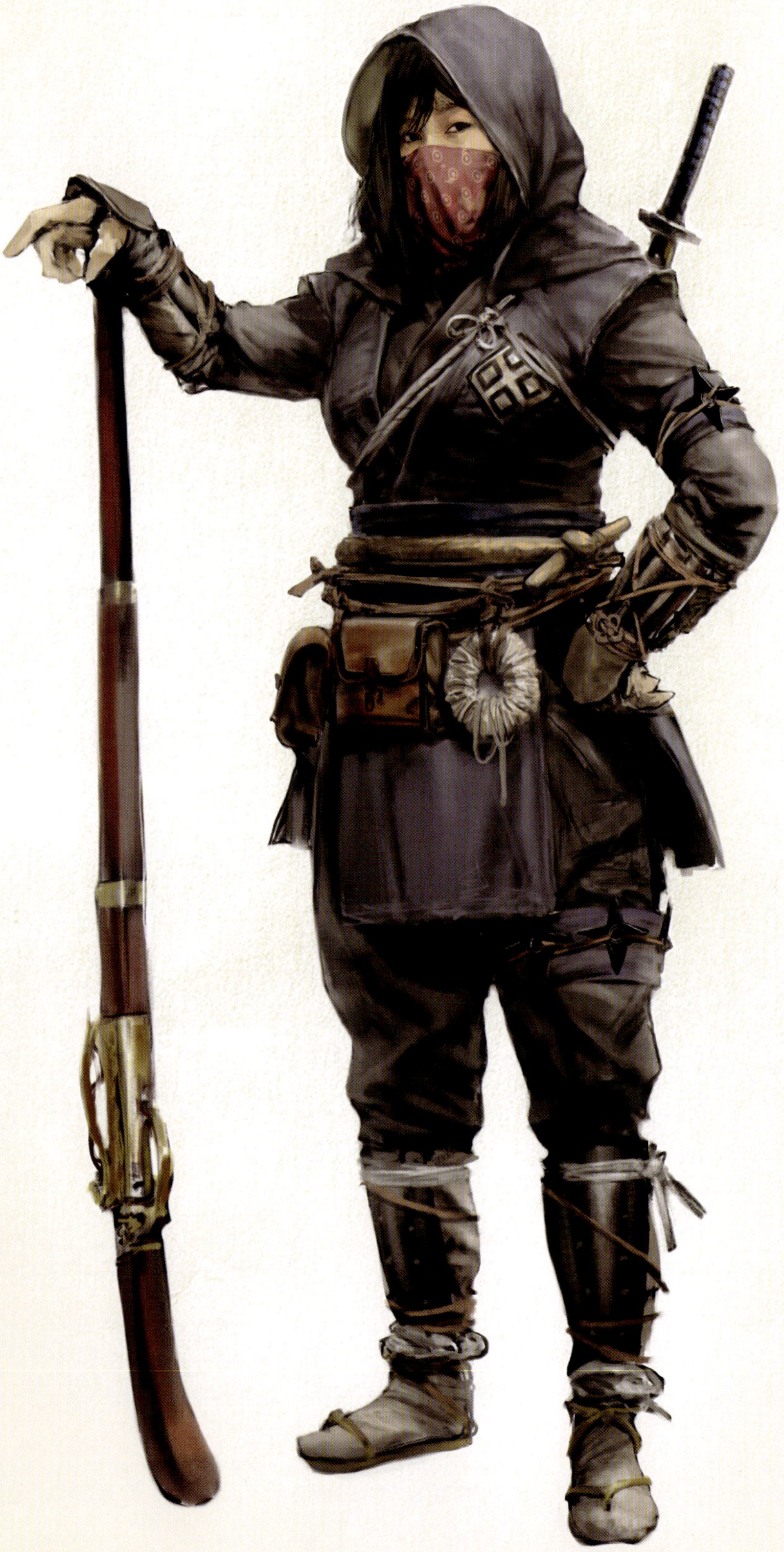

KATSUHIME

One of the *shinobi* allies Naoe can recruit, Katsuhime is a skilled sharpshooter with her rifle, or *teppō*. A native of Omi, she spent an idyllic childhood as a daimyo's daughter until Oda Nobunaga conquered the province. Now she's known to many as the "Teppō Lady"—clad in Portuguese military attire, passionate about gunpowder and firearms. She can be brash and irreverent, with a fiery personality aptly described as "explosive."

ART BY KATE CRUZ

GENNOJO

Impulsive, charming, and reckless, Gennojo plays the classic Robin Hood role as a thief who robs the rich blind, gives the loot to the poor, and delights in wreaking general chaos throughout his home province of Yamashiro. Recruitable as an ally in Naoe and Yasuke's league, he tries to find more constructive ways to silence his personal demons.

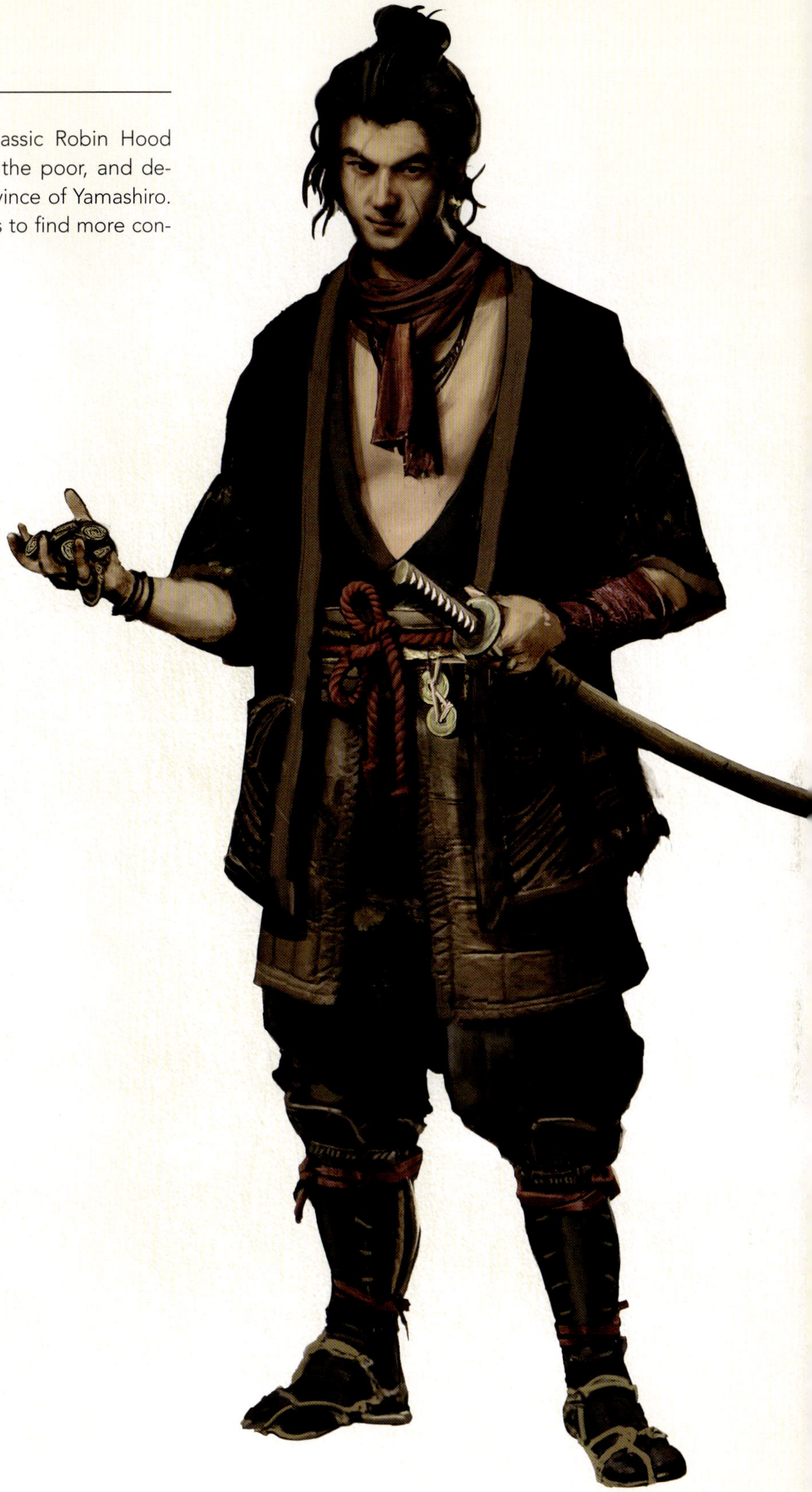

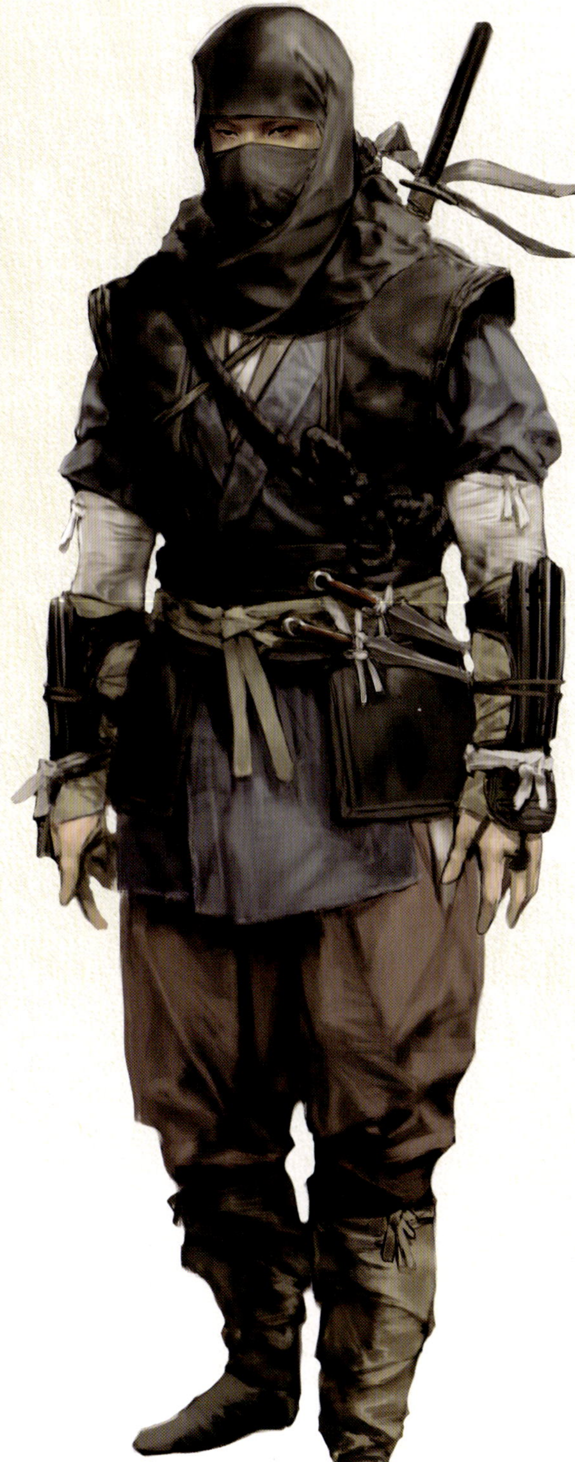

ART BY VINCENT GAIGNEUX

NAGOYA YAGORO

Another recruitable *shinobi* ally, Yagoro comes from a mining village in Tamba. Cheerful and idealistic, he feels a strong sense of justice as well as a deep disdain for oppression. His response is to become a self-taught Assassin equipped with a Hidden Blade that he fashioned himself. Once recruited, he can gain more formal training in the Creed.

ART BY FRED RAMBAUD

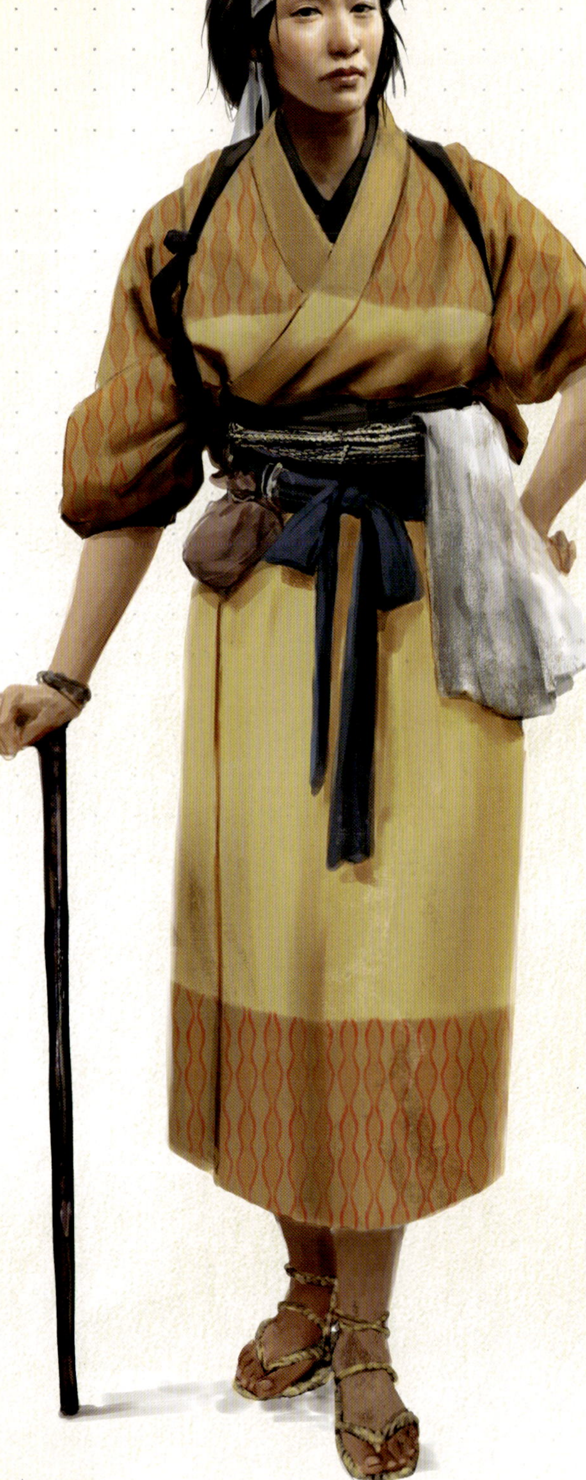

TOMIKO

Tomiko has lost almost everyone she cares about to the raging wars of Japan's Sengoku period. But she is a hardened survivor, and her farm becomes the hideout site for the growing network of *shinobi*. Tomiko also helps in recruiting new members into the league.

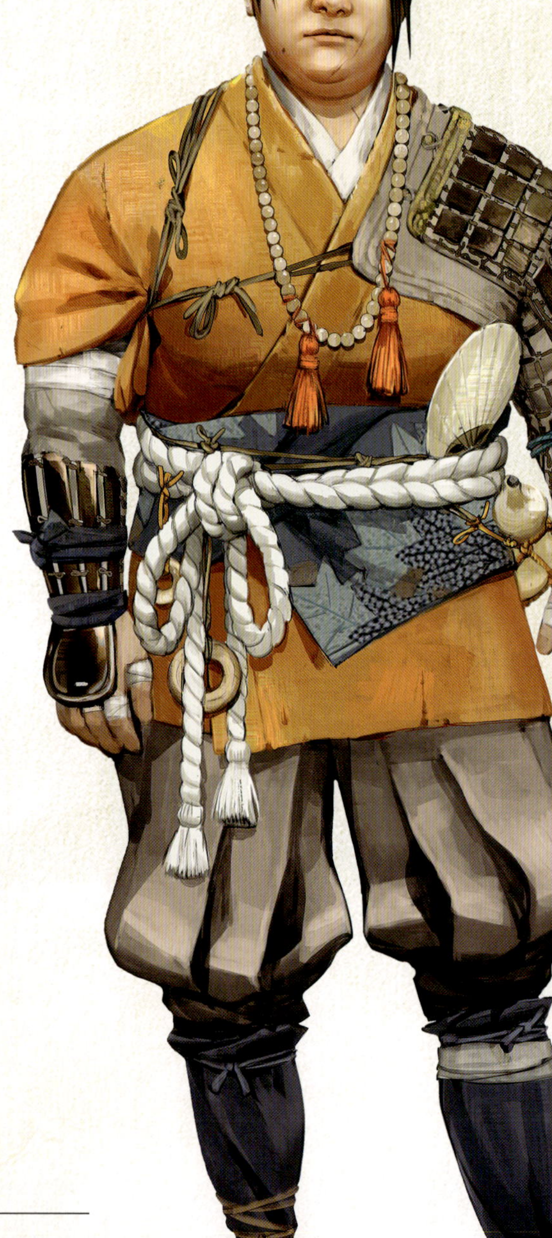

YAYA

Yaya brings formidable strength, both physical and spiritual, to any cause. As a dedicated *sōhei*, a Buddhist warrior-monk, she became a fierce fighter. But time spent in various monasteries, including Hongan-ji, helped Yaya be more at peace with herself as she learned the value of meditation. As a recruitable ally, she passes on her centering calm and self-regulating practices to Naoe.

ART BY KONI (AMANDINE GIRARD)

ART BY SINA HAYATI

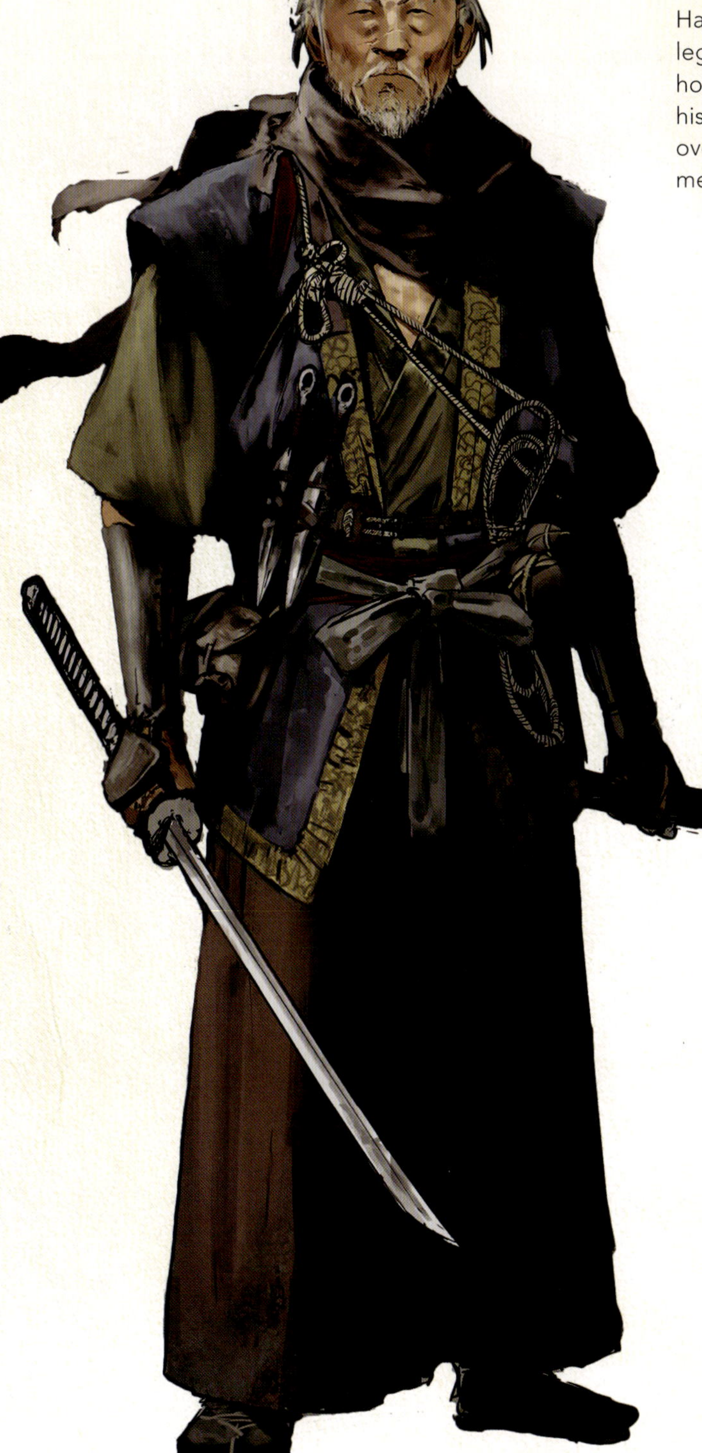

MOMOCHI SANDAYU

Harsh and uncompromising but always fair, Momochi Sandayu is a legendary *shinobi* warrior who has been fighting to protect his Iga homeland since he was a boy. He holds the atrocities inflicted on his people deep in his heart, and then transforms the pain into an overwhelming fury on the battlefield. Sandayu does nothing in half measures; every act is decisive.

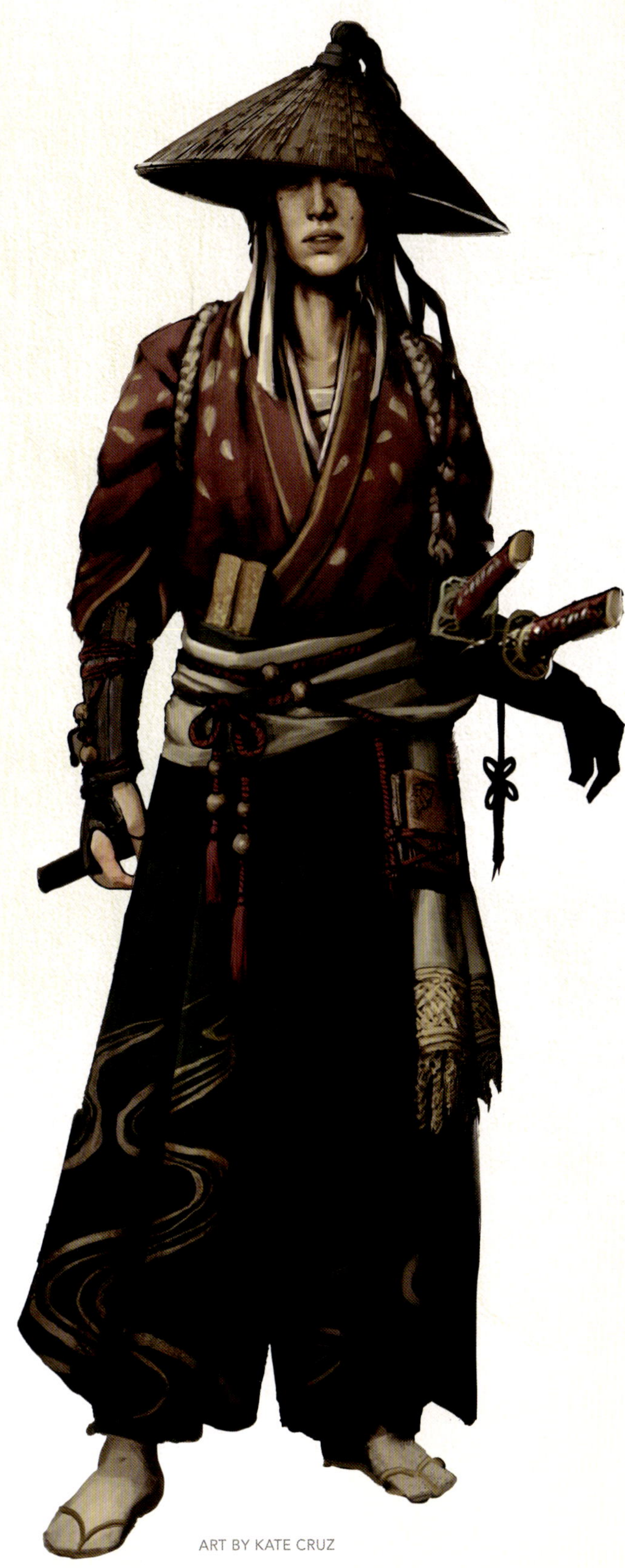

ART BY KATE CRUZ

IBUKI

Free spirited, rebellious, yet joyful by nature, this recruitable ally is a solitary ronin who came from a clan of obedient samurai but now follows a unique moral compass. They were well trained and excel in combat but always felt constrained by the strict rules and stoicism of the samurai class. Typically clad in a classic kimono and *hakama* pants, Ibuki harbors a deep reverence for poetry, art, and nature.

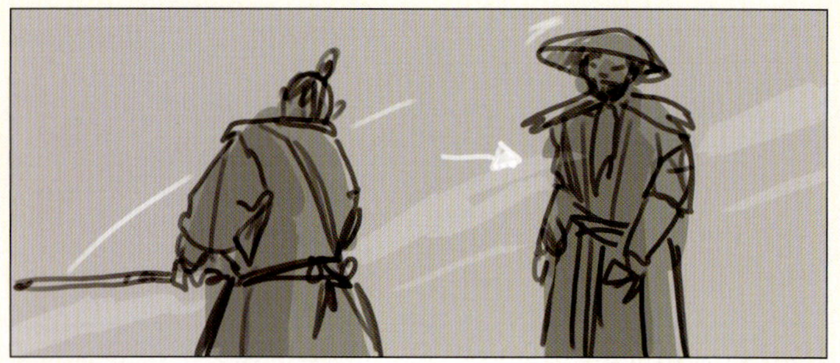
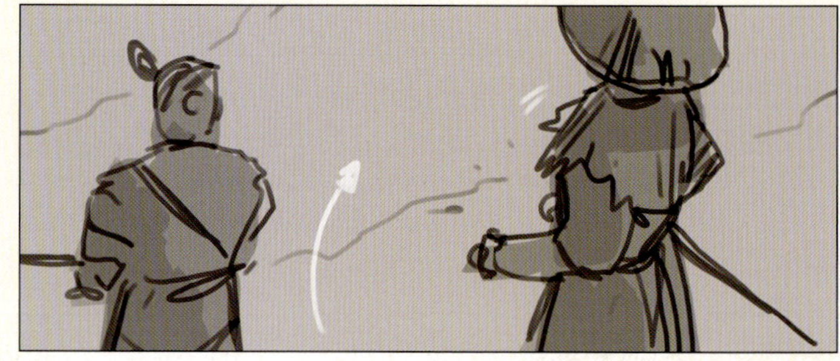
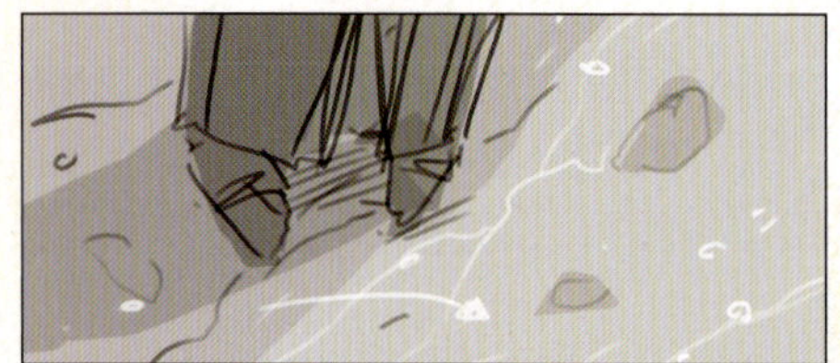
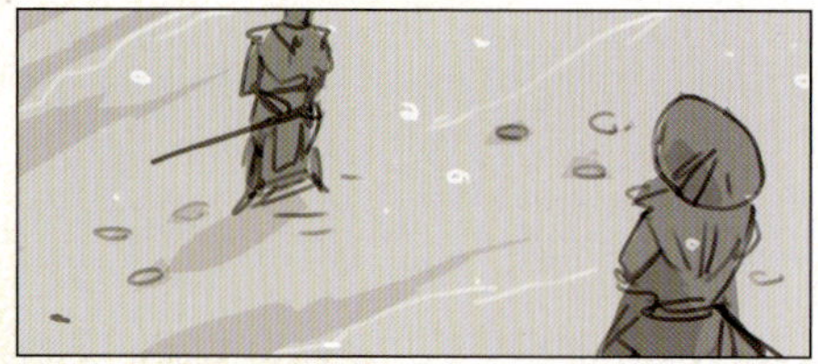
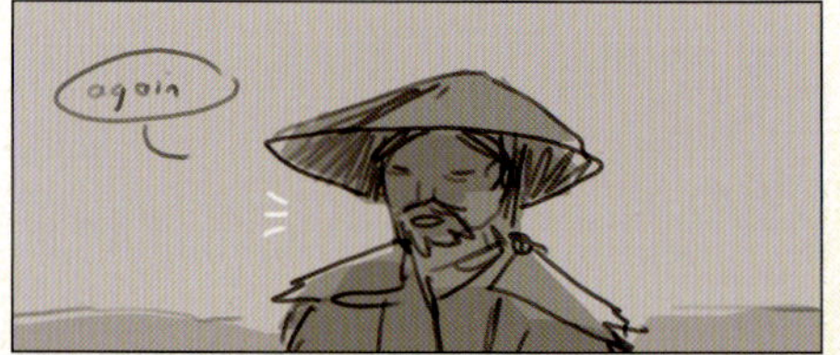

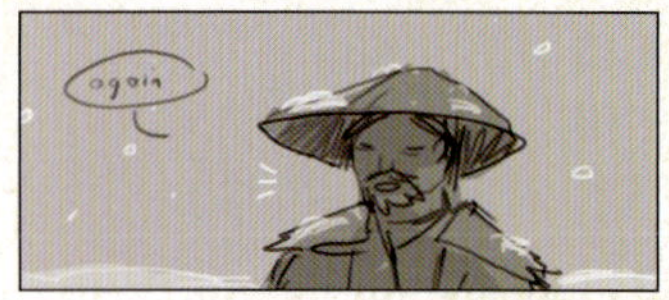

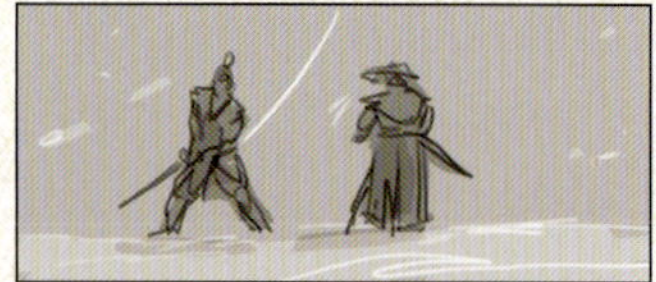
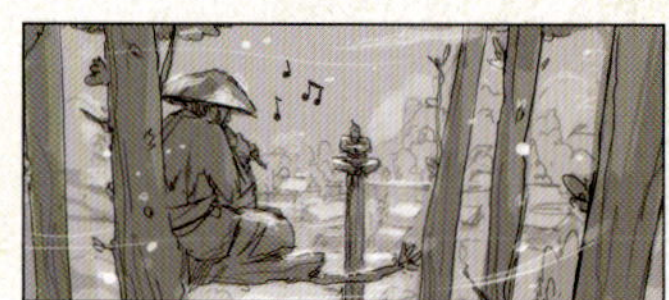
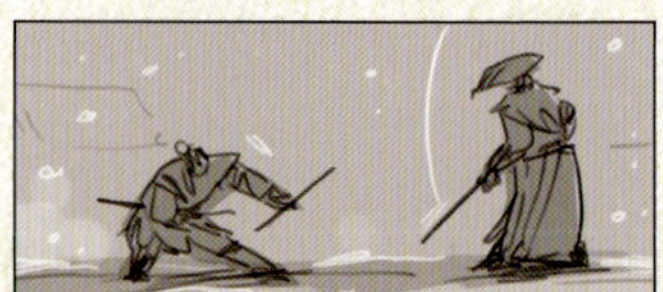
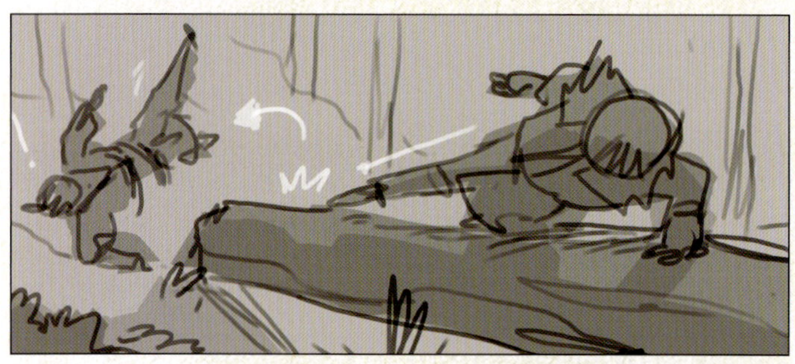
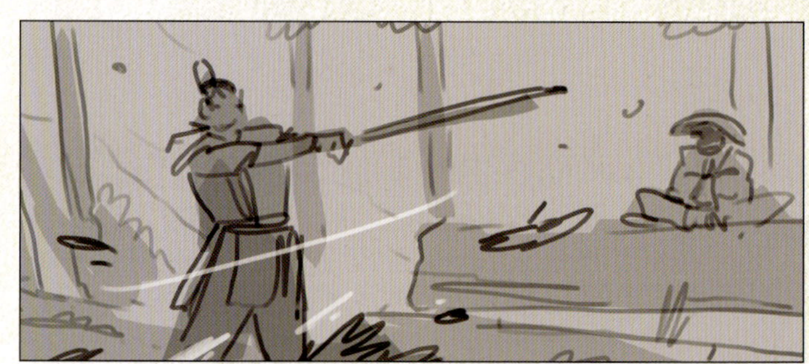
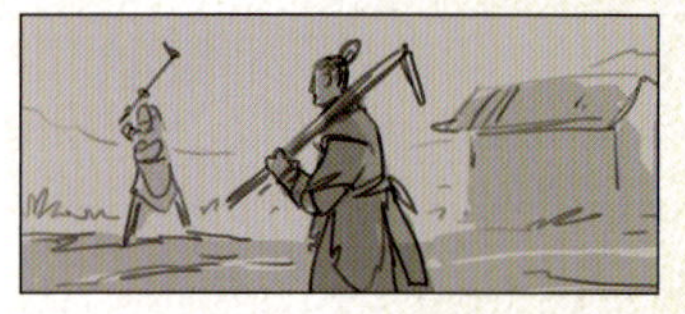
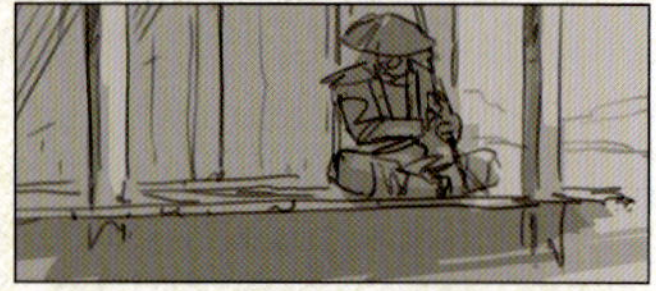
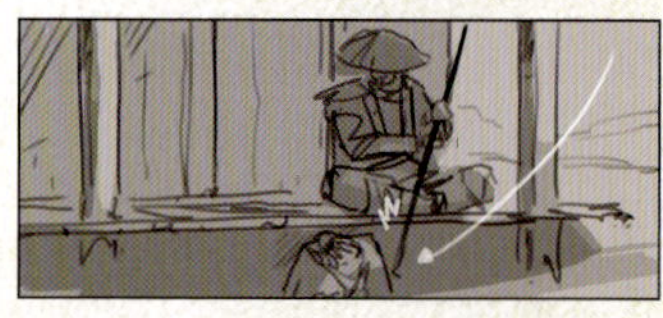
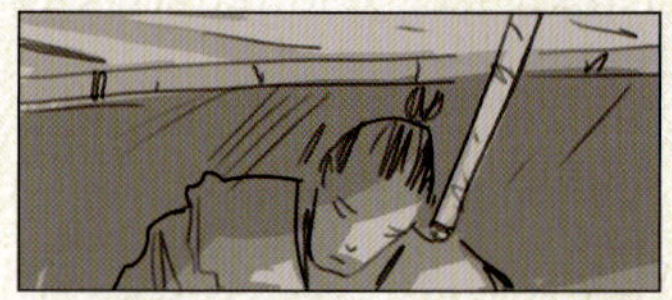
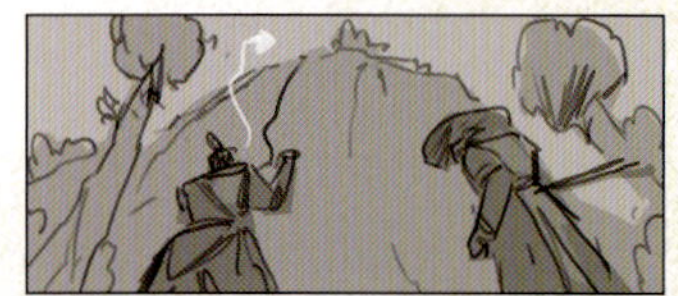
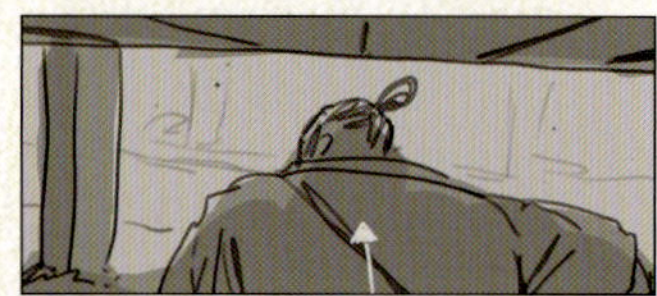
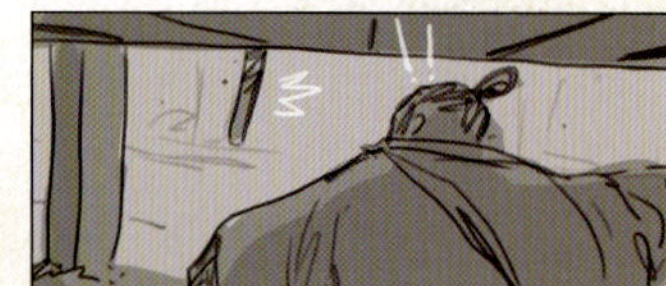
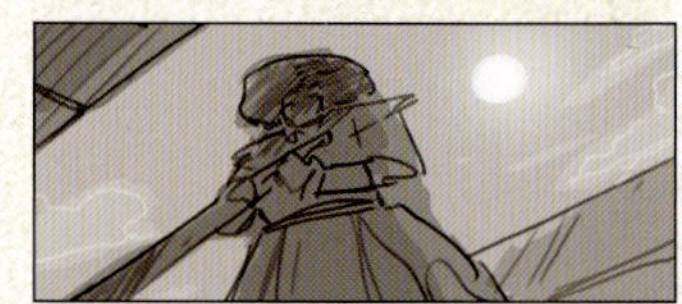
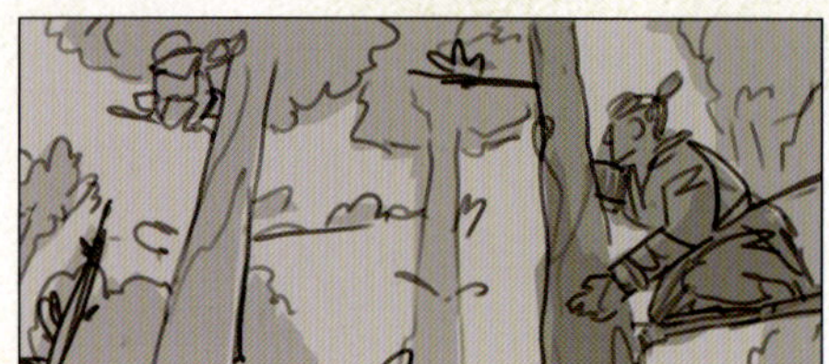
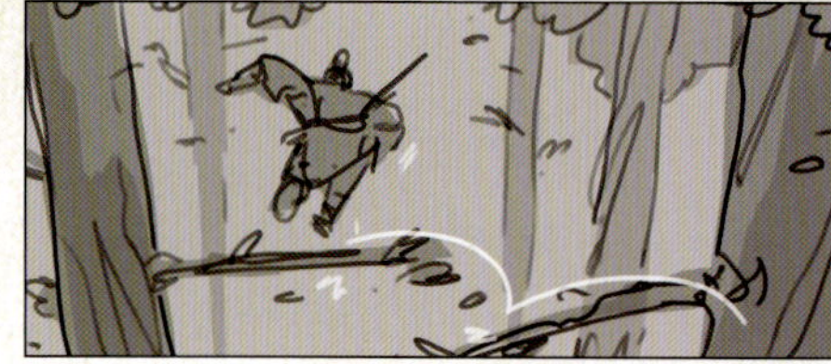
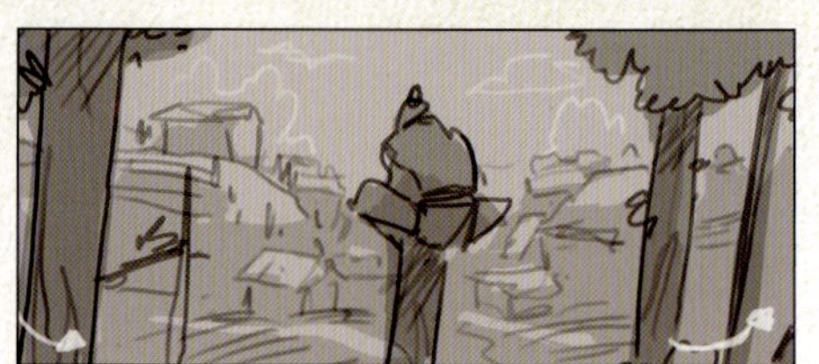

STORYBOARDS

The *Shadows* art, story, and level design teams collaborated closely to create the look and feel of individual scenes within the game's narrative flow. One efficient way to facilitate that process was to start with storyboards—simple panel sketches that lay out the key moments, or "big beats," of a scene. According to Luc Plante, the game's quest director, storyboards help calibrate the best pacing of a sequence, with certain key panels turned into full-color concept art to help convey the scene's proper tone or mood.

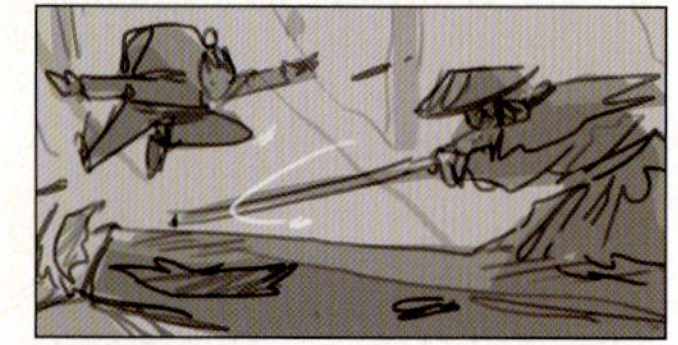
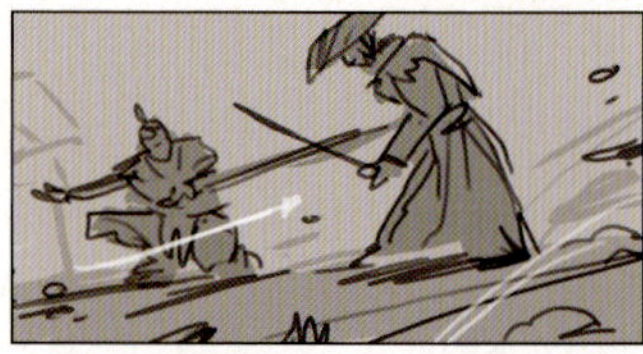
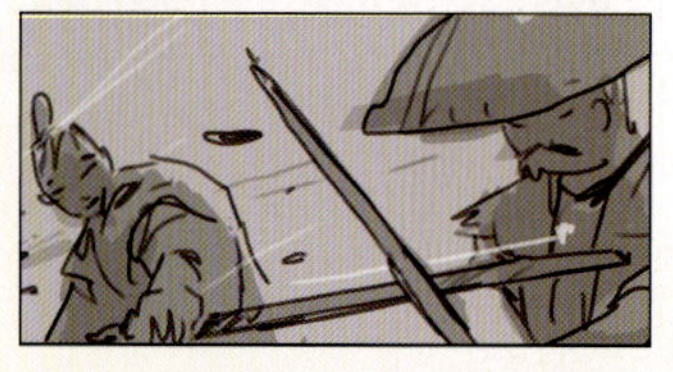
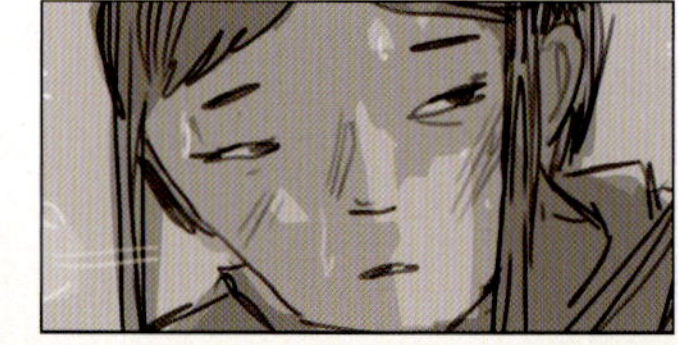

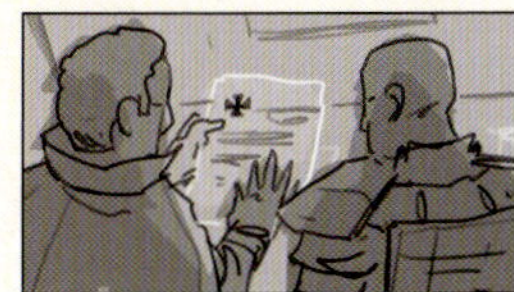
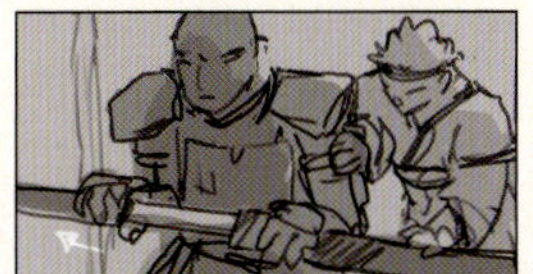
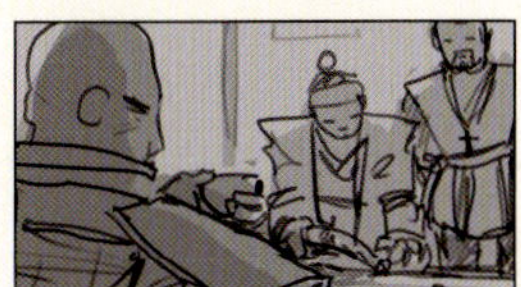
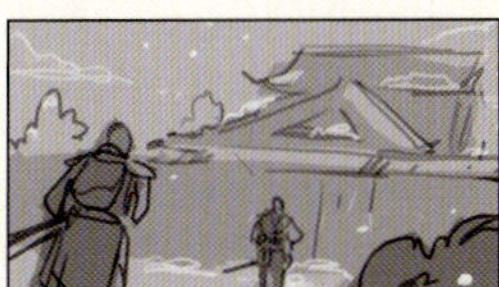
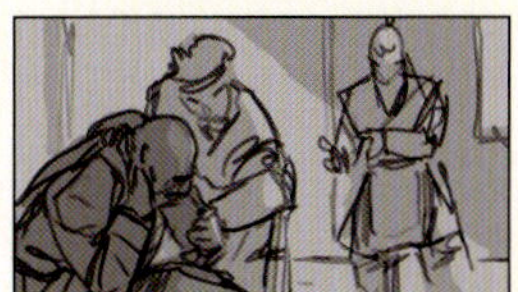
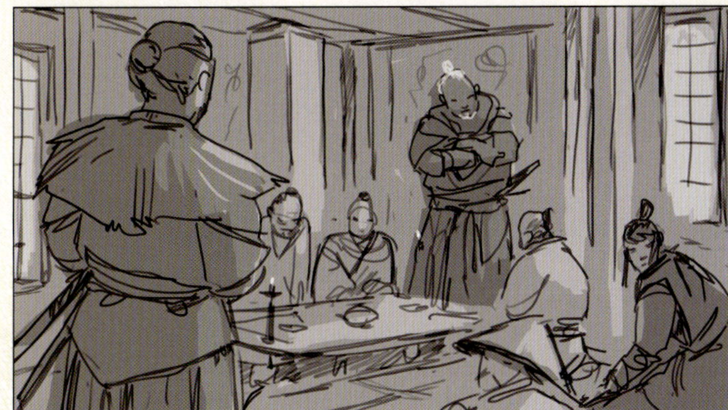
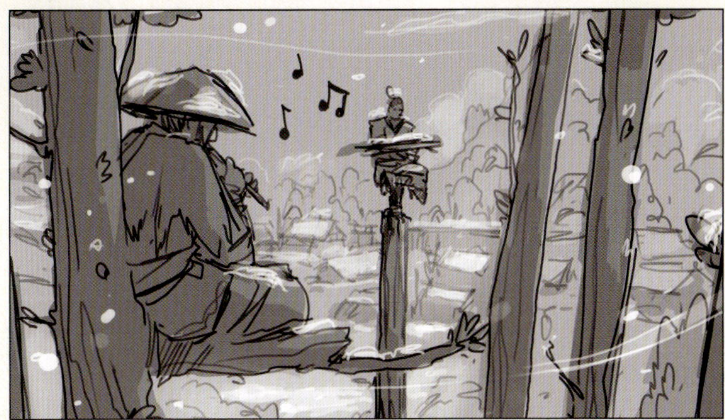
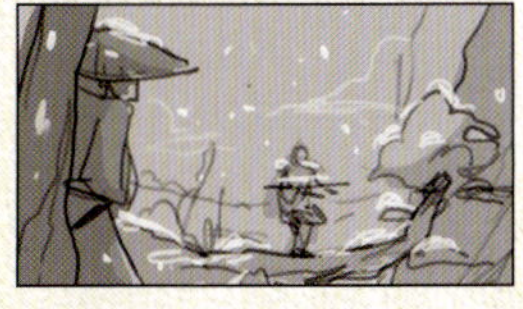
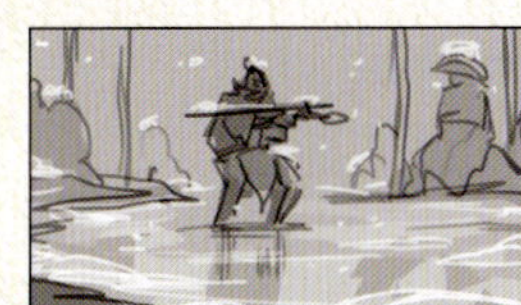
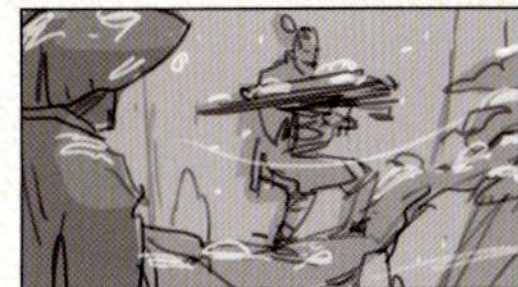
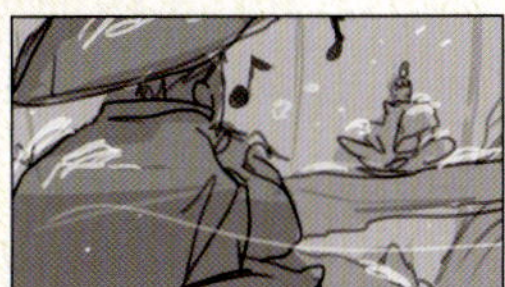
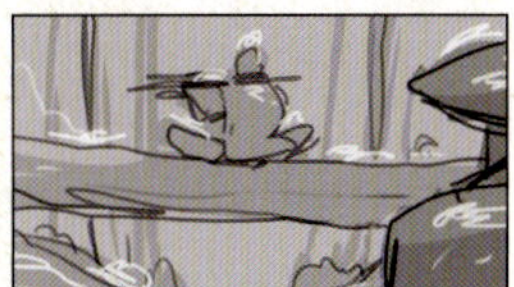
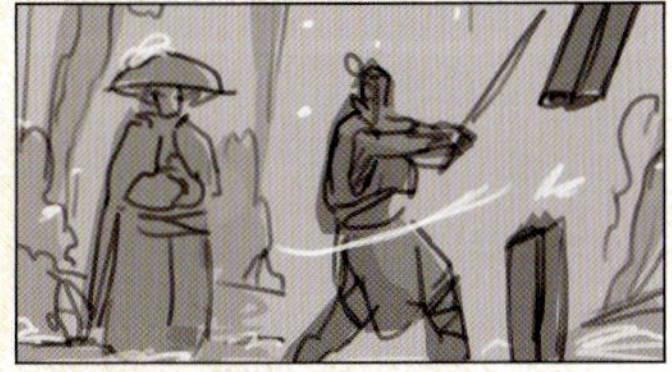
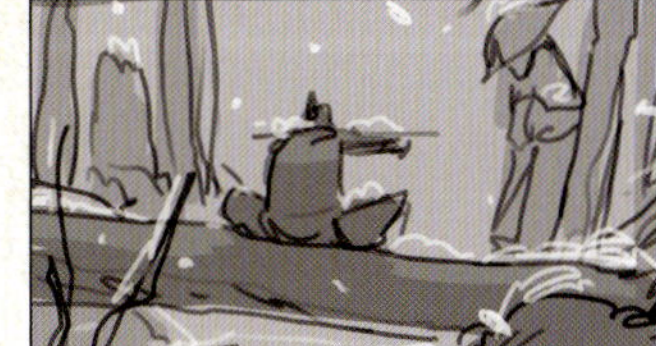
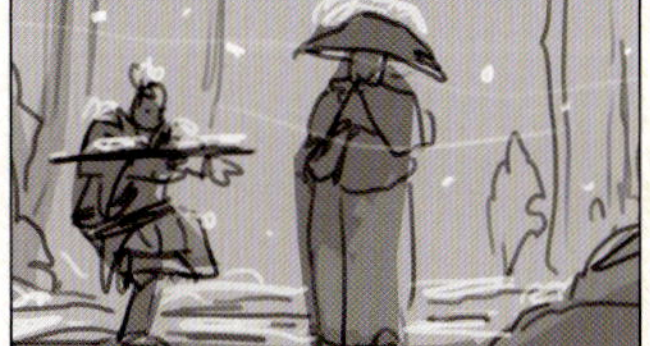
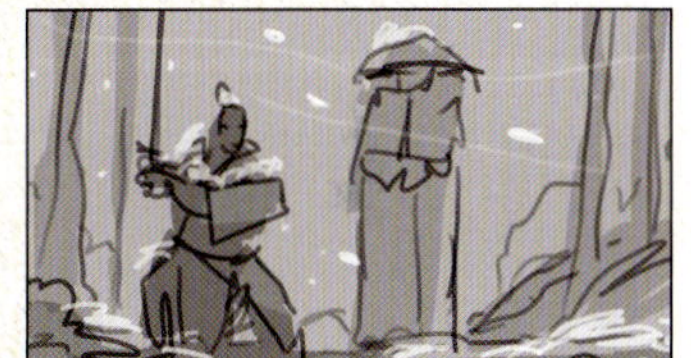
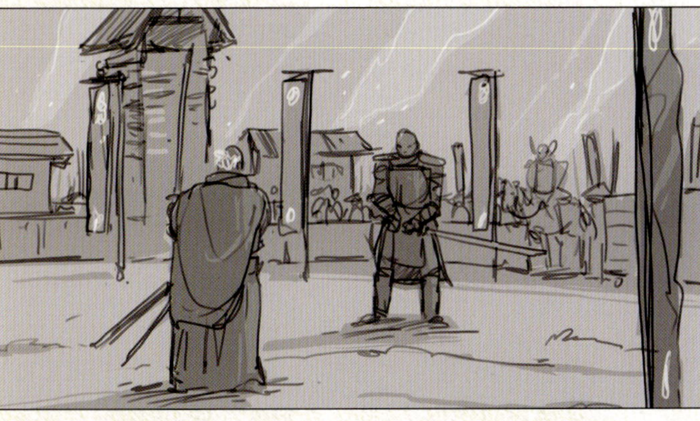
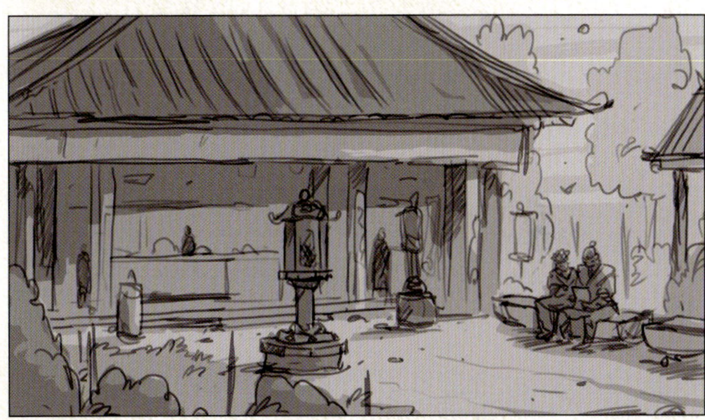
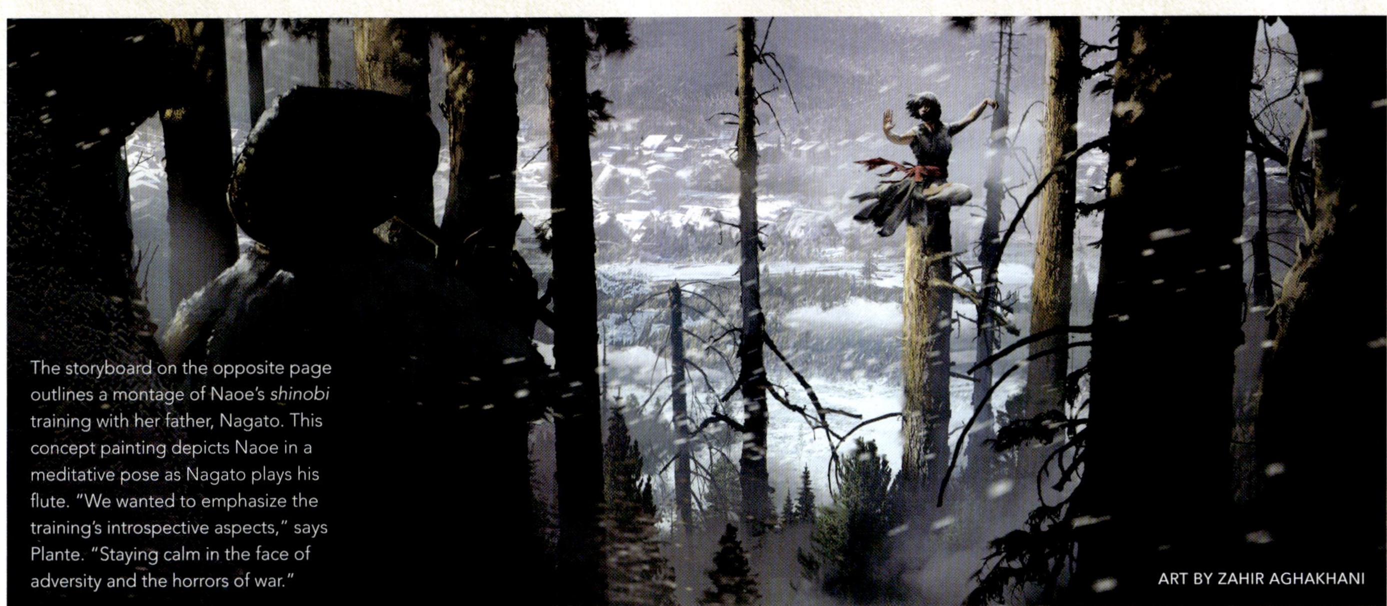

The storyboard on the opposite page outlines a montage of Naoe's *shinobi* training with her father, Nagato. This concept painting depicts Naoe in a meditative pose as Nagato plays his flute. "We wanted to emphasize the training's introspective aspects," says Plante. "Staying calm in the face of adversity and the horrors of war."

ART BY ZAHIR AGHAKHANI

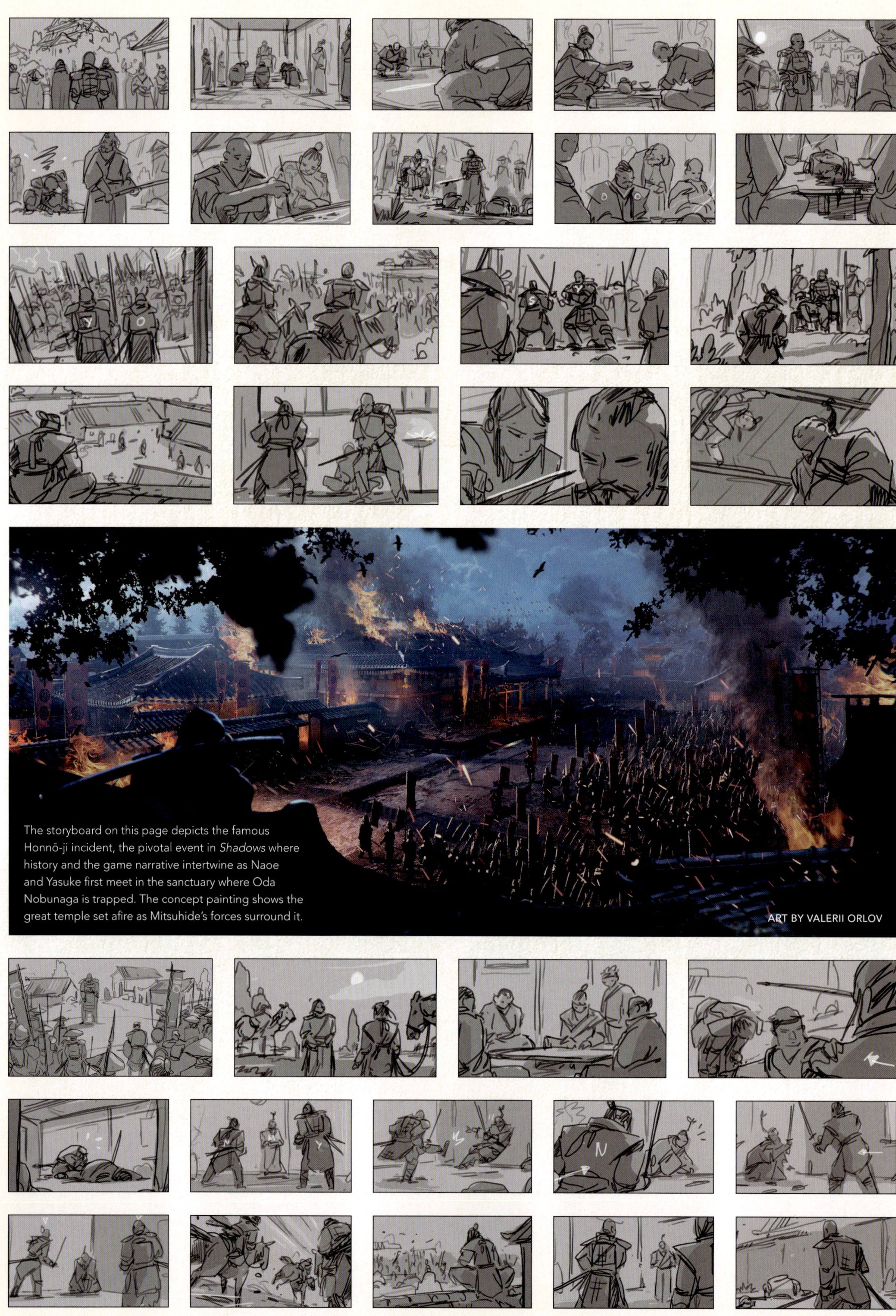

The storyboard on this page depicts the famous Honnō-ji incident, the pivotal event in *Shadows* where history and the game narrative intertwine as Naoe and Yasuke first meet in the sanctuary where Oda Nobunaga is trapped. The concept painting shows the great temple set afire as Mitsuhide's forces surround it.

ART BY VALERII ORLOV

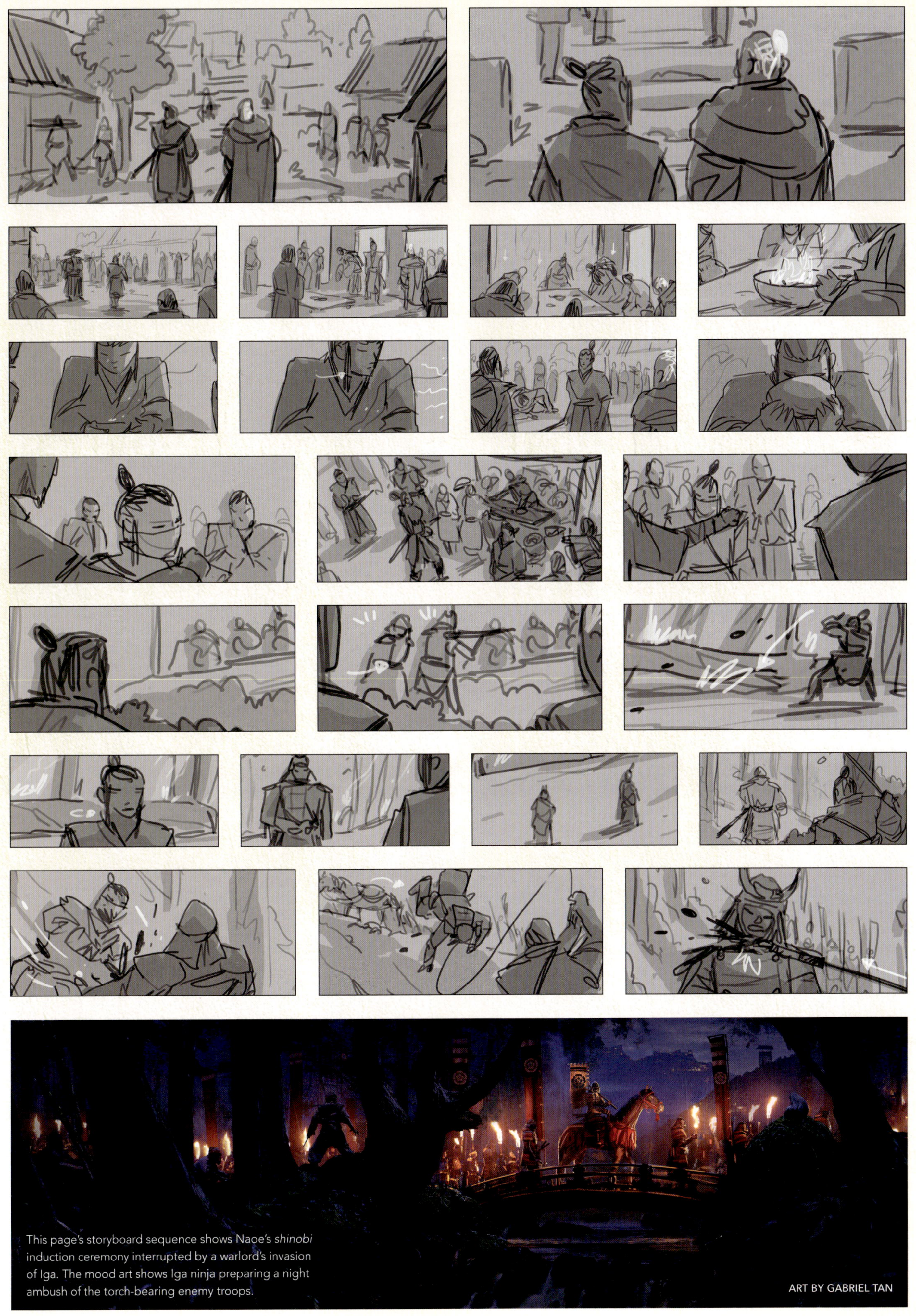

This page's storyboard sequence shows Naoe's *shinobi* induction ceremony interrupted by a warlord's invasion of Iga. The mood art shows Iga ninja preparing a night ambush of the torch-bearing enemy troops.

ART BY GABRIEL TAN

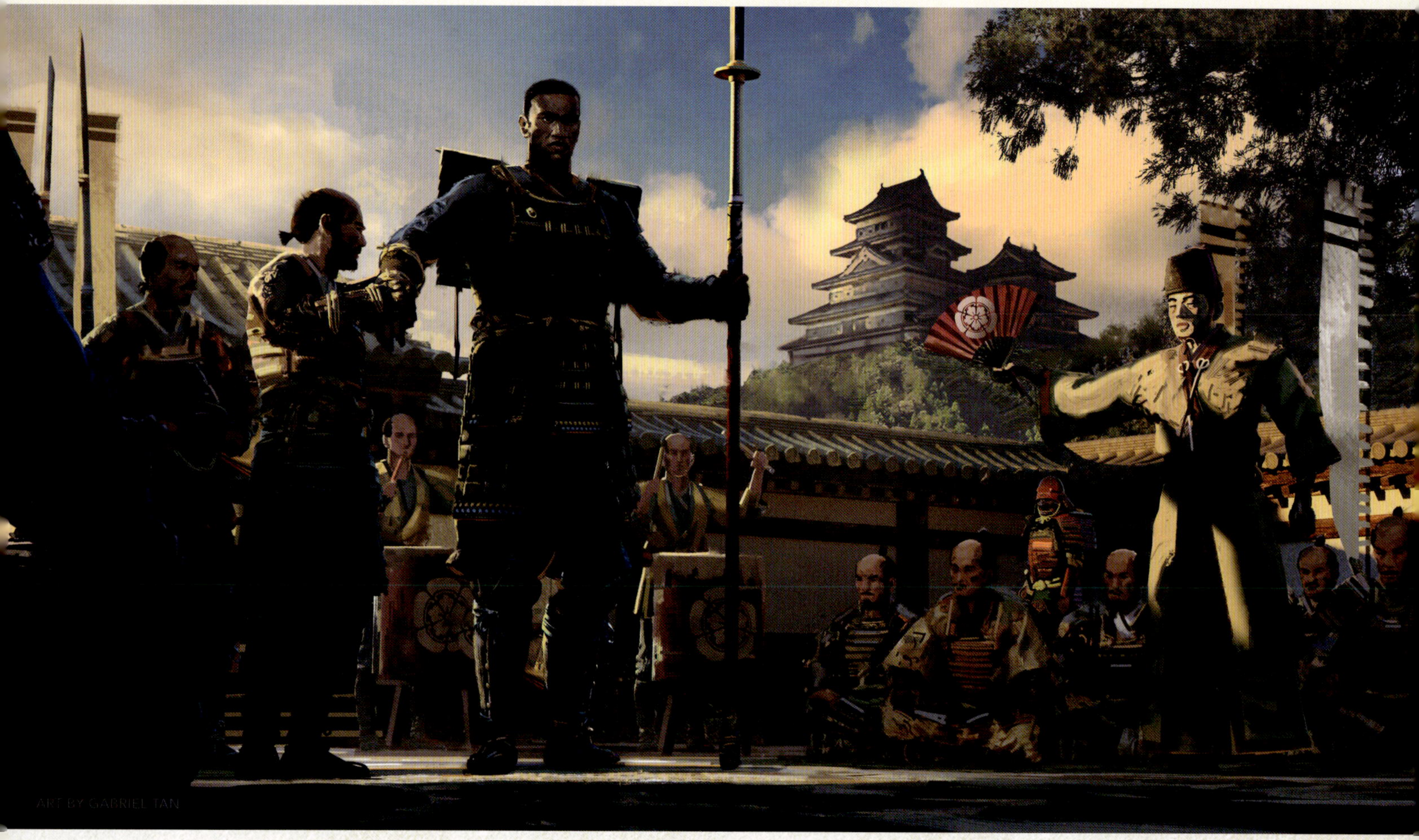

ART BY GABRIEL TAN

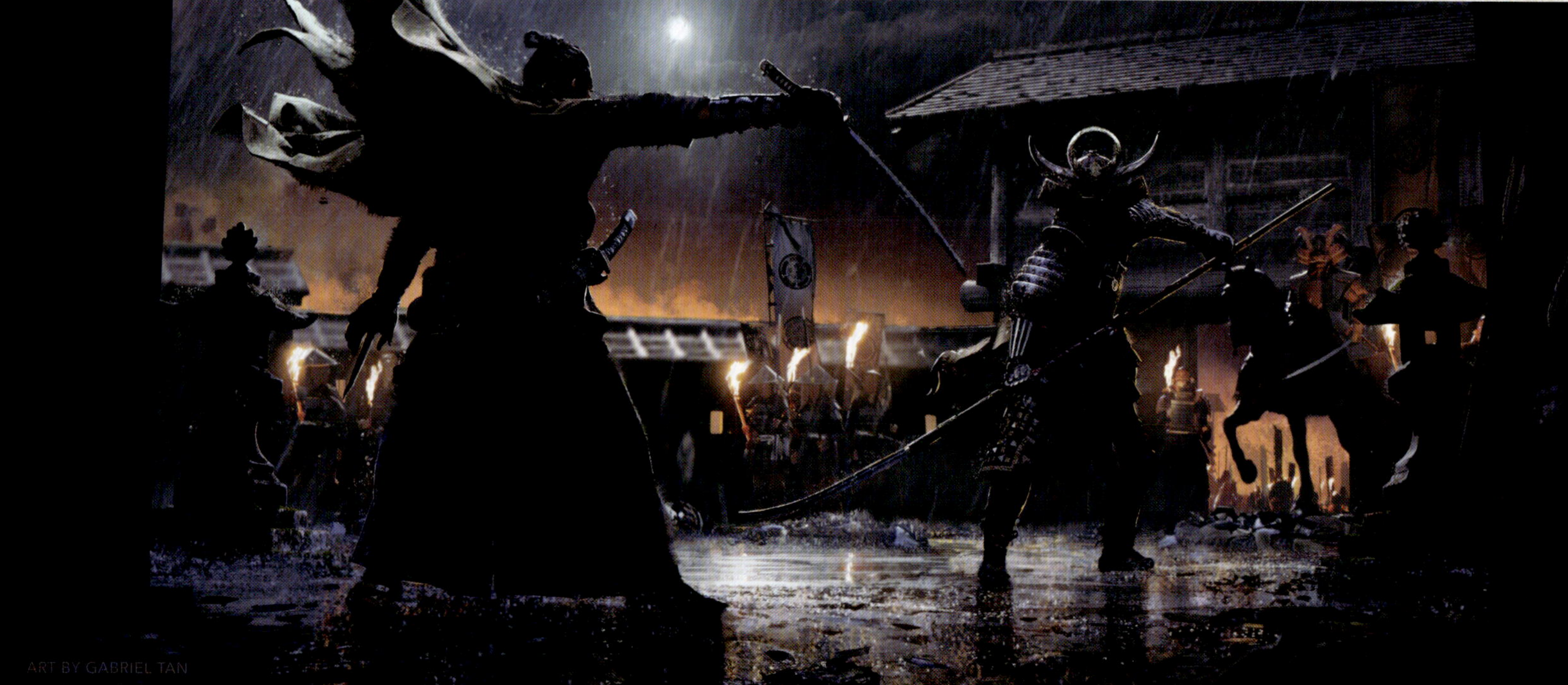

ART BY GABRIEL TAN

NARRATIVE CONCEPT ART

Narrative concept art is created to nail down the look, feel, and mood of significant scenes in the *Shadows* story line. The story team generates notes on how a key moment should be depicted; a concept artist conjures a vision of that moment using color, contrast, lighting, and perspective; the design team weighs in on how best to physically stage it in the game environment; and then, based on that input, the story team may revise the scene's structure or elements for a more dramatic effect. "Again, it's a very collaborative, back-and-forth process," says Luc Plante. "We inspire each other to expand the way we think about important scenes."

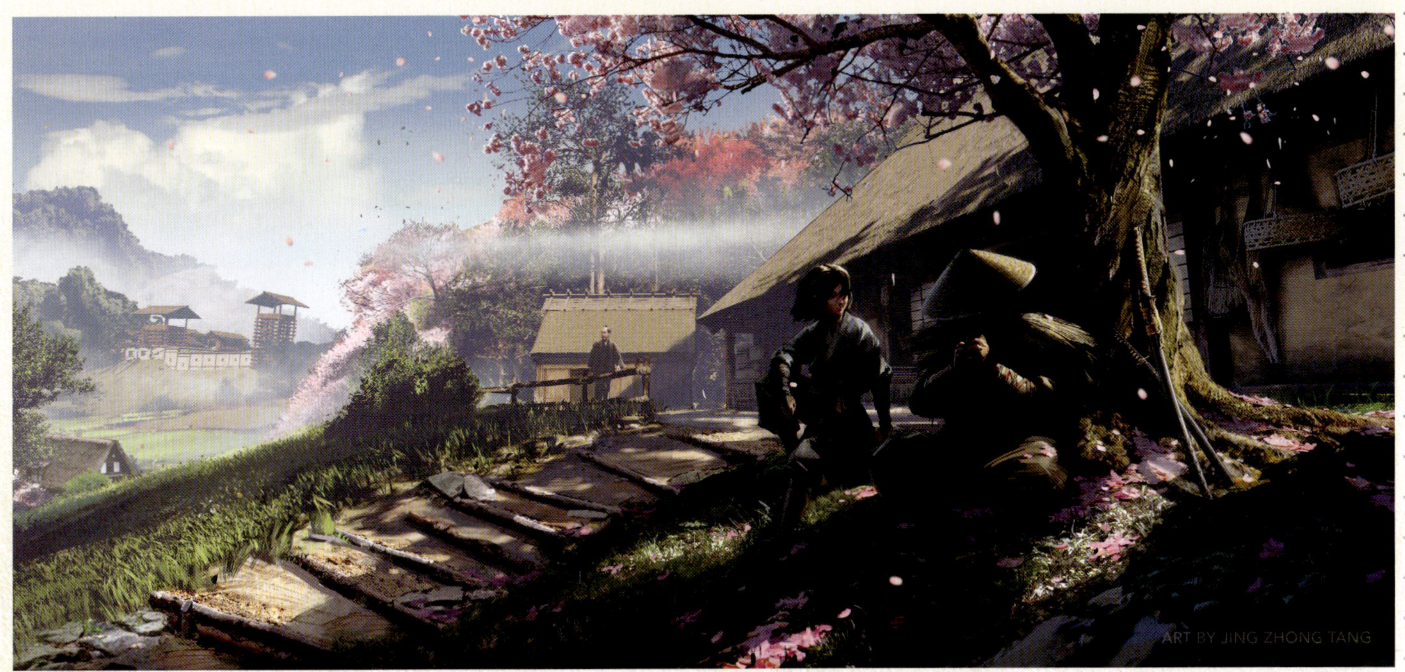

ART BY JING ZHONG TANG

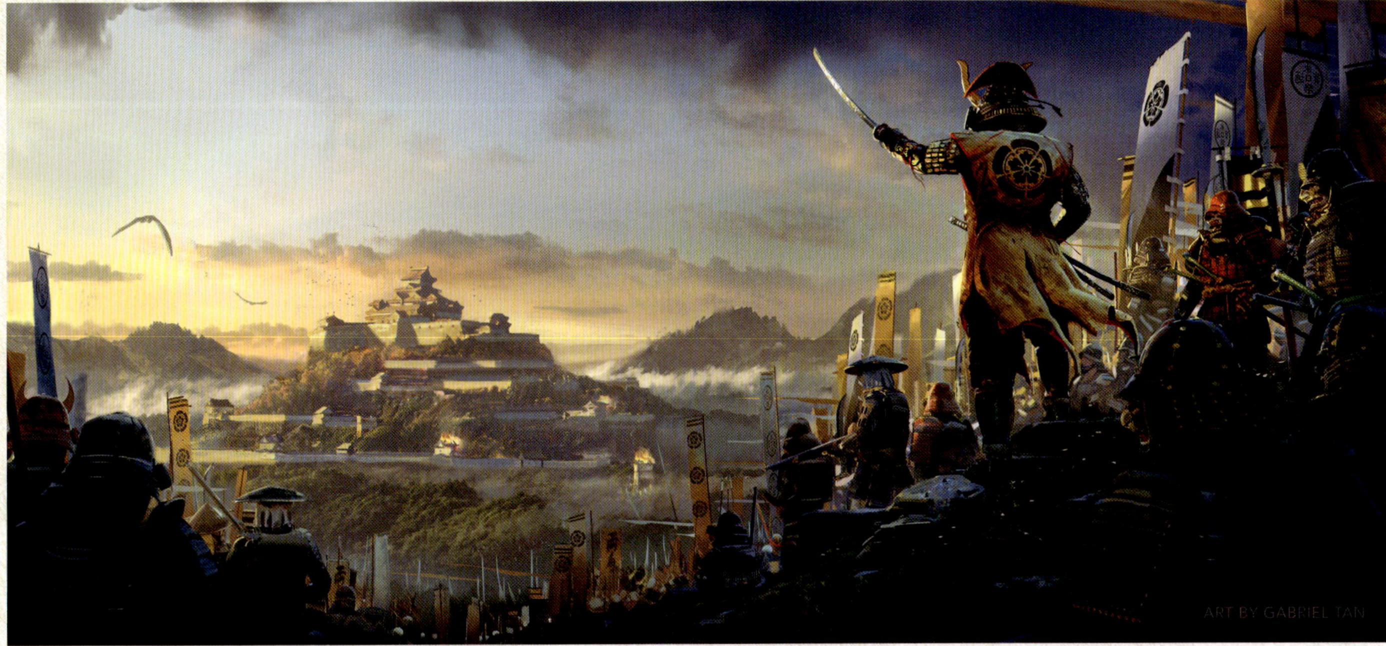

ART BY GABRIEL TAN

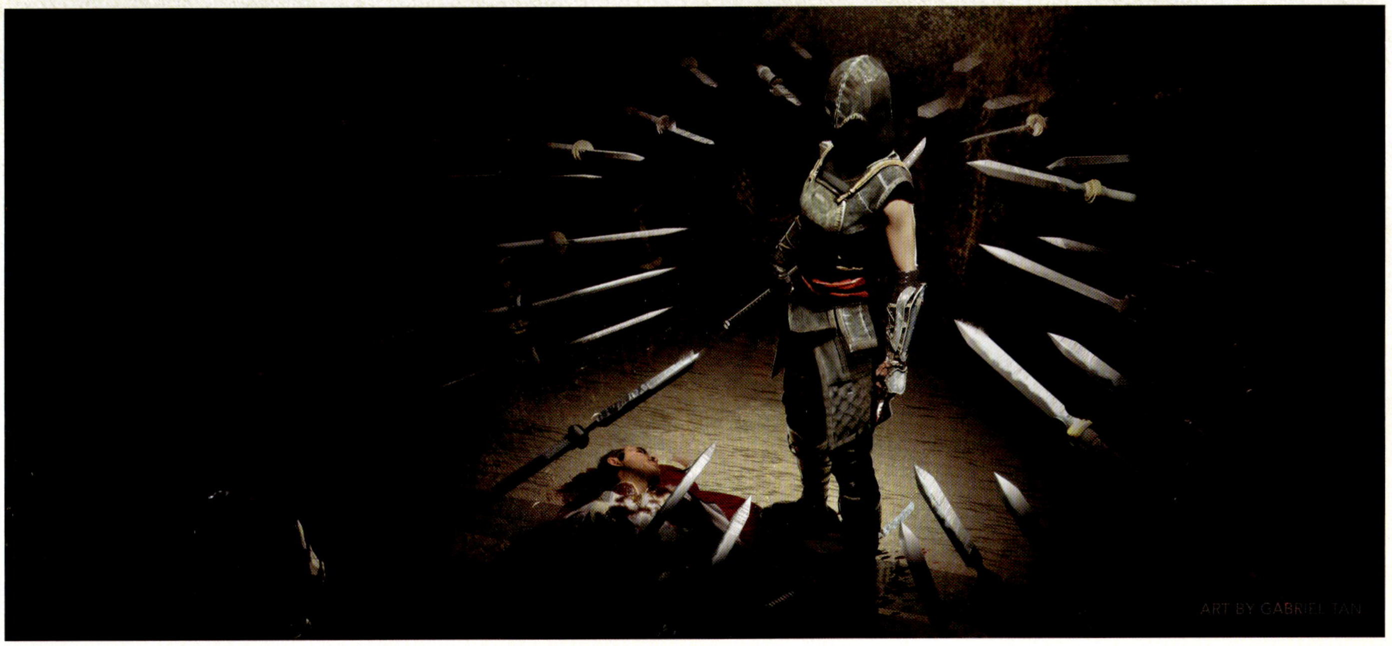

ART BY GABRIEL TAN

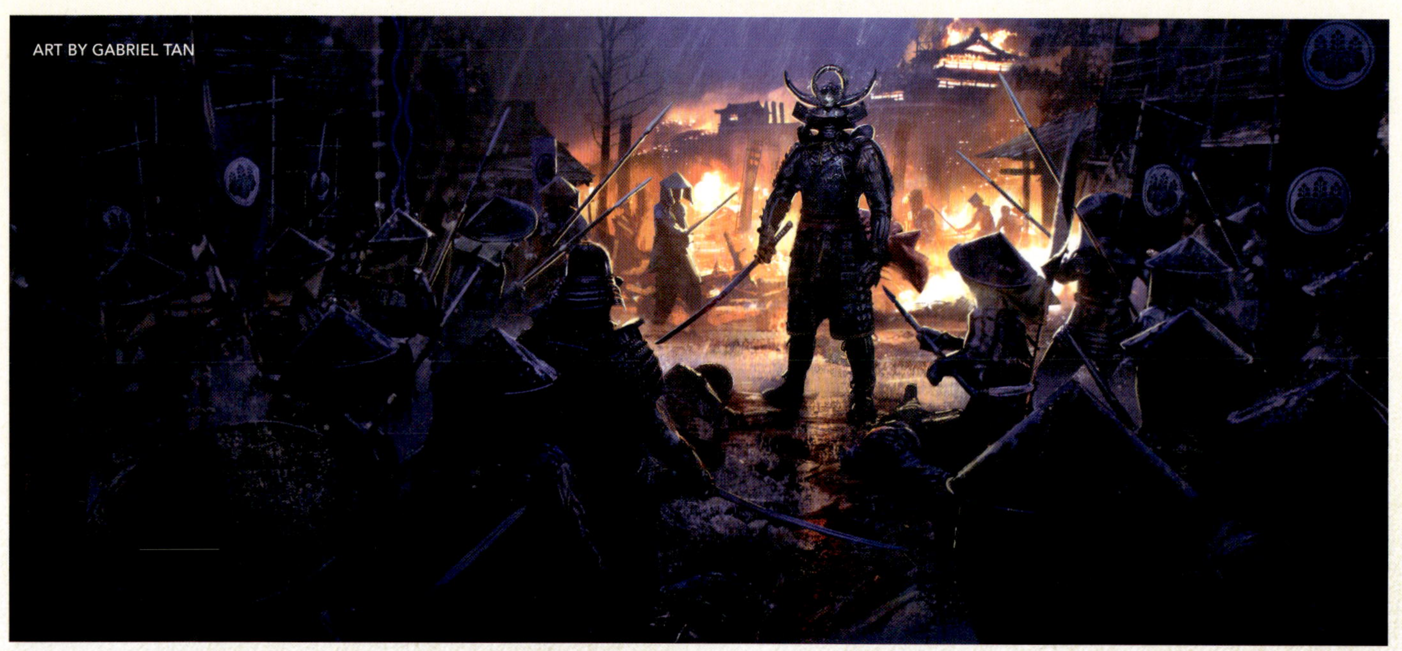

ART BY GABRIEL TAN

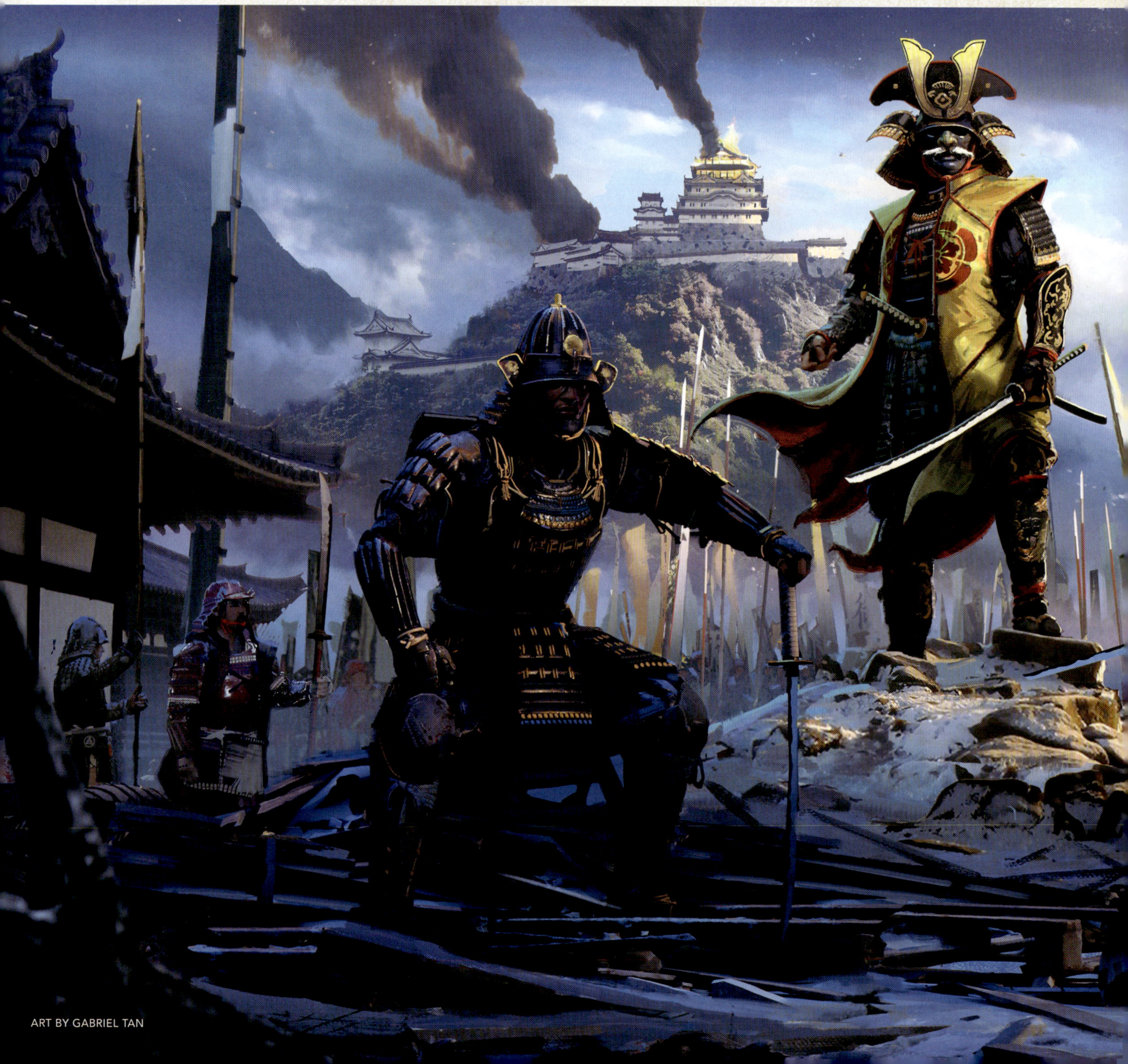

ART BY GABRIEL TAN

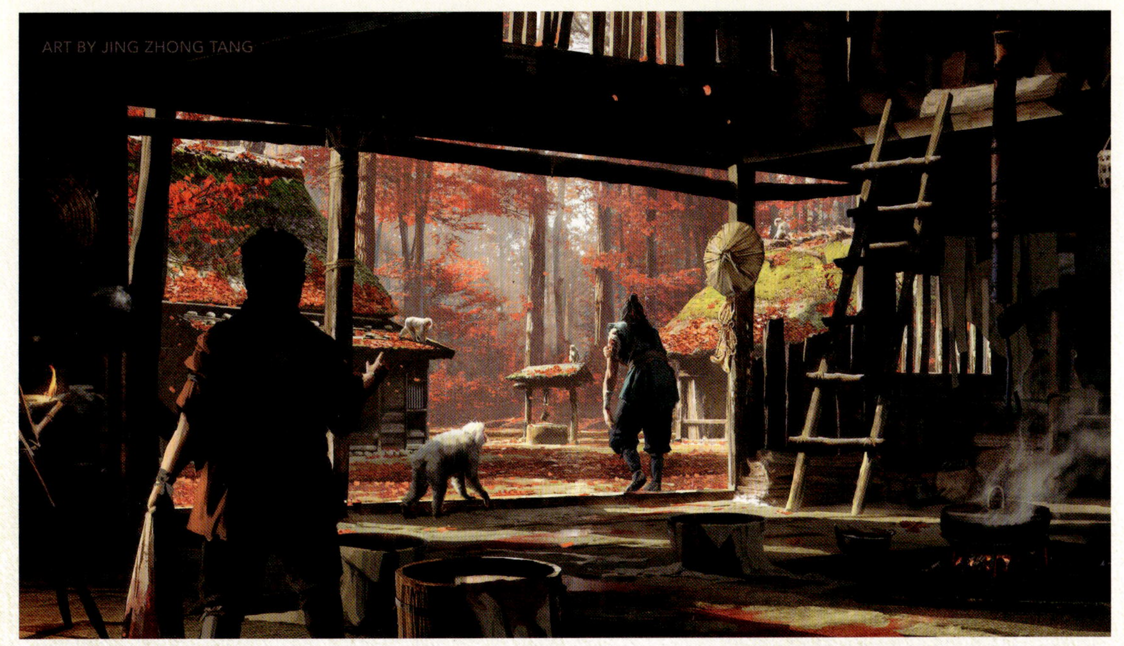

These concept pieces provide vivid examples of how lighting and shadow can be used to summon powerful dramatic effects. "Concept art is often less concerned with scenic details and more focused on emotional impact," says Plante. *Left:* An autumn portrayal of the temple where a grievously wounded Naoe recovers under the care of Junjiro and the monk Sorin. *Opposite page:* The towering figure of Yasuke is framed by flames during the Iga invasion. *Below:* As a besieged castle burns on the ridge beyond, Oda Nobunaga pronounces harsh judgment on vanquished foes with his champion Yasuke at his right hand.

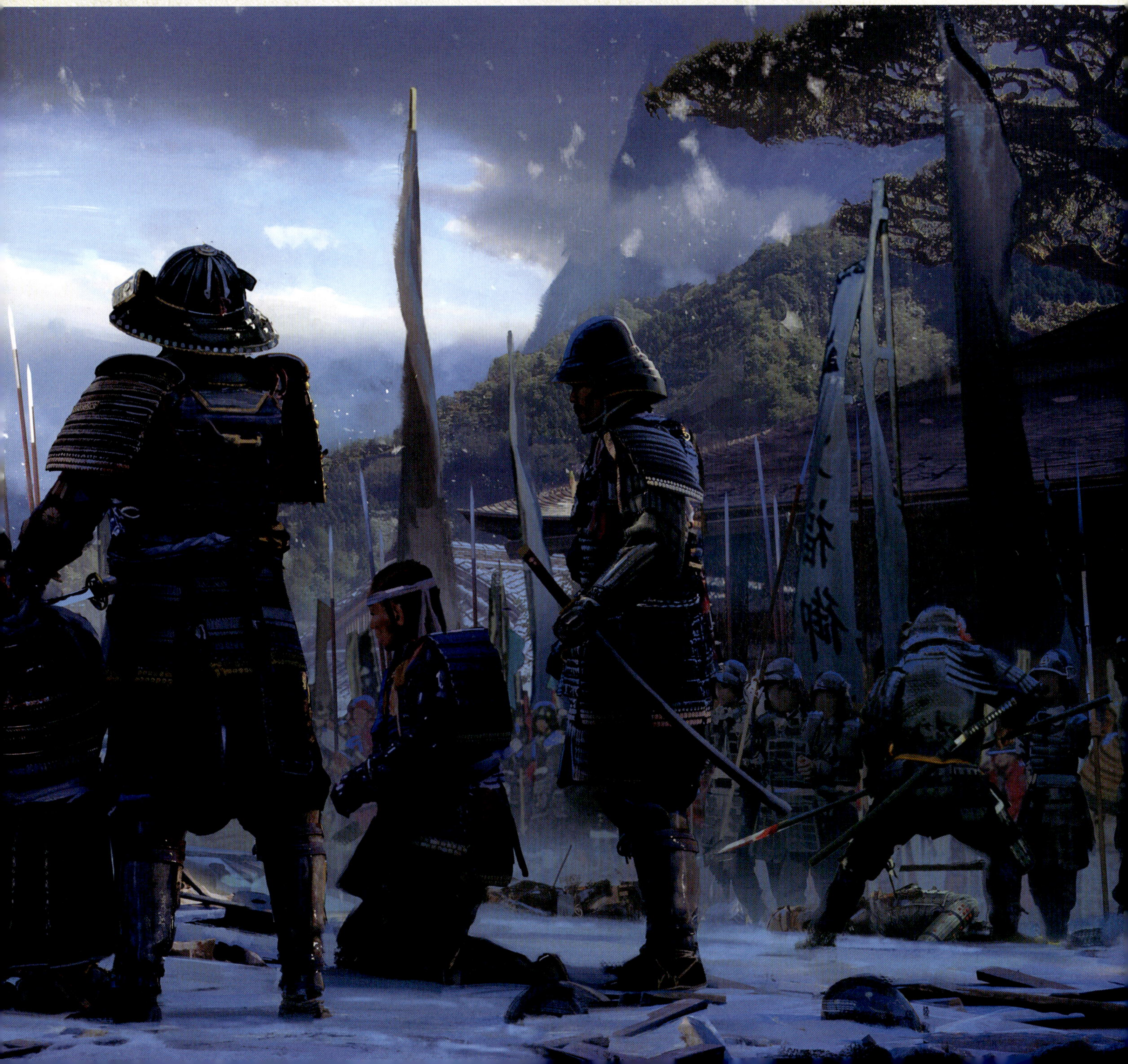

Below: Concept art depicting the ceremonial *shinobi* tradition where Naoe drinks water mixed with the ashes of her signed pact pledging her skills to the defense of the community. *Opposite page:* Yasuke engages an enemy target in a garden setting under the blossoming *sakura* tree and a sunset that creates what Luc Plante describes as "an almost poetical mood." *Bottom:* Naoe confronts one of the game's more elusive, manipulative foes in a candlelit setting that conveys a sense of secrecy and conspiracy.

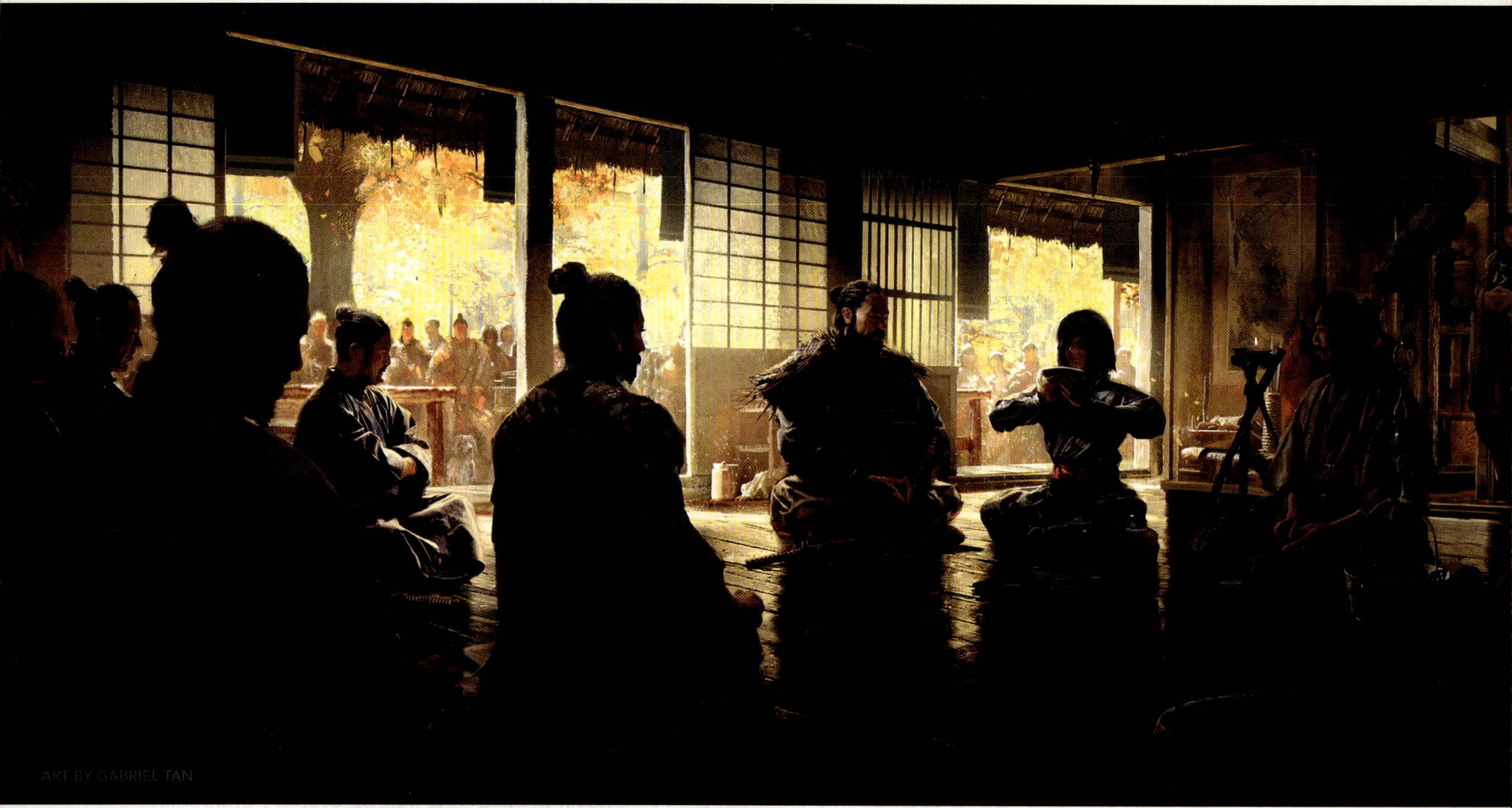

ART BY GABRIEL TAN

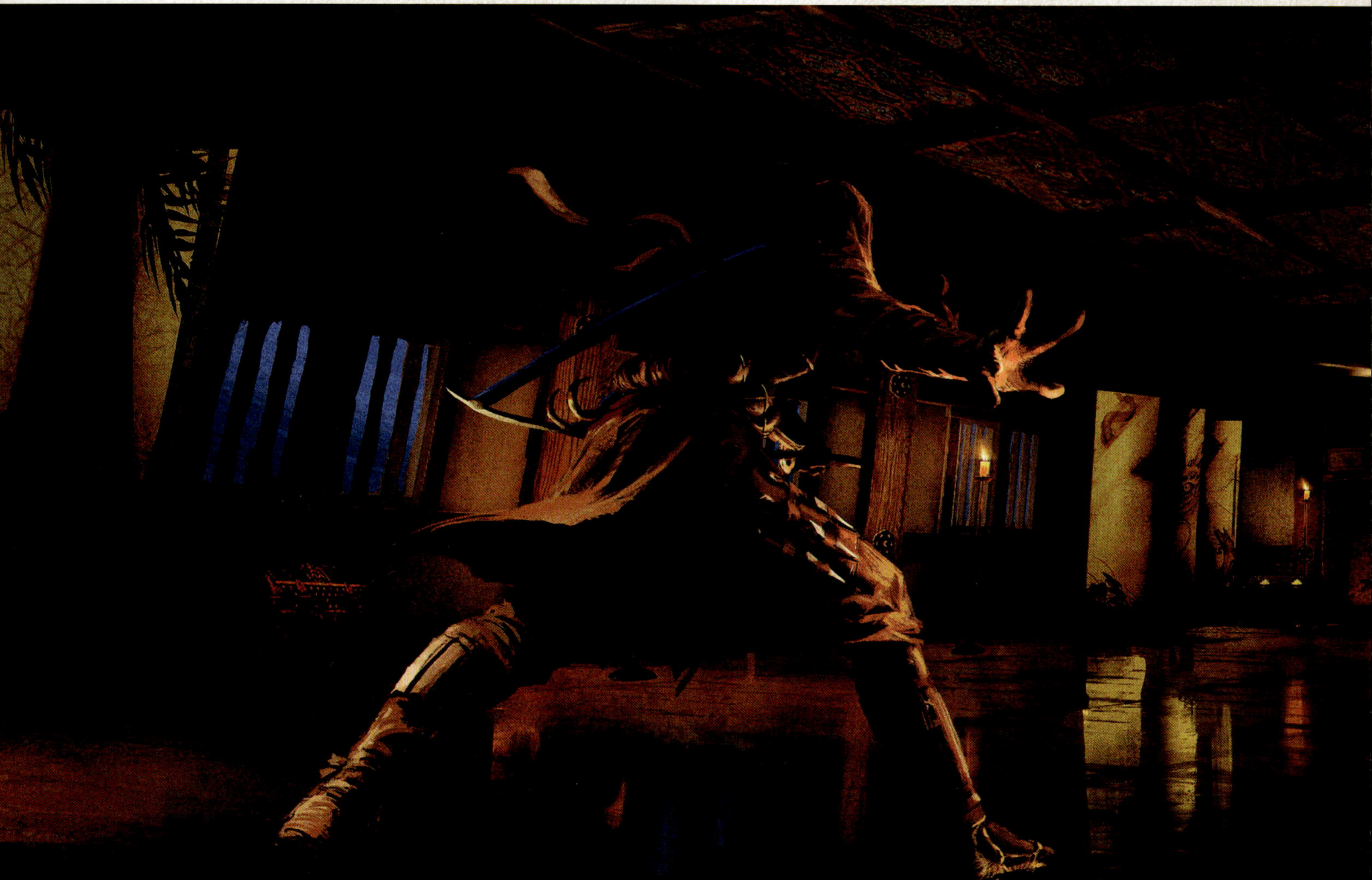

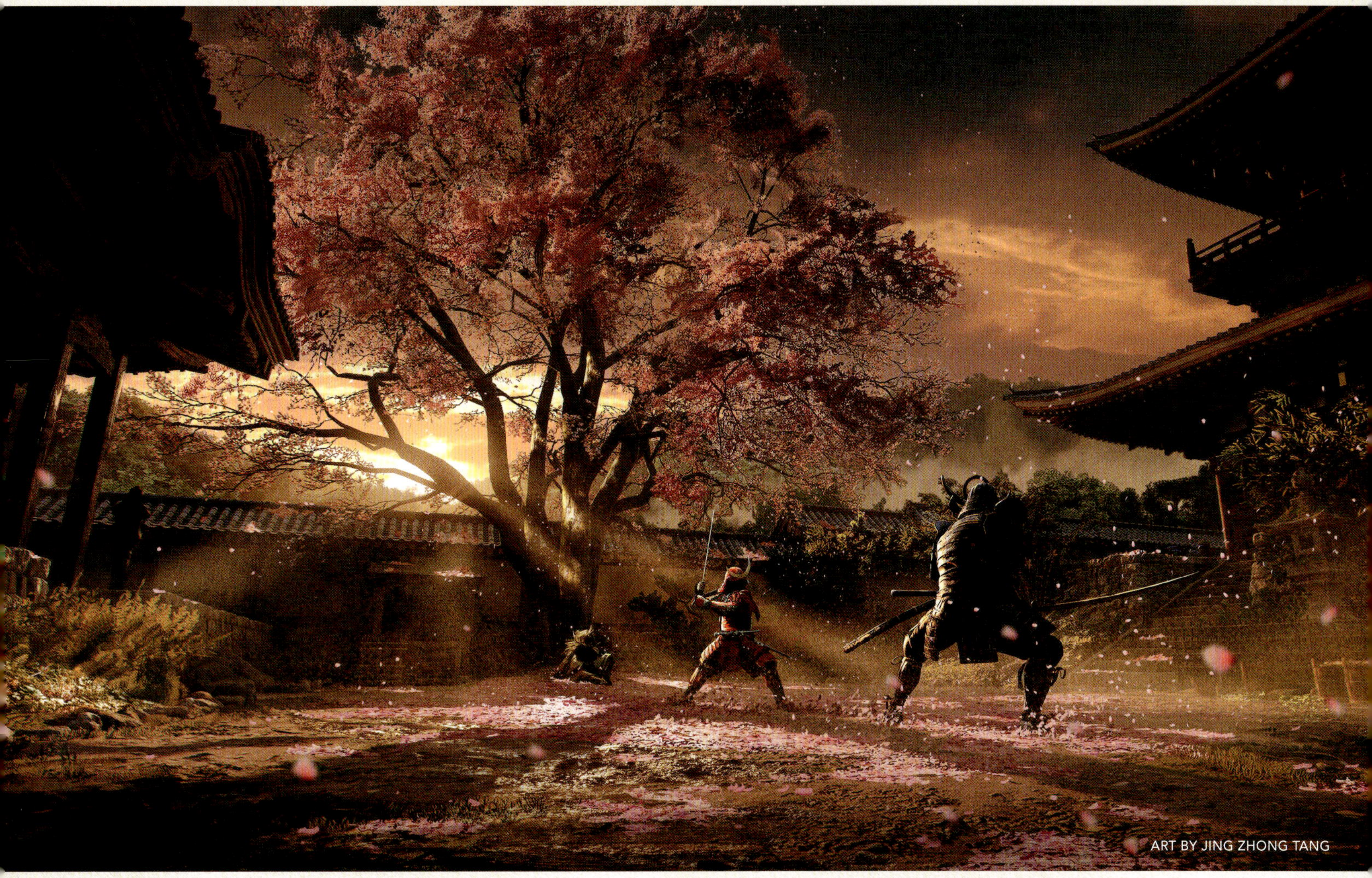

ART BY JING ZHONG TANG

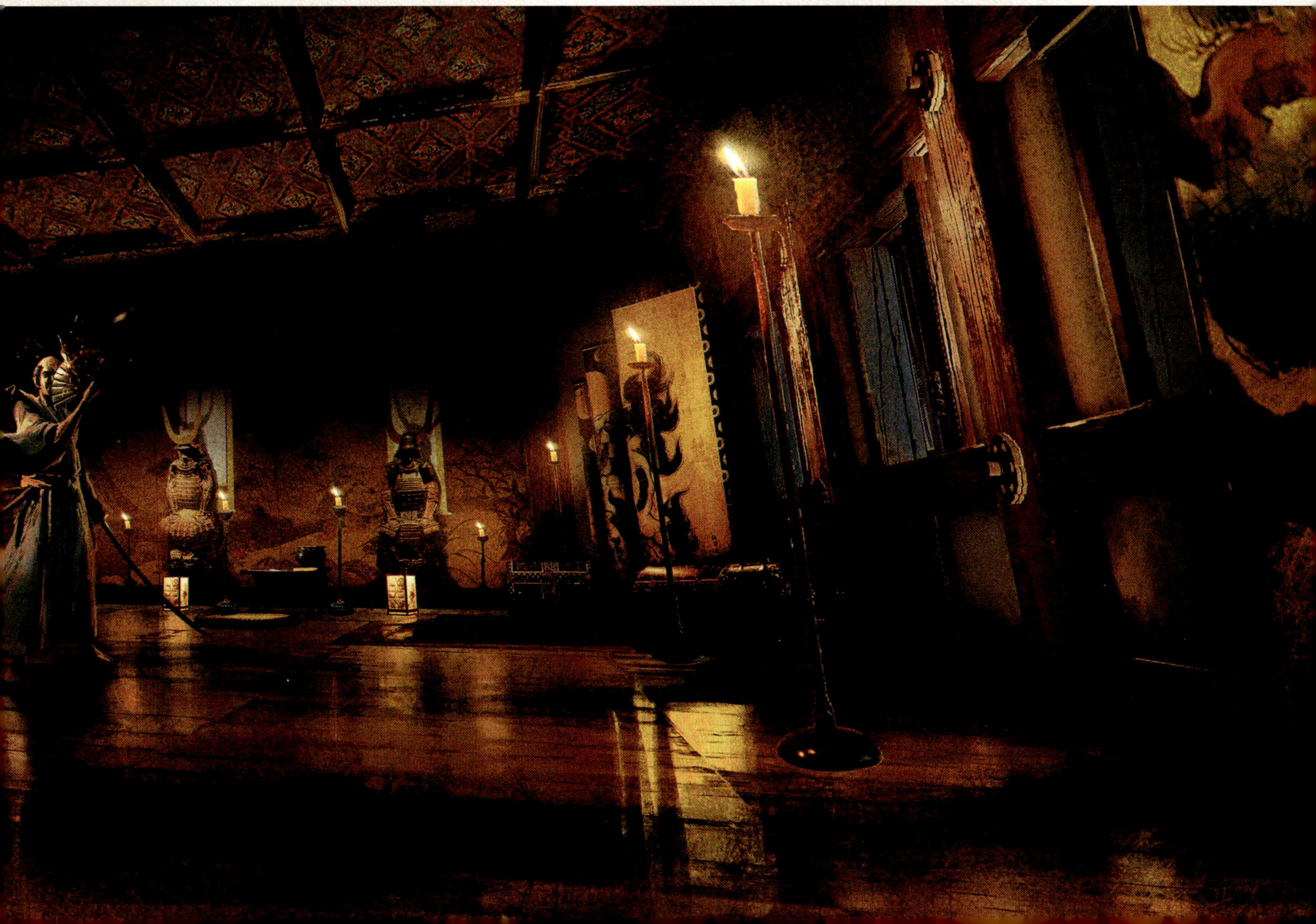

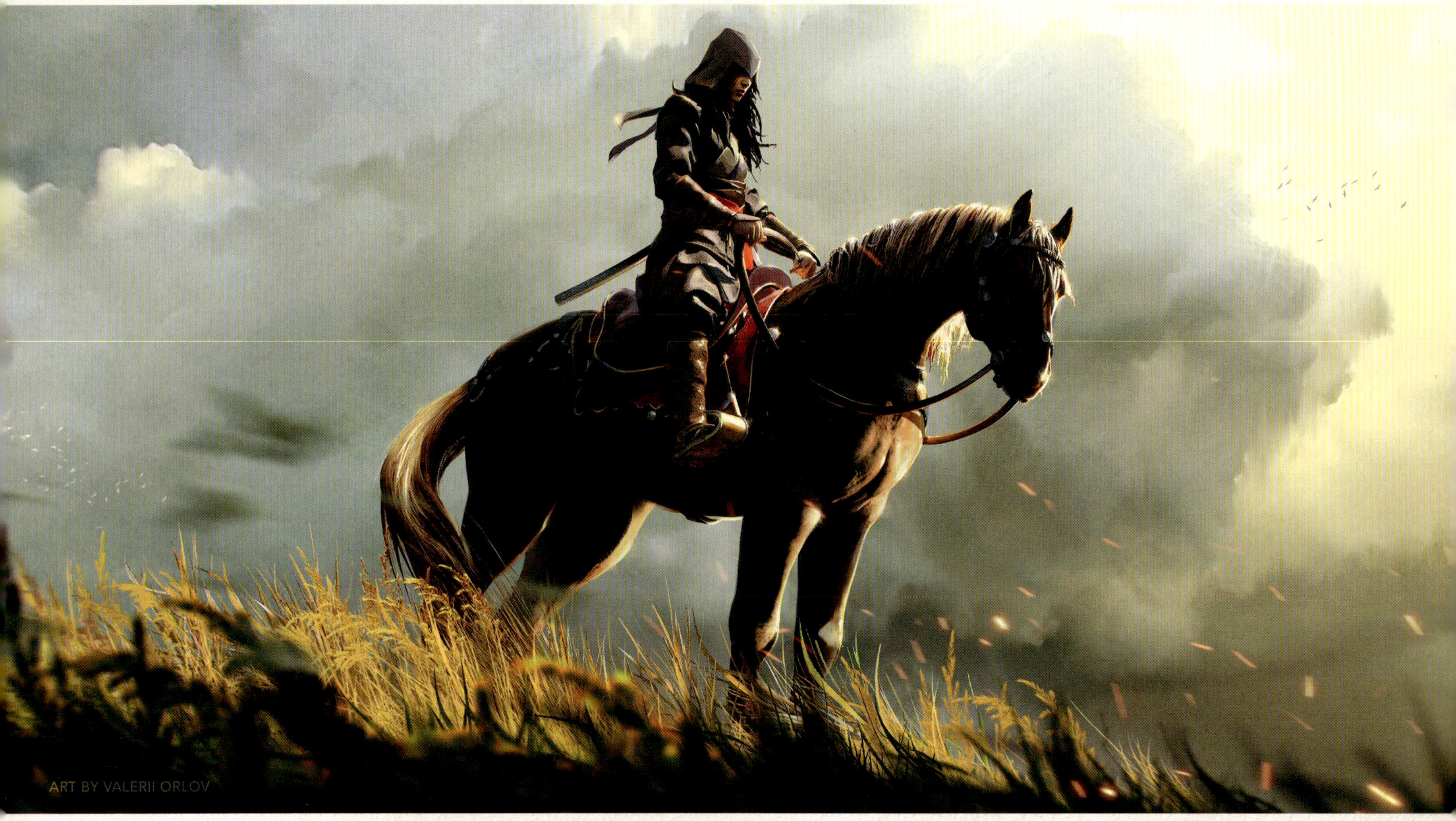

ART BY VALERII ORLOV

The concept art team created a striking shot of Naoe on her mount *(above)* to showcase her emergence from the vengeful shadows to become a heroic archetype. *Opposite page, top:* Yasuke and a Portuguese delegation (shown bowed and kneeling) meet Oda Nobunaga (in the doorway) for the first time; Plante describes it as "dramatic ambiance to match a game-changing moment," a scene devoted to authenticity in its portrayal of tradition and the code of hierarchy in feudal Japan. *Right:* Naoe and Junjiro sketch the red-crowned crane that's perched atop a centerpiece structure in the village plaza.

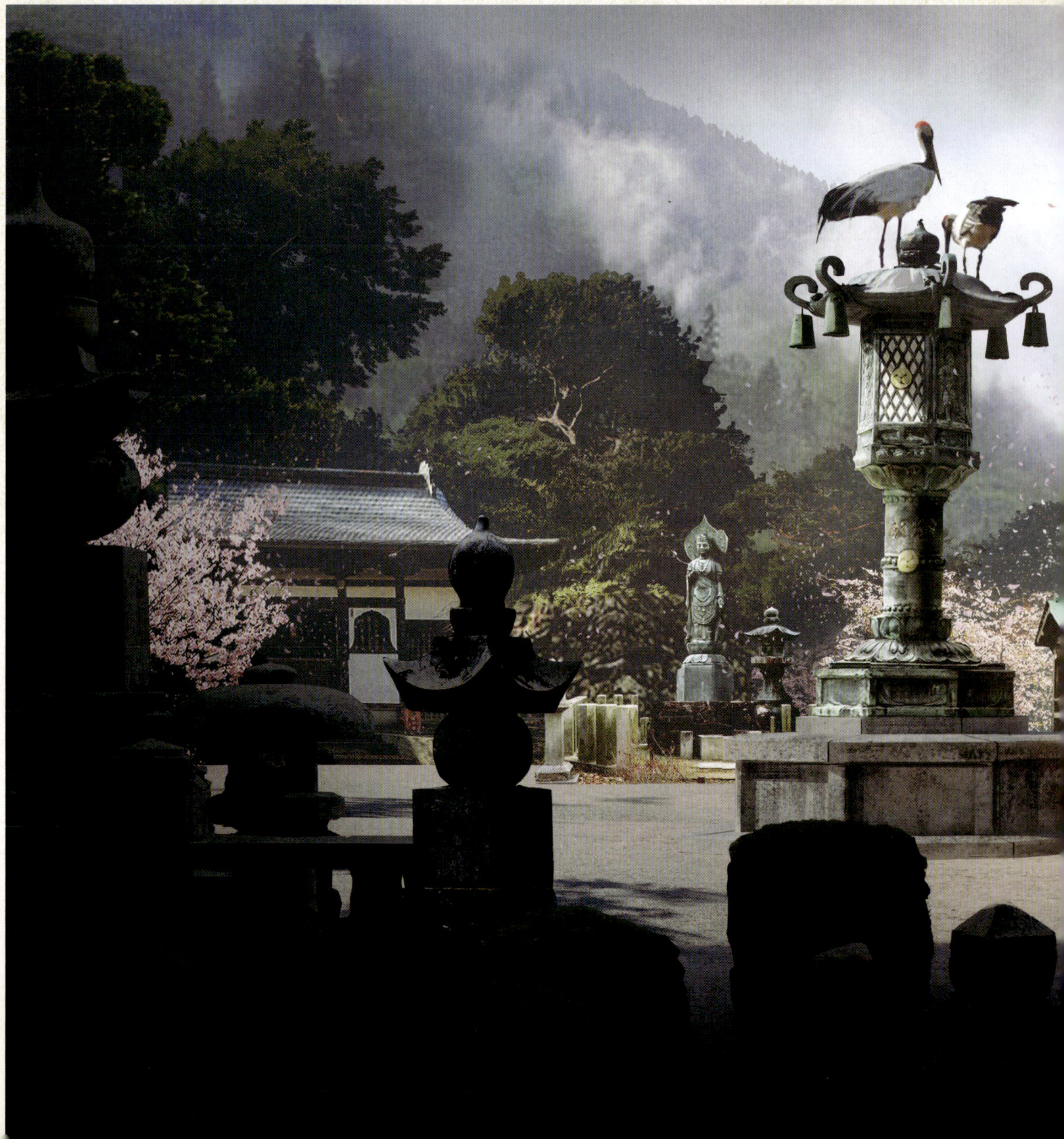

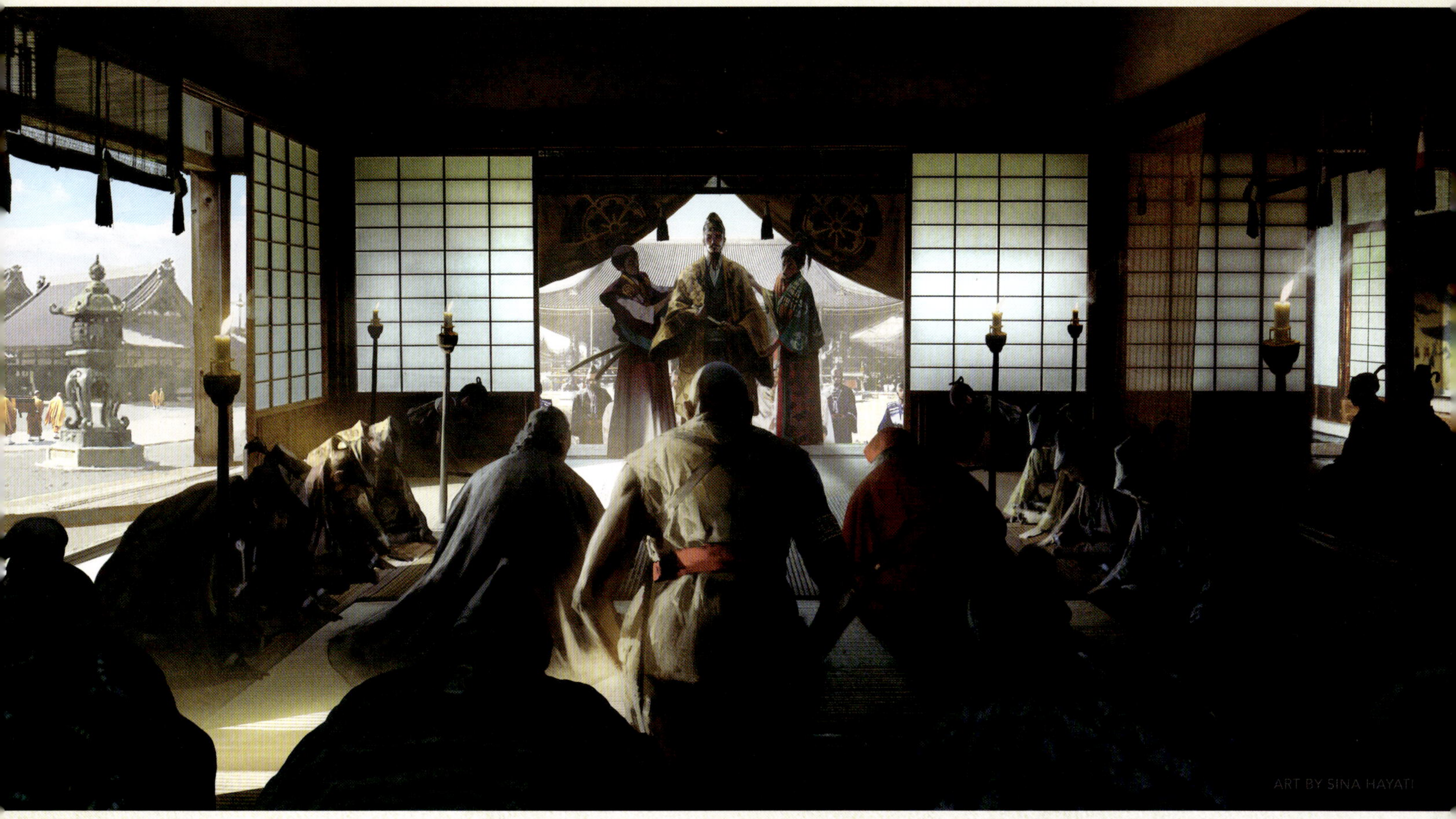

ART BY SINA HAYATI

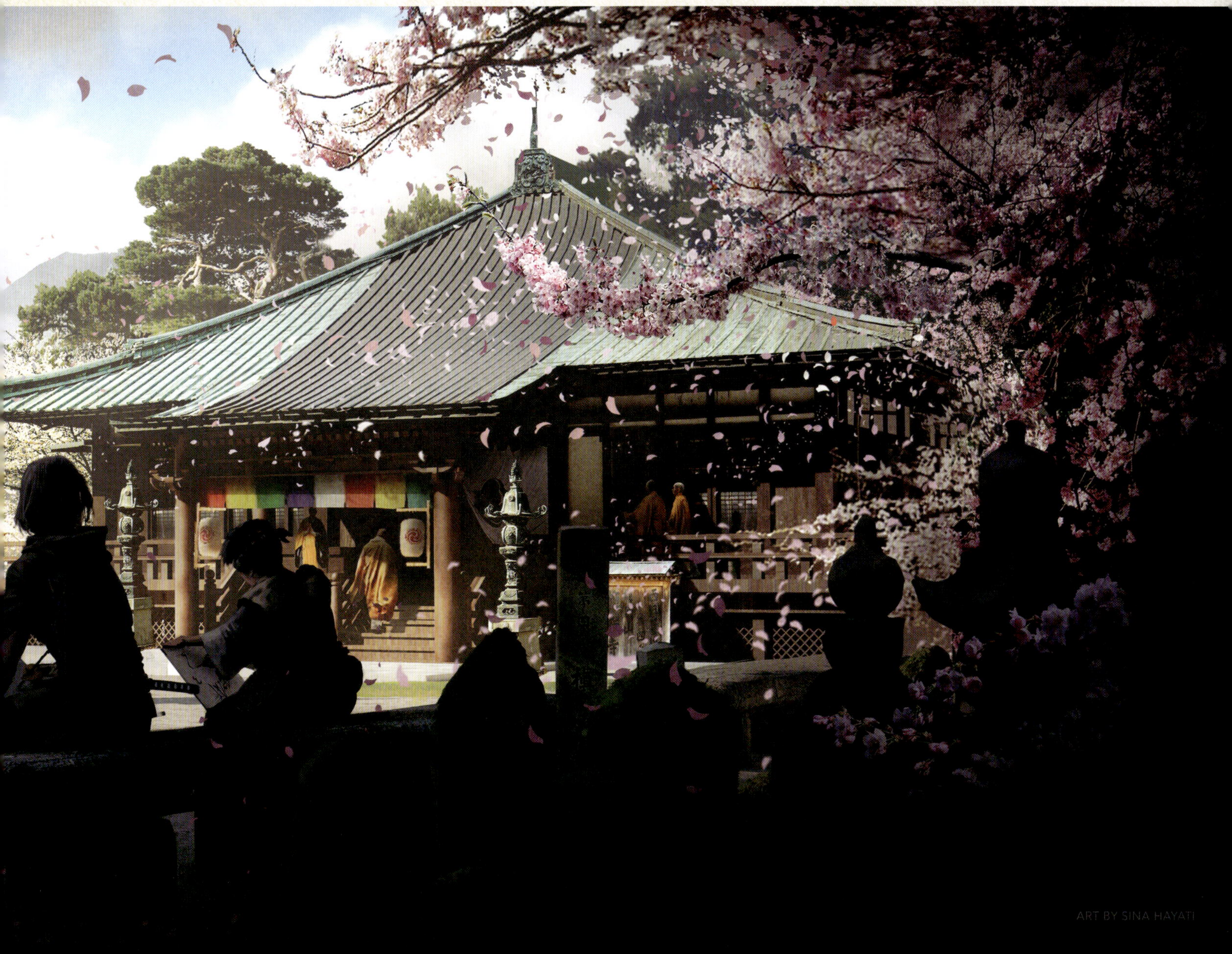

ART BY SINA HAYATI

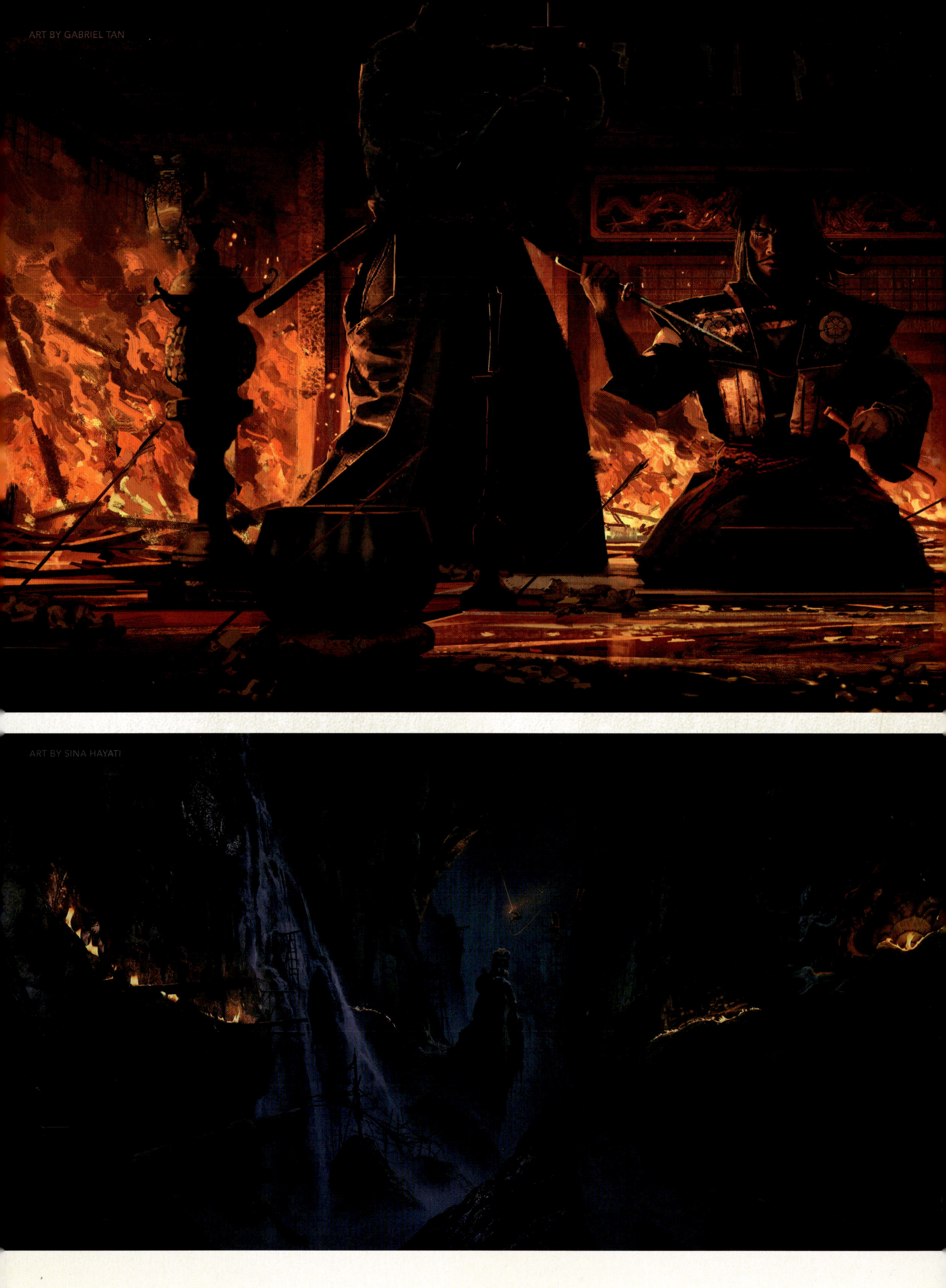
ART BY GABRIEL TAN

ART BY SINA HAYATI

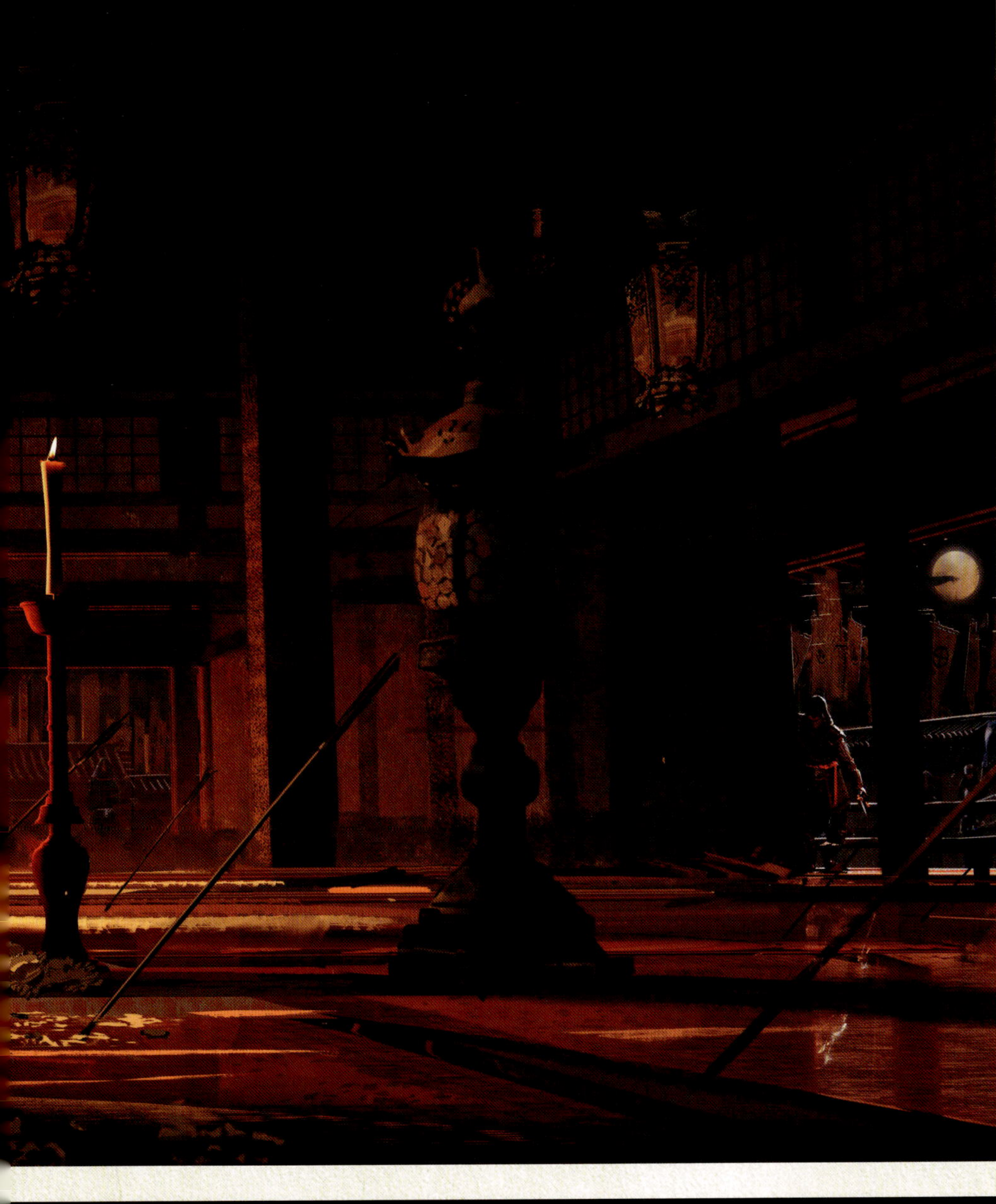

The moment that Oda Nobunaga commits seppuku *(left)* as the Honnō-ji temple burns down around him—with Yasuke serving as his second and Naoe lurking in the far-right doorway—is certainly one of the most intensely dramatic in the entire game. *Opposite page, bottom:* Using parkour to explore spectacular, dimly lit cavern environments. *Below:* The design team wanted assassinations to be more visceral than they were previously in the series, so this concept piece features harsher contrasts and a bloody outcome; Naoe wields a gore-stained *kusarigama* in one hand as she finishes a grim slash with her Hidden Blade.

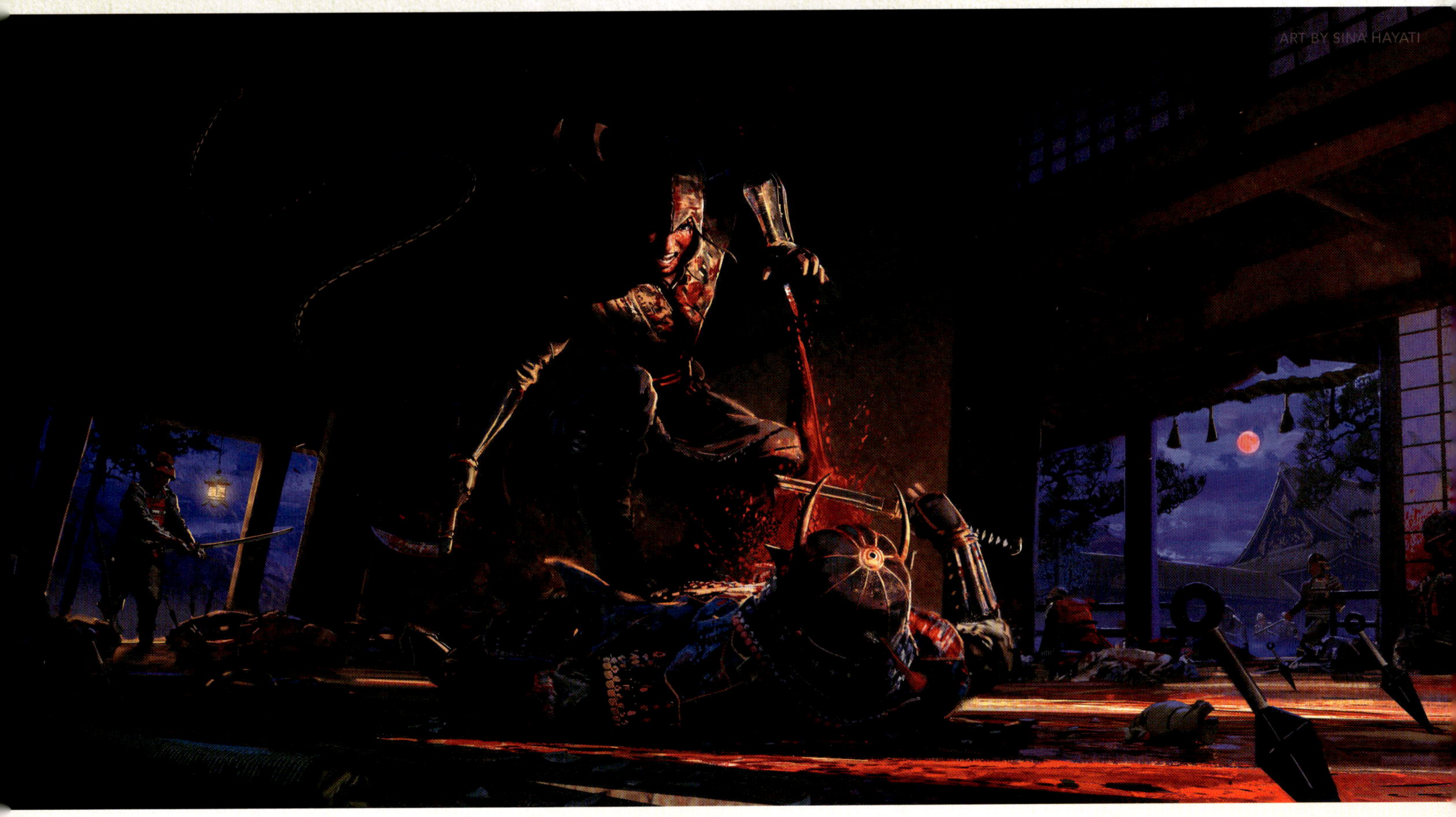

ART BY SINA HAYATI

Plante says the narrative department wanted the concept art team to explore key sequences in various environments with a range of ambient conditions. *Right:* In a misty forest, Yasuke wreaks havoc with his *naginata* on the bodyguard detail of a conspirator. *Below:* Naoe stealthily escorts a victim out of a rainy, muddy outlaw encampment. *Opposite page, bottom:* The precarious assassination of a target surrounded by samurai in a military training ground.

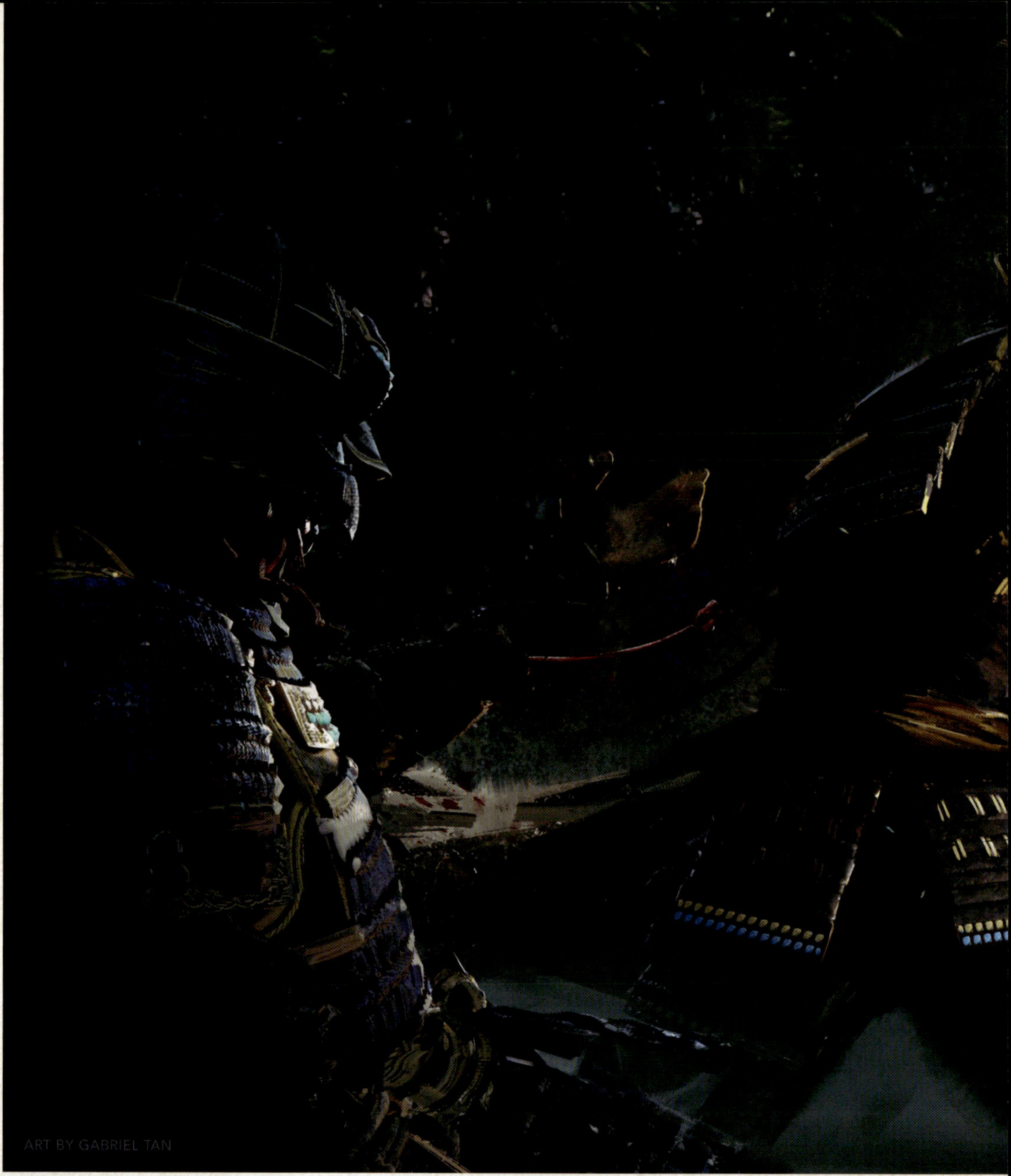

ART BY GABRIEL TAN

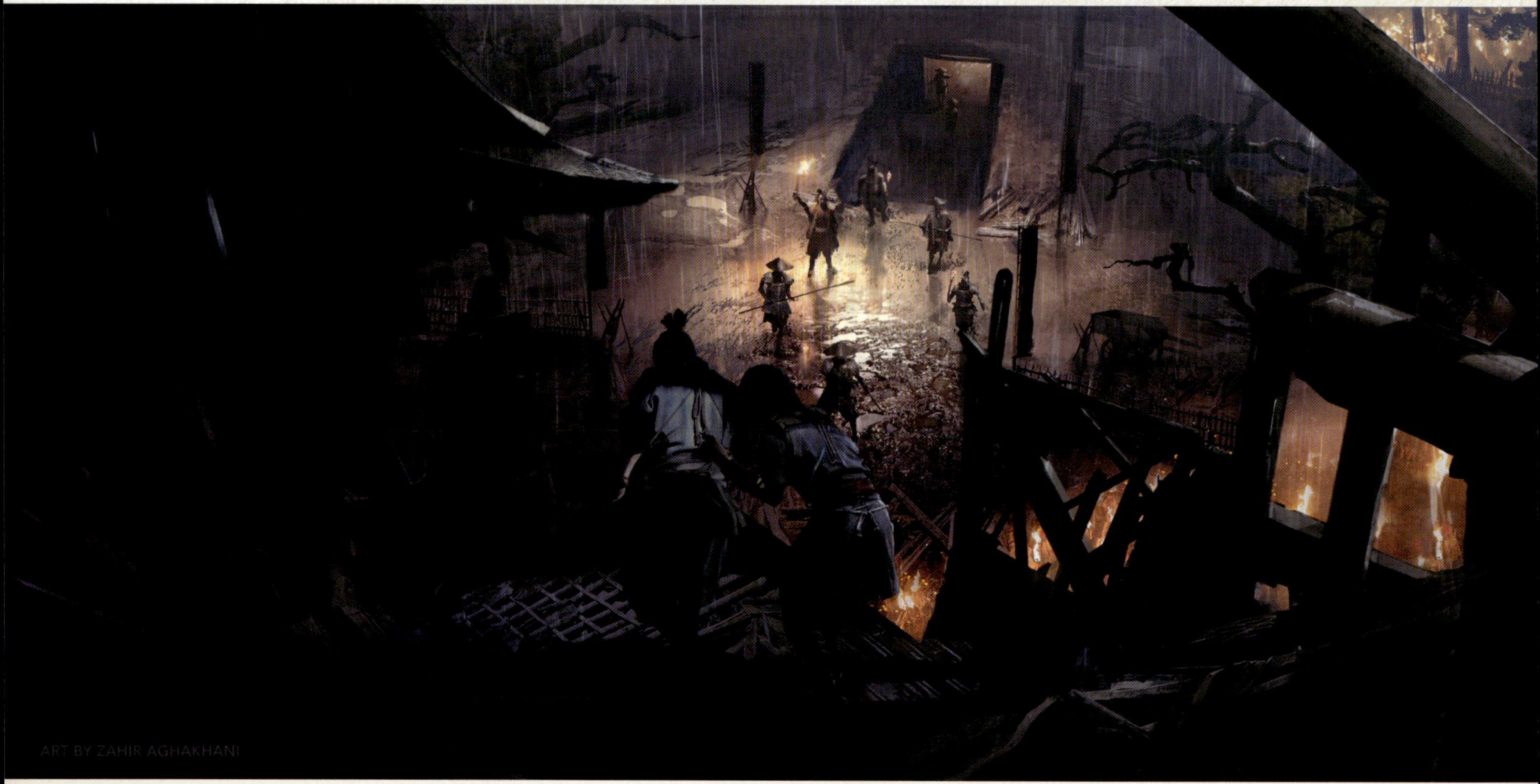

ART BY ZAHIR AGHAKHANI

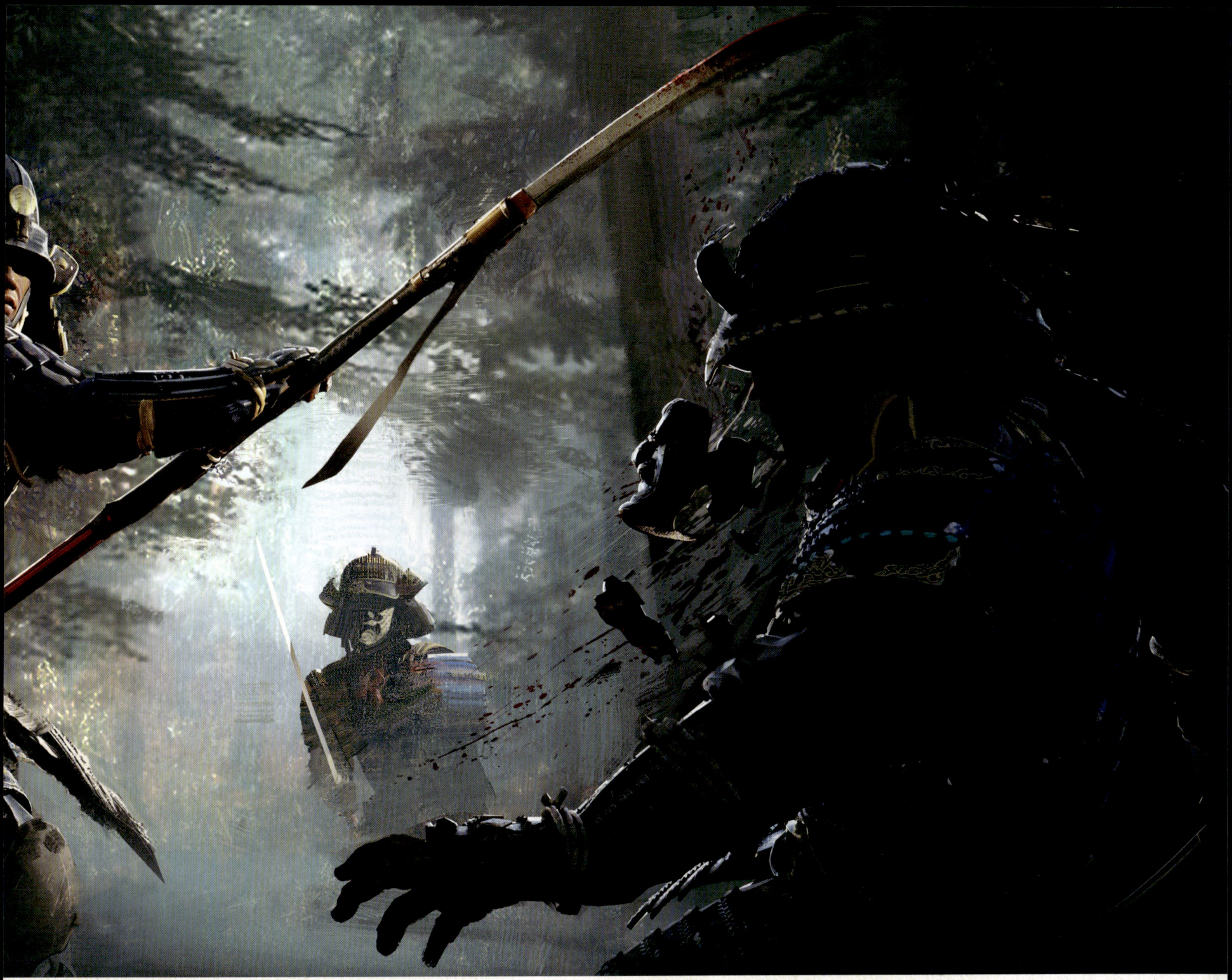

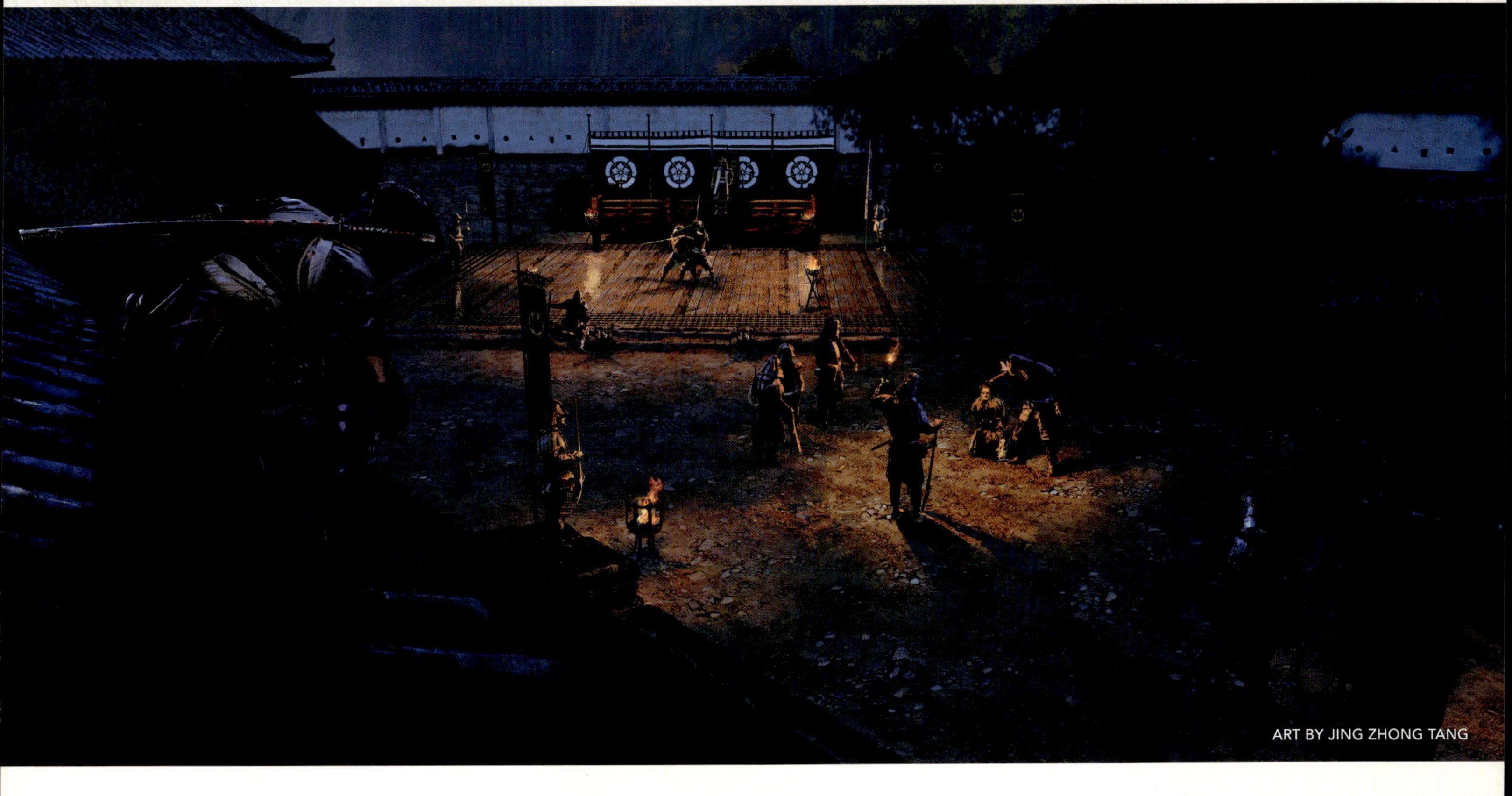

ART BY JING ZHONG TANG

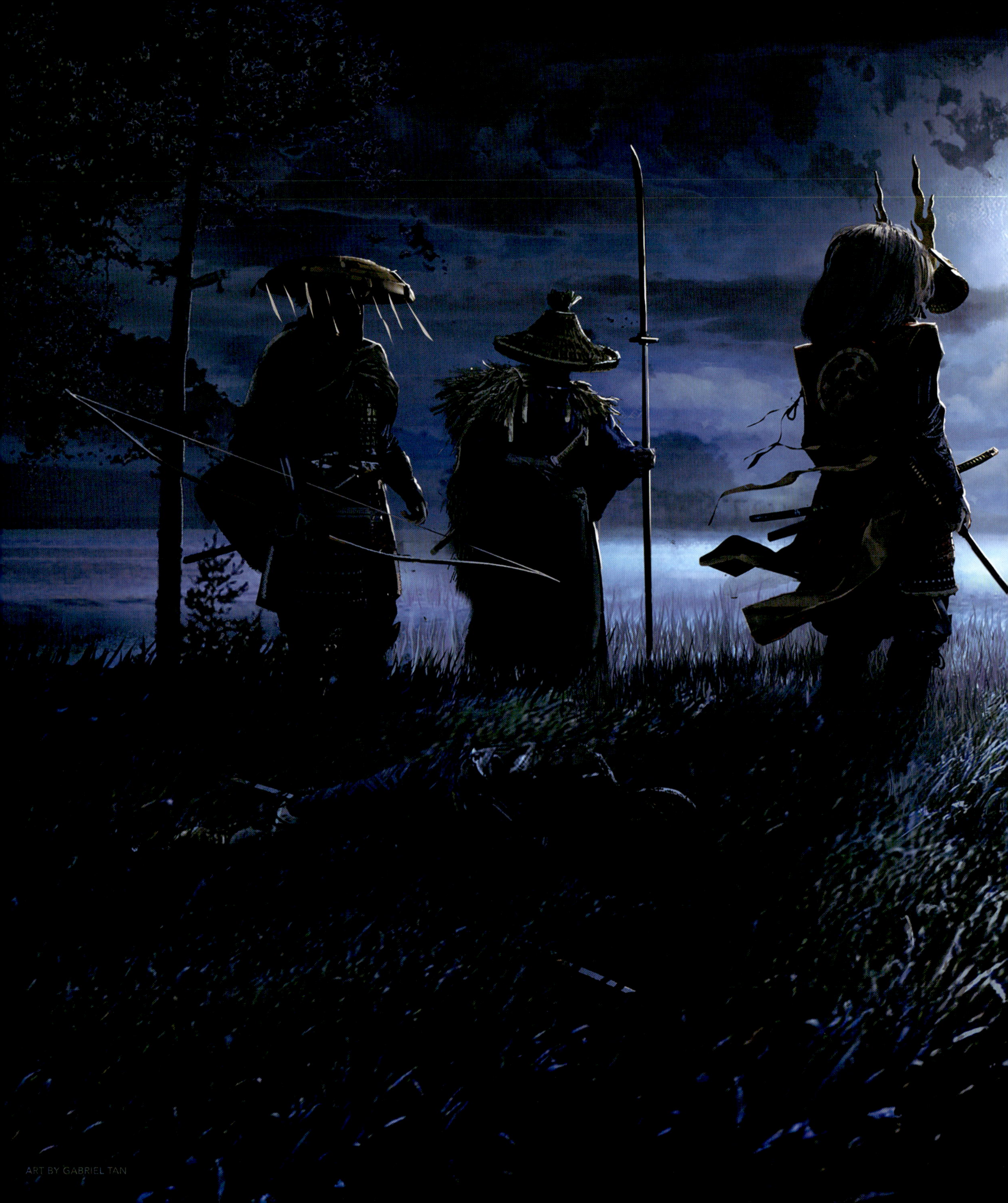

ART BY GABRIEL TAN

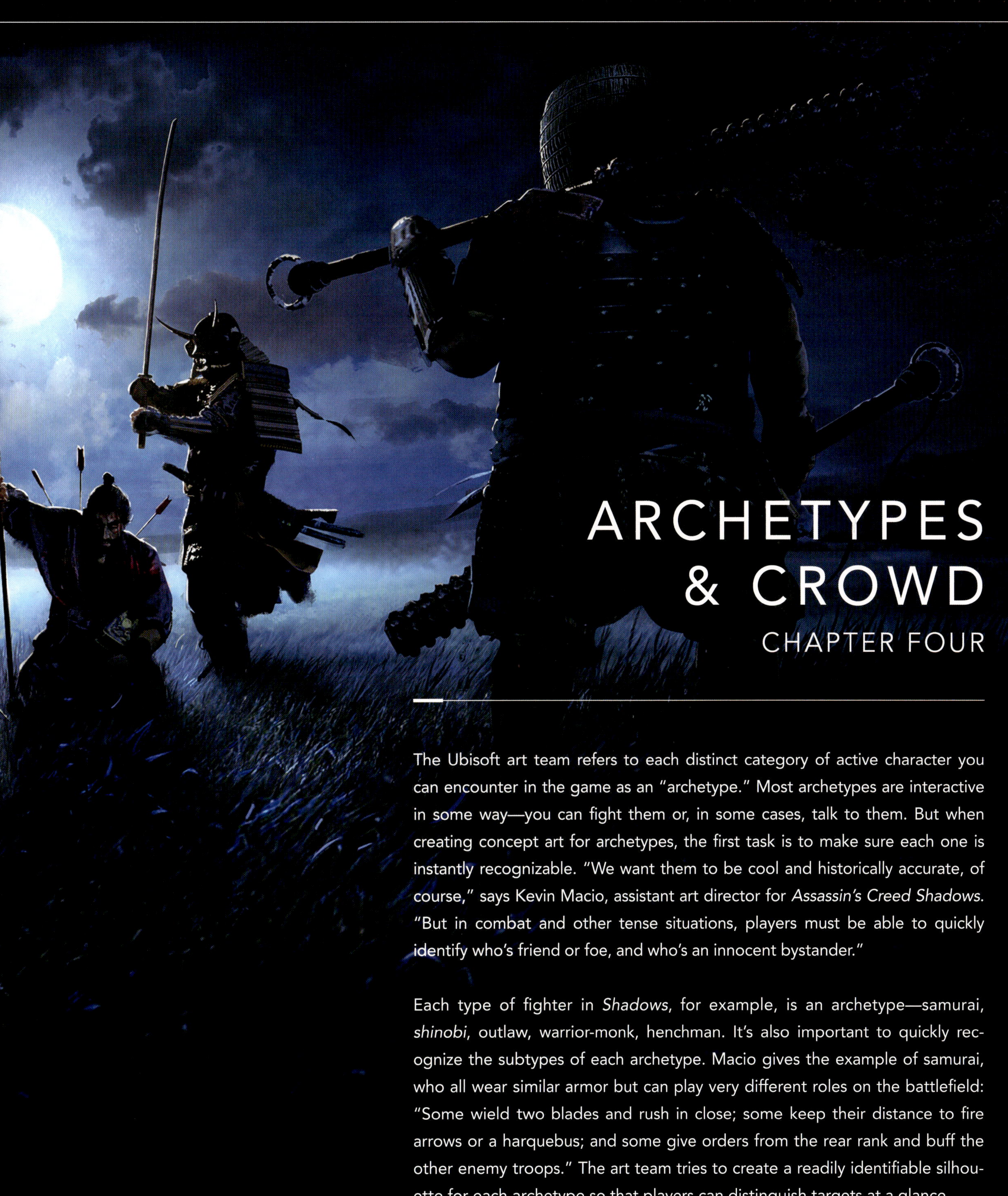

ARCHETYPES & CROWD

CHAPTER FOUR

The Ubisoft art team refers to each distinct category of active character you can encounter in the game as an "archetype." Most archetypes are interactive in some way—you can fight them or, in some cases, talk to them. But when creating concept art for archetypes, the first task is to make sure each one is instantly recognizable. "We want them to be cool and historically accurate, of course," says Kevin Macio, assistant art director for *Assassin's Creed Shadows.* "But in combat and other tense situations, players must be able to quickly identify who's friend or foe, and who's an innocent bystander."

Each type of fighter in *Shadows*, for example, is an archetype—samurai, *shinobi*, outlaw, warrior-monk, henchman. It's also important to quickly recognize the subtypes of each archetype. Macio gives the example of samurai, who all wear similar armor but can play very different roles on the battlefield: "Some wield two blades and rush in close; some keep their distance to fire arrows or a harquebus; and some give orders from the rear rank and buff the other enemy troops." The art team tries to create a readily identifiable silhouette for each archetype so that players can distinguish targets at a glance.

ART BY TYLER RYAN

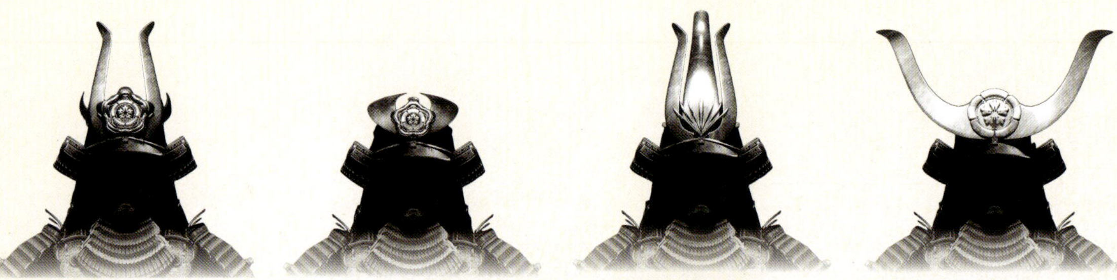

One way to clearly differentiate samurai warriors from one another is the distinctive and unique metal crests called *maedate* fastened atop their helmets.

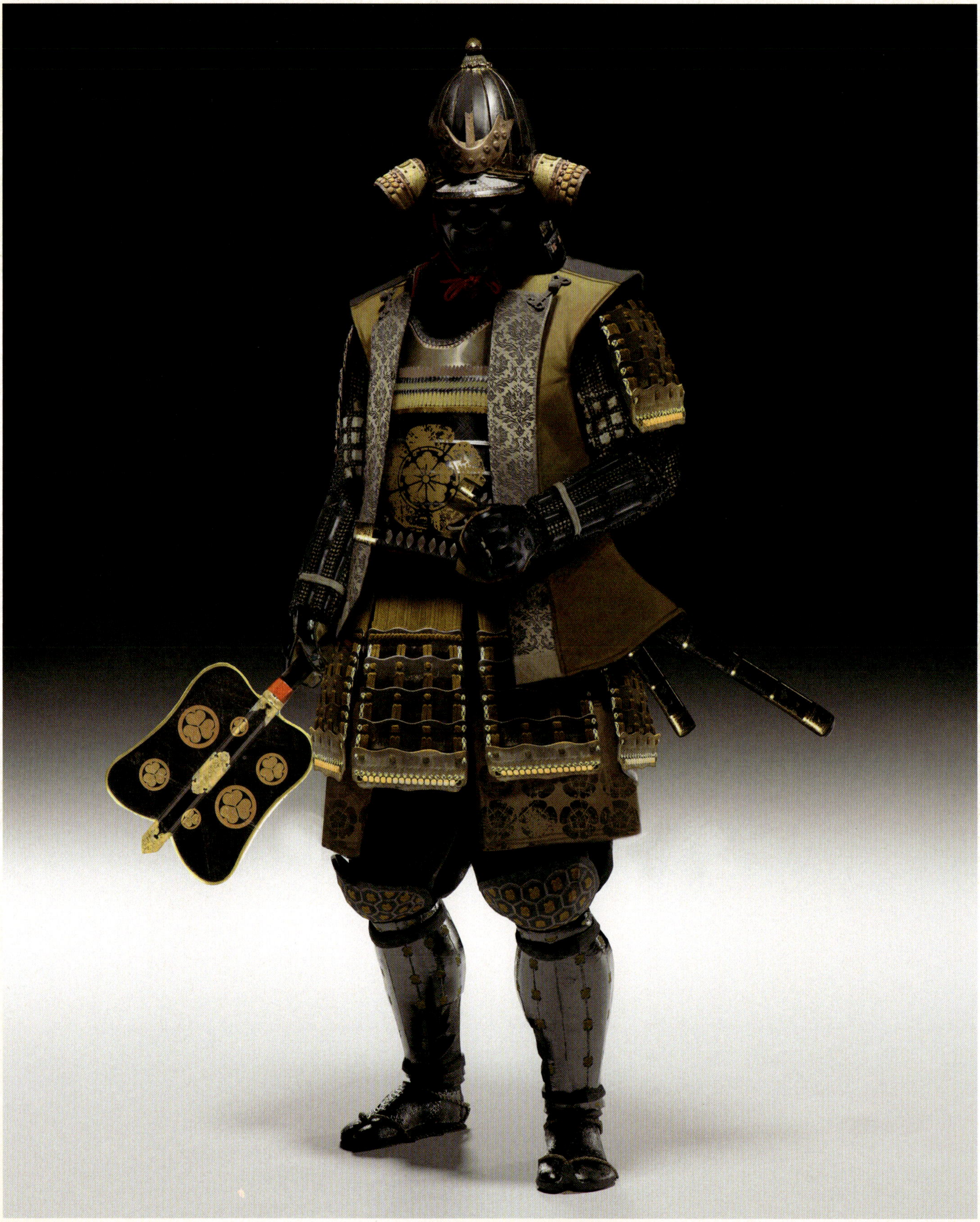

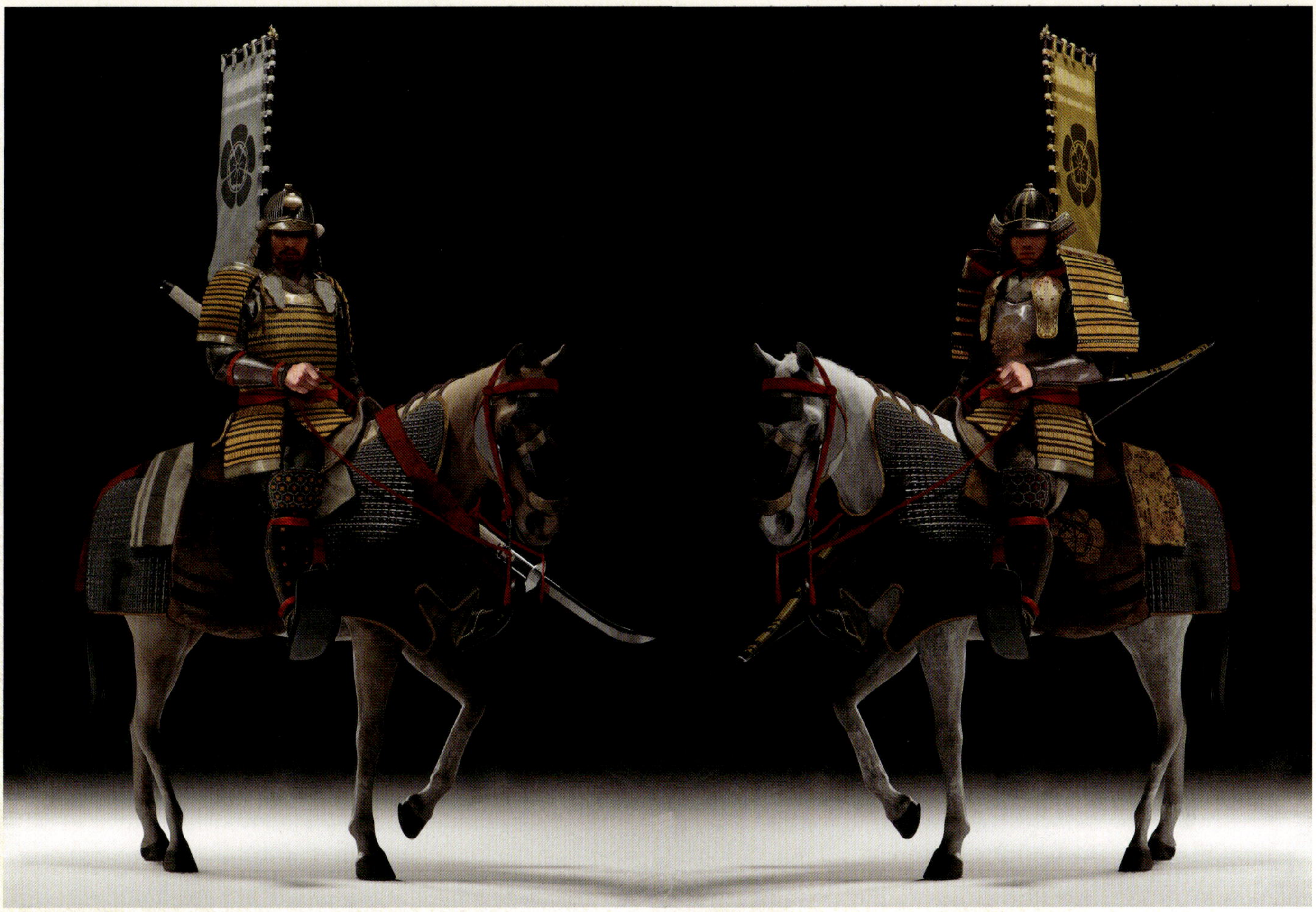

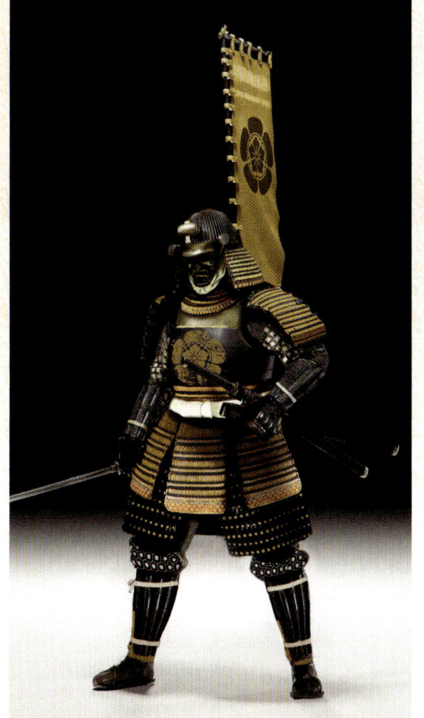

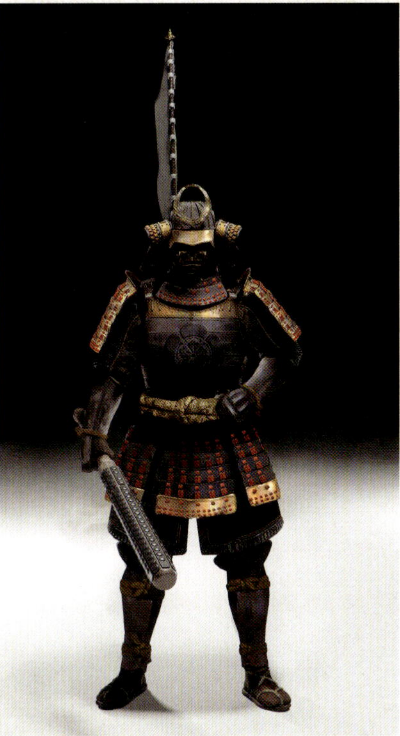

Samurai variants include mounted units carrying war banners associated with certain daimyos to help organize and identify individual clans and factions on the battlefield.

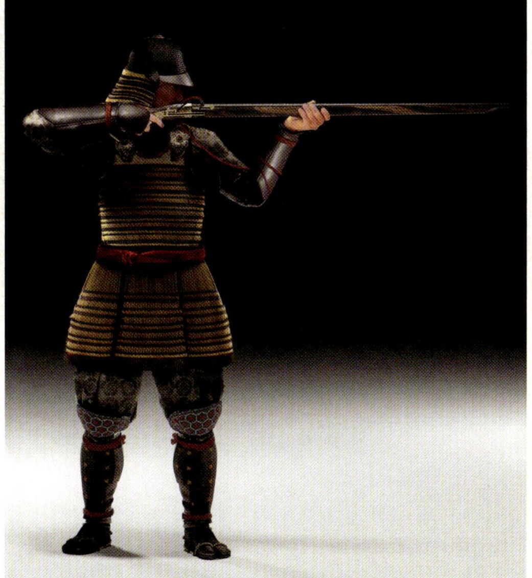

SAMURAI

Samurai are well known as some of the most formidable warriors in history, and of course the same is true in *Shadows*. From the harquebus-armed sharpshooter to the massive, powerful brute wielding a *kanabō* club, each samurai subtype is highly distinctive on the battlefield. The samurai field tactician seen on the opposite page wears the classic *jinbaori* jacket over his armor and signals his orders using a war fan called a *gunbai*.

ART BY TYLER RYAN

CASTLE GUARD

The imposing castle guard archetype is an elite samurai warrior assigned primarily to castle defense, as the name implies, and is typically the biggest threat within a fortress. The castle guard features three different variants: the big-horned katana master *(right)*; the huge, powerful *kanabō* warrior *(below)*; and the field leader wielding a razor-sharp *naginata* spear *(bottom)*.

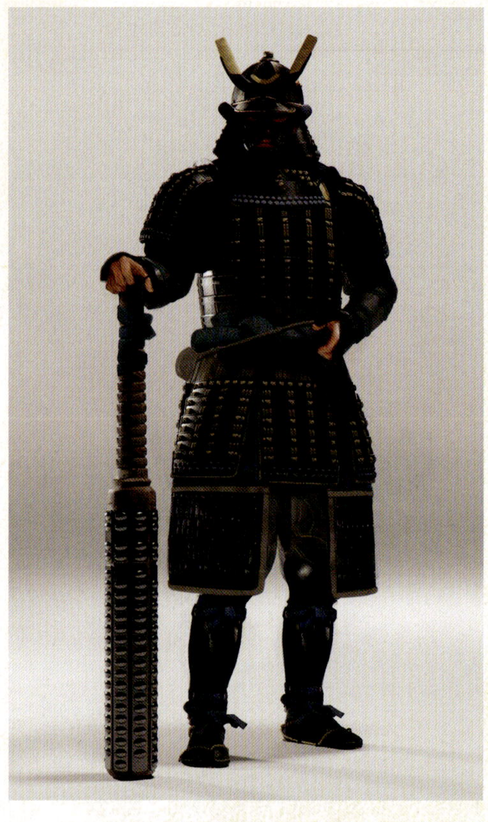

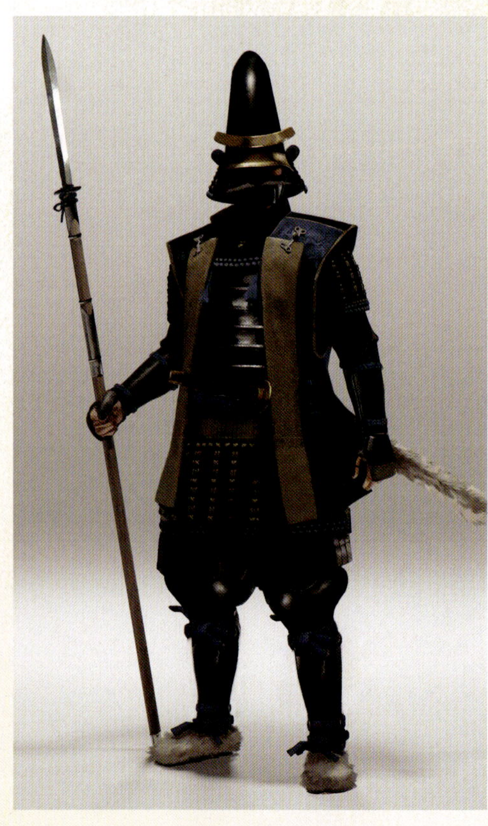

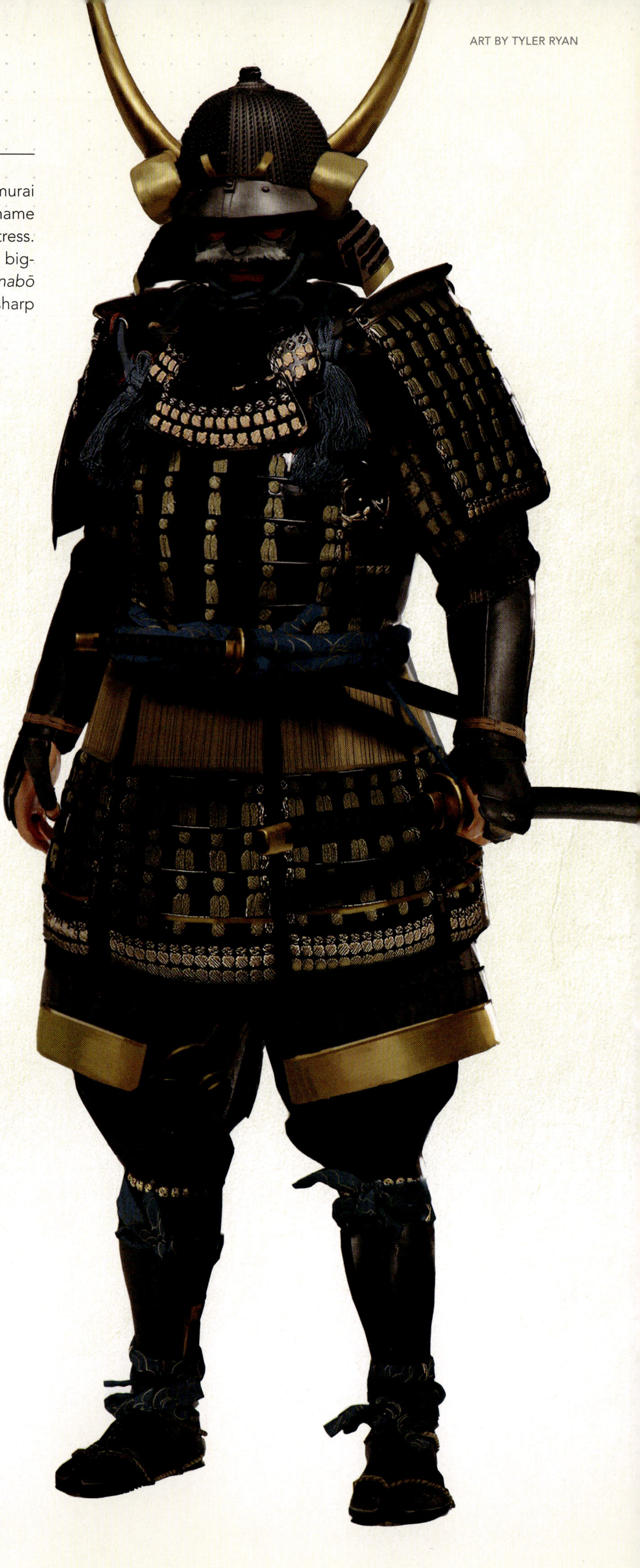

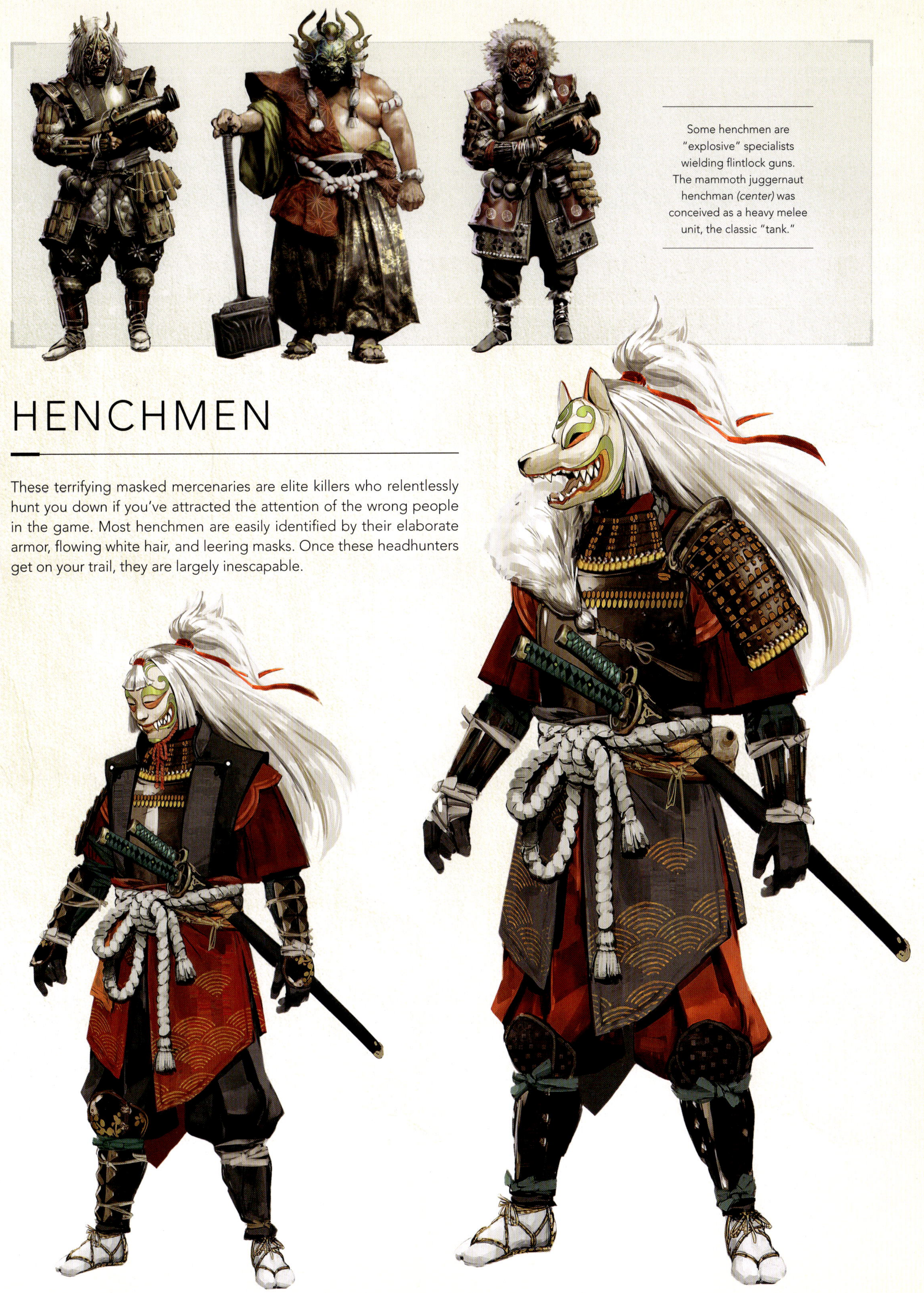

Some henchmen are "explosive" specialists wielding flintlock guns. The mammoth juggernaut henchman *(center)* was conceived as a heavy melee unit, the classic "tank."

HENCHMEN

These terrifying masked mercenaries are elite killers who relentlessly hunt you down if you've attracted the attention of the wrong people in the game. Most henchmen are easily identified by their elaborate armor, flowing white hair, and leering masks. Once these headhunters get on your trail, they are largely inescapable.

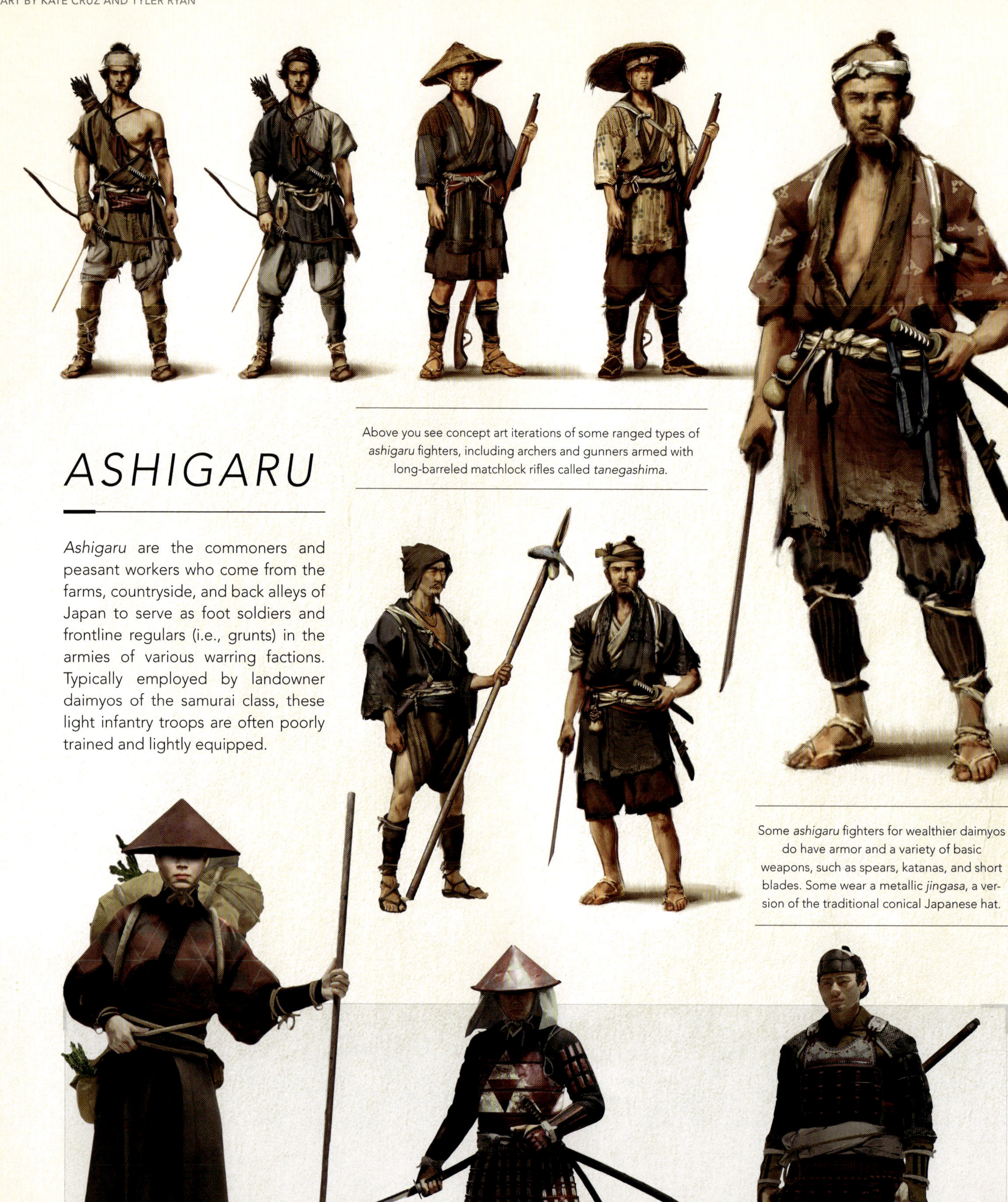

Above you see concept art iterations of some ranged types of *ashigaru* fighters, including archers and gunners armed with long-barreled matchlock rifles called *tanegashima*.

ASHIGARU

Ashigaru are the commoners and peasant workers who come from the farms, countryside, and back alleys of Japan to serve as foot soldiers and frontline regulars (i.e., grunts) in the armies of various warring factions. Typically employed by landowner daimyos of the samurai class, these light infantry troops are often poorly trained and lightly equipped.

Some *ashigaru* fighters for wealthier daimyos do have armor and a variety of basic weapons, such as spears, katanas, and short blades. Some wear a metallic *jingasa*, a version of the traditional conical Japanese hat.

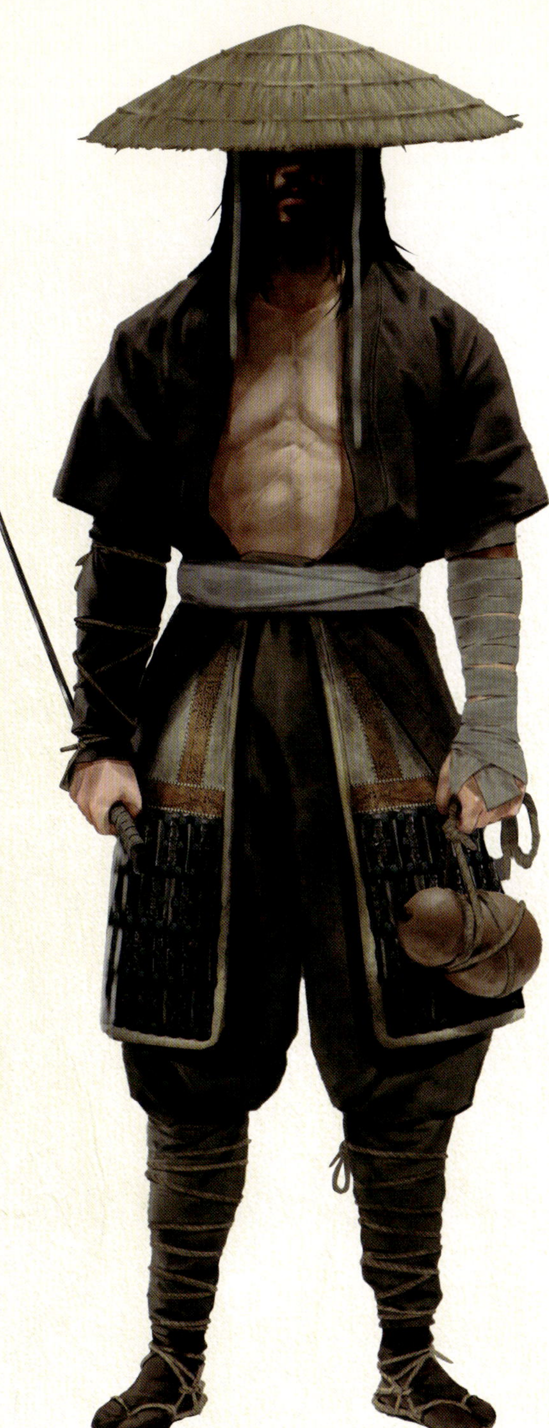

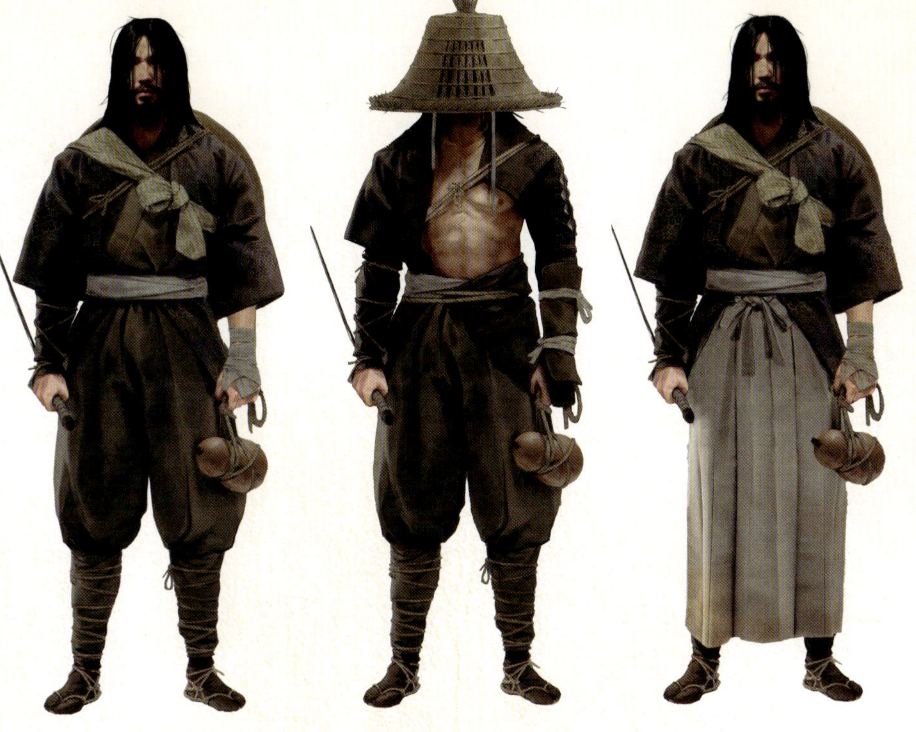

Here you see concept art of ronin equipped with wakizashi, one of which wears a distinctive roningasa, a hat made of woven bamboo that covers the face and is worn to hide his identity.

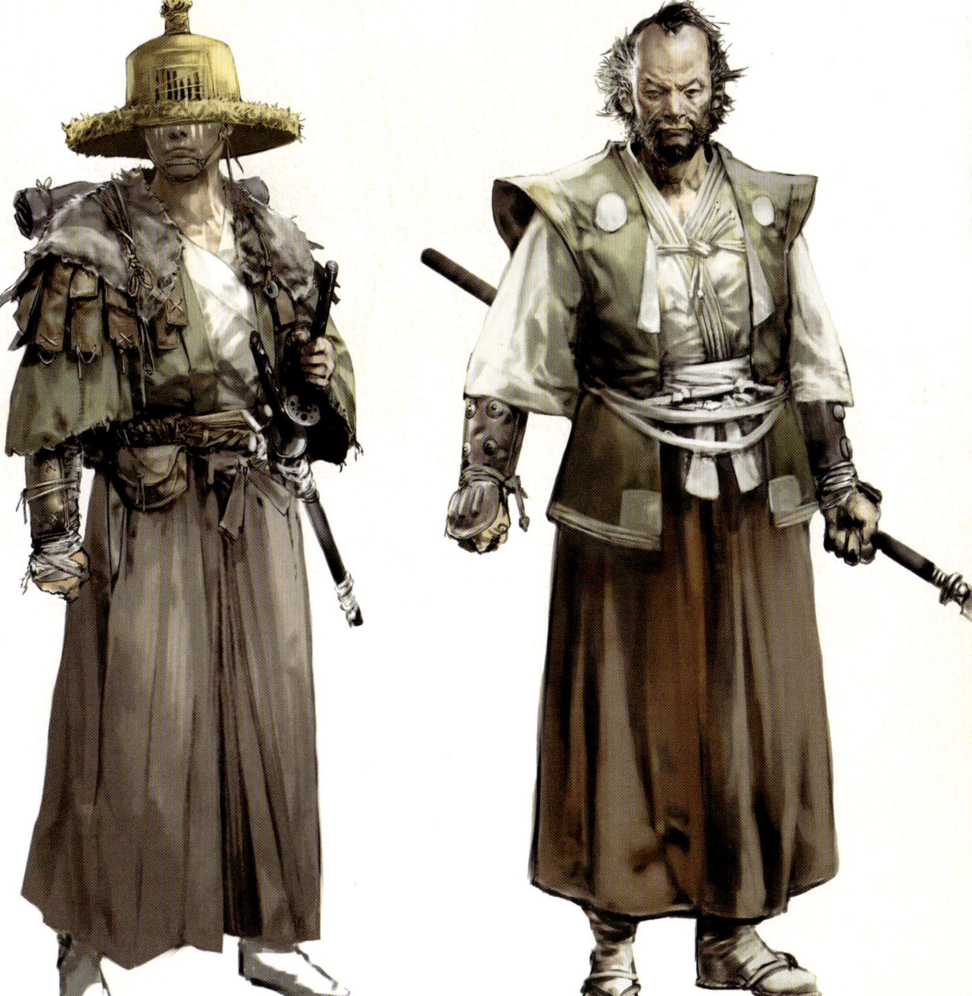

RONIN

Ronin are "free agent" samurai, lone wolves whose masters have either died or disavowed them. This makes them wandering warriors, often available (especially in the war-torn Sengoku period) to serve new lords as bodyguards or mercenary soldiers for hire. The ronin, in their traditional garb, are not as fashionable as the samurai landowners and masters.

OUTLAWS

These ragtag bands of brigands haunt the uninhabited countryside, roaming forests and roads looking for victims. Although similar to *ashigaru* fighters in terms of their equipment and capability, *Shadows'* outlaws operate independently and do not serve as military fodder for nobles. All travelers should beware these brutal, lawless gangs.

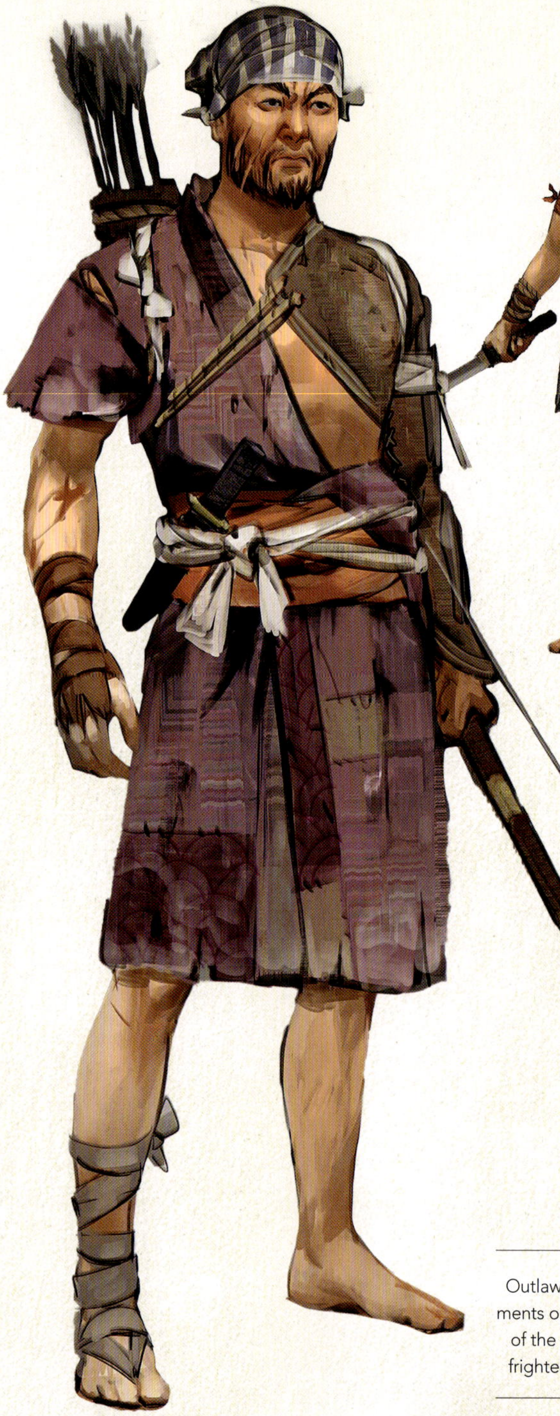

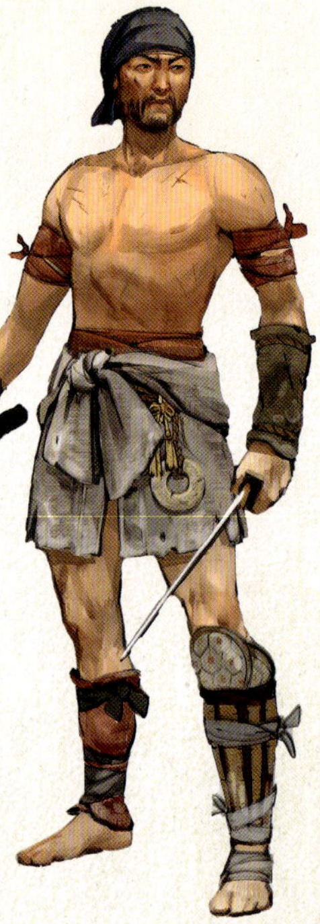

The short, scythe-like *kusarigama* blade is a favorite close-range weapon of many regional outlaw gangs. Some have scavenged a few mismatched armor pieces from various robberies too.

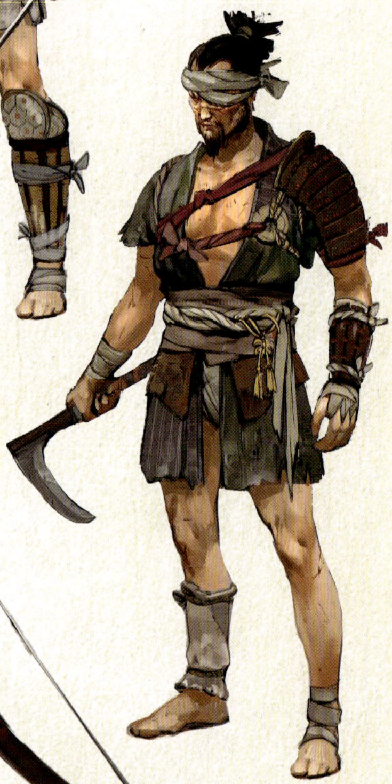

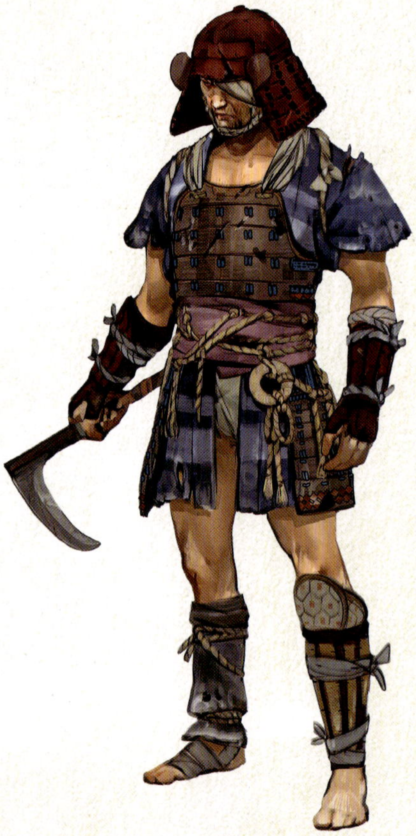

Outlaws often congregate in encampments outside of towns and cities. Some of the camp inhabitants can be quite frightening, like the ones seen below.

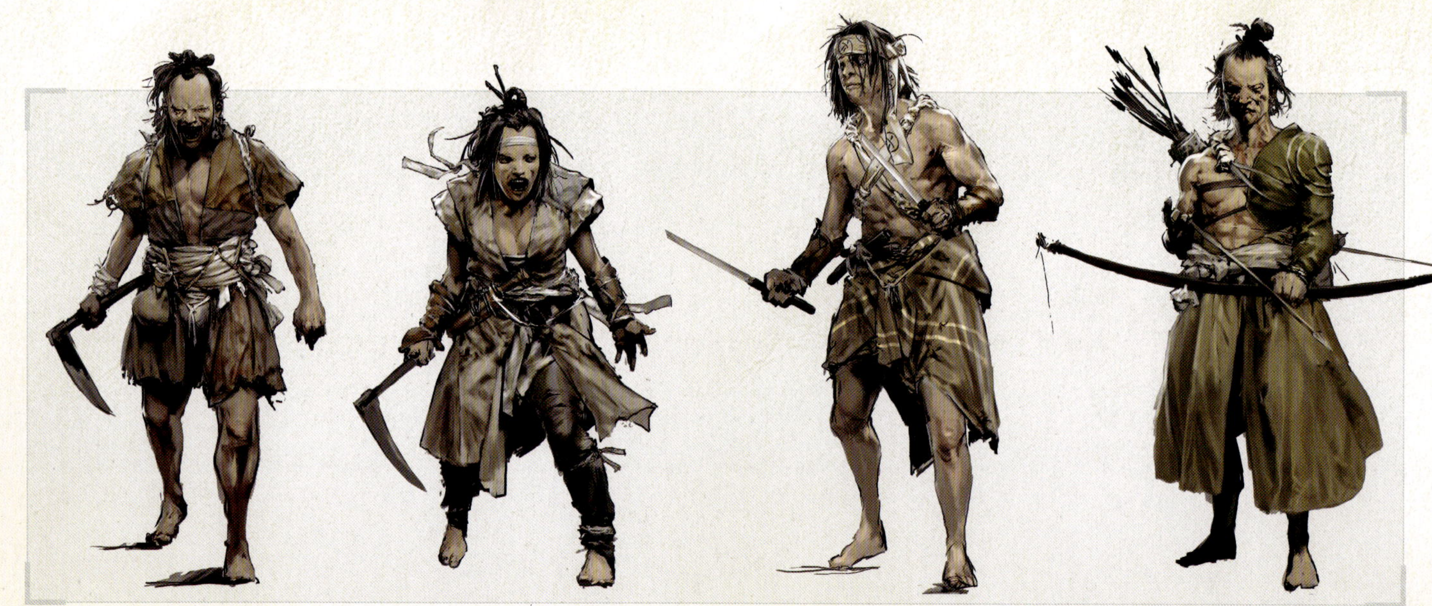

WARRIOR-MONKS

The name speaks for itself—warrior-monks are trained as skilled combatants, fiercely fighting those who would threaten their sanctuaries, lands, religious cause, and customs. Yellow, white, gray, and dark blue are the predominant colors of monk outfits, and these holy warriors inhabit temple complexes in every province.

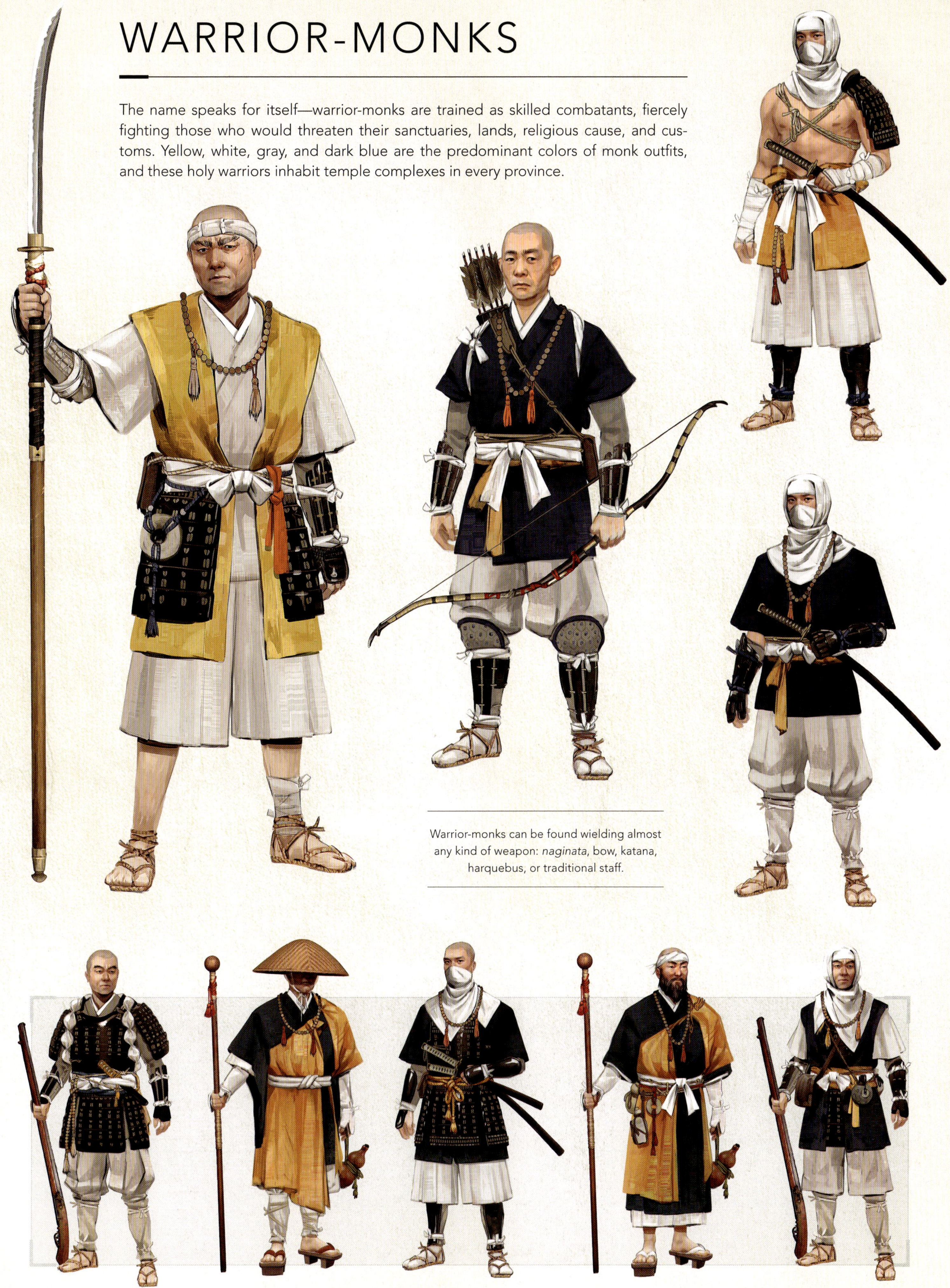

Warrior-monks can be found wielding almost any kind of weapon: *naginata*, bow, katana, harquebus, or traditional staff.

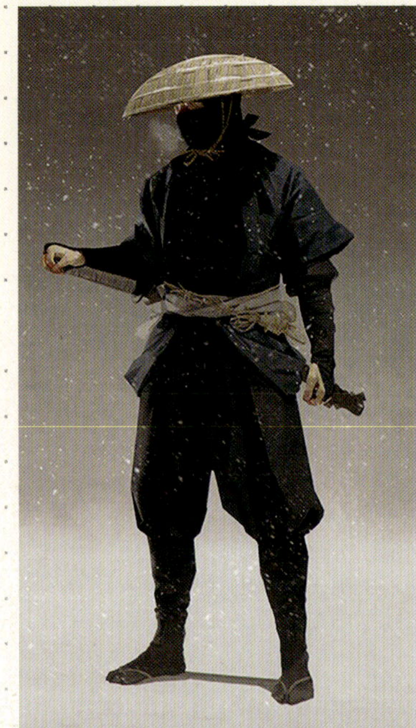

Masked and mysterious, *shinobi* are light on their feet. They prefer smaller, swift weapons like the katana, *kusarigama*, *tanto*, and *shuriken*. A well-tossed smoke bomb can also help a ninja melt into the shadows.

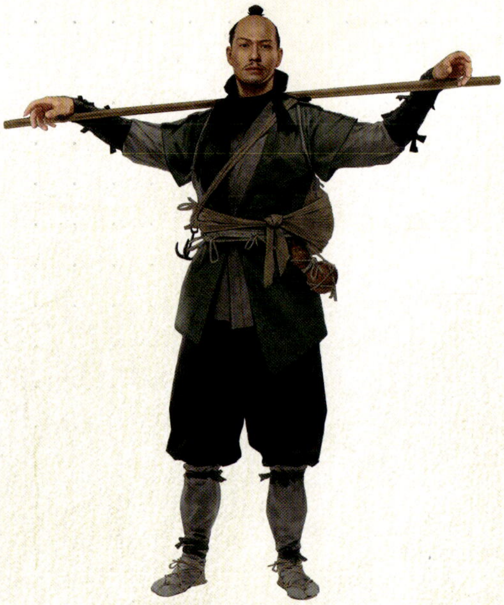

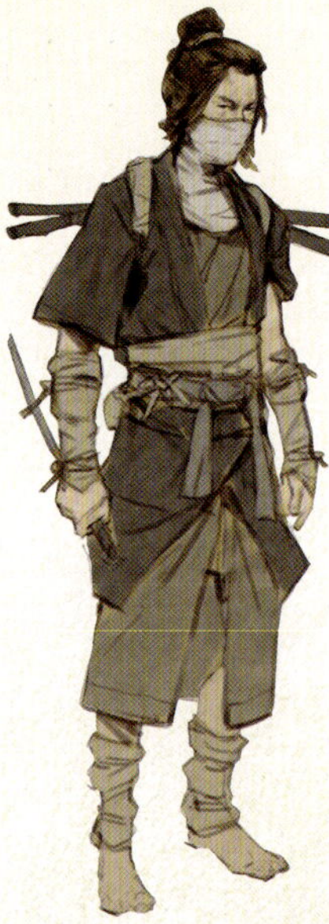

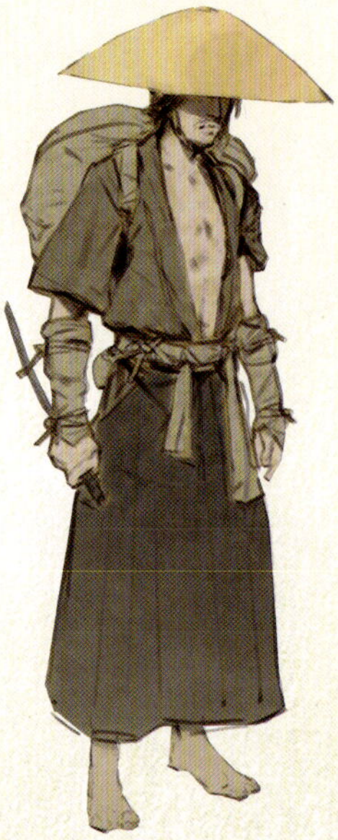

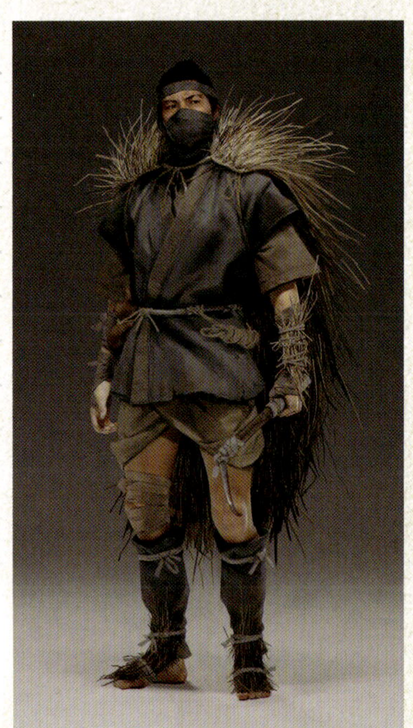

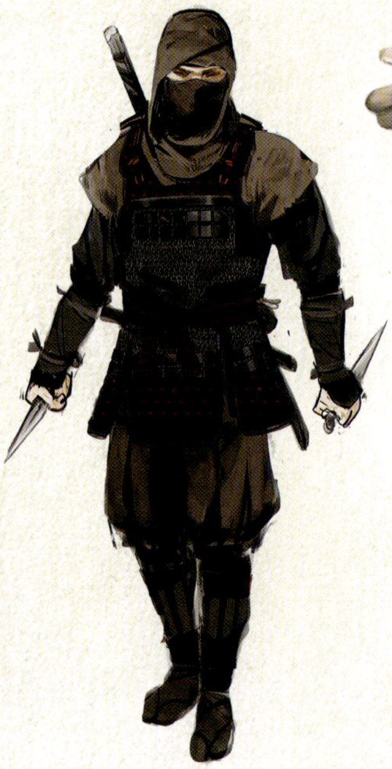

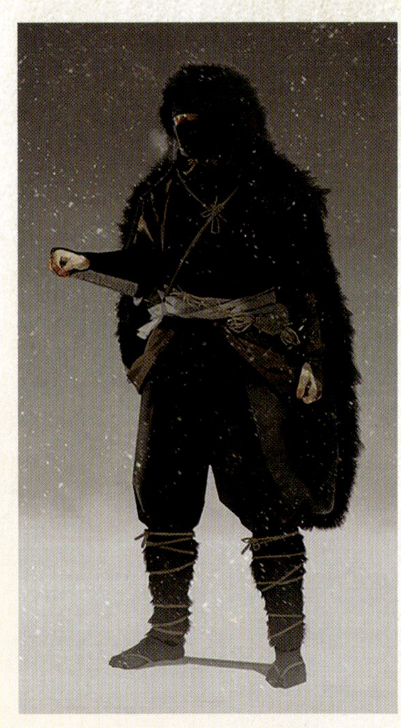

SHINOBI

The classic *shinobi* warrior is a master of martial arts and many other things—stealth, deception, infiltration, espionage, ambush, assassination, and all forms of guerrilla warfare. Extremely agile and highly mobile, these ninja fighters will use terrain, tools, and tricks to gain whatever advantage is possible in combat.

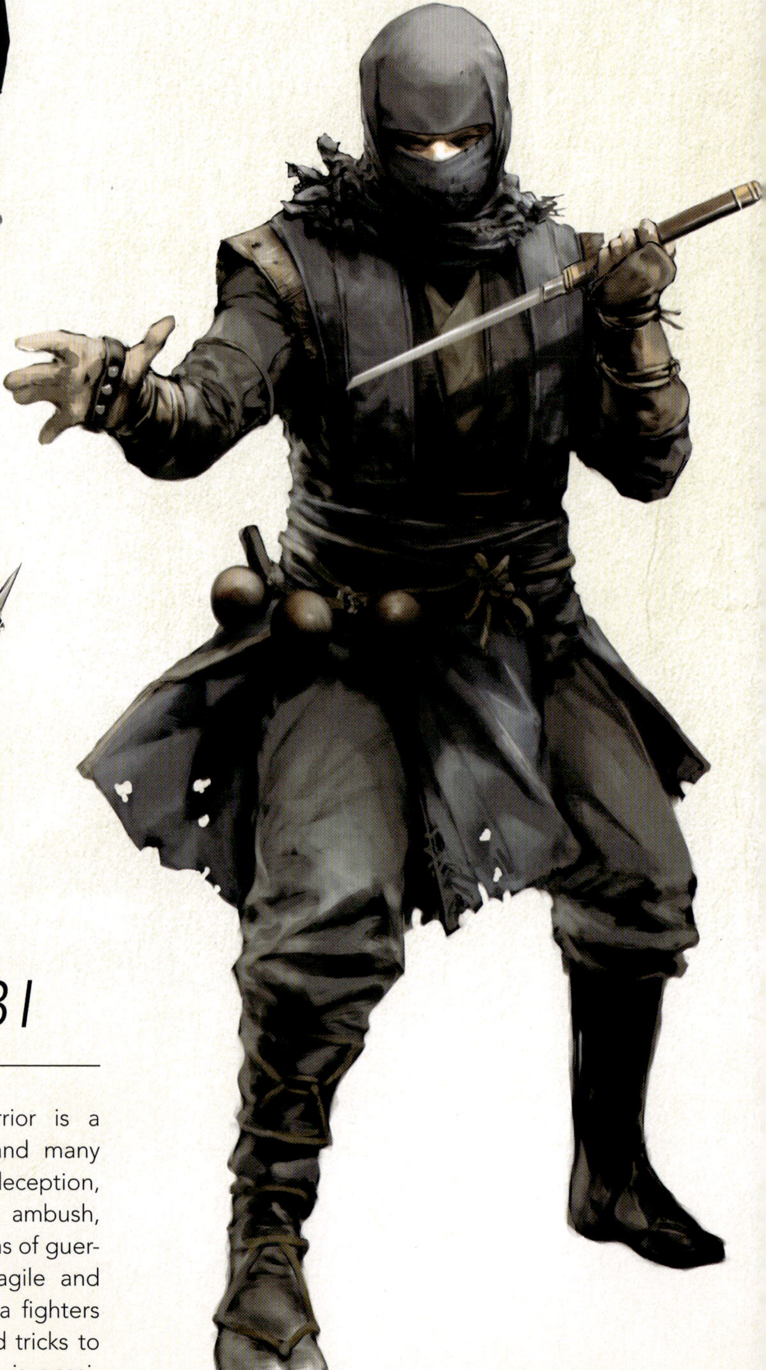

ART BY TYLER RYAN AND VINCENT GAIGNEUX

ART BY KATE CRUZ

PORTUGUESE

Found primarily on the docks of Japan's port cities or aboard towering merchant vessels, the Portuguese are the primary Western power making inroads into Japanese commerce and cultural exchange. The main points of contact are traders and Catholic missionaries, but other Portuguese variants include sailors, riflemen, and armored soldiers.

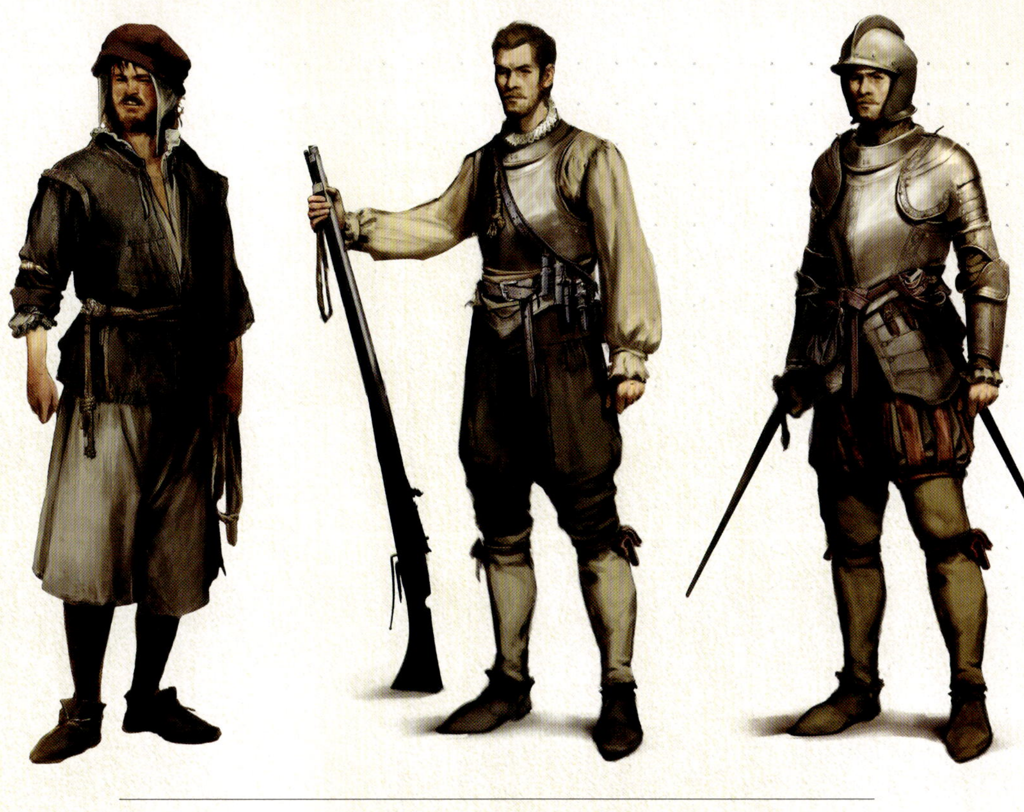

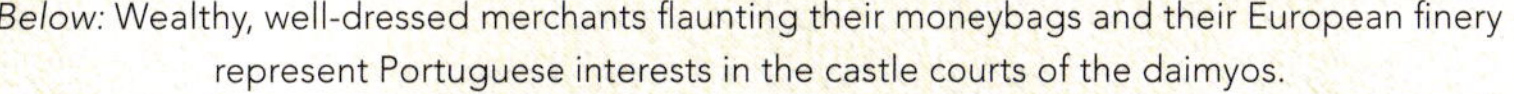

Below: Wealthy, well-dressed merchants flaunting their moneybags and their European finery represent Portuguese interests in the castle courts of the daimyos.

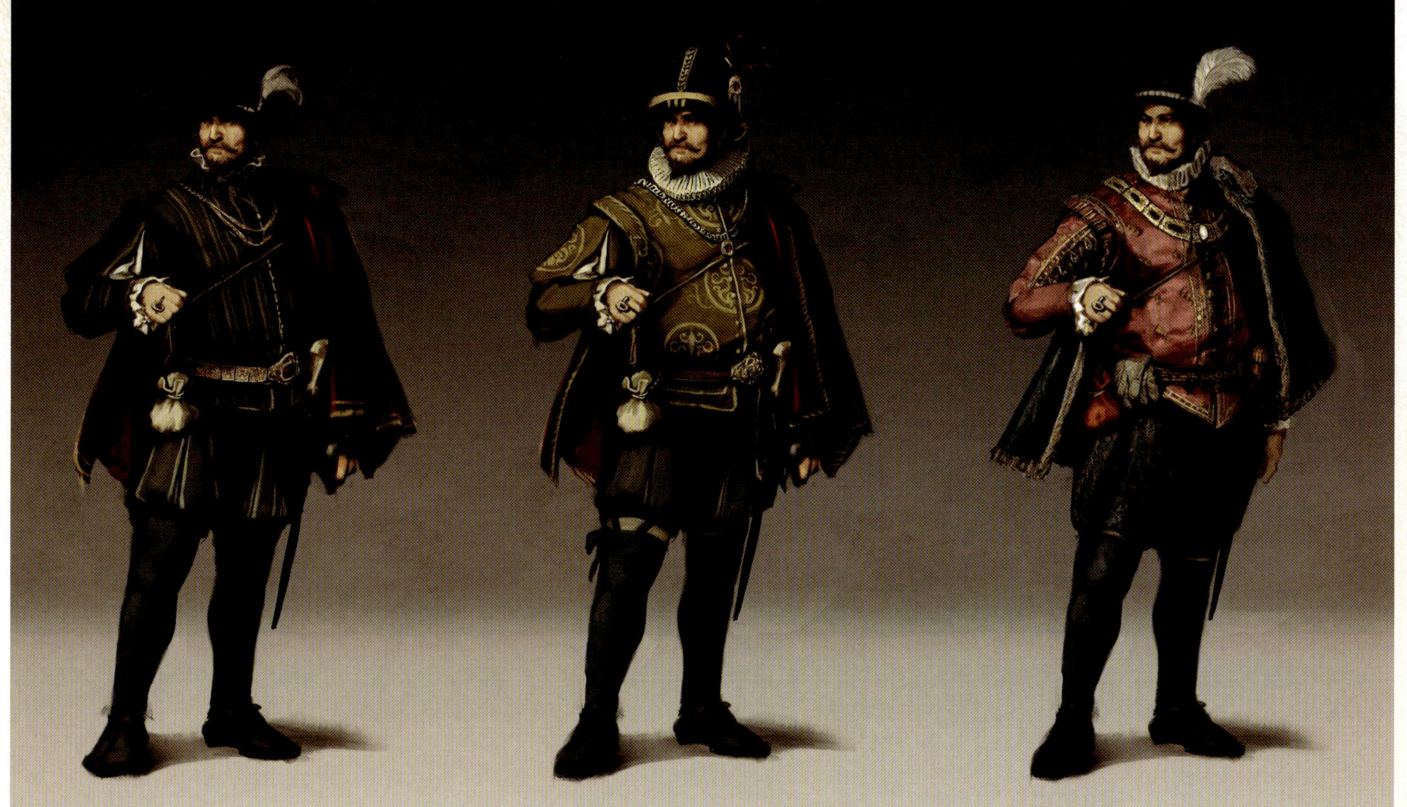

Here you can see an interesting range of clothing associated with various character roles and levels of affluence—merchant, monk, artisan, middle class, nobility, worker, and servant.

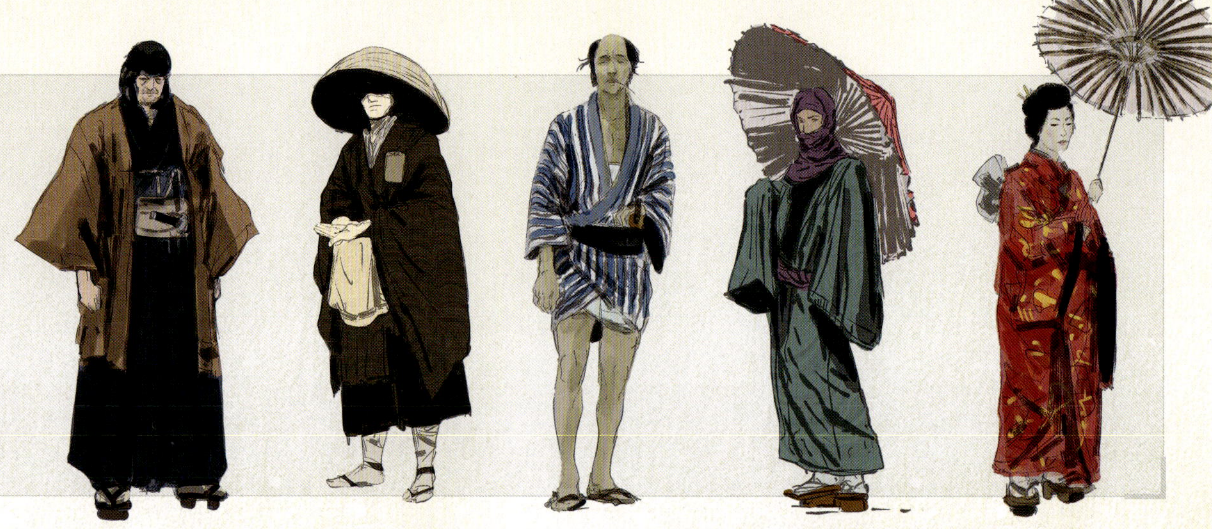

CROWDS

The *Assassin's Creed Shadows* character art team worked hard to populate the game world with a rich variety of local crowds—e.g., residents, travelers, merchants, shoppers, workers, and all manner of pedestrians—all clad in historically accurate garb. "A tremendous amount of work and research went into this effort," says Kevin Macio.

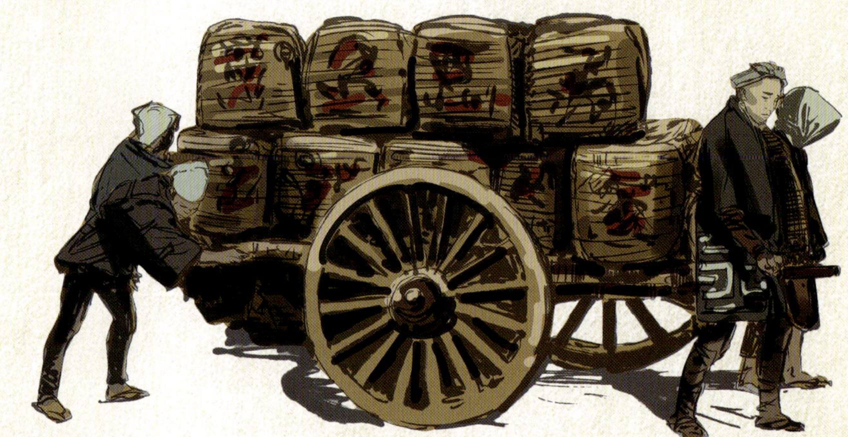

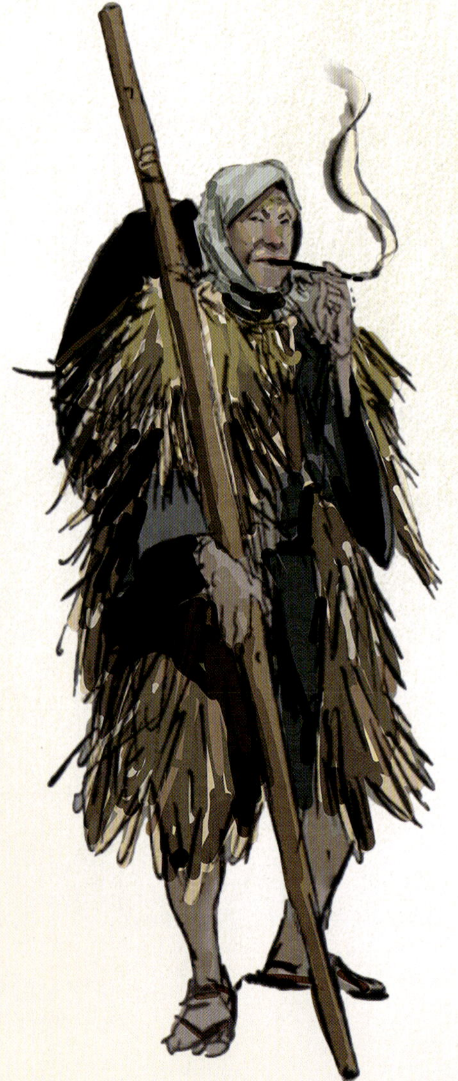

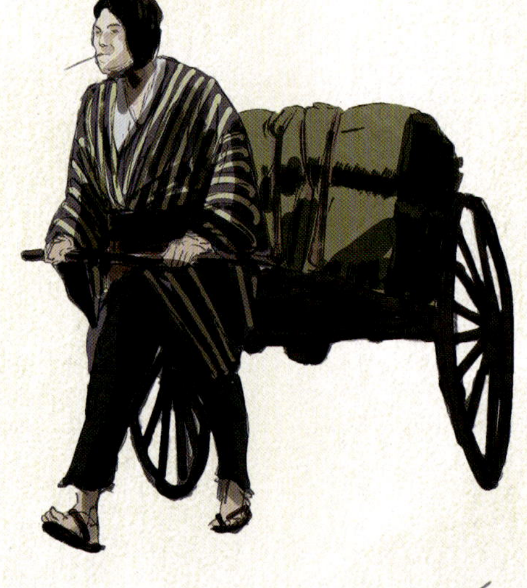

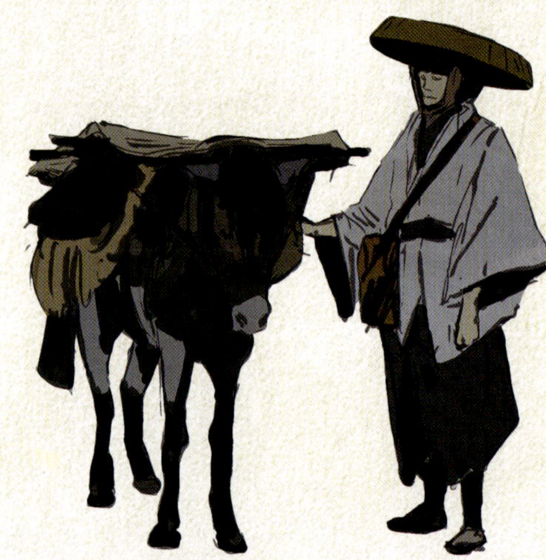

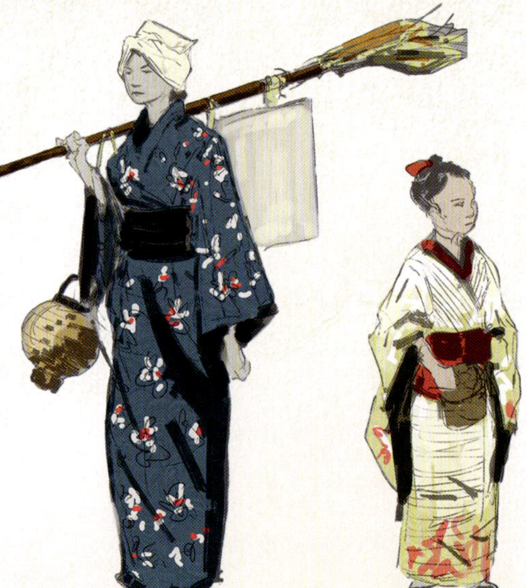

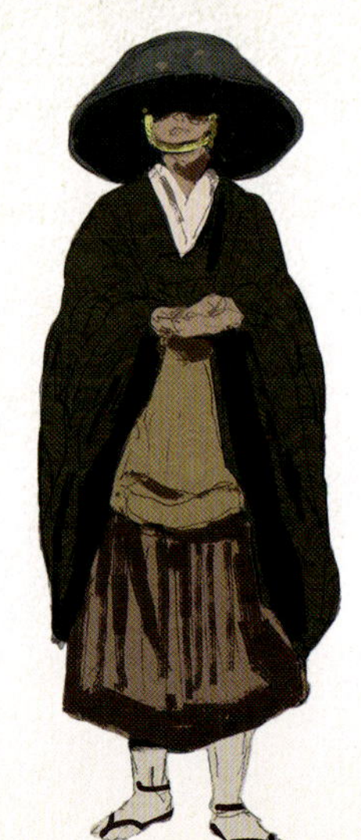

Social classes in feudal Japan were easily differentiated by attire.

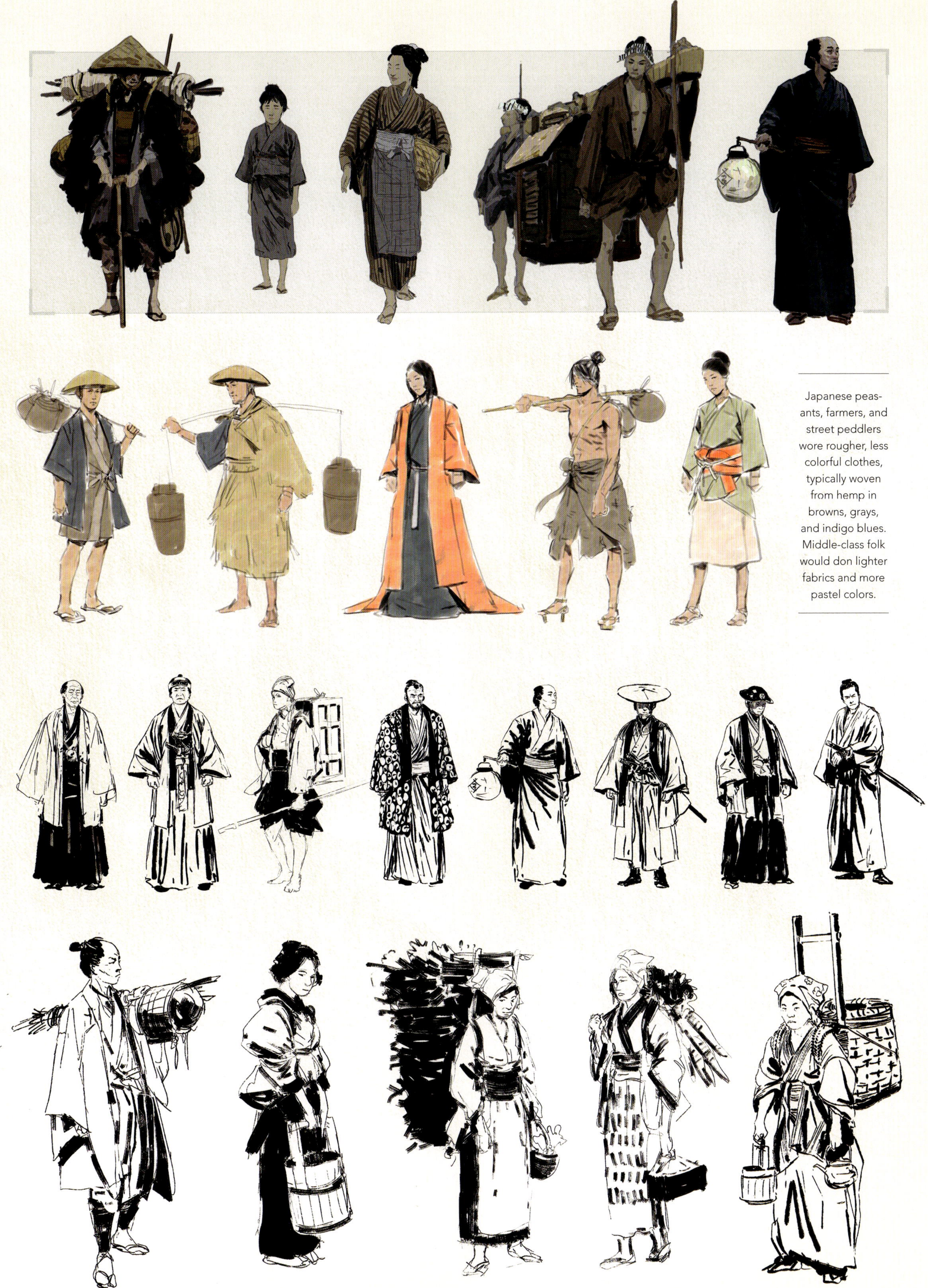

Japanese peasants, farmers, and street peddlers wore rougher, less colorful clothes, typically woven from hemp in browns, grays, and indigo blues. Middle-class folk would don lighter fabrics and more pastel colors.

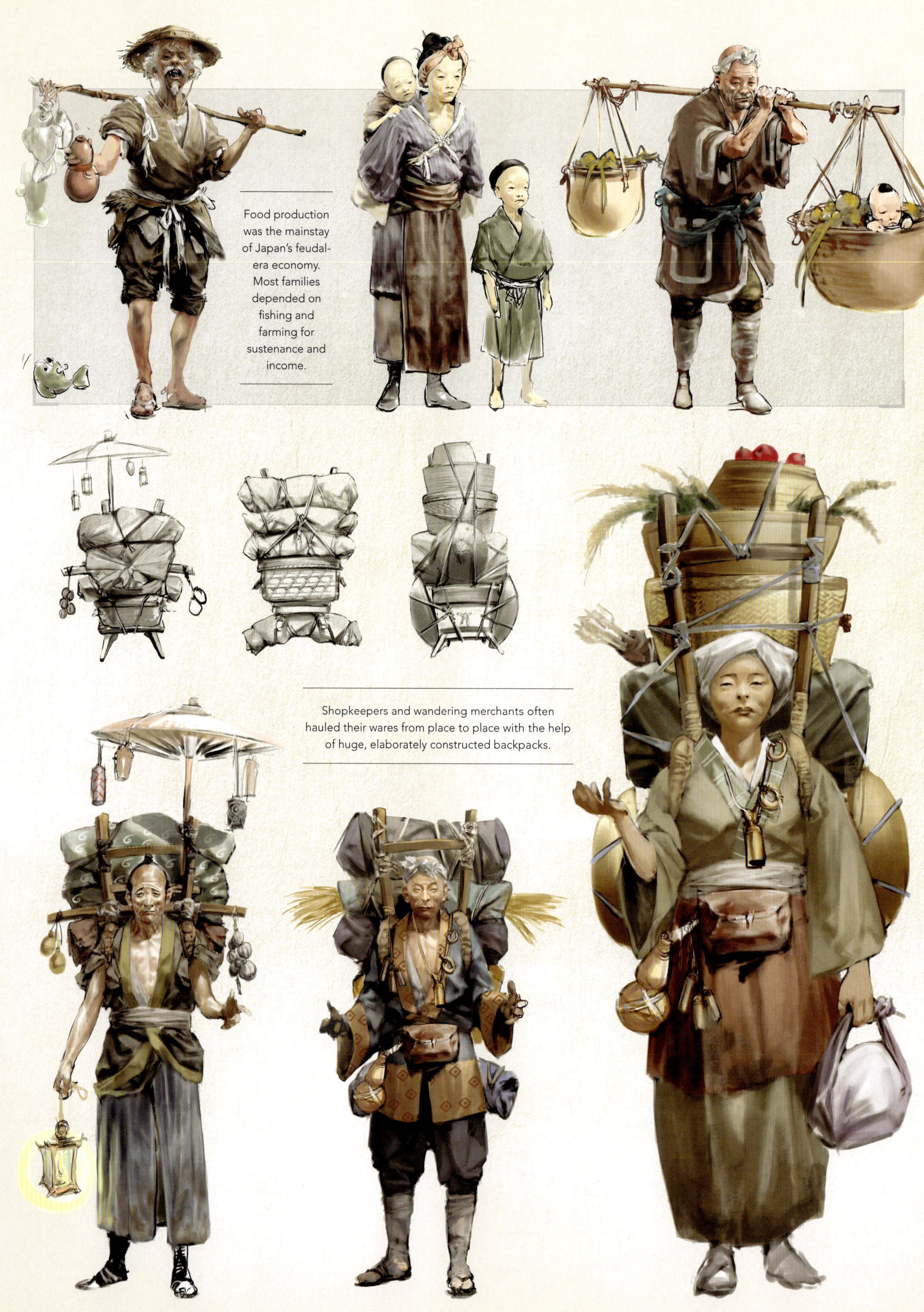

Food production was the mainstay of Japan's feudal-era economy. Most families depended on fishing and farming for sustenance and income.

Shopkeepers and wandering merchants often hauled their wares from place to place with the help of huge, elaborately constructed backpacks.

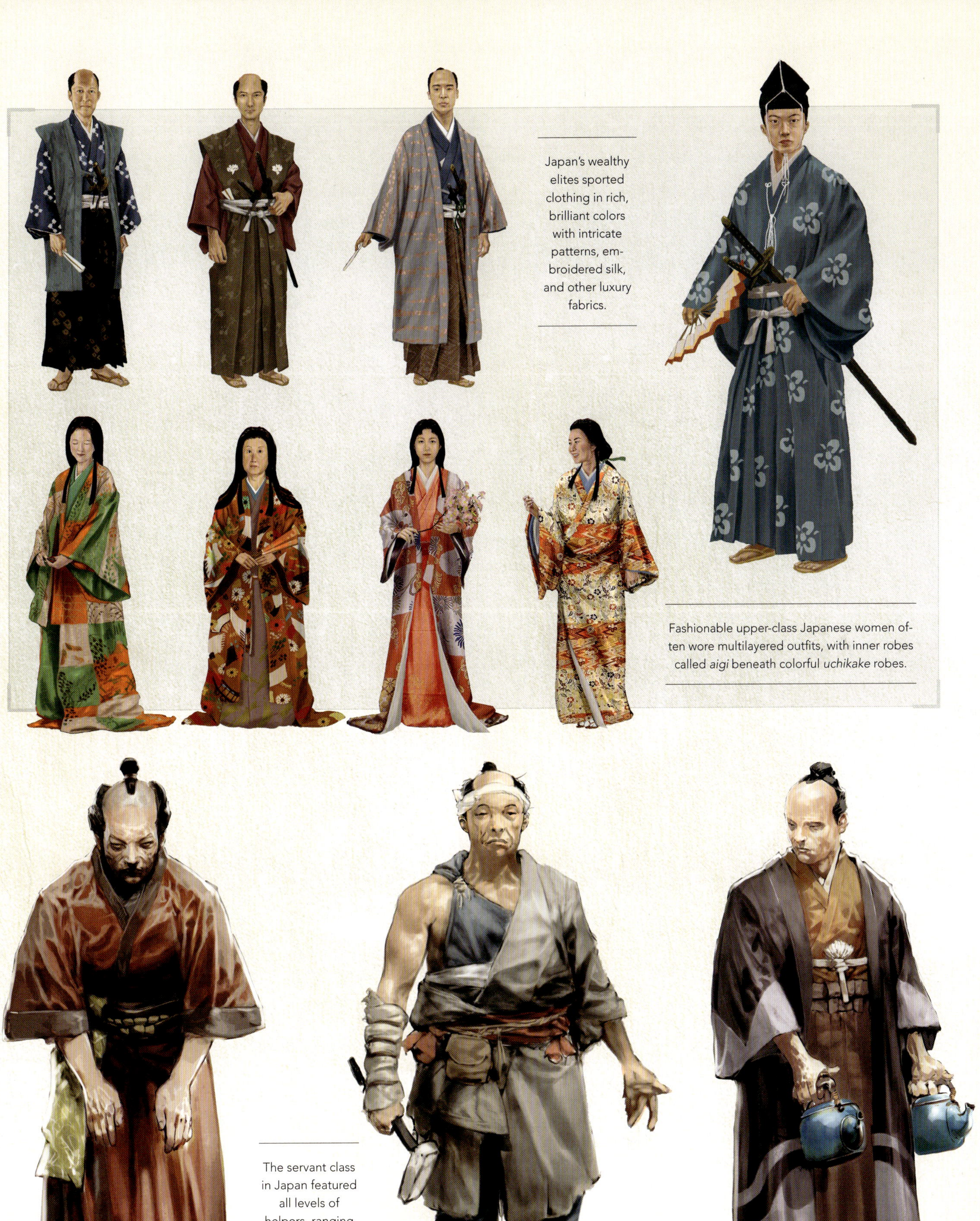

Japan's wealthy elites sported clothing in rich, brilliant colors with intricate patterns, embroidered silk, and other luxury fabrics.

Fashionable upper-class Japanese women often wore multilayered outfits, with inner robes called *aigi* beneath colorful *uchikake* robes.

The servant class in Japan featured all levels of helpers, ranging from well-dressed domestic workers to roughly clad skilled laborers like the hammer-wielding blacksmith seen here.

MOUNTS

Horses in *Assassin's Creed Shadows* are differentiated by their saddlery—i.e., the saddles, pads, blankets, harnesses, reins, breast collars and plates, headgear, and decorative items worn by the mount. Naoe and Yasuke each acquire an in-game mount that can be accessorized with a wide variety of custom items. Each saddle set in the game is designed to match one of the protagonists' outfits.

This page features concept art for Naoe's custom saddlery. The saddle set at right is designed to complement Naoe's ghostly Onryō outfit.

ART BY XIAO LUO

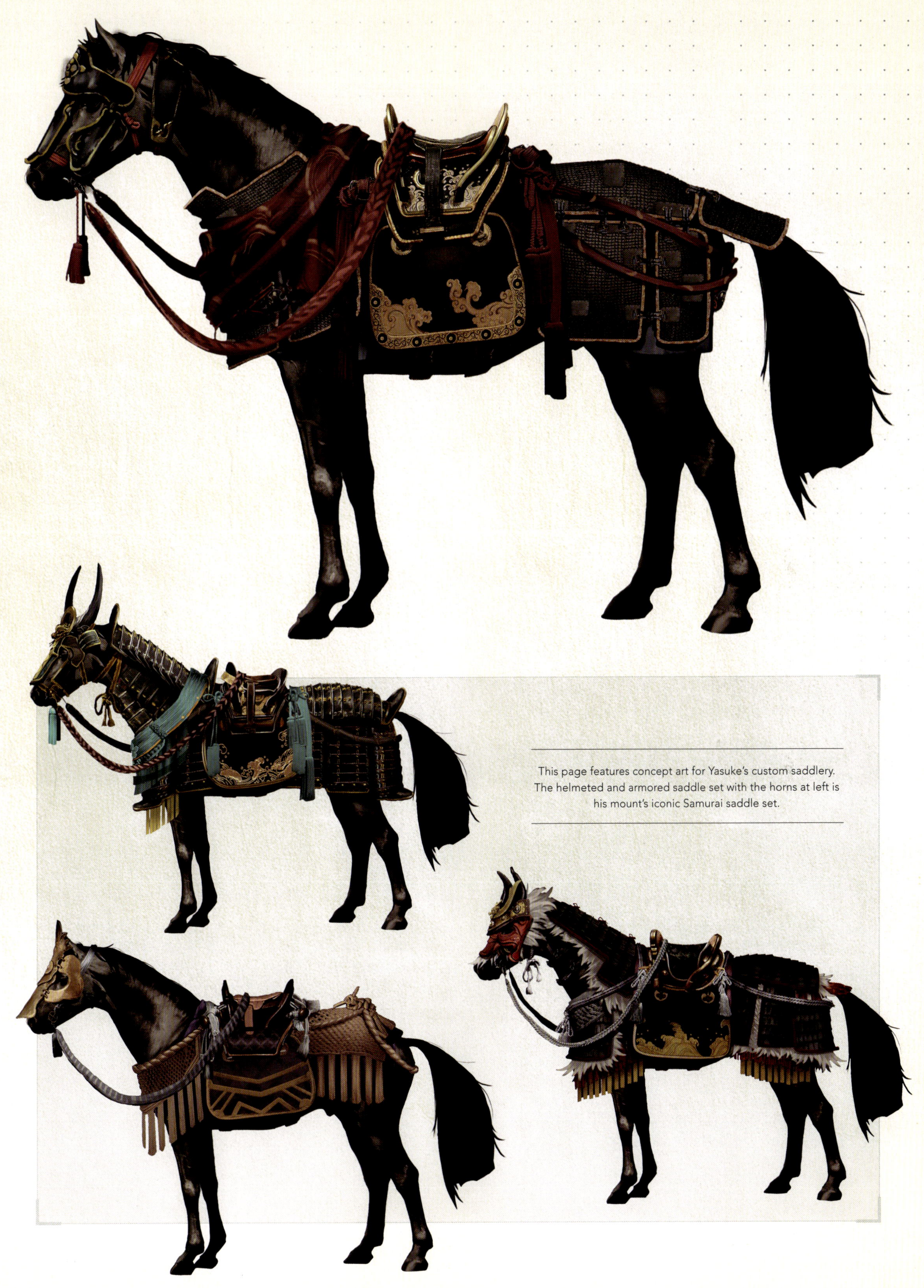

This page features concept art for Yasuke's custom saddlery. The helmeted and armored saddle set with the horns at left is his mount's iconic Samurai saddle set.

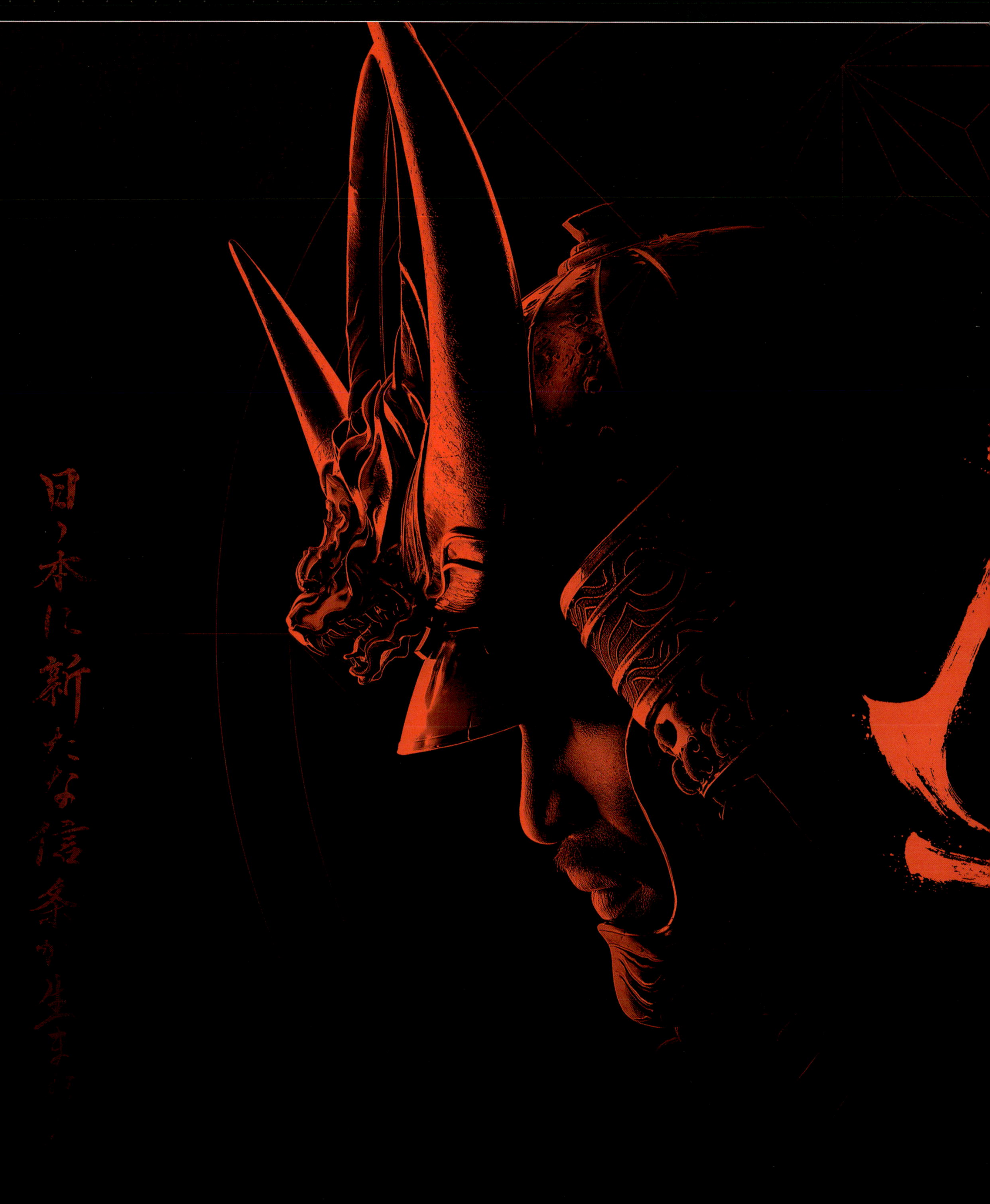
日ノ本に新たな信条が生ま

VISUAL IDENTITY & INTERFACE

CHAPTER FIVE

Much of the concept art for *Assassin's Creed Shadows* focused on creating the look and feel of the game world, conjuring characters, environments, and key narrative moments. At the same time, a whole team of artists and developers was spearheading the *Shadows* branding effort—shaping the game's unique visual identity with an emphasis on authentic images true to the game's era. From the distinctive red slashes of the crest to the dramatic intensity of the dual heroes seen in profile, the team fashioned an unforgettable look for a game that had been known for years simply as "Codename Red."

Another core aspect of the *Assassin's Creed* identity lies in the user interface (UI) and user experience (UX). The visual design team worked alongside the UX, integration, programming, and audio teams to craft the visual features and iconography that players use to interact with the game and navigate its world. Much care is given to the development of this UI/UX interaction and the way it looks and feels when a player crosses the threshold into the game universe.

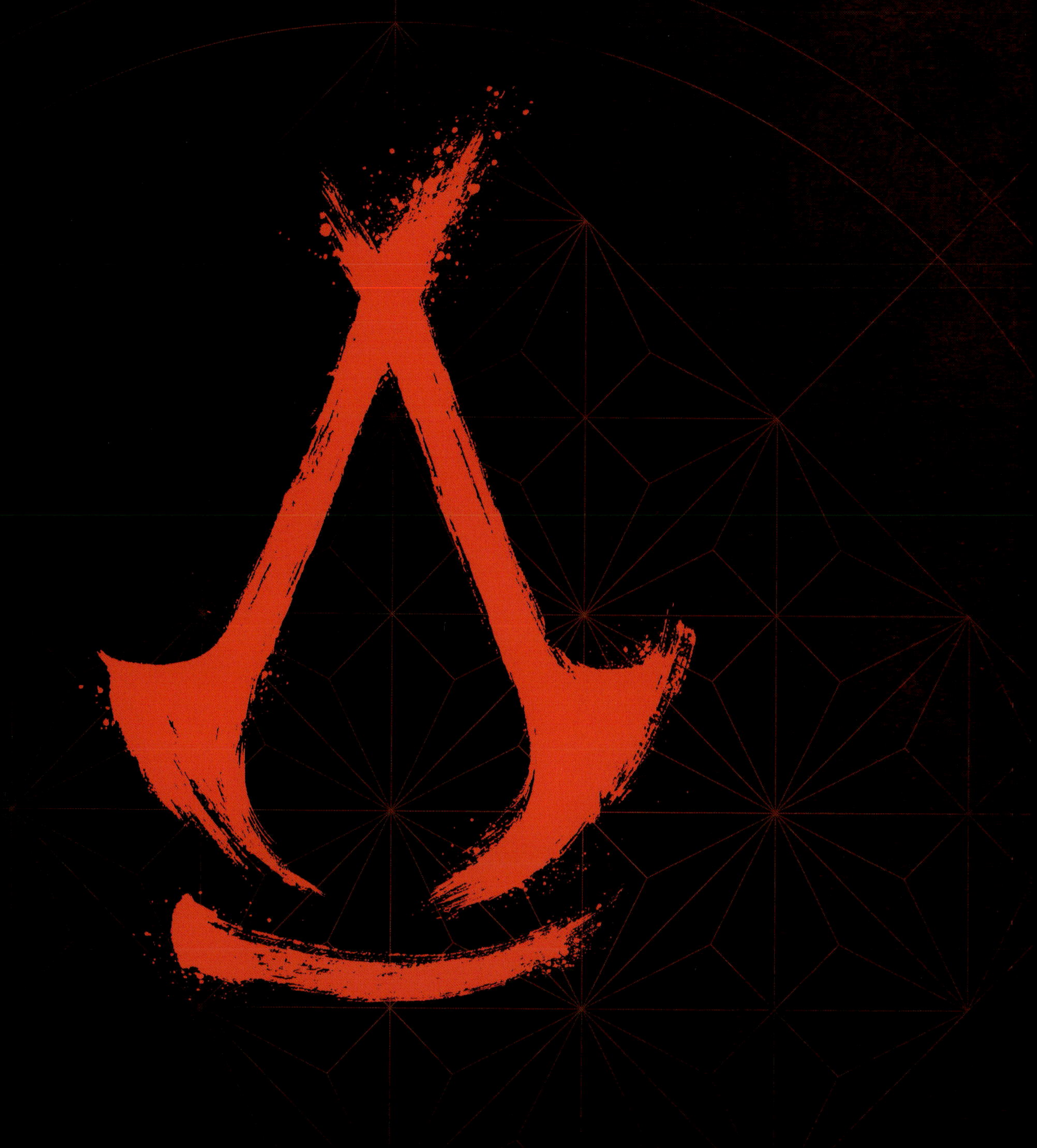

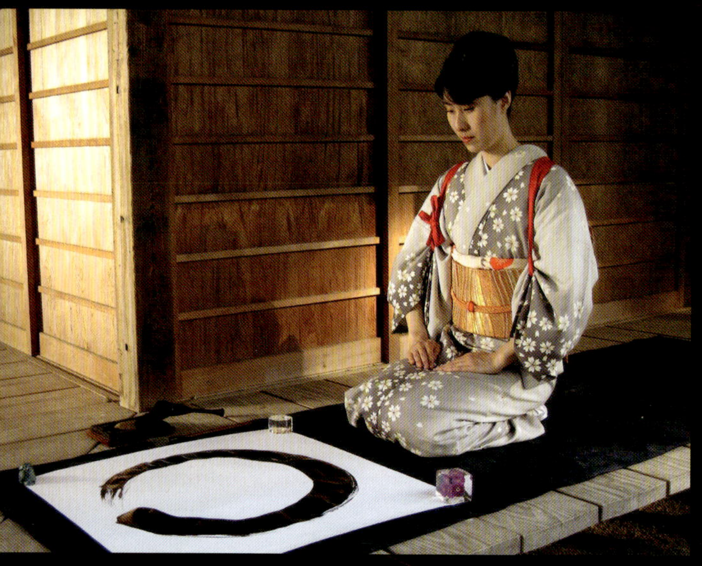

THE CREST

The *Shadows* crest *(above)* was designed in close collaboration with the award-winning Japanese master calligrapher Shoho Teramoto *(left)*. With Shoho's help, the team struck a perfect balance between the historical authenticity of the setting and the *Assassin's Creed* fantasy. The raw aggressiveness of Shoho's brush strokes in the crest creates a striking contrast to the overall elegance of her calligraphy—a contrast aptly representative of the beauty and brutality of feudal Japan.

KEY ART

Generated early in the development process, key art displays dramatic renderings of central game images—for example, the protagonists, Naoe and Yasuke, depicted here in stirring action poses—that help convey the game's essential vision to the art and design teams. Key art also typically serves as the basis for images used in advertising and box art.

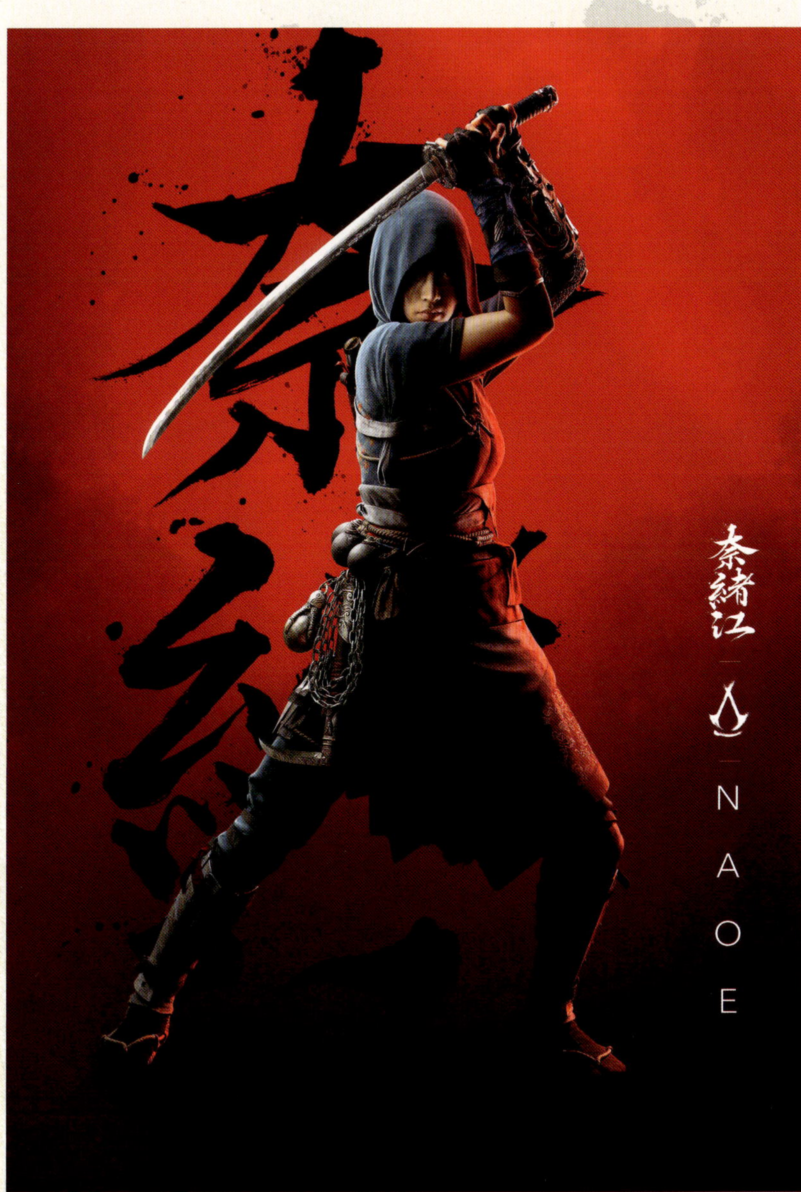

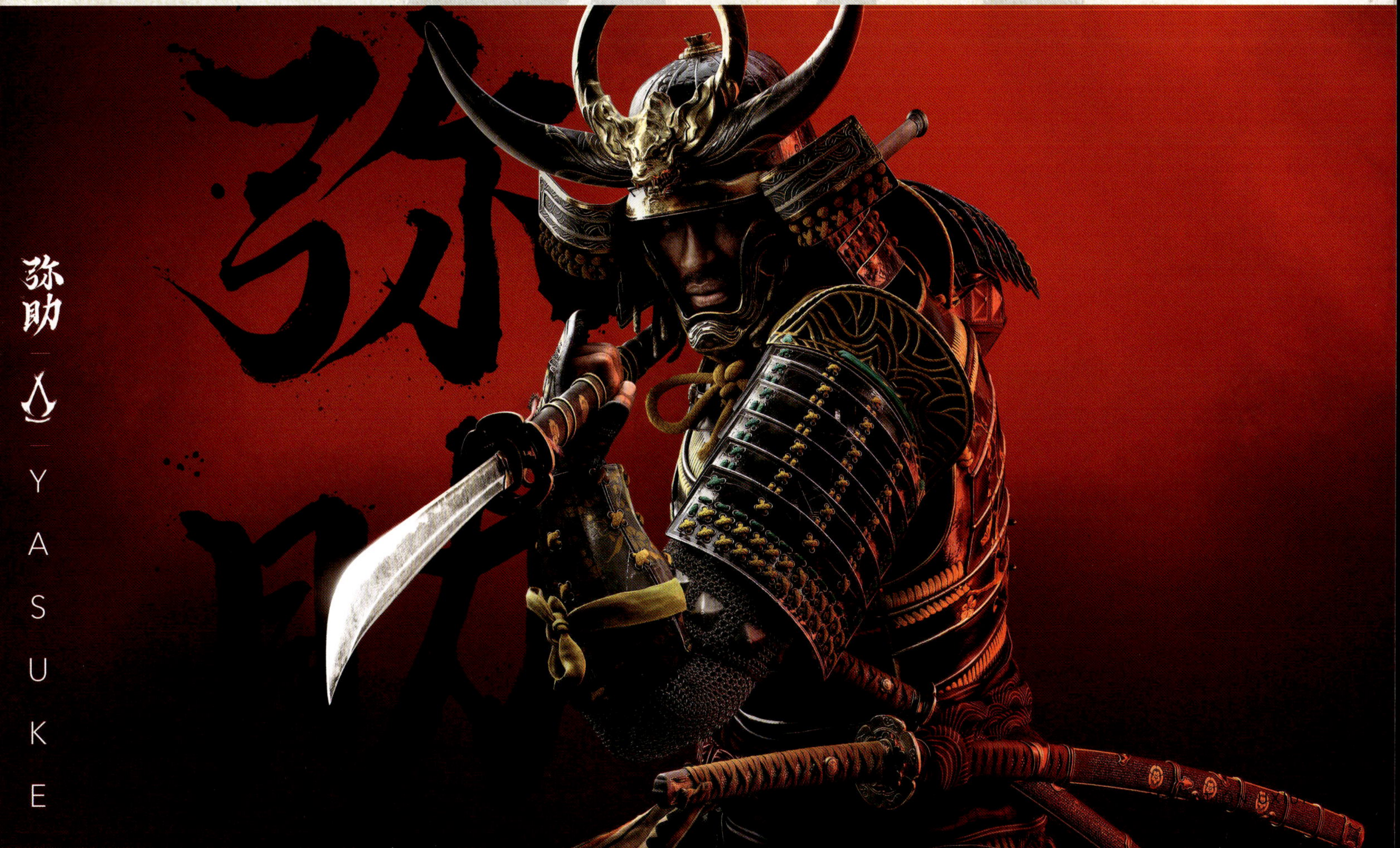

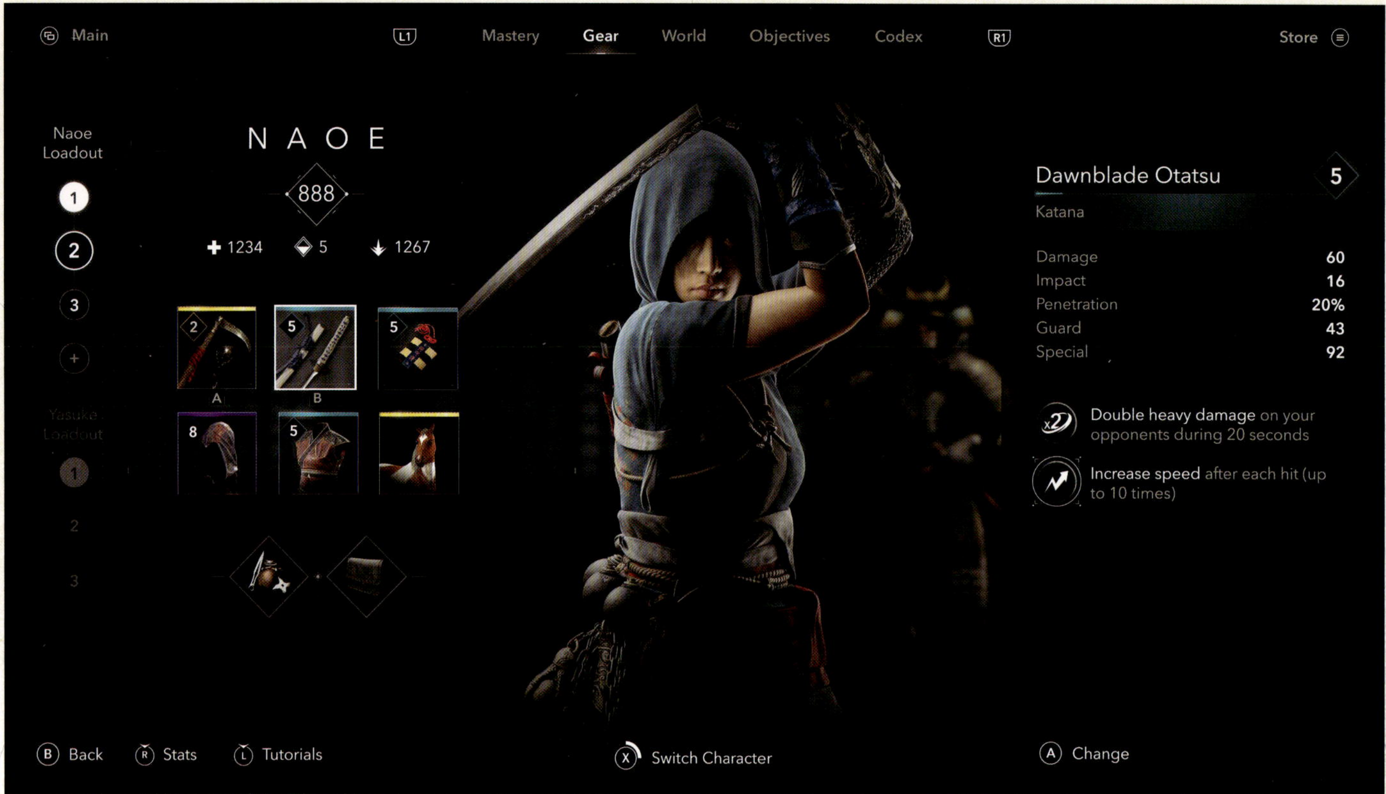

UI/UX

The interface of *Assassin's Creed Shadows* aligns with the franchise's reconnection in recent games to the Animus as a pillar of the brand. The team's goal was to subtly infuse the interface with the essence of the Animus—a sleeker and more technological look—without overshadowing the historical fantasy of the traditional Japanese imagery. Through minimalist layouts accompanied by clean animations, the visual design team sought to highlight the ambiance and assets of the game within the menus. A constant guideline for the team during the development was to envision the Animus as a contemporary museum, with feudal Japan being the showcased exhibition.

The preliminary mockups in this section may still change before the game is made final, but they serve as a strong example of the team's coordination and shared goals.

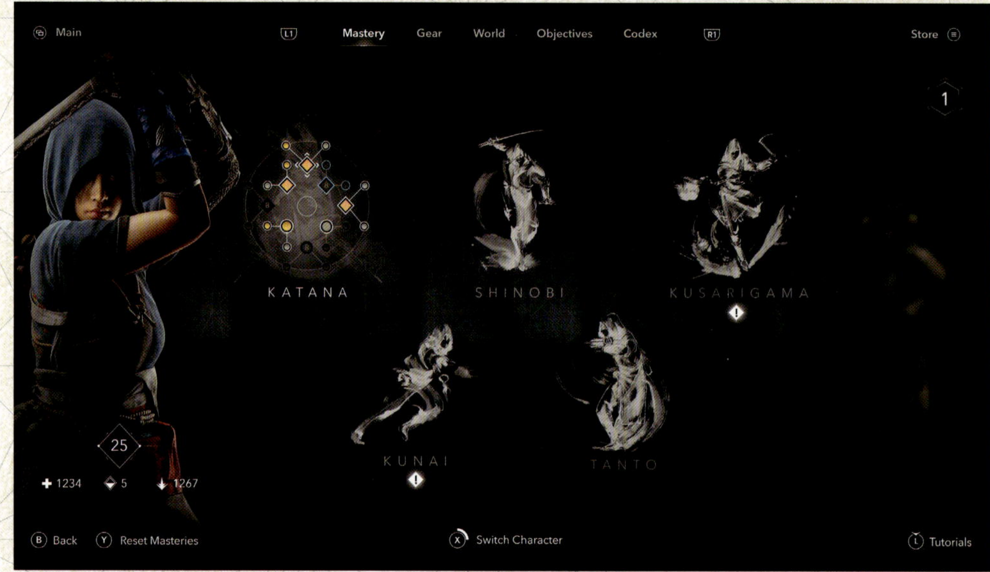

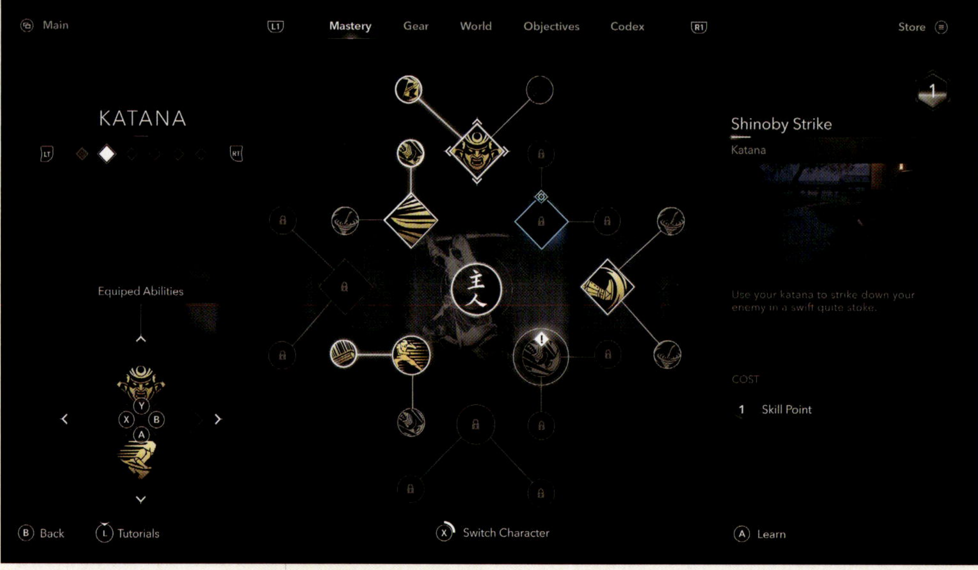

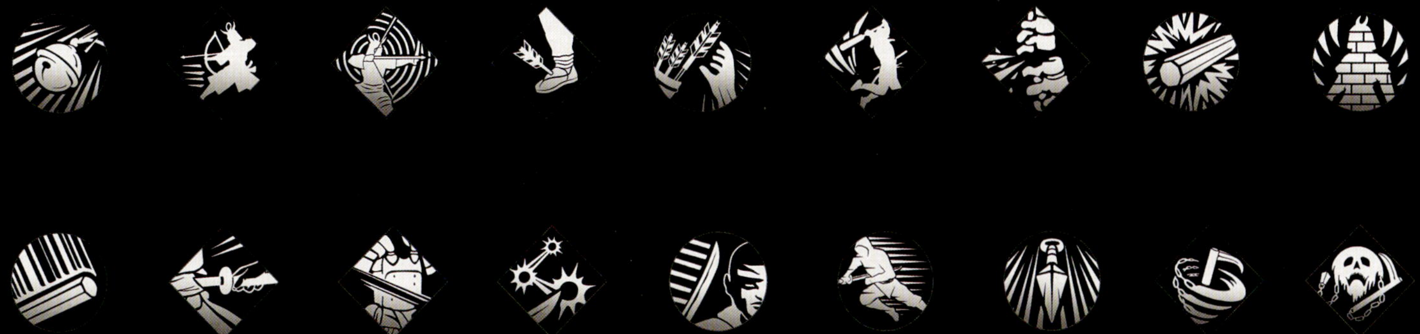

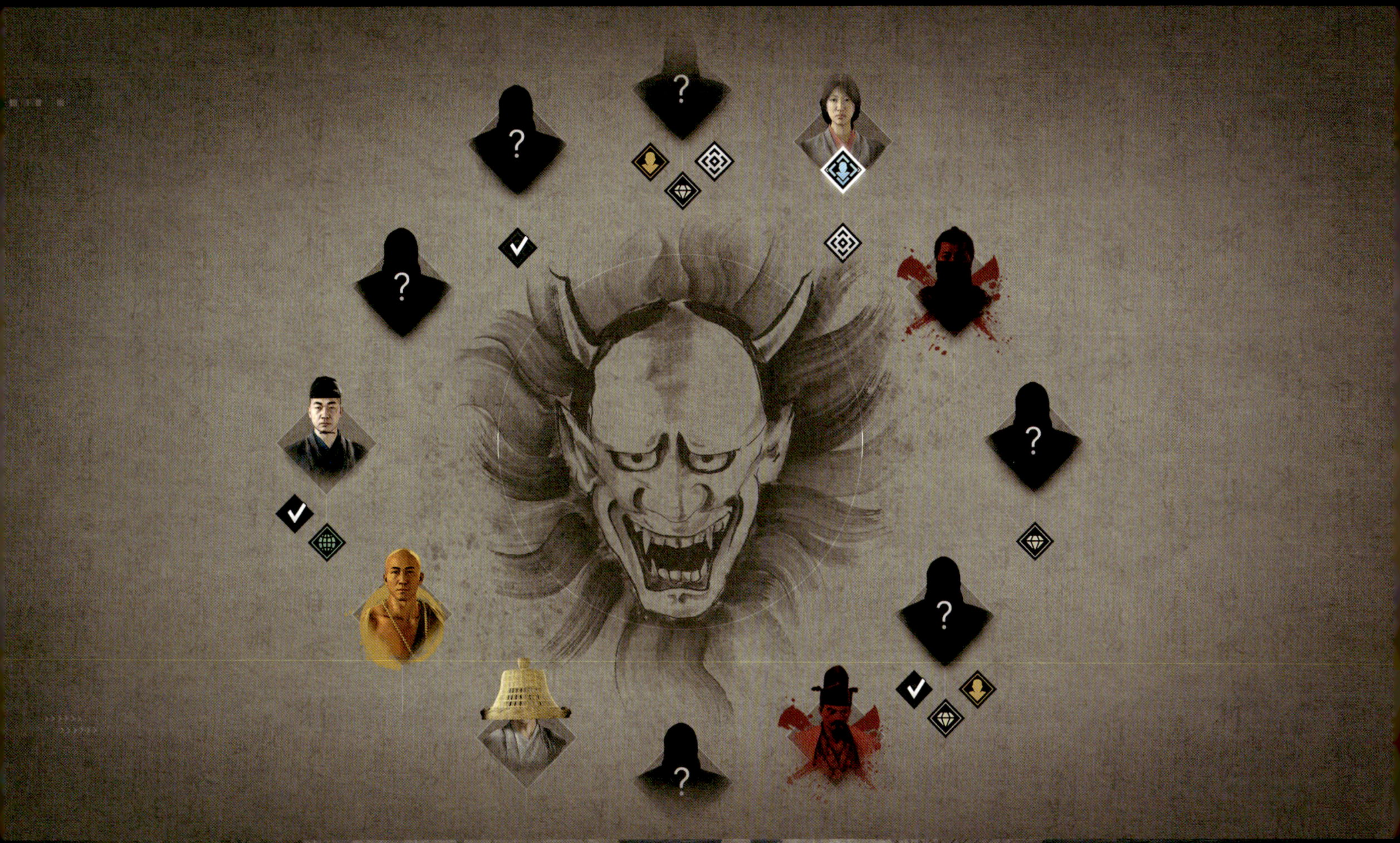

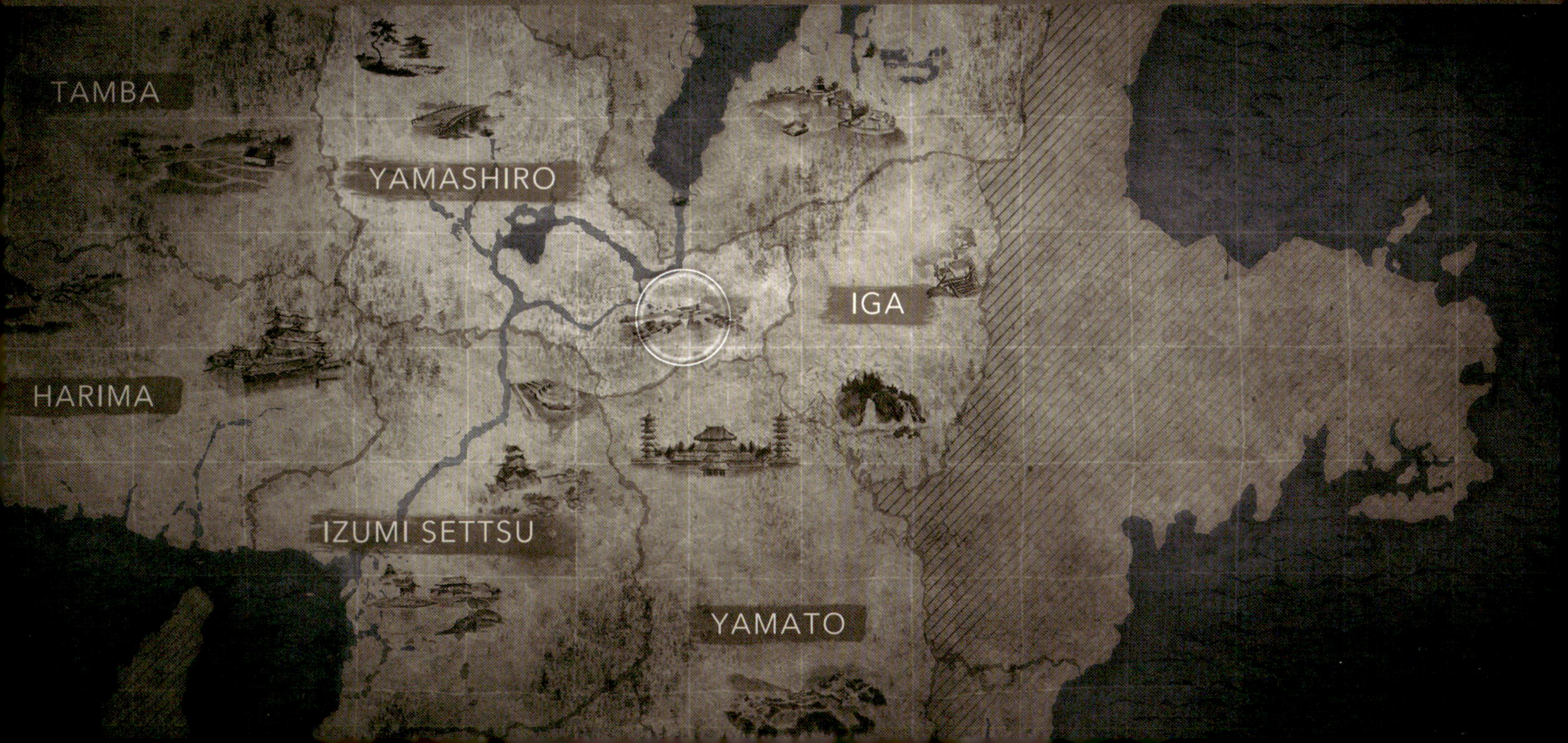

TAMBA
YAMASHIRO
IGA
HARIMA
IZUMI SETTSU
YAMATO

UBISOFT QUÉBEC

MARC-ALEXIS CÔTÉ // VP & Executive Producer
KARL ONNÉE // Producer
JONATHAN DUMONT // Creative Director
CHARLES BENOIT // Game Director
STEPHANIE-ANNE RUATTA // Historian / World Director
LUC PLANTE // Level Design Director
MARIE CAUCHON // Product Marketing Director
THIERRY DANSEREAU // Art Director, Graphics
JONATHAN VEILLETTE // Assistant Art Director, World
GUILLAUME CROTEAU // Assistant Art Director, World
VINCENT LAMONTAGNE // Assistant Art Director, Biomes
MICHAËL LEVASSEUR // Assistant Art Director, Presentation
DOMINIC GLADU-DESPATIS // Team Lead, Architecture
DIMITRI ALEXIS // Team Lead, Materials
ANTOINE BARBOT // Team Lead, Props
SIMON WEANER // Concept Artist
JAMIE CHANG // Artist
KEVIN KOK // Artist
FELIX ROBITAILLE // Artist
QUENTIN LE GOFF // Artist
HUGO LAMARRE // Artist
THIBAUT REIMEL // Artist
VINCENT DÉROZIER // Artist
ALEXANDRE RODRIGUE // Artist
PABLO BLANES // Artist
SVITLANA KOVALCHUK // Artist
ELIE PAQUIET // Artist
MAKSIM KUTSENKO // Artist
OLIVIER TREHET // Artist
FRANÇOIS LARRIEU // Artist
DAVID THERRIEN // Artist
JULIEN MANON // Artist
ADRIEN GUIGUES // Artist
DMYTRO MOTUZ // Artist
JUSTIN VAILLANCOURT // Artist
BROOKE DAVIES // Associate Narrative Director
ALISSA RALPH // Lead Scriptwriter

UBISOFT MONTRÉAL

NICOLAS RIVARD // Art Director, Visual Conception
KEVIN MACIO // Assistant Art Director, Characters & Weapons
ARIANE TROTTIER // Assistant Art Director, Characters
ÉLYSE CANUEL // Product Marketing Manager

UBISOFT CHENGDU

GABRIEL TAN // Art Director
SINA HAYATI // Senior Concept Artist
ZHOU YOU // Senior Concept Artist
ZAHIR AGHAKHANI // Concept Artist
JING ZHONG TANG // Concept Artist
XU XIAO TING // Lead Character Artist, Animal
YE WEN XIANG // Senior Character Artist
CHEN QIAN // Senior Character Artist

UBISOFT SINGAPORE

FRANCO PEREZ // Art Director

UBISOFT OSAKA

SIDONIE WEBER // Art Director
GENSEKI TANAKA // Senior Concept Artist
JULLIUS GRANADA // Concept Artist
ALBERT LIN // Senior Concept Artist

UBISOFT UKRAINE

VALERII ORLOV // Senior Concept Artist

UBISOFT MANILA

KATE CRUZ // Senior Concept Artist
ARNYLL DALE GACUSAN // Senior Hard Surface Artist
JOSHUA PEDRON // Concept Artist
JILLIAN YOUNG // Concept Artist
REN GOMOS // Concept Artist
FRANCIS FAURILLO // Artist
NIKO SABERON // Artist
JEMA MANALLO // Artist
DALE GACUSAN // Artist
KURT NUÑEZ // Artist
RUBY LOPEZ // Junior Concept Artist
DANI VILLACORTE // Junior Concept Artist

HELIX MONTRÉAL

OLIVIER AMMIRATI // Artist
EVE BERTHELETTE // Art Director, Visual Conception
MYLAINE BLAIN // Artist
DELPHINE BOCCARD // Graphic Designer
ALICE BRUYNEEL // Production Manager
PASCAL CAPLETTE // Art Director, Visual Conception
SARAH CHAMAILLARD // Illustrator
HUGO DESCHAMPS // Art Director, Visual Conception
PATRICE DUFRESNE // Art Director, Visual Conception
CAMILLE FACHE // Graphic Team Leader
LEO FULFORD // Artist
CATHERINE GAGNÉ // Production Director
SIMON GASTIN // Art Director, Visual Conception
SALLY GOTTSCHALK // Illustrator
ANTHONY GUEBELS // Art Director, Visual Conception
MASSIVA HAMICHE // Illustrator
MAUD LE GUENNOU // Graphic Designer
CASSIDY LERMAN // Production Manager
JEAN-PAUL MAGEREN // Production Manager
ALLAN MATUDIO // Artist
BENOIT PERREAULT // Art Director, Visual Conception
MARTIN PORTAIS // Artist
RENATO REBOUÇAS // Artist
LAURENCE ROBERTS // Content Specialist
PHILIPPE SAVOIE-LEMAY // Artist
FABIEN TRONCAL // Creative Director
ZACHARY VIEL // Production Manager
HERNAN VIETRI // Assistant Art Director, Graphics

UBISOFT TRANSMEDIA TEAM

AYMAR AZAÏZIA // Transmedia Content Director
ETIENNE BOUVIER // Senior Transmedia Content Manager
FATIHA CHELLALI // Publishing Project Manager
JULIEN FABRE // Director, Global TV & Transmedia
CAROLINE LAMACHE // Business Development Director, Transmedia

SPECIAL THANKS

YOHEI ASO, FATMA ZOHRA BENSOUDA, MARC BRASSARD, VINCENT GAIGNEUX, EDUARD GODLACH, GENTARO KAWAGA, SADAYUKI KISHIDA, KONI (AMANDINE GIRARD), FRANCIS LAFLECHE, JUAN HUGO MARTINEZ, ISMAEL PADDACK, FRED RAMBAUD, TYLER RYAN, PR. SACHI SCHMIDT-HORI, CAROLINE SOUCY, PR. PIERRE-FRANÇOIS SOUYRI, SHOHO TERAMOTO, PR. SENDA YOSHIHIRO